Introduction Summaries

Woman of Valor by Jill Stengl
England 1631 - Helen has come to Marston Hall to care for three neglected children and a household in disarray. Both the gardener and the lord of the manor admire her inner beauty, but only one man will win her love.

A Duplicitous Facade by Tamela Hancock Murray
England 1812 - In obedience to her father, Melodia agrees to marry a man she has never met. But when a masquerade ball is held to celebrate the marriage, Melodia suspects she has more enemies than friends.

Love's Unmasking by Bonnie Blythe
England 1814 - Matthew is certain a godly girl does not exist among London's moneygrubbing debutantes. He imitates a fop at society functions to repel them, but his own ruse traps him in an engagement.

A Treasure Worth Keeping by Kelly Eileen Hake
England 1827 - Paige is thrilled to hear her father has been hired to restore one of the country's largest collections of antique volumes—until she learns the mysterious earl is hosting a house party during their stay.

Apple of His Eye by Gail Gaymer Martin
England 1851 - Sarah is curious and independent for a young woman of her day, which leads her to fall in love with a man who would never be invited into the family manor as a guest.

Moonlight Masquerade by Pamela Griffin
England 1865 - Letitia, an unassuming lady's companion to her cousin, quickly finds herself the possessor of incriminating information and the focus of attention from two mysterious men.

Fayre Rose by Tamela Hancock Murray
Scotland 1358 – Fayre was brought to Kennerith Castle to tend the duke's rose garden in payment for her father's taxes. When the Laird Kenneth falls ill with the plague, only Fayre is brave enough to play nursemaid.

Fresh Highland Heir by Jill Stengl
Scotland 1748 - When Hermione's stepfather takes over Kennerith Castle, he retains Allan for Hermione's bodyguard. She is determined to think the worst of Allan, until someone is out to get rid of him and the true heir of the castle comes into question.

English Tea and Bagpipes by Pamela Griffin
Scotland 1822 - When Fiona's sister and Alex's brother run off to marry, the families oppose the match between a poor highlander and an English nobleman. Fiona impulsively goes after her sister, and Alex follows.

9 Romances from the Home
of Austen and Dickens

The BRITISH
Brides
COLLECTION

Bonnie Blythe, Pamela Griffin,
Kelly Eileen Hake, Gail Gaymer Martin,
Tamela Hancock Murray, Jill Stengl

BARBOUR BOOKS
An Imprint of Barbour Publishing, Inc.

Print ISBN 978-1-64352-024-7

eBook Editions:
Adobe Digital Edition (.epub) 978-1-64352-026-1
Kindle and MobiPocket Edition (.prc) 978-1-64352-025-4

Published by Barbour Books, an imprint of Barbour Publishing, Inc., 1810 Barbour Drive, Uhrichsville, Ohio 44683, www.barbourbooks.com

Our mission is to inspire the world with the life-changing message of the Bible.

 Member of the
Evangelical Christian
Publishers Association

Printed in the United States of America.

Contents

WOMAN OF VALOR

by Jill Stengl

Dedication

To Kim, Phyllis, and Ruth:
When I think of England, I think of you and the experiences we shared there as military wives. Friendship like ours is blessing beyond measure.

Chapter 1

"O ut, woman. This be as far as my coach goes. The road past here is all mud." The driver wrenched open the coach door, placed the step in front, then proceeded to haul down Helen Walker's small trunk and dump it upon the side of the road.

"I paid you to drive me to Biddlesham Fen." One hand on the door frame, Helen peered out.

"And here you be." The driver waved a gloved hand to indicate marshy fields on every side. "This crossroads is nigh the village. Make haste, woman. There be a fog comin' in."

Helen opened her mouth to protest further, but the coachman narrowed his eyes and lifted a brow. His bristly, pockmarked face reminded Helen of an ill-tempered pig. Shaking in every limb, she stepped down. Her shoes sank into mud. Lifting her petticoats, she sloshed over to her trunk.

"God be with you." Kind words, spoken in a voice of lead. The driver climbed back to his seat.

"You cannot leave me here!" Helen cast a fearful glance skyward. Across the way, strategically placed at the crossroads to catch the attention of any traveler, an iron cage swayed in the crisp spring breeze. Racing clouds released a brilliant sunset ray to highlight its resident criminal's decayed condition. Helen clapped a hand over her mouth.

Without another word to her, the driver coaxed his team into a sidetrack, turned the small coach around, and headed back to Thetford.

Gaping in disbelief, Helen watched until the coach passed out of view. Casting a glance down each vacant road, she felt tightness in her belly. A wind gust cut through her woolen cloak and stung her cheeks. Ropes and chains creaked. A ghastly shadow bobbed near Helen's trunk until a cloud mercifully obscured the sun. Helen kept her gaze averted from the atrocity across the way.

Clutching her cloak at her breast, she sat on her trunk, closed her eyes, and begged God to send help quickly. "Not that I believe You unaware of the situation, Lord. I know that Your eye is upon them that fear You and hope in Your mercy. I ask to be delivered from all my fears and to have my feet placed upon solid ground." She peeked at her soggy shoes, then squeezed her eyes shut. "As You know, my cousin expects to meet me in the town of Biddlesham Fen tonight and—"

A mournful cry drifted across the fens. Helen's mind told her it was a bird, but her imagination insisted it was the ghost of her putrefied companion. Her face crumpled as she fought back hysterical tears. *Am I doomed to spend the night in this place? I would walk to town, but I do not know which path to take. God, You promised not to allow trials too great for me to bear! Why did I ever leave Surrey? I might have married Wilmer the butcher and raised his six children. Anything would be better than going mad here in this marshland with no one to see or care!*

A rhythmic beat caught her attention. Was the poor wretch on the gibbet rattling about again, or was a horse coming?

Screwing up her face, she peeked with one eye. A horseman approached from the north. Relief slackened Helen's taut nerves until she realized the rider could be a highwayman. . .or worse, a phantom.

Trotting hooves splattered mud. The puffing horse pulled up several feet from Helen, sparing her skirts. Huddled within her cloak, she cast an anxious gaze upon the rider. He looked substantial enough in brown leather doublet, plain gray breeches, and cuffed boots. Unlike many men of fashion, he wore his hair short—falling just above his shoulders—yet a flowing cape gave him a dashing air.

"Helen Walker?" The brim of his hat shaded the man's face. Helen beheld only an imposing hawk nose and a clean-shaven chin. Could this be. . . ?

"Cousin Cyril?"

"Surely you did not expect him to meet you in person. Have you been waiting long? I never thought of a trunk. Need a cart for that." His mount, a fine palfrey, stamped a hoof and whipped its cropped tail from side to side.

"Where is my cousin?"

"Who, Biddlesham?" He sounded scornful. "The *master* is away on business. We will not see him for a se'ennight, I expect."

"I–I see," Helen replied.

After a short pause, the horseman said, "I shall return for the trunk tomorrow." He dismounted in one motion and handed her his horse's reins. Helen and the horse regarded one another uncertainly; then the animal lowered its head to graze.

Helen's rescuer hauled her trunk into the brush and concealed it. Helen disliked the idea of leaving her possessions unattended overnight, but she was in no position to object.

"I shall give you a leg up. You will ride behind me."

Helen accepted his outstretched hand and, rising, gazed into his eyes. "I must ride a-pillion?" she said, hating the wobble in her voice. Something about the man sent warning signals racing through her veins. She clutched her cloak at her throat. "You will be safe."

The padded pillion strapped behind the saddle gave little confidence of solidity, but Helen had no choice. Placing a hand on the man's shoulder, she let him boost her to the seat. The horse shifted beneath her. Her skirts tangled around her legs, and for a flustered moment she sat astride, hands gripping the cantle between her knees.

"Put your feet to the off side; you will find a platform." Once again she detected amusement in the man's voice. Smoothing her rumpled petticoats, Helen drew a deep breath in an attempt at composure. Her rescuer climbed back into his saddle. His broad back was close; his cape nearly engulfed her. Pushing it aside, she clutched the saddle's high cantle and tried to rise above her circumstances.

Warmth emanated from both man and horse. Helen's nostrils twitched. Along with the expected pungency of horse, leather, and male body, she caught a spicy fragrance that made her think of summer and gardens. "Better hang on to me," he said.

The horse started walking. Helen found it easy enough to balance her body, but her mind reeled with alarming speculations. The man's elegant carriage, cultured voice, and the hint of gallantry in his manner were at odds with his plain garments. Was he, in fact, a highwayman? Was she allowing herself to be abducted? Her head felt light from exhaustion even as a thrill swept through her.

"What is your name?" she demanded.

"Oliver Kirby. This wind is pushing the fog inland. We must hasten." The horse moved abruptly into a canter. Falling backward, Helen grabbed at Kirby's shoulders and hauled herself against him. Terror clutched her throat.

"I told you to hang on. Wrap your arms about my body."

Helen obeyed, keeping her hands fisted. His blowing hair tickled her face. His cape was cold and damp from fog or rain. She wanted to lash out at the man, but she held her tongue. He might decide to set her down beside the road and let her fend for herself. Which would be worse, abduction or desertion?

It was entirely improper for a lady to be so close to a man, on or off horseback. *What would Papa think if he were to see me now?* But the situation was oddly exhilarating—Oliver Kirby's shoulders looked enormous from this angle, and it was not unpleasant to lean against his solid back. He seemed cleaner than most men; she hoped he carried no lice.

Kirby? The name was familiar.

Not far ahead, the road disappeared into a murky gray cloud. A similar cloud of uncertainty oppressed Helen's soul. *Dear Lord, guide me into Your paths. I know not what to do! Are You here with me?*

"So you are the master's cousin?" Oliver Kirby called back.

"Aye, Master Kirby, we share grandparents." She lifted her face and voice against the wind.

"I am not your master; I am but a hired servant. Call me Oliver, as befits my station."

Astonishment rendered Helen silent. A hired servant? Surely not! To address such a man by his given name would seem brazen.

"What of your other family?" he asked.

"My parents died one year since."

"I am sorry. The plague?"

Helen was surprised to hear genuine sympathy in his deep voice. "Nay. They were both stricken in years. I was the child of their old age."

"And you have traveled here alone from. . .London?"

"Surrey. I traveled first on horseback in a caravan, then by river to Thetford. There I hired a coach."

"And the driver left you at the crossroads? The swine."

Helen thought this characterization apt. "Does my cousin often travel on business?"

"He has always liked to travel, both for business and for pleasure. These past few months he travels even more."

Helen found it difficult to imagine anyone traveling for pleasure. "Since his wife, Sarah, died, you mean. Her death devastated him, I know from his letters. But are there not three children yet living? Surely he must care for them," she protested.

Helen felt Oliver's shoulders move. "Now they have you." The horse slowed to a jog, then a walk. "It becomes too dark for the horse to run. Wrap my cloak about you. I hear your teeth rattle from the cold."

Helen thought he might actually be hearing the pounding of her head or the throbbing of her backside. She was far too chilled to disobey. Enveloped beneath the silk-lined cloak with only her face exposed, she refrained from further conversation.

Mist drifted along the ground. Above, lowering clouds concealed every star. Not one bird chirped a friendly good evening. No foxes yapped; not even a dog barked. Helen heard only the horse's muffled hoofbeats. She could feel Oliver's steady breathing. His back was warm. Helen could not determine which of her reactions to him took precedence, trepidation or security.

An unearthly cry floated through the fog. The horse snorted in response. "No self-respecting highwayman would be out on such a night," Oliver said firmly, as if to convince himself. At first Helen thought he was addressing her, but when he continued speaking she realized that he was talking to the horse. "Almost there. Soon you'll be back in your warm stall. However, you must be patient while I deliver the governess."

What manner of man spoke to a horse as if it could understand?

"We have arrived," Oliver announced.

The horse continued walking up a tree-lined drive, through an open gate, past several outbuildings. Torches lit the approach, yet light shone in only two of the manor house's many glass windows. Helen extricated herself from Oliver's cloak and scanned the looming brick building. "This is my cousin's home?"

Without bothering to answer, he dismounted and reached for her. She placed her hands on his shoulders and swung her legs over the saddle. His gloved hands nearly spanned her waist, sending hot waves of alarm through her body.

Oliver tossed the reins over the horse's neck and gave its haunch a slap. The animal trotted away, disappearing into the mist. "Enter." Taking Helen's arm, Oliver hurried her toward the house.

"Where are the other servants?" Helen planted her feet. "Where have you brought me?" Frost showered from her hood when she gripped it beneath her chin, and her quickened breath added to the surrounding fog.

He made no attempt to conceal his annoyance. "This is Biddlesham Hall, I warrant it. Wherefore no one has come to greet you, I know not. . .although, household matters have been in disarray since the mistress passed on and the house-steward left us. Now if you will but step inside, I shall find a maidservant who will relieve your fears."

Helen lifted her chin and tugged her arm from his grasp. "I am not frightened," she quavered.

"Oh, not in the least." He opened the door and ushered her inside.

The great hall was dark except for glowing coals on the hearth, which did nothing to warm the icy expanse. A portrait hanging over the fireplace fixed Helen with a disdainful stare. She shivered. How could anyone live in such a tomb?

"The fire needs stoking."

Helen followed at his heels to the stone hearth and watched while he blew the fire back to life. When the flames were crackling and bright, Oliver turned to face her, brushing off his breeches. "I'll go find Jenny or Maggie to show you to your room. Or Gretel. She is the housekeeper and a veritable dragon." A smile did little to soften his features.

Still gripping her cloak at her throat, Helen nodded. Frightening though it was to be so close to a man, the surrounding darkness was worse. How she longed for something, anything, familiar and secure!

"Once I find someone to show you to your room, you will feel better."

The words were kind, yet Helen sensed contempt. She crept toward the fire and lifted shaking hands to seek its warmth. "I am grateful. You are very good."

"Sit yourself nigh the fire. I shall return forthwith."

Helen felt panic rise in her throat. "Mayn't I come with you?"

He blinked. "To the kitchen? I suppose you may. You will need to learn your way about the house."

As one in a dream, Helen followed him along a hall to the back door, then along a covered walkway to the detached kitchen. Two elderly servants looked up from their tankards when Oliver entered. "Where you been, Master Oliver?" The plump man sounded well into his cups.

"Don't call me master," Oliver growled. "This is Helen Walker, the new governess. Helen, meet Cook and Gretel. Has anyone prepared the nursery room? Where is Maggie or Jenny?"

The iron-eyed woman called Gretel said, "If you ain't a master no more, you've no call to bark orders like one." She summed up Helen in one glance. "Puny, ain't she? Whiter than a ghost. I forgot she was coming."

A huge mastiff rose from the hearth and shoved its muzzle into Oliver's hand. Helen backed toward the doorway. Her mouth went dry. At any moment the dog might see her.

Oliver patted the animal absently. "Where are the maids?" he asked again.

"This is Friday; the others are gone to town or their homes, as you might recall if you would but settle your mind for a moment."

Oliver rubbed his chin. "Then you must help, Gretel. Helen needs a woman's care lest she take a chill and die ere she claps eyes upon the children."

Gretel's scraggly eyebrows rose. "She's a servant, same as us. Let her make up her own room, I say." She glared at Helen. "You'll find clean bed linens in a chest. The mattress is fresh stuffed."

Helen could not drag her gaze from that dog. Her feet were lead weights. Her mind seemed detached from her body.

Gretel tossed back her drink and wiped her mouth on her own plump shoulder. "If you're hungry, take whatever food you find."

At that moment, the mastiff noticed Helen. With a thunderous bellow, it rushed to investigate.

As from a distance, Helen heard Oliver shout at the dog. Enormous white teeth in a slavering red mouth loomed like approaching death. Her body went slack. First the beamed ceiling then the flagstone flooring flashed before her eyes. Dimly she expected to impact upon the stones, but something broke her fall. A deep voice repeated, "Helen?"

Chapter 2

Helen opened heavy eyelids and blinked. No light met her straining eyes. She lay adrift in total darkness. Panic filled her chest. *God? Are You here?* A quilt fell away when she struggled to sit up. Billowing softness surrounded her.

She sat in a feather bed, fully clothed.

At last, her eyes caught the dim glow from a banked fire. A muffled wail brought her fully awake. Somewhere nearby a child was crying. Helen flung off the quilt and put her feet to the floorboards. Groping with shaking hands, she discovered a bedside table, a tray, and what felt like cold meat and a roll. There it was—the hoped-for candle.

Helen slipped out of bed and knelt on the hearth, touching her candle's wick to the coals. Her heart pounded and her hands trembled—she could scarcely grip the taper. At last the candle flared to life, and Helen pressed it firmly into its holder. Protecting the feeble flame behind her cupped hand, she searched her chamber for a door. Did no one else hear those pitiful cries?

Two doors led from her bedchamber. The weeping came from behind the door nearest the windows. When Helen pushed it open, the creak of its hinges sent chills down her spine.

The stench of bodily waste made her clap a hand over her nose. Disgust overcame her fear of the dark. Did no one empty chamber pots in this house? Steeling herself, Helen lit a sconce on the wall and set her candle on a stool. As light filled the chamber, her knees gathered strength and her breathing deepened.

Three small beds lined the walls, each with a blanket-covered lump. The farthest lump reared up to reveal wide eyes in a round face. As Helen approached the child's bed, two skinny arms reached for her. She dropped to her knees and took the child in her arms. "I am Cousin Helen. Did you have a bad dream?"

The small head nodded against her shoulder. "A bad dog eated me, Cousin Helen."

Helen could relate to that nightmare. She patted the bony little back and encountered one source of the foul odor—the child's bedclothes and shift were soaked.

15

" 'Twas only a dream, little one. I think you will sleep better if we get you into dry clothing and a clean bed." Helen lifted her small charge and stripped the trembling body of its clinging gown. Every rib showed beneath the child's pale skin. Scars dotted her body. Helen's memory began to return. "You are Patsy?"

Patsy nodded. Her lower jaw shook with cold. "I can sleep with Avril."

"Where are your clean clothes?"

Patsy wrapped both arms around her thin body and shivered.

"Patsy, where do you keep your clothes?"

Realizing that the little girl would not or could not give her an answer, Helen began to search the room. She found a clean shift, several sizes too large, on a wall hook. "This will have to do."

"That is Avril's. She will be angry," Patsy stated as Helen enveloped her in the gown. The child's eyes were large and apprehensive in her thin face. Her hair appeared to have been chopped off at chin level.

"We will worry about that tomorrow, little one. Now is the time for good girls to sleep."

"You will be here when I wake?" Patsy reached small fingers to touch Helen's face. "I like you, Cousin Helen."

Helen scooped Patsy into her lap and rocked back and forth. "And I like you. I will be here in the morning. I am your new governess. I will care for you and Avril and your brother from now on." At the moment, the boy's name escaped her.

"My brother is Franklin. Joseph died of the spots. He was my other brother. My mother died too. Our old nurse went away and got married. Do not die, please, Cousin Helen?"

"I shall strive to remain alive for a long while yet, Patsy." Helen began to hum a little tune, pressing her cheek against the child's matted hair.

"I am hungry." Patsy's cheeks were sunken. Helen decided it would be wise to give her food whenever she craved it. She led Patsy into the other chamber and allowed the child to eat heartily from the loaded tray on the bedside table. After building up her fire and setting lighted candles about the room, Helen nibbled on a date and watched the little girl drain a cup of milk.

Her stomach nicely rounded, Patsy popped a thumb into her mouth as Helen carried her to Avril's bed. The child was asleep before Helen tucked her in. Avril frowned in her sleep and rolled toward the wall. The older girl's hair was as tangled and dirty as Patsy's—shorn during the recent bout of illness, Helen surmised. Had no one cared for these children since their mother's death?

Helen snuffed the light and returned to her chamber. She blew out her candles, leaving only one lit beside the bed. After removing her gown and petticoats, she crawled beneath her quilt, mentally listing the changes she would make on the morrow. "Dear Lord, give me strength to bring Your glory and love into this house," she whispered. "And please help me to endure this wretched darkness."

—⁓—

Morning light awakened Helen. Delighted to see streaks of sunshine on her bed-clothes, she climbed out of bed, pulled back the heavy draperies, and let light stream into her chamber. After stretching her stiff arms and shoulders, she poured water into her basin and began to splash her face. "Good morning, Lord Jesus."

She unbraided her hair and began to comb out its tangled length. Last night's fog had made ringlets out of the fringe on her forehead and around her ears. Helen tried to comb them out, creating puffs of curls. Lacking a mirror, she could only feel the disarray she had caused.

Someone knocked at the door. Probably a maid. "You may enter," Helen called.

Silence. Curious, she opened the door, then slammed it shut. Waiting in the hall was the man with the scornful smile and hawk nose. She had just shocked the life out of him, no doubt, answering the door in her smock, with her hair hanging loose! "One moment, please."

She pulled on her wrinkled gown. Tossing aside an assortment of petticoats, she hunted for her cap. *Where was I when I took it off?* Pausing abruptly, she wrinkled her brow. *I don't remember coming to this room last night. How did I get here?*

Another knock at the door. "I have your trunk," he explained in an overly patient tone.

The cap was nowhere in sight. Helen sighed. *I recall there was a huge dog. . . Or did I dream it? Or was that Patsy's dream?*

The next knock was harder.

Helen lifted the latch and pulled the door wide open.

"God give you good day, Helen Walker. I trust you slept well after your disturbing experience."

As usual, his deep voice hinted at derision. Helen's face burned. "My disturbing. . . ? Oh, aye. Thank you, um. . ."

"Oliver," he supplied. "I promised to bring your trunk today. Where would you like it placed?"

She stepped back and fixed her gaze upon the floor. "Against the wall between the windows, if you please. You must have risen before dawn. You are exceeding kind." She could not bring herself to address him by his first name. Did governesses often allow male servants to enter their bedchambers? Helen found the situation uncomfortable.

He hefted the trunk, crossed the small chamber without bumping into any furniture, lowered the trunk, and shoved it against the wall. "Is there anything else you'll be needing?"

Helen remained near the open door. She tried to sound friendly yet indifferent. "I'm sure I shall straightaway learn to feel at home here now that I have my trunk. It contains not only my clothing, but also my Bible and other items that belonged to my parents. Everything I own is packed inside."

"I, too, cherish a Bible among my belongings. Its translation was one of the few beneficial acts our late king accomplished. Do you read it often?"

She was startled into looking at him. "Every day. Are you a disciple of Jesus Christ? I mean, do you truly know God?"

This time Oliver lowered his gaze. "I do. Knowing Him is my only boast."

"And does the vicar in this parish teach from the Scriptures?"

"He does. There are many true believers in the community." Oliver shifted uneasily. A flush stained his high cheekbones. "You find it difficult to believe that I am a Christian."

Helen floundered for a moment. Ignoring his comment, she tried to speak brightly. "I must confess, I feared that I would find no one in East Anglia with whom to fellowship, but God has provided for my every need just as He promised. Please accept my apology. I was uncivil to you last night. Had I known you were a Christian, I would not have mistrusted you so."

Helen could not read his expression.

"It is I who should ask pardon," he said softly. "I should have perceived that you were nigh unto swooning and been more solicitous of your welfare."

"Swooning?"

He shook his head slowly, his eyes searching her face. "You do not remember?"

Helen swallowed hard. "Wha–what is it I should remember?"

The door to the nursery creaked open, and Patsy staggered into the room, rubbing her eyes. She lifted the hem of her borrowed gown to keep from tripping over it. Oliver greeted her. "What have we here? Good morrow, little lady."

Helen would never have believed the man could speak in such affectionate tones. He seemed to welcome the child as a reprieve.

Patsy blinked up at him. "Uncle Oliver, wherefore are you here?" Then she caught sight of Helen. Her face lit up, and she dashed across the room to fling herself into Helen's open arms. "You're not a dream!"

"No, darling, I am real," Helen assured the child, holding her close.

"Did you bring Cousin Helen for me, Uncle Oliver?" Patsy twisted around in Helen's arms to inquire. "She says she came to take care of us. I think God must have sent her. I prayed for a new mother, although Avril told me not to. Maybe Father will marry her and we will be a family again."

"This cannot be, Patsy, for I am your close relation," Helen hastened to inform the child. "Cousins may not wed by order of the church."

Patsy's face fell. "But I do so want a mother."

"I understand. Would you like to hear me read a story? I have a Bible in my trunk. It has the most wonderful stories you ever heard."

"I will take my leave, ladies. Enjoy your cousin while you may, Patsy."

On that remark, Oliver closed the door behind him.

———

Jenny entered the kitchen, carrying an empty tray. "Those children were eating like trenchermen when I left the nursery. Must have worked up appetites with all the screeching and howling that went on this morn." After discarding the tray on a worktable, she ladled pottage into a bread bowl and joined the other servants for the noon meal.

"She's a glutton for work, this governess," Maggie complained around a mouthful of pottage. "Such a wee thing to be spouting orders like a queen!"

"And how she did handle that Franklin when he tried to escape the bathin'!" Jenny added, giving a snort of laughter. "Took the lad by the back of his neck, she did, and popped him in the tub pretty as you please! Not even the late mistress could make that one do as he was told. I wonder how long it will be before the young knave starts his usual tricks and makes this governess wish she had never heard of Biddlesham Hall."

Gretel frowned and shook her gray head. "Weak as the children be, she'll be the death of them with this washing and this opening of windows. The master will return to find his offspring dead of lung fever, for certain."

"I do wonder what he will say," one of the gardeners agreed. "However, this Helen be a friendly enough wench. Leaned out her window to compliment me on the gardens today whilst I was trimming topiaries. Not above her station, that one."

Jenny scoffed. "So you say! Thinks she's mistress of the hall, she does. How my arms ache from toting water up and down, up and down so's she could wash."

Maggie laughed, displaying gaps between her yellowed teeth. "Puts me in mind of Oliver and his fancy for soap and water!" She dug an elbow into Oliver's ribs. He continued eating.

Jenny ranted on. "She had me digging through chests and trunks for clean clothing. Says she is taking the children out for fresh air. As if the nursery ain't awash with cold air from the windows hanging open all the day!"

"She will be good for them."

All eyes turned to Oliver. "What did you say?" Gretel demanded.

He rose and tossed his soggy bread bowl out the window to the waiting chickens and geese. Eyeing the other servants coldly, he said, "Helen is exactly what those children need—someone to love them and give them hope for the future. Attend upon me now: We must keep Diocletian out of Helen's way until the master returns. Quincy," he addressed the undergroom, "I place you in charge of the dog. Do you hear?"

Quincy nodded.

Gretel gave a cackle. "Gone soft on her, has our master-of-horse. Today I asked her how she liked being put to bed by Oliver, and she looked nigh unto swooning all over again."

Laughter rippled about the table, then suddenly hushed. Oliver cast a glare around the room. After one slap of his gloves against the tabletop, he strode outside into the brilliant sunlight.

Speculative glances and whispers followed his exit.

—⁓—

Helen paused to pray before selecting a pheasant leg from the noon trays. "Why did you do that?" Avril demanded, her gray eyes sullen.

"Why did I pray? I always thank the Lord for His provision. Look at this fine meal! Certainly we have much for which to thank Him." Helen smiled at the eight-year-old but received a blank stare in return.

Avril hunched her shoulders and munched on a crusty loaf. Soap and water had revealed a pretty child with pearly skin, luminous eyes, flyaway brown hair, and an aura of despair.

Franklin had not spoken a word since his enforced bath. Chewing with no effort to keep his mouth closed, he consumed only a few bites of meat and a handful of raisins.

Beside Helen, four-year-old Patsy gnawed on a cold meat pasty. Her exuberant hugs had lightened Helen's burden several times that morning.

Exhausted by the battle of wills and the physical labor, Helen began to doubt her own judgment. She now had three clean charges and a tidy nursery, but she feared she had created at least one lifelong enemy. Franklin's gaze held even more venom than Avril's, and the servants had seemed less than pleased by her requests for their extra labor. Had she not been the master's cousin, she suspected they would have refused outright.

To make matters worse, her thoughts kept returning to Oliver Kirby. He was, by his own admission, a fellow believer, yet his presence inspired in Helen a confusing blend of admiration and apprehension. Not that Scripture prohibited manliness while encouraging godliness; Helen had simply never before encountered a man possessed of both qualities in full measure.

If only she were well enough acquainted with Gretel to know whether or not to believe the housekeeper's astonishing report. Whenever she tried to envision her unconscious self in Oliver's arms, her mind flitted away in denial while her face grew hot.

Brushing her hands on her apron, Helen rose, strolled to the window, and looked down upon the terraced garden. Raised beds and pebbled walkways, paths that disappeared beneath bowers of interwoven tree branches, and a sunlit sweep of lawn reached as far as the distant woods. Pressing both palms against her warm cheeks, Helen drank in the perfume of evergreens and herbs.

Her heart expanded. "Thank You, Lord Jesus," she whispered. "If the children can learn to love me, I shall be content to live here. Please help me to find my place."

She turned back to the children with a bright expression. "After luncheon we shall walk in the gardens. It is a fine day, and we all need fresh air."

Chapter 3

One sunny afternoon more than a week after her arrival, Helen headed for the stables. Finding a groom cleaning stalls, she inquired, "Where might I find Oliver Kirby?"

The young man removed his cap. "In the pasture by the orchard, training the master's green colt. I'm Quincy the under-horseman, just so's you know. Your company will pleasure Oliver. He watches you take the children out to play every day. He says he's watching the children, but I know better."

Helen didn't like the way he smiled. "Thank you. Good day." Lifting her skirts, she picked her way through the stable yard, scattering chickens and ducks.

She met Oliver on his way back to the stable. Helen maintained a respectful distance from his lively mount. Oliver had removed his doublet, wearing only a full-sleeved white shirt above his loose breeches and cuffed boots. Although his hat bore no plume, he resembled the most dashing of cavaliers. Helen was uncertain which intimidated her more, Oliver or the horse.

"Braveheart, meet another valorous soul." Patting the colt's sweaty neck, Oliver grinned at Helen.

"I have come to enlist your aid," Helen announced in a nervous tremolo.

"Indeed? Where are the children?"

"With the head gardener. Guy is teaching them to plant parsnips. I would not leave them alone."

"My mind is now at rest. In what manner may I help you, Helen Walker? Will you climb up behind me here on Braveheart? We can better converse while in close proximity."

Wishing she could smack him, Helen backed away. "I will walk." She fell into step beside the tall horse, keeping a wary distance. "I find that the children have few outdoor playthings," she began.

"Franklin cares little for sport. Nevertheless, I will find a ball for you, and we can obtain hoops from the cooper. Is this the aid you require?" He sounded disappointed.

"Cousin Helen!"

Helen turned to see Avril running up the path. "Look what I found in the kitchen garden!" She held out a rock. "It has gold streaks in it. Guy says it isn't gold, but how would a gardener know? I want my doll to have it."

Helen heard stamping hooves and snorting behind her. Gripping Avril by the shoulders, she hurried the girl toward the gardens. "That would be nice, dear. Now return to Guy—he must wonder what became of you."

Avril peered around Helen. "Franklin says he will ride away on Braveheart someday."

Squeals and grunts from the horse roused Helen's curiosity. She turned to find Oliver wrestling with the rearing animal. Hooves, tail, and powerful quarters whirled past her at close range.

"Off the path!" Oliver ordered.

Helen pressed against a hedge while Braveheart thundered past. Avril sighed from the shelter of Helen's arm. "Is he not magnificent?"

"Aye, and his steed is fine also," Helen breathed.

—∿∿—

"I beg pardon for Braveheart's misconduct," Oliver said while hanging the colt's bridle upon a hook. "He is but newly broken to ride and finds it arduous to submit his will unto mine."

Still somewhat breathless, Helen simply returned his smile. Oliver touched her elbow and escorted her from the stable. "Avril is like unto a different child since your arrival."

Helen avoided looking at her companion. "Aye, she has become a veritable magpie. Poor child—how she mourns her hair! I assured her that it will grow as does her strength. The girls enjoy being clean and neat, and they love to learn and hear stories."

Oliver noticed an omission. "Has Franklin given you trouble?"

"I know not how to think of him. He keeps to himself unless provoking one of his sisters. The child never smiles or laughs. He seems unnatural. Does he talk to you?"

"Seldom. Since Sarah's death he has retreated into himself. Does he respond to your attentions?"

"Embracing him is like embracing a stone. And one more thing. . ."

"Aye?" Oliver encouraged.

For once Helen did not feel as if Oliver were inwardly ridiculing her. She stopped and faced him, studying her hands. "I have discovered. . .problems in the nursery. Once the ropes supporting my bed gave way suddenly. One night there was little water in my pitcher—it was all on the foot of the bed. Once I found my clothing strewn about the room. I hate to suspect one of the maids of such childish tricks, but I also dread to believe that Franklin would be so cruel."

"Someone should have warned you. Be aware that Franklin has a knack for finding a weakness and exploiting it. If it helps at all, know that I am on your side in this conflict."

Helen smiled and looked up. "You have no idea how much it helps! I have felt alone here, with no one to pray with or talk to except the children."

Oliver regarded her for a long moment. His lashes were so thick and dark she could scarcely see his eyes. "You can talk with God."

"I do. He is my constant confidant."

"I believe you. But have you ever before confided in a man, Helen?"

"Only my father."

Oliver's lips twitched. "I thought as much. You are as jumpy as a fawn whenever a man approaches. Or is it only me?"

"I–I don't know what you mean." Helen slipped her hand up to finger her neckcloth.

"Even as you illustrate my point." Oliver caught her fidgeting fingers. "Do you suspect me of dire intentions? A man tires of being regarded as a ravening wolf."

Helen tugged at her hand, her gaze fixed upon the brown hollow at the base of his throat. He allowed her fingers to slip through his grasp. "Why must you make sport of me? I cannot be at ease around someone who thinks ill of me no matter what I do or say!" Helen blurted while backing away.

She turned and ran toward the house.

—⁓—

Two days later, a breeze rippled the surface of the lake, sending sparkles of sunlight into Helen's eyes. Four white swans floated near a stand of cattails and rushes, ignoring the children's attempts to entice them with bread. Wildflowers carpeting the lakeshore shaded up a knoll into the verdant lawn. New leaves clothed overhanging tree boughs.

"Altogether lovely!" Helen breathed deeply. "This is my favorite artwork—God's masterpiece of creation."

"You smile a lot, Cousin Helen," Avril observed. "Do you find everything comical?"

Helen couldn't restrain a chuckle. "Not everything. But I do find joy and amusement in many things. The Bible tells us to 'rejoice evermore.' God wants His children to be joyful."

"He must be pleased with you," Patsy said, bouncing in Helen's lap. "Except that you're not a children."

Helen hugged the little girl. "In God's eyes, I will always be a child."

"I guess He's pretty old," Patsy stated.

Helen lay back on the grass and laughed aloud. "Patsy, dearest, you're a treasure."

Franklin knelt on the lakeshore, poking with a stick at something down in the water like any other nine-year-old boy might. But, unlike a normal boy, he did not join the conversation.

"Cousin Helen, are you going to marry our father? He said he would find us another mother."

Helen answered the challenge in Avril's eyes. "Your father asked me to come because you children need someone to care for you. I came because I need a family to love since my parents died and left me alone. The Lord provided for everyone's needs at once. If your father does choose another wife, I'm sure he will marry a woman who will love his children."

"If he marries again, will you have to go away?"

"Let's not worry about the future, Avril."

"Father doesn't like us since Mother died. Uncle Oliver plays with us sometimes, though," Patsy announced. "He throwed the ball to me yesterday, and I catched it bunches of times. Franklin said I never could."

Pleased that the subject of Oliver had arisen, Helen tried to question delicately. "Why do you call Oliver 'Uncle'?"

"He is our uncle," Avril said. "Our mother was his sister."

"He is your—" Helen was too surprised to continue. No wonder Oliver was so obviously a gentleman. No wonder "Kirby" sounded familiar—it had been Sarah Biddlesham's maiden name. From everything Helen could recall hearing, Cousin Cyril had married into a propertied family of good repute. She longed to ask why Oliver now worked as horseman for his brother-in-law.

"May we wade in the lake?" Franklin asked abruptly. His knees were damp, and mud smeared his jerkin. "I want to catch tadpoles."

Helen hated to disappoint the boy the first time he requested anything of her, but. . .

"What's the matter, Cousin Helen? Don't you like tadpoles? They grow up into frogs." Patsy patted Helen's hand. "Franklin likes to catch frogs and toads and newts."

Helen struggled to turn her grimace into a smile. "How interesting! However, I fear it is too cold for wading as yet." Casting about for an alternative, she brightened. "You could climb these marvelous oaks." She plopped Patsy upon the grass and leaped to her feet, brushing grass clippings from her skirts and peeling off her gloves.

The children stared as Helen patted a sprawling oak's lowest branch. "Come," she coaxed. "Have you never climbed a tree? I often climbed trees during my childhood. From the branches of this one, I'm sure you could touch the sky!"

Helen helped Patsy find a secure place on one of the tree's massive support branches, while Franklin and Avril headed for a nearby oak. "Is this not enjoyable?"

Patsy grinned. "I'm a squirrel." She wrapped both legs around the limb.

"You're a bright-eyed red squirrel with tufted ears." Helen patted the child's knee and savored Patsy's adoring smile.

"Cousin Helen, look at me!" A call came from the next tree.

Helen shaded her eyes and gazed at Avril. "My, but you're high like a bird on the wing!" she said. The girl smiled in satisfaction from a perch no more than ten feet from the ground.

Franklin appeared determined to out-daring-do his sister. Helen saw his foot slip and gasped inwardly, but the boy caught his balance and continued upward.

"Franklin, that is high enough. Can you touch the clouds from there?" Helen tried to keep alarm from her voice. "Franklin, please stop climbing now. Franklin?"

The boy ignored her. At last he settled into a fork between branches and hollered down, "Look at me!"

Helen forced admiration into her voice. "Franklin, you must be higher than the church tower! Can you see all the way to Cambridge?"

He laughed. "I can see all the way to France."

Studying his position, Helen nibbled a fingernail. "Maybe you'd better come down now. Let's explore the maze."

Avril obediently slid toward the tree's trunk. A gust of wind made the trees groan and sway, leaves aflutter. Helen heard Franklin give a yelp. "Are you all right up there?"

Not a word in reply.

"Franklin, do you need help getting down?" Helen lifted Patsy from her perch and, with the child on her hip, trotted toward the other oak.

Avril scooted down the trunk and landed with a thump on her backside. Hopping up, she brushed herself off and joined Helen. Her cheeks and eyes glowed. "What else may we do, Cousin Helen?"

"We must wait for your brother before we try anything else," Helen said. She peered upward, shading her eyes. The topmost branches swayed back and forth. "Franklin?" Moving to the other side of the tree, she caught sight of his face. His eyes were squeezed shut. Both arms and legs gripped the tree. "Can you hear me?"

No response. The sisters echoed her call. Their shrill voices filled the air. "Come down, Franklin!"

"You girls stay here with your brother while I go for help," Helen ordered quietly. Franklin had sharp ears. "No! Don't leave me!" he screeched.

"I saw Guy, the gardener, mowing the grass only a short distance from here," Helen tried to assure him.

Franklin shook his head. "You can't go; I'll fall. You must come and catch me."

"But someone must get help. I cannot climb a tree!" Helen protested.

"Help me!"

26

The panic in his voice prevailed over fear and propriety. "Avril, find someone to help."

Avril nodded. "Do you want me to take Patsy?"

"Aye." Catching hold of a stout branch, Helen swung into the tree and began to work her way upward. "Hurry, girls!" Tree-climbing was not as easy as she remembered. Her shoes slipped on the rough bark. Her cumbersome skirts snagged on twigs and bark.

A stout branch beneath Franklin's perch supported Helen's weight. Gripping another branch with one hand, she stood on tiptoe and touched the boy's ankle. "You could slide into my arms, Franklin. I am here to catch you."

Freckles looked dark upon his white cheeks. His face scrunched into a mass of wrinkles. "You're too small. You would drop me!"

"I am stronger than I look," Helen said.

"Helen?" A deep voice inquired from below.

Helen looked down. The world tilted. Oliver Kirby's upturned face appeared distant, and the girls' faces were small dots.

"I'm coming up."

Helen tried to focus on a distant hill, but that one downward glance had destroyed her equilibrium. No wonder poor Franklin was afraid to move! "Dear Lord God, please strengthen our fainting hearts and bring us safely back to earth," she prayed aloud. "Thank You for sending Oliver to our aid."

Closing her eyes, she slithered her feet along the branch until she could hug the main bough. Another gust of wind made the tree wave and groan. Helen's groan followed shortly thereafter.

"I'm right beneath you." Oliver said. "Can you move to that fork in the branch there? Otherwise I must climb around you to reach Franklin."

"I can move." Helen extended one shaky foot and tried to release her death-grip on the bough. Oliver guided her foot to a safe place, then shinnied up far enough to hold her waist while she shifted her weight to the other branches. He held her arm even after she was securely seated.

"I will be all right now. Please help Franklin."

"You are certain?" His fingers squeezed gently. Today he wore no gloves. His sleeves were rolled up, revealing hairy forearms. Resisting the urge to grab hold around his neck, Helen nodded.

Through a haze of dread, Helen watched Oliver coax Franklin into his arms. With the boy hanging like a sack on his back, Oliver climbed down the tree. Although Helen could not distinguish Oliver's words, his kindly voice gave her comfort.

"Come down, Cousin Helen. Franklin is safe now." Avril's shout penetrated Helen's fears.

Four faces looked pale against the green grass far below. Helen felt a tear spill over and hated herself. "I can't!" she whispered.

Oliver gathered the children around. Helen opened her eyes in time to see her three charges dash across the lawn, giggling and shouting. Patsy tripped over her dress and fell but she hopped up without a cry and chased the others.

Oliver scrambled up the tree. "I sent the children to gather wildflowers," he confessed while still several branches beneath her. She noticed how he avoided glancing upward lest he inadvertently look up her skirts. "I thought you might find it easier to descend without an audience. Are you injured, Helen?"

"No." A sob escaped. "I am a fool."

"I suspected as much," he said in that bantering tone she despised. "How do you come to acknowledge it?" He panted slightly as he pulled himself to her level. His hands each gripped a branch, one on either side of her legs. His hair glistened with strands of gold and silver where sunbeams touched it. Deep lines framed his mouth.

Helen wiped away a tear. "I did well until I looked down."

He chuckled, showing white teeth. "You will notice that I avoid looking down. Such height would frighten any person of sense. Franklin chose the largest tree in the park for his first attempt at climbing."

"The fault is mine. I encouraged them to climb. I thought it would be good exercise." Knowing that sooner or later Oliver would have to touch her, Helen felt her heart rate increasing. His kindness was more unnerving than his derision.

"And so it is. You are the best thing to come to this manor in many a long year, Helen."

Doubting his sincerity, Helen looked into his eyes. They were blue, she realized. How dark they had seemed beneath his thick brows! Beautiful eyes in an otherwise hawkish face.

Releasing her grip on the branches, she reached a hand toward him. His palm was warm and rough. One of her feet slipped, but Oliver caught her by the elbow. "Take care. If you fall, I am here to catch you."

Oliver coaxed her to follow his lead. His arms and legs were like a safety net around her. He seldom touched her, but she felt his body heat at all times, he was so close. Helen frequently clutched at his arms and found herself leaning in order to feel his solid chest against her back.

"Hold to the tree, Helen. It is stronger than I," he reminded her more than once. Helen began to wonder if she were dreaming.

At last Oliver hopped to the ground and reached both arms toward her. Interpreting this as an invitation to jump, she let go of the tree and dropped. Oliver managed to break her fall, but her impetus landed him flat upon the grass. Locked together, they rolled over like a log and came to rest side by side. Helen stared into his eyes. "I beg your pardon!"

Oliver stared back. Silence stretched long until Helen felt her face grow hot. She attempted to get up, but Oliver's encircling arms restrained her as if she were a butterfly, using just enough force to keep her from fluttering away. She placed both hands against his chest, yet she did not push. His heart pounded against her palms.

Then he released her and quickly stood, facing away from her with his arms crossed. "Here come the children. I must warn you that Franklin will not like your knowing about his fear."

"And I am not pleased that he knows about my fear," Helen admitted shakily. "I hope this is not something he can use against me."

Laughing and chattering, two little girls trotted across the green lawn. "We brought you flowers, Cousin Helen!"

Avril dropped daisies into Helen's lap. Patsy showered her with dandelions and tiny blue flowers that had already wilted beyond recognition. Franklin approached more slowly, wearing a smirk that should have put Helen on her guard.

"Let's make daisy chains," Helen suggested. Crossing her legs to make a table of her lap, she began to sort through the flowers. She hoped the children had not witnessed that embrace. *Did it really happen or did I dream it?*

Oliver turned. "I must return to work. I am pleased to see you and the children enjoying these gardens. I have often lamented the fact that only Diocletian and I appeared to appreciate their beauty. The gardeners work hard to keep this place up."

Helen scanned her surroundings and slowly shook her head—the brilliant hues of spring bulbs, the pale green of new leaves like a mist upon every tree, the smooth lawns. " 'Enjoying' scarcely begins to express how such beauty affects me. This place is a tiny foretaste of heaven."

Looking up at Oliver, she added, "Many thanks for your aid, and God be with you, Oliver Kirby." His name was pleasant upon her lips.

"And with you, Helen Walker. Helping you affords me unparalleled diversion." His eyes twinkled, but this time Helen did not mind.

"Did Avril run all the way to the stables to find you?" she suddenly thought to ask.

"I was working with the colt again in the pasture just beyond the fence," Oliver explained. "I heard the shouting and came to investigate."

"Do you need help, Uncle Oliver?" Franklin asked.

Oliver gave Helen an inquiring glance. "Do you mind if Franklin joins me for an hour or two?"

"Not at all." To Helen's amazement, Franklin talked animatedly until he and Oliver disappeared around a hedge. "Does Franklin often help your uncle?" she asked.

Avril shook her head. "He doesn't help anyone, ever. But he likes horses."

Helen smiled while threading one daisy's stem through another. This day was a tremendous answer to prayer, even to prayers she had never dared utter.

"I like playing in the garden, Cousin Helen. May we play here every day?" Patsy tucked dandelions among Helen's braids.

Helen felt as if her chest might burst with the fullness of joy. "Aye, every sunny day!"

Avril chuckled. "You're making God happy again," she said. "You make Uncle Oliver smile. I wonder if you can make Father smile. He hasn't smiled much since our mother died."

Helen touched the girl's slender arm. "I can't make anyone smile, Avril. Only God can put joy into people's hearts."

Avril shook her head. "I still think He uses you to do it, Cousin Helen."

Chapter 4

Sleep well, children." Helen kissed each child in turn. The girls returned her hugs, but Franklin endured his kiss and hug stoically. After blowing out the candles, Helen closed the nursery door and leaned against it. Tonight her room seemed friendlier, even though shadows flickered in every corner. The day's sunshine, flowers, and fresh air lingered within Helen's soul.

A heavy knock at her chamber door brought her back to the present with a start. "Master Cyril has returned. He requests your presence in his drawing room." It was Gretel's voice.

"Cyril has returned?" The man must have sneaked into his house like a thief, Helen decided. Although now that she thought about it, there had been unusual commotion in the house while she prepared the children for bed. "He wants to meet me tonight?"

"He awaits you now."

"I shall come presently." With trembling hands Helen smoothed her hair—picking out a few wilted dandelions—inspected her face, removed her apron, and straightened her skirts. At last her questions about Cyril Biddlesham would be answered.

She opened her chamber door to find Gretel waiting. By the light of the house-keeper's candle, the two women traversed a long hallway past the stairwell, past rows of Biddlesham family portraits, to the other wing of the house. Gretel rapped on a door and pushed it open, stepping aside to allow Helen's entry.

The chamber was well lighted, although smoke and a sickly-sweet odor filled the air. As Helen entered, her cousin rose from a chair, then bowed over her hand. "Well met, Cousin Helen." Looking down from his considerable height, he smiled, crinkling his blue eyes. A pointed beard concealed his chin while his cheeks were clean-shaven. Dark hair curled softly on his shoulders with one beribboned lock hanging upon his broad chest. The froth of lace edging his falling band collar and the gold brocade of his doublet merely emphasized his air of romantic masculinity.

"Cousin Cyril," Helen murmured. She saw a remarkable resemblance to Avril in his countenance. Absorbed in her examination of his features, she forgot to remove her hand from his grasp. One of his brows lifted, and his moustache twitched.

A rumbling growl stopped Helen's breath. Turning her face toward the fireplace, she beheld the mastiff of her nightmares standing on the hearth. Its dripping flews quivered to reveal ivory tusks.

"Down, boy. Cousin Helen is family." Cyril patted her stiffened shoulder. "Never fear; Diocletian will not harm you. Reach out to him."

Helen could not move. Hackles bristling along a spine the height of Helen's waist, the dog held her in a fixed stare.

"Are you deaf, child? Show the dog that you do not fear him, or he will despise you."

"But I do f–f–fear. . . ," Helen faltered.

"Nonsense. A nobler beast than Diocletian never lived. Reach out your hand and touch him."

Silently claiming every protection promise in Scripture, Helen obeyed. As soon as her fingers stroked his. head, Diocletian relaxed. His heavy tail wagged, and his ears drooped.

Thank You, Lord.

"Now come and sit across from me here before you topple to the floor." Cyril indicated a second carved oak chair. "Tales of your endeavors have already reached mine ears. Is it true that you applied soap to my son?" Cyril took a clay pipe from the mantelshelf, sucked on it, and puffed smoke.

Trying not to cough, Helen settled into the chair. "Aye, cousin."

"You must possess more fortitude than is now in evidence. Although, it is true, Franklin is a weakly child." A melancholy expression filled Cyril's eyes. "His brother was robust and intelligent, a true Biddlesham. If illness can take a boy like my Joseph, I hold little hope that the others will survive to become adults. However, I am thankful you have come to take charge of them while they live. Since your father was a man of the cloth, I'm sure you will help prepare their souls for eternity."

Helen scooted forward on the chair until her feet touched the floor. "I see no reason why your children should not live to maturity, barring some unforeseen illness. I shall certainly strive to train them in godly ways and guide them into all truth. They are intelligent, resourceful children, especially Franklin. I believe that—"

Cyril continued as if she had not spoken. "For some reason, we have always had difficulty keeping a nurse or governess in our employ longer than the requisite year. Perhaps the problem is our remote location. . ." His voice trailed off, and he sucked on the pipe again.

Helen dared to break the silence. "I believe it would benefit Franklin to be oft in your company. The boy craves the guidance of a man. I will bring the children to call upon you each day at whatever time you choose."

Cyril puffed for a full minute before replying. "I have no desire to attend my offspring every day. It would, perhaps, be advisable for me to observe their progress each week. Let us say you bring them to me here in my drawing room for a brief interview each Saturday evening. I do wish to see them tomorrow morning, however, to inspect the progress you have made during my absence. I plan to marry soon; I am newly betrothed to the widow of a wool merchant from Ipswich. Courtship and business will demand the majority of my time in these coming months."

"You—you plan to marry? You never wrote of this intent. . ."

Cyril's lips twitched. "I was unaware of it myself until last week. The bewitching creature has convinced me that man was not meant to be alone."

"I see." Concern for the children filled Helen's thoughts. Would the "bewitching creature" make a good stepmother?

Movement at her side startled Helen. Pressing one hand to her heart, she stared down into beseeching eyes. Diocletian laid his black muzzle upon her skirt, leaving streaks of drool upon the fabric. In her peripheral vision Helen saw his tail waving, but she could not lift her gaze from the dog's face.

"Hmm." Cyril sounded mildly pleased. "You have found favor in Diocletian's eyes—a rare honor. He must recognize a relative; there is a Biddlesham look about you. I dimly recall your mother, my aunt. She lived here until her marriage—a comely woman. Your father was a diminutive, bookish sort. Her acceptance of his suit puzzled the family. But then, in neither a vicar nor a governess is height a requirement." A sardonic smile curled his moustache.

Helen laid a trembling hand on the dog's head and saw the thick tail increase its tempo. A pink tongue, nearly as large as Helen's hand, swiped over the dog's lips and nose. The head on Helen's lap felt as heavy as Patsy's entire body. Although the hair on Diocletian's head was rough, his ears were warm velvet.

Perhaps her cousin was right and this dog named for a cruel Roman posed no threat. It was difficult to believe that a body so large, possessed of such teeth, could contain a gentle heart.

She spoke quietly. "My parents loved each other deeply—"

"Your parents married late in life." Cyril dropped into his chair and stretched his long legs toward the hearth. Firelight reflected from his forehead. Helen now noticed his receding hairline and the lines framing his mouth and eyes. She heard the creak of stays whenever he moved.

"And I was their only child. We had a happy home in Wyttlethorpe parish. My father was schoolmaster as well as vicar, so I received an excellent education."

"The quality of your letters told me as much. I trust you will pass on that education to my progeny as long as you are in my employ. I do not wish them to attend the school in Biddlesham Fen village. It has been my observation that congregating in masses brings on illness. My apothecary advises keeping the children apart from others of their age and feeding large quantities of white meats."

"Milk and eggs?" Helen translated the term in puzzlement. "What benefit does he hope to acquire from such diet?"

"Their good health." Cyril puffed rapidly at his pipe. "Have a care; I do not relish being questioned, cousin." Giving her a sidelong glance, he suddenly asked, "Have you seen our haunting spirit?"

Helen's blood ran cold. "Did you say. . . ?" Her spine stiffened. "Nonsense. I do not believe in ghosts."

"Be that as it may, an apparition walks the grounds of Biddlesham Hall. Some say the specter is my grandfather who walked every evening in the gardens. Since he is your ancestor as well, he might appear to you." A glitter in Cyril's eye told Helen that he baited her.

"Taunt me not with spectral tales. I am no child to be tormented so."

He grinned. "You seem a veritable infant, with those trusting eyes and dimpled cheeks."

"I am twenty-eight years of age and no babe," Helen snapped.

His eyes flashed sparks. "And I say you are a child. I warned you not to question me. Have done with you!" With a dismissing wave, he slumped back in his chair and puffed smoke.

Helen slid from beneath the mastiff's jowls. "Good even, Cousin Cyril."

He glowered into the fire. "Sleep well, cousin."

The dog escorted Helen to the door. Although she recognized the acceptance in his drooping eyes, the animal's presence made her knees go weak. "Good even, Diocletian," she murmured, reaching out to give his broad head a farewell pat. *You, at least, are a gentleman. Who behaved like a child just now? Not I and not you.*

"Take the dog down to the kitchen when you go," Cyril ordered without turning around.

After shooting a glare at her lounging cousin's back, Helen ventured to touch the dog's head once more. "Come, Diocletian."

The mastiff's head and tail lifted, and he rushed into the hallway, nearly knocking Helen off her feet. She heard soft laughter from the drawing room as she pulled the door shut. The passage was dark and silent, lighted only by an occasional wall sconce. Although she knew that men's disembodied spirits did not walk the earth— such a thing was entirely unbiblical—Helen found that her imagination had a will of its own. Lifting her chin, she swallowed her panic and trotted past all those closed doors toward the stairwell.

The dog waited at the back door when Helen caught up with him. "Here you are," she gasped. Diocletian was reassuringly solid and alive beneath her hands. He willingly escorted her to the out-buildings, waiting politely while she opened the doors.

A roaring fire warmed the kitchen. Cook lounged at the table with both feet on a bench. He gave her a glance, then looked again from Helen to the dog. He exclaimed something unintelligible as his feet hit the floor, and Helen wondered if the man might be foreign.

"Does the dog stay with you, Cook?" Helen asked.

"But the dog. . . We are to keep the dog away from you since he makes you swoon! How is it that you walk with him so calm?"

"My cousin introduced me to Diocletian tonight." Helen patted the dog once more, feeling pride in her accomplishment.

"Ah." Cook still looked mystified. "Master Oliver will not believe me when I tell him." His jowls flopped as he shook his head.

"You say the dog made me swoon? I do not recall. . ." Helen wrinkled her brow in the effort to remember.

" 'Twas the night you came. Master Oliver caught and carried you away. No one else was to touch! Romantic, eh? All the servants talk about how he watches over the little governess and defends you from harm. Always he keeps to himself, but now he finds reason to be near you. A good man he is for a good woman. It gives him shame that King James stole away his lands." Glancing furtively about, Cook crossed himself and winked soberly at Helen.

Smiling to hide her confusion, Helen excused herself and backed out the door.

Once in her chamber, she prepared for bed, panting from her frenzied run up the dark stairs. When her dress and petticoats lay in a heap on the floor, she splashed her face and neck with water from the basin, then rubbed her face with a towel. "I wish Cousin Cyril cared more for his children. I had parents who adored me—a blessing I would not trade for any amount of wealth or beauty. Perhaps his new wife will be the mother for which Patsy prays. Lord, I must trust You to provide for these children."

She paced across the room while taking down her abundant hair. Her candle flickered. Helen stopped and stared until the flame straightened.

Ashamed of her inordinate alarm, she heaved a sigh. "As if darkness could harm me. Lord, why must I be so fearful? 'I sought the Lord, and he heard me, and delivered me from all my fears,' " she quoted. "You did enable me to overcome my fears many times today, Lord Jesus. There was the tree—although Oliver in effect had to carry me down, I don't believe he realized the extent of my fear. And I actually befriended a dog! Only You could provide such courage. Cousin Cyril did not appreciate the magnitude of my victory, but You do."

Instead of picturing her handsome cousin, Helen dwelt upon memories of Oliver's rugged face. Smiling, she pulled her hair over one shoulder and stroked its length. "I wonder if Oliver would like my hair. It isn't a pretty color, but it is soft."

Warmth invaded her body and heart.

Leaning over, she braided her hair into a thick rope. "Oliver said I was the best thing to come here in many years." Not a particularly romantic statement, to be sure, but at the moment any positive remark from Oliver nourished her runaway fancy. "The servants say he watches over me."

A breeze from her open window made Helen shiver. After tying off the braid, she hurried to her bed and pulled back the quilt. Something dark lay upon the white ticking. Helen paused with one foot lifted. Teetering, she fell forward with hands braced on either side of the invading object.

At close range she beheld four outstretched legs, empty eye sockets, and a gaping mouth. A scream caught in her throat. Everything went dark except for that ghastly gray nightmare. She could not shift her gaze. Her body seemed frozen except for the throbbing beat in her ears.

At last she caught a gasping breath and flung herself away from the bed. Huddled on the floor with both arms wrapped around her folded legs, she rocked back and forth, whimpering. As her mind began to clear, her lips whispered psalms. " 'Yea, though I walk through the valley of the shadow of death, I will fear no evil: for thou art with me. . . The Lord is my light and my salvation; whom shall I fear? The Lord is the strength of my life; of whom shall I be afraid?' "

Wiping her eyes with the backs of her hands, Helen took a deep breath. "Certainly not of a toad. The creature has been dead for eons, from the look of it." She clambered to her feet, tripping on the edge of her smock. Her gaze avoided the bed. "But what shall I do now?"

A handkerchief provided her deliverance. Averting her eyes as much as possible, she gripped one of the toad's stiff legs with the folded cloth, carried it to the open window, and dropped it, handkerchief and all. The handkerchief unfurled and floated down like a falling leaf. Helen leaned over the sill but could see nothing of the toad in the bushes far below.

Stars glittered overhead, and nocturnal creatures chirped. Helen wished she were not afraid of the dark, for the gardens appeared enchanting by starlight. Spirals of mist drifted across the lawns and lurked behind hedges. In a few short weeks, the trellises and fences would be cloaked with sweetbriar and blooming vines, and the heady perfume of jasmine might rise even to Helen's window.

A dark figure near the lavender hedge caught Helen's attention. She recalled no bush or statue in that location. Craning her neck and squinting, she leaned farther out. Her hand slipped, and she gave a little cry before ducking back inside. *How foolish I am!* she berated herself while waiting for her heart to stop its thundering. *Come morning, I shall be able to see the statue clearly instead of breaking my neck while trying to see in the dark.*

A chilly wind made her reach to close the window. Her hand stopped short. Her widening eyes searched the lavender hedge in vain. The dark figure was gone.

Seconds later she was huddled beneath her quilt in the middle of the bed. The breeze caused by her wild rush had extinguished her candle, leaving Helen to shiver in complete darkness.

Chapter 5

As dawn lit the eastern horizon, Helen pulled her dress over her head, bound her hair, and donned a cap and shawl. After scooping up her Bible, she marched downstairs with eyes straight ahead, determined not to run like a rabbit from invisible predators lurking in dark corners of the house.

She lifted the bar and opened the back door. Gray morning light touched her face. Smoke trickled from the kitchen chimney—*Cook must already be at work.* Helen stepped outside into a wonderland of silvery mist, dewy grass, and sleeping flowers. A spiderweb shimmered between two shrubs, its weaver waiting patiently for the sun to awaken a prospective meal.

Helen searched the back of the house for her bedchamber window, then hurried to hunt through the bushes below it for her handkerchief. The square of white cambric was nowhere to be seen. Might a bird have carried it away? There had been no wind last night. She searched behind and beneath the topiary hedges to no avail.

Giving up at last, she entered the formal gardens in search of a bench. Her footprints were dark on the grass, and the hem of her dress became damp. She saw other, smaller prints in the dew; a rabbit or a fox had traversed the garden earlier that morning.

Beneath a trellis she found a wooden bench. After wiping it dry with her apron, she settled down and opened her Bible. Daily readings had taken her to the book of Isaiah, where she had become somewhat bogged down. Beginning with chapter forty-one, she buckled down to read. Two verses on, her mind and her eyes wandered from the page.

She sucked in a deep breath and released it in a tremulous sigh. Another sleepless night consumed in terror of the unknown.

A bird began to warble from a nearby beech, and sunlight pierced the mist, turning dewdrops into diamond-drops. Helen's lips quivered; tears overflowed. Wiping her face with an already soggy apron corner, she mourned aloud. "Why, Lord, do I doubt You whenever darkness falls? I have no trouble believing while the sun shines; but as soon as trials enter my life, my courage fails. I read Your Word daily, yet I draw little sustenance from it. How I long to talk again with my father and mother, to emulate their wisdom and soak up their strength!"

In the silence following her outburst, Helen considered her words. *Do I have faith of my own, or have I relied upon my parents to have faith in my stead? Is God truly my Father? He is never a grandfather—I cannot depend upon my parents' faith to save me.*

Discouraged, she again began to read. The tenth verse widened her eyes. She read it again, aloud. " 'Fear thou not; for I am with thee: be not dismayed; for I am thy God: I will strengthen thee; yea, I will help thee; yea, I will uphold thee with the right hand of my righteousness.' "

With a moist smile, Helen lifted her gaze to the sky. "Lord Jesus, You have promised to be with me always, even unto the end of the world. I know that You created all things and that nothing is too difficult for You. You promised to hold me in the palm of Your almighty hand. I shall not fear things that walk by night. I shall not fear the beasts You have created. I shall not fear the wrath or mockery of man. I shall not fear the future. You are the Lord, and beside You there is no savior."

She read on, finding promises and assurance in every chapter.

Some time later, sensing another presence, Helen lifted her head. Oliver leaned one shoulder against a stone archway and watched her. "I wondered when you would notice me."

Helen snapped her Bible shut and rose quickly. His hair dripped water, and his shirt clung to his damp torso. His booted feet were crossed, and his head was bare.

Was he impervious to cold? Helen gathered her shawl closer to her shoulders and tried to restrain a shiver that was not entirely induced by the morning chill. "How long have you been there?" she demanded.

"Not long. I, too, often come to the garden to commune with my Lord." Despite the twinkle in his eyes, Oliver's voice held a tender note that soothed Helen's nerves. "Upon returning from my daily ablutions in the pond, I saw your footprints leading away from the house and followed them here. I apologize for disturbing your meditation."

Helen shook her head and took a few hesitant steps toward him. The gateway he blocked was her only exit from the enclosed garden. "You wash in the lake?"

"I swim on all but the coldest of days."

"In your clothing?" she asked before thinking.

"Nay, to walk about in wet attire would invite illness."

After contemplating his answer for a moment, Helen felt her face flame.

Oliver laughed softly, then sobered. "Are you well, Helen? Does aught trouble you?"

Startled by his insight, she glanced up, met his probing eyes, and again dropped her gaze. "I have brought my troubles to the Lord. Now I believe all will be well. But I thank you for the inquiry."

Pushing away from the archway, he took a step toward her. "You carry a heavy burden on your slight shoulders. Franklin alone is more burden than many could bear. He is my sister's child; I would share that load with you if will allow it."

Emboldened by her concern for the children, Helen searched Oliver's eyes. He seemed sincere. "I am grateful for your offer," she whispered, unable to find her voice.

He approached and reached a cold but dry hand to touch her cheek. Helen closed her eyes. "You were weeping," he said. "Why?"

Helen swallowed hard. "I am learning how little faith I have," she admitted. "I find it difficult to trust the Lord with my life. Always I have had my parents to depend upon; now I have only God. I know that He is sufficient and that only He can truly meet my spirit's deepest longings. Yet in the darkest hours of night, when fears assail me, I find it hard to realize His presence."

He nodded. "I struggle with similar trials, Helen. Since the day of your arrival, I have come to realize that others can see little of Jesus in my life. Your amazement that I, too, was a believer shocked me to my senses."

Her eyes widened. "Oh, but I did not intend—"

A smile touched his lips. "I understand that you meant no offense. I cannot imagine you intentionally hurting anyone. Your surprise was genuine, the very reason it was effective. You struggle against fears; I fight daily, hourly against overweening pride." Blinking, he studied the top of a distant oak. "It is a fierce battle."

Helen touched his arm. "I will pray for you, Oliver."

He lowered his gaze to her hand. It looked small and weak against his sinewy forearm. Embarrassed, Helen started to pull it away, but he quickly clapped his other hand over hers and held it in place. "And I will pray for you, Helen."

—ᴡ—

From the tiny white temple in the middle of the rose garden, Helen could see over the top of the maze and glimpse the pasture beyond. Two distant figures held her interest—a horse trotting in measured circles and the man on its back.

"What are you staring at, Cousin Helen?" Avril asked, joining her at the window. "Do you like Braveheart? I like his two white legs and pink hooves."

"It is a beautiful horse," Helen agreed.

"Uncle Oliver used to own Braveheart's mother, Glorious. Father bought Glorious for my mother. He bought lots of Uncle Oliver's horses, then hired him to care for them. Glorious died last winter of the colic, and Uncle Oliver cried."

"Oh!" Helen exclaimed.

"He cried more when my mother died, though, because she was his sister. Everybody else in the family died except us children. Jenny says the Kirby family was cursed because they were papists. What are papists, Cousin Helen? Am I one too?"

"Nay. You mustn't attend to gossip from the servants. You live under God's protection, not under a curse. 'Papist' is a term used to describe Roman Catholics.

I was unaware that Oliver was Catholic." The idea troubled her. His life must be in constant danger.

"He isn't, and neither was Mother. I'm glad Father bought the horses. He did it to make Mother happy—she was afraid Uncle Oliver would go to the New World after he lost his property. He won't leave as long as his horses are here. It looks wondrous fine to ride upon a horse. I wish we could go for rides sometimes. We never get away from the house. Even the gardens are walled in. Franklin says he is going to run away someday and become a highwayman."

"Oh?" Helen cast a glance over one shoulder at Franklin. Instead of studying equations, he was on the floor, absorbed in using a stick to tease a crawling beetle. Helen knew she should demand that he return to the bench and complete his lessons, yet she dreaded the inevitable battle. Patsy had fallen asleep on one of the benches, her soft lips parted and her cheeks rosy.

"You talk too much, Avril," the boy grumbled.

"Cousin Helen doesn't mind." Avril leaned against Helen's side. "This morning when we visited Father in his rooms, he told us he plans to marry again. Patsy told him he should marry you. Franklin said he'd go live in the stable with the grooms if Father marries again. He said he wants to grow up to be like Uncle Oliver and tend horses. He never wants to sell wool. Then Father got all red in the face and called you to take us away."

Helen's arm tightened around the girl's slim shoulders. Sighing, she buried her nose in Avril's fluffy hair and breathed in its lavender scent. "I thought he seemed vexed, and no wonder. He cares about you children. He misses your mother and brother. I believe he is frightened of losing you as well." At least she hoped Cyril cared. He must care. "I am sure his new wife will be a good stepmother. Your father chose your mother, didn't he? Therefore, he must be a good judge of women."

"I should have died instead of Joseph."

The low voice from behind gave Helen a shock. "Why do you say that, Franklin?"

He continued poking at the beetle. After a long silence he said, "Father wishes it was me that died. I heard him say so."

Pain gripped Helen's heart. "Oh, Franklin, you must have misheard him."

The boy shrugged as if to reject her pity. "He doesn't care about anyone but himself. He thinks we should be glad that he's bringing another woman here to take Mother's place. I hate him."

Helen silently prayed for wisdom. "You might feel that way now, but in time I believe you will come to love him again. From this day on, my prayer each morning and night is that your father will recognize the treasure he has in you children. He should be proud. Now, Franklin, I must insist that you complete your lessons, or we will never again use the temple as a schoolroom."

To her surprise, Franklin crawled back to the bench and resumed his equations—but not before Helen saw a wet spot appear on the wooden floorboards beneath his face. Tears burned her eyes as she began to comprehend the depth of Franklin's despair. *How can I help these children, Lord? What can I do? I need to talk with Oliver as soon as possible.*

—᠁—

That night Helen found a snail making a trail of slime across her bed linens. She performed a dance of horror, waving her arms and screeching silently. This time, anger joined her disgust and gave her courage to deal with the situation immediately. After gripping it by the shell and holding it at arm's length, Helen dropped the snail out her window to join the toad.

She refused to look toward the lavender hedge. " 'I will strengthen thee. . .yea, I will uphold thee,' " she quoted to herself. A day of constant communion with the Lord had done wonders for her spiritual fortitude. Last night's terror now seemed absurd, yet she knew that even one unguarded thought could again send her reeling into the pit of fear.

How had Cyril known that the mere suggestion of a phantom would be enough to start her imagination spinning? Was her craven character so evident? Not that she suspected her cousin of staging a ghostly promenade; Helen knew she must have imagined the entire episode. Rogue that he was, Cyril would delight in discovering the success of his ploy. She resolved he would never know.

Like father, like son. Somehow Franklin had discerned her dread of crawling things and now intended to use it against her—just as Oliver had warned. Should she drag the boy out of bed and chastise him for the prank, or should she pretend it never happened? Would either choice dissuade him from further escapades?

"Lord, You know how I despise these crawly creatures. . .and now Franklin knows it too. What am I to do? I must talk with Oliver."

Chapter 6

Summer approached, bringing to the gardens the glory of blossoming fruit trees, climbing vines, and budding roses. Days of romping with her young cousins should have been among Helen's happiest, yet she struggled against discontent.

One Saturday evening during her free time, Helen sat in the terraced garden with her Bible open in her lap. Pondering and praying, she attempted to put her troubles into words.

"Lord, sometimes I catch glimpses of Oliver, and more than once I have discovered him watching me play with the children, but each time he hurries in the opposite direction without a word. I thought I must be imagining his avoidance, yet time has proven otherwise. I can date his attitude of formality to the day after Cyril returned to Biddlesham Hall. Has my cousin forbidden him to address me? I cannot imagine why."

She paused, thinking, then began to shake her head. "I was foolish to have read more than casual amiability into Oliver's remarks and behavior. He said nothing that could lead me to expect more from him." But then she recalled the strength of his arms about her and the warmth of his eyes and voice. "He said he would help bear my burdens, yet when I need him he is nowhere to be found." Her shoulders began to quake, and she mopped flowing tears with her apron. The Bible slid off her lap and fell closed upon the bench.

"I feel so dreadfully alone! Because I must always be with my charges, I seldom see the other servants. Cyril does not crave my company. He knows I disapprove of the way he neglects his children." Shaking her head back and forth, she whispered to herself. "I dare not question him about my future as governess to his children. Perhaps it is best this way—I am not fit for my position. You know all about Franklin, Lord." Helen rolled her eyes and dissolved into fresh tears.

Franklin daily became bolder in his disrespect. He had not yet attempted outright defiance, but Helen knew he was biding his time. Every night she found some token of his aversion in her bed—dead fish, living beetles, worms, spiders, newts, nettles, and burrs. Once she had pulled back her quilt only to release a bat from its confines. Eventually the creature had found its way out her open window, but not before fouling the rush floor mats and the clothes chest lid. Helen had cried herself to sleep that night.

Her voice quavered as she spoke once more. "I understand that You allow these trials for Your purpose. I beg only Your care, provision, and comfort for my wounded spirit."

When dark spots appeared upon her skirts, Helen at first thought they were teardrops. But pelting drops upon her cap and shoulders sent her running across the lawn with her shawl over her head. Inside the house, servants scurried about like so many ants. Maggie rushed along the hallway, bearing an armload of bed linens and quilts.

Helen found the children unsupervised in the nursery. Wooden blocks lay scattered across the floor. In the middle of the room, Patsy crouched in a heap, sobbing. Avril sat on her bed, cradling the rag doll Helen had made for her. Kneeling on a chest beneath a window, Franklin rested his chin on his folded arms and stared out at the pouring rain.

"What has happened? Why are you not with your father?"

Avril launched into an explanation. "Father sent us away. He said he could not endure children because he must prepare for Lady Lillian's arrival."

"Lady Lillian? Cyril's betrothed is coming here?" Helen gasped. "When?"

"Today. Jenny couldn't watch us because she was busy. She said we were to wait here for you. Then Patsy bumped Franklin's block castle and made it fall, so he hit her."

Helen helped Patsy to her feet and inspected her for injury. The child appeared more hurt in spirit than in body, so Helen laid Patsy upon her bed and smoothed tear-wet hair from the little girl's flushed cheeks. "I said I was sorry." Patsy's rosy lips trembled.

Rising, Helen tried to keep the irritation she felt out of her voice. "I am disappointed in you, Franklin. Patsy is smaller and weaker than you are. A gentleman never hits a lady."

"What can you do about it?" Franklin asked bluntly without turning around. His voice dripped insolence. "You'll be gone soon, when my father marries that woman."

Helen was unprepared for confrontation, yet she could not allow open rebellion to go unchecked. She gripped Franklin's shoulder and tried to make him face her. In one motion, he threw off her touch, spun around, and kicked her shin a glancing blow. "Leave me be!"

While Helen collapsed on the floor holding her leg, Franklin ran for his life.

"Are you all right, Cousin Helen?" the girls asked, wide-eyed.

Helen staggered to her feet, puffing in wrath. "I will live, but Franklin is doomed. Avril, watch over Patsy for me." She skimmed down the stairs and stopped in the great hall, uncertain of the boy's flight path. The front door stood slightly ajar. Helen rushed outside in time to catch a glimpse of the boy disappearing around the corner of the house, headed for the stables. Helen took off in pursuit.

Rain pounded on her face and soaked her cap. She slipped on the wet gravel and fell headlong, skinning both palms and her knee. Immediately she scrambled up and ran, panting and sobbing.

The interior of the stable was dark, in keeping with the dismal weather. Helen rushed through the open door and stopped, hearing Franklin's voice although she could not yet see him. Oliver emerged from a stall, restraining a squirming boy.

"She'll kill me! Don't let her get me, Uncle Oliver! She's a monster!"

Helen felt like a dragon at the moment, ready to breathe fire. Her face streamed water, her dress dripped mud, and her smock clung to her body, so wet that her skin showed through the fabric. Her neckcloth and cap had disappeared sometime during that wild dash. Pressing both hands against her chest, she shivered even as she fumed.

Oliver spotted her before Franklin did. Stopping short, he gave the boy a shake. "Whatever have you done to Helen, you young whelp?"

"Nothing, I swear it! She is crazy!"

Helen clenched her jaw and enunciated slowly. "He kicked me in the leg."

Franklin's head popped up, and he met her gaze with defiance. "I did not. She's just a poor relative that Father took in out of pity. She's afraid of everything. Why should I obey her?"

Helen flushed beneath Oliver's scrutiny. Without a word to her, he turned back to Franklin, gripping the boy by the front of his doublet. "While I have a word with your governess, you pick up a rake and shovel and begin cleaning stalls. The dung cart is nigh the back door. Ask Quincy where to begin."

Franklin's jaw dropped. "I shan't do it! I shall tell Father."

With one hand, Oliver hoisted the boy to his eye level. "You will, and without another word unless you wish me to find a switch. You and I will exchange words in the near future."

Franklin wilted and nodded. When Oliver released him, the boy slumped off to collect his tools. Oliver watched him move out of sight.

Helen wrapped her arms around herself and shuddered, dimly aware that her palms were stinging. While Oliver spoke with Franklin she had furtively attempted to pull her bodice higher on her chest, but it failed to conceal her drenched smock. Although most women would have considered her attire modest, Helen felt improper. Her neckcloths usually covered her almost to the chin. Embarrassment only fueled her fury.

Crossing his arms, Oliver regarded her soberly. "Tell me."

"Do not insult me by offering again to share my burdens," she said. "These many days I would have welcomed your listening ear, but no more."

Some emotion she could not identify rippled across Oliver's face. Stepping toward her, he reached out a hand. Helen slapped at it and backed away.

Oliver stopped short. "Helen, let me see your hands."

She looked down to see red streaks on her smock, blood from her scraped palms. Her bruised knee ached. Sobs kept her from speaking, which also fanned her wrath.

Oliver gripped her wrists, and Helen panicked. "Unhand me!" Flailing with both arms, she struggled to free herself. She lifted her foot to kick his shins but could not bring herself to hurt Oliver as she had been hurt. He had done nothing to merit such treatment.

"I set the boy to work, Oliver." Quincy, the under-horseman, sauntered into the walkway, recognized that he had blundered into an interesting situation, and paused to observe.

"Helen, my dear woman, calm yourself," Oliver said. "I mean you no harm."

"Dost wish that I should tie her down, Oliver?" Quincy offered.

"Get hence," Oliver growled, glaring at the younger man over one shoulder. When Helen's frenzy did not abate, he released her and held out both hands in entreaty. "I desire only to give you aid, Helen. Let me bathe and anoint your wounds."

His solicitous tone confused her further. Covering her face with both stinging hands, she wept. Words began to spew from her lips, garbled by sobs that jerked her frame. "I am a fool! You have shown me nothing but kindness, yet I misunderstood your intent. I am but a plain and humble spinster, never to expect notice from such as you."

One arm encircled her shoulders. His fingers pushed damp curls from her forehead, slid down to her ear, then cradled the nape of her neck. He rested his nose atop her head and sighed. "Nay, you are right to chide me. 'Twas I, not you, who played the fool. Lord, forgive my senseless pride," he groaned. "How blind I have been!"

Helen could not comprehend his words inasmuch as his touch was sending exquisite fire through her veins. Feeling vulnerable and indecent, she was in no mood to be patronized. This splendid man could never want her as his bride; therefore his caresses were not rightly hers to savor.

Oh, how I love Oliver Kirby.

The terrifying realization gave her strength to push away. Shaking and panting, she stared into his face. "I–I scarcely know you! We are mere acquaintances. How long ere you once again forget my existence?"

"She carries the field there, Oliver. You've spoken nary a word to her these three weeks. All us servants noticed. Seems a heartless way to behave toward a choice wench." Leaning on the farthest stall partition, Quincy chewed the end of a long straw and gave Helen a broad wink.

"Begone!" Oliver wheeled upon his assistant. "This is none of your affair."

Helen made a dash for the open doorway and plunged back into pouring rain. In her wake followed Quincy's laughter.

A shadow fell over her. Still running, she glanced up to find a cape fluttering above her head. Oliver jogged beside her, holding his cape at arms' length.

Helen stopped in the middle of a puddle on the entry drive. "Leave me be!" she shouted, pushing at his arms.

"Not until you are safe inside," he shouted back. "You will come ill after such a soaking."

"And the children need me, I know," she said bitterly. She turned to run, but he caught her arm, tossed the cape over his own shoulder, and pulled her close. She felt his hands cupping her face; then his lips pressed against hers. Helen went limp. Her hands crept up his chest.

"I need you, Helen." He spoke against her forehead. His hat's broad brim protected her face from the rain; his embrace restored warmth to her frame. "Come." Pulling the cape from his shoulder, he wrapped it around her and escorted her to the front door.

She turned in the doorway, still in a daze. He smiled tenderly and touched her chin with his knuckle. "We will talk later when you are dry. I will send Franklin to you when he completes his labors."

She nodded and watched him fling the cape back over his shoulder as he strode toward the stables. Quivering hands covered her cheeks. Oliver had kissed her in plain view of anyone in the house who might have happened to be near a window. Fear and delight warred for prominence among her emotions.

—⁂—

Lady Lillian's entourage was late in arriving. "Muddy roads slowed our travel to a crawl," Helen heard a hearty female voice proclaim as she watched and listened from the stair landing. The future mistress of Biddlesham Hall seemed to accept the delay without dint to her high spirits.

"Cyril, this place is a delight! What a magnificent hall! The ideal surroundings for a magnificent man. I brought my faithful old nurse Middy and a few retainers." Helen smiled at the description of a swarm of attending servants. "I hope we are no trouble."

Helen's smile widened. No trouble to Cyril, perhaps, but she could imagine the turbulence in the kitchen. At least Helen had no immediate worries, for Cyril desired only that she keep his children unseen at present.

While returning to her room, she thought she heard a door click shut. Franklin! Was that boy up to mischief again? Helen jerked open her chamber door to find. . .

nothing. A small fire glowed on her hearth, and candles flickered in the draft from the doorway. She marched across the room, hauled open the nursery door, and extended her candle. The sound of peaceful breathing met her ear. Each bed held a motionless lump.

Shaking her head, Helen returned to her room and prepared for bed. Her scraped hands still hurt, and her knee was turning blue. Recalling Oliver's concern, she sighed. Reluctant though she was to pin her hopes upon a man who had proven himself less than dependable, she could not prevent dreams of marriage and family from creeping into her thoughts. Oliver had captured her interest from the first, she admitted. What woman would not find such a man irresistible? Not even his sarcasm had sufficed to discourage her interest.

Slowly she combed tangles from her hair, frowning in thought. What if Cyril and Lillian wished her to remain as governess to the children? Would Oliver want his wife to work at the manor? Not that he had proposed marriage, she reminded herself.

The idea of leaving Patsy and Avril brought pain to her heart. If only Cyril would learn to care for his children. Visions of her cousin as she had glimpsed him in the great hall that evening, clad in full regalia—lacy boot tucks, falling band collar, and beribboned lovelock—pranced through Helen's mind. The peacock. Why did he not cherish his children? Did the man even know the meaning of love?

And Lillian—would she love Sarah's children? Franklin might be lovable if he tried, but Helen pitied any woman in the position of stepmother to that child.

Catching herself in the midst of resentful thoughts, Helen squeezed her eyes shut. *Lord, help me to respect my cousin, and please teach him to love his children. Bless Lillian, and help the children to like her. Much though I love them, they are not my children and I cannot direct their future. I cannot even direct my own.*

Helen wandered to the window and rested her forearms upon its sill. Tonight the garden was clear and calm. The rainstorm had passed; moonlight silvered topiaries, walls, and statues. She could hear the garden's fountain and the faraway cry of an owl.

Helen's thoughts drifted back to the night she had seen the "ghost." A little smile twitched her lips. *What a coward I am!* Since her arrival at Biddlesham Hall she had encountered many frightening circumstances—among them several daunting people, an enormous dog, countless crawly creatures, a mysterious apparition, pervasive darkness, a recalcitrant boy, and one terrifyingly attractive man. *Notwithstanding, I am yet living, sane, and functioning as a member of the household.*

Still contemplating this revelation, she pulled back her bed quilt to check for prior inhabitants. Her horrified gaze traveled around speckled coils to meet an unblinking reptilian eye.

Chapter 7

Dropping the quilt, Helen swallowed a wave of nausea. Franklin had out-done himself. Of all creatures, Helen most dreaded snakes.

Taking deep breaths, she told herself repeatedly that the snake must be dead or Franklin could not have carried it to her room. Using the edge of her apron, she scooped up the slender creature and shook the cloth until the snake lay coiled in its center. Just as she reached the window, her heart nearly stopped—it could not be... Surely the snake's tongue had not flashed out for an instant! Cold and inert, the scaly nightmare lay limp upon her apron, but Helen knew in her heart that the beast was alive. Not even a snake should be dropped alive from a first-floor window. She must carry it downstairs and release it into the garden.

Keeping one eye on the bundled apron, she donned her dress. At this hour she was unlikely to meet anyone in the hallway, but she would not take the chance.

The great hall was still lighted. Cyril and his guest must be sitting up late. Like a wraith she passed the doorway, but Cyril spotted her. "Cousin Helen, come and greet my betrothed."

Shrinking inwardly, Helen obeyed, clutching her bundle beneath one arm. Cyril and Lillian sat near the fire; a gray-haired woman occupied a seat in the shadows. When Helen stepped into the hall, Diocletian rose from the hearth and approached her, tail waving. Helen patted his head, but he insisted on more petting. Pressing his nose against her bundle, he snorted.

Without budging from his chair, Cyril waved an idle hand in Helen's direction. "Lillian, this is my cousin Helen Walker who traveled here from Surrey to care for the children."

Helen curtsied, and Lillian nodded. "Good even, Helen." The woman surprised Helen with a friendly smile. "I am pleased to make your acquaintance. Have the children retired for the night? I look forward to meeting them."

Helen's heart warmed. "They are asleep, mistress. I will bring them to you on the morrow."

Lillian turned to Cyril. "She is a pretty thing, dear. Far too attractive to remain a governess. I am certain she could marry well if given a respectable dowry." She spoke as if continuing a conversation.

"And I am sure your beloved Middy would be an excellent nurse to my children. I told you before, beloved, that I am trying to convince my brother-in-law to take Helen to wife. The two would make an ideal match."

Helen kept her jaw from dropping with some effort. Fascinated by her bundle, Diocletian pushed against Helen's side until she staggered. He gave another snort. Helen felt movement inside the apron. Her heart skipped.

"But is he the best match for our Helen? I have heard rumors about the Kirby family. Did not King James confiscate their estate?"

"Aye, but it was a trumped-up affair. Verily, Oliver Kirby never was Catholic. No Kirby was Catholic to my knowledge. That tale originated with Lord Holmquist—a neighbor who coveted the Kirby lands and discerned a way to obtain them at no cost."

"And King Charles has never amended the error?"

Cyril waved his pipe. "He cannot be bothered."

"May I be excused, Master Cyril?" Helen quavered.

"Not as yet." Cyril turned back to Lillian. "I purchased many of Oliver's horses to pacify Sarah. He has remained in my employ these several years, yet I know that he longs to move on. I have heard him speak with animation of the New World, the Virginia colony."

Lillian's curls bobbed as she nodded. "Mayhap you could give him aid. It is unseemly to have a former gentleman working as servant, let alone the brother of your first wife. I would be uneasy in his presence."

Cyril puffed at his pipe and stared toward the vaulted ceiling. "An honest sentiment. I shall approach Oliver again. You may go, cousin. Take Diocletian out to the kitchen."

"Blessed dreams, Helen," Lillian said.

Helen curtsied and hurried from the room with Diocletian at her heels. As she reached to unlatch the back door, something touched her wrist. She looked down and nearly screamed. The snake had found an opening among the folds of her apron. Its head emerged, tongue flickering. Cringing, she shoved the narrow head back inside and tightened her bundle.

Diocletian snuffled against her arm. Pushing his bulk away, Helen opened the door and stepped outside. At last she could be rid of her nightmare. But when she reached for the bundled apron she felt a sharp pain. Startled, she threw out her arm. The snake hung from her thumb.

The door closed behind her just as Helen emitted a scream releasing all the pent-up horror of weeks of torment. Waving her hand and shrieking, she ran barefoot across the lawn with the two-foot-long snake streaming behind her. Barking in a thunderous bass, Diocletian raced beside her until a scent in the nearby shrubs jerked his head to one side. He skidded to a stop while Helen pounded on.

"Helen!" Oliver called from somewhere behind. "Helen, what are you doing? Stop!"

Running blindly, puffing labored sobs, she blundered across pebbled walkways and velvet lawns. Oliver caught her around the waist. She stepped on his boot and lost her footing. He staggered and fell, bringing Helen down upon the wet grass with him.

Rolling over, he came to his knees and pinned Helen to the ground by her wrists. "Have you lost your mind, woman? Did you run from the dog?"

Helen shook her head, still gasping and whimpering. At that moment, the snake released her thumb and slithered across Oliver's hand. He let out a yelp and pulled away. "A snake?"

"It bit me," Helen moaned and began to cough.

Oliver helped her sit up, then pursued the snake and snatched it by the neck. After a quick inspection, he released it. "A grass snake. Undoubtedly more frightened than we are." He glanced around. "It should escape before Diocletian returns. He is a poor hunter."

Helen tucked her knees and curled into a ball. "I care not what happens to it. Just keep it away from me!"

"Let me see where it bit you." He squinted at her hand, turning it back and forth in the moonlight. "Plenty of scratches, but no bite mark. Grass snakes have small teeth. Now come, get off the wet ground, my dear. Let us talk."

Helen allowed him to pull her up. "I have never before visited the garden after dark. Is it safe?"

Oliver placed an arm around her shoulders and led her to a bench beneath a bower of climbing roses. "Quite safe when taken at a moderate pace. I walk here with Diocletian every night."

Helen looked up. "You do?"

Oliver sat beside her. "Aye. Head dog-keeper I am as well as head horseman. Diocletian likes Cyril, but he spends more time with me and Quincy than with his master."

"You walk here every night—even in the rain and the fog?"

"Aye. This surprises you? The dog needs exercise."

"I believe I saw you near the lavender hedge one misty night and mistook you for a ghost."

"A ghost?"

Helen bowed her head. "Cyril told me that night of a spirit that haunts the garden. I know better than to believe in such things, yet the sight of you sent me cowering to my bed."

"Typical of Cyril. Was that the night you dropped a handkerchief from your window?"

"You saw me?" Helen's head popped back up. "Franklin had put a dead toad in my bed. I used the handkerchief to pick it up but accidentally dropped the kerchief out the window with the toad."

"A toad in your bed?"

"Tonight it was the snake. I find some creature in my bed nearly every night."

"I shall throttle that young rascal," he declared grimly. "I have oft seen you at the window of a night and wondered why. I thought. . ." He sounded embarrassed. "I confess, that first night I thought you saw me. But when I approached your window and called, you had disappeared."

"I was quaking beneath my quilts in fear of the haunting spirit." Helen chuckled at her own foolishness.

Oliver reached into his doublet and pulled out a lacy bit of fabric.

Helen touched it lightly. "You kept it? But why?"

"I thought you dropped it for me." His voice was gruff.

"But why would you want it?"

He shrugged, then leaned forward and rested his elbows on his knees, head bent. "Have you not guessed? I adore you, Helen Walker." Suddenly he rose and paced a short distance away. "I wish to ask your cousin for your hand in marriage and have the banns published as soon as possible. If this is not agreeable to you, let me know at once, and I will never again bother you with my foolish hopes."

Helen could scarcely speak. "Even though Cyril advised you to marry me?"

He turned abruptly. "You know? Oh Helen, it was pride that turned me from you for a time. I would not allow Cyril to choose my bride, yet I was miserable without you."

"I thought my heart would break when you seemed to forget my existence."

He rushed back to kneel before her on the wet grass. "Then you do care for me? Today you said we were mere acquaintances."

"I spoke in anger. It is true that we do not know one another well, but we will have ample time for acquaintance while the banns are being read."

"And after we wed, for the rest of our lives," Oliver added. "Kiss me, Helen, and I will believe that you love me."

"Do you think it wise? We cannot marry for six months." Although she longed to kiss him again, the very intensity of her desire made her hesitate.

"Unless I carry you off to Newgate." The teasing note in his voice no longer annoyed her. He persisted, "Helen, I love you enough to honor you and keep you pure until you are mine in the eyes of God."

She touched his forehead with trembling fingers and traced his dark eyebrows.

"Where will we live, Oliver? Here with Cyril?"

His eyes caught the moonlight. "For a time. I often think of sailing to the New World. Would you be willing to embark on such an adventure?" He pushed his head against her fingers like a dog begging to be petted.

"With you, I would go anywhere. But what about the children?" Helen caressed his wavy hair.

"I hope to have several if you are strong enough to bear them."

She felt her face grow warm. "I meant Cyril's children. I shall miss them."

Oliver paused. "God will provide for them."

"I like Lillian. I pray she will be a good stepmother."

He sighed and clambered to his feet. "As do I. We must accept the fact that Sarah's children are Cyril's to raise, not ours."

A voice called from across the grounds. "Oliver, are you out here? Come straightaway!"

Hands cupped around his mouth, Oliver shouted back. "Over here."

Helen heard running footsteps in the grass. Quincy panted as he spoke. "It's the colt—Braveheart. He's missing. Gone from his stall, and a saddle missing too!"

Chapter 8

Mincing on tender feet, Helen rushed to the house. Cyril leaped up at sight of her face. "What is it? The children?"

She shook her head, still panting. "Your horse—Braveheart. He is missing from the stable. Oliver sent me to tell you."

Cyril's face hardened. "Begone, woman, and tend to the children." Helen heard him conversing with Lillian as she returned to her room. A few minutes later, the front door slammed.

Helen sat limply on the cold bed, exhausted. Her fire burned low, and her candles had nearly guttered. She picked up a candle and entered the nursery. Avril slept with her mouth ajar and arms flung wide. Patsy resembled a lump of blankets. Helen patted the child and frowned. She pulled back the quilt to find. . .a lump of blankets. The little girl was gone.

Panicked, Helen checked Franklin's bed to find a similar bundle of bed linens. A moment later she had hauled on her shoes and started downstairs, flinging a shawl over her shoulders as she ran. Lillian and Middy were no longer in the great hall, and the fire burned low.

The front door opened and a figure stepped inside.

"Oliver?"

He pushed the door shut with one foot, and Helen realized that he carried Patsy's limp figure. She pressed a hand to her heart. "No!"

"Never fear; she sleeps. I found her in an empty stall."

Helen's legs gave way. She dropped upon a nearby bench. "I was coming to tell you—Franklin is also missing."

Cyril entered behind Oliver, carrying a lamp. Its rays lighted Oliver's drawn face and Cyril's marble countenance.

Helen hurriedly explained. "Cousin, I believe Franklin took the horse. Patsy must have followed him to the stable. He has often threatened to run away, but I never dreamed he would do it. But then, after today, I should have watched him more closely."

"What happened today? Lillian's arrival?"

Helen related Franklin's earlier behavior and punishment. "Although in the past

Franklin has harried governesses and threatened to run away, I have reason to believe that this latest prank denotes desperation of soul."

"How so? The child lacks for nothing," Cyril protested.

Seeing cracks in his facade, Helen answered bluntly. "He believes you do not love him, Cyril, and his heart is breaking."

Her cousin looked to Oliver, who nodded silent agreement. Cyril drew a shaky breath. "I must find my son," he said and rushed back outside.

"Take her," Oliver ordered, dumping Patsy into Helen's arms. "Fear not; I will ride with him. Pray, my dearest."

Helen met Lillian in the upper hallway. Burnished auburn locks streamed over the woman's lace dressing gown. Her voice held concern. "What has happened?"

"Franklin has taken the horse and run away. Oliver found Patsy in the stable."

Lillian opened the nursery door for Helen and helped her tuck the child into bed. Holding her candle aloft, she studied the little girl's face. "She is adorable."

Helen smiled. "She will love you."

Lillian returned the smile. "I pray so. I have long desired children but can bear none of my own. God has blessed me beyond measure. I will remain here and wait for Franklin's return."

Rejoicing even as she prayed for Franklin, Helen returned to her room, leaving Lillian with her new family.

—⁂—

Helen lay upon her bed for hours, fully clothed and listening. Occasionally she dozed; frequently she prayed. Memories of Franklin flashed into her thoughts. How that boy loved horses! Why had she never approached Cyril about obtaining him a horse?

Helen awoke to gray darkness. Bumps, footsteps, and hushed voices from the nursery sent her rushing to the door before she had completely regained consciousness. She flung the door wide and stood blinking. Oliver laid Franklin upon his bed and pulled blankets over the boy.

By the dim morning light Helen saw Cyril bend to kiss Avril's cheek and smooth wispy hair from her forehead. Beside him stood Lillian, a shining angel in white lace.

Oliver left Franklin sleeping and approached Helen. "You are still awake?" he whispered.

"I was asleep. He is well?" She indicated Franklin.

Oliver grinned; Helen could see his teeth gleaming in the gray shadow of his face. "He is well. Your prayers are answered, Helen. Come, let us find a quiet place to converse and leave Cyril and Lillian with their children." Taking Helen by the hand, he led her into the hall and down the stairs. Unmindful of her bare feet and frazzled hair, she followed.

Oliver revived the fire in the wide stone fireplace, just as he had done the night of Helen's arrival. Watching him as he squatted on the hearth and blew upon the coals, she suddenly felt joy sweep over her. "I love you, Oliver."

He stopped blowing and chuckled. "Fine time to tell me so. Wait a moment until I can join you."

She made room for him on the bench and snuggled beneath his arm. "First tell me what happened."

Oliver picked up her hand and gently kissed its scraped palm. "We found Franklin and Braveheart together about four miles the other side of town. They were both unhurt. Apparently Franklin dismounted, then could not remount the horse without a mounting block. Braveheart is not yet fully trained, you know, and he would not long endure a young boy's futile attempts to regain his seat."

"And Cyril?"

"We talked tonight, during both the ride out and the ride home." Oliver sounded pensive. "It had been long since we conversed. I believe the threat of losing another child has shocked him into understanding how precious are his daughters and son. Cyril pledged tonight to be a better father—to love them openly and give them time and attention."

"It is truly the answer to my prayers." Helen sighed in delight. "Lillian loves the children already."

"Furthermore, your cousin gives our union his blessing and will have the first banns read this very morning in church. He has promised Braveheart and several of my mares as your dowry. We can establish a horse farm in Virginia as I have often dreamed."

"God is good to us." Helen laid her head upon Oliver's chest. "I will miss the children. I do love them, Oliver."

"Your love for them and your courage were the first traits I admired in you."

Her head popped up. "My courage?" She laughed. "What courage? Oliver, if you only knew. . ."

"I knew how terrified you were that first night, left alone on the fens with a rotted corpse. One glimpse of your sweet little face, and I wanted to scoop you up and assure you that nothing would ever frighten you again—yet at the time such behavior from me would have frightened you more than anything!"

When Helen smiled, Oliver gently touched the dimple in her cheek. "I know how difficult it must have been to leave the only home you had ever known and travel across the country to care for a strange relative's children. I saw the abject terror in your eyes when Diocletian rushed you that first night. I can only imagine your reaction to finding dead toads and snakes in your bed—"

"Among other things," she murmured.

"Then there was the oak tree, and the ghost. . . You have encountered terrors sufficient to slay many valiant souls, yet you persevered. And I? Far from protecting you forever, I abandoned you when you needed me most."

Helen reached up to stroke his cheek. "Yet you overcame your pride, darling. We all struggle with sin. Sometimes the Lord prevails; sometimes our old nature prevails for a time. Do not condemn yourself—I think you are wonderful."

"Ah, Helen, your courage rises to every occasion, and you never give up. Not one woman in a thousand can boast such tenacity and valor."

"It was the Lord, not I," she admitted.

"I know." Oliver lowered his face until their lips softly met.

A DUPLICITOUS FACADE

by Tamela Hancock Murray

Dedication

To my talented coauthors, friends, and sisters in Christ:
Pamela, Jill, and Bonnie.

An hypocrite with his mouth destroyeth his neighbour:
but through knowledge shall the just be delivered.
PROVERBS 11:9

Chapter 1

England, 1812

Melodia Stuart stood before her father in his study. She tried not to shiver. Winter's chill hung in the room despite flames burning in the gray stone fireplace. Shivering would indicate weakness, which Father despised. Since he considered the space a man's domain, Sir Cuthbert Stuart seldom summoned her there. Her requested presence bespoke the profound importance of his news.

He studied her, no doubt regarding her slim frame that he had often told her needed to be fleshier to attract a suitor. Yet tonight, he smiled.

"I have news for you, Melodia. Good news." He drummed his fingertips on the armrests of his mahogany chair, in which he had positioned himself in a grand posture more befitting the prince regent than a landed gentleman.

"I am sure if you believe the news to be welcome, I shall share your sentiment."

"Of course you shall." He looked at her with eyes as blue as her own. "I have triumphed, finally. I have made arrangements for you to become betrothed."

"Betrothed?" She took a moment to let the horrific word and its implications sink into her mind. She clutched her hands together in a feeble effort to brace herself before she spoke. "But, Father, I had no idea you were thinking of promising me to anyone."

"Neither did I. While I was visiting London, the occasion presented itself as a surprise even to me," he admitted. "But since the match is such a good opportunity, I could not let it pass."

Visions of their acquaintances paraded through her head. None of them appealed to her. "Who...who is the man?"

"Sir Rolf Tims."

"Sir Rolf Tims?" Melodia searched her memory. "I seem to remember that name, but no face comes to mind."

"Ah." A moment of quiet penetrated the brisk air before he continued. "Yes. It was not you but Felice who met him during her stay in Normandy last fall."

"Oh." Melodia recalled how a fever had kept her from vacationing abroad with her sister and father the previous year. "Now that you bring him to mind, I believe

Felice mentioned Sir Rolf." A sly idea crossed her mind. "Since she has made his acquaintance, why not betroth her to him instead of me?"

"I have someone else in mind for Felice. Someone more suited to her temperament. A man who is strong enough to rein in her impetuous will."

Melodia remained silent. Despite his admiration for her intellect, Father had always considered her gentle spirit a sign of weakness. If he sought a hard man to control her younger sister, then perhaps his misperception would be to her benefit. She took in a breath and tried not to flinch as she presented another argument.

"I know many fathers match their daughters with men they have never met, but I never thought you would actually do such a terrible thing." Melodia tried not to whine. If she hoped he would grant her a hearing, she had to force herself to take on the calm demeanor of a woman and not display wild emotions of a spoiled little girl. He would indulge Felice in such antics, but not Melodia. "You just cannot!"

His stare caught her attention. "I can, and I will." As he tensed his jaws, graying mutton chops on both cheeks inched forward. "You must understand that my actions are to everyone's benefit."

Since Father prided himself on his logical ability, she sought an appeal to reason. "But surely you would not expect a rational person to agree to a match with an unseen husband."

"Sir Rolf is a reasonable man, yet he has agreed to marry you without a meeting. You should count yourself lucky, at that." Father surveyed her. "Had he seen your stringy hair that cannot hold a ringlet, your lips that are far too red for a lady, and your large feet, he might not have given his assent. I am only thankful I had the foresight to procure a flattering portrait of you from an artist I paid well. And that Sir Rolf did tell me he prefers a woman with dark hair and fair skin—qualities you possess."

Though his description rang true, Melodia's reflection showed that the features God formed to compose her face worked to her advantage. Rather than a bland beauty, her countenance held the benefit of expressiveness. "But how will my betrothed and I converse? We may not have the slightest thing in common."

"Oh yes, I am glad you bring me to the subject. It is more than evident that Providence granted you a strong mind, but not every man is as appreciative of your intellect as I, your lenient father."

"I would hope any man to whom you would betroth me would be as understanding as you."

"A likely fantasy," he responded. "You are far too high-minded for your own good. If he is a typical man of this age, your husband will not be seeking to engage in intelligent conversation with you when he surely can take advantage of conversing with men. Instead of holding such ideas, you will act as a proper lady—speaking when spoken to, being seen, not heard, and exercising the utmost obedience to your husband."

She flinched.

"I implore you not to resist." He wagged a cross finger. "You know full well that our family name is our first and foremost interest, and your marriage will strengthen our ties to important concerns here and abroad. Through this connection with the Tims family, your offspring will be heirs to one of the most powerful family lines in the empire. You should be grateful for the favor that Providence has bestowed upon you."

"You speak of Providence. Certainly you know I had contemplated giving my life to the Lord rather than becoming a wife and mother."

"I am aware of your childish fantasies, but the time to abandon those has come. If you would read your Bible with more care, you will learn that you can serve the Lord as a wife and mother. Case in point, a young virgin girl named Mary." He tilted his head at her as he made his point.

"I will gladly serve the Lord as a wife and mother, if that is His plan for me."

"Since you and Felice are the only daughters I have to offer, I believe this is indeed His plan for you. And since you are the elder of the two sisters, Sir Rolf has agreed to wed you. You should be thanking God instead of bemoaning your fate."

"I would not be, as you say, 'bemoaning my fate' if you were not marrying me off to the highest bidder."

"Enough!"

"I am sorry, Father. I should not have spoken so boldly." Melodia stared at the edge of his desk rather than letting her gaze touch upon his face.

"Please do not debate me. I only have your best interests—and those of the Stuart name—at heart."

"Yes, Father."

If only her mother were still alive! Perhaps she could have spoken to Father and asked that he not subject Melodia to such an arrangement. She often wondered what her mother had been like. A slip of a woman, like a songbird, she had been told. No wonder Melodia's lanky frame and large feet—despite the fact that both traits had been inherited from Father's side of the family—did not please him. She knew another reason why he found her appearance lacking. Convinced his wife contracted a chill from little Melodia soon after the birth of Felice, he blamed Melodia for such an untimely death.

"Of course you will obey me," Father said, interrupting her musings. "The wedding is set for the first day of February."

"But that's in less than a week!"

"Precisely. I suggest you begin preparations today."

—m—

The moment after Father excused her, Melodia rushed up the front stairs to Felice's bedchamber in the south wing and knocked on the door.

"Come in, Mandy."

Melodia entered to find Felice's maid brushing her hair in front of the vanity mirror. The silver handle of the boar bristle brush glistened underneath the candlelight.

"It is not Mandy. It is I," Melodia said.

"Well, I do wonder where Mandy is with my warm milk. She does dawdle. But welcome, sister." Despite the fact that the maid continued to brush Felice's hair, she twisted her waist to face Melodia. "Why are you visiting my bedchamber at this late hour?"

"Father has told me the most dreadful news."

Felice set her brush on the table. "What is it?"

"He. . .he has betrothed me to a man I have never met."

Felice didn't seem as surprised as Melodia thought she would be.

Melodia rushed to her sister's side. As the maid stepped back, Melodia took Felice by her woolen-clad shoulders. "Felice, did you know about this? Why did you not tell me?"

"No, I did not. I promise you that. But you know Father. He has always wanted us to marry to his advantage—and to ours."

Melodia let go of her sister. She clutched her hands together and paced in front of Felice's vanity. "I did not think he would be so cruel."

"Cruel? No, I think he is a generous man who wants the best for our family and our future heirs."

Melodia groaned. "Only you, his favorite daughter, could make such a proclamation."

"But my dear, fathers everywhere betroth their daughters to the best and brightest men available. It is our custom. Surely you are not such a babe in the woods that you are ignorant to our ways."

Melodia stopped pacing long enough to face her sister and to set her lips into a tight line. "I have no taste for your sarcasm."

"And I am sure Father had no taste for the argument you undoubtedly presented to him." Felice leaned her chin against her palm.

"Yes, you do know me too well."

"And knowing Father, he won."

Melodia lifted her forefinger. "He only thinks he was victorious."

"Oh, I suspect he won handily. And I venture you will be married by this time next week. So who is the lucky bridegroom?"

Melodia stopped her useless pacing. "Sir Rolf Tims."

The smile disappeared from Felice's face as she took in a breath. "Father betrothed you to Sir Rolf? The very Sir Rolf I met in Normandy?"

Melodia shrugged. "I do believe Father mentioned that in passing." Suspicion mingled with curiosity. "What do you know about Sir Rolf?"

"Not much. Not much at all." Felice turned back around and motioned for the maid to resume brushing her hair. She stared at her reflection. "But what about your desire to serve the Lord? Does Father not care about your heart?"

"He believes I can serve God as a wife and mother."

"That is what he said?"

The maid set a piece of hair against her palm and smoothed honeyed strands with her brush.

"Not exactly. But I am sure that is what he thinks."

"And you acquiesced."

"I did try to get him to listen to reason, as you guessed. But in the end, how could I not submit? I am his daughter. Even if I were not bound to obey him according to the Ten Commandments, I am duty bound by law to do as he wishes."

"That will be all, Cassie."

Cassie stopped brushing, nodded, and curtsied. "Yes, milady."

As Cassie made a silent exit, Felice folded her arms and pouted, then looked into the mirror and addressed Melodia's reflection. "I am not so sure I would. Perhaps I would run away and find my own destiny."

"Perhaps your high-spirited nature would permit you to take such a course," Melodia speculated. "We shall see when Father announces your fate. Since we are so close in age, I have no doubt that will happen soon after my own nuptials. In fact, if you have a gentleman in mind who has caught your eye, you might implore him to speak to Father now with thoughts of your future. Otherwise, he might saddle you with someone with whom you would not care to share breakfast the remainder of your days."

"I—I am sure Father will consider my feelings." Felice rubbed her hands together.

"Then you might mention Lord Farnsworth. I notice he looks your way wistfully whenever you are near."

"That old pig?" She scrunched her nose.

"That 'old pig,' as you call him, is not so displeasing to look upon, is he?"

"Not if you like a rotund frame and sanguine cheeks."

"Bespeaking of enough food to eat and a jolly disposition—both aspects not to be taken lightly in a marriage," Melodia pointed out. "And he is a church deacon with a significant title and fortune."

"You sound like Father."

"Be prepared, for you will have to face Father regarding your feelings. Only I wish you more success than I encountered."

"Do you really think Sir Rolf is so bad?"

"You know I have never met him. I am hoping since you became acquainted with him in Normandy that you can tell me more."

Felice reached for a bottle of powder scented with the pungent but sweet scent of lily of the valley and dabbed it on what little flesh on her wrists her gown exposed. "Yes. I met him."

"What does he look like?"

"I should think a spiritual person such as yourself would care not a whit what he looks like. Especially since you recommend a match for me with a so-called jolly fellow."

Melodia ignored the snide portion of her sister's observation. "I cannot help but wonder since I will be staring into his countenance for the rest of my days."

Felice shrugged. "I suppose he appears well enough. I do not remember so much about him. A vague image comes to mind of a tall person with fair hair and an indistinguishable face."

"And his ability to converse?"

"As well as the next man, I suppose. He said nothing memorable to me."

"Oh. Well then, you should be grateful that Father did not pursue my suggestion that he betroth you to Sir Rolf instead of me."

"You suggested such?"

"Yes, but he said he has someone else in mind for you."

"I wonder who?"

"I know not. Perhaps I should have made more of an effort to find out for your sake, dear sister, but I confess I was too involved in considering my own fate—and composing arguments opposed to it—to ask."

"Do not let your omission vex you, Melodia. I will learn of his plans soon enough."

"And there is no one you desire for yourself, no one you can bring to Father's mind? I dare not venture another suggestion."

She didn't hesitate. "No. No one. So when are your nuptials?"

"February 1. Father has arranged for us to marry the day after Sir Rolf arrives."

"So soon?"

Melodia winced. "I suppose he is in hopes that Sir Rolf will not have time to change his mind once he sees me."

Felice didn't offer the comforting assurances Melodia sought. Nevertheless, Melodia pressed on with her next request. "Felice, will you be my maid of honor?"

Felice pounced on the offer, which didn't surprise Melodia since Felice loved the idea of romance. "Of course. I shall wear a lovely shade of sapphire, with ivory lace at the neck, cuffs, waist, and hem."

Melodia laughed. "Sapphire blue?"

"Is that not one of your favorite colors?"

"Yes. That and pink."

Felice leaned against the back of her chair. "Well, which should I wear? Blue or pink?"

"I do not think we can afford to be too particular. We need to consult the seamstress to see what fabric is available."

"True." She peeked at her reflection. "Which color do you think flatters me more?"

"You will look beautiful in either."

"Well," Felice responded. "We shall have to decide as soon as we can. With the nuptials upon us, my bridesmaid's dress must be sewn."

—∽∽—

The night for her to meet Sir Rolf had arrived. Melodia was packed and ready to leave the only home she had ever known to embark on a journey halfway across England to live out the rest of her days. Why her father wanted to claim lineage to a family living so far away was beyond her, but he had his reasons. He always did. Or at least, so he said.

As her lady's maid, Rachel, styled her hair, Melodia attempted no conversation. She was in no mood for idle chatter. At least Father had agreed to allow Rachel to accompany Melodia to her new home. Becoming acclimated to a new home and husband as well as a staff of servants would prove troublesome enough. She didn't need to be stranded without her well-loved maid.

"Are you pleased with the way I have styled your hair, Miss Melodia?" the young girl asked.

Melodia concentrated on her reflection and noted meticulous rows of curls set around her face. "Yes. This will do."

"Will Miss Melodia be wearing silver or gold earrings tonight?"

"Neither. The pearls. And I want my pearl necklace."

Rachel took the jewels out of the unlocked silver box on Melodia's dresser. Melodia caught a glimpse of silk, a mask decorated with feathers and pearls given to her twenty years before by Madame Justine Girardeau, a beautiful and elegant French woman, when Melodia was but five. With the help of Father, madame and her husband had escaped Paris before the Reign of Terror and now lived far away in Canada.

Justine and Melodia exchanged letters from time to time. She enjoyed the contact even though news was months old by the time a letter arrived from Canada. Melodia had learned that Justine and Émile had been blessed with a large family. The orphan they adopted, Luc, had recently married. Melodia smiled to herself as she recalled holding a scrawny infant whose large voice defied his diminutive size.

Rachel shut the box with a snap, taking Melodia's thoughts away from her friends living across the sea. "An excellent choice, Miss Melodia. These pearls will look well against your fair skin and contrast agreeably with the green dress we have chosen." She handed the earrings to her mistress and then hooked the necklace around Melodia's neck.

"Thank you, Rachel."

"Shall I have tea brought up? And perhaps some biscuits?"

"No. I am not hungry. Thank you."

"I don't blame you for feeling a bit nervous. I'd be, if I were meeting my future husband for the first time."

"I wish you had not reminded me." She tightened her hands together.

"I'm sorry, Miss Melodia."

"No. I am sorry. I did not mean to be irritable." She thought about the little necklace with a gold cross that remained in her jewel box. "I wish I could wear my favorite piece, but Father told me not to wear any religious items. Apparently he doesn't want me to scare off my suitor."

Rachel shrugged. "Your future husband might be well advised to find out about our faith now as later. Surely Sir Cuthbert has not betrothed you to someone who doesn't profess to being a Christian."

"No, I think he would make sure he is a professing Christian." A pang of doubt shot through her chest. She could only hope. "But his faith is not as important to Father as his family name, I am sorry to say. Father's most ardent desire for the evening is for all to go well, and for this marriage to take place. After that, no doubt I am on my own."

Chapter 2

Rolf waited in the drawing room and studied green velvet draperies framing large windows that revealed the wealth of the occupants of the Stuart estate. Larger-than-life oil paintings—one of a man and the other of a woman—graced each side of the fireplace. Rolf surmised the portraits of the couple, dressed in the fussy style of finery his parents wore when they were young, depicted his future bride's parents when they were in the bloom of newly wedded youth.

Aside from the portraits, a large piano crafted from wood polished to a deep hue dominated the room. Rolf judged from such accoutrements that his heirs would be moneyed indeed. Still, he wished for the hundredth time that he hadn't agreed to such folly. Yet Father, battling illness in his London apartment to such extent that he could not travel to witness the nuptials, had spoken to Rolf of honor and duty. Apparently both, considered the highest of virtues, were enough to convince Rolf to promise his father that he would marry a woman he had never met. His sister, Martha, had married and was in her time of confinement as she awaited the arrival of a child. But that was not enough for the elder Tims. By agreeing to the marriage, Rolf was most of all fulfilling the desire to make his dying father happy in the knowledge that through his son, a new generation of heirs would carry forth the family name.

A picture of Melodia playing a tune by Mozart on the piano entered his head unbeckoned. Surely a woman granted such a name was gifted with a talent for music. He would enjoy watching her long fingers move along the ivory keys with deftness and grace. Perhaps he might be moved to join her, strumming his lyre in accompaniment. He took in a breath as the image faded.

Heavenly Father, was I a fool to fall in love with Melodia based on a small portrait? He contemplated the thought, not for the first time.

Perhaps. But her father assured me his elder daughter prays to Thee with fervor each night, that she blesses each meal, and does not have to be prodded from bed to rise for worship each Sabbath. Otherwise, Thou knowest I never would have acquiesced to such an arrangement. And yet, Father, I pray for Thy strength and guidance, that I am not making a mistake.

Rolf wondered how Melodia could be devout when her sister seemed anything but. He remembered what Felice had been like during her visit to Normandy. According to his memory, she was attractive enough—gathering single men around her with a bat of an eyelash—but too coquettish and flighty for his tastes. When Rolf's own father had first mentioned him being matched to a Stuart, Rolf was afraid that Felice was the one he had in mind. So when Father uttered Melodia's name, Rolf had felt relieved. Yet what if Sir Cuthbert Stuart had exaggerated her love for the Lord? What if she proved to be just as capricious as her sister?

Cuthbert's voice cut into his thoughts. "So sorry for my delay, my boy. It couldn't be helped, I assure you." He extended his hand, and Rolf accepted the gesture.

"Not at all, sir. I have been quite comfortable by the fire."

"Good." Cuthbert eyed the tea table. "I see my servants are also tardy this evening. I had requested that refreshment be brought in to you."

As if on cue, a maid entered carrying a tray filled with biscuits and tea.

"I do not appreciate your tardiness," Cuthbert reprimanded her.

The young girl made haste to set the tray on the low-lying tea table. She turned to them, quaking, and managed a curtsy. "I beg your gracious pardon, milord, but Cook accidentally let the fire go out and we had to restart it."

He harrumphed. "See that does not happen again."

"Yes, milord. May I pour tea, or will you be waiting for Miss Melodia to join you?"

"We shall not wait. Our guest no doubt would welcome a cup of tea to warm his body and spirit after his journey." He motioned for Rolf to sit on a diminutive sofa across from the plush chair he took for himself. Rolf obeyed.

"My elder daughter should be presenting herself momentarily. I trust you are not too nervous, my boy?"

"No." He wasn't sure if he was nervous or not. He hadn't learned enough about Melodia to discern if he should be.

Cuthbert took a sip of his drink. Studying him, Rolf noticed he seemed more like the nervous bridegroom. What was wrong with Melodia? He remembered the portrait and a realization struck him. Melodia had been too ill to go to Normandy with her father and sister. Was she a sickly little thing, unlikely to produce the heir Rolf's father so wanted? Or perhaps she limped. Or was her face pockmarked? Such a detail was guaranteed to be omitted by any artist. Could it be that her ability to speak well had been impaired in some fashion? In a flash, he wondered if he discovered that his future bride bore any of these afflictions, could he get out of his promise?

Just as quickly, shame filled him. How could he be so shallow?

Heavenly Father, I do not ask Thee for the woman with the most stunning outward appearance but for one of healthy body and mind. A woman who loves Thee, a woman who will teach our children to love Thee. I do not ask for happiness. I have been granted too much privilege and too many blessings in this life Thou hast given me to ask for everything. Prepare me to meet with whatever circumstance Thou thinkest fit for me to endure. May I be the meet and right husband for this woman.

"You seem contemplative," Cuthbert said. "I hope you are not thinking of changing your mind." He slathered clear red jelly on a plain scone.

Glad he wasn't prone to blushing, Rolf stirred one lump of sugar into his hot tea with more vigilance than required. The pressure he applied to the handle of the spoon caused the silver filigree pattern to dent his fingertip. "Indeed not. Why would you contemplate such a thing?"

Cuthbert laughed, but his mirth didn't seem sincere.

Melodia entered. When introductions were made, Rolf stopped himself from taking in a breath as he took in her face. The portrait had been accurate. Her eyes were bright, and a thin, pointed nose gave her face a dimension lacking in the countenances of other women he knew. Dark brown ringlets fell against smooth skin. He found her tall, lean frame appealing as well.

"I hope you are not too disappointed." The edge in Cuthbert's voice superseded the playful tone.

"I am not." Rolf found no difficulty in keeping his voice strong and steady since he spoke the truth.

"Good." Was it relief he saw on Cuthbert's face? "Then we may proceed with the nuptials."

Rolf had not even spoken to Melodia, but based on her beauty, he was ready to acquiesce. He swallowed.

Lord, I pray I will not regret this leap I am about to take. May our marriage be in accordance with Your divine will, despite its less than auspicious beginning.

Guilt visited Rolf like a vulture circling a dying beast. He had agreed to the marriage to please his father. The bargain was a desperate attempt to merge the Stuart fortune with the Tims expertise in business affairs. Without the influx of Stuart money to give the business a boost, the Tims family fortunes overseas—in France and Germany in particular—could well become as extinct as a woman wearing a powdered wig on the street.

Melodia gave him a charming curtsy. "I am pleased to meet you, Sir Rolf." Her voice matched her name—melodious.

"And I am enchanted."

Was that a blush he saw on her cheeks? Surely in this ribald day and age, he hadn't happened upon an innocent. But the way she refused to let her gaze meet his, the shy way she held herself, indicated she was no worldly woman. Perhaps she was a prize.

Though he wanted to talk more to her that evening, Melodia's father kept him otherwise occupied. Cuthbert seemed afraid, somehow, that Rolf would back out of his promise. He wondered why.

He had no time to linger on such thoughts when Felice entered.

"You remember my younger daughter from the time we visited the summer home of our mutual friends in Normandy." Cuthbert nodded toward Felice.

"Indeed. A pleasure to see you again, Miss Stuart." Rolf took her hand in his and brushed the back of it with his lips. Felice looked more pleased than she should have. He regretted the gallant gesture. He didn't want to do anything to encourage her. He had seen her look at him in a furtive manner when she thought he wouldn't notice. He prayed the actions were his imagination or her disposition lent itself to flirtation with many men.

—⁓—

"Oh, how lucky you are!" Dressed in her woolen night shift, Felice sat on the edge of Melodia's bed after the happy evening had transpired. "Sir Rolf is even more handsome and witty than I remembered."

"Yes, your enthusiasm for him seems to have grown considerably since I first told you about our betrothal," Melodia observed. "I could see that you enjoyed his company. One might think you were the bride rather than I."

"Silly goose! I will not be seeing him—or you—once you leave here. Is it so wrong for me to be friendly to my future brother-in-law? After all, I may be visiting you soon, and he may have many handsome friends who are looking for a wife."

Melodia shook her head. "That is you, Felice, always looking for an opportunity." Her voice held more of an edge than she intended. Melodia had felt overshadowed by her vivacious sister all evening; her resentment showed.

"Oh, do forgive me, my dear sister," Felice begged. "I only wish I were as lucky as you are. You do like him, do you not?"

"I—I cannot tell. I suppose he is as amiable as I can expect. I really cannot pass judgment yet."

"True. Perhaps Father should have promised him to me since we met in Normandy." Felice laughed.

"Do you really think so?"

"Well, you are the oldest, and he has promised him to you. So now we shall see what Father has planned for me. He still refuses to reveal anything. I confess to not a small bit of fear."

Melodia embraced her sister. "You know you are Father's favorite. Surely he will find a wonderful match for you. You must learn to trust your earthly father as you trust your heavenly Father."

"Perhaps you should listen to your own sermon," Felice suggested. "Then you would not be so vexed about your wedding day."

Melodia knew her sister was right. After Felice left Melodia's bedchamber, dressed in an air of more excitement than Melodia herself felt, she dropped to her knees beside her bed. She rubbed her hand across the quilt, realizing this would be the last night she would sleep in her own bed, the bed she grew up with from her childhood. After the festivities, she would be leaving for her new home, blessed with a new name.

She recalled the last wedding she had attended. She remembered how the couple kissed after they were proclaimed man and wife. A flush of heat warmed her body as she realized the kiss from her groom would be her first. The kiss would take place among people she had known all her life, and Rolf's groomsmen who had journeyed to witness their nuptials. The idea of such an intimate moment occurring in front of everyone left her feeling nervous. She almost wished she had convinced Rolf to walk with her on some excuse—to see the garden statuary, perhaps—so she could practice a kiss in private. But she hadn't, and that was that.

Still, no regret nudged her that Rolf's kiss would be her first. She longed for no other man and had not been curious during her earlier years. The men of her acquaintance were more like brothers to her than suitors. She would be giving Rolf, this man she didn't know, but a man chosen for her, the gift of herself.

Father in heaven, I beseech Thee to take away my fears, and to help me be a good wife in spite of my doubts, since judging by my new situation, Thou hast called me to family life. I thank Thee that Rolf seems to be kind, and that he is not disappointing to look at—handsome, even. I pray that he is a godly man, and that we can make a life together that will be pleasing to Thee.

She rose and climbed into the bed of her maidenhood for the last time.

Chapter 3

Three weeks after they had exchanged vows, Melodia was thoroughly ensconced in her new home on the other side of England and adjusting to an extent that she shocked even herself by how well she took to being a new wife. She had been surprised to discover how well the household was run. Before her arrival, Rolf had lived alone at the estate since his sister, Martha, had long married and moved to Dover, leaving no related woman available to offer him assistance.

Martha had been confined with a delicate condition at the time of the wedding so they had not met, but at the soiree Melodia and Rolf hosted early on to meet the neighbors, she heard nothing but good reports about his sister. She looked forward to the trip Rolf had promised they would take to London after Martha's child was born. Melodia wondered how long the Lord would tarry in granting her a child. A blush of happiness filled her at the thought.

At the moment she sat in the library, rocking in a comfortable chair situated near the fire that warded off early spring's chill. No matter how urgent household duties seemed, she never neglected to indulge in her quiet time each morning. Since her marriage, she had been drawn more than usual to the Song of Solomon. So many of the passages reflected her developing feelings of love for Rolf. She had been warned by more than one experienced matron not to assume love would follow the wedding, but already it had for her, and she could see by Rolf's tenderness that he had developed fondness for her as well. For that, she was grateful.

Most of Melodia's friends had already begun corresponding with her, and Felice's daily missives had kept her up-to-date with news of home. So far, Father hadn't made any announcements about his plans for her. Melodia knew Father felt less insecure about Felice's chances of making a good match than he had felt toward hers. Felice, with her coy wit and appearance of a classic beauty, had many potential suitors. She didn't hesitate to report her current prospects to Melodia, and though any of the men she mentioned would have made a fine husband, Felice always seemed to be waiting for someone better. Melodia prayed Felice would find that elusive man.

Rolf's voice cut into her thoughts. "You appear so peaceful, I am loath to interrupt."

Melodia looked up from her Bible. "Even if you interrupted me a thousand times, I know this passage well enough to recite it by heart, so it matters not. You have something to tell me?"

He drew closer to her. "Yes. I will be spending the next few nights at the Howard estate."

She tried not to pout. "Oh. A hunting party?"

"Yes. I wish you were included, but as you know, Henry is a bachelor and never considers offering diversion for the ladies."

"Then I suspect he shall evermore remain a bachelor."

Rolf chuckled. "And I suspect that prospect is not entirely displeasing to him."

Melodia bit her lip to keep from complaining. If only he were present more. First, business affairs kept him occupied. As for leisure, hunting, fishing, and gatherings with his gentlemen friends seemed to hold more allure than her charms. She supposed Rolf's behavior was normal for a man of his station; after all, how could she expect him to forego the pursuits he enjoyed just because he had placed a wedding ring on her finger?

"You do not mind terribly, do you?" he asked.

What could she say? She felt she had no right to object. "I want what makes you happy, Rolf."

He leaned over and kissed her on the forehead. "You have thus far proven to be the perfect wife."

As he turned to exit, she didn't let him see her wry expression. Perhaps she should consider being less "perfect," as he called her, and more outspoken about her feelings. In the meantime, she resolved not to feel sorry for herself.

But she did.

—⁂—

The next day, a maid interrupted Melodia at the end of her midafternoon toilette and presented her with a calling card the hue of cream and fashioned from thick paper. "Lady Eustacia Cunningham to see you, Miss Melodia."

Standing next to her vanity, Melodia ran her fingers over the imprinted letters on the card. She had met Eustacia at the soiree, but their time together had been too brief for her to learn much about her. Melodia really was in no mood to receive a visitor, but since she couldn't honestly claim to be indisposed, decorum demanded that she accept Eustacia's call.

She glanced at the mantel clock and saw that teatime had arrived. "Bring tea into the drawing room," Melodia instructed in a voice that, to her surprise, betrayed no anxiety. "I shall meet her there."

"Yes, milady." The maid curtsied.

Melodia glanced at her reflection in the mirror. She hadn't designated that particular day as one when she would be receiving visitors, so she was pleased when she noted that her appearance was presentable enough. Rachel had curled her hair, and though the ringlets weren't as tight as they had been at breakfast, they hung around her face in an attractive manner. The white bandeau she wore in her hair contrasted well with her curls and brought out the natural blush in her cheeks. Her white dress, though an everyday frock, was one of her better and more flattering outfits. She took in a breath and prepared to face her visitor.

As she walked down the large front hallway flanked by oil portraits of Tims ancestors on either side along with occasional tables that displayed ceramic vases, she knew she never need worry herself about the appearance of the Tims estate. She discovered soon after her arrival that the staff was plentiful, efficient, and reliable. The housekeeper and butler who headed the rest of the servants proved competent if not always warm. As long as they held their positions, no dust would be allowed to linger on the furniture.

When he first showed her the estate, Rolf had told her that his sister, Martha, had decorated the home within the past three years during her period of engagement. The fashions and fabrics still looked fresh, and Melodia estimated that they would continue to look well for several more years.

A little smile quickened her lips when she recalled how Rolf asked if the décor was to her taste. She assured him in truth that as long as she felt comfortable and the colors weren't too garish, she could make do in any room. Still, she was glad he had considered her feelings enough to inquire.

Striding over the threshold of the drawing room off to the right of the center hall, she eyed an attractive woman resting on the sofa upholstered in a brocaded fabric the color of clotted cream. Dressed in deep green as she was, with hair a lighter blond than Melodia had ever seen on anyone else over the age of four, the wispy woman cut a striking figure. Had Melodia not been married, no doubt a pang of jealousy would have visited her.

They exchanged greetings. "I was just about to take tea. Will you join me?"

Eustacia tilted her chin toward the tea table and inspected the refreshments, which to Melodia's eyes looked especially delectable that day. "I always have time for tea at the Tims estate. I was great friends with Rolf's sister, Martha, you know."

Melodia took a seat across from her visitor. "Yes, I do believe you mentioned that when we met at the soiree." Which was why Melodia had made a special effort to accept Eustacia's unannounced call and to make sure tea was served. She picked up the teapot and began to pour.

Eustacia inspected her but with kind eyes. "I see you are just as beautiful when caught off guard as you are when ready for an occasion."

Melodia nearly spilled a stream of tea on the table but managed to lift the pot upright in time to avoid a mishap. "Beautiful?" The word escaped her lips unbidden.

Eustacia cocked her head. "Do you mean to say that you are not accustomed to such compliments?"

"Well, no, in fact." She set the pot down for good measure.

"And modest, too. No wonder Rolf likes you."

Melodia considered that Eustacia displayed not a small bit of effrontery to try to catch her unawares and to admit it at that. "Thank you," she managed.

Eustacia took a sip of her beverage and swallowed. "Your cook stocks excellent tea. See to it that she continues."

" 'Therefore I say unto you, Take no thought for your life, what ye shall eat, or what ye shall drink; nor yet for your body, what ye shall put on.' " She hadn't meant to blurt the verse from Matthew. She clapped her mouth shut. Then she saw Eustacia's quizzical look. " 'Is not the life more than meat, and the body than raiment?' "

"Are you quoting scripture to me?"

She stared at her half-filled cup of black tea. "I—I beg your pardon. Force of habit, I suppose."

"Not a very good habit unless you plan to live in the church. Few people enjoy a sermon unless it is from the vicar. And often, not even then."

"I beg your pardon." Melodia stiffened. This was not going well.

Eustacia took a small fruit tart. "So how do you like it out here in the country?"

"I grew up in the country myself, so I am accustomed to it. This estate is pleasant."

"Pleasant? Is that the best word you can find to describe where you live?" Eustacia looked about the room. "That is not how the other nearby women would describe such a grand place."

Jealousy tweaked her heart. What other women had caught Rolf's eye while he was still unattached? She decided not to stray into such territory. "I like it very much."

"Good." She eyed a portrait of Rolf. "No doubt you will be putting your own touches on the décor soon."

"I think I shall keep it as it is."

Eustacia's eyebrows shot up. "Indeed? Well, Martha will be delighted to learn that. She put quite a bit of effort into furnishing this estate in a proper manner."

"Her taste is exquisite, and I am grateful to be the beneficiary of her knowledge of colors and fabrics."

Eustacia smiled as though she meant it. At that moment, Melodia could see that Eustacia had decided they could be friends. She sent up a silent prayer of thanks to the Lord. Melodia had a feeling she would need all the friends she could cultivate.

Chapter 4

A few days later, Rolf hovered by the door of the library and watched his new bride absorb the wisdom of scripture. Since her arrival at his estate, he had been encouraged by her example to increase his own reading of the Word.

Since Melodia didn't lift her head, he knew she hadn't heard his footfalls hitting the thick wool runner on the hall floor. He was glad, since her intense concentration gave him the opportunity to drink in her beauty.

Earlier reservations about his new bride had vanished. She had more than lived up to the exquisite image in her portrait. Her form looked pleasing—neither too wide nor too wispy. Her voice didn't grate on his ears. She stood erect and walked with grace. Had Melodia not debuted only this past season, Rolf imagined she would have been wooed and taken by an attentive suitor long before he met her. He had wondered why Cuthbert had seemed so eager to make a match for her and why he had wanted to rush the wedding after their initial meeting, an arrangement Rolf agreed to only because of Melodia's devout reputation and his father's poor health.

Rolf's first impressions of Melodia did nothing to answer his questions about Cuthbert's odd though unexpressed fears that his daughter was in some way unmarriageable despite her attractiveness and large dowry. Only after Melodia and Rolf had been wed a few weeks did she hint about her father's resentment of her that was nursed by how he blamed her at least in part for her mother's death. Rolf suspected that Cuthbert's contained rage closed his eyes to Melodia's true assets. No wonder she had given more than a passing thought to running away to a secluded life dedicated to God's purpose. Still, as she shared these family secrets, obviously not wanting to show her father disrespect, nothing in Melodia's expression or voice asked for Rolf's pity. If anything, he had a feeling she would rebuff any attempts to make her take on the role of victim.

He admired her strength and was grateful to his father's lucidity in the midst of his own struggle for health that he had suggested a match with Melodia instead of waiting for her younger, coquettish sister. Indeed, Rolf had enjoyed the freedom of bachelorhood, and he had met few women intriguing enough to spur him to more than an idle thought of altering his situation. But as he watched Father grow increasingly ill—his coughing fits growing closer and closer together despite treatment—Rolf felt his obligation as a son weighing too heavily upon his mind to ignore.

During one of his trips to London to see his ailing father, situated in a small apartment where he could be near his doctors and druggists, Rolf broached the subject of marriage. Father's ready response indicated he had contemplated the possibilities. His strong voice demonstrated his joy that Rolf had asked. Melodia Stuart's name fell from his lips, followed by a smile. The answer didn't come as a surprise to Rolf since Father and Cuthbert had been boyhood friends.

Encouraged by Father's response to his query, Rolf took quick action by approaching Cuthbert the following week when they were guests at the same dinner party. After his future father-in-law's acquiescence, Rolf took the news to London. To his delight, Father's face took on a glow for the first time he could remember in months, perhaps even in a year. The look of happiness and, Rolf had to admit, approval told him that the match was well timed and taken in wisdom.

Honour thy father and thy mother: that thy days may be long upon the land which the LORD *thy God giveth thee.*

Not for a moment did Rolf regret taking this commandment to heart.

Another verse from the second chapter of Genesis came to mind: *Therefore shall a man leave his father and his mother, and shall cleave unto his wife: and they shall be one flesh.*

His wife. Enough of spying on her, however lovingly.

He cupped his hand over his lips and let out a warning cough.

—⁓—

Melodia heard Rolf clear his throat. She stopped reading in midverse.

Her husband was home!

She tried not to look as though she had been waiting for him with eagerness akin to a lover in Song of Solomon. Would he notice that in anticipation of his arrival she wore his favorite dress—or at least one upon which he had commented? She agreed that the yellow frock foretold the advent of Easter, with its meaning of redemption and salvation—the new beginnings promised by spring with its blooming flowers and hospitable weather. Just donning the color made her feel warmer and cheerful.

Despite her attempts to appear indifferent, she knew her enraptured expression upon seeing his fine features must reveal her feelings. As she noticed her heart beating rapidly, she wished he would tell her he loved her. He hadn't yet. But that was too much to expect. The closest he had ventured toward such a declaration was the day he told her she was the perfect wife. She clung to that sentiment for all it was worth.

Though he read scripture each day and conducted himself in a godly manner as far as she could see, Rolf was a man of reserve. Besides, she didn't want him to confess to feelings he hadn't yet developed. She knew he wouldn't in any event. He was too honest for such duplicity.

He smiled, adding to her emotions. "There you are. I thought you would be here."

Melodia closed her book but restrained herself from rising. To her delight, he strode over to her chair, bringing along with him the smell of outdoors—a mixture of new plant life, manure, dust from the road, and sweaty horseflesh. He bent over her for an all-too-brief kiss on the lips, then touched her cheek with manly fingertips before he moved his hand to the back of the chair. She wanted him to linger, wishing he hadn't concluded the contact.

"How was the hunting trip?" she asked.

"Excellent." He stood in front of her straight and proud with remembrance. "I garnered no new mountings for my study, regrettably, but our catch was good enough. We shall be feasting on game for at least a week."

"Good."

"That pleases you."

"Why would it not?"

He chuckled. "Many London women would turn green in the face at the prospect of consuming wild meat even for one dinner, let alone for an extended period of time."

"As you know, I am not a London woman."

"Indeed. And I am glad you are not." He grinned as he took the seat across from her. He settled into the back of the wooden chair and crossed his legs. "No doubt you recall Suffolk?"

The image of a short, stocky man just past his thirtieth birthday came to mind. "Yes."

"He proposed an excellent idea, one I think we should pursue."

"Oh?" She leaned forward.

"After Easter, I should like us to host a masquerade ball."

She gulped. The welcoming soiree had been enough of a crowd for her. She had been relieved when the last guest departed. At the prospect of yet another event, a feeling of shyness overwhelmed her. "Should we be hosting another gathering so soon? Especially an event that promises to require complicated arrangements?" Her brain formed a large list of errands to be accomplished for such an affair—engaging musical entertainment, composing a menu for an exquisite dinner within Cook's capabilities and talent. Or should they hire a caterer? And then the most important—compiling the proper guest list. Her mind whirled.

He chuckled. "Truly you jest. Did you not entertain often at your father's? After all, as the elder daughter, would you not be his hostess by default?"

"Yes, but Father was never one for hosting parties. And I suppose though our standing would have been improved had we been known for lavish affairs, he preferred quiet evenings. I suppose if Mother had been alive. . . ."

"Yes. Forgive me." He leaned over and patted her on the knee. "But you have a new life here, one that promises to be engaging and even exciting if you will allow yourself to enjoy your opportunities to the fullest. I say it is high time that you turned over a new leaf and learned how to be an elegant and popular hostess. And I suggest our first major event should be, as my friend suggested, a masquerade ball."

She tried not to let a frantic look cross her face. "Perhaps as a bachelor, you were not aware of the many preparations that such an event will require."

"Do not worry, my dear. I am confident you are up to the task."

"I—I—"

"Do not tell me you are too shy, because that excuse will not work with me. Especially not since you will be hiding behind a mask. Too bad, since you are such a beautiful woman."

She felt her cheeks blush. Was everyone here in the habit of calling women beautiful? The idea of herself being considered lovely still left her feeling uncomfortable. She had never visualized herself as magnificent, and wondered how others could.

"You have my permission to order an exquisite costume to be sewn for yourself," he continued. "Eustacia's seamstress is sure to take you on as a client. I understand she called upon you while I was away?"

"Yes." A thought occurred to her. "Upon your urging?"

"Not at all. Eustacia never has to be urged to do anything, and if such a thought had crossed my mind and I mentioned it to her, she would have stayed home out of spite."

"Really, now, spitefulness does not seem to be the right word to describe her."

"Perhaps not. High-spirited is more like it. Which is why she has not yet found a husband. For who could tame her?" He winked.

"Despite your levity, you seem to think high-spiritedness is a fine quality."

"In her, yes. But I like my wife demure, as you are, my lovely." His voice softened on the word *lovely*. A warm flush filled her as she recalled their intimate moments, moments that as a maiden she never dreamed she would come to anticipate for their sweetness. She shook thoughts of his hot kisses out of her head. Married though she was, lingering on matters of the flesh could lead to vulgarity.

Such thoughts served to soften her attitude to any idea he might suggest. "I have to say, a masquerade ball might have its advantages. You spoke of a mask. I have one

I can wear. It was given to me by a French woman long ago. So it is an heirloom of sorts."

"I am not so lucky. I shall need to have one made."

"I can sew one for you."

"You would do that for me?"

"Of course. You are my husband." The word caused her to look down at her skirt.

"So I have been successful in persuading you to host a ball, then."

"Yes, you have." She gazed into his eyes, knowing he could convince her of almost anything.

Chapter 5

The night of the ball arrived sooner than Melodia could believe. As she watched the partygoers feast on the food, she recalled how for weeks she had immersed herself in preparations, wanting to please Rolf by making a good impression. Over time she had become more comfortable around his friends and neighbors. The soiree they hosted had broken the proverbial ice, and Melodia had formed light bonds with several of the women living nearby. As tradition warranted, Melodia called upon her neighbors, and they returned the favor. She knew the guests on their list would be giving the anticipation of an evening full of lively entertainment priority over criticizing the music, food, drink, and conversation. That fact helped to ease her anxiety.

Still, the ball was only the second event she was hosting as Rolf's wife. The winter soiree had been informal, so this was her first foray into entertaining on a grand scale, and she didn't want anything to go awry. Thankfully the household staff knew how to procure the best ingredients for dishes such as roast beef, stuffed quail, sugary confections, buttery fruit tarts with flavored icing, and other delicacies sure to impress. Melodia was all too aware that a poorly executed party could result in ruin for her reputation as a hostess. The restrictions of the day—the importance of impressions, connections, social rankings, appearances, and style—were some of the reasons why life as a secluded religious had seemed appealing. Until she met Rolf. The temptation to thank her father for making the match crossed her mind.

She stood near the fire that warded off evening's chill. Spring had arrived dressed in her usual array of greens, reds, pinks, yellows, and blues, so the fire's task of keeping the partygoers warm was less arduous than it had been at the soiree only weeks ago during winter's gray pall. A crackle from the fire almost made her jump, reminding her that she wore white silk that would not fare well should it make contact with dark ashes and especially not a stray ember. She moved a step away from the heat and regretted her decision to wear white yet again. Amid vibrant hues of the other ball gowns, she felt colorless. Even worse, would people guess her identity before the unveiling at midnight, perhaps guessing—wrongly—that she had chosen white since she was yet a bride. Instead, she had chosen a color befitting the heat of July because the material went well with her heirloom mask.

True to Rolf's promise, Eustacia had introduced Melodia to her seamstress, who proved more than competent in fashioning a flattering cut for the gown. In matching the mask, she had wisely omitted feathers but had sewn pearls around the neckline and cuffs. The buttons were also fashioned of pearl. Rachel had needed an inordinate amount of time, and no doubt much expenditure of frustration, to dress Melodia in a fashion containing a long row of buttons on the back of the dress and then four on each cuff. Yet the effect had been worth the effort. She touched a dark curl just to be sure it remained in its strategic place peeking out from underneath her pearl-embossed bandeau, the motion leaving her confident she still appeared unruffled.

As she ran an indifferent forefinger over the edge of her saucer, her gaze set itself upon the refreshment table. Several dishes were becoming sparse, a good sign attesting to their popularity but a worry considering she wanted to make sure everyone had enough of the precise offerings they wished to eat. She nodded to a maid and, once she garnered her attention, nodded toward the table to indicate the need for attention. The graying woman bobbed her head and scurried into the kitchen. Melodia had instructed the caterer not to be sparse with the amount of food he prepared for the evening. She was determined not to run out of any delicacies at her affairs—a development that would lead to the most catty gossip the next day and set her reputation as a stingy and disorganized hostess for as long as she remained at the Tims estate.

As she waited for the maid to obey her order, Melodia watched the partygoers flit, chat, and flirt among each other, satisfied that her evening was proving to be a success. She eyed Rolf. Even wearing the black mask she had made him, complete with feathers from a peacock she had retrieved from the grounds, the fine shape of his countenance was unmistakable. Pride in the fact that he was hers and hers alone swelled through her chest even though she didn't beckon such an emotion.

At that moment a tall woman wearing a bold red dress slid through the crowd. Watching her, Melodia admired her mysterious guest's head covering, an elaborate concoction set so closely to her head that Melodia almost wondered if the woman could have been bald. Shaking the ridiculous idea from her mind, she set her admiring gaze on three elaborate feathers that stood from the crest of the headdress. Melodia noted that if she were as tall as the mystery guest, she would have omitted the placement of anything that would add even more height to such a statuesque frame. But since the woman, who even in costume appeared striking, wore red, Melodia could only guess she didn't mind garnering more than her share of attention.

She felt amused until she noticed that the woman drew near to Rolf and reached toward the top layer of a three-tiered sterling silver tray for an egg with creamed filling. Melodia thought the woman's only objective was to acquire the food until she noticed that the woman's skirt touched the thigh of Rolf's velvet pant leg. Before Melodia could react to the close contact the woman's leg made with her husband's, the female turned toward him and laughed in the counterfeit manner of a coquette. Melodia's stomach lurched as she witnessed her whisper in his ear. He chuckled in return. Was he putting on a polite front, or did he find the woman amusing?

Her heart thumped.

Who was the woman in red?

And what had she said to her husband?

She watched for Rolf to move away, hoping he would make a hasty retreat. Just then her view was blocked by a gentleman. Gray curls peeked out from underneath a tricorn hat, and he wore a distinguished costume. She surmised him to be Lord Harrington but resisted calling him by name lest she be wrong—or right.

"I must say, I am having quite the extraordinary time this evening," he observed. "And what of you, my lovely? Are you finding the ball to your liking?"

An instant before, such a compliment—especially given to her by a man who probably didn't realize she was his hostess—would have offered her sufficient pleasure to float for a week. But now, his words seemed inconsequential. Nevertheless, she put on a smile and waved her fan. "Yes, it is. I am having a wonderful time. Have you tried the quail?"

He eyed the table. "Is it good?"

"Splendid."

"As a general rule, quail is not to my liking, but you have convinced me to give it a try." He wagged his finger. "I hope this is not your way of getting rid of me."

She tittered. "Indeed not."

A squat woman wearing a multicolored frock made of silk and decorated with random blue, white, and green oval beads made of glass approached Melodia and shared a few inane but pleasant observations. She guessed her to be Mrs. Snidow, but she couldn't be sure since she wore a blue and green mask with white piping. Melodia tried not to fix her gaze on Rolf, but in her jealousy, keeping her eyes averted from him proved difficult. She did notice that he had moved away from the woman as she had hoped he would and was at that moment conversing with a man wearing a plain black mask and an equally severe black costume. She watched Rolf off and on throughout the evening, but the woman didn't reappear. She felt relief.

Until she realized that perhaps that was their plan. If Rolf were seen talking to the same woman too much—and wearing red made her easy to spot—they might attract suspicion. Melodia wallowed in self-inflicted doubt. The fact that the woman seemed to have vanished left her with little comfort.

Midnight drew near. At that hour, the guests were destined to strip their faces of the masks that concealed their all-important eyes, presenting an unencumbered view of their identities for all to see. Melodia decided to watch for her rival.

"Are you quite ready for the masks to come off?" someone asked.

"I am ready." Her voice reflected the determination she felt. "More than ready."

The grandfather clock bonged the hour. Amid happy music played by the five-piece orchestra that had added much to the atmosphere all evening, the masks were taken off to reveal an array of faces amid gasps of delight, chuckles, and exclamations, Melodia kept her features fixed into a pleasant expression as she scanned the horizon for the unknown woman. Yet no tall woman was to be found. Instead of offering comfort, her absence left Melodia feeling more unsettled.

The brief moments that comprised the rest of the evening seemed inconsequential to Melodia. She remembered people flattering her person and her party, but alarm kept her from basking in well-earned praise. All she cared about was getting Rolf alone so she could question him.

After what seemed like an eternity, the last guest departed, and the butler shut the front door. Amid the last utterances of farewells, whinnying of horses, hooves clomping against gravel, and the occasional squeak of a turning wheel, Melodia watched the Harrisons board their carriage, the vehicle tilting inches to one side and back again as each person encountered the steps and then disappeared inside.

Rolf turned to face Melodia. He let out a triumphant sigh. "The ball was a complete success. I am very, very proud of you, Melodia, my dear." He ventured toward her. Melodia could see from the expression on his face that a kiss occupied his mind. She forced herself to ignore how handsome he appeared and how, at any other time, she would have received the gesture eagerly.

She stepped back. "May I see you in the library, Rolf?"

"The library? After such a successful night, I would think that you might want to enjoy your triumph with me—elsewhere." A mischievous grin played upon his lips.

"No." The word sounded sharp. She decided to soften the blow. "Not until we talk."

"Ah. You want to relive the night by sharing a bit of gossip. Very well. Shall I have tea brought in?"

Her stomach felt so sour with emotion that the thought of eating tempted her not in the least. "None for me."

He shrugged. "Then none for me, either."

As he followed her down the hall, Melodia almost felt guilty that she had allowed him to think he would be enjoying a rundown of the evening's events with her when the conversation instead promised to be unpleasant. Still, she had to know the identity of the scarlet-clad woman. The touch against the thigh, obviously staged by the woman to appear accidental, was not. Melodia knew. She just knew.

Melodia shut the door behind them in the library and held on to the doorknob as though it contained some life-sustaining fluid that would help her keep her balance. She watched Rolf settle into a seat with the ease of a man anticipating an evening with a fine book. She wanted to sit, wanted to appear casual, but no amount of good breeding could keep her from displaying the tip of the poison arrow of jealousy. "Who was that woman, Rolf?"

"Woman?" He clutched the chair's arms. His eyes widened, and his head shook in such a slight manner it almost seemed to jerk. "The question seems absurd when one considers that every woman in the parish was in attendance tonight. With the exception of Mrs. Deal. You were aware that a sudden bout of illness kept her from attending?"

"Yes, and I sent my good wishes for this evening and have every intention of having Peter deliver her a pot of chicken soup tomorrow for luncheon as a sign of our goodwill."

"An excellent idea. She is sure to appreciate the gesture. She's a lonely old woman, and no doubt she was quite distressed upon missing the ball."

"No doubt." Melodia wished they could remain on the topic of chicken soup all evening, but she had to insist they return to her original question. "Indeed, there were many women here tonight. But one in particular caught my eye when she spoke with you."

"Oh? I had no idea you would care so much now that we are an old married couple." His eyes sparkled with indulgence.

She refused to let him distract her. "The one wearing the red dress."

He chuckled. "There were a lot of red dresses."

"Not like this one."

Obviously sensing that she thought the question to be no laughing matter, he turned more serious. "I beg your indulgence, but you will have to remember that as a man, I have honed little skill in the way of powers of observation regarding women's dresses. I am more interested in you, the woman wearing a perfectly lovely white dress."

She wanted to give in to his flattery, but she couldn't. If she allowed this opportunity to escape, it would be gone forever. "Let me see if I can better enable your powers of recall. The woman was wearing an elaborate head covering with three bright red feathers protruding from the top. Certainly you remember that."

He thought for a moment. "Yes. I do remember that as an unusual hat."

"An unusual hat." She pursed her lips. At least he hadn't insulted her by pretending not to remember such a ridiculous costume. "And what of this woman?"

"I—I did not care for the way she brushed against you, or the way you seemed amused by her conversation."

"My darling!" He jumped out of his chair, rushed over and, before she could protest, took her by the waist. "Certainly you are not jealous. Are we not still in the throes of newly wedded bliss?"

"I would hope so. But after tonight, I have developed the distinct impression that someone else wishes we were not." She stepped back within his embrace.

"I think not. Everyone wishes you—and us—well. I have never heard the least bit of negative utterance said against you. Please believe me."

"But surely you know who this woman was."

He blanched. "I cannot say with certainty that I do. And that is the absolute truth."

"You know everyone on our guest list. Have known most of them for years. Can you not offer me a clue?"

"I cannot." He took his arms away. Though her speech had been hostile, Melodia regretted the symbolic loss of his fondness. "Do you want to know what I really think?"

"Y–yes." She braced herself for a lecture on how not to be a suspicious shrew.

"I believe the guest crashed our party."

"What? How could something like that happen, especially when the woman was wearing such an outlandish costume?"

"That is just the point. The woman most likely chose a larger than life gown and headdress with the idea that no party crasher would dare appear in such bold attire, and therefore no one would stop her."

Melodia contemplated his idea. "I can see the logic in that." She wanted to believe it. She wanted to believe that the woman attended the ball uninvited, taking full advantage of the fact that all the guests' faces would be concealed by masks. The thought gave her comfort. At least then the woman wouldn't be one of the friends she had recently made. "Yes. I believe you have something there."

"So you see, there is nothing to fear."

"Well then," she ventured against her better judgment, "since you have no idea who the mystery woman might be, can you tell me what she whispered in your ear?"

"I. . .it was hard for me to hear anything amid all the talk and music."

"But you laughed."

"My, but you were watching closely."

She could no longer look into his eyes. "I beg your indulgence. I suppose I am a bit of a shrew, and I have no right to be. You married me even though you knew me only by name and reputation, and you have shown me nothing but kindness since my arrival here. I surmise that not every husband would have been so considerate. Especially since I am so far from my home and family, and no one would ever know if you were cruel."

He took his hands in hers. "I am considerate because I want to be. You are a woman who deserves everything I have to offer as a husband. Now if you will allow me, I would prefer to put aside anything having to do with any mystery woman and concentrate on the lady before me." He caressed her cheek. "I love you, Melodia. And I always will. Remember that."

She gasped. The words she had been waiting to hear! "I love you, too, Rolf."

He took her into his embrace, urgently this time. She didn't resist his kiss.

Chapter 6

O h Melodia, I am so glad you sent for me!" Felice ran into her sister's arms, forgetting all expected restraint in front of the maids witnessing their exchange in the parlor.

Melodia broke the embrace but took her sister's hands in hers. "You must be exhausted after your journey. Come. Let us take tea in the drawing room. The view from the windows is so lovely. You can see the gardens."

"That sounds delightful." Felice inspected her traveling suit sewn from service-able cotton the color of an afternoon sky just before the first strike of a thunderstorm. "But I am not dressed for tea."

"Indeed not, but teatime is upon us. You can dress in your best for tea tomorrow to make amends for your lack of decorum today, can you not?"

"To keep you from delaying your teatime, I shall. Thank you for overlooking my drab attire."

"Of course," Melodia said. "And while we partake, Peter will carry your trunks to your room just down the east hall. The Gold Room. I will show you later myself. I assure you, your room is the best guest suite in the house. Not too far from mine."

"That is kind of you, sister."

"I would never let you stay in any but the best room," she commented as Felice followed her. Moments later, they were sitting together on the sofa. Felice didn't delay in sharing all the news about their friends.

After Felice had exhausted all avenues of tittle-tattle, Melodia posed her own query. "So how is Father?"

"He misses you. But you know how reserved he is. He would never admit to it."

Melodia swallowed. "He must be even more lonely now that you are here. Did you have trouble convincing him to let you visit me?"

She shrugged. "He knows that visiting you would make me happy, so he agreed."

"Are you really so happy to see me, or are you just glad to escape that awful Sir Arnold that Father is determined you are to marry?" Melodia teased.

"Both! Oh, if I can make a good match here, maybe Father will change his mind." Felice looked around the room. Melodia saw that she seemed to notice wallpaper of bucolic scenes and that the windows were framed in damask. Felice's gaze rested upon an original oil painting of a pastoral scene, framed in rich wood. Her observation traveled to the tall pendulum clock, then to the fireplace mantel carved from Italian marble, then to the costly rugs, and around the room to take in the details of each piece of imported furniture. "And I do think I might be able to do well here. Very well."

Melodia chose to ignore Felice's bold observation about her hopes for increased wealth. "And we could live just minutes from each other and visit every day. A splendid prospect, indeed."

She nodded. "So is that why you wanted me to visit? So I would ultimately live here near you?"

"Perhaps."

"Now, dear Melodia, as lovely as such a prospect sounds, I sense that you have some other reason for summoning me here. I hope it is not the result of any unhappiness with your handsome new husband. Is he secretly cruel?"

"No, indeed." She paused. "Although I have reason to believe that at least one of his friends might be."

Felice gasped. "What do you mean?"

"Remember how I told you we were hosting a masquerade ball?"

"Yes. And you also wrote me it was a great success—in the same letter in which you asked me to visit. Surely you did not exaggerate the truth?"

"No. It was a success. Except. . ."

Felice leaned forward. "Except what?"

"A mysterious woman flirted with Rolf."

Felice let out a laugh. "Oh, is that all? Why, women flirt all the time—especially when masks conceal their faces. No doubt many batted their eyelashes at Rolf during the night. You happened to see only one of them."

"I am not sure such a declaration does anything to console me."

"You are much too sheltered from the ways of romance." Felice touched her fingertips to her curls. "Why, even I have been known to flirt now and again and mean nothing by it. If I did, I would have been wed at least thrice by now."

"Yes, I have witnessed such, and I am sure you could give this particular coquette quite a contest. But there was more to the flirtation than mere frivolity."

"What a ridiculous notion."

"Ridiculous? I think not. A wife can sense these things."

"And you called me here to—to what? Rescue you? How?" Felice stirred her tea. "I was wondering who she is."

Felice set her silver spoon on her saucer. "And you think I will be able to help you? My dear, I certainly know none of these local people. Why, you would have a much better chance at solving the mystery yourself."

"So the facts would demonstrate, but your mind is sharp, and so are your powers of observation."

"And my common sense as well, apparently. Why did you not make a point of observing this woman at the unmasking?"

"I tried," Melodia said, "but she was gone."

"Oh." Felice stiffened and set her half-empty cup on the table. "Certainly you confronted Rolf?"

"Yes." Melodia set down her own cup. "May I warm your tea?"

"Please do." Felice nodded. "I hope you waited until after the party to ask him about this woman."

"Of course." Melodia's voice betrayed her irritation. "But he offered no clues."

"I am sorry you are so vexed, but I still think I can offer only limited assistance. Someone who knows Rolf's group is much more likely to be of help. I know you have had little time to cultivate friendships here except for perhaps that woman you mentioned." She paused. "Eustacia?"

"Yes."

"Surely she has lived here forever, and I am merely a passerby. Why not ask her?"

"And confide my feelings to her? She has visited me often, and I do consider her a friend, but I still prefer to share my innermost thoughts with my sister."

"Well then. What did this woman look like?"

"She wore a stunning ensemble of red. Her headdress covered her hair, so I have no idea what color it was, or even if it was styled with the curls that are all the rage in Paris. She was tall, about your height." Melodia sent her sister a disgusted shake of her head. "You would have much better sense than to wear large plumage on top of your head to add even more height. Obviously the woman followed poor advice from her seamstress—or someone." She shuddered.

"Indeed." Felice's voice sounded taut. "I suppose then, you should be on the lookout for a woman with a dreadful sense of fashion."

"Or maybe you can advise me to the ways of the world."

"Yes, we are an unusual pair. You, the elder sister, seeking advice from me."

"But you have always wanted to marry. Unlike me. So you have schooled yourself in the ways of romance whereas I paid them little attention all these years."

"True."

"And your visit here will help me be less lonely."

"Lonely?" Felice's brow crinkled. "How can you be lonely?"

"In addition to the woman I told you about, I'm afraid I have other competition for Rolf's attention. Namely, business. And hunting, fishing, and gatherings with his gentleman friends. In fact, he is away on such a trip as we speak. He will not be returning until the night of our next soiree."

Felice's eyebrows rose. "So he enjoys frivolities. He seems not to be home unless a party is planned or in progress."

"I beg your pardon. I did not mean to sound harsh. He is in London visiting his father, who is quite ill."

Felice's lips tightened into the type of tight little smile that showed she wished she hadn't spoken so soon. "I am so sorry. Yes, I did hear he is ill and is not expected to recover. I am so glad you decided not to go and put yourself at risk of contracting his illness."

"Do you not remember what I wrote to you only a fortnight ago?"

"Ah, yes." She nodded. "You did go to see him and found him looking wan and coughing terribly. I suppose I merely skimmed such a depressing portion of your letter. Do forgive me. I much preferred to concentrate on the fine bonnet you wrote of procuring at the milliner's. You must tell me which shop so I can take a peek at her wares the next time Father and I journey there."

"Madame Jullienne's. Yes, her work is exquisite. And I am not surprised that you concentrated on the happy part of my letter, being such a cheerful soul yourself." Melodia took a sip of tea. "I am glad I took advantage of the opportunity to visit with my father-in-law. I had not seen him in years and would not have recognized him had we not been reacquainted."

"I am sorry to hear he seems so ill. I do hope you have not developed a cough since your return." Felice flinched.

"Do not worry yourself. I would never invite you to my home at a time when I thought I could put your own health at risk. I do believe his maladies are caused by old age. I suppose such a condition is contagious for those who live long enough to catch it."

"And the meeting went well?"

"Yes. He was kind to me."

"But Rolf did not see fit to have you accompany him a second time?"

"No. I have seen enough of London to last me for a time. And in any event, Rolf is going to take care of some errands for his father and return home after that. I would only encumber him. Though I do wish I could be with him."

"Ah yes. Loneliness. The plight of many an aristocratic woman. But would you rather be a poor peasant too busy plowing the fields to worry about such trifles as loneliness and jealousy?"

Melodia shuddered. "Indeed not."

"I only hope the woman in red is not from London and that Rolf is not stopping by to see her when he is town to visit his father."

"I am sure the woman in red is not from London." Nevertheless, Melodia wished

Felice hadn't brought up the possibility.

"If so, she would have traveled a distance just to brush against your husband and feign it was an accident." Felice chuckled. "But I would not worry about any other woman if I were you."

"Why not?" Melodia hoped Felice would impart some comforting words—perhaps commenting on the couple's devotion to God's commandments or on Melodia's fine character being enough to keep Rolf from straying.

"He would never discard you. As his wife, you are afforded a status that no mistress ever can. You will remain secure, my dear. I am sure of that. But in what state you wish to live the remainder of your days is up to you. You can choose to remain chaste and miserable, or you can choose to carry on great love affairs in a discreet manner and enjoy much frivolity. Once I am safely married, I know I can trust you not to confide in anyone that finding romance on my own is what I plan to do."

"Felice! How can you say that?"

"Easily. You know how much I despise the man Father has chosen for me."

"And you are his favorite daughter," Melodia reminded her.

"That does not seem so, does it? I think Rolf is a much better husband than Arnold can ever hope to be. I know he is much more handsome."

"I would hope that, if you do plan to make a better match while you are here, it will be with the intent of being a good wife and not a faithless one."

"Perhaps with the right man, I can be swayed."

"You are incorrigible!" Melodia tapped her spoon against the rim of her cup. Though her sister enjoyed talking in a daring manner, Melodia knew her well enough to see beyond her boasting. Felice was much like her. She only wanted a happy home and family. Though she flirted now, she was unlikely to live a wanton life as a single woman and certainly not after marriage. Not as she claimed some of the other women did.

As they moved their conversation on to other subjects, Melodia tried to block Felice's warning out of her mind. But the words kept spinning in her head.

I will not give up without a fight. I will be the best wife I can. I shall start by taking Rolf at his word that he will not succumb to another woman's charms.

Still, in the future, she would eye every tall woman who could have been at the ball with the utmost care.

Chapter 7

A week later, Melodia found herself searching the manor house for Rolf. He had been late in making his return from London. Before the soiree in progress that night, she had only been able to discover the most broad details about his father's health—that he was neither better nor worse—and to utter mention of Felice's arrival. At the latter intelligence, she had expected him to react with indifferent pleasantness. She wondered why the news of her sister's stay seemed to annoy him.

Melodia worried. Rolf wasn't in the habit of abandoning his guests in the middle of a night's entertainment. Lord Suffolk had been in the midst of playing a lively tune he had composed himself only the past week. Their audience was the first to hear him perform his work. She couldn't imagine why Rolf wouldn't be present to hear the tune played with immense skill on the piano.

Even worse, her concern about him caused her to forget her manners. She slipped into the dim hallway to search the rooms and gardens for where he might have gone. He was not to be found. The longer she searched, the more alarmed she became. Disgust at having to slip out from their guests, proving herself to be a poor hostess, grew into anger at him for putting her in such a position, then dissolved into fear. Perhaps he had been overtaken by illness. Perhaps even at that moment he was in pain, hoping she would find him so she could administer aid. Or what if something even worse had transpired? She clasped her hand to her throat in horror but nevertheless forced her feet to keep moving. She had to find him!

As she passed a rounded archway leading to the north wing, a woman's voice floated from the turret stairs. ". . .annulled."

The voice sounded familiar, but she couldn't place it. The word made her even more curious. She stopped. "Annulled?"

"I will not have my marriage annulled. And that is final."

Her hand flew from her throat to her side and clenched itself in fear and anger. The man's voice belonged to Rolf. He was defending their marriage to this woman, whoever she was. But why? What could the woman have said that could even give her the boldness to suggest that Rolf's marriage should be annulled?

Curiosity overcoming fear, Melodia peered up the stairs, even though the action risked her getting caught. She had to identify the woman. A hem of gold material told the tale. The woman whispering to Rolf was none other than Eustacia! Her friend!

Why would Eustacia want to spread rumors strong enough to suggest that her new husband annul their marriage?

Unless. . .

Unless she had been the one who was flirting with Rolf at the ball! But was Eustacia tall enough to fit the description? And hadn't her ball gown been pale blue rather than the striking red gown that the flirt had worn?

Trusting Eustacia was her friend, Melodia never thought before about how tall and regal Eustacia stood. Perhaps she had worn a blue gown, then changed into the red one, then back into the blue one, just to fool Melodia. If Eustacia wanted Rolf for herself, such an effort would be a small concession to make to keep her identity concealed.

Rolf had said Eustacia was high-spirited. Perhaps risk offered excitement she could find no other way. Perhaps Eustacia had deliberately cultivated her as a friend to gain her confidence. A smart move.

But then again, Rolf had told Melodia that he admired her character, not Eustacia's. Was Rolf to be believed?

More thoughts, both logical and preposterous, flooded her head until she thought they might pour out of her ears. She rubbed her palm on the side of her head as though such a motion would help contain them. At the moment, she only knew she felt too confused and befuddled to think about anything. She had to get out of sight before Rolf—and Eustacia—caught her spying on them.

Like the child she suddenly felt she was, Melodia took the only action she knew. She fled to her bedchamber, threw herself on the down-filled mattress, and sobbed.

Moments later, someone entered. She had been missed! Melodia stiffened, shut her eyes, and pretended to be asleep. As the figure drew near, she heard the rustle of a dress. The intruder was female. The strong odor of lily of the valley fragrance revealed her identity. Felice had come to comfort her, but Melodia didn't want to be comforted. She kept her eyes shut.

Melodia felt Felice's soft hand brush her exposed cheek. "Melodia, dear, what is the matter?"

Her eyes remained shut.

"You cannot fool me. I see your eyelashes fluttering. You are not asleep." Melodia felt the mattress sink in one spot as Felice sat on the side of the bed.

Melodia tried to keep her eyes shut but to no avail. Once her sister had determined that she was fooling, there was no turning back. She allowed her eyes to flutter open but remained in a prone position. "I do not wish to speak to anyone, not even you. I am ill. Please give my excuses to the remainder of our guests."

"I will do no such thing. You are to come downstairs with me right this instant. You cannot have it said all over the parish that you abandoned your own party."

"Illness is an acceptable excuse."

"I would not recommend it. And I do not believe you are ill." She inspected her. "You. . .you are crying. Tell me. What is really the matter?" Felice held out a clean handkerchief in a way that reminded Melodia of a carrot being dangled in front of the nose of a horse.

Melodia sat and took the offered item. "I noticed Rolf was missing from the party so I went to look for him. I thought he might be ill. But instead I found him on the turret stairs with. . .with. . ." She sniffled.

"With whom?" Felice rubbed her open palm on Melodia's back.

"You will never believe it."

"Eustacia."

Melodia felt her eyelids widen as far as they would go. "How did you know?"

"I saw him leave the concert and her follow not long after. I had my suspicions that the timing of their departures was no coincidence. And then when I noticed you left in the middle of Lord Suffolk's song, I knew something must be amiss." Felice patted Melodia's back. "So where were they?"

"On the turret stairs."

Felice took in a breath. She opened her mouth to speak but shut it. Clearly, she was afraid to ask what had transpired.

"They were just. . .talking," Melodia assured Felice. "It was what they talked about that concerned me. She said something about annulling our marriage."

Felice gasped. "No!"

"I thought she was my friend." Melodia dabbed the handkerchief against her eyes. "Maybe she still is."

"Indeed?" Doubt dripped from Felice's voice.

"Perhaps Rolf has done something to warrant her suggestion. As I told you, he. . .he is absent a great deal."

"You would think that about Rolf?" Felice paused. "Well, he is a man, after all. But what if he is? Would you really want to leave your marriage?"

"No. No, I do not."

Felice dropped her hands to her lap and looked into Melodia's eyes. "You have come to love him."

Melodia looked into her own lap and nodded.

"Then we must stop Eustacia. She must not be allowed to play the coquette with your husband any longer."

"I was thinking, and wondering—could she have been the woman behind the red mask that night at the ball?"

"Yes. Yes, I am convinced of that now," Felice said without missing a beat. "I am your sister. You can trust me, and only me, to tell you the truth. Let me prove it to you. Let me help you prove that Eustacia was the masked woman you saw with Rolf that night—a woman hiding behind a duplicitous facade."

"But I asked Rolf—"

"And he lied. He lied to you before, and he will lie to you again."

Melodia swallowed. "No."

"I know such a possibility is heartbreaking to consider, but you must. I regret heartily that I am the one to break your heart, but for your own good, you must face facts," Felice implored.

"I know what we have to do. There is one person we can confront. And we will do so now."

—⁓—

As Rolf listened to Mrs. Snidow play a flute duet with her young daughter, the tune swirled around him but missed his ears and his mind.

Where was Melodia? He looked for his wife, eyeing the door every few moments in hopes that she would reenter. Surely she knew how her absence must appear odd. She had, much to his delight, established herself as an exemplary hostess, yet her reputation wasn't so secure that she should absent herself from the performances.

If only he hadn't allowed Eustacia to pull him away from the gathering! He had been suspicious of her willingness to befriend Melodia but had put aside his reservations in hopes that Eustacia was displaying maturity in spending time with his lonely wife. Rolf wasn't a conceited man, but he knew that not so long ago Eustacia would have welcomed his offer of marriage. And she had many attributes to recommend her—just not attributes that appealed to him. He wanted a woman of spiritual depth, something Eustacia lacked. The longer he stayed married to Melodia, the more convinced he became that their marriage was God's will.

Confident in his union with Melodia, Rolf had believed Eustacia when she said she had something important to share. Like a stunned fly whirring into the spider's web, he had flown onto the turret stairs and heard Eustacia whisper things to him—things he never wanted to hear. Surely they couldn't be true! Surely Melodia didn't harbor some secret love back where she came from and wasn't carrying on with illicit love letters to him at this very moment. Why, she even suggested that the man had been circulating among them at the masquerade ball. That could not have been possible!

The worst confession from Eustacia was that the rumors suggested that Rolf himself was seeking an annulment to their marriage. He was too much in love with

Melodia not to forgive her anything.

As Mrs. and Miss Snidow completed their song, he clapped along with the guests and then halfway watched Miss Jane Laurel take her place in front of the audience for a solo. As she struggled to hit notes too high for her natural range, Rolf went over the guest list for the masquerade ball that had been the source of such distress for Melodia, distress he wished she hadn't been forced to endure. He matched a masked guest with each name. He didn't remember seeing any uninvited guests among them—except the woman in red who had flirted with him.

If only he had seen her motive and had fled from the refreshment table the moment she made contact with him! But like a fox cornered by the hounds, he could only stare in disbelief when she whispered in his ear that she loved him. Unwilling to embarrass the woman, he had responded in the only way he knew in public. He chuckled. No matter that he exited as quickly as etiquette allowed. He never should have appeared to enjoy her words. But everyone knew he had recently married. Surely the woman didn't mean what she said. Idle words of flirtation, meant to bolster the emotions of the speaker as much as the receiver.

Heavenly Father, forgive me my slip. I have been wed only a short time, and I still do not know how to act as a husband should. Forgive me! I ask Thee to take away any desire that any other woman except Melodia may still harbor for me, for though I am strong enough to resist their wiles, I wish not to break any hearts. Thou hast seen fit to give me Melodia. Let me be worthy of her.

Chapter 8

Later that evening, as the concert given by their friends and neighbors was still in progress, Melodia and Felice waited for their guest to enter Melodia's private study. She chose the room for the confrontation on purpose, knowing the familiar and intimate setting would make her feel more confident.

Before exiting her bedchamber, Melodia had taken a few moments to compose herself. Rachel had been summoned to touch up her hair, and though the maid's eyes held a curious look, Melodia resisted confiding to her trusted servant. Rachel had brought a few chips of precious ice to help reduce the puffiness of Melodia's tear-stained eyelids, yet despite those efforts the skin around her eyes still looked enlarged from sobbing and her face remained splotched with red. In spite of these disadvantages to her personal appearance, she sat upright in the most thronelike chair available.

"Are you nervous?" Felice asked.

"Yes," Melodia admitted. "But I shall try not to reveal my feelings."

"I am distraught to see you so vexed."

Melodia dabbed her eyes, pleased that the motion was successful in preventing new tears from falling. "I cannot bear the thought of my husband keeping secrets from me—secrets that could affect our marriage. Especially now that. . .now that. . ."

"Now that what?" Felice looked at her with widened eyes.

"Do you promise you will not reveal what I am about to say to anyone?"

"Yes."

Melodia felt herself blush as she peered at her lap. "I think I may be presenting Rolf with an heir this winter."

"Oh Melodia!" Felice rose from her chair so she could embrace her sister. "How wonderful for you!"

"I—I thought it was wonderful. Now I am not so sure."

"Of course you are sure. A baby is a beautiful blessing." Felice's eyes darkened. "How dare he! How dare he take part in romantic intrigue when he has a wife of whom he should be mindful!"

Melodia didn't have time to answer before Eustacia entered. "You wished to see me?"

"Yes," Melodia answered from her seat, refusing to rise.

Her voice displayed irritation. "I wish you had not summoned me at the peak of the festivities. Lord and Lady Ellingworth were just about to sing a duet when I was summoned here." She stared at Melodia as though thunderstruck. "Are you quite all right?"

"She will be soon, I hope," Felice snapped from her own chair situated near Melodia's.

Eustacia eyed both women. "So you both wished to see me?"

"You might say so," Felice said.

Melodia wanted to elaborate, but suddenly her throat closed. She took a sip of lemonade, but the cool liquid did nothing to open her vocal cords.

Felice looked over at Melodia, then back to Eustacia. "What my sister wants to know," Felice said, "is why you were lingering on the turret steps with her husband and what vicious rumor you were spreading to him."

Eustacia turned as white as a snowflake. "I beg your pardon?"

"You heard me," Felice prompted.

Eustacia drew herself to her full height and eyed both women. "There must be some mistake. I do not know what you think you heard, but I assure you, I have done nothing improper in relation to your husband, nor do I wish to do so. He has been my acquaintance for many years. Indeed, we were childhood playmates. I would never wish any harm upon him."

"So you do not deny you spoke to Rolf this evening?" Felice asked.

Eustacia crossed her arms. "I know what you imply, and I will not dignify such a question with an answer. And I suggest, Felice, that you not make a pursuit of such prurient pastimes as gossip."

"I beg your pardon," Melodia said, "but despite your protests otherwise, I would guess that you are the one who was engaged in gossip on the turret steps—or worse."

Eustacia's lips tightened.

"I am giving you an opportunity to clear yourself," Melodia said. "If you choose not to accept it, I will be forced to ask you to leave and never expect to return here as my guest again."

"You would say no such thing. I am the only friend you have here."

Melodia clenched her teeth behind closed lips to keep herself from showing emotion. Indeed, at that moment, she had never felt more abandoned. Yet she knew she had gained many companionable acquaintances since her arrival in the country. She felt sure that, given time, she could cultivate many friends.

"And you know full well that Rolf would be sure to object should you try to ostracize me," Eustacia said. "We were once close, you know. And I do not refer to our time together as children."

"No, I did not know he had piqued your interest. But that explains much. Thank you," Melodia said. "You have just confirmed my suspicions about a mystery that has been puzzling me ever since the masquerade ball."

"A mystery? Do tell."

"You." She pointed at Eustacia's nose even though she knew that the gesture was the height of rudeness. "You are the woman in red."

"The woman in red?" Eustacia uncrossed her arms and inched her head toward her. Her mouth slackened into an uneven *O*. "I beg your pardon?"

"Oh, I saw that you were quick to change back into your blue dress in time for the unmasking. But you made quite an impression in your red dress and feathered head covering during the ball."

Eustacia laughed. "Your mind has certainly taken a flight of fancy, Melodia. I am flattered that you think I would devise such an elaborate scheme, but I did no such thing. In fact, I saw the woman you mention. Who would not? She was certainly stunning, and I noticed that all the men seemed enraptured by her presence. In fact, I envy her, whoever she is."

The confession left Melodia shaken. "You. . .you mean that woman really was someone else?"

"Truly. Bring me the Bible you love so much, and I will put my hand on it and swear that I speak the truth."

"No. I do not require such dramatics. I will take you at your word."

"Really? When you have just threatened to banish me from your house forever?"

"I am so sorry, Eustacia. But will you please tell me what you were saying to Rolf while the two of you were on the stairs?"

"Are you saying you have absolutely no idea?"

"No."

Eustacia turned to Felice. "May I speak to your sister alone?"

"I should be privy to anything you have to say to my sister."

"Please." Eustacia sent Melodia a pleading look.

Melodia glanced at Felice, who wore a pout much like the one she would wear as a child when she didn't get her way. Father would always give in to that pout. Melodia decided that since she was in the process of testing an important friendship, she would not be as vulnerable as their father to Felice's wiles. "Felice, I would like to be alone with Eustacia."

"And have my own reputation ruined?"

"What I have to say has nothing to do with you in the least," Eustacia promised.

"I believe her," Melodia assured Felice.

"If I break my word, Melodia is free to tell you," Eustacia added.

Felice let out a dissatisfied sigh but rose from her seat and exited without another word.

"Thank you," Eustacia said.

Melodia motioned to the seat that Felice had vacated.

"I am sorry you saw Rolf and me on the stairs. I never meant for that to happen."

"Obviously."

"I beg your forgiveness for my outburst about my former interest in Rolf. I admit I once wished he would become a suitor. I thought such an arrangement would be a fine thing, especially because of my deep fondness for his sister, Martha."

"I understand." Melodia nodded.

"Good. And now that the two of you are wed, the happiness he wears on his face is something I have never witnessed in him before. I could never have caused him to look like that. Not ever. And because he is a fine man, I am pleased for him. And for you." When Eustacia placed her hand on Melodia's, she decided not to move it. "Please believe me when I say that I am your friend."

"Though moments ago I thought you were not, I believe you now. I can see the sincerity in your face. And you have been a friend to me since my arrival here. I shall never forget your kindness," Melodia assured her. "But you must realize I have not been married to Rolf long, and appearances. . ."

"Yes. We must have looked as though we were in the throes of a love affair. I am sorry that I put Rolf in that position. But I had to speak with him."

"About what?" Melodia kept her voice gentle.

"I wish I did not have to say this, Melodia, but you apparently have enemies here. Someone is spreading rumors that you are in the midst of a passionate correspondence with a secret love you have hidden away—possibly a suitor from home. And of course, since Rolf, as a normal man, is often absent, that only adds fuel to the fire."

Melodia concentrated on Eustacia's declarations, wishing she could laugh and sob simultaneously. "Whoever is saying such nonsense does not know me at all. In fact, do you not remember that I told you myself that I had not even expressed interest in any suitors before my marriage to Rolf?"

"Yes. You had quite a different life planned for yourself. And I believe that. I have seen in your demeanor, the light in your face, the way your love for the Savior shines through you, that you would never deceive Rolf. And that is why I felt I had to tell him what was happening. I wanted to spare you hurt."

"By suggesting an annulment?"

Eustacia gasped. "I suggested no such thing. That is only a tangent running through the rumor mill. You must have heard the end of our conversation when Rolf was expressing to me how preposterous such an idea is. And I agree with him." A tear trickled from Eustacia's right eye. "Melodia, I humbly beg your forgiveness for causing you distress. Please, please find it in your heart to forgive me."

Melodia squeezed Eustacia's hands. "No. Please forgive me for doubting you."

"You have not known me long, and what you thought you overheard was enough to vex any matron. Your readiness to pardon me only proves yet again the depth of your character."

The women embraced, knowing that no rumor would ever come between them again.

Chapter 9

Melodia made her way back to the party, but Felice approached her from the side and grabbed her sleeve before she could return to her seat.

"What happened?"

"Eustacia is not the woman in red, and she was only trying to protect me by speaking to Rolf."

"Is that so?" she hissed. "I am not so sure I would trust her if I were you. So who do you think the woman was?"

"I do not know. I will pray about the situation. Now we must return to the party." She attempted to do so.

"This is an outrage!" Felice whispered. "Rolf is not conducting himself in a proper manner, especially considering your delicate condition. If I were you, I would pack my bags and leave tomorrow. You and I can go back home. You can say you miss Father and want to visit him. Just do not tell Rolf you are never returning."

Melodia thought for a moment. "If I do, then the woman in red may return."

"So what if she does? Rolf does not deserve you."

The night's events had drained Melodia to the point of surrender. "Oh, all right. I will go home for a time with you. Perhaps getting away for a fortnight is just what I need."

Minutes after the soiree ended, Rolf met Melodia in the parlor. Even after the night's events, his touch upon her hand made her feel reluctant to part from him.

"Felice told me you are planning to leave," he said.

"Not for long. Just to visit Father."

"And your sister is returning with you."

"Of course. Why would she stay here?"

"Why, indeed?" He sighed. "Eustacia told me to be sure to see you as soon as the evening ended. Apparently you have something important to share?"

"My, but you have been busy conversing." Her voice sounded sharper than she intended. She jerked her hand from his almost involuntarily.

"You are upset. Please tell me what has happened to vex you so. I will have nothing distress you if it is within my power to stop it."

"I believe you now, but I was not so certain earlier this evening when I spied you and Eustacia on the turret stairs."

He gasped. "What did you hear?"

"Enough. And then I confronted Eustacia, and she explained the full conversation. I know about the rumors. Rolf, I promise you they are not true."

"Of course they are not true. I regret that she told you. Such vile accusations were not meant for your ears."

"Who do you think is saying these awful things about me? The woman in red, perhaps?" Melodia's stomach lurched.

"I can promise you no one is saying anything negative about you now. I started another rumor, only this one is true. I am making it clear that anyone who tries to sully your name will have to face my wrath."

Love for him surged through her. She took his hands. "But how can you stop them from saying things behind our backs?"

"Perhaps I cannot. But my name and reputation mean something around here. I doubt anyone will want to cross me." He squeezed her hands. "I will defend your honor now and forevermore. And as you are my wife, you will obey me as you agreed in our vows, yes?"

She looked at her toes, clad in kid leather, peeking from underneath her soft green skirt. "Yes."

"Then I want you to obey me now. Stay here. With me."

She looked up. "Do you really want me to?"

"I would not ask if I did not." His eyes took on a sad cast. "Why do you doubt that I would want you to stay?"

"I. . .the rumors."

"No. I never want you to mention such a thing again. Do you understand?"

For the first time, Melodia saw Rolf's eyes narrow and his features tighten in anger. She could see why Rolf had a reputation as a great hunter—and why he was feared by his enemies.

"I cannot bear the thought of your departure under such circumstances." He clutched her waist and pulled her toward him. She surrendered with abandon to his urgent lips.

She forced herself to pull away from him. "I will stay but only on one condition. You must tell me the truth. You say you spoke to the source of the rumors. Who is it?"

At that moment, Felice rushed into the parlor. "No. Do not tell her."

"You were listening to us?" Melodia asked.

"Yes. But it is for your own good." She placed an urgent hand on Rolf's arm. "Do not tell her. She is in no condition to be upset."

"No condition?" Rolf looked at Melodia. A smile of cognizance flooded his face.

She averted her eyes. "Yes, it is as you guessed. If all goes well, I will be presenting you with a gift from God—an heir—this winter."

"Melodia!" He lifted her in his arms and whirled her around.

"Careful!" she jested.

Laughing, he squeezed her in an embrace. "Oh Melodia, this is one of many moments in our marriage I have been dreaming of! An heir! I hope his eyes are as bright as yours."

"And his form as fine as yours," Melodia said.

"No doubt he will be beautiful," Felice said. "But, Melodia, we must prepare for our departure on the morrow."

"No," Rolf said as he sat Melodia back on her feet. "I do not want her to leave. Especially not now. She is in no condition to travel. Undoubtedly you suggested such folly, Felice?"

"I—I thought visiting Father would do her good."

"You thought nothing of the sort." Rolf's eyes took on an anger Melodia didn't expect. "Felice, it is time your sister knew the truth."

"No." A light of fear visited her eyes, and she clutched her throat.

"I have been protecting you all this time but no longer."

"Protecting her?" Melodia asked. "Rolf, what do you mean?" She looked at Felice. "What is happening here?"

He looked at Felice with a cold sternness. "You should be ashamed of yourself, Felice. If I were you, I would rather die than let my sister know how little I thought of her."

Melodia felt more confused than ever. "The truth, Felice. I want to know."

Felice concentrated her attention on Melodia and looked at her with flashing eyes. "Rolf has never belonged to you, Melodia. He is mine, and you do not deserve him."

She pressed her hands to her heart. "What?"

"You were supposed to live the life dedicated to God, remember?"

"Yes. But Father forbade it."

She regarded the floor. "Yes, I am aware of that. Even though I am his favorite daughter, he would not listen to reason."

"Are you saying that Father knew you wanted Rolf for yourself but insisted that I marry him?" The thought was too much to bear. Only a few months before, Melodia would have been more than happy to throw Rolf straight at Felice and never look back. Now the thought left her throat dry and her heart heavy. She looked at him, a fresh wave of love rushing to her being.

"I am indeed." Felice crossed her arms. "You were more than happy never to marry, yet he was not willing to, as he said, 'waste' an opportunity to marry you to

Rolf to bind our family's fortunes. Then that would leave me free to marry Arnold." She grimaced.

Melodia felt shamed. While Rolf was no fool, to have him spoken about as a commodity left her with embarrassment. "Stop it, Felice."

"Do not worry about sparing my feelings," Rolf assured her. "I know the ways of the world."

"Remember Normandy? How we dined and danced?" Felice reminded Rolf. Her voice held a tantalizing tone that left Melodia cold.

"I dined and danced with many lovely ladies. I am sorry that what I thought was polite behavior on my part was interpreted as much more by you, Felice." Rolf's voice held an edge Melodia had never heard.

"But. . .but. . ." Felice stopped herself and sighed.

"That is correct. You cannot think of any promise I made or anything else I said that would have led you to believe I harbored any feelings for you beyond the pleasures of polite conversation. I am sorry, Felice. I have come to love your sister. No matter how many masquerade balls you attend uninvited or how many rumors you spread, you cannot change my mind—or my feelings. And I do not want you to try."

Realization struck Melodia. "Felice, you are the woman in red!"

Felice countered with more rage than Melodia knew her sister possessed. "You!" She shook her finger in Melodia's face. "You ruined everything."

"I? I ruined everything?" Melodia paused to bring down the tension in the room. "Just what do you think you were trying to do to my marriage? I suppose you told Father you were visiting a friend."

"Of course." Her voice held no remorse. "Although Father did insist that I bring three servants."

"And you chose three who fear you too much to reveal your secret," Melodia guessed. "Father always lets you have your way, regrettably."

"I must say, the Goat's Head Inn proved quite a disappointment. I never saw so much riffraff in one place at the same time."

Rolf shuddered. "I never would have allowed my sister-in-law to stay at such an establishment."

She shrugged. "It was only for one night."

"But why, Felice? Why did you go to so much trouble just to come here in secret and whisper to my husband?"

"Do you want the truth?"

"If you are capable of telling it."

Felice flinched. "I suppose I deserve that. I flirted with Rolf because I assumed you were not in love."

"Oh, but we are in love!"

"Yes, I can see that now. And I never should have interfered. Only. . ."

Melodia could see the hurt of lost love in her sister's face. "I am sorry, Felice. I never wanted to be the cause of any unhappiness for you. I love you too much."

"You do?"

"I know she does," Rolf said. "And you should be grateful for such a wonderful sister. I know I am thankful that God gave me a gift in Melodia far greater than I deserve."

Melodia took Felice's hands in hers. "You are my sister, and you shall always have my love. But for now, I think it is best if you return home to Father. I will write him a letter imploring him not to betroth you to Arnold. I cannot promise he will comply, but I can try."

"You would do that for me?"

"Yes."

Obviously overwhelmed by Melodia's forgiveness, Felice kissed her sister on the cheek. "I shall be taking my leave of the estate on the morrow."

Seeing Felice's sincerity, Melodia nodded. Felice exited the room, her demeanor humble.

Melodia turned to Rolf. "I beg your forgiveness for doubting you."

"No, I am the one who should be asking forgiveness. I allowed myself to appear faithless when nothing could be further from my mind—or my heart."

She smiled, knowing they could forgive each other anything for the rest of their lives. "I must ask one favor. Can we dispose of the costumes we wore to the masquerade ball? The memories they evoke—ones of doubt and torment—are too great to bear."

"I agree. I never want to see the dress you wore or that mask or my costume ever again. I promise I will donate both costumes to charity—somewhere in London, where we are unlikely to attend an event where we would find anyone else wearing them."

"And I certainly never want to see a crimson dress again. Never."

"Crimson would not be becoming on an expectant mother in any event." As Melodia giggled, he caressed her curls and took in a happy breath. The kiss they exchanged let Melodia know they truly would enjoy a happy ever after.

LOVE'S UNMASKING

by Bonnie Blythe

Dedication

To my husband, who is everything a hero should be.

Acknowledgments

Special thanks to Tamela for recommending me for this anthology and
to Pamela and Jill for making me feel so welcome. As always,
I am indebted to my critique partners in the Crits and ACFW#11 and to my
main writing buddy, Vickie McDonough, for her unwavering encouragement.

Man looketh on the outward appearance,
but the LORD looketh on the heart.
1 SAMUEL 16:7

Chapter 1

London, 1814

Oh dear! Is everyone in London so intimidating?

Amaryllis Sinclair peered up at the face of the butler while standing on the front steps of her aunt's West End London townhouse. Fatigue made her limbs leaden after the long journey from Dorset to London. Lady Agatha's traveling carriage had not been particularly well sprung, and Amaryllis looked forward to a quiet nap after her trip.

"You are expected," the butler said in sepulchral tones. "Step inside."

Amaryllis took trembling steps into the dim hall, noting the black-and-white tiles and a hall table flanked by two heavy Jacobean chairs. A large painting on one wall depicted a stag being savaged by hounds.

"This way, Miss Sinclair," the butler intoned. "My lady is in the Blue Room."

Following the butler's stately tread, she heard the sound of barking somewhere deep inside the house. She nibbled her lip in anticipation of meeting her great-aunt for the first time. In point of fact, she'd never known of Lady Dreggins's existence until a week ago when a crested letter arrived at her home, offering the sponsorship of a season.

At twenty summers and busy with the needs of a small church parish, Amaryllis had begun to lose hope of marrying. The letter had seemed like an answer to prayer. Perhaps in London, she would find a godly man for her husband—a man not swayed by the dictates of fashion or pleasure but with his attention turned toward what was most sober and worthy.

The butler pushed open a door and preceded her into the room. "Miss Sinclair, my lady."

Amaryllis stepped across the threshold. Her gaze fastened on a woman reclining on the arm of a backless sofa, and she put a gloved hand to her mouth.

Here was no diminutive lady with the sparkling eyes and white locks she'd envisioned during the long trip. Instead, a squat woman, powerfully built with freckled arms and a bulldog jaw, stared back at her with small, bearlike eyes. Two tiny pug dogs shuffled forward, barking and wheezing. Amaryllis took a step back, not wishing to be bitten.

"You Sinclair's daughter?"

"Yes, my lady."

"Is he still too busy with botany to spare time for his flock?"

"Er, well—"

"Are you mealymouthed? Speak up!"

She took a deep breath. "My father is very fond of flowers, my lady."

The woman smiled smugly and petted one of the dogs on the head. The dog seemed to have an asthmatic fit. Amaryllis struggled to compose her expression, not daring to give away the shock that assailed her.

"Not planning to give you a season, was he?"

"No, my lady."

She patted the cushion next to her. "Well, Lady Agatha will take care of that."

Clutching her reticule in her hands, Amaryllis crossed the room and perched on the edge of the sofa. Her smile felt more like a grimace.

"I think you'll do," Lady Agatha said. "Maria Ashbury has a young charge, whey-faced and with red hair. Most unfortunate hair color, red. The Duke of Wellington even went so far as to shave his son's red eyebrows off. What do you think of that, hey?"

"I—"

"Your opinion's not important. The key is to stay quiet and smile prettily. Men hate intelligent women, so if you're unfortunate enough to have much book learning, keep it to yourself. A lady only needs to be able to write her name so she can sign her dressmaker's bills. Beyond that, her sole occupation is to be a pretty ornament to a man and bear him heirs."

Amaryllis glanced at her aunt's puce-colored gown, constructed with many gores, flounces, and bows, and wondered if she had ever married and had children. "It's very kind of you to offer me this opportunity, my lady," she ventured.

Lady Agatha touched her mop of curls tinted an improbable gold color. "That's me, generous to a fault. You may repay me by marrying well."

A frisson of alarm skittered down her spine. "My lady?"

Lady Agatha sat up and fixed her beady gaze on her. "My boon companion, Maria, and I have something of a wager. She insists she can make a superior match with her charge. Because the girl has an ample dowry, she thinks she can puff her off to a duke."

Alarm mushroomed into panic. Amaryllis worried that her rate of breathing might soon match the wheezing of the dogs.

"She won't be able to compete with your looks, however. I had a notion Sinclair's daughter might be a diamond of the first water. Your mama was a reigning belle of London in her day."

"Thank you," Amaryllis said faintly.

"And the icing on the cake will be the tidy dot I'll settle on you if you do as I say. No one will be able to say you don't have a dowry." She peered closely at her face. "You don't, do you? Poor as a church mouse, hey?"

"No dowry, my lady."

She leaned back, seeming satisfied. "Well, we'll put a spoke in Maria's wheel this very night. Colette, my maid, will be able to alter something. I took the liberty of choosing a few gowns for you. That's me, generous to a fault. Now off with you."

A petite woman entered the room, with dark hair, darker eyes, and sallow skin.

"Go with Colette. She's French, so ignore her prattle."

Amaryllis rose from the couch and swallowed. "Am I to understand we are to attend an event this eve, my lady?"

Lady Agatha turned to her, her face an angry purple. "Now didn't I just say that?"

"I had thought to rest after my journey from Dorset—"

"Pah! There's no time to be wasted. You ain't one of those milk-and-water misses, are you?"

"No, my lady," she said with an inward sigh.

"Good. Now show your appreciation by going with Colette. Make haste, girl! There's a wager to be won!"

—⁓—

"A curse on all these newfangled ways to tie a cravat!" Lord Matthew Leighton snarled, tearing the offending garment from his neck and tossing it onto the floor where several others lay piled in a heap.

He heard his friend, the Honorable Peregrine Haddon—Perry to his friends—chuckle from where he sat in the corner of the bedchamber.

"Faith, I've never seen you in such a pother. Surely you don't suffer from a case of the nerves. This is hardly your first ball!"

Matthew peered at his expression in the cheval glass and wondered if his plan to appear as a fop was worth the effort. His dark hair had been teased so high he resembled a Friesland hen. His face still bore marks from the recent scrubbing he'd given it after deciding he couldn't bring himself to wear paint.

Matthew wrinkled his nose at the pungent musky cologne with which he'd liberally doused himself, and the lurid red-and-magenta stripes of his waistcoat made him cringe. His brown-eyed reflection stared back at him as if he'd gone mad.

Maybe I have.

"Tonight's ball," he said evenly, "is my first since the lengthy convalescence from my leg wound at Salamanca. Naturally, I want to look my best."

Perry scoffed good-naturedly. "What I think is now that you hold the title of viscount, you plan revenge on all those debs who ignored you when you had no money."

"Now, Perry," Matthew said with a note of sarcasm in his voice, "you know I would never stoop to such levels. I am rather too bookish, too religious a man, to involve myself in such a Machiavellian scheme."

"Much to the dismay of those pretty *señoritas* who plied for your attention back in Spain. I wish I'd garnered such attention, but I possess neither your figure nor your fortune."

"Spare my blushes, Perry," he said, glancing at his rather chubby friend. Perry had round blue eyes and a mop of black curls. "You're well enough in your own way. And it goes to prove the fickle, petty snobbery of London females. They pass over a heart of gold for some old lecher with moneybags. Or in my case, ignore the fact that I had to bear the loss of my father and brother to get the title, never mind that I'm barely out of mourning. To the fairer sex, I'm nothing more than a means to an end. It's enough to send me back to the fighting."

"It's the way of the world, Leighton. Only you seem not to understand that. Too sensitive for your own good."

Matthew made a final pleat in his cravat. "Then all the more reason to stiffen my backbone and accept my fate as a rich, eligible bachelor. I shall enjoy the hurly-burly spectacle made to secure my newly acquired fortune."

Perry sighed loudly. "By courting the simpering misses, that's what you'll find. Better to look out for a sweet girl, unspoiled by avarice or cynicism."

Matthew placed a ruby stickpin into the snowy folds of his cravat and regarded his friend with a mocking smile.

"It is you who are the romantic, Perry. Such a girl does not exist!"

Chapter 2

A maryllis trembled on the threshold of a mansion, waiting to experience her first ball—something she never had imagined would happen.

A red carpet had been rolled down the steps. Blazing torches flanked the entrance. Light from hundreds of beeswax candles poured out from the doorway, and the scent of hothouse flowers hung in the air. She followed her aunt into the ballroom.

"Lady Agatha Dreggins and Miss Amaryllis Sinclair," the butler announced. After curtsying to Lord and Lady Taylor, the purveyors of the ball, she followed Lady Agatha to the rows of rout chairs lining the dance floor.

Amaryllis gazed about with wide eyes. As Lady Agatha settled onto one of the chairs, her avid gaze ranged the room. "Hmmm, Maria has not made an appearance. Mayhap she realizes the futility of trying to compete with such as I!"

Amaryllis perched on the edge of the chair, trying not to allow her benefactress's words to alarm her further. The idea that this whole undertaking was based on a wager!

She glanced across the crowd. Dancers swayed to and fro in a cotillion. Ladies dressed in every color of the rainbow flashed and twirled around men dressed mostly in black evening garb. Amaryllis glanced down at her celestial blue gown worked with silver embroidery, and a portion of her dread eased. Perhaps she would meet a worthy man here, someone who would be kind and cheerful. Someone who shared her faith in God.

Suddenly, Amaryllis became aware of a huffing and puffing beside her. She looked over to see Lady Agatha breathing hard and fastening a gimlet eye on a bony, long-faced woman who was leading a wispy-haired girl toward the chairs.

As the two older women glared at each other, Amaryllis chanced a smile at the young lady. The girl, who had gray eyes and light red hair, smiled back. Warmth flooded Amaryllis at the response. Surely this girl was as sweet-natured as she appeared, and Amaryllis very much desired a friend.

"Maria," Lady Agatha said gravely as they came to a stand before them. "Meet my charge, Miss Amaryllis Sinclair."

"And meet mine, Miss Fanny Elwood."

Curtsies were traded all around. Fanny sat down on the chair on the other side of Amaryllis. "Are you as nervous as me?" she whispered behind her fan.

Amaryllis felt instantly comfortable at the girl's merry expression. "I'm terrified," she confided.

"Well, don't worry too much. You'll undoubtedly win the wager."

"You know about that? I don't mean to disparage my hostess, but it seems a rather odd way to go about things."

"It's dreadful! But when you've got pots of money and no husband to keep you in check, I guess there's a risk of becoming totty-headed!"

"Shh!" she whispered, horrified Lady Agatha might hear.

Fanny gave her a conspiratorial wink. "I may be a trifle blunt, but it's the truth. Anyway, there's no contest. With your looks, you'll be engaged within a week!"

Amaryllis felt her cheeks warm. "Don't talk fustian! Even I know blonds are unfashionable." She waved her fan in the direction of the dance floor. "That woman there is in the current mode of beauty." A dancer with dark brown hair, liquid brown eyes, and a tiny, pouting mouth, swished past them in the arms of her gallant.

Fanny shrugged. "I suppose." She leaned close. "What do you say about having our own wager? *We* could see who gets engaged first!"

Amaryllis fanned herself. "No, thank you." She shuddered at the notion of making a game of finding a life partner.

Fanny grinned. "You must be the only one who doesn't gamble in this town. Just the other day, I overheard two men bet on which fly would climb a wall faster. Ludicrous!"

"Indeed!"

A party of men strolled past. Amaryllis gazed at them with interest. Most were soberly dressed in black coats, white waistcoats, and clocked stockings. One, however, stood out like a peacock among crows. He wore a pink satin coat over a garish waistcoat set about with an absurd assortment of fobs and seals. Purple silk breeches, striped stockings, and red-heeled shoes completed the unbelievable ensemble.

She had read about such excesses in the newspapers but assumed they'd been exaggerated. Here before her stood what she could only describe as a dandy. His voluminous cravat nearly covered the lower part of his face. A quizzing glass swung idly from his slender fingers. She hid a smile behind her gloved hand.

"Leighton," she heard Lady Agatha boom. "Meet my charge, Miss Amaryllis Sinclair."

Amaryllis looked up with expectation, wondering which man her aunt addressed. The colorful fop put up the quizzing glass and stared at her with a horribly magnified eye.

"La! She's a beauty, but I can't be bothered," he said in a mincing voice. "Your servant, Lady Dreggins."

When he started to walk away, Amaryllis sucked in a little breath. The man had cut her! The rude, uncouth—

"Ah, I must insist. The girl needs a bit of town bronze, and one dance with you will establish her in society."

Amaryllis was even more shocked by Lady Agatha's coercion. *What a dreadful moment!*

The man called Leighton stopped and gave Lady Agatha a haughty stare.

"Your mother would've wished it," she pressed, dabbing a lace handkerchief to her eye. "We were great friends, as you know."

The man dropped the quizzing glass and turned back to Amaryllis. She cringed under his scrutiny, glancing at Fanny for support. Fanny gave another wink and whispered, "He's rich as Croesus."

Amaryllis hoped the floor would open beneath her and swallow her up. A look at the man, and the frown marring his features, told her he'd heard Fanny's comment.

He made an elaborate bow, flicking a delicate handkerchief, his nose almost touching his knee. "Would you do the honor of dancing with me, Miss Sinclair?" he drawled.

There was nothing for Amaryllis to do but accept. She rose and put her fingertips on his proffered arm. She avoided looking back at Lady Agatha or Fanny, knowing they were somehow delighted with the turn of events.

On the dance floor, they took up positions for a Scottish reel. Amaryllis hoped she could remember the steps. She and the housekeeper at the vicarage had practiced to while away winter afternoons. As they waited for the music to commence, she studied the man before her. His heavy-lidded expression and mocking smile didn't seem to match the absurdity of his clothes.

"Is this your first season, Miss Sinclair?"

"Yes, my lord."

"And you are on a hunt for a rich husband?"

Amaryllis gasped. Before she could respond, the music began, and she was forced to follow his lead. The dance lasted half an hour, and the figures kept them separated for the most part. She took a measure of relief from each reprieve, but whenever they met, his glinting gaze seemed to find her wanting. Amaryllis experienced a savage urge to cry.

By the time the dance came to an end, she felt tears well up in her eyes. Exhaustion from her travels made her want to collapse, and her head ached from trying to remember all the steps. As Lord Leighton promenaded her around the room, the dancers blurred into a dizzying swirl, and she stumbled.

"Are you unwell, Miss Sinclair?" he asked in a deep voice at odds with his earlier falsetto. His surprisingly strong arm encircled her waist.

Amaryllis pressed a hand to her forehead as the floor seemed to heave beneath her. "I feel faint."

She was vaguely aware of being hustled from the dance floor. A rush of cool, musty air hit her face, and she realized the viscount must've taken her into an unused room.

"The crush in the ballroom was such that I could not return you to Lady Agatha quickly enough," said Lord Leighton, depositing her onto a sofa. He took a branch of candles and lit them from a smoky sea-coal fire in the grate.

Amaryllis lowered her head in her hands and concentrated on taking deep breaths. After a moment, she glanced at the door and was relieved to find it open to the hall.

"Now that you've established the conventions are being observed, you may forget your plan to compromise me."

She stared up at the viscount in wonder. He stood with his arm along the mantel of the Adams fireplace, glaring at her.

"My lord?"

"Don't play the country innocent with me," he snapped. "I heard your friend mention the state of my finances. Well, I can tell you, you shan't get your hands on it!"

Amaryllis shot up from the sofa. "That's absurd!" The room lurched crazily. She staggered. As if from the wrong end of a telescope, she saw Lord Leighton lunge for her—and saw his leg buckle from beneath him when he tripped on the edge of the sofa. He fell forward, knocked her backwards onto the sofa, and landed on top of her. The air whooshed out of her lungs.

In her supine position, blood rushed back to Amaryllis's head. She blinked owlishly at Lord Leighton's face only inches from her own. He scrambled to his feet, glowering down at her, his handsome face flushed a dark red. He brushed his sleeves in a finicky manner as if to remove all traces of their encounter from his person. *It wasn't my fault!* Amaryllis bit her lip.

"Well, Miss Sinclair. Was that one of your little tricks?"

Before she could answer, Lady Dreggins stumped into the room. She waved her fan at Lord Leighton in a menacing manner.

"I saw the whole thing, Leighton! You compromised my charge, and now I demand satisfaction. You will marry Amaryllis to save her reputation!"

Chapter 3

A maryllis sucked in an icy breath. She put her gloved hands to her cheeks, unable to believe her aunt's accusation.

Lord Leighton's words dripped with venom. "You are mistaken, madam. I have no intention of allying my name with that of your charge or anyone else at this time."

Lady Dreggins peered up at his tall form, apparently unmoved by his stature. "On the contrary, you placed Miss Sinclair in a delicate position and were caught." She thumped her cane on the floor. "That sort of behavior will have to wait until after the honeymoon."

Amaryllis let out a low groan. She longed for the poky little Tudor pile she had called home her entire life, despite the threadbare furniture and damp patches on the walls. Her father, a timid, bespectacled man who cared for nothing but flowers, transformed in her mind from an emotionally absent parent to a loving one with his arms outstretched. Surely, any place was a haven compared to the likes of London and its inhabitants!

She peeked up at Lord Leighton. As if aware of her attention, he turned and fastened his gaze upon her. Amaryllis shrank back against the cushions of the sofa.

"What do you have to say for yourself, you scheming little minx?"

His dark eyes glittered in the pallor of his face. His lips were thinned in a white line. He appeared to be in pain, as well as justifiably angry. She remembered the way his leg had collapsed from under him. She clasped her hands together.

"Are you hurt, my lord?"

––⁓––

Matthew scowled. Was he that obvious? The vixen peered up at him with wide blue eyes, looking admittedly fetching with her flushed cheeks and blond hair in disarray from their tumble. He fought the sudden temptation to believe her concern was genuine. Her air of innocence was an act, of that he was certain. Despite his inclination to believe the worst, he found his senses quickening at the girl's loveliness.

"La, my Amaryllis is all solicitation," Lady Dreggins said, waggling her fingers. "She'll make a fine viscountess."

Matthew opened his mouth to deliver her a stinging set-down. He heard a disturbance in the hall. His cousin Bertie Snell ambled into the room, gazing about with obvious interest. A brunette floated alongside him, her limpid gaze taking in every detail. Matthew remembered her as Lady Olivia Thorpe, a dazzler with whom his cousin had made him promise to dance.

"What's to do, Leighton? Lady Thorpe is simply pining for you. Remember, you are engaged with her for the supper dance."

Matthew looked with disfavor upon Bertie. His oily behavior and darting dark eyes gave him the manner of a horse trader.

Bertie raised his quizzing glass at Miss Sinclair and sent her a haughty stare. Although Matthew had done the same only a short time before, Bertie's action irritated him. Miss Sinclair's color was high, but she held herself with quiet dignity.

"Well, Leighton," Lady Dreggins thundered. "What are you going to do about my charge, hey?"

"What's this?" Bertie squawked. He gave the older woman an outraged glare, flicking his handkerchief as if to shoo her away.

Matthew's bad leg throbbed and burned from his stumble. The room seemed to close in on him. Lady Thorpe glided up to him and slid her hand around his arm. Her liquid brown gaze threatened to swallow him up. He glanced at Lady Dreggins, whose humorless smile and hard eye boded a scandal if he refused to come to heel.

Miss Sinclair kept her gaze averted to her clasped, gloved hands. Only the quick rise and fall of her chest indicated her high state of emotion. The bugle beads of the cap in her lap winked in the low light of the room.

Matthew breathed a silent prayer for forgiveness for what he'd done—for what he was about to do. *My vanity has brought me to this point. Now I must suffer for it.*

The pressure of Lady Thorpe's hand on his arm increased. Lady Dreggins's wheezing breaths quickened in tempo. Bertie flicked the lid of his snuffbox and took a generous pinch.

Matthew made a decision. He must choose the lesser of two evils. And perhaps he might find a way out of his conundrum before he found himself wedded to a stranger.

Straightening, he looked at the older woman and cleared his throat. "Lady Dreggins, permit me to pay my addresses to Miss Sinclair for her hand in marriage."

Lady Dreggins thumped her cane on the floor, swelling up until she looked about to burst from the confines of her corset.

"Done!" she boomed. "My charge accepts!"

That was when Miss Amaryllis Sinclair fainted dead away.

—⁂—

Returning from an early morning ride in Rotten Row before his staff had arisen, Matthew strode into the hall of his London town house and stripped off his gloves.

His butler, Steves, took his gloves and hat, and inclined his head.

"I hear congratulations are in order, my lord."

Matthew started. "Congratulations?"

"On your forthcoming nuptials."

He thinned his lips. "News travels fast in this town."

"Actually, I ascertained the information from the morning newspapers."

Matthew ground his teeth as a fresh wave of fury washed over him. "No doubt that Lady Dreggins inserted it *seconds* after she trapped me into marriage with her equally conniving niece!"

"My lord, this is not joyful news?"

"No, it is not," he snapped. "I find myself affianced to some country bumpkin who set a neat trap for me." He tried to make Amaryllis Sinclair's image into a cunning, shrewd female. Instead all he could remember was the way her blue eyes filled with alarm when she woke up in his arms after her faint. He also remembered the purity of her skin, the light fragrance of her perfume. . . .

He grimaced. Surely such an innocent countenance was just a ruse. He'd seen it before when his male friends had been enslaved by belles of the ball only to find themselves married to empty-headed harridans.

"The Honorable Peregrine awaits you in the breakfast room, my lord."

Matthew's frown eased a bit. He entered the breakfast room to find Perry filling a plate with kippers and a rasher of bacon from the chafing dishes. He looked up with his usual cherubic smile.

Before he could speak, Matthew put up his hand. "Do not congratulate me, whatever you do, Perry."

Perry grinned and brought his plate to the table. "Still huffy, eh? Thought you might've settled down by now."

Matthew grabbed a plate and began filling it with eggs and toast. "Your wits have gone wandering, my good friend. I'm still quite livid and will make every effort to escape this debacle."

Perry grunted. "Don't see what all the fuss is about. Miss Sinclair is a pocket Venus. A real shiner. Make a fellow proud to have a girl like her on his arm."

Matthew raised a brow as they sat down at the table. "Looks can be deceiving. I'll grant that Miss Sinclair is, as you so delicately put it, a 'real shiner,' but I also know she's sly, scheming, underhanded, tricky—"

"Are you sure about that?" Perry interrupted with his mouth full. He stabbed the air with his fork. "Maybe she's as sweet as she looks. Maybe it's that dragon aunt of hers who's behind any scheming. Give the girl a chance."

"Give the girl a. . ." Matthew pursed his lips and shook his head, deciding he'd had enough talk of Miss Sinclair. "By the way, is there a reason you stopped by this morning? Although I'm always happy to receive you."

"Breakfast," Perry mumbled around his food. "I'd starve on what my cook prepares."

Matthew sent him an amused smile. "Fire her. Hire another."

"Can't. She terrifies me. Easier to come here."

He laughed. "You're welcome anytime, Perry."

His friend drained his teacup. " 'Sides, thought you might want to know what Snell said in his cups after you left last night. Mumbling something about seeing you dead before he'd see you wed."

Matthew leaned back in his chair, drumming his fingers on the tabletop. "That cousin of mine bears watching. He's been acting awfully strange lately."

"He was certainly surprised when you returned to London a fortnight ago from Spain. Like he'd seen a ghost." Perry blotted his mouth with the edge of the tablecloth. At Matthew's raised brow, he belatedly noticed the folded napkin next to his plate.

"Can't get used to these newfangled French inventions."

Matthew chuckled.

"Enough of your creeping cousin. This is a beautiful day and as such deserves a visit to a beautiful girl."

"Forming a *tendre* for someone, eh, Perry? Who's the lucky lass?"

He turned red. "No such thing, Leighton. I'm talking about us paying a call on your fiancée."

Chapter 4

Amaryllis winced as pale light flooded the room when the chambermaid pulled the curtains open. She struggled to a sitting position, her brain fogged by something dark and ominous lurking just outside her memory. Her throat ached, whether from crying or a cold, she didn't know.

"What time is it?"

The maid bobbed a curtsey. "Just past one, miss."

"One in the *afternoon*?"

"My lady and miss didn't return home until after four this morning."

Amaryllis slumped back against the pillows as the shadow hovering over her burst into unhappy brilliance—she was being forced into marriage to someone who didn't want her. And her aunt had insisted they stay for the duration of the ball to make sure *everyone* had heard the news.

She put her hands over her face and began to cry.

"Your chocolate, miss."

Amaryllis looked up to see the placid face of the maid through a blur of tears. She accepted the cup and saucer with trembling hands, struggling to compose herself.

"My lord the viscount is accounted a good catch, miss."

She stared in surprise. "You know about it?"

The maid lowered her gaze. "The announcement was in the papers this morning. Mr. Biggs, the butler, told the staff."

I doubt Viscount Leighton sent that announcement to the papers. It had to be Lady Dreggins! She sniffed mournfully, wondering how to cope with such a cascade of humiliations.

The maid fluffed her pillows behind her. "And they say he do be a brave man."

Amaryllis looked up after venturing a sip of the chocolate. "The butler?"

The maid's lips firmed. "No, miss, the viscount."

She thought back to the foppish dress and mocking gaze of her supposed fiancé, wondering if they were speaking about the same person. "Brave? How?"

"In the campaigns. The battle in Salamanca was written about in the papers,

125

and my lord was mentioned especially." The maid bobbed another curtsey and left the room.

He was a soldier? She tried to imagine the fribble she danced with last night leading troops into battle. A hysterical giggle escaped her lips.

The momentary merriment faded away. *How can I ally myself to such a man? Dear Lord, surely this is not Thy will for my life. Surely Thou wouldst not have me yoked together with an unbeliever!*

Colette swept into the room and began laying out an ensemble. "Time for miss to arise. Lady Dreggins wishes you to be ready for callers."

"Callers?" she said faintly. "Does anyone in this town ever rest?"

"No, miss. They are here for one purpose and one purpose only—to marry well."

Amaryllis sensed an underlying mockery in the tone of the lady's maid. She swallowed a shaky sigh and got out of bed.

—⁓—

Lady Agatha Dreggins visibly preened over her apparent coup as they sat in the drawing room, awaiting callers. "Maria was fuming, Amaryllis. I tell you, it was my finest hour."

Amaryllis bit her lip. "Aunt, I'm not sure it is wise to take glory in gambling."

"Stuff. It's the way of the world."

The way of the world meaning the city of London. Amaryllis eyed the wheezing pug dogs in her aunt's lap, wishing with all her heart she was back home in Dorset. Her gaze fell on the skirt of her morning gown of green crepe edged with blond lace. On the other hand, she could never have afforded such a wardrobe back in the parish, and she was feminine enough to enjoy a pretty frock.

Worries about her supposed fiancé suddenly eclipsed the beauty of her dress. She leaned forward. "Aunt, I beg of you, do not hold me to this engagement. What happened was purely an accident."

Her aunt's expression became mulish. "Doesn't matter. Besides, Leighton needs to marry and set up his nursery, not prance around throwing away his fortune on himself."

"I'm sure that is for the gentleman to decide."

"Have no fear, Leighton will do what's expected of him."

Amaryllis experienced a pang of pity for the viscount in the face of her formidable aunt.

"And it's important that his cousin does not inherit. Leighton *must* have sons."

Lady Dreggins stared at her as if Amaryllis could present sons by sheer force of her will.

"Cousin? That man who came into the room when. . . ?" Her voice trailed away as renewed mortification rushed to the fore.

"Bertie Snell is a wastrel," her aunt said, "and would run the Leighton estates to rack and ruin. He almost got his hands on them when your fiancé nearly died. Leighton is the last of his family." One of the pugs lumbered onto her lap. "He does have an older married sister whose daughter, Regina, is due to make her come out next season, and a good thing, too. The girl is beautiful, but positively wild. She needs to be matched with someone with a strong hand to keep her from doing something scandalous. When you and Leighton marry, perhaps you can befriend her."

"Of course," Amaryllis murmured. "But what's this about my fiancé almost dying?"

"Took a ball in the leg during a campaign. Was invalided home, and a fever almost finished him off. It's amazing he's alive." She patted the asthmatic dog on its head. "Might not last much longer though if his dandyism extends to lead paint. But t'wouldn't be a bad thing if he departed for foreign shores after you've produced a couple of heirs."

"Travel to America?"

"I'm talking about death, child."

"Aunt!"

"Tish. My Leon had the good sense to pop off six months after we were married. I have done a much better job with the estates than he would have."

Amaryllis wondered if her dreams of love, marriage, and children were just that—a dream in this world of unions as business contracts and heirs merely a guarantee that fortunes remained in the family. She began to feel sorry for the viscount.

The butler entered the room. "Lord Leighton and the Honorable Peregrine Haddon, my lady." He stepped aside to allow the two gentlemen in.

She caught her breath when her gaze met her fiancé's eyes. He wore a blue morning coat of Bath superfine stretched across his broad shoulders, nankeen breeches, and glossy Hessian boots. His dark hair was styled in the windswept, and his conservatively pleated cravat exposed the clean lines of his jaw. There was no sign of the fop in the imposing figure that stood before her.

Amaryllis almost wished for his return.

His friend Mr. Haddon peeked around from behind and smiled beatifically. "Good morning, ladies. The weather is fine, is it not?"

Lady Dreggins waved them to the couch opposite. "Do sit down, gentlemen. Biggs, tea and cakes, if you please."

"Yes, my lady."

As the butler quit the room, Amaryllis peeked at Lord Leighton. He sat ramrod straight, resting his hands on the knob of a silver-topped cane. His dark eyes surveyed her with an air of disinterest. She felt her cheeks growing hotter by the minute.

He turned to her aunt. "Lady Dreggins, I must say you were most prompt in sending the betrothal announcement to the papers."

Aunt Agatha wiggled her fingers at him, a toothy smile stretching across her face. "Tol rol, you fellows are so forgetful when it comes to such things. No need to thank me."

Mr. Haddon cleared his throat. "How did you find your first ball, Miss Sinclair?"

Amaryllis's gaze flew to the viscount's friend. *Is he mocking me?* She glanced at Lord Leighton. He returned it with a limpid gaze of his own.

She took a deep breath. "I found it most singular, sir."

—⁓—

Matthew regarded his apparent fiancée with something approaching appreciation. *That's an understatement, if I ever heard one.* And though her beauty captured his attention, he hardened his heart when he remembered the way she had trapped him. How to get out of it? He'd chosen not to appear as a fop today because of the disastrous result on the previous evening, though he might revisit the ploy at some future date.

His gaze dropped to her lips. *Perhaps I should take some premarital license.* His conscience panged him, but the injustice done to him burgeoned in his mind.

She sent him a seemingly shy smile. "How is your leg, my lord?"

Matthew jerked in surprise. Lady Dreggins harrumphed. He notched up his brow. "My, what free and easy manners must thrive in the country. My, er, *leg*, as you so delicately put it, is much improved. I thank you for your concern."

His temporary fiancée bit her lip, her blue eyes wide. She looked down as a blush mantled her cheeks.

"Lady Dreggins, might I have a few moments alone with my betrothed?"

Miss Sinclair looked up, her lips parted.

"No, Leighton, you may not."

Mr. Haddon cleared his throat, eyeing his friend. "I say—"

"Alas," Matthew said coolly, "I must insist."

Lady Dreggins thumped her cane and rose to her feet, decanting the dog onto the floor. "Ten minutes and not a moment more."

When Mr. Haddon, who darted nervous, meaningful looks in his direction, and Lady Dreggins left, he regarded the young lady where she sat with her gaze fastened squarely on her clasped hands.

"That is a vastly fetching hair ribbon, Miss Sinclair."

She snapped her head up. "I beg your pardon?"

"I meant that I was only able to view the top of your head. I prefer this aspect much better."

Her cheeks turned fire red. *Quite the little actress,* he thought cynically. "Do take a turn of the room with me."

She stood and slowly took his arm, careful not to touch him any more than she had to. It struck him as odd behavior if it was true that she'd planned to trap him into marriage. Perhaps she *had* been forced into it by her aunt, as Perry had suggested. A plan to repulse her materialized in his mind as he thought once more of her lips. "Miss Sinclair."

"Yes?" She looked up at him, her eyes the color of a warm summer sky.

He felt his own face heat at what he was about to do, but he stiffened his spine, rationalizing that it would be unwise to succumb to a sham of a marriage with a stranger—even if she was pretty. "May I kiss you?"

She pressed her hand to her chest and took a step back. Her frozen expression matched the ceramic gaze of the shepherdess on the mantle. "I barely know you!"

Matthew was unable to keep the irony from his voice. "And yet we *are* engaged to be married."

He moved closer, effectively blocking her into a corner between the fireplace and an escritoire. She backed up until she bumped into the wall.

"Are. . .are you really going to kiss me?" she squeaked.

He placed a hand on the wall next to her and lowered his head, wondering if becoming unengaged might be more pleasant than he thought. "Perhaps."

Miss Sinclair gulped. "Are you healthy, my lord? I fear I woke up with a bit of a sore throat."

He raised his brows.

"Because," she rushed on, "Aunt Agatha said you were once quite ill and might even pop off right after we're married."

Matthew raised his head and narrowed his eyes, regarding his oh-so-innocent fiancé. Was this part of her game? To cast herself as an unwilling victim, to make him somehow sympathetic to her plight and allow the engagement to stand?

Well, I won't be a pawn in some matchmaking busybody's scheme. Despite the delicious temptation Miss Sinclair presented, he decided he wouldn't attempt to kiss her. It could actually cement their betrothal in *her* mind. Better to stick to playing the part of the fop.

He pulled out a handkerchief and held it up to his nose. "La! Stand back, Miss Sinclair. I do not wish to be a victim of your contagion." He flicked the handkerchief at her. "Get thee hence!"

Amaryllis glared at him in surprise and marched over to the sofa. She sat down, her back stiff with outrage.

The drawing room doors opened. Lady Dreggins lumbered in. "Well, Leighton, not up to anything havey-cavey, I trust."

"Here now," Perry sputtered as he walked in behind her. "Leighton doesn't resort to such goings-on."

"In fact," Matthew said in a falsetto voice, "this Miss Sinclair is quite a forward girl. She got close enough to kiss me, then informed me of her contagious status. Really, Lady Dreggins, you should choose charges only from the healthiest stock if you plan to loose them into society."

The older woman puffed up with anger, her gaze darting from him to Amaryllis. "What's this all about? Are you bamming me, Leighton?"

"I had it from her own lips." He let out a shriek of laughter at his pun and glanced at Amaryllis for her reaction.

Distaste had curdled her gentle features, which gave weight to the notion that Miss Sinclair had no more interest in this marriage than he. A reluctant admiration for her sprang up within him. Still, he needed to disaffect her to the point of begging her aunt for a release from the engagement.

Even if it meant playing the fool.

—◆—

Once Lady Dreggins had delivered herself of the stern dressing-down on the impropriety of mentioning the word *leg* in polite society—*nether limbs* being the appropriate term—Amaryllis was given leave to go to her room.

At the window of her bedchamber, she pressed her forehead against the cool panes and looked out at the jumble of rooftops and birds wheeling against the cloudy sky. *This is not at all what I expected, Lord. Is there still hope that I can find a husband this season? It will be dreadful if I don't marry, and Aunt has to endure the expense of the season for nothing.*

But to marry some coxcomb who minced and pranced in that disgusting way? She closed her eyes. It was either him or some man in his dotage back in the parish.

Amaryllis released a weary sigh and wandered over to the fireplace, where a cheerful applewood fire crackled against the chill of the day. She sank down onto an upholstered ottoman and thought of her surprise when Lord Leighton had arrived in somber morning dress. The tall, masculine man had been far and away divergent from the fop she'd become engaged to—until it served his purpose to play the fool again.

So which was the real Lord Leighton? The dandy or the dashing man of fashion?

A plop of rain fell down the chimney, landing on a fire castle with a hiss and crumbling it into a pile of embers. Was that happening to her dreams? Because dandy or dashing, what remained of import was finding a godly man to take as husband.

Chapter 5

Amaryllis was allowed to rest the following day before a busy schedule of evening events, and she was thankful for the reprieve. She spent the time in her bedchamber reading a Minerva Press novel. While she enjoyed the distraction of the gothic romance, Amaryllis felt the heroine was rather trying, always swooning and fainting about the place.

Remembering her own swoon in that musty room with many avid spectators made her cheeks grow warm. But that reaction had been real. Surely a mere apparition was no match for the discovery of being betrothed to a ridiculous stranger.

She thought once again of seeing Lord Leighton without the popinjay veneer. She had actually found herself attracted to him—actually had wondered if she would like it if he kissed her.

Amaryllis set the book down and jumped up from the chair. *This is not the proper direction for my thoughts. Marrying the viscount will surely never come to pass—somehow the Lord will spare me from such a poor match.*

But what if He doesn't?

Amaryllis groaned. Somehow she had to stop this farce of a betrothal. Besides, the viscount didn't want her any more than she wanted him. And to help him along, perhaps she might even dabble in a little masquerade of her own. Something to give him a disgust of her.

Her restless gaze landed on the cover of the novel, reminding her of the cloying, clingy heroine who was prone to faint at every little noise. She blinked. Of course! The perfect way to repulse someone who didn't want her was to cling and pine and wheedle—and to press her unwelcome attentions on the skittish object of her pretend passions.

She giggled at her own melodramatic thoughts, but images of clutching the viscount's arm, of gazing into his eyes—of risking a kiss—assailed her untried senses. It would be a dangerous game—a deep game where she might be burned instead of spurned.

But do I really have a choice? Imagine a lifetime joined to a posturing fop. Think of the consequences!

Amaryllis firmed her lips and raised her chin, her heart pounding in her ears. *I'll do it!*

—~~—

Butterflies took flight within Amaryllis's stomach as the carriage stopped in front of a large mansion later that evening. Flaming torches lit the entrance, and once again, she felt the frightening thrill of venturing into the unknown. What would be the result tonight?

She took a measure of comfort in the fact that she was in looks—at least that's what the cheval glass had told her. Colette's choice of a round train-dress of rose Moravian muslin and silk roses nestled among her curls made her feel like a princess—and a little wistful that she had yet to meet her special someone.

"You know, we neglected to set the amount of a wager because I surely owe you some money!"

Amaryllis turned to see Fanny Elwood approaching with Maria Ashbury. She impulsively reached out to give the young woman a hug.

Fanny regarded her with a mischievous twinkle in her eyes. "I knew you'd get engaged soon, but this surprised even me. Congratulations!"

Amaryllis bit her lip, hesitant to divulge the details of her bizarre betrothal to her new friend. "Thank you."

As they sat down and arranged their skirts, Fanny leaned over. "I want all the details, you know. It must be romantic to receive an offer on one's first evening in town!"

Fiddling with the lace of her reticule, Amaryllis wondered how to answer in such a way as not to be dishonest. "Um, well—"

"I spy the fair charmer now," someone shrieked. "Make way!"

Amaryllis looked up in the direction of the disturbance to see Lord Leighton tittupping toward her on high boot heels. He made an elaborate bow with many flourishes of a lacy handkerchief in front of her and straightened, regarding her with a mocking smile.

"I am come," he said in that absurd voice, "to claim your hand for the waltz."

The viscount had outdone himself tonight. His coat of a virulent purple was worn over a waistcoat embroidered with a pair of showy peacocks. His cravat foamed up over his chin, and the points of his collar nearly touched his nose.

Out of the corner of her eyes, Amaryllis saw Fanny holding up her fan to hide most of her face, but sensed her friend was laughing at the outrageous spectacle of this Pink of the Ton. The grand plan to shame her fiancé into breaking the engagement suddenly seemed imperative.

Lord Leighton held out his arm. Closing her eyes briefly to summon strength, Amaryllis stood and accepted his escort. He led her to one side of the room, sweeping her into the crowd as the strains of the waltz began.

She spent most of the time adjusting her steps to the crush of dancers, while trying *not* to notice the pressure of the viscount's hand at the small of her back. Despite the fact that the Prince Regent had given his blessing to the once-forbidden dance, it still seemed disgraceful to be so closely entwined with a member of the opposite sex. Finally, the dance came to an end. Amaryllis remembered her plan to cling to her fiancé. *It's now or never.*

As he promenaded with her around the room, she hung on his arm and gazed up into his eyes. "I just dote on the waltz, don't you, Lord Leighton? It is a rather scandalous dance, I suppose, but don't you think it was *made* for us?" She batted her eyelashes for good measure.

The viscount blinked rapidly. "Er, yes, Miss Sinclair."

She pressed up against his side and lowered her voice. "I cannot wait to see your home, my lord. Pray tell me, does it have a large ballroom? I simply dote on dancing and will want to have many balls and parties. I look forward to redecorating your—our—home."

She stopped and faced him, peering up at him with her most appealing expression. "*Do* say you'll get a special license so we may marry as soon as possible. I simply dote on quick weddings. Not the pomp and circumstance of a Hanover Square wedding for me. On the contrary, a small, intimate wedding of modest proportions will suffice. What say you, my lord?"

Lord Leighton tugged at the top of his collar, his face flushed a dark shade. "Really, Miss Sinclair, I wouldn't dream of marrying you in such a hole-in-wall way. You deserve the grandest of weddings. Take a year or two to plan, you know, no rush and all that."

Amaryllis rapped his knuckles with her fan. "Silly boy! You act as if you are getting cold feet, which is surely far from the truth. Admit it, you long for immediate nuptials as much as I."

"Ah, here is your aunt, Miss Sinclair. Deary me, I see Mr. Haddon frantically waving me over. Must be some kind of emergency. Your servant."

He bowed quickly and scuttled off into the crowd.

Amaryllis released a pent-up breath and leaned back against the chair, wondering if she'd laid it on too thick.

—⁓—

Matthew strode outside to the balcony facing the back of the property. He nearly bumped into Perry, who followed him out.

"I say, where's the fire, Leighton?"

Matthew ground his teeth then forced himself to inhale a deep draught of cool night air. He took out his handkerchief and mopped his brow.

"Is anything the matter? You look affright."

Tucking away the handkerchief, Matthew gripped the iron railing. "Perry, I'm in trouble. Apparently Miss Sinclair wants me to obtain a special license and marry right away."

Perry slapped him on the back. "That's capital news. Just capital."

Matthew gave him a haughty stare. "Are you mad?"

"Miss Sinclair is all that is suitable. She'll make a beautiful bride."

"Perry, may I remind you my sole intent this season was to avoid matrimony, not find myself deep in the middle of it!"

His garrulous friend shrugged. "Got to get married sometime, you know. Set up a nursery, carry on the family name, eh what?"

"You're missing the point!"

"Here now, no need to get huffy."

Matthew raised an eyebrow and straightened his shoulders. "I never 'get huffy,' Perry. Please do see reason."

"What I see is a perfectly charming young lady who you, mind you, proposed to. Look around at the debs. Won't find one like Miss Sinclair. Sad crop of debs this year, sad crop."

Matthew shook his head, realizing he was getting nowhere. He replayed Amaryllis's little performance in his mind, wondering what her angle was. "She's already talking of redecorating Leighton Hall, the grasping female."

"Place could use a bit of sprucing up. Last time I was there, it smelled of dust and damp dog."

"Perry, are you on my side or what?"

"Think about it, Leighton. If you don't snap her up, someone else will."

"Tcha!" Matthew spun on his heel and stomped from the room, regretting the pain shooting up his thigh—which did little to improve his mood.

As he headed back into the ballroom, someone passing by clipped his shoulder.

"Hey, coz, we were just looking for you."

Matthew turned and saw Bertie and Olivia Thorpe on the fringes of the crowd. Desiring to avoid conversation with his annoying relative, he bowed to Lady Thorpe.

"I believe I still owe you a dance from the other night, my lady."

She smiled and took his proffered arm. As they began the steps of the cotillion, he studied the woman with whom Bertie seemed to want him to become better acquainted.

Her deep brown eyes matched his in color, and her pomaded hair shone in the candlelight. He wondered what she saw in Bertie.

"How do you find the season, Lady Thorpe?"

"Very well, I thank you."

The measures of the dance separated them for a time. When they met again, she smiled. "And how do you find the prospect of marriage, my lord?"

He remembered Amaryllis's words. "Singular, my lady."

His dancing partner emitted a silvery laugh and sent him an understanding smile. "These misses out of the schoolroom can be a trifle *farouche*. . .and rather forward, if you ask me. Even to the point of trickery."

Matthew frowned at the tone in her voice. She had been witness to the disastrous proposal and surely knew he'd been backed into a corner. But for some reason, he was offended by her judgment of his fictional fiancée. Something prompted him to tease her a bit.

"I admit the matter presented itself most awkwardly, but now that it's accomplished, I confess, I look forward to love in a cottage, surrounded by doting children."

Lady Thorpe cast him a sly look. "Ah, you are funning. Love in a cottage, indeed."

The dance came to an end. He smiled stiffly and returned her to his cousin, who was leaning against a pillar at the edge of the ballroom, watching them.

As Matthew walked away, Lady Thorpe's words plagued him, echoing the throbbing wound in his leg that refused to completely heal.

Love in a cottage. For some reason, the notion echoed something in his heart, something unidentifiable at the moment, while Amaryllis Sinclair's face rose to mind.

Chapter 6

A t least here, Perry, we may find refuge from the trials of women." Lord Leighton ushered his friend ahead, and they filed up the aisle of the rapidly filling church to the private box. He looked forward to focusing on God and forgetting his troubles over a country miss.

As he settled himself in his private box, he gazed across the way to see others who were in attendance. When he saw the owner of a smart chip straw bonnet adorned with cornflowers, all his expectation of a peaceful service fled.

"What is *she* doing here?" he grated.

"Who?" Perry asked in a disinterested voice.

"That woman!"

Perry leaned over the box to view the one below. " 'Pon rep, that's Miss Sinclair."

"I am aware of the identity of the person, Perry," he said in freezing accents. "She is here to torment me, to rob me of my last refuge, to—"

"Why are you in such a taking, Leighton? Perhaps she's here to commune with the Lord as you are."

"Pah!"

Several people turned around at the noise, including his fiancée. When she caught sight of him, her eyes widened, and her lips thinned. She sent him an irritated glare before turning back around.

"Well!" said Matthew, offended despite himself. "She acts if she's the one who is put out, when I have the prior claim."

"Oh, do hush," admonished Perry. "The service is about to begin."

Matthew failed to bring his rioting thoughts under control—anger and attraction warred within him. Regardless of her pretty face and well-turned ankle, he would not succumb to entrapment. He would *not*.

"Well, that was a fine service, just fine. Might I repair to your place for luncheon?"

"Of course," Matthew said distractedly. He was ashamed to admit that his fixation with Miss Sinclair and the troubles she presented had blinded him to the entire service.

"Going to greet your fiancée?" Perry asked cheerfully.

"No, I am not. Why give her the satisfaction since she followed me here to torture me?"

As if he didn't hear, Perry waved to Miss Sinclair and Lady Dreggins and hurried to meet them out on the steps of the church.

Matthew followed, seething with a fresh wave of anger—then belatedly felt a sense of shame for his unrighteous attitude. *Dear Lord, I pray for Thy forgiveness for the darkness of my heart in Thy house.*

After greeting several parishioners, trading bows for curtsies, and exchanging innocuous remarks about the weather, Matthew finally made it out onto the steps where he could hear Perry talking with Miss Sinclair about her friend, Fanny Elwood. Schooling his expression into one of blandness, he headed toward them.

—∞—

Amaryllis sensed Lord Leighton before she saw him. Then, from the corner of her eye, she spied him approaching their group. Despite her angst at seeing him this morning, she couldn't help but notice his fine appearance.

She flushed when she remembered the verse the vicar had used for his sermon. Still, the short frock coat with brass buttons worn over a tan waistcoat with matching breeches made her wonder how she ever thought him a fop. His shiny top boots, beaver hat tilted at a rakish angle, and walking stick completed the picture.

Amaryllis released a breath, sternly reminding herself the truth from God's Word: "Man looketh on the outward appearance, but the Lord looketh on the heart."

"What was that, Miss Sinclair?" Lord Leighton asked, raising her gloved hand to his lips in a perfunctory greeting.

She felt herself blush as she realized she'd spoken the verse out loud. Lifting her chin, she cleared her throat. "I was referring, my lord, to the scripture text used in this morning's sermon from the first book of Samuel."

His lean cheeks seemed to darken as he raised a brow. "And you are, er, familiar with the books of Samuel?"

"Indeed, my lord. I especially enjoy reading the exploits of David."

"What are you prosing on about, Leighton?" her aunt demanded. "Of course Amaryllis is familiar with the Bible. Her father is a vicar!"

"But I also enjoy perusing God's Word, Aunt Agatha."

Lady Dreggins bridled. "What's this? You ain't turned Methody, have you, hey?"

Amaryllis refrained from rolling her eyes. Before she could answer, Lord Leighton leaned forward.

"And what, pray tell, is your favorite book of the Bible?"

She regarded him, determined not to let his proximity affect her senses...much. "I take great comfort in the Psalms, naturally, but I hold the Gospels dearest to my heart."

The viscount straightened, his gaze considering. Amaryllis wondered what he was thinking, wondered how he could make her feel hot and cold by turns.

"And the scripture today was?"

Returning his steady gaze, she said in a low voice, " 'Man looketh on the outward appearance, but the Lord looketh on the heart.' "

"Apt, Miss Sinclair. Very apt." He sketched a brief bow and walked away.

Amaryllis watched him go, having no idea what he'd meant with his cryptic statement.

"Wonder what's up with Leighton," her aunt groused. "Must be a disordered spleen. Remind me to have my footman take round some rhubarb pills."

—∾∾—

The following day, Lady Dreggins took Amaryllis to tea at Maria Ashbury's home in Berkley Square. Regardless of who'd won the wager, Mrs. Ashbury maintained the better address and accordingly lorded that fact over her friend.

"Lady Dreggins! So good of you to come all the way from Green Street," she said archly. "I trust you passed a pleasant journey?"

Lady Dreggins removed her cloak and handed it to the butler. "Indeed, I take much comfort in Amaryllis's betrothal to such an eligible *parti*. How goes the hunt for Miss Elwood?"

Mrs. Ashbury's heavily rouged cheeks turned a deeper red. "My drawing room has been filled with many callers—"

"Ah, how many offers has she received?"

Mrs. Ashbury affected not to hear and led the way to the drawing room. Amaryllis suppressed a sigh at the behavior of her elders.

In the drawing room, decorated with a great quantity of Egyptian furnishings after the current mode, she saw Fanny and several other ladies.

"Lady Dreggins and Miss Sinclair, allow me to introduce to you some here whom you may not have met. Mrs. Barton and her daughters, the Misses Tabitha and Jane."

An elegant older woman sat next to two dimpled daughters with butter blond ringlets and china blue eyes. They bobbed curtsies at the introduction.

"And Lady Olivia Thorpe. Unfortunately her mama is unwell today and could not be with us."

The pleasure at seeing Fanny faded somewhat when Amaryllis saw the woman who'd witnessed the sordid proposal scene at her first ball. The young woman, with her brown eyes, straight nose, and perfect rosebud lips, nodded from where she sat regally on a backless striped sofa.

"Pray be seated, ladies, and I shall ring for tea."

Fanny patted the cushion next to hers, and Amaryllis thankfully crossed the room and sat down next to her.

"I'm so glad you're here," Fanny whispered. "Perhaps we shall be able to have a real visit. You're always too busy dancing at the balls for us to have a comfortable coze."

Amaryllis blushed and regarded her friend, who wore a pretty apple green morning gown with a fringed shawl, which brought some color to her pale eyes. "You are funning me, Fanny. Now, tell me all about your prospects. Is there a gentleman you favor above all others?"

Fanny covered her mouth with her hand and giggled. "Indeed, and you shall be shocked to hear his identity." She glanced around the room as if afraid of being overheard. "Your fiancé's friend Mr. Haddon."

Amaryllis smiled. "I am not shocked but rather pleased. Mr. Haddon is all that is amiable. Unlike—" She bit her lip against the unkind words about the viscount. Clearing her throat, she continued. "Does Mrs. Ashbury attend church? Mr. Haddon attends with Lord Leighton at St. George's."

"Oh!" Fanny bounced on the cushion. "I must get her to take me next Sunday."

The tea service arrived, and cups were passed all around. Amaryllis's aunt and Mrs. Ashbury talked exclusively with one another. The two Barton girls lisped and giggled their way through several cups of tea and plates of cakes.

Suddenly, Lady Thorpe approached Amaryllis. "Miss Sinclair, I have long wanted to make your acquaintance. Do take a turn about the room with me."

Fanny sent her a rueful smile. Amaryllis stood and followed the woman to the perimeter of the room, her heart pounding at the certain direction of conversation. Lady Thorpe linked arms with her and smiled as if they were boon companions.

"As you know," she said in a low voice, "I was witness to what happened with Lord Leighton. And I want you to know you have my gravest sympathies."

"Um, well, that is very kind of you—"

"Of course, there's no doubting that the viscount is accounted rich and is fiendishly handsome, but sometimes that is not enough to make up for other things."

The ominous tone of her voice made Amaryllis stop. "Other things? What do you mean?"

Lady Thorpe increased her grip on her arm, tugging her forward. "Far be it from me to gossip, but rumors have been circulating for some time. . . ."

Amaryllis's respiration increased, mixed with a growing sense of annoyance. "Rumors," she said flatly.

Olivia peered around to confirm their privacy. "A string of mistresses," she whispered. "And 'tis said his heart is as hard as stone, and society shudders at the poor victim he will take as wife."

"What I've seen of society," Amaryllis said tartly, "is that many are hard-hearted, yet that stops no one from marrying."

"But I've heard he beats his servants, his horses, and I fear he will beat you, too!"

Lord Leighton might be a slave to fashion, but she could not imagine him beating anyone. "Fustian!"

Olivia Thorpe's smile faded. "My apologies for trying to warn you, Miss Sinclair. Beatings you may endure, but you will wish you had heeded my words when you learn he has left you for the arms of his mistress after your marriage. That will surely be beyond bearing, even for you!"

Lady Thorpe abruptly dropped her arm and walked away. *Managing female,* Amaryllis thought crossly. Yet as she returned to Fanny's side, the image of Lord Leighton in the arms of another woman seared itself into her brain. She balled her hands into fists as an unexpected emotion slithered into her heart.

Jealousy.

Chapter 7

Do you really think Amaryllis Sinclair has any intimacy with the Holy Scriptures?"

Perry leaned on the pommel of his saddle, gazing out to the foggy green distance as they wended their way through Hyde Park. "Stands to reason. Vicar's daughter and all that."

Matthew grimaced, patting the neck of his roan. "Perhaps she learned of my interest in that direction and is using the knowledge to further her hold on me."

"Perhaps if you took the scriptures to heart you'd stop mincing around like a coxcomb and simply ask Miss Sinclair outright."

Matthew felt as if he'd been struck, made doubly painful by the truth in the words. "I'll thank you to keep such observations to yourself," he said in a chilly tone.

Perry let out an apologetic grunt. "Think on it, Leighton. You haven't been yourself this last week."

His conscience panged him. He *had* been behaving badly lately. "Perhaps you are right, but I don't always find myself forced into an engagement!"

"Then break it if you are so set against it."

He sighed. "You know very well I cannot break the engagement. If I did, doubtless that Dreggins woman would have me in court. That is why I must give Miss Sinclair a disgust of myself so *she* will initiate the break."

"It's a lot of nonsense if you ask me."

Matthew shook his head as if to clear it. "My apologies, friend, for snarling at you. Let us endeavor to forget such 'nonsense' for a time, eh? We've been trotting sedately along long enough. What say you to a bit of a race?"

Perry grinned. "You're on!"

He pointed with his whip. "To that tree yonder."

Nodding, Perry yelled, "Heeyah!"

Matthew spurred his mount, and together they flew across the greensward. The wind in his face was exhilarating, freeing him from the confines of his troubles.

Suddenly his horse jolted to a stop—and he went sailing through the air—sky, clouds, and grass, spinning before his eyes.

Matthew landed on his back with a dull thud, the air evacuating his lungs. The thundering hooves of another horse approached. Dazed, he closed his eyes, willing himself to draw in air.

"Leighton! Are you all right?" Perry skidded to a stop and knelt at his prostrate form.

Matthew held up a hand as little by little air seeped into his lungs. He took a gasping breath and struggled to a sitting position. After a moment, he clambered to his feet, holding on to Perry's outstretched hand.

"How's the leg?"

Matthew gingerly twisted his previously injured leg, noting no new pain. "I'm all right," he croaked. After a few more minutes, he walked to where his horse stood, its eyes rolled back and muscles quivering.

"Easy, boy." Matthew gripped hold of the reins and ran his hand along the horse's neck, speaking in soothing tones. Something wasn't right. As he examined the animal's legs for any sign of injury, he noticed a wetness on its flank. When he touched the substance, his fingers came away sticky with blood. "Perry, look at this!"

Matthew checked under the saddle and blankets and found a large thorn embedded in the horse's flesh. Perry calmed the horse while Matthew pulled it out. The animal whinnied, then stilled when the object had been completely removed.

"What do you make of it? This is bigger than anything I've ever seen. And how did it get under the blankets?"

Perry took the thorn. "Wicked looking thing, I'll warrant that. Show it to your groom and see what he makes of it."

—⁂—

After a long, hot bath to ease his aching muscles, Matthew felt more the thing. Not only had his body taken a beating, but his conscience, as well. Perry was only speaking the truth that he'd been treating Miss Sinclair shamefully. Fiancée or no, she deserved better.

Later, as his valet brushed his evening coat, Matthew determined to behave with impeccable manners tonight at the rout where he would surely see her. Regardless of whether he'd been tricked or not, he must treat her with delicacy and kindness, especially as she was an apparent sister in the Lord.

After presenting his invitation to the long-faced butler at the mansion and entering the evening's festivities, Matthew mentally prepared himself for the crush of fighting his way up the stairway among the other rout goers to greet the host and hostess at the top, then fight his way back down the other side of the stairs, all without the added benefit of refreshment or entertainment.

He craned his neck, looking for a diminutive blond among the pushing and shoving guests. *Now where is she?* His groom had heard from the Dreggins's groom that they'd planned to attend tonight. Matthew made it all the way up the stairs, greeted the hosts, and was almost all the way back down before he spotted her.

—⁂—

This is madness. Amaryllis struggled to breathe amid the mass of perfumed, unwashed bodies of the ton. A wizened old man with a pink scalp to match his satin pink evening coat leered up at her from his smaller stature. She pressed herself backward, hoping to eel through the crush without damaging her new gown embroidered with gold thread.

Her formidable aunt seemed to be in her element, conversing with practiced ease in the press. Amaryllis fought down a rising feeling of panic. *Lord, please help me get down these stairs!*

"Miss Sinclair!"

A familiar voice drew her attention downward. *Lord Leighton!* Remembering Olivia Thorpe's words that had festered overnight, Amaryllis turned her shoulder and refused to face him. Her heart pounded, and she felt dizzy—whether from the crowd or from pique, she didn't know. Regardless, she wanted to be well away from that philanderer.

"Miss Sinclair, take my hand and allow me to lead you out of the fray."

She peeked back at him only to see one old dowager rap him on the head with the sticks of her fan for getting too close. Amaryllis winced on his behalf but edged upward away from him. The ancient man who had given her a fright moments before leaned closer and clicked his false teeth at her in a terrible leer.

Oh, for pity's sake! Desperation made her turn toward Matthew and grasp his outstretched hand. His grip was warm and strong as he gently threaded her through the crowd, down the steps, and out to the hall. Breathing a sigh of relief, she sent a sideways look up at her benefactor.

Once more he had forgone the foppish attire and was resplendent in a black double-breasted wool coat with tails worn with gray trousers. A diamond winked from the sculpted folds of his cravat. She hardened her resolve, remembering to look beyond the appearance and to the heart.

"Forgive me, Miss Sinclair. I have not yet bid you a good evening."

Amaryllis flicked open her fan and shielded the lower half of her face in an attempt to gather her wits. His open expression and seemingly genuine smile made her feel more out of kilter than when she'd been on the staircase.

She averted her gaze. "Good evening to you, Lord Leighton. Are you alone tonight or did you bring a friend?"

"Unfortunately Mr. Haddon is feeling a trifle under the weather and elected to remain home."

"I'm sorry to hear that, but I wasn't referring to Mr. Haddon." Amaryllis almost choked on a fresh wave of jealousy.

He raised his brows. "Whom are you referring to, I pray?"

"A lady friend, perhaps?"

"A lady friend." His brow arched upward.

"Of cracked reputation?"

Blood rushed to the viscount's face, and his expression was like thunder. "I beg your pardon!"

That's torn it. Amaryllis too late realized one of her aunt's rules of decorum: never, ever mention a man's mistress to his face.

Lord Leighton took hold of her upper arm and marched her to a less populated area. His voice sounded like a hiss. "What on earth could compel you to allow such filth to pour from your mouth?"

"Are you going to beat me next?"

White to the lips, he stared down at her with eyes that smoldered like coals. "Would you mind explaining to me how you came to believe such a farrago of lies?"

She bit her lip, realizing she was in deep trouble. *If Aunt Agatha catches wind of this, I'll be packed off to the country quicker than a wink.* But the poison of Lady Thorpe's words had infected her heart and mind. Amaryllis's eyes filled with tears of mortification.

"Did someone tell you this?"

She nodded, unable to speak.

"What utter rot! I demand to know who."

"Is it true?" she asked just above a whisper.

He pulled her close, his face only inches from hers. "Miss Sinclair, I am a man of faith, and as such I do not fraternize with ladies of certain reputations, neither do I beat anyone! Now, I want to know who is spreading such lies about me."

"You're a Christian?"

His features softened somewhat. "Yes, Miss Sinclair."

"Oh. I didn't know there were any in London."

A smile tugged the corners of his lips. "Yes, even in London." He gave her a gentle shake. "Now will you tell me who gave you such wicked information?"

Amaryllis gazed up at him, taking in the details his proximity afforded. He had long, thick lashes and a small scar over one eyebrow. He smelled of soap and cologne, and even better, he was a believer. "How did you get that scar?"

"Miss Sinclair," he growled. "The name, if you please."

There's no going back now. "Olivia Thorpe told me you had a string of mistresses and that you beat them as well as animals and servants."

His expression grew grim. She wondered how she ever thought him effeminate.

He tucked her arm through his and drew her from the shadows to where Lady Dreggins stood waiting for the carriage.

"There you are, you naughty child. I have been looking for you this age. Leighton, be so good as to call for our carriage."

He bowed and, as he straightened, sent Amaryllis a look she was unable to decipher. "As you wish, madame."

After he left, her knees felt decidedly weak. She took a deep breath to calm her nerves and grabbed hold of the revelation that Lord Leighton's heart was in the right place after all.

Chapter 8

I tell you, Perry, I felt as if she'd slapped me." Matthew paced in front of a window in the library of his townhouse. He looked up to see his friend taking his ease in a large, leather, winged chair and regarding him with twinkling eyes.

"Was it that she mentioned it to your face or that she imagined you to have a mistress in keeping?"

Matthew stopped and took a breath. "Both. To hear such language from her lips." He slapped his gloves against his thigh. "Dash it all, it's her look of innocence that gulls me. I keep forgetting she's not what she seems."

Perry grunted. "To Miss Sinclair, neither are you. What would the young miss think if her foppish fiancé had once considered the curacy?"

"I told her I was a Christian."

"Fan me ye winds! What did she say to that?"

Matthew slumped onto the facing chair. "Said she didn't know there were any in London."

Perry chuckled. "Can't say that I blame her for such a supposition. And when she finally meets one, he's a far cry from anything she's seen in her parish." He leaned forward. "Do you know what I think?"

Matthew leaned against the back of the chair. "You will tell me regardless," he said dryly.

"I think that the Lord orchestrated this meeting with Miss Sinclair."

"What!"

Perry put up his hand. "She's apparently a believer, and you did not think they existed. Well, here's one right under your nose. Couldn't be more perfect."

"You've got windmills in your cockloft, Perry. I doubt very much that Amaryllis Sinclair is a believer. Don't forget she tricked me into a betrothal." When his friend raised a supercilious brow, Matthew cleared his throat. "Besides, why would she tell me Olivia Thorpe said such lies about me? Lady Thorpe would have no reason to act that way. Another strike against Miss Sinclair!"

"Fiddle," Perry said pleasantly. "Olivia Thorpe is an intimate of your obsequious cousin, who can't be trusted under the best of circumstances."

"It's probably just a coincidence."

Perry stood and went over to the bellpull, giving it a tug. "Not like you to be so stubborn, Leighton. You act as if you're in love with Miss Sinclair."

"Love!" Matthew expostulated, jumping to his feet.

"You rang, sir?"

"Ah, Steves," said Perry rubbing his hands together. "Got any of that seed cake about?"

"I shall ascertain if the cook has any in the larder, sir."

When the butler left, Perry grinned. "All this argufying makes me hungry, and your cook's seed cake is sublime." He sat back down.

Matthew shook his head, half-amused, half-exasperated at his friend's behavior. "Love, indeed. When I marry, if I marry, it will be to a sweet-natured girl from a good family far away from London, I can tell you that."

"You've described your fiancée to the letter."

Matthew put up his hand. "Enough! We are getting nowhere. And still the question remains, why would Lady Thorpe say such things about me, if Miss Sinclair can be believed."

The butler appeared with a tray of cakes and two dessert plates along with tea. Matthew watched as his friend piled several cakes on his plate and bit into one with a look of exaltation on his face. "Stands to reason she's doing it on behalf of Snell," he mumbled around a mouthful. "If you don't marry and produce a son, he inherits."

Matthew sank down onto the edge of the chair, unwilling to allow such a thought to flourish. "I cannot believe such a gothic scheme, Perry. Been reading Mrs. Radcliff's novels, have you?"

Perry set down his teacup after taking a noisy drink. "Don't need to. Watching you and Miss Sinclair is more novel than anything I could read."

"Droll, my friend. Very droll."

"Well, what if it's true? Snell doesn't want you to marry. Say he tells the Thorpe female to drip poison in your fiancée's ear so she'll break off the engagement."

Matthew eased back against the chair, surveying his friend from under heavy lids. "And how do you come up with such a Banbury tale?"

"Just popped into my head. After your groom told me that the thorn must've been placed under the blanket of the horse deliberate-like, well, it just adds up."

"My groom said that?" he asked faintly.

"You were still wobbly from being thrown. Must not have heard."

Matthew closed his eyes, unwilling to acknowledge such madness. *Dear Lord, it cannot be true! Please help me find out the truth.*

"Yes," Perry said after demolishing the last of the cake, "looks like your cousin has murder on his mind!"

Amaryllis gazed out the window down to the street below, watching the carriages fly over the cobblestones. Would Lord Leighton call today? She longed to look in his eyes again and ascertain if he spoke the truth.

Could the viscount truly be a Christian? And if he was, was he the man God intended for her? She blew out a breath and smoothed the folds of her morning gown trimmed with Valenciennes lace.

"You are not attending, child!"

Amaryllis jumped at the gruff sound of her aunt's voice. The dog wheezed in agreement. "Yes, my lady?"

"You must help me address these invitations."

She moved across the room to where her aunt sat at the escritoire. "Invitations to what? Are you to have a rout?"

"Don't be silly. These are for your wedding."

"My wedding," she said in a colorless voice. "Has a date been set?"

Lady Dreggins harrumphed. "Not yet, but I'll pin Leighton down next time I see him. Regardless, there is much to be done. No one will say Agatha Dreggins does not do right by her charges!"

Amaryllis wondered at the anxiety mixed with longing that filled her. *Will I really marry Lord Leighton?* A delicious shiver went over her until she remembered his strange behavior.

She glanced at her aunt. "What is the viscount's Christian name?"

Lady Dreggins peered at her with her small eyes. "His Christian name? Why, it's Matthew, I believe." She looked up as the butler entered the room with a letter on a salver.

"Yes, Biggs?"

"The post has arrived, my lady."

Amaryllis retrieved it for her aunt and watched as she broke the seal and read the contents.

"Make haste, Amaryllis. Leighton is to call at five. You are to join him for a carriage ride at the fashionable hour."

A dizzying assortment of feelings swirled within Amaryllis—excitement, fear, and a suffocating longing for the unknown. As she hurried up to her bedchamber to change into riding dress, she thought of the viscount's Christian name.

Matthew. His name is Matthew.

Matthew helped Miss Sinclair up onto his curricle. He'd forgotten what a fetching creature she was. She wore a scarlet velvet spencer over a fine muslin gown, and a dashing shako hat was perched atop her golden curls. The cool afternoon air lent color to her cheeks.

With an effort, he forced himself to remember she might not be all she seemed. As he climbed up next to her, he sent her what he hoped was a charming smile. He planned to test her, to test Perry's assumption that the girl was religious.

Matthew nodded to the boy who held the horses' reins. "Stand away, Jimmy!" He snapped his whip above the team of matched bays, and the curricle lurched forward as Jimmy hopped onto the back.

They headed for the ring, where many of the nobility drove at this hour, and he wondered how to broach the subject and discern a genuine response from his fiancée.

"The day is very fine," he ventured. "Even here in London, one can see the beauty of God's creation."

She gazed up at him, her searching look seeming to divine the secrets of his soul. "Yes, my lord."

Matthew cleared his throat, determined not to become befuddled by a mere slip of a girl. *He* was the one doing the investigating.

They entered the gate to the ring and joined the queue of carriages making the circuit around the loop. Quizzing glasses were raised, and people craned their necks to see who was with whom. Matthew nodded to a few acquaintances before turning his attention to Miss Sinclair.

"I've been thinking about our conversation. The one where we discussed Lady Thorpe telling you some untruths about me."

She glanced at him and blushed.

"Do you have any idea why she would do such a thing?"

Miss Sinclair furrowed her brows for a moment. "If she did lie, then it must be that she wants to thwart our marriage." Her face turned an even deeper shade of red. She looked away.

Matthew considered her words, which echoed Perry's. If they were true, then just about everyone was attempting to thwart his marriage to Amaryllis—including himself.

"Hmm. An interesting perspective. Here's something else to consider. The other day I was thrown from my horse."

"My lord!" Miss Sinclair put her gloved hand on his arm, her eyes wide. "Were you harmed? Was the war wound in your, um, nether limb, aggravated?"

Matthew bit the inside of his cheek to keep from laughing as his defensiveness eased. Surely he wasn't misreading the concern in her eyes. If she was acting, she'd be fit for Drury Lane.

"I was unharmed, Miss Sinclair. But a large thorn was found under the saddle blanket, giving rise to the notion that it was no accident."

She gasped. "Who could do such a thing and why?"

"That's what I'm trying to discern."

Matthew guided the horses to a nearby park and stopped under a stand of oak trees. "As a matter of fact, I thought we could work together to solve the mystery, and I hoped we could begin by beseeching the Almighty for His aid."

—⁓—

Amaryllis stared at the viscount, wondering wildly if he was mocking her. She gazed into his eyes, longing to discern the truth in their dark depths.

Deciding that prayer was the best option regardless, she swallowed and nodded her head. When he took her hand in his and smiled, her heart fluttered like a trapped bird. Suddenly his lashes swept downward, and it took a moment for her to realize he'd begun to pray.

Amaryllis caught her breath and closed her eyes, striving to focus on the Lord instead of the viscount's deep voice.

". . .We ask for Thy favor to discover any plot intended to harm me or Miss Sinclair. And help my cousin and Lady Thorpe to seek Thee in all their ways. Amen."

"Amen," breathed Amaryllis. She looked up at Lord Leighton, astonished that a simple moment of prayer could establish a sweet intimacy with a man she longed to trust but still feared. Would she ever learn the whole truth about him?

Chapter 9

Amaryllis was no nearer to the truth a week later. Lord Leighton, back to his mode of a dandy, sat at the long dining table crowded with guests, wearing a black- and yellow-striped coat and yellow silk breeches that made him look absurdly like a wasp. His dark hair was teased to a ridiculous height, and he spoke in that high, mincing voice that so grated on her nerves.

What had happened to the seemingly godly man who sought the Lord on her behalf?

She frowned at him from where she sat down at the lower end of the table, away from the higher ranks that included Lord Leighton's cousin and Lady Thorpe. He caught her glance and his cheeks darkened as if he'd been caught doing something unseemly.

Amaryllis looked away and scowled down at her turtle soup, wishing something made sense about this season. Had she really been silly enough to indulge in dreams of romance and marriage to a good man? At this rate, she worried she was well on her way to becoming just another cynic who filled the salons and ballrooms of London.

She glanced at the footmen who stood at attention along the back of the room. One of them, a tall and broad-shouldered Adonis, placed a second bowl of turtle soup in front of Lord Leighton, who continued sipping spoonfuls and talking a great rate, interspersed with dreadful shrieks and giggles.

Just above her, Mr. Haddon also frowned at his friend. Was he thinking the same thing? Next to her sat Fanny, who was attempting to get Mr. Haddon's attention with the vigorous application of her fan. Amaryllis sighed. It seemed everyone's hopes this eve were destined to be thwarted.

Two hours later, the dinner came to an end. The hostess stood and nodded her head for the ladies to retire to the drawing room and await the gentlemen.

Lord Leighton jumped up. "Let us dispense with ceremony and join the ladies, shall we?" He waved his fan in Amaryllis's direction. "I positively pine to be with my ravishing fiancée."

Amaryllis flushed. His tone made the words sound like an insult.

The other gentlemen looked resigned. Since the viscount was of the highest rank, they couldn't refuse and appeared to acquiesce with bad nature.

Once they were all settled into a large drawing room painted a pale green with frescoes on the ceiling, Amaryllis found a quiet corner out of the glare of the flaming branches of candles. She played with the sticks of her fan, wishing the evening were at an end so she could lie down in her bedchamber with a cool handkerchief on her forehead.

"My cousin and Lady Thorpe acquit themselves well, wouldn't you say?"

She looked up into the glittering, dark eyes of her fiancé. "My lord! I didn't hear you approach."

Lord Leighton flicked up the tails of his coat and settled beside her on the sofa. "No doubt you were lost in dreams of planning our wedding?"

Amaryllis clenched her fists, longing to box his ears. Despite his occasional attractive manners, how could she for even a moment consider opening her heart to such a hardened fribble—especially one who played fast and loose with his faith? She shook her head, too angry to speak.

He waggled his fingers at her. "Tol rol. Mayhap you should, since I have reconsidered a long engagement. A love like ours must not be made to wait, so I shall acquire a special license from the bishop that we may marry with haste."

"You shall do no such thing," Amaryllis said in a quavering voice. She swallowed, finally realizing what she must do. A glance at her aunt, who would go into histrionics at the broken betrothal, made her shudder. But she could not, would not marry such a man!

"My lord, I fear I must inform you of a sudden change of circumstances." She glanced up at him to see if he ascertained the direction of her words.

The viscount blinked several times and pulled at his neck cloth. "Faith, 'tis hot in here."

Amaryllis bit her lip as her courage ebbed. She took a deep breath and stiffened her posture, resolved to follow through on what was right. "I'm sure you would agree with me that we would not suit—"

The viscount stared at her, his eyes taking on an odd, glazed aspect. Suddenly, he subsided to one side of the sofa and slid onto the floor.

"Lord Leighton!" Amaryllis fell to her knees next to him and chafed his wrists, half-furious that he might be playing a prank to shame her, half-terrified he was truly ill.

Her shout had roused the other guests, who rushed to her side as she cradled his head in her lap. One of the ladies waved a vinaigrette under his nose. The viscount blinked once, turned sheet white, and passed into unconsciousness. Mr. Haddon lightly slapped his friend's face to no avail, then yelled for a doctor.

Some of the men laid bets as to when he'd recover, several ladies fainted, and still the viscount lay unnaturally still in her lap. Amaryllis began to pray.

"My lord is resting now."

Amaryllis twisted around when she heard the doctor's words. She jumped up and hurried to where Mr. Haddon stood next to the small man who wore a bag wig, an old-fashioned frock coat, and buckled shoes.

"I have given him a purge," he said in a low voice, "and in time the fever will most likely abate."

"Fever?" she asked, clasping her hands together, not caring if she appeared rude to the guests still assembled in the drawing room an hour later.

The doctor peered at her through his spectacles. Mr. Haddon intervened. "This here is the viscount's betrothed."

The doctor nodded. "Ah, yes, you must not worry, young lady. Men home from the battlefield are often beset by fevers."

"Who is with my lord now?"

"A chambermaid of the house, I presume."

Amaryllis stood trembling, engulfed by a fear she could not identify. Without waiting to speak to her aunt, she rushed from the room and ran out to the hall.

"The viscount!" she said to the butler. "Where is he?"

The butler raised his brows and swept her with a disapproving look. "Is there something I can help you with?"

She stamped her slippered foot. "I am his fiancée, and I demand to see him!"

"Very well," he said frostily. "Follow me."

Amaryllis followed him, longing to scream in frustration at the slow pace as they traversed long corridors toward the guest wing.

A movement to her left caught her eye. She turned to see what it was. Down a short hall, ending in a shadowed alcove, she saw Bertie Snell drop several guineas into the hand of the footman who'd served the viscount's turtle soup.

What are they doing in this part of the house?

The butler gave a discreet cough. "We have arrived, miss."

Amaryllis glanced at the butler, dismissed both him and the consequences of her actions from her mind, and entered the bedchamber. She found a chambermaid sprinkling rose water in the room, who stopped at her entrance.

"Would you please bring me several strips of cloth and a basin of water? I shall now sit with my lord."

The chambermaid bobbed a curtsy and quit the room. Amaryllis looked at her surroundings. A branch of candles on a toilet table flickered in the gloom, casting eerie shadows. The red bed curtains were closed. Stepping quietly to the bedside, she pulled them back.

She put her hand to her mouth. Lord Leighton looked so pale, she feared for his life. The frilly nightshirt he wore lay open revealing the strong column of his throat, but the white color of the garment heightened his waxy pallor. All her angst fled before a rush of unexpected affection.

She dragged a chair over to the bed and sat, taking his icy hand in her own in an attempt to warm it.

"Heavenly Father," she whispered, "I beseech Thee to make my lord well. Bring him comfort and healing."

The maid returned with the requested items. Amaryllis released the viscount's hand and turned to the toilet table. From her reticule, she produced a small flask of cologne, which she emptied into the basin of water. She placed the strips of cloth into the water and, when they were soaked, took one, gently wrung it out, and bathed the viscount's forehead.

Matthew opened his eyes, and he took her hand in a weak grip. His sleepy gaze held hers for a long moment. "You look like an angel, Amaryllis, with the candlelight glowing on your hair."

A blush heated her cheeks at the compliment combined with the use of her Christian name, making her wonder if she had a fever herself. *And yet his skin is not warm but cool.* She forced her features into a smile. "Flirting even from your sickbed, I see."

He gave a little tug to her hand. "Not flirting, but proud to be affianced to one as beautiful as you."

She swallowed, longing to believe his loverlike words were genuine but fearing he was playing with her emotions despite his illness.

Voices echoed up the hall. Amaryllis eased her hand from his and went out into the hall, closing the door behind her. Mr. Haddon, with Fanny on his arm, and Lady Thorpe accompanied by Bertie Snell approached the chamber. Lady Dreggins brought up the rear.

"How's the fellow?" Bertie drawled. "Turtle soup is too rich for some, eh what?"

"The doctor said he had a fever," Amaryllis said quietly. "But his hands are like ice."

"Tut tut, Miss Sinclair," Lady Thorpe said. "The fact is you should not be in a man's bedchamber at all. Leave the viscount to the servants, and he shall do very well."

Amaryllis regarded Lady Thorpe, knowing she was right, then directed her gaze to Bertie, who fidgeted with his snuffbox. The memory of him paying the servant lent a suspicious air to his actions. She remembered what Lord Leighton had said about the thorn hurting his horse and about Lady Thorpe's lies. What if there had been something put into the viscount's soup? She suppressed a stab of alarm.

Fanny sent a small smile, and Mr. Haddon's expression revealed worry for his friend. Lady Agatha harrumphed that it was all a rum do.

Amaryllis firmed her lips. "Nevertheless," she said clearly. "I will sit with my fiancé until he is quite recovered."

———∞———

Matthew slowly opened his eyes and for the longest time didn't have any idea where he was. Candlelight wavered on red bed curtains, but otherwise the room was shrouded in darkness.

Images flickered through his mind—images of Amaryllis glaring at him, then seeing her mouth go slack with distress. He remembered many voices and a lot of fuss, and now he was here—but here wasn't his home.

Matthew turned his head slightly toward the candlelight and was rewarded with a breathtaking pounding in his skull. He closed his eyes, waited for the pain to subside, then risked moving his head a little more. After a sensation of dizziness faded, he saw someone else in the room.

He blinked to bring the vision into focus and realized Miss Sinclair was in the bedchamber. She sat in a chair next to the bed, her head pillowed on the mattress by her folded arm, asleep. Her other arm was stretched across the counterpane, her fingers wrapped around his own.

Well, now that her reputation has been compromised, I will have to marry her after all. The notion did not depress him in the slightest. Instead, he came to the unexpected realization that he'd fallen in love with her.

From her contempt at his dandyisms, to her knowledge of the scriptures, and now her compassion at his bedside, Miss Amaryllis Sinclair had clearly demonstrated she was no gold digger determined to trap him into marriage—and he was ashamed he'd ever entertained such thoughts.

He tried to squeeze her fingers, but his grip faltered. He blew out a sigh and closed his eyes, praying for a speedy recovery. What had landed him in this bed anyway? He could only remember his stomach suddenly roiling combined with a feeling of overwhelming confusion.

A little gasp drew his gaze back to where Amaryllis sat. She had awakened, and her eyes were filled with tears.

"Lord Leighton," she whispered. "You're awake!"

Chapter 10

A knock sounded at the door. Amaryllis tore her gaze from the viscount's and brushed the tears from her eyes with the back of her hand.

Mr. Haddon popped his head in the door. "Lady Dreggins is demanding your presence in the drawing room, Miss Sinclair."

"Please give my compliments to my aunt, Mr. Haddon, but I cannot leave until I am assured of the viscount's health."

"Go ahead, Amaryllis," the viscount said in a low voice. "I believe I am much improved."

She turned and gazed at him, noting that a touch of color had returned to his face. "Are you quite certain, my lord?" The nightmare she'd woken from moments ago in which he had died clung to her with frightening intensity.

Lord Leighton inclined his head ever so slightly and offered a feeble smile. "Perry will apprise you if there is any change in my recovery."

Amaryllis released his hand, suddenly embarrassed to be caught holding it. She dropped her gaze and rose on unsteady legs. Smoothing down the folds of her dress, she sent a shy smile toward her fiancé and turned to leave.

Mr. Haddon stood outside the door. "How long have I been here?" she asked him.

He pulled a watch from a pocket in his waistcoat. "About five hours, I should think."

"And did my aunt leave and return for me?"

"No, she has been here this age along with all the other guests. They have been playing cards as was planned."

"What!" Amaryllis stared at him in shock. "Entertaining themselves while my lord was at death's door?"

"Well, er, yes, Miss Sinclair. In fact, they didn't seem to believe Leighton was all that ill."

She grabbed hold of his arm. "Yes, he was, Mr. Haddon, and I think he may have been poisoned."

Perry's eyes bulged. "Steady on! How can you be sure?"

"The footman who served my lord his soup was later seen by me receiving money

156

from Mr. Snell. I know it's circumstantial, but can it be a coincidence? No one else got sick, and Lord Leighton did not have a fever."

"I say, Leighton was right. Gothic goings-on and all that." He patted her hand. "Tell you what, you put in a good word for me regarding Miss Elwood, and I'll send round notes to you keeping you apprised of Leighton's condition. Have we a bargain?"

Amaryllis smiled. "Yes. Thank you."

He sketched a bow and disappeared inside the bedchamber. She sagged against the wall next to the door, exhaustion assailing her. Surely she'd only nodded off moments before Lord Leighton had awakened. She remembered long hours keeping watch, fervently praying for his recovery.

Amaryllis heard a muffled shout through the door. Realizing it had not been latched, she eased it open a few inches. She squelched a stab of guilt at eavesdropping and inclined her ear to the conversation inside.

"And based upon Miss Sinclair's suspicions," Mr. Haddon was saying, "tonight's events may not be a coincidence."

"I believe you have the right of it," Lord Leighton said in an angry voice. "And the time has come to confront this once and for all!"

—m—

"Isn't it exciting? I confess I'm in high alt and don't know how I shall be able to wait a whole week!"

Amaryllis smiled at Fanny's enthusiasm. Everyone was talking of the masquerade ball at Lord and Lady Ackers's Berkley Square mansion. At first Lady Dreggins and Maria Ashbury had pooh-poohed the notion of their charges attending, as masquerades were known to encourage loose morals, but Mrs. Ashbury had been overheard admitting high hopes that Mr. Haddon was *epris* in Fanny's direction and might use the occasion of the ball to propose.

All that remained was the choosing of fripperies to complement their costumes. Amaryllis decided to stop worrying about Lord Leighton's health and enjoy the sunshine of their outing to Exeter Exchange. Mr. Haddon had been faithful with his missives, but she wondered if he were too quick to assure her. If he could be believed completely, Lord Leighton had improved immeasurably and was planning to attend the masquerade.

Gazing about the shops from the windows of the carriage, Amaryllis couldn't suppress her own hopes of dancing with the viscount to test her tender new feelings when she wasn't terrified for his health. The carriage came to a stop, and a footman opened the door and let down the steps.

Exeter Exchange on the Strand quivered with the noise and bustle of shoppers and stalls filled with every imaginable ware, including scarves, cheap jewelry, toys, and fans.

"Amaryllis, do come here!" Fanny cried. "I found the perfect mask for my costume!" She held up a satin sequined affair with rainbow feathers.

"I agree, Fanny. It's perfect!"

"And a mask for you, miss?" the vendor asked. He had swarthy skin and a bushy black mustache and sideburns.

Amaryllis looked over the selection, trying to decide which would be the best match for her white gown. She had decided against the usual shepherdess, gypsy, or Turk costumes that were so popular and planned to wear a pretty mask with regular fancy dress.

"May I be so bold as to ask what will you be wearing, miss?"

She told the vendor, whose fingers flew over the selection. He picked one up and showed it to her with theatrical flair. "For a night of mystery, this will be the best. This is not just any masquerade mask but one worn during a ball as the wearer fled the Terror in France. And later, by a lady who thought her lover false. Be not alarmed, their paths led to true love."

"And just how did you come by all this information?" Amaryllis asked, biting the inside of her cheek.

He closed his eyes. "The mask, it speaks to me, I sense this intrigue and romance in the glint of the pearls and—"

"The gossipy servant what gave it to him told him all about its owners, that's what," said a ruddy-faced woman who was apparently the man's wife. "Blimey, Jem, you an' yer stories."

Amaryllis laughed as his face turned red. Covered in white silk with seed pearls and white feathers, the mask was pretty and would be just the thing to match her gown. She paid the price of five shillings and couldn't help wondering what might be in store for her when she wore the mask.

After another hour spent choosing ribbons and gazing at everything offered, they headed home. When Amaryllis arrived back at her aunt's town house, Biggs held out the salver. On it was a note folded like a cocked hat.

Her heart beat a little harder. Mr. Haddon only sent plain letters sealed with wax. Amaryllis took the note to her bedchamber and opened it with trembling fingers.

Miss Sinclair,

Mr. Haddon and I launched upon an investigation, and after searching for the servant you saw receive money from my cousin, we discovered him in his cups as he apparently has a weakness for drink. We found out that he had been paid to put arsenic in my soup and had also been paid earlier to put the thorn under my saddle, all 'for a lark.' I decided to speak to the groom at Leighton Hall about the carriage accident that took the lives of my father and brother. He believed

*there was evidence that the ridge poles had been sawn through, but I had earlier
dismissed such a notion as he was known to be rather touched in the upper works.*

Amaryllis put her hand to her mouth. *Murder?*

*All together, this is simply too much to ignore. Apparently, Bertie thought
I had died when I was wounded in the war and so assumed he was heir to the
title. When I appeared in London, he had to find a way to get rid of me, and in
part thanks to you, he has not succeeded.*

*I do not have direct evidence except for the ramblings of a drunk man and
the mutterings of an old groom, so I cannot involve the local magistrates at this
time. I have, however, decided to embark on a plan which I will carry out at the
masquerade ball Thursday next.*

*I tell you this so you will not worry if events seem odd that night. I covet
your prayers for the endeavor to be successful and for my cousin to be brought to
justice. Please destroy this letter after you have read it.*

I remain humbly yours,
Leighton

Amaryllis bit back an exclamation. Worry that the viscount was embarking on
a foolhardy scheme conflicted with disappointment that his words contained not a
trace of affection.

Shoving the letter through the grate into the fire, she watched as the paper
curled and turned into ash. She hoped her dreams would not follow suit.

As if confirming the theme of the masquerade, a thick yellow fog crept through the
city streets, masking the night of the ball. Amaryllis shivered and pulled her cloak
more closely around her frame to protect her gown of white spider gauze over a
white silver embroidered satin slip with paste diamond clasps.

Her heart beat erratically at the eve to come, not from debutante nerves but
from worry over Lord Leighton's plan—a plan to which she was not privy. She
glanced at her aunt, who dozed as the carriage clip-clopped over the cobblestones to
the mansion in Kensington.

Dear Lord, please protect Lord Leighton—Matthew—from any harm tonight. The
prayer seemed somehow incomplete but worry fragmented her thoughts. Amaryllis
glanced out the window and saw the flambeaux outside the mansion. They had
arrived.

She looked down at the satin mask winking in the gloom, wondering what the
night might reveal. Taking a deep breath, she quickly tied on her mask. The carriage

door opened, and the footman let the steps down. Lady Dreggins awoke with a snort. Amaryllis alighted and marshaled her reserves for whatever lay ahead.

—∿—

Matthew leaned against a pillar and watched the dancers in their glittering, feathered masks and colorful costumes. He wore a simple black domino over his evening clothes and a plain black silk mask.

I hope my plan works. If it doesn't, I will be made the fool. He had the idea put about that he was considering wearing the costume of a Renaissance gentleman before making it known he would be unable to attend. Matthew regretted using deception to achieve his aims, but this had become a matter of life and death.

He stiffened. A man clad in a doublet, hose, and plumed hat strolled past.

"La," the costumed figure said in a high falsetto. "I just pine to waltz with my fiancée, Amaryllis Sinclair. Have she and that dragon aunt arrived yet?"

Bertie! He took the bait! His cousin was of a similar height and physique and spoke in that ridiculous voice, making it easy for someone to take the imposter as the viscount. He cringed as Bertie continued to make a complete cake of himself. *Poor Amaryllis! Did I disgust her as much as my cousin disgusts me? Faugh, what a coxcomb!*

He continued to watch his cousin prance and simper. *Now, if only Bertie will take this charade all the way.*

"Matthew!"

The soft utterance made him twist around. He saw Amaryllis, a vision in shimmering white and silver satin, looking past him to the Renaissance imposter she obviously thought was her real fiancé. Despite her mask, he saw her rigid stance and the high color of her cheeks.

Bertie approached her, flickering a lacy handkerchief in her face. "Remember my rank and title when you address me, my pert country miss."

Amaryllis's lips firmed, and she sank into a low curtsy. "My lord viscount."

Matthew glared at his cousin for his impertinence, only to realize Snell was just mimicking what he'd seen.

Bertie held out his arm. "Your manner pleases me, therefore I shall deign to dance with you for the cotillion. No, I shall accept no words of gratitude. It is enough to know you will cherish this for years to come."

Matthew seethed, breathing through his teeth as they whirled away in the figures of the dance. *Posturing popinjay!*

—∿—

Amaryllis bit her lip, fighting against a wave of tears. Her fiancé was behaving like the veriest fool! Surely he didn't need to act so when they were together. To think she'd allowed her feelings for him to grow warmer.

How can he be party to any plot while he's leering at me like any half-pay captain?

She lowered her gaze. *But Matthew never leers. He plays the part of the fop, but he has never taken such license.*

Amaryllis studied her cavalier when they met in the figures of the dance. Dark eyes glinted from his heavily sequined mask. Despite the similarity of color, something wasn't right. Could it be someone else? Could this be part of Matthew's plan?

Deciding to do a little investigation of her own, she smiled at her partner. "Such a comfort to join you in prayer the other day, my lord."

"Prayer!" he scoffed. "Waste of time, Miss Sinclair. Religion is naught but for women and fools."

A wave of relief washed over Amaryllis. Even in jest, Matthew wouldn't speak so. Heart pounding, she confined her comments to harmless prattle for the remainder of the dance.

At last it came to an end. Before she could scan the ballroom for a glimpse of her true fiancé, a man in a black domino approached her and bowed over her hand. Suppressing a surge of disappointment, she bobbed a curtsy and joined him in the waltz.

Chapter 11

Looking for someone, miss?" Matthew asked in a purposefully husky voice, watching as Amaryllis's masked gaze swung back to him.

Coloring up, she shook her head and stared at his cravat as they whirled about the room. Silk flowers with jeweled centers winked in her hair, and the stuff of her gown floated around her body. He thought of the sweetness of her spirit, and the quiet dignity with which she comported herself.

The newness of his feelings, discovered when he was at his weakest, had been shaken in the cold light of day by the incessant worry that she was marrying him for his money. If only he could be sure.

"Your fiancé, perhaps?" he pressed. "You are fortunate in securing such a prize. 'Tis said he's rich and you naught but a poor parson's daughter."

"Sir," she said through clenched teeth, "your manner is most unbecoming."

A savage desire for the truth urged him on. "It's more becoming than that of a scheming adventuress."

Amaryllis stopped and stared at him with a fiery gaze and clenched fists. "You go too far, sirrah! I would marry Viscount Leighton if he didn't have a farthing!" She spun on her heel and pushed her way through the dancers.

Matthew watched her go until she disappeared from view, the meaning of her words heaped like burning coals on his head. He cursed his hard heart—and his lack of trust—and feared his harsh words might have cost him the woman he loved.

———

"Aunt Agatha," Amaryllis said breathlessly when she reached that lady's side, "have you seen Lord Leighton?"

Her aunt stared at her. "Are you blind?" She pointed with her fan. "There he is, heading for the card room."

Amaryllis saw the man with whom she'd danced the cotillion. How could she voice her doubts that he was her real fiancé?

Lady Dreggins turned to a dowager, with whom she'd been conversing. "Imagine, a girl not even recognizing her own betrothed!"

Amaryllis loosened the strings of her mask and removed it, intending to find the ladies repairing room where she could sort through her jumbled thoughts. Had she really just declared herself to a complete stranger?

Had she really fallen in love with her own fiancé?

The motion of the crowds heaved like waves of the sea, making her dizzy. She wanted nothing more than to find Lord Leighton and—

And what? Tell him you love him? Tell him you want to marry him? Tears burned her eyes. *He's made it plain he doesn't want you!*

Amaryllis put her hand to her head, taking deep breaths to clear her mind. *If I tell him, his reaction will be that of the man in the domino—cynicism and suspicion.* She glanced up to see Fanny being led by Mr. Haddon in the figures of a Scottish reel. She envied their simple courtship. They had no secrets between them.

Suddenly she knew she must tell Matthew the truth, regardless of his reaction.

—⁂—

More than anything, Matthew longed to find Amaryllis and reveal himself, but at that moment, his cousin sauntered by, heading in the direction of the card room. Matthew threaded his way through the crowd at the edge of the dancing, barely able to keep sight of the florid hat bobbing ahead of him. Bertie disappeared into the card room.

Matthew tried to go faster but was impeded by the ball guests gathering to watch the leaps of the more talented dancers. One dancer jumped up only to lose his balance and careen to one side.

A wave of people was pushed back from the impact. Costumed guests stumbled in his direction. A man, obviously drunk, reeled against Matthew, knocking his mask askew, crashing him to the floor, and landing on his bad leg.

Ladies shrieked and went into faints while others chanted the showy dancers to greater heights. Ripping off his mask in fury and pain, Matthew pushed the sodden man off his leg and struggled to get up.

A gasp right above him caught his attention. He looked up.

Amaryllis!

—⁂—

"Matthew," she whispered, hardly able to believe her eyes. His dark gaze and flushed face seemed to mirror her own thoughts. Beyond them, a kaleidoscope of humanity twirled past, oblivious to the quiet tableau in their midst.

She stretched out her hand, attempting to help him up. He took it and slowly rose. Leaning against her, he staggered out into the hall, where he collapsed onto a bench and struggled to catch his breath.

"I fear this wound will not heal completely," he said in a low voice. "I feel like a doddering old man!"

"I'm sure you just need more time, my lord, and. . .and I shall offer my prayers on your behalf." Amaryllis twisted her hands together, knowing her face was scarlet.

The real issue was not Matthew's leg but what he must think of her after her declaration. His steady gaze gave her no answers.

"Who was that man I danced with earlier?" she ventured as he remained silent. "He said he was you."

Matthew looked away and shook his head. "It's too late," he said in a choked voice. "I can barely walk right now."

She stared at him, frowning. "What's too late? Why would that man say he was you? I don't understand."

"Make haste, man!" Perry Haddon appeared, as out of breath as his friend. "I just heard that Snell insulted Lord McAlister in the card room."

Suddenly, the fog cleared in her brain. Bertie! The plot! Amaryllis turned and dashed toward the card room, ignoring the oaths that followed her as she rudely shoved past the bodies congregating around the card tables.

The man in Renaissance garb struck a man in a red silk domino, Lord McAlister. "Name your seconds!"

Amaryllis felt faint as she understood Bertie's intention of masquerading as Matthew in order to get him killed in a duel. McAlister would expect Matthew, not Bertie, to meet him on the field of honor—and when Matthew didn't show up, the man would be even more incensed and challenge him personally. Even if Matthew survived, his reputation would forever be in ruins. She struggled to formulate a plan, knowing she had to do something.

"Stop!"

Her clear voice rang out. Everyone turned toward her. Several men eyed her and made lewd comments about her appearance in a man's domain. Amaryllis suddenly wished for the anonymity of the mask but didn't have time to put it back on.

"It is a trick!" she continued, struggling to get air into her starved lungs amid the cloud of tobacco. "That is not Lord Leighton whom you have challenged, but his cousin Bertie Snell!"

The man in the red domino bridled like a horse. "What's this, Leighton, some kind of schoolboy prank? Remove your mask!"

Bertie impaled Amaryllis with a hate-filled gaze before spinning and bursting through the crowd surrounding him.

"Get him!" someone yelled.

Suddenly all the languid, drawling London bucks acted as one man and went after the escaping imposter. Shouts of *Halloa Halloa!* rent the air, as though it were a fox hunt.

Amaryllis gripped hold of a drape as they rushed past, needing something to keep her anchored. She closed her eyes, striving to regain her composure. *Please, Lord, let Bertie be discovered and Matthew kept safe!*

Finally, when all was quiet in the card room, she opened her eyes and walked out to the hall on trembling legs. The noise inside the ballroom took on a fevered pitch when Bertie was caught. She heard her name, along with the viscount's and his cousin's, among the babble of excited voices.

It worked! Thank You, Lord.

Amaryllis turned and saw Matthew where he sat on the bench in the deserted hall, his head in his hands. He looked up at her approach, his eyes dark and unreadable. She paused, unable to think beyond the thundering of her heart. A tenuous thread of emotion seemed to hover between them.

Matthew put out his hand. Amaryllis quickly closed the space between them and took it. He pulled her down next to him.

Her mouth dry, she took a deep breath. "I think Bertie has been exposed."

Matthew gripped her hand. "Miss Sinclair. . .Amaryllis," he said in a low voice, "what you said, was that true?"

She knew he wasn't referring to his cousin or the foiled plot. She gazed down at their clasped hands, her heart swelling with a suffocating longing for him to return her feelings—and with fear that he might be readying to make a mockery of her.

Deciding to unmask the burgeoning truth of her heart regardless of the consequences, she looked up at him and nodded. "It is true that I have fallen in love with you, my lord—"

"What's this I hear about you interfering with a duel, Amaryllis?"

They turned to see Lady Dreggins stumping into the room, her features crumpled and sour. "I told you it's unpardonable—that a man will never forgive such an insult even if it's a case of false identities. Ain't that right, Leighton?"

He opened his mouth to speak, but she cut him off with a wave of her cane.

"I suppose you'll be calling on the morrow to break the engagement. Well, for once, I can understand. What Amaryllis has done is beyond the pale, and should you cry off, it would be rightly so. Imagine such widgeon-like behavior, after all I've done for you, Amaryllis—"

Matthew cleared his throat. "If I might interrupt, Lady Dreggins."

He looked down at Amaryllis. The sweetness of his smile took her breath away, and the glimmering emotion in his eyes surely echoed the sentiment in her own heart.

Drawing her hand to his lips, his gaze caressing, he murmured, "Alas, I have fallen in love with your charge, my lady, and the engagement most certainly stands."

A TREASURE
WORTH KEEPING

by Kelly Eileen Hake

Dedication

For my fellow library lovers!

Chapter 1

England, 1827

W e had a deal!" Stephen Montebourn, Earl of Pemberton, turned from the window to glare at Emma. Grown military men blanched under the force of his gaze, but not his younger sister.

Far from cowering, she met his gaze steadily. Only the telltale red of a blush betrayed her guilt.

"How many are there?" No sense wasting time on anger. For now, he needed a plan to avoid the approaching danger.

"Nine."

"Specific threats?"

Her hesitant pause underscored the gravity of the situation. "Four," Emma confessed apologetically.

"Modus operandi?" Stephen regretted the curt way he ground out the words, but information was vital—the enemy was closing in. As well versed in military strategy as his captaincy had left him, he still found his mother, who'd waged many a campaign on the home front, a formidable opponent. The countess's current mission: to see her only son leg-shackled as quickly as possible. From the moment Stephen arrived home after his father's death, his mother had begun foisting "marriageable" females on him at every opportunity. It constantly ruined his plans.

"You know, the usual." Emma paced over to the window. "Although there are some unknown quantities—"

Their mother sailed into the room, effectively cutting Emma off.

"Stephen, it's time. We need to be ready for them!" His mother's expression could have been hewn from granite as she set herself for battle. She knew very well that the expert he'd hired to organize and restore the once-magnificent library of Pemberton Manor would be arriving tomorrow.

Stephen collected rare and valuable tomes during his travels and had anticipated the coming month. Finally, after a year of tending to the various properties his father had left him and evading simpering misses with frills and gewgaws—not to mention their determined mamas—he would be able to devote time to his books.

He'd thought he'd survived the worst of her marital campaigns. Early on he'd enlisted his sister, Emma, as an ally and sort of spy in the feminine camp. Unfortunately, Mother had apparently discovered the arrangement and, in a brilliant last-ditch effort, sprung a house party full of eligible females upon them without either of her children knowing until it was too late.

"Mother, I would have been ready for them, had you informed me they were expected."

The countess skewered him with a steely gaze. "I know. That's precisely why I didn't. For this to be a success, you can't be miles away!"

Too true. The impossibility of a dignified retreat loomed before him. As the occupants of the first coach emerged, he eyed them with despair, then blinked. Twins? Did his mother really think that mirror images would increase the odds he would choose one as his wife? These young girls couldn't be his mother's candidates—surely there must be an older sister. . .but no. The carriage door shut behind a woman whom he assumed was their grandmother. He bristled. He wanted no schoolroom miss whose head was full of giggles and gowns. When he decided to marry, he would choose a woman to share his life—his heart, his home, his family.

Then again, he reconsidered as his mother glared determinedly at him, *we could take a continental tour. . . .* But all of that would be very far into the future. For now, he had to deal with the present ordeal of actually welcoming young women into his home with the pretense that they would be welcome company. In truth, he felt they were all assassins with one target: his bachelorhood.

—⁓—

Paige Turner leaned back against the squabs of the well-sprung hired coach. Papa, despite his protests against the cost of such luxury, snored softly in the opposite seat. Usually, Paige bowed to her father's wishes, but in this she'd stood firm. When they'd used a less expensive conveyance to visit Lord Linbrooke a scant two months ago, her father's rheumatism flared with a vengeance. He never complained, but she could always tell when the pain grew. This time, Papa himself decided it was *she* who needed the extra comfort. She didn't bother to disabuse him of the notion so long as it would spare his pride and his joints.

Standing five feet, seven inches tall, Paige knew no one else shared her doting papa's view that she embodied the phrase "delicate blossom of womanhood." At the advanced age of four-and-twenty, she accepted her status as a spinster, though her father seemed determined to ignore social convention in this regard.

Ever since Mama had died three years ago, Papa had immersed himself in the quest to find a suitable helpmate for his only daughter. Unfortunately, his requirements reflected an elevated estimation of her matrimonial worth. Her father's determination to see her espoused to one of the gentry sprang from the roots of his own marriage.

When Papa first met Mama, she'd come in to have an old copy of *Canterbury Tales* rebound. Four months later, their whirlwind, forbidden romance culminated in a quick trip to Gretna Green. Once Mama's family became aware she had eloped with a commoner, they relinquished her dowry and washed their hands of her forever.

Father determined Paige would receive all the luxury he hadn't quite been able to give his beloved wife. The only solution was for Paige to "take her place" in society, although she protested her place remained alongside him with the books and work she'd learned to love, not among the callous aristocracy whose cruelty to her mother cut deeply. He stubbornly closed their rare books and bookbinding shop to travel the country, renovating run-down manor libraries in hopes of finding Paige her husband.

"I know what you're thinking, daughter." Her father lazily opened one eye to peer at her. "You place too low a value on yourself."

"Oh, Papa." She shook her head. "When will you believe me when I tell you that I'm happy? Besides, you're the only one who doesn't think I'm on the shelf!"

Her father gave a derogatory snort. "You're an intelligent young minx with a sense of humor, and I am not the only one to notice. What of Lord Linbrooke? You two got along rather well. It's a pity there was nothing more I could do. . . ."

Paige's eyes narrowed at the cryptic comment. "For his library, or to push us together?"

"Both." His wide grin faded somewhat as he looked at her speculatively. "It's a pity you won't wear something other than gray, Paige. . .blue or green does you much better."

"Gray doesn't show the dust, Papa. It's very serviceable."

"Makes you look like a maid."

She hadn't weathered this same conversation dozens of times only to lose now. She craved no wardrobe crammed with fashionable garments practically impossible to put on without assistance and just as difficult to move around in. She didn't need to waste time carefully packing, washing, pressing, and repairing expensive, colorful fabrics.

"Look on the bright side, Papa. At least everything I own matches!" *Even my eyes.* Occasionally, she had to stifle a pang of remorse when she read a book where the heroine had eyes of gorgeous green, sparkling hazel, deep blue, or even intriguing brown. Still, it wasn't as though she'd never had an offer.

James Tuttle, the baker; Otis Boggs, the blacksmith; and even Lyle Jessup signaled interest at one time or another. Perhaps she was just too exacting. So what if the baker thought bringing a bag of flour every bit as romantic as a bouquet of flowers, or the blacksmith's idea of a bride price was his earnest offer to shoe her father's horse free of charge for life, or that the cobbler's apprentice insisted on taking her for long walks in the new shoes he'd made for her—two sizes too small. They'd all make fine husbands—for someone else.

Paige enjoyed the freedom she'd gained as a spinster, and besides, her father needed her. *If* she ever married, she wanted a man strong in the Lord, who would love his family and could carry on an intelligent conversation. Papa would also prefer him to be rich, titled, and handsome. Only a complete dunderhead could think matchmaking mamas any worse than a plotting papa!

—⁓—

Matchmaking mamas are a blight. Stephen stepped into the library for a brief respite as the guests prepared for dinner. For the most part, their daughters were just pawns. And to think, he'd actually been looking forward to the next few weeks! Freddy Linbrooke spoke so highly of Samuel Turner and his assistant, Stephen couldn't wait until they arrived to begin the categorization and renovation of his library. During his military travels, Stephen had greatly enlarged his collection of rare and ancient manuscripts.

There was something about books, especially older books, that appealed to him. He could hardly explain it even to himself. All he knew was that each volume contained not only the knowledge of its author, but also the skill and love of those who translated, scribed, printed, and bound it. Every tome represented the transmission of thoughts, beliefs, and ideas that connected mankind from one end of the continent to the other.

If only men could live up to the ideals found on treasured pages, there would be no war or murder or any of the unspeakable things human beings do to one another. Stephen had long ago made peace with it all, giving his anger and disappointment to God, but he still found himself longing for a world where people weren't so self-involved. To his way of thinking, these books were tangible evidence that man could look at himself and society critically and attempt reformation.

But one couldn't live in books forever, and for now, he had a situation to deal with. How could he avoid the trap of marriage to a woman he didn't, and possibly couldn't, love?

He brightened as Emma strode into the room. She was already nearing nineteen, years past the age when most debutantes made their coming out. Stephen privately agreed with their mother that young girls fresh from the schoolroom were not ready for marriage, but his sister had long passed that stage. Perhaps this house party would provide her an opportunity to hobnob with some of the people she'd meet in London.

He and his sister had formed a sort of partnership since his return. She'd warn him when Mother planned to throw an eligible female in his path, and in return, he'd arrange for her season. He couldn't really blame her that Mama had figured out their partnership and made this last ploy to entangle him in matrimony. Father's death had made Mama aware of her own age, and she was very determined to see her grandchildren.

"You've already met most of the guests, so your first impressions are probably accurate." Emma got to the point.

"Still, I'd like your opinion. The twins?"

"The Misses Pertelote are seventeen years of age, accompanied by their grandmother, Lady Pertelote. To be honest, none of them seems overly heavy in the brainbox, Stephen. I don't think you have a lot to worry about there. They're not meanspirited or fortune hunters, and they made their come-out a year ago. The only trouble will be telling who is who, since they dress identically, and you don't want to insult them."

Stephen took a moment to think it over. *Well, it could be worse. . . .*

"Miss Abercombe, accompanied by her cousins, Mr. Flitwit and Mr. Ruthbert, is nearing her majority and rather independent. Most think her past her prime, but I believe Mother invited her because she has the reputation of a bluestocking, so she might share your interest in books."

Why a woman in her early twenties merited the status of unmarriageable was beyond Stephen. Older women were more mature, confident, and interesting. He might enjoy the company of the bluestocking, but he'd take pains to make sure his attention wasn't misconstrued. He relaxed a bit. He could handle a pair of young twins and an intellectual.

"Why have only two parties arrived?"

"Mother arranged for a rather intimate party in the hopes that the fewer females, the more time you'd have to spend with each of them. She knew Lord Freddy would be coming a bit later after the Turner party arrived for the library, so she didn't invite many gentlemen."

"So she only invited three girls and their entourages?" Emma wasn't meeting his gaze any longer, and Stephen sensed she was avoiding something. "That's a bit odd."

"Well. . ." Emma faltered, cleared her throat, and pushed on. "There is another party."

Something clunked into place in the back of Stephen's mind. "She didn't. She *wouldn't*. Not. . ." His heart plummeted at the misery etched on Emma's face.

"Arabella Poffington." His sister spoke the foul name in a single breath, as though getting it over with quickly would diminish the horror of it.

Arabella Poffington. She was, in a word, a menace.

"And. . ." Emma gulped. "Her father and brother."

"A title doesn't make a man a gentleman!" Despite his resolve to keep a cool head, Stephen's temper got the better of him. "I can't believe I have to spend so much time with people like that. It's such a waste, and all for the sake of appearances. Who cares? The library. . ."

Chapter 2

Paige didn't need to hear another word. She'd wandered down to sneak a peek at the library and had heard far more than she'd anticipated.

"I can't believe I have to spend so much time with people like that. . . ." The words rang in her ears as she hurried back to her room on the fourth floor. Obviously, the earl was more than slightly peeved that he'd have to rub shoulders with commoners such as her father.

The man exemplified the vanity of his class. That type of thinking prompted her grandparents to disown her mother! How dare he judge her father without having so much as met him? Lord Freddy had urged them to take this commission, citing the new earl's love of books and lack of pomposity. Perhaps the earl was only judgmental of those from other stations.

Lord, she prayed, *I know I tend to believe the worst about those with titles, but I've just heard that the earl holds us in disdain! The condemnation in his tone angers me. How can I look past words overheard when I loathe all he said? Help me to be strong, God, and not ruin all Papa has worked for. Amen.*

———

Early the next morning, Stephen sought the solace of his library. After a dinner full of gossip, titters, innuendo, and barely veiled animosity among some of the guests, he'd gratefully retired to bed last night only to have his sleep filled with nightmares of harpies—whose faces looked suspiciously like Arabella Poffington's—chasing him with rings.

As he strode toward his desk, the swish of a skirt caught his attention. Not again! It wouldn't be the first time a fortune-hunter had tracked him into an empty room to claim she'd been compromised in order to force an engagement. Drusilla Dalrumple's attempt two months ago had been the last. Unfortunately, retreat was the only option to avoid the trap.

Before her partner could burst in and raise the cry, he executed a hasty about-face to quit the room, only to run into his sister.

"Good morning, Stephen! I knew I'd find you here. I wanted to know why I haven't met Mr. Turner yet. I know he and his assistant arrived, but they weren't present for dinner last night."

Stephen heard her voice trail off as he paced toward the bookcase where his would-be fiancée hid. Now that his sister's presence gave legitimacy to the scene, he could confront the schemer.

"What are you doing here?" As she came into view, he realized he'd made a tactical error. This pigeon presented no threat. Her gray dress proclaimed her a servant. Was he suffering from paranoia, that he would suspect a maid of nefarious schemes? Servants were trained to be invisible, and he'd all but yelled at the poor girl. She turned, and he caught a flash in her stormy gray eyes.

"I'm sorry. I mistook you for someone else." The apology sounded lame as he found himself caught in her gaze. The anger that blazed but a moment ago faded into politeness, but he fancied he could still detect a trace of it. Why was she in here? The fire would have been lit hours ago, and he'd already overseen a full-scale cleaning of this room in preparation for the library renovation. Perhaps one of his guests sent their personal maid to check up on him. He couldn't very well interrogate her now, not after barking at her scant moments before.

"Oh," Emma interrupted, coming up behind him. "Did you suspect an intruder, Stephen?"

He nodded briefly, watching the maid's face for signs of subterfuge as his sister added kindly, "I haven't seen you before; you must be new. What's your name?"

"Paige Turner." The woman curtseyed. "Sorry to disturb you, milord, milady. I didn't think anyone would be here so early."

"Turner? Are you any relation of Samuel Turner?" It couldn't be. Of course, a book restorer would name his daughter Paige Turner. He appreciated the clever play on words, but it faded behind the truth he would be faced with another female. Surely Freddy would have warned him.

"Stephen, you didn't tell me his daughter served as his assistant!" Emma laughed. "Lord Freddy thinks so highly of you, and we've been looking forward to having you and your father look at our library, haven't we, Stephen?"

Grateful his sister stepped in to smooth the situation, he bowed. "A pleasure to meet you, Miss Turner. I regret that I was unable to greet you last evening. I trust your journey went well?"

"Yes, thank you, milord. I apologize. Lord Linbrooke mentioned how extensive your collection is, and I couldn't resist a quick peek."

Well, well, Miss Turner has an independent streak, as well as an obvious enthusiasm for her work. If she gets past my abominable manners, the next few weeks in the library might well prove more interesting than I'd expected.

"What's your professional opinion, Miss Turner?" The words weren't mere courtesy; he genuinely wanted to know.

She turned her head, and her expression softened as she took in her surroundings. "From what I've seen, the collection is impressive and in fair condition. You have every right to be proud of it, and it will be a pleasure finding ways to properly display it."

Her sincerity touched him. He respected that she hadn't merely flattered his books but had given an honest appraisal that work needed to be done to do them justice.

"Has your father risen yet, Miss Turner?" Emma's voice broke in. "I'd love to meet him."

"Yes." Miss Turner's eyes clouded over again, and he wondered why. "If you'd like, I'll go fetch him."

"That won't be necessary. I'll just ring someone to request that he join us." He pulled the cord, and a maid hurried into the room.

She curtseyed. "You called, your grace?"

"Please ask Mr. Turner to join us. You'll find him in the Blue Suite on the third floor." The maid looked distinctly uncomfortable.

"Is there something wrong, Mattie?"

"Um. . .forgive my impertinence, milord, but Miss Poffington has settled into the Blue Suite. She claimed it yesterday, saying it's where she stayed in the past. I promise she's still there, milord. I lit the fire in that suite earlier this morning."

Stephen turned to Miss Turner. "I'm sorry the arrangements were altered without my knowledge, Miss Turner. Would you point Mattie in the right direction?"

"He'll be on the fourth floor, second room on the right-hand side of the east wing." She smiled warmly at the maid. "Thank you."

Stephen was sure Emma's frown mirrored his own. The fourth floor was much too far for an older gentleman to travel every day. The library was on the first!

"A mistake has been made. If it won't disturb you and your father, I'd like to move you closer to the library." Upon her nod, he added, "Mattie, is the Green Suite on the second floor available?"

"I believe so, milord. I'll see to it." Mattie curtseyed and left the room.

A few moments later, Samuel Turner entered the library and dipped his head. "Good morning, milord."

"Good morning, Mr. Turner. It's come to my attention that you were placed in the wrong quarters. I apologize for the oversight."

"Quite all right, milord. There was nothing wrong with the rooms we were given."

"I beg to differ, Mr. Turner. I trust you will find your new arrangements more comfortable and conveniently close to the library."

"Thank you, milord. I see you've already met my daughter."

"Indeed. May I present my sister, Miss Emma."

"Lovely to meet you, Miss Emma."

"And you." Emma curtseyed. "I'm afraid I'll have to be off. Mother will be wanting me. Things are so hectic, what with the unexpected houseguests who also arrived yesterday. I'm sure I'll see you both at luncheon, so I'll leave you to your business."

Chapter 3

P aige watched the earl's sister leave with regret. The young woman was unaffected and sincere, a refreshing contrast to the earl.

From the snippet of conversation she'd heard last night, Paige had thought he'd be older. This man's discerning gaze took her aback. Even more disconcerting was her own dismay that he'd thought her a maid. The Earl of Pemberton was a walking contradiction—self-absorbed and careless with the feelings of those of lower station, yet polite and concerned for the welfare of his library and her father. Which was reality and which the facade? Even now, as her thoughts roiled back and forth, he led her father to what was surely the most comfortable chair in the room and began enthusiastically discussing the library.

As the next few hours passed with the three of them exchanging ideas and information, Paige decided she must have been mistaken. After all, she'd only overheard the middle of a conversation, and it was the earl's right to question any strangers who wandered around his home. Besides, he treated her father with respect, and there was no denying the enthusiasm lighting his features as he spoke of his books.

Before they'd even looked over most of the extensive library or taken stock of the more valuable pieces, the butler regally announced luncheon.

Paige smiled at the butler. "Where is the kitchen?"

"You misunderstand," the earl clipped in an affronted tone. "Did you eat with the servants at Lord Linbrooke's?"

"No, milord. Lord Linbrooke was most welcoming, but he wasn't formally entertaining a house full of guests at the time." Paige quickly realized her mistake and tried to rectify it. It wasn't as though the assumption was unwarranted. They had been hired to complete a project, not to attend a house party.

"You are to eat with the rest of the guests and family." His smile erased all doubts. "Be assured your company will only add to the quality of our table."

"Thank you. We'd be pleased to join you," Papa agreed.

"No, Papa," she whispered in protest as her father whisked her out of the library. "Lord Freddy's was one thing, with just his parents and aunt, but a whole room full of strangers? I didn't bring anything to wear. Wait, I don't own anything suitable to wear!" She knew she was babbling, but if she didn't do something, she'd have to face a table of people looking down their collective aristocratic noses at her and her father at least twice a day for the duration of their visit.

"Nonsense. Weren't you telling me how there was nothing wrong with your wardrobe?" Her father trapped her neatly. "I don't want you worrying. You're just as good as anyone else, and I want you to remember it, Paige."

The earl led them to the dining room. It appeared as though almost everyone was already seated for a casual, buffet-style luncheon.

A servant handed her a plate, and she stared blankly at the table filled with delicacies. Delicate steam wafted from various dishes, the tempting aromas of seasoned potatoes and succulent ham making her mouth water.

"It all looks wonderful, doesn't it?" The earl's sister stood beside her and reached for a bun as Paige selected some fresh fruit, cheese, and sliced ham.

"It certainly does, Miss Emma." Faltering a bit as she looked at the long dining table, Paige was relieved to see her father already pulling out a chair for Emma, then gesturing to the one on his other side. Her father shot her an I-told-you-they-were-just-people-and-they-would-like-you grin as the earl took his seat at the head of the table—right next to Paige.

She began to relax and took a bite of the ham, surveying the other guests. She'd already met the earl and his sister, and the dowager countess at the far end of the table seemed genial enough.

The earl noticed her inspection and began a whispered list of the guests.

"Miss Turner, you've already met my sister, Emma. The fellow to her left..." He nodded toward a rather rotund gentleman. "Is Sir Ruthbert, who accompanied his cousin, Miss Abercombe." The bespectacled young lady, Paige noted with interest, wore gray.

A soft voice to the earl's right carried on the litany. "The next is Mr. Flitwit, Sir Ruthbert's brother." The woman gave a titter. "Such a shame he couldn't pick a better hairpiece...."

Paige was shocked to hear such venom come from such beauty. The speaker boasted golden hair teased into ringlets around a face blessed with sparkling hazel eyes and rosy cheeks. It brought to mind how just the Lord was to look within rather than upon outward appearances.

"This, of course, is Miss Arabella Poffington," the earl interjected grimly, "accompanied by her brother, Lord Arnold Poffington. Their father holds the place next to my mother at the end." His dry tone left Paige no doubt he disapproved of the girl's vicious remarks.

Her brother, Lord Poffington, had the effrontery to peruse Paige through a quizzing glass, then drop it with a dismissive snort. Paige could see why her plain attire wouldn't garner the approval of a gentleman dressed to the nines in canary yellow. Curious to see what sort of father raised children so lacking in manners, Paige saw a sallow man with a haughty expression. *Well, that explains it*, she thought uncharitably. Determined not to sink to the level of a snob, she asked, "And the kindly looking lady in purple?"

"Lady Pertelote. She accompanies her granddaughters, the Misses Pertelote." The Misses Pertelote were twins blessed with blue eyes and auburn hair. Paige couldn't suppress a smile when she realized they were the only ones presented without their first name. Perhaps she wouldn't be the only one who found it difficult to tell them apart.

One of the twins caught her smile and gave a jaunty little wave before turning back to her grandmother. Overall, Paige decided, with the exception of the three Poffingtons, it looked to be a pleasant group.

At that moment, Miss Poffington, apparently unused to being ignored for long, captured the earl's attention. "Now that you've introduced your little friend to all of us, perhaps you'd share her name?" The sweet voice warred with the sharp glance she shot at Paige.

"Certainly," the earl obliged stiffly. "I'm most pleased to introduce Mr. Samuel Turner and his daughter, Miss Paige Turner."

Paige noticed a hint of a smile playing around the edges of the earl's mouth. Good. She loved her name and was glad to see he appreciated her father's whimsy.

"Mr. Turner," the girl murmured thoughtfully. "Odd, but I'm certain I've never heard that name before. And to think, I've practically memorized *Debrette's Peerage*!" She gave another mirthless laugh, and Paige felt anger rise.

"That's quite all right, Miss Poffington. Perhaps you've heard of Paige's mother, Miss Fortescue." Her father's comment fell on fertile ground.

Miss Poffington smiled eagerly, an avaricious gleam in her eyes. "That does sound familiar. If I'm not mistaken, there was a bit of a scandal years ago—"

Paige closed out the malicious woman's delighted recitation and quickly prayed, *Lord, please help me to hold my temper and not give this woman any cause to malign my father for his daughter's behavior. The way the aristocracy relishes tearing apart those who saw past class issues to find love angers me. You know Mama served You as best she could. Help me to remember that I must do the same.*

"I'm delighted to have enlisted the Turners' expert advice in renovating the library this month." The earl's quick intervention halted Miss Poffington's gossip.

"The library, you say? And I believe I heard the woman's name is *Paige Turner*. Why how provincial! Don't you think it quaint, Arnold?"

Emma leaned forward. "It really is quite clever, but then, one would expect such inventiveness from people who are well read. It is refreshing to have an original name, is it not?" Emma smoothly supported Paige.

"Why, yes. I do prize originality. It is so wearying to see the same old thing time and again." Miss Poffington glanced toward the twins. "To my way of thinking, gloves, shoes, and horses are the only things that should come in pairs."

Paige couldn't take it any longer. She opened her mouth to respond to the vicious comment, only to be silenced by a sharp elbow in the ribs from a papa who knew her only too well. She wasn't the only one outraged by the girl's spite. As the last of the spread was carried away and the desserts brought out, the earl took advantage of the opportunity.

"I disagree, Miss Poffington. After all, two helpings of sweet is far more desirable than one of sour."

Chapter 4

P lease?" The next day, Arabella Poffington peeked up at him through lowered
lashes. Stephen supposed she was attempting to look sweet and demure, but
the overall effect was closer to a nearsighted squint that anything else.

"I'm afraid not, Miss Poffington. I've been planning the restoration of the library
for months now." Her resulting scowl confirmed his opinion of her changeable
disposition.

"But Stephen, I already have the servants setting up the croquet field on the
south lawn."

How like her to order *his* servants and then demand his approval. "I hope you
enjoy yourself." He disentangled his arm from her grasp, gave a slight bow, and left
the room. He gladly escaped to the library. Paige stood by a large oak shelf on the
east wall, frowning.

"Is something wrong, Miss Turner?" He strode over to meet her.

"Do you see anything wrong with this bookcase?" She looked at the large oak
piece enigmatically.

Stephen scrutinized it carefully, seeing no cracks or splits in the wood. He
stepped back to see whether any shelves had bowed due to too much weight, and
suddenly, he understood.

"It doesn't match the other bookcases in the room. The stain is a lighter hue."
Odd how he'd never noticed before. She certainly had an eye for detail.

"Exactly. It's also narrower than any of the others. Is there a reason why this was
added?"

"It's been there for as long as I can remember."

Samuel Turner came over to join them and studied the fixture at considerable
length. Stephen watched in fascination as father shot daughter a questioning look
and received a slight nod in answer.

"Would you object to removing it, milord?" Samuel asked.

"No, but why?" He was obviously missing something.

"This wall receives the least amount of direct sunlight. If these shelves were
removed, it would be easy to construct a display case for some of the older manuscripts

you mentioned," Miss Turner explained.

Her father added, "Since we're going to need very special displays, it's best to order them from the beginning of the process, so they're ready along with the rest of the room."

"All right," Stephen readily agreed, "but I'm afraid my collection is far more extensive than you know. It will require more than one fixture this size. We'll empty this one and remove it today. After the remainder of my books arrive tomorrow, we'll decide how many others need to be removed."

With that arranged, they went about emptying the highest shelves first. Not about to let a lady or her older father upon the rolling ladder, Stephen climbed up. Carefully, he passed the books down for Miss Turner's inspection, and she then gave them to her father for sorting.

"You have marvelous taste," she applauded when he handed her a copy of *The Decameron.*

"Thank you. Of course, some of these have been here for decades, and I had no part in their selection. I'm particularly interested in legends, fables, and tales passed down through centuries." He found a copy of *Beowulf.* Their thumbs brushed as she took it, sending a wave of heat up his arm. He cleared his throat. "Shakespeare and Marlowe shouldn't be ignored, though." He hoped she hadn't noticed his distraction.

"I enjoy the contemporaries, but I must admit, the older the manuscript, the more fascinating I find it." She gestured toward a stack by her father. *"The Rape of the Lock* is wonderful satirization."

"I agree, though if you want something a bit out of the ordinary, I'd recommend John Donne. Especially—"

"The Flea!" She spoke the title just as he did, and their eyes met. The shared humor made the time pass quickly as he and Miss Turner enthusiastically took down the plethora of volumes occupying the space while her father began separating them according to subject. They'd already agreed to organize first by genre, then by author as was necessary. Any sets would remain with their fellows and be placed in a separate section. The older and more valuable volumes that were the crowning glory of his collection would fill the new cases they'd design.

Hours later, Stephen had a greater appreciation for the sheer time that would be involved completing the process. This was the smallest bookcase, but it still stood as high as all the others, which stretched to the sixteen-foot-high ceiling.

As they finished the last row, Emma swept into the library, closely followed by a servant carrying a pitcher of lemonade and four glasses.

"Perfect timing, Emma!" Stephen grinned as Miss Turner eyed the lemonade longingly. "How'd you know?"

"I didn't. I simply couldn't take any more of Miss Poffington's croquet tournament.

After Miss Abercombe won the first game, Miss Poffington decided that whoever won the most out of five earned the status of grand champion. So at the end of game four, I hit my ball over the hill. I'll have to apologize to the groundskeeper later. They're still searching for it." She looked around. "Why did you start in the middle of the wall?"

"We plan to remove this shelf and install display cases for more delicate manuscripts," Miss Turner explained, accepting a glass. "Thank you."

"The collection itself is magnificent and well preserved," Mr. Turner offered. "The real work won't be in restoration but organization. By the time we've catalogued and separated the books, little else will need to be done. Aside from the display cases, the layout already provides ample space."

"I'd thought we'd be doing a bit more than adding display cases," Stephen broke in. This was his favorite room in the house, but the ancient furniture gave off an oppressive air. The large walnut desk situated beneath the window boasted sharp corners and clawed feet. Uncomfortable high-backed wooden chairs flanked the massive stone fireplace. The real draw of the room would always be the knowledge and mystery it contained, but he'd like to make it more inviting.

"I want to make this room. . .better. Less depressing," he clarified.

"I'd hoped you'd say that!" Miss Turner burst out. "I know just what it needs." Stephen didn't miss the conspiratorial grin she shot at Emma.

"Wait a minute. I didn't mean lace and rocking chairs or little glass whatnots!" He put his foot down before further damage could be done.

"Credit us with better taste than that!" Miss Turner folded her arms across her bosom, but the sparkle in her eyes let him know she wasn't insulted.

"What will happen if I unleash the two of them?" Stephen sought wiser counsel from Samuel Turner, who smiled and shook his head.

"It's too late, milord. But I wouldn't worry. Paige always did have a knack for making a place comfortable."

"The key is going to be color," Emma assured him.

Stephen wasn't sure he approved of the direction things were taking. He gazed suspiciously at his sister's lavender daydress.

"No pastels," he ordered.

"I should think not. I said the room should be inviting." Miss Turner scanned the room. "I wasn't thinking it should appear feminine."

He was grateful for her support until his gaze fell on the drab muslin of her gown. Would bland be any better than frills? "What did you have in mind, Miss Turner?" He figured that forewarned was forearmed.

"No pastels, nor white nor black. More along the lines of reds, blues, and browns. I was thinking of maybe a burgundy plush rug trimmed with deep blue in front of the fire, to set off armchairs in soft tanned leather. The tables would be a bit darker, perhaps mahogany, with plenty of candles for extra light." The picture she painted was warm, cozy, and masculine without being oppressive.

The sparkle in her eyes made him wonder why he'd ever thought gray could be bland, and he found himself smiling. Her enthusiasm pleased him. She'd lost the stiff formality of this morning and the tight expression she'd maintained through lunch. He suspected she'd been restraining herself from giving Arabella a putdown she'd never forget.

"Supper will be served in one hour." The butler's voice echoed solemnly from the doorway. Anything else would have to wait, as they filed out the door to freshen up.

The next day, they resumed their conversation, tying up loose ends.

"That leaves only one question. A single display case won't bear the entirety of my collection. We'll need to construct some others. Where would you want to place them, Miss Turner?" the earl asked as he turned around, surveying the room in its entirety.

"How much room will be needed?" She stepped back hurriedly as the footmen, having removed the shelves from the bookcase, hefted the emptied shell and made for the door.

"I've several manuscripts I'd like to see displayed. If at all possible, they should be opened, face up. . . ." He let his thoughts trail off as he realized she no longer paid attention to him. While he spoke, she'd made her way to the far end of the room, standing where the irregular bookcase once had been.

"What's this?" she asked as she gestured to the wall. He noticed the small door for the first time as she grasped the handle and turned.

Chapter 5

L ocked." Paige couldn't quite keep the disappointment from her voice. "Do you know what it is?"

"No, I've never seen it before. That old bookshelf stood in front of this door for as long as I can remember. It hasn't been opened in decades."

The surprise in his voice sparked her imagination. After all, it wasn't every day one stood in an ancient manor house in front of—

"A secret room! How wonderful!" Emma's exclamation voiced Paige's own excitement.

"I wonder," Paige's father murmured. "Not to be a wet blanket, but is there another entrance?"

The earl shook his head. "The music room is on the other side. It may just be a connecting door." Everyone followed as he strode to the music room, where silk hangings obscured the wall in question. Paige watched in fascination as the earl began thumping along the wall, searching for a door frame.

"Don't just stand there!" Paige exhorted as she joined him. It didn't take long to ascertain the wall possessed no door. Her excitement rising, Paige watched as the earl walked the length of the room, then counted the paces again from the hall.

"Well?" Emma burst out.

"After counting the steps and taking into account the library measurements we gathered earlier, I'm certain that is no connecting door. There must be a small room, about eight feet wide. The rooms on either side are so large, it wouldn't be apparent unless someone actually measured. It could be an old storage room." Everyone trooped back to the library to stare at the mysterious door.

He pulled the bell, and another maid appeared immediately. She scampered off to fetch the housekeeper. A few moments later, an older woman bustled into the room, brandishing a large brass key ring.

"What may I do for ye, milord?" she asked breathlessly after a rather creaking curtsy.

"Do you know anything about this door, Mrs. O'Leary?" The earl's gentle, unhurried tone impressed Paige even as she fought her own impatient nature. So many of the nobles they'd visited hardly even bothered to glance at the help.

"Nay, m'lord. I've ne'er seen it afore. Here are the keys. I reckon ye'd like to see if we con open it?" Affection warmed her Scottish burr as she offered the earl her key ring.

"Thank you, Mrs. O'Leary. This may take a while." He fingered dozens of keys, searching for those made of iron. "But if we can open the door, we will have need of light. It would be a great help if you'd fetch some lamps and such." He began trying various keys as she left the room.

Paige held her breath as key after key failed, until she resorted to counting to pass the time. It was either that or pass out for wont of air, which certainly wouldn't do. She would be ready when the door opened.

Meanwhile, Mrs. O'Leary rejoined them. It appeared as though word of the secret room had spread, since she brought along enough candles to light a chapel—each one with its own attendant. The library became quite crowded, and Paige couldn't help but smile. Twenty-two keys after the first, a sort of sharp *snick* sounded, and the earl cautiously pushed the door open. A rush of stale air greeted the onlookers but thankfully carried no hint of damp or mold.

"Candle." The earl reached back without taking his focus from the dark doorway, only to be practically pushed off his feet as no fewer than six servants hastened to light his way. Regaining his balance, he straightened to his full height and turned around. The glare faded quickly as he shook his head and gave in to a grin.

"All right." He accepted the nearest candle. "Thank you for your earnest dedication, one and all. Now, I'd appreciate it if everyone but the Turners would step back. And snuff most of those candles, lest we lose the library!" Everyone obeyed, good-naturedly jockeying for position as the earl, Paige, and her father moved in to explore.

Heart pounding, Paige followed the earl closely. She raised her candle as high as possible, trying to see everything at once. Instead, she bumped into him as he stopped suddenly, her candle dripping hot wax onto the nape of his neck.

"Watch it!" he hissed, rubbing the back of his neck.

Paige's apology faded from her lips as her eyes began adjusting to the dim light. Old trunks and crates littered the floor, tossed in with old pieces of furniture leaning glumly against the walls. A large chest lay directly before them, the cause of the earl's sudden stop.

"What a mess." The earl obviously didn't share her enthusiasm. Incredible how one family could lock up a room full of possessions and forget them while others lived in simple cottages scarcely larger than this secret room. Paige couldn't contain her excitement. Who knew what they'd find in one of these trunks?

Paige knelt in the dust to open the chest and pulled out a leather-bound copy of *L'Morte d'Arthur*. Opening the manuscript, she noted the date proclaimed it to be more than a century old. The earl strode by, snuffing her spluttering flame.

"I'll have the servants clean the place out. We'll burn whatever is in bad shape and put the rest in the attic," he decided aloud. "Then we may be able to put this room to use."

"You must be joking!" Paige couldn't stop the exclamation, although she practically felt her father's warning glare. *Ouch!* Well, she certainly felt the warning elbow, at any rate.

"I beg your pardon, Miss Turner?" The chill tone belied the earl's polite words. Luckily, she was spared the devastating effect of his expression with so little light to illuminate it. Even so, she could feel the heat radiating from him.

"My apologies, milord. I just. . ." She gave up as he raised his lantern to peer at her. It was no use trying to explain away her impetuous outburst. Dissembling never was her forte. She sighed. "Aren't you at all curious? I can't imagine finding a room that's been sealed for a century or more only to shovel its contents into the attic and use antique furniture for kindling." Silence greeted her, and Paige wondered miserably how soon they'd be asked to leave as the earl frowned at her.

Why were the upper classes so full of their own importance they couldn't abide listening to the opinions of others, even when honestly and sincerely expressed? She meant no offense. The anger rose even as she desperately tried to tamp it down before she gave their employer a serious reason to dismiss them.

"Please forgive her, milord. It's my own fault I never made her learn to keep her thoughts to herself." Her papa's voice only fanned the flame. Why should he have to apologize for a comment she'd made just to appease wounded vanity?

"Not at all. Maybe your daughter has a point." The softly spoken words startled her out of her silent reflections. What? She was right? Well, of course she was right, but an earl was admitting he was wrong? She peered up at him in the glow of the lantern, realizing the frown she'd seen as condemning was really thoughtful. He swung his arm around to better illuminate the contents of the room.

"What made you say a century?" The question was sincere. "I know some of it's old, but I'm not sure it's all that old. Are you an expert on furniture as well as books, Miss Turner?" He sounded genuinely interested rather than mocking, and appreciation for his lack of pomposity flooded her. It wasn't often a nobleman valued her input. Most of them pretended she didn't exist, preferring to address only her father.

"This." She held her find up to the light. "The print date is 1697, milord." He gently took it from her, his thumb brushing her palm. The shivers racing up her spine owed nothing to the temperature of the room. The light of the lantern bathed his face in a soft glow as he perused the book, showing an expression of wonder.

"It's beautiful. And in the original French." His enthusiasm warmed her heart even as the look of respect in his eyes as he spoke to her roused something more dangerous. She realized she'd been holding her breath as he shifted his gaze to her father.

"Would you mind helping me go through these trunks? Your daughter has a keen eye, and we may yet find more treasures. I know it's not part of the original commission, but I'd like to see this room as an addition to the library." Rather than order them to perform more work, he invited them to explore a treasure trove of family possessions, asking whether or not they had the time and inclination.

Now was Paige's turn to not-so-subtly grab her father's arm. She let go when she caught sight of his self-satisfied grin.

"To be honest, milord, my joints aren't what they used to be, and sitting on the floor opening old crates isn't wise at my age. It would be time well spent, though. Since this room has no windows, it would be perfect for your older and more valuable collectibles. We've spoken enough that I feel I've a good idea what you'd like done, so what say you and Paige go through this room while I continue on in the library?"

That's why he looked so pleased. Paige vowed she'd speak to him later about his matchmaking. She should have known he'd jump on the opportunity. Well, he had a surprise coming. After lunch, Emma had confided the reason for the house party, and Paige knew the last thing his grace wanted to do was spend time alone in a dark room with an unattached female. She waited for the earl's response, wondering how he would phrase it. Something like, "I'd really appreciate your expert opinion, Mr. Turner." Or, "You could probably use your daughter more than I. My sister would be delighted to help, you know."

"That sounds like a fine idea to me. Shall we continue tomorrow? I'm certain it's almost time to change for dinner." His deep voice, slightly amplified in the small room, sounded anything but horrified or desperate to be rid of her. On the contrary, he sounded almost excited.

Her brow furrowed as she followed her father out of the room and thought over the situation. The conclusion she reached sent pangs through her heart. Obviously, the earl did not consider her a threat to his bachelorhood. *Is it because I'm of lower station or simply that I'm old and plain?*

Chapter 6

Stephen whistled as he changed for dinner. Things were definitely looking up. Just yesterday he'd decided the next week would be horrendous. It was a forgivable assumption, given that he'd been facing days on end filled with prospective brides whom he thought held no prospects. Of course, that was before he'd cornered a feisty miss whose intriguing eyes discovered a secret room and a valuable volume languishing in an old trunk.

At first, he'd been angry. He'd realized that, even in the sanctuary of his library, he wouldn't be able to avoid eligible females. How had his friend managed to forget mentioning that the talented and knowledgeable Mr. Turner brought his daughter with him?

Her fire delighted him. How long had it been since someone bothered to disagree with him? Not while he commanded his troops, and certainly not since he'd joined the ranks of a society only too pleased to fawn all over him due to a title and fortune he'd never earned. No. This was no simpering debutante or sly diamond he need tread carefully around.

Miss Paige had spunk, in addition to an active mind and an honest streak. Not to mention abominable fashion taste. It would be interesting to see what she'd look like with that heavy, dark hair curling around her shoulders instead of pulled back so tightly. The candlelight in their secret room picked out rich strands of mahogany in her brown tresses even as she glowered at him, brandishing a book.

His gaze fell on the volume he'd carried up to his chambers. One thing was for certain. Even if they found nothing else of value the next day, he would enjoy the search. He could feel the grin spread across his face.

"You look awfully pleased with yourself." Freddy Linbrooke strolled into the room and sprawled on a chair.

"So you had the nerve to show up, after all," Stephen countered lightly.

"Well, I thought I'd give you a day or so to get over the surprise before I showed up." Freddy let loose a grin of his own. "Still, I assure you there will be no cause for disappointment. I'd forgotten what it was like to enjoy an intelligent conversation without innuendo and being rapped with a fan. Paige Turner's a most. . .unusual young lady. Bang-up to the echo, if you ask me."

"I noticed." Stephen quelled a spark of jealousy over the fact that his friend had gotten to know Miss Turner so well. "But you should have prepared me."

"You wouldn't have hired Mr. Turner if I'd told you he'd bring his daughter." Freddy idly twirled his pocket watch. "Seems you've suffered a bit of paranoia regarding the fairer sex lately."

"Paranoia, eh?" Stephen muttered grimly. "Wait until dinner."

"I already told you she's not that kind."

"And I agree. My mother made other plans."

"Your mama's a worthy opponent," Freddy agreed. "But she won't find an ally in Miss Turner. Not angling for a rich husband."

"Reassuring as that is, you mistook my meaning. Mother knew I'd be here to oversee the library, so she planned a surprise house party—an intimate gathering of eligible women and their escorts." Stephen relished watching as comprehension darkened Freddy's face.

"Stormed the manor, have they? Sorry, old chap." He heaved a sigh. "Bother. Now I'll have to do the pretty, too." Horror widened his eyes as he asked, "Miss Merryweather wasn't invited, was she?" Freddy, as another eligible peer of the realm, had his own share of female admirers. Estelle Merryweather made no secret about the fact she'd set her cap for the wealthy viscount.

"Now who's overanxious?" Stephen teased, then shook his head. "No, but Arabella Poffington wrangled an invitation."

"Well, on to the battle, I say." A relieved Freddy marched out of the room. "It should be an interesting stay."

—◦—

There'd be reckoning for this bit of matchmaking, Stephen vowed. Now that the numbers were even, his mother had taken over the seating arrangements. Rather than a casual buffet as they'd enjoyed at luncheon, he'd have to endure a seven-course meal. How had she not realized he'd need to be next to the Turners, since they were his honored guests?

He eyed Freddy enviously. Sure, he could enjoy himself, sandwiched between Emma and Miss Turner. To be fair, Stephen himself enjoyed the place on his sister's other side, but the menace of Miss Poffington to his left far overshadowed that comfort. *Two courses down, five to go.*

Stephen winced as Arabella daintily slurped another bit of split-pea soup. He'd withstood cannon fire. How could the challenge of stoically enduring Arabella's piercing titter prove a heavier burden? He wasn't sure, but he knew it to be true.

Silently, he disparaged the social dictates allowing one only to politely converse with the guests seated directly to one's left or right. How long could a man feign interest in his plate? The footman placed a serving of capon in front of him, and he stabbed it with his fork with far more violence than necessary.

He struggled to pay attention as Arabella recited various snide on-dits with malicious glee, but found his mind wandering until the words *hidden for ages* brought him back. He realized immediately what had happened.

Miss Turner had mentioned the secret storage room, and Emma enthusiastically corroborated the report to an interested Lord Freddy—along with everyone else at the table. Despite the convention of concentrating solely on the conversation of one's partners, everyone stilled at the mention of a secret room.

Stephen suppressed a groan. Why hadn't he warned everyone not to mention it? He should have known better. Now everyone at the table began buzzing excitedly. He caught the words *heirlooms, treasure hunt,* and *mystery* at random.

"Ooooh, how interesting." Arabella laid her hand on his arm, ostensibly overwhelmed with excitement. "You're so clever to find a secret room everyone else missed."

He reached for his glass to dislodge her touch. "Actually, Miss Turner found it." He wanted to give credit where credit was due, and after Arabella's catty words the night before, he would not pass up an opportunity to praise Paige.

"But I'm sure you were the first one to look inside. You're so brave." He couldn't believe she was actually batting her eyelashes at him.

"Yes," he replied shortly, manfully resisting the urge to spill his water as a pretext to leave the table when she scooched her chair nearer.

"I'd love to explore it. It's so exciting to see things no one has for years."

He briefly considered offering to avoid her for the next twenty years in a gallant attempt to please her, then discarded the tempting notion. Instead, he pasted a concerned expression on his face.

"Why, Miss Poffington, I must say I'm rather surprised. I'd hate to think of your ruining one of your lovely gowns in the dust."

"You're right." A frown wrinkled her brow. "I haven't anything suitable. Perhaps I could borrow something from Miss Turncoat." She cast a disdainful look at the second gray dress Paige wore in the same day.

Stephen wasn't fooled. If Arabella considered Miss Turner to be competition, she knew her rival's name. It was a deliberate insult, just as was the remark about her dress. Such idiocy made his blood boil.

"Why, Miss Poffington, I doubt that would do." He stabbed another bit of succulent capon. "The two of you are as different as night and day." She preened at the comment, though Stephen thought she would do better to remedy that as soon as possible. This stuck-up wench would do well to cultivate the sincerity and intelligence Miss Turner displayed. True, Paige had spoken before she thought earlier, yet her artless honesty and conviction were to her credit, in sharp contrast to Arabella's blatantly catty remarks.

"Besides," Stephen spoke loudly enough to garner the attention of the entire table, "I wouldn't permit anyone access to the room until we ascertain both its condition and contents. We have yet to find proof that the floorboards are in good shape and the place isn't infested with spiders and other distasteful insects that thrive in such places." He disciplined himself not to grin at the expressions of terror gracing the faces of his guests.

"You know we are in the process of renovating the library. I'll be more than happy to give everyone a detailed tour after the work has been completed." This promise placated even the most recalcitrant of his guests, whose romantic ideals of treasure hunting easily gave way in the face of cobwebs. At least he could rest assured that he and the Turners would be able to proceed with the library in peace.

Mother rose, signaling the end of the seemingly interminable meal, and the women followed her into the parlor as he led the gentlemen to the billiard room. He vastly enjoyed the reprieve until Sir Ruthbert cornered him, asking when he planned to lead them on a hunt. Making some vague response, he headed for the door.

"About time we joined the ladies, don't you think?" When he walked into the parlor, he noted Emma's harassed look as she sat between Miss Turner and Miss Poffington. Miss Turner's snapping gaze betrayed her bland expression as Arabella nattered on.

"Why, it's so interesting to talk to someone who *works* for a living. You know, Father has always shielded me from any of the tradesmen at our home, so I never had the opportunity to interact with someone like you before."

Stephen realized he'd caught the tail end of what must have been an unbearably long and insulting monologue. Arabella excelled at that dubious skill.

Miss Turner pasted on a smile and turned to face Arabella. "And I do not hesitate to tell you, I've never enjoyed company such as yours."

Stephen suspected the words were not intended as a compliment, yet they could be interpreted as such. He had to credit her for being clever enough to avoid falsehood while avoiding a faux pas.

"Now, as I've so much to do tomorrow," Miss Turner said as she rose, "I think I'll excuse myself to get a good night's sleep."

At least Miss Turner could hold her own. Stephen envied her easy escape even as he wondered whether he'd fare so well as she had for the remainder of the evening.

Chapter 7

I can't believe we've already been here almost two weeks! Paige stretched as she awoke. She and her father had established a sort of pattern during the days, although by no means had they settled into anything mundane.

Since the discovery of the secret room, a certain anticipation colored their work. Before anything else could be done, a day was lost airing out the room. Then the process continued at an agonizingly slow pace. The servants, already overly busy meeting the needs of the houseguests, came only in pairs rather than the excited crowd present for what Paige thought of as the grand opening.

Another five days plodded by as the servants scrubbed the walls free of dirt and cobwebs, attached wall sconces to provide adequate lighting, then dusted items and moved them to rest against the walls before the hardwood floor could be swept and mopped.

Paige jumped out of bed, relishing the warmth provided by the fire as she dressed. Finally, she and the earl could begin looking through the mysterious trunks! The long wait hadn't been the only test of her patience. The rest of the work in the main library did not show the typical progress. The sheer size factored into this, but most of the cause lay with the time wasted on social niceties. The servants delivered breakfast directly to their chambers. Luncheon, however, took more time, although since they'd begun adjourning to the cheerier morning room, the company improved.

The three smaller tables provided a welcome change, as Paige enjoyed the company of Lady Emma, Lord Freddy, and Miss Abercombe. Whenever possible, the earl joined them, but Arabella Poffington and her party determinedly waylaid him on a regular basis. Paige couldn't help but sympathize with the distressed and longing looks he sent toward their table as Arabella let loose her high-pitched titter. By now, Paige knew this signaled a cutting observation or direct insult aimed at some poor, maligned soul.

The elaborate multi-course dinners and requisite entertainments, varying from cards to music, monopolized the entire evening. She even lost a precious hour having to "dress" every night for the formal ordeal. What with all the distraction of the house party, she and her father lost almost half of every day! She harbored a sneaking suspicion the earl shared this sentiment with her, although her father certainly didn't mind foisting her into the company of "others of her station."

It did no good to dwell on what Arabella Poffington would say to that idea! Paige shook her head. It didn't really matter—not when the earl and a dozen mysterious trunks awaited her belowstairs.

She resisted the impulse to scurry down the staircase, instead choosing a more decorous pace. Her heart sank when she realized the earl wasn't in the library yet. *Of course, that's only because I was so ready to explore, and he has to be here.* She ignored the small voice in the back of her head that tsk-tsked and remembered all the kind things he'd done.

Long ago, she'd decided she must have misunderstood the first words she'd overheard him speak. The earl exhibited none of the snobbery she'd braced herself for. Instead, he not only let the servants know he appreciated their efforts, but he also called each one by name. He displayed no patience for Arabella's snide comments and went out of his way to make Paige and her father feel welcome among his upper-class guests.

She let her thoughts continue along this vein as she wandered toward the secret room. The earl's uncommon enthusiasm for knowledge and books warmed her heart. Why, she could almost see those fascinating green eyes light with interest—

"Good morning, Miss Turner." The deep timbre of his voice pulled her out of her reverie, and she realized she hadn't been imagining those intriguing depths—she'd been staring into them.

"I'm so glad you're here!" she blurted out without thinking. At his wide grin, she swiftly amended, "When I didn't see you in the library, I thought I'd have to wait, and I must confess, my patience is at an end. Have you already begun?"

"I'm hurt, Miss Turner. I wouldn't dream of beginning our exploration without you. After all, if you hadn't such a keen eye, we wouldn't be standing here. Shall we?" He gestured toward the trunks.

"Yes, please." She resisted the urge to peer over his shoulder as he opened the first trunk. Instead, she walked a short ways over and picked another. "Hmm. . . Old ledgers and accounting records in this one. How about yours?"

Paige smiled at him. She should have known that he'd share his findings immediately rather than make her wait. "It looks like old primers. Yes, here's an English text. . .math problems. . ." She laughed. "One of your ancestors had horrible penmanship!" She passed the practice sheet to the earl.

"Wait a minute. This looks a lot like mine!" He chuckled. "One of the reasons I became so fascinated with older, handwritten manuscripts is that I could never duplicate them."

Paige vividly imagined a young earl painstakingly copying lines, frustrated and intrigued to find something he couldn't master. She moved to the next trunk.

"You write beautifully, Paige. I've peeked at some of your notes. It's an enviable talent."

"It's more of a skill," she consoled. "One needs a deft hand to restore and mimic script, and I practiced for years at our old shop." She hoped he didn't hear the wistfulness that crept into her tone. If he had, he gallantly ignored it.

"Before we search any others, I should move these aside." She watched as he hefted the heavy-looking trunk, noticing the breadth of his strong shoulders as he carried it across the room. After he repeated the feat, they continued.

So many choices. Each chest held a promise she couldn't wait to reveal. She reached for another, only to pull up short at his disappointed groan.

"Ugh. Clothes. Why would anyone put clothes in an old teaching room next to a library?"

She reached out to stop him when he made as if to close the lid and move on. "Wait a minute! I never thought you'd give up so easily. You have to look through the entire thing."

He pulled out article after article of clothing. Layers of doublets, gloves, voluminous folds of farthingale dresses appeared. She ignored the I-told-you-so look he shot her as he reached to stuff the beautiful fabrics back inside. Something clunked as he dislodged a hat from the top of the pile.

"What do we have here?" Paige picked it up and looked inside. After fishing out a small black bundle, she tossed the discarded velvet cap toward the earl.

"Ahem!"

She looked up from unraveling the fabric to see she'd hit her target: The cap hung drunkenly on his head and over one eye.

She tilted her head and surveyed him critically. "I suppose we should be grateful your valet has a more refined sense of style than you do." Through teasing him, she plucked it from his head and dropped it into the chest. His deep rumble of laughter caught her off guard. She'd thought his rare smiles to be special, but when he gave happiness free rein, the result took her breath away.

After his laughter had run its course, he gestured to the bundle in her hands. "So, what treasure did you find?"

She hastily finished unwrapping it to discover two small paintings. "Miniatures. I'd say this fellow was an ancestor of yours."

When he looked at the brown eyes and blond hair depicted, he shot her a doubtful glance. She elaborated, "The shape of the nose and chin are similar. It looks like his young bride gave you your green eyes." The lovely woman, rather than staring solemnly as was customary, had been painted smiling. She looked happy and radiant.

"I'll bet these dresses belonged to her," Paige murmured, "and you're right. It's a bit odd they were stored here."

"Maybe not. Old rooms collect the strangest things."

"Like what?" The overly warm voice sent chills down Paige's spine as Arabella Poffington invaded their secret room. Her cloying perfume filled the air, the heavy scent making it difficult not to sneeze. Out of the corner of her eye, Paige saw the earl surreptitiously shut the lid on the chest of clothes.

"We've found stacks and stacks of old papers and ledgers," he answered. "Boring things no one bothered to get rid of but didn't actually want to read. So tell me, to what do we owe the pleasure of your company?"

"Well," Arabella heaved a dramatic sigh, "I suffered an absolutely dreadful headache all night and simply couldn't sleep. No one else is up and about, so I hoped for some pleasant company." The adoring look she shot at the earl made it clear Paige wasn't included in her estimation of "pleasant company."

Something had to be done, lest they be saddled with the harpy for the rest of the day, nay—the remainder of the party! Arabella Poffington would spend one hour in their workroom and consider it open ground from then on.

"Oh dear." Paige stifled a pang of guilt. *Lord, forgive me for believing the worst of this woman. Maybe I can help.* "No wonder you're so pale. Do you know, the cook kindly made my father a headache draught a few nights ago, and I'm sure she'd be glad to do the same for you."

"How sweet." The fire in Arabella's eyes proved Paige's hunch that the headache was only a pretext to win some attention.

"You do look a bit peaked, Miss Poffington," the earl joined in, the very picture of concern. "I know fair complexions are all the rage, but it won't do for any of my guests to become ill. Why don't you make your way back to the comfort of your room?"

"All alone?" The tremulous note positively rang with vulnerability and demanded a knight in shining armor.

"It wouldn't be proper for me to escort you to your chambers. You really must be ill to so forget, Miss Poffington. I'm certain Miss Turner would assist you if you wish."

"Oh, such a fuss is hardly necessary," Arabella gushed, and Paige felt a spurt of gratitude toward her for the first time. "Your concern is so kind, milord."

"Of course, I'll immediately send word to the kitchen, ordering the cook to make all due haste with that healing draught. I trust you'll be much recovered by supper."

Paige watched the solicitous manner in which he herded the intruder out of the library with a mix of admiration and, at the sight of Arabella leaning heavily on his supporting arm, a hint of jealousy. She ignored it. She'd never willingly play the role of cosseted-beauty-turned-manipulative-harridan. Why the upper classes rewarded physical charm over kindness, compassion, or intelligence was beyond her understanding. For now, while the earl rid them of the problem, she would practice patience rather than give in to her curiosity and explore the contents of that promising crate in the corner.

She grinned at the earl as he returned to the library.

"I don't suppose," he drawled lazily as he leaned against the doorsill, "that draught Cook is making for Arabella is a tasty beverage?"

"Sadly, though its restorative powers are undeniable, Papa did lament its acrid flavor."

"Well, imagine my surprise," the countess spoke from the doorway, "when I went down to confirm tonight's menu and Cook told me Miss Poffington is ill. The news is so distressing, I knew the other guests would be in sore need of cheering up." The sparkle in her eyes belied the words. "I decided it's a fine day for a picnic luncheon. Follow me."

After our long wait, we hardly even began to explore this room before being dragged away! Paige stifled a groan, and she respectfully followed her hostess toward a dismal afternoon of fresh air and delicacies.

Chapter 8

The next morning, Stephen strode into the library to find Paige staring wistfully at the door to their secret room. Stephen held the only key, and the room was always locked to prevent the likes of Arabella pawing through things and causing irreparable damage.

He smiled, remembering the previous morning and Paige's outburst of "I'm so glad you're here!" Her thoughts mirrored his so often, yet she constantly surprised him. For a routine library renovation, the past two weeks had been anything but dull.

"Good morning." She shot a conspiratorial smile at him. "If we continue this trend of getting here a little earlier every day, maybe we can actually finish! You know, since he begged off the picnic yesterday, Father is almost done cataloguing your collection already."

"Could you believe that picnic took up the whole afternoon?" The earl shook his head in disbelief. The trek to the old abbey ruins made it so everyone returned to the manor just in time to change for supper. The only bright spot was Arabella's absence.

He noticed the daisies Paige had picked yesterday now graced the mantel. The other women snatched up lilacs and roses for their own bedchambers, but it was so like her to leave the simple blossoms where others could appreciate them.

"I enjoyed the abbey, but I must confess to some frustration that we waited six days to open these trunks, and we only managed to get through three before stopping." Paige traipsed in behind him as he unlocked the door. They fell to the task at hand with unbridled enthusiasm.

"Let's try that one." She gestured to a rather long crate resting in the corner under a stack of other boxes.

"We'll have to get to it first." He hefted another box off the pile and set it on the old school table.

Paige couldn't resist peeking inside. "Oh, look at this!" The china doll with its exquisite painted features, beautifully stitched clothing, and tiny ringlets deserved admiration. Paige held it up to catch the candlelight.

"A doll?"

"Sorry, but there are a few things in here you might find interesting." Paige moved aside to allow him room. In moments, Stephen animatedly dug around in what looked to be an old toy chest. He set down a spinning top, some crooked samplers, and a few carved animals before pausing.

"Would you look at this? Someone had a talent for whittling." He drew out handfuls of figures, each about three inches tall.

"What are they? Toy soldiers?"

"Prussian soldiers. Look at the detail! Their uniforms are perfect right down to the last detail. And these chess pieces— Wait a minute. . . ." He dove into the toy chest once more and emerged with more chessmen and a board of contrasting light- and dark-hued wood.

"Truly exceptional workmanship," she agreed. "We should find a place for this in the library."

Years fell away from him as he pulled out an intricately carved, life-size sword. "The one I played with as a child couldn't hope to compare with this." Stephen ran an admiring hand down the dull blade. "We'll have to find a place to display this, too." He placed both beside the doll on the table, which would hold the wonderful things they found. The next crate proved more difficult to open.

"I think Mrs. O'Leary left a crowbar in here, just in case." He watched as Paige rummaged in the corner and emerged triumphantly.

With her hair slightly mussed, a streak of dirt across her cheek, and her right arm enthusiastically brandishing a heavy crowbar, she looked like a librarian warrior queen. If every other trunk held only clothing, it didn't matter. Stephen knew he'd already found the most precious thing in the entire manor. He took the crowbar and worked at the lid until it popped off.

"I think it's more clothes. Let's look at them later and move on." He shook his head as she pulled at the cloth. What was it about women and clothes? Reaching for another chest, he pulled up short at her admiring gasp. He turned to find a real warrior queen, complete with helmet and shield, woven into an intricate tapestry Paige held aloft. She came back into view as she laid the piece on the table.

"You really do have to stop rejecting anything that isn't paper, milord! Isn't she magnificent?" The same glee as had been evident when she waved the crowbar lit her face, and he couldn't help but smile.

"I've never seen anything so wonderful." His reply had less to do with the tapestry than its champion, but Paige didn't notice.

"I think it's Deborah, one of only two female judges to rule Israel. Am I right?" Her question made him take a closer look.

"I believe so. This would be a depiction of when she rode with Barak to defeat Sisera. She was supposed to be his talisman of God's favor."

"See? Behind every great man is a determined woman." Paige's eyes sparkled with humor.

No self-respecting man could leave it at that. "The trick is that the man chooses the woman."

She chuckled in acknowledgment of his comeback. "Deborah would look marvelous over the mantel, don't you think?"

"Certainly. I wonder who made this and where she came from." He lifted the now-empty crate to make room for the next and found a slim volume sliding around. "What's this? I can't read it, but it looks like German."

Paige came to read over his shoulder as he opened the book. He caught a whiff of sunshine and honeysuckle as concentration furrowed her brow.

"It's a diary. And you're right; it is German. Wait a minute! Annalisa of Ravenhurst," she murmured and scurried off to one of the trunks they'd opened yesterday. "Yes, that's right." She brought over the miniature of the woman and traced the name on the back.

"It's her diary, and she probably wove the tapestry!"

"It makes sense. Germany has a strong warrior heritage." He flipped through the diary, curious. "Why don't you read it to me?" He handed her the diary, and she perched on the edge of the table next to the tapestry. He caught a glimpse of trim ankles and dainty feet enclosed in worn leather half-boots before she adjusted her skirts. He settled on one of the sturdier trunks as she began to translate.

> "*Fifth of April, Year of Our Lord, 1763*
>
> *Today the Mother Superior called me to her office. After Papa's death, I was certain I'd stay here the rest of my life as I have no other relatives.*
>
> *I did not know Papa arranged a betrothal for me until this afternoon. This diary is a gift from my intended, the first Earl of Pemberton, whom I am told received his title in service to his king.*
>
> *It is kind of him, and I hope bodes well for the future. He also sent a miniature of himself. He seems a handsome man, not dissolute, so I pray he not be given to drinking, gambling, or any other vice. . . .*"

An elusive memory niggled in the back of Stephen's mind. He concentrated, content just to hear the soothing tones of her voice. Then he remembered.

"Wait a minute!" His sudden exclamation startled her, and she almost dropped the diary.

"What?" Disgruntled, she was absolutely adorable. He completely understood; whenever he began reading, the world faded away.

"This is family legend. I remember my grandfather telling me when I was just a boy." Interest flashed in her silver eyes, encouraging him to continue.

"The first earl of Pemberton was appointed in the early eighteenth century for service to the crown. I believe he uncovered an assassination plot. This manor always belonged to the family, but we only bore a viscountcy until then. As the story goes, the first earl, my great-grandfather, agreed to a diplomatic, arranged marriage with a younger German noblewoman whose father bore no sons. It's rather poetic that a woman with no more family was given a new family with a new name—almost like they'd start off on more of an equal footing."

"So the miniatures are the very first earl and his young bride?" Paige clutched the diary in her excitement.

"It looks like that's the case," he agreed.

"How wonderful. To think all of this came from Germany when they were wed." A troubled frown creased her brow. "But why would everything be locked in here?"

"My ancestor went to fetch his bride in autumn, and they were wed immediately in Germany. They stayed for the winter rather than travel and didn't leave for England until late summer, after she'd born his heir. Supposedly they loved each other deeply, but she died on the trip to England. By all accounts, losing her grieved the first earl deeply, and he never remarried."

"That's terrible." Regret lined her expressive face. "Well, now we know the secret of the hidden room. I imagine he couldn't bear to look at the things that reminded him of her, so he sealed them in a spare room. Such a pity. She seemed like a lovely woman." Paige traced the flowing script with one finger.

"Why don't you read a bit more before we continue looking through the trunks?" he encouraged, loathe to leave the story on such a disheartening note. It made the place a bittersweet treasure—bitter from its poignant past, but sweet because he shared it with Paige. Stephen didn't want her to regret their special room, especially not the time they spent in it together.

Paige began translating again:

> "*Seventh of April, Year of Our Lord, 1763*
>
> *My betrothed is on his way to fetch me. I pray daily for peace and strive to give my concern to the Lord, though it is difficult when I think of how I will be marrying a man I've never spoken with and moving to another country.*
>
> *The tapestry of Deborah I began takes on a new meaning for me. Since my great-great grandmother Lorice, weaving has been a skill and comfort to the women of our family. Now, the task deepens, reminding me to trust in God's plans for my life. I take comfort that Deborah was another woman the Lord took far away from everything she knew to lead her country to victory on the battlefield.*

My marriage is to strengthen my country, and I, too, will be going some-place I'd never imagined I'd belong. I hope to finish the tapestry before the earl arrives. I harbor hopes it will hang in our home someday. I do not bring much to this man save a good name and my determination to be a good wife.

I have a few baubles, this tapestry, and my most precious possession—the Gutenberg Bible passed down through our family for generations. I cherish the thought that I may have children who will use it to further their walk with the Lord. . . ."

Paige's voice trailed off as she looked up from the diary to meet his gaze.

"If he really did put everything of hers in this room, then is it possible the other items mentioned are in here, as well?" Even in her excitement, she didn't articulate the hope of finding an original Gutenberg Bible.

"There's only one way to find out." He followed as she hopped off the table and headed for the remaining unopened trunks.

"This one. I don't know why, but I'm positive." Paige shoved a large trunk off the smaller crate she'd singled out earlier.

"Move back a second."

She stepped back as he used the crowbar to open the crate. Paige couldn't help but notice the play of strong muscles beneath his blue superfine overcoat. When he moved aside, she squeezed in for a better look, her heart pounding.

Chapter 9

They'd found it. She reached for the large object at the same time he did. She tried to convince herself the tingles racing up her spine were due to the excitement over finding such a treasure. He held it as she unwound the old cloth, revealing brown leather.

Beautifully made, the leather-covered studs across the front formed a cross. Awestruck, she touched them, smiling as his hand covered hers. Neither of them spoke, their silence a mark of reverence for the cherished Bible.

Papa walked into the room. "It's awfully quiet in here." His voice boomed around them.

"Papa, look!"

"What's this?" Her father became quieter as he suspected the magnitude of the find. "Can it be?"

"An original Gutenberg," the earl confirmed. He opened it, and the pages fell to Psalms.

" 'Thy word is a lamp unto my feet, and a light unto my path.'" Paige translated the Latin aloud, marveling that they should find this verse so naturally.

The first letter of each chapter was written in red, with exquisite rubrication in still-vivid hues of green and gold embellishing the thick pages.

"Here." Stephen gently flipped through the volume until he reached the verse he sought. " 'Let the word of Christ dwell in you richly in all wisdom'—Colossians."

"Surely the Lord intended for you find it," Papa said softly. He reached out and returned to the front of the volume. " 'The fear of the Lord is the beginning of wisdom: and the knowledge of the holy is understanding'—Proverbs."

"That brings to mind another of my favorite verses." Stephen turned a few precious leaves. " 'A wise man is strong; a man of knowledge yea, increaseth strength.' Also Proverbs. Wisdom and understanding from the Lord strengthens us not only as individuals, but as His children."

"Turn to Romans chapter nine, verses thirty-eight through thirty-nine," Paige requested. She laughed. "I forgot they hadn't numbered the verses yet."

The earl scanned through the book of Romans and finally read aloud, " 'For I am persuaded, that neither death, nor life, nor angels, nor principalities, nor powers, nor things present, nor things to come, nor height, nor depth, nor any other creature, shall be able to separate us from the love of God, which is in Christ Jesus our Lord.'"

"This is one of my favorites because it reminds me that no matter where I am, He is with me," Paige said.

"And He loves us," Papa added. "Let's see if we can find First John chapter four, verses seven through eight, please."

"No need." Stephen closed his eyes. "I know them by heart: 'Beloved, let us love one another: for love is of God; and every one that loveth is born of God, and knoweth God. He that loveth not knoweth not God; for God is love.'"

The holy words of love spoken in Stephen's deep bass sent tingles down Paige's spine once more. She darted a look at Papa, and his raised eyebrows told her he'd intentionally brought up the subject of love.

"Oh, you know your favorite verse isn't here, Papa. After all, the commandment, 'Honour thy father and thy mother' is in Exodus." She ended the disturbing topic of love, only to realize something. "The diary only mentions the Gutenberg Bible. I wonder if she possessed both volumes, or if she refers to this alone."

"I don't know. There's not another in the crate, and I'd imagine they would be packed together to prevent separation if she owned both."

"But they were traveling. Could it have been to prevent the loss of both if one went missing?" She hated to sound as though she were ungrateful for what they'd been given, for they now held a blessing from heaven.

"We'll write to the abbey where she stayed and see if they know anything about it. I don't see any other matching crates." Stephen still didn't sound disappointed, merely fascinated.

"Paige! I knew I'd find you here." Emma shattered the tranquil feeling.

"Look at this, Em!" Stephen tried to show her the precious Bible, but Emma would have none of it.

"We haven't the time right now, brother." She caught Paige's arm and headed for the door. "The ball is tonight, and we must get ready!"

Alarm shot through Paige as she dug in her heels. How could it already be afternoon? "I'm not going to the ball! It isn't my place!"

"Balderdash." Stephen stopped his perusal of the Gutenberg to glower at her. "You're a lady through and through. Besides. . ." His smile banished any thoughts of arguing. "I want you to be there."

"But, um, I. . ."

Emma marched her toward the door as Paige struggled for a plausible reason to avoid her fate. Desperate, she played for time. "It's hours before the ball! Surely we could wait a bit."

"Every lady takes hours for her toilette before such an occasion."

"Why?" The question escaped before Paige could think it over. Her curiosity always managed to find her at the most deplorable times.

"You'll see." With a gamine grin, Emma whisked Paige upstairs before she could utter another word of protest.

—⁓—

"I haven't a thing to wear." Paige spoke the realization aloud as she stood before the armoire, looking critically at a sea of gray cotton and serge.

"I know." Emma's self-satisfied pronouncement held no reassurance. She opened the door to the sitting room between Paige's room and her father's.

"Miss Rosebrawn will see to it that this isn't a problem. I gave her your measurements as best I could figure them. I borrowed one of your other gowns, but I've noticed they're a bit large on you. Of course, there will be a few alterations needed, so she'll have just enough time to finish it for tonight!"

Miss Rosebrawn held up a shimmering creation of white cloth overlaid with sheer silver.

"Come on, love. We'll have it on in a trice, then you'll let old Rosey see what needs be done!"

Paige couldn't voice the protests welling up inside her: It was too expensive, she didn't deserve it, they were too kind. . . . The simple truth was, she couldn't stop imagining what it would be like to meet Stephen at a ball dressed in this ethereal gown.

"Oooh, how marvelous!" Emma gave a little clap as Paige twirled a bit.

Fit for a princess, the high-waisted gown fitted closely at the bodice, then gathered beneath her bosom to fall in graceful folds to the floor. Tiny, ruched sleeves, which Paige would have thought simply ridiculous in their frivolity, flattered the line of her neck and gave dignity to her height. *Really,* Paige mused, turning to look in the large cheval mirror Emma had thoughtfully produced, *it's not all that different from what I usually wear. Silver just sparkles a bit more than gray, and it's slightly tighter in the chest than I'm used to, but it's not overly fitted. . . .*

"It's too large in the waist," Rosey muttered, pinching the fabric and sticking in a pin.

Paige couldn't stifle the gasp of dismay at the dramatic change. "No, that won't be necessary. I love it just the way it is." Paige groped in vain to find the mischievous pin wreaking havoc on her dress. "This way it's simply too. . ." For the first time in her life, words failed her.

"Flattering?" Emma supplied helpfully, amusement coloring the word. "Really, Paige. It's neither improper nor ostentatious, though it showcases your figure quite nicely. Why have you been hiding behind those old gray dresses? This suits you far better. I can't wait to see Stephen's reaction!"

Paige couldn't respond, didn't know how to explain that the dress made her feel vulnerable. Simply by cinching in the fabric at the waist, Miss Rosebrawn turned the garment from lovely to stunning. The dress, no longer the focus of the ensemble, served to accentuate. . .her. Although, if she were to be perfectly honest, it wasn't overly revealing, nor did the fabric cling because the overdress skimmed the other fabric.

Coward, Paige chided herself. *Who are you to dictate fashion, anyway?* She remembered how Stephen had at first thought her to be a maid. Then her mind filled with other memories. Stephen, his eyes alight with earnest interest when she spoke. How he never made her feel like a giant when he stood next to her and how he valued her company. *"I want you to be there."* The words echoed sweetly in her thoughts, and she realized for the first time how much she wanted to be there for him. In this dress.

She squared her shoulders, stifled her qualms, and smiled at Emma and Rosey. "It's perfect. Thank you so much for your kindness." Tears swam in her eyes as Emma enveloped her in a hug.

"Here, now!" Rosey pushed them apart. "It won't do to wrinkle it afore you ever wear it!"

"That's right." Emma composed herself. "We'd best get on with it. Please tell Alice to come in, Miss Rosebrawn."

For the next three hours, Paige gave up protesting. The mysterious Alice smeared some concoction—smelling suspiciously of cucumbers—all over Paige's face, instructing her to let it sit as she luxuriated in a warm bath. Before her hair dried, the formidable lady's maid wielded a pair of scissors. Here, Paige wouldn't be overruled. She allowed only a trim rather than a more stylish cut. After her hair dried, she regretted her stubbornness, for surely if she had less hair it wouldn't have taken so long to curl.

Finally, after she'd been primped, powdered, draped in her mother's pearls, and popped into a pair of Emma's slippers, Paige allowed the maid to help her into the lovely gown. As she made her way toward the receiving platform at the top of the grand staircase, she felt a strong kinship with Deborah and Annalisa, all of them women venturing where they felt they didn't belong.

Chapter 10

Tonight's the night, Freddy." Stephen threw the sixth ruined cravat on the bedside table, narrowly missing his friend. He just couldn't concentrate.

"So you've finally figured out you're in love with her?" Freddy took mercy on him and constructed an elaborate knot.

"I asked Samuel's blessing this afternoon while Emma kept her busy, and Mother gave me the Pemberton engagement ring, looking like the cat who swallowed a canary." Amazing how not even that bothered him. After Emma stole Paige, he'd read their Bible for hours. But every chapter somehow reminded him of her.

He ran across the "noble woman" passage in Proverbs and felt a stab of longing to be the man who gave her children. Flipping the pages, he came to verses about love. "Love is patient. . . ." He felt anything but patient. He couldn't wait to see her again.

"You couldn't do better than Paige, old man. Still piqued I didn't warn you?"

Stephen decided he must be in love, since the I-knew-it-all-along tone of his friend's voice didn't bother him. He left the room to join his mother and sister in the receiving line. His mother must have invited every neighbor within five miles.

Stephen's smile froze after twenty minutes, and his mind wandered. Where was Paige? He'd seen no glimpse of her since Emma had whisked her off. She should have been among the first ones in the receiving line.

Of course, part of her beauty lay in her unpredictability. No other woman he knew would allow dirt to smudge her cheek, traipse around in baggy gray dresses, brandish crowbars, discover secret rooms, enthuse over books, care diligently for her father, and love the Lord like his Paige. Her versatility reflected in those marvelous gray eyes of hers, stormy, deep, lit with the fire of her inner loveliness. A man could get lost in such eyes.

He welcomed the news that this would be the last guest. He bowed to yet another debutante, the shining silver of her gown reminding him faintly of Paige. He smiled into her gray eyes, and his own widened in shock.

Behind this shimmering creature, the epitome of sophisticated elegance and taste, lurked the mischievous minx he'd come to love.

"Good evening, milord." Her dulcet tones sent his pulse racing as she curtseyed gracefully. He longed to rip the ribbons from her hair and run his fingers through those mahogany curls. The style, while lovely and all that was proper, did not showcase her uniqueness as did the queenly braided coronet she typically wore. How could a man want a woman's hair to be up and down at the same time?

He offered her his arm and escorted her as they descended the grand stairwell toward the ballroom. Tonight, he'd ask her to be with him forever. He knew exactly where he'd propose, too—in the place he'd first seen her: their library.

—⁓—

Heart hammering a wild beat, Paige concentrated on the steps. It simply wouldn't do to fall down the stairs, no matter how Stephen made her head spin.

Papa led her to the ballroom, and she hardly knew where to look. The chandeliers gave a glow reflected in the fabulous jewels and clothes of the guests. She smiled, remembering the first time she'd seen this place, when Stephen began thumping the wall in their hunt for the secret room.

"May I request your hand for a cotillion later this evening, miss?" She glimpsed at a freckled face blushing hotly as the youth bowed.

"Certainly." As he scrawled his name on her dance card, another fellow took his place. *Amazing what one little dress can do,* Paige thought bemusedly as her tiny card filled more rapidly than she ever would have thought possible. Years ago her mother had insisted Paige learn to dance, though she hadn't practiced in quite a while.

"My turn." Stephen's voice cut through her reverie, and he snatched up her dance card with unneeded ferocity.

"I may not be of nobility, milord, but even I know one isn't allowed to waltz unless given the nod by a patroness at Almack's!" Paige felt scandalized and more than a little pleased as he signed his name next to all three waltzes planned for the evening.

"That's only for young debs making their come-out." His words both thrilled her and sent a pang of regret coursing through her body. The pain of not being a lady of his class would be mitigated by the fact he'd singled her out.

"Ahem, Ahem." The orchestra stopped playing as Lord Poffington stepped onto the dais and cleared his throat purposefully.

"I just wanted to make a toast. Let's all raise our glasses to the Earl of Pemberton and his bride-to-be, my only daughter, Miss Arabella Poffington!"

Gasps met his pronouncement as Arabella stepped next to her father, simpering smile in place. "Lord Pemberton—although I suppose I can call him Stephen now," she cast a smitten look toward him, "simply insisted. Thank you all for wishing us happy."

As Stephen moved toward the platform to join his fiancée, Paige made a beeline for the door. Excited whispers buzzed in her ears as she tried to leave without bursting into tears.

"So romantic. . .they make a lovely couple."

"Perfect match, both of high station. . ."

"I'm so relieved. You know, I'd heard rumors he spent far too much time with some little commoner. Can you imagine a nobody being the next countess?"

"Of course not. He knows what's due his station."

Paige finally reached the hall and ducked into the library, closing the door and giving in to the tears. *I'm being silly. I knew he'd never choose me. "Some little commoner," "a nobody." They are right. I would never fit in, anyway. How could I have been so blind as to think he despised Arabella's catty comments? Since when did a man care about words when a woman offered beauty and status?*

She'd have to leave. It would be impossible to see him in their library, their secret room again. She couldn't pretend happiness when her heart lay shattered and her pride sorely bruised. Before she left, she'd see the Gutenberg one last time, though, as a reminder of God's love.

—⁂—

The moment of frozen disbelief cost him dearly. Even as Stephen stormed toward the dais, he saw Paige make her way out the door. He longed to go after her but knew if he didn't expose this engagement as a sham, he'd be duty-bound to wed Arabella Poffington.

"You are mistaken, sir." He used his height to tower over Lord Poffington.

"Oh no, I'm not." The older man drew his shoulders back. "I have it on very good authority you two reached an understanding after spending the afternoon unchaperoned," his voice lowered, "in the caretaker's cottage."

"Impossible. Such a situation never arose, Lord Poffington. And don't you suppose I would be gentleman enough to approach you if I desired your daughter's hand?"

Clearly, his firm tone gave Arabella's father pause, and for the first time, the older man cast an uncertain look at his daughter. "But I was told two days ago. . ." His voice trailed off.

Lord Freddy broke in. "Inconceivable. Two days ago would make the day in question Wednesday, and I personally can vouch for the fact that the earl spent the day in his library with me, the Turners, and his sister, Emma."

Stephen watched with satisfaction as the smile dropped from Arabella's face.

"How dare you accuse my son of even a hint of impropriety!" Stephen's mother rapped Poffington on the chest with her fan.

"I apologize for the. . .misunderstanding. We will, of course, be leaving immediately. My daughter. . ." Lord Poffington spat out the word, "has some explaining to do." As they left the ballroom, everyone burst into conversation.

Stephen made for the door, only to be blocked at every turn by guests expressing their relief he'd escaped marriage to "that Poffington chit."

As each person offered condolences, he edged around them, desperately wishing for the first time there was no secret room but instead an adjoining door to the library. He would give almost anything to escape so he could find Paige and explain what happened.

He burst into the hallway and was heading for the library when he saw Samuel Turner just ahead of him. "Wait." Stephen put a restraining hand on the older man's shoulder.

Samuel turned around, shaking his head. "You don't know how bad this is. She heard all those people saying how you and Arabella were the perfect match. I warned you earlier you'd have to convince her that our station didn't matter. It may be too late."

Stephen refused to give up. "No, it's not."

The older man's eyes darkened in resignation. "I'll pray for you both. But so help me. . ." Fire flickered in his gaze. "If you make this worse, you'll hear from me, earl or no." Paige's father crossed his arms and leaned against the wall. "I'll be waiting right here."

Finally, Stephen made it to the library, and his heart stopped. She wasn't here. But the door to the secret room stood open, although he'd made sure to lock it when he left. Stepping over several bent hairpins, he strode in to check on the Gutenberg.

Paige sat on a short stool, traces of tears still on her face, with the Gutenberg on the table before her.

"Paige. . ."

"Don't." Her shoulders stiffened. "I can't hear it, not now. I'll be leaving in the morning. I–I–I wish you happy, Stephen."

His heart leapt as she spoke his name. "Paige, you don't understand. Arabella lied to her father, and they've been publicly denounced. I never wanted her. If you really wish me happy. . ." He knelt and took her hand in his. "Marry me, Paige. I love you."

"I can't." Her voice broke as she began to weep. "I heard what everyone said. They'll never accept me as your bride. I'm unfit to be a countess."

She looked so forlorn, he wrapped his arms around her and let her cry on his perfectly knotted cravat. "Darling, I love you. You're everything I've ever wanted in a wife. The nobility is a fickle crowd, anyway. Right now they're tearing Arabella to shreds with their words. What does their opinion matter if you care for me, too? The Lord doesn't divide us by class but by the contents of our hearts. Yours is beautiful to me. Can't you make room for us?" He held his breath, waiting for her answer. If she refused him, he could never stand in this room again, never hope for a family of his own.

"I love you, too, Stephen. Are you sure?" Her eyes, once sparkling gray, stared up at him, red and puffy.

He'd never seen anything more beautiful. "I've never been more certain. Be my wife."

"Can we pray about it?" she asked. "I came in here for guidance, and I wanted to see the Bible one last time. I'm just not sure."

Stephen looked more closely at the open page and smiled as he read aloud: " 'Whoso findeth a wife findeth a good thing, and obtaineth favour of the Lord'— Proverbs." He took her into his arms. "I think God's will is quite clear." He slipped the family engagement ring on the third finger of her left hand.

"Let's go downstairs so I can show everyone my treasure." Stephen took her hand as they left the room, thanking the Lord for his blessings. God gave him not only the gift of His Word but also the love of a lifetime. Amidst the trunks of a forgotten room, he'd truly found a treasure worth keeping.

APPLE OF HIS EYE

by Gail Gaymer Martin

Dedication

To my wonderful English cousins
in Rowledge Farnham in Surrey
Paul, Jennifer, Nicola, and Scott Gaymer

And to my Gaymer ancestors, founders of England's
Royal Warrant Gaymer Cyder, whose true story inspired me.

*"With men this is impossible,
but with God all things are possible."*
MATTHEW 19:26

*"Keep my commandments, and live;
And my law as the apple of thine eye.
Bind them upon thy fingers,
write them upon the table of thine heart."*
PROVERBS 7:2–3

Chapter 1

Victorian England, 1851–52

Sarah Hampton peeked through her lacy bedroom curtain into the flower beds along the garden wall. "Who is the stranger tending the flower beds, Dulcie?"

The young maid eyed the stranger. "The new orchard keeper, miss."

"The orchardist? But. . .if he is the orchard keeper, why is he in the garden? Where is Benson?" Sarah was fond of the old gentleman who brought her apples from the orchard and rosebuds from the garden.

"He's ill, miss," the maid said, fastening the buttons of Sarah's chintz morning dress, though the clock had already chimed twelve noon.

"Very ill?" Sarah asked, peering through the lace.

Dulcie shrugged. "Ill enough to need time to mend."

Sarah faced her. "Then the young orchard keeper will do the gardening until Benson returns, I suppose."

"You ask a passel of questions, Miss Sarah." The servant shook her head and patted the dressing table stool. "Now if you'll sit, I'll dress your hair."

"No, Dulcie, I'll just tie it back with a ribbon, please." She pulled a ribbon from a wooden chest on her dresser. "See. It's cherry, the same color as the ribbons on my dress."

Dulcie made a tsking noise. "Let me at least make the bow. Your mother will be after me if I let you out of your room looking like a ragamuffin. You're a young woman, now—enjoying your coming out."

"Piffle, I'm but a child." She waved the ribbon like a flag, wishing her coming out had never been thrust upon her.

The maid snorted at her comment and caught the red streamer in her hand.

Acquiescing, Sarah pivoted on the dressing stool, allowing the maid to tie the ribbon, but her mind rested on the new orchard keeper whom she'd seen from the window.

Filled with anxious curiosity, she yearned to run into the out-of-doors and see the man more closely. Even from above, he looked like a giant, much taller than her father who seemed a tower in Sarah's eyes.

Dulcie completed the bow, then turned to dispose of Sarah's discarded nightgown.

After one last look in the mirror at her white gown and bright ribbons, Sarah hastened from the room and down the stairs. With the dining room empty, she snatched a piece of bread from the sideboard, smeared it with jam, and hurried through the side door to the garden.

To her disappointment, the new orchard keeper had vanished from the border beds. Intrigued, Sarah slipped through the garden gate and sank onto the stone bench inside the wall, cooled by the dappled shade. She bit into the thick slice of bread and licked the fruity spread from her lips, her gaze darting from one side of the garden to the other. Suspecting the stranger had gone to the orchard, she nibbled the bread and waited.

Having overlooked her morning prayers in her exuberance, Sarah closed her eyes and asked God's blessing on her family and country. . .and for strength to face her eighteenth birthday. Soon her parents expected her to be courted and married, but Sarah had little desire for the convention. She'd danced and accepted callers, but none had won her interest. Not one had sent her heart on a merry chase. Squeezing her eyes closed, she prayed for God to guide her to the man of her heart.

When she lifted her eyelids, a shadow had stretched along the ground to her feet. Timidly, she tipped her head upward and looked at the mountainous man. Her heart jolted with such force it took her breath away. She gaped at him as he neared.

His attention did not settle but passed her by. He moved away to distant beds and went about his business, adding compost around the base of the budding flowers. She observed him and ate her jam and bread.

Sarah had always talked with the older gardener, Benson. She'd known him from childhood, and with his white hair and leathery wrinkles, he seemed like the grandfather she'd never had. When she'd grown to nearly a woman, her mother scolded her for lingering in the garden and bothering the gardener. But he seemed kind, and Sarah loved to smell the earth and blossoming flowers, all God's handiwork.

Now, knowing she behaved improperly, Sarah couldn't help but stare at the tall, lanky man. While his size seemed almost fearful, his gentle face and handsome features calmed her scurrying pulse. He so concentrated on his work that he seemed to ignore Sarah until she wondered if he'd even seen her at all. But she could tell one thing: he loved the earth as much as she did.

Swallowing her upbringing and the last of her breakfast, she rose and stepped away from the bench into the sunlight, calling to him. "Good morning."

He dropped the trowel and jumped to his feet, towering above her head. Instead of speaking, he only gave a bow and tipped his cap, then retrieved the garden tool and returned to his work.

Feeling ignored, Sarah scowled. Yet, she understood his hesitation. The young man belonged in her father's employ and knew his station. Regardless, she longed to hear his voice, venturing it would be deep and vibrant, coming from the depth of his massive chest.

"Do you have a name, gardener?" she asked.

He turned to her, removed his cap, then shifted toward the house and back again as if he waited for the hand of God to smite him if he should speak. "John Banning, miss." His resonant voice sparked on the air.

"Don't be apprehensive, Mr. Banning. If my father is about, I'll explain that I spoke to you first."

He gave her a grateful look, slipped on his cap, and turned back to his compost and trowel.

With daring, she moved closer and scooped up a handful of moist earth, breathing in the loam's rich aroma.

He faced her fully and a frown settled on his brow. "Please, miss, don't dirty your hands." He pulled a kerchief from his pocket and handed it to her.

"Thank you, Mr. Banning. You're a gentleman." She brushed her hands with the cloth, but viewing the soiled fabric, she did not return it. Instead, she clutched the kerchief and drew in a deeper breath. "I love the earth. Everything in nature. You too, I would imagine."

He nodded, seeming to avoid her gaze.

"We come from the earth, you know," she said. "Ashes to ashes and dust to dust."

" 'And the Lord God formed man of the dust of the ground.' " John glanced her way, then lowered his gaze.

Sarah's pulse tripped. She studied the man's sensitive profile, feeling something sweet and lovely happening in her chest. "You've quoted from Genesis. You are a Christian man."

He nodded and wiped the perspiration from his brow with the back of his hand, his nervousness evident in his shifting stance.

Sarah tilted her head to capture his gaze. " 'And the Lord God said, It is not good that the man should be alone.' "

John faltered backward and shook his head. "I must return to my work, miss."

Good sense washed over her, and she nodded, withdrawing to the garden wall and letting the man continue his tasks. But instead of leaving, she lowered herself to the bench and fingered his soiled kerchief. No grown man had ever been so gallant toward her. He had treated her as if she were a true lady.

In silence, she watched him work, wondering about his age and background. Did he live in Barnham? If so, why had she never seen him? Sarah let her mind play on his name. *John Banning?* She'd heard his family name before, but the time and place failed her memory.

Finishing, John gathered his equipment and strode across the garden toward the tool shed. He gave her only the faintest nod.

Sarah watched him go, the sunlight reflecting on his broad back, his dark hair curling at the nape of his neck. The man's gentle manner stirred her. She could see his love for the earth—his kindness, offering her his kerchief and his respect. Benson had been thoughtful as well, but he had not stirred such unknown feelings within her.

Recalling the fearful look in his questioning eyes, she admitted she'd been wrong to speak with him without a proper introduction. With a whispered prayer, she asked God's forgiveness.

—⁓—

John stood inside the tool shed, staring into the darkness and calming his pulse. What had he been thinking to allow the young woman to carry on a conversation with him? He'd begun his employment only today and had not earned the family's trust.

Riddled by uncertainty, John wondered about the young woman. . .girl who'd pestered him. He assumed she was Sarah, the Hamptons' only daughter. Calculating what he could recall, he speculated she would be in the middle of her teen years—almost ready for courting.

Despite her presumptuousness, her lovely face had impressed him—her raven black hair and eyes the color of a hedge sparrow's eggs. Beneath her youthful innocence, her attention had jarred unwanted thoughts. She had been born a woman of rank, not one who should enter his thoughts in such a beguiling way.

His first glimpse of her had sent the nerves shimmering down his back. Like an angel, she had sat in the shade dressed in a white frock. Bows the color of ripe apples trimmed her gown and captured her long dark hair. He recalled the sunlight flickering through the foliage and sprinkling her with fairy lights.

Not only her loveliness, but her disposition, as well, clung to his memory. Though a young woman of breeding, she treated him as an equal. A man. Her direct gaze and love of the earth. . .love of God had wrought the strange feelings that tripped through him.

John pulled his mind from the charming girl, wiped off the tools, and stowed them. The shed held the afternoon heat, and he slipped off his cap, then reaching into his pocket, he sought his kerchief to mop the moisture from his brow. The cloth had vanished.

He remembered. He'd given it to her. *Sarah?* The name lilted through his thoughts. A woman of breeding. A woman with pluck, yet gentleness. He'd seen it all in her soft blue eyes. He drew in a ragged breath and stepped into the light. His eyes were blinded by the afternoon glow, and John paused a moment before he closed the shed.

The Hamptons' gardens burst with life in the June sunshine. He had much to do to keep the hedges and shrubs pruned and trimmed, the flowers and vegetables fertilized, and the orchard maintained. Grateful, he knew a full crew would arrive in time for harvest.

Still, his work wasn't finished. In respect to his parents, he owed his father time and energy on the family property. His labor also served as rent for the use of the small cottage on the family farm. Though he was only twenty-five, John's back ached like an old man's from the bending and digging he'd done since he'd come back to Barnham.

He broadened his pace and stepped beyond the garden wall, but the sight caused him to falter. Near the side porch, Edward Hampton stood on the lawn with his daughter. John noticed his employer's impressive stature as he stood beside the petite young woman. Though nearly as tall as John, Hampton's girth and posture presented a man of dignity and prosperity.

Withdrawing his gaze, John hurried to pass by unnoticed but hesitated when he heard the man's voice.

"Big John. How did you fair your first day?"

John pulled off his cap and clutched it in his left hand. "Fine, sir. Thank you. I'll return tomorrow early. There's much to do." He kept his focus away from the fair face that stared at him.

"Sarah, this is our new orchardist, Big John Banning," Hampton said, his eyes beaming as he gazed at his daughter.

"How do you do?" Sarah asked, without disclosing their earlier meeting.

"Very well, miss. Thank you." John stepped back, longing to make his escape. "Until tomorrow, sir." He tipped his cap and propelled his long legs to carry him away with haste, but once a safe distance away, he glanced over his shoulder and saw Sarah watching him.

—⁂—

"Why do you call the man Big John, Father?" Sarah asked, her focus still tied to the young man.

"His stature, my silly Sarah. Can't you see the man is a Titan?" He patted her arm and walked with her toward the house. "I've heard once during the yeomanry review in Norwich, the duke commented on his great stature. Big John may be a yeoman, but he is a man to be reckoned with."

Surprised at her father's words, she suspected she saw admiration in his eyes. "Is he from Barnham? I recall the name Banning, but I have no recollection why." She grasped her father's arm as they ascended the stairs.

"Robert Banning, John's father, leases a parcel of my apple orchard. He produces cyder as we do." He pulled open the door and allowed Sarah to enter first.

"But their cyder is not the fine quality of ours, is it, Papa?" She grinned at her doting father, knowing what she said would make him laugh.

He chuckled. "My girl," he said, then paused. "Young woman, I should say." He stood back and gazed at her with a look of pride. "You know, Sarah, you've been presented to many eligible men of the community. You must consider yourself a woman."

"Fiddle-faddle. I love being your daughter, Papa. I need no other man to care for me. I'm not eager to be a woman. Let me be your little girl awhile longer." She sent him a playful grin, but in her heart, she meant every word.

Her father thrust a hand behind his back and shook his head. "My Sarah, I might be willing to keep you here longer, but your mother has other plans. She wants you to be a lovely bride one of these days." He stroked her cheek and strode from the room.

Sarah watched his departure until he vanished through the doorway. *A bride. A wife. A mother.* All those things were distant frightening dreams.

She had been prepared for adult proprieties. She'd learned proper etiquette and conversation in polite society. With her mother's encouragement, she'd learned to sing and dance, to read literature and speak a little French, and to do needlework. Now the season had arrived when she would be presented to the young men for courtship. Yet her heart was not in it.

Despite her assured proclamation, Big John Banning towered in her thoughts. His chestnut hair, his gentle eyes, his humble manner. A man of the earth and the sky. His shoulders in the clouds, his hands in the soil, and his feet secured to the earth.

Chapter 2

W hat is this cloth?" Dulcie asked, holding up John's kerchief.

"It's the orchard keeper's. He offered it to me so I could wipe dirt from my hands." Sarah eyed the clean kerchief she'd washed and hung on the towel stand. "I must return it to him."

"No, miss, I'll return it. Your mother will be angry if she finds you too cordial with the man."

"Piffle." Sarah snatched the handkerchief from the maid's hands. "I will take care of it, Dulcie. . .and I'll speak with Mother." She arched her eyebrow, hoping to make her point with the servant.

Dulcie backed away. "It's your choice, miss."

Sarah sank into her window seat and clutched the white kerchief, while Dulcie finished her tasks and left the room.

Spreading the cloth in her lap, Sarah brought the corners together to fold it but, instead, paused. Struck by an idea, she rose and located her sewing box, opened the lid, then plucked out a needle and brown silk thread.

To find more light, she carried the items back to the window seat and looked toward the garden wall. Today no one tended the garden. After she threaded the needle, Sarah selected a corner of the kerchief and began small embroidery stitches, creating John's monogram.

A tap on her door startled her, and she slipped her needlework beneath the pillow behind her back. "Come in," she called.

The door opened, and her mother stood in the threshold. Sarah watched her mother sweep into the room. Tall and trim, her straight back and long neck announced an air of elegance and breeding. "Why are you inside, Sarah? It's a lovely day. Come let us sit in the shade so we can discuss your party. Time is fleeting."

"We have nearly two months. . .until August." Eyeing her mother's determined face, Sarah's stomach tightened.

Her mother sank beside her on the cushion. "Preparations must be made properly. We must make our guest list and prepare the invitations. Then we'll select the menu." Her mother touched her hand. "I want to please you, dear."

"You could please me by not insisting upon another ball. I've danced enough and accepted too many young men callers. None piqued my interest. I don't want to think about courting and. . .marriage. I would rather be a spinster, Mother. Please."

With fire sparking in her eyes, her mother bolted upward. "Sarah, what has gotten into you? A woman must have a suitable husband. Do you want to be an old woman with only servants for company in your old age?"

Before Sarah could respond, her mother sank to the cushion beside her. "Dear Sarah, you are a beautiful young woman, and you may take your time finding the young man who captures your heart. But we will hold your ball." Her look pleaded with Sarah. "Marriage can be a beautiful experience. Fulfilling. . .and exciting."

Her mother's face flushed, and Sarah wanted to ask questions. She'd never seen her mother's life filled with more than tending to servants and accepting a party invitation on occasion.

"And babies, Sarah. You'll want children." Her mother's features softened, and she caressed her daughter's cheek. "What would I have done without you to bring me such joy?"

Sarah looked at her mother's misty eyes and could no longer argue. She would have the ball. But what young man would capture her heart? Sarah's fingers slipped beneath the pillow and touched the cotton handkerchief. "I'll be down shortly."

Her mother wrapped her arms around her daughter's neck, pressing her cheek against Sarah's. "I'll go now. We'll talk outside." She rose and slipped from the room.

When the door closed, Sarah released a rattled breath and looked out the window, her mind wandering. For years, she had known the young men who attended the parties. Awkward, proper men whom she'd met at church and social functions. Breeding had trained them well, but each had lost the naturalness Sarah found appealing. None had left a lasting impression or sent warmth rushing through her veins like the poets proclaimed. None. . .

She faltered, remembering the unexpected sensation that riffled through her in the garden. The tenderness that tugged against her heart when she spoke to the quiet dark-eyed orchard keeper. Holding her breath, Sara panicked as a deep fear stabbed her. She came from landed gentry. John had been born a yeoman. A farmer.

Yet with stubborn persistence, she pulled the kerchief from behind the pillow and looked down at her stitches. With the *J* completed, she lifted the needle and finished the *B*. Yeoman or not, John Banning behaved as a gentleman. She broke the thread, folded the cloth, and tucked it inside the sleeve of her wrapper before disposing of the needle and thread.

Moving across the room, Sarah stopped at the door and grasped her courage. She must cooperate with her mother. . .behave properly as society and her parents expected.

Still she clung to her mother's words. *You may take your time finding the young man who captures your heart.* Sarah would take her time.

—⁂—

John hunched over the boxwood that formed a low maze in the formal garden. Pruning the new growth, he shaped the shrubs into perfect cubes. In each corner of the garden, the greenery formed four intricate patterns. In the hub of the adjoining paths stood rows of iris, delphinium, foxglove, and in the center, a sundial. The formality reminded him of society—everything in its appropriate place.

Concentrating on his work, John trimmed the outer hedges beside the displays of peonies and rosebushes. When footsteps crunched on the gravel, he sprang to his feet. "Miss Hampton," he said catching his breath.

"Good afternoon, Mr. Banning. The garden looks grand."

She stood beside him with a pale pink parasol opened to block the sun. The color matched the trim on her pale gray dress.

"Thank you." Nervousness stiffened his stance, and he looked toward the opening in the gate, knowing her father would consider it inappropriate for him to converse with his daughter.

"I so much enjoy the sunshine instead of spending gloomy hours in the arbor. My mother insists I attend one more ball. Men are so blessed to be excused from such foolishness."

Startled by her comment, John hesitated. While she seemed to wait for his response, he sorted through words that would be proper for a man in his position. "I'm sure it will be a wonderful party. Your parents are eager to present you to the young men of the community." He swallowed, imagining the suitors who would gather around her, awed by her loveliness.

"Fiddle-faddle, I'll oblige if I must. But consider this, Mr. Banning. What do you do if you visit a shop for a new cap. . .and none meets your expectation?"

He struggled with her thinking, wondering how she had moved the conversation from admirers to caps. He could only answer her honestly. "I would not be interested in a new cap, I suppose."

"Yes, that's my thinking exactly. If no suitor meets my expectation, I'll not be interested."

Thinking of what had been said, John finally thought he understood. "I'm certain one gentleman will catch your fancy, miss."

She shrugged and traipsed away toward a row of blossoming perennials. "Perhaps, but I can't imagine it."

Her voice caught on the breeze, and John hid the grin that curved his lips. He bent again to the trimming, though his concentration centered on the vision of gray and pink who strutted nearby.

"Look at the peonies," she called, moving closer to the row of flowering stems. "The ants have done their work. They're open wide and very delicate—like flounces on a ball gown."

Eyeing the fragile blossom, he could imagine Sarah dressed in a dainty frock covered with ruffles and lace, accepting the offer of a dance from a young gentleman. As she moved from flower to flower, her graceful manner delighted him. Her delicate parasol bounced above her head while sunshine spread around her feet like liquid gold.

Without thinking, he stepped to her side, bent down, snipped a blushing peony blossom from the plant, and presented it to her. Sending him a sweet smile, she accepted the stem between two long pale fingers and nestled it against the bodice of her frock.

Her direct gaze lowered to the blossom. "It's so beautiful. Look at the tinge of pink." She extended the petals beyond the shade of her parasol and in the full sun, the color seemed ethereal.

Before she drew the peony into the shade, a large white butterfly lit upon the bloom. Sarah paused, and her face filled with delight.

John watched as the airy insect flitted above the flower, its wings wafting like a lady's fan, intriguing and enticing.

When the butterfly floated away, Sarah gasped and drew in a full breath. "I forgot to breathe," she said, her laughter as airy as the insect. "Such a lovely moment. Thank you, Mr. Banning."

Her delight had given him a lovely moment as well. "You're welcome, miss. . .but God provided the butterfly. I only offered you the flower."

"Indeed, but I still want to thank you." As if struck by a thought, she faltered and slipped her fingers beneath her lace-fringed sleeve. "Lest I forget. . ."

She withdrew a white cloth from beneath the pink ruffle, and John stared at it in amazement. Could it be his kerchief? And if so, why had she tucked it into her sleeve?

She presented the handkerchief to him. "Here. It is yours. Remember? You offered it to me to wipe my hands."

He stood frozen, unable to move.

"Don't fear, Mr. Banning. It's clean. I washed it for you." As if encouraging him to accept it, she jiggled her hand, and the cloth splayed downward, fluttering on the breeze.

He grasped the clean kerchief, noticing the neat stitching in the corner; the cloth could not be his. When he lifted the end, his pulse surged, seeing the letters *J B*. His initials. His monogram.

He pulled his amazed gaze from the white fabric and looked at Sarah. "But this isn't. . .did someone—"

"I embroidered your initials. There is no *B* for Big. I hope you don't mind."

B? A soft chuckle rippled from his throat, followed by his concern. "I'm touched by your generosity, miss. . .but it's not at all proper."

"Piffle, Mr. Banning. It's my way to make you beholden."

He tensed, speculating what she might mean.

"Now I'll expect flowers from you. Vases of them for my pleasure. Our ailing gardener, Mr. Benson, presented me flowers often. Might I expect the same?"

Shamelessly, John gazed at the woman, wanting to remind her Benson was elderly and married. But how could John tell her he could not give her flowers because he might also give her his heart?

—⁂—

Sarah carried the flower inside, filled a small vase, and carried it to her bedroom. Setting it on her dressing table, she sank onto her bed and gazed at the blossom. Her hands trembled with the awareness of her shameless behavior toward the young man. She had been flirtatious with the orchard keeper—totally improper and unforgivable to her parents. She prayed God would not find her indiscretion unpardonable.

Sarah lifted the hem of her skirt and slid her feet onto the bed. Through the lace curtain, a blue sky filled the window, and she lifted her prayer toward the heavens, asking God if the feelings that struggled inside her were the Lord's bidding or her own evil direction. No matter, she needed God's forgiveness.

"Sarah." Her mother's voice sailed through the doorway.

"Come in," she called, watching the door until it opened and her mother stepped inside, her mauve skirts swishing against the door frame.

"Are you well? You look flushed." Her mother bustled across the floor and pressed the back of her hand to Sarah's cheek.

"I'm well. I walked in the garden, and I became heated." Sarah could never tell her mother what brought the blush to her cheeks.

"Perhaps that's all it is." Her mother rose and drew a cloth from the washstand, then wet it with water from the pitcher. Returning to Sarah, she pressed the damp towel against her daughter's forehead. "I have exciting news."

From the enthusiasm in her mother's voice, Sarah's interest was aroused. "What news, Mother?"

"Father has agreed we will all go to London to visit the Crystal Palace Exhibition. I suggested the holiday to celebrate your birthday."

"To London—but how long would we be gone?" Her mother's expression sent a fearful sensation skittering down Sarah's back. She should have expressed excitement, not disappointment. "How lovely. Thank you." She prayed she had hidden her obvious concern beneath her new exuberance.

"My—my, Sarah, for a moment you sounded as if you didn't want to go." She fanned herself with her hand, then rose and lifted the window to allow a cooler breeze to drift into the warm room. "There, now that's much better." She sent Sarah a gentle smile. "While in London, we'll purchase new gowns, especially for the ball."

Instead of returning to Sarah's side, her mother pulled back the curtain and peered outside. "The new orchard keeper is certainly making wonderful improvements to the landscaping." Facing the room, her gaze lit upon the flower on Sarah's dresser.

Sarah swallowed her guilt.

"Who gave you the peony, Sarah?"

Controlling her vulnerability, Sarah sat up and swung her feet to the floor. "It's from the garden."

"But you didn't pick the flower. Peonies have strong stems and must be cut," her mother said as her back stiffened.

Feeling helpless again, Sarah's shoulders sank. "I asked Mr. . . .the orchard keeper to cut the blossom for me."

"The orchard keeper?" Her mother's lips puckered with disapproval. "The Banning boy is a farmer."

"He is not a boy, Mother. He's a man. . .and. . ." Sarah realized her error too late. The words had already slipped from her lips and struck her mother's ear.

"Yes, Sarah, John Banning is a man. Please use good sense and proper conduct when dealing with such matters." With a final look, she turned and strode from the room.

Sarah stared at the empty doorway, then turned to the lovely peony on her table. Did good sense and proper behavior have anything at all to do with her? She cringed, knowing the unwelcome answer.

Chapter 3

Sarah passed through the garden gate and wandered among the flowers, longing to see Mr. Banning. His work took him to both the orchard and the gardens. Perhaps today, he labored among the apple trees.

She sensed he'd been avoiding her. As soon as she appeared near the stone bench, he scurried toward the shed or to another area of the garden. Still from a distance, she noticed his gaze turned toward her, and Sarah wondered if he felt the same stirring excitement as she did.

Her mother guarded her incessantly. They had spent hours together planning the August ball. At times, Sarah had longed to be stricken with some disease— the plague maybe—so the ball could be canceled. Then the seriousness of her wish struck her, and she would retract her thought, asking God to forgive her foolishness and to proffer a way to solve her dilemma.

In only a few days, her family would head for London. Her father, who had gone a month earlier on business, had viewed a small part of the amazing industrial exhibition and had told her about the wonders of the display. Though Sarah looked forward to exploring the new Crystal Palace, she did not look forward to buying the gown for her ball. She loved new frocks, but the ball gown affirmed the immediacy of her birthday. . .and her August gala. If she were truly honest, she preferred to remain in Barnham near the orchard keeper, even though he pretended not to see her.

Sarah quickened her pace, returning to the garden gate, holding the spring-green parasol to cover her fair skin from the summer sun. Perhaps Mr. Banning had not come to the manor at all today. She shrugged and stepped briskly across the lawn, up the stairs, and closed the parasol.

When she entered the house, Sarah ambled down the hallway with no idea how she would occupy her time. Passing her father's study, his voice rang out to her. She spun around and stood in the doorway. "Good afternoon, Papa. It's a lovely day."

"You've been walking in the garden?" From his desk, he looked at her over his spectacles.

"Only a few minutes." Did he suspect her interest in the orchard keeper? She waited for his reprimand.

"Where are you off to now, Sarah?"

His questions caused a guilty shiver up her spine. She shrugged. "Nowhere in particular. Perhaps I shall read."

He slipped off his spectacles and rubbed his nose. "Would you do your papa a favor, please?"

Relieved, she stepped deeper into the room. "Certainly."

He slid on his eyeglasses. "Mr. Banning is in the conservatory. Would you tell him to see me before he leaves today? He can ring the servant's bell and have someone show him the way to my study."

Her heart leaped at the news. "Yes, I'd be happy to deliver your message." She monitored her excitement, longing to dance from the room and head for the conservatory. She forced herself to cross the floor and kiss her father's cheek before leaving his company.

Once beyond her father's gaze, she dashed past the family parlor and dining room, through the large formal sitting room, and out the French doors toward the conservatory. Stepping beneath the glass dome, she stood in place, making a circle and peering through the palms and ferns. When she heard a noise from the left, her attention focused on the greenhouse, and she followed the sound.

When she stepped inside, the orchard keeper lifted his head from his work.

"Good afternoon, Mr. Banning," she said.

He shifted, his gaze darting toward the doorway. "Why. . .have you come here, miss?"

"Looking for you." Gesturing toward him, Sarah realized she still carried the parasol.

"Looking for me?" His jaw tensed. "But why?" His brows knitted.

"I will tell you soon enough, but first, I need you here." She beckoned him to follow.

Clearly concerned yet curious, John wiped his hands on a ragged cloth and walked behind her into the conservatory. Inside the dome, she sank to the stone bench and patted the seat beside her.

He eyed her frilly parasol.

"I came from the garden," she replied, answering his questioning look. "Please sit here." She pressed her palm against the bench. "I cannot see you up there."

"Miss, I. . .I can't sit with you." He glanced toward the glass enclosure of the greenhouse. "I'm working." His thoughts jumped to the garden. Had he trimmed something improperly? What had been so urgent in the garden to cause her to search for him?

"Please," she said, looking into his eyes and causing him to tremble. "Father is in his study and Mother is indisposed. Don't be apprehensive."

"Has my work displeased you?" He studied her face, seeing no unpleasantness.

"Your work? Not at all, Mr. Banning. I admire your ability in the garden."

"Then, why have you looked for me?"

"I have a message, but first, I am curious. I desire to know more about you."

"Me? No. . .miss, being alone with you is improper."

"I'm weary of being proper, Mr. Banning. I'll go away if you will sit beside me for only a moment." She gestured again to the empty place at her side.

He eyed his dusty clothes, then her lovely green- and white-striped wrapper and matching parasol, her hair knotted and pinned at her neck. He should not allow himself to submit to her, but winning the battle seemed hopeless.

The young woman's determination awed him. Such strength and honesty in one petite frame. He sank to the farthest corner. His voice tightened in his throat, and he could not look in her eyes; they were too close. . .too intimate. "What do you want to know, miss?"

"I wish you would call me Sarah." Her voice seemed more a whisper.

He could never call her by name. *Sarah*. It played in his mind like a love song. Perhaps she could ignore propriety, but his position allowed him no options.

"I understand your family lives in town," she said.

"A farm on the outskirts of town, miss."

"Who tends the farm?" She plucked at the pleat in her skirt.

"I do. . .and four brothers, miss."

She drew in a gasp of breath. "You toil here all day, then—"

"Yes, evenings and the hours I'm not in your father's employ," he said, recalling how weary his life had seemed before meeting. . .Sarah.

Her eyes widened. "Do you not have time for leisure?"

"On occasion," he said. But the occasion had been very rare. While her life abounded with social engagements, parties, and excursions, he toiled. . .but not forever. Someday he would own a business. . .if God honored his dream.

"Work is not meant to fill each hour," Sarah said. "I'm sure God has provided a verse to assure us that pleasure and leisure are important, too."

John searched his memory. "My knowledge of Scripture is limited, though I would presume the Lord allows some leisure."

"But. . .you quoted me a verse, don't you remember?" A frown marred her face. "I thought—"

"I know there is a God in heaven who controls the universe and directs the seasons, but. . .a man of my means has no time for church and little time for Bible reading."

She shifted to face him more squarely, a quizzical expression on her face. "Then how did you know the Bible verse the day we met?"

"From my mother. She always reminded us if God found the earth perfect enough to create people, then we should never be too proud to till the soil." His pulse raced as he looked into her tender eyes.

"Such meaningful words. . .your mother's." She lifted her head toward the light streaming through the overhead glass. As if kissed by heaven, the sun's rays beamed upon her.

"But why have I not seen you before. . .until that day in the garden?" she asked.

"I've been away working as an apprentice. I dream of owning my own cyder business one day. A cyder of such fine quality it will receive a warrant from the queen." Embarrassed at his admission, he paused. She would probably think him foolish to have such high hopes.

"Mr. Banning," Sarah said, her voice as tender as a whisper, "that's a wonderful ambition. Please don't call it a dream. Dreams don't always transpire, but ambition. . . that is different."

"Thank you kindly for your confidence," John said, rising. "Now I must return to the greenhouse." He extended his hand to help her rise.

"You are a gentleman, sir," Sarah said. "I have more than confidence in you—I have faith. I shall pray for God's blessing on your endeavors. With God, Mr. Banning, all things are possible."

John gave Sarah a polite bow and backed away, with her words hanging in his thoughts. *With God all things are possible.* Could she be correct? Would God be interested in a lowly man's hopes? Wouldn't the Lord be too busy saving people for eternity to worry about a simple man's plans?

He grinned, realizing he'd said plans, not dreams.

"Mr. Banning, I nearly forgot," she said, pivoting toward him like a lithe dancer. "My father requests you see him in his study before you leave. Pull the cord and a servant will show you the way."

Surrounded by ferns and palms and washed in sunlight, she sent him a bright smile and moved with grace through the doorway into the house. John stared at the empty opening, longing to be released from the feelings that stirred in his chest. She was a woman to be cherished.

Though she had vanished, he drank in her enticing scent of lavender and chamomile that clung in the air. Sweet. Young. Fresh. She appeared to be a dreamer as he was. He read it in her eyes. Though she tugged on his heart, he felt certain even God could not make this dream come true.

Saddened by the thought, he hurried back to his work, riddled with concern. Why did Mr. Hampton want to see him? Had he displeased the man? If God had a special plan for even the simplest of men, John prayed the Lord would be with him now.

The servant tapped on Edward Hampton's door, and when admittance had been granted, John entered. Hampton sat at a spacious walnut desk, matching the paneling that covered the walls.

"Please," Hampton said, rising and gesturing toward a chair, "have a seat."

John hesitated, scrutinizing his rough work clothes. "I'll stand, sir, as not to soil the upholstery."

"Don't be absurd, lad, sit." He gestured again.

"Thank you." John accepted the chair and waited, his hands twitching in his lap. He struggled to keep his eyes forthright and confident.

"Let me be direct. I have two reasons to speak with you. First, since your position at the manor, I have had no opportunity to discuss at any length the gardens and orchards with you. You mentioned you arrived home from an internship. I would enjoy hearing your new methods."

"My methods?" John faltered, amazed at his employer's interest.

"I trust you, John. You are a man of vision. You have come to me highly recommended. I've known your father for years and respect him."

John relished his sincerity. "I hesitate to interfere with my untested approach."

"Come now, I am only asking your thoughts," Hampton said. "First let us discuss the orchard. I would like your opinion on the cyder apples." He eyed John over his spectacles.

John hesitated, knowing his father leased acres of the Hamptons' orchard. "Sir, I'm not certain what you—"

"Let me be totally frank. I've heard from some of the townsmen that your family's cyder has a sweeter taste and higher color. Are you responsible for this?"

John nodded. "I have experimented with a variety of apples, sir, and I am pleased with the balance of flavor."

"And I've heard you are producing a small batch of specialty cyder." He waited with the look of expectation.

"Yes, sir. It is woodruff."

Hampton stared at his desk, nodding thoughtfully. "Woodruff? Yes, it has a distinctive flavor." He focused on John. "Let me consider what you've said, Big John. Now, tell me about the gardens. What news do you bring us?"

Reviewing methods he had recently learned, John described ways he'd been taught to improve the vegetable gardens. Then he recalled his excitement in working with new exotic flowers being grown in England.

Hampton drew back. "What of this 'bedding out' I've heard so much about? Have you seen the phenomena yourself? They tell me the origin is Aztec."

"That's correct, sir. I have seen it used for growing plants to create the intricate mosaic pattern of flower beds."

"And pray tell, what are they?" Edward asked.

"Flowers bedded in varying colors that form pictures. Before returning home, I took a carriage ride past the new Crystal Palace in Hyde Park and saw the wonderful gardens there."

"Ah, yes, I did catch a glimpse. Did you go inside?"

"No, sir, time did not permit a viewing. But it is a sight," John said, recalling the amazing glass building he'd heard covered seven hectares on the ground and thirteen kilometers of display tables.

"Would you like to see the inside, Big John?" Edward asked.

John studied his employer, wondering why he had asked about an impossibility. "Certainly, sir. Visiting the industrial exhibit would be a man's dream."

"If you would like, you will have your dream. . .with one condition."

John closed his gaping mouth, embarrassed at his addled state. "Sir, I don't understand."

"I am asking you a favor. I have promised my wife and daughter a trip to London to see the Crystal Palace—a brief trip that will include a shopping excursion for the ladies. I can no longer travel with them, having pressing business here at home."

"How might I assist you?" John asked, his mind whirring with possibilities.

"I trust you, young man. Not wanting to disappoint my family, I would like you to accompany them to London. You and the coachman will be paid and accommodations arranged."

I trust you. Obviously, Mr. Hampton had no knowledge of Sarah's visits to the garden or conversations with him. The man had no idea how John struggled to control his feelings for the intelligent, lovely young woman. A woman presented and ready to marry.

John grappled with his employer's offer. Saying no seemed impossible, but spending such luxurious hours with Miss Banning would be John's undoing.

"So will you consider my offer, John? I will be ever in your debt." Hampton slid his spectacles from his nose and ran his fingers along the bridge, eyeing him with a persistent gaze.

"I will do whatever you ask, sir."

Hampton rose and rounded his desk, then clamped his hand on John's homespun shirt. "You are a good lad. I will inform my family."

Speechless, John could only nod. His mind raced with questions. Now he faced the reality of hours. . .days in the presence of the lovely Miss Hampton.

Chapter 4

Sarah studied her father's face all through dinner and sensed he had unpleasant news for them. His look sent a chill down her arms. The dining room hung with silence while the servants removed the china and silver, then brought on the sweet course, warm pudding with sugar and butter.

When all had retired to the kitchen except the butler, her father cleared his throat, and Sarah slid to the edge of her seat, waiting to hear the message that had bothered him through dinner.

"Excellent meal, Mary," he said.

"Thank you, dear. Cook made the pudding especially for you. She knows you love it."

"I'll have to properly thank her." He cleared his throat again and clenched his fingers together against the table edge. "I have something to discuss with you both. It concerns our trip to London."

"Oh dear, I hope nothing has occurred to change our plans." Mary daubed her mouth with a napkin.

Tension knotted along Sarah's spine and settled between her shoulder blades.

"Unfortunately, there has been a minor change." Her father shifted with discomfort. "Lord Beckenridge will arrive in the village while we are to be gone. Since he must speak with me on business matters, I find it impossible to leave."

"But what of Sarah's birthday. . .and her gown?" Her mother's concern etched across her face.

"You and Sarah shall go as planned. I've made arrangements."

"No, Papa, not without you." Sarah prayed this was the long-awaited solution for which she had hoped. No holiday from the manor. No new gown for the ball she didn't want.

"You will be in good hands. Both of you," he said.

When he straightened his back, Sarah observed her father's determination. No one could be quite so stubborn. . .except perhaps her own obstinate nature.

"But how without you, Papa?"

"John Banning will be your escort," he pronounced.

"Mr. Banning?" Mary said, her attention shifting from Sarah to her husband. "But Edward, is this appropriate? Should we not delay our trip and—"

"I cannot promise a journey to London before the ball, Mary. . .and you wanted to select Sarah's gown." He arched a brow at his wife.

"Well, yes," she murmured.

Sarah sat speechless. She could ask for nothing more wonderful. . .or more agonizing. For days she would be under her mother's watchful eyes. How could she avoid holding conversation with Mr. Banning during the journey?

"You have nothing to say, Sarah?" her father asked.

"I'm disappointed you won't be with us, Papa."

"You'll have a wonderful holiday without me." Her father moved aside his dessert and leaned forward on his forearms. "I have talked to this young man, Mary. John is a reliable fellow. I realize he is a laborer, but I see a future in the lad."

"You do, Papa?" Sarah's heart tripped.

"What do you mean, Edward?" Mary asked.

"He has learned some grand techniques while away, and he's shared them with me—ways to make our cyder more appealing to our buyers, and Big John has offered valuable advice about new apple trees I will add to our orchard."

Sarah sat back amazed at her father's excitement.

"We are removing the Sheep's Nose and Court Royal trees to make room for Yarlington Mill and Dabinett. The lad is filled with ideas." Her father stared beyond his family, his thoughts seemingly in the future. "I will reward the young man. . . somehow."

Her mother vocalized a disapproving harumph. "He is rewarded by a trip to London. I would think that is enough."

He gazed at her over his spectacles. "Mary, Sarah is present. We will discuss this later if you don't mind."

Watching her mother's shoulders tense, Sarah longed to ask questions. How could John be rewarded? Why did her father trust his wife and daughter to his care? But she knew better than to ask. At this moment, she could hardly contain her joy. Somehow she would enjoy John's company despite her mother's watchful glare. If she couldn't find a way, she would leave her destiny in her heavenly Father's care.

—∞—

Sarah breathed a relieved sigh when the public carriage returned them to their London hotel. She'd spent tedious hours with the dressmaker selecting her ball gown and other frocks for the social engagements following her birthday celebration.

The trip from Barnham had been tiring and uncomfortable. She sat with her mother in the carriage while John rode outside with the driver. What made her think they would have an opportunity to converse? She wondered if her father had traveled with them if he might have allowed John in the carriage and enjoyed conversation, learning more about his ideas for the plants and orchard. A foolish speculation. If her father had come, John would be at the manor, tending the garden.

Encouraged, Sarah could barely believe how fondly her father had spoken of John. He saw John's worth—his talent and quick mind. Her mother, on the other hand, only saw a lowly farmer.

Because of the time constraints, Sarah's dresses would be delivered to their home, an extravagance Sarah thought unnecessary but her mother deemed important. When the carriage door opened, the driver helped them to the ground with their few packages.

Her mother paid the driver, while Sarah hurried ahead of her to the lobby and waited by the staircase. She'd never considered her father would arrange for John and the driver to stay in a less choice hotel. She sighed. Another propriety.

Since they'd arrived in London, Sarah had garnered enthusiasm for the Crystal Palace. People spoke of nothing else. At least at the exhibition, she and John might have a moment outside her mother's vision to speak a private word. Sarah eyed the grandfather clock on the broad staircase. John would arrive in a few moments to take them to the exhibition.

Sarah darted up the stairs, her mother trudging behind her. On the first floor, she rushed to their suite and waited until her mother arrived, breathless, with the key.

Tossing the packages on the settee, Sarah poured water from the pitcher, bathed her face to remove the street grime, then looked into the mirror. Her face glowed but from more than the exertion of the climb. The excitement of seeing John had tinted her cheeks a rosy hue.

Her mother had plopped onto the tapestry lounge and fanned herself from the midday heat. Her mottled red cheeks softened Sarah's heart. Going to the wash-stand, Sarah dampened a cloth to soothe her mother's flushed face.

"Thank you, Sarah dear," her mother said, continuing to fan. "You must remember to use the language of the fan, Sarah. Practice lest you forget."

"Mother, I have watched ladies and their fans forever, it seems. I don't need practice. I'll do what is natural."

"Sarah," her mother's voice raised to an unfamiliar pitch, "you will do what is proper. What has come over you, daughter? Since you have approached eighteen years, you have lost your gentler ways."

"I'm sorry, Mama," Sarah said, crumpling to the floor beside her and pressing her cheek against her mother's skirt. "I know you and Papa have only my well-being in mind, but I am having difficulty accepting what I must do."

"You will enjoy it in time, Sarah."

Sarah doubted it, but she did not disagree. She had no desire to be admired and courted by the young men of the surrounding area of Barnham. Sarah swallowed her thought, not wanting John's image to surface in her mind.

Why did this man stir her like no other? She'd wrestled with her thoughts over and over. Though roughened by physical labor, John had qualities that the eligible young gentlemen of the area did not. Maturity, tenderness, ambition, ingenuity, and a simple godliness. Those qualities rose in her mind when she thought of him. Yet her eagerness frightened him. She saw the look in his eyes. She must garner self-control. John would certainly avoid her if she showed him her true admiration.

Her mother rose from the lounge and appeared to have gained composure to make their way downstairs. With eagerness, Sarah waited, and when a tap sounded on the door, she opened it.

"The driver is downstairs," John said. His focus locked with Sarah's for a heartbeat, then slid to the carpet.

"The carriage is waiting, Mama," Sarah called over her shoulder.

Since she had only seen John dressed for gardening, Sarah admired his Sunday clothes. He looked more handsome than she had ever imagined, and the sight warmed her. Hearing the rustle of her mother's skirts, Sarah stepped away from the door to grasp her parasol and reticule.

Her mother swished past, handing John the door key. He stayed behind to lock the suite, then hurried forward to assist her mother down the long staircase. Sarah went ahead, imagining how it might feel to have John's arm linked to hers.

At the carriage, John assisted them both inside. His hand lingered a moment on Sarah's glove, and when she drew away, the pressure of his fingers lived in her thoughts.

The carriage rocked and bounced along the cobbled streets, and when traffic became heavier, Sarah noted they were nearing Hyde Park. The driver guided the horses down North Carriage Road, approaching the north entrance of the park leading to the Crystal Palace. Through the iron gates, Sarah saw the giant glass edifice with the flags of all nations floating above. Transepts jutted from each end of the building, and in the distance, she viewed people on foot and riding in carriages traveling toward the entrance. As they neared, the sight astounded her—elegant palms, statues, flowers, and the gigantic fountains.

"It's lovely," Mary said, her voice sounding awed by the splendor. "Your father chose Friday for our excursion. It is the favored day of the gentry with tickets going for a half crown. With smaller crowds, we'll have time to linger over the exhibits."

"What will the driver and. . .Mr. Banning do while we're inside, Mother?" Sarah's heart pitched, waiting for the answer.

"Your father is generous, Sarah. He has allowed them to attend today as well."

"Very generous," Sarah said, monitoring the thrill in her voice. She closed her eyes, sending a thankful prayer to her Father in heaven.

At the grand entrance, John stepped down and gave them assistance. While her mother spoke with the coachman and arranged an agreeable time to depart, Sarah longed to tell John she would find him inside, but her mother's keen ears would hear even the smallest murmur.

When all had been agreed upon, Sarah and her mother went on ahead while John followed. Sarah gave a longing look over her shoulder, listening to her mother's prattle about the vast array of magnificent displays.

The exhibit appeared more than they could enjoy in one day. They moved from one display to another, marveling at the merchandise from all over the world, but Sarah's thoughts were behind her. Occasionally, she looked over her shoulder to see John an acceptable distance behind them.

Focusing on the exhibit, Sarah inspected elegant furniture, ornamental silver pieces, decorative boxes covered with japanning or decoupage, and spinning machines weaving hand-spun cuffs, but always, her mind centered on John. Watching her mother's eyes widen, Sarah inched forward to admire the majolica ceramic earthenware— brightly glazed vases and sculptures in all sizes and shapes. When they reached the talk of the exhibition, the Patek Phillipe watches, her mother halted to study the lovely timepieces. News had traveled that Queen Victoria had purchased two of the creations during her visit.

When her mother insisted she sit for a silhouette portrait, Sarah had a small respite, while John observed from a distance. She had been more intrigued by the daguerreotypes. The thought of her actual portrait etched on a metal plate intrigued her.

For high tea, Sarah followed her mother to the refreshment tables where they nibbled on tea sandwiches and scones with jam. Sarah observed fashionable women and men ambling past, overhearing their praise of the Crystal Palace and the exhibition, but she longed to discern what John concluded about the amazing array.

When Sarah felt she could endure no more waiting, her mother straightened her shoulders. "Look, Sarah, it's Lady Hughes and her sister, Penelope. Remember, they came with Lord Hughes to visit last spring."

"Yes, Mama." Only a year younger than Sarah, Penelope had provided good company during her visit. Her appearance gave Sarah hope.

Before her mother acknowledged them, the woman sent her a friendly wave and hurried to their table. "Hello, Mrs. Hampton. Sarah. Isn't this glorious?"

"It is, Lady Hughes. Would you and Penelope care to join us?"

"That would be so kind," the woman said. "Will we inconvenience you?"

"No, Lady Hughes, please accept my chair." Sarah rose, taking advantage of the opportunity. With her plan in motion, she touched her mother's shoulder. "Perhaps,

Penelope and I could view the displays nearby. Do you mind, Mama?" Would her mother refuse with Lady Hughes in her presence?

"Two young ladies without an escort?" her mother responded. "I think not."

Eyeing Lady Hughes, Sarah was unable to read her thoughts. "Please, Mama. We'll stay nearby, I promise."

Her mother's arched brow silenced her pleading.

Chapter 5

D isappointed, Sarah conversed quietly with Penelope about the displays, while her mother and Lady Hughes prattled about something called McCormick's reaper and the giant cannon; eventually, her mother turned the discourse to Sarah's coming out.

When the tea had vanished and only crumbs lay on their plates, Lady Hughes and Penelope made their good-byes and wended their way through the crowd.

"Before we had tea, I noticed the most amazing spinning machine, Mama." She beckoned her mother to follow and led the way back.

Pausing to view the automated spinning machine, Sarah scanned the crowd, praying that John had not vanished. Her heart lifted when she saw him. He stood deep in the assemblage, his height jutting above the others.

"I see Mr. Banning, Mama. May I move forward? I'm unable to see well." Without waiting for an answer, she shouldered her way between two patrons, leaving her mother behind.

"Mr. Banning," Sarah said, breathless with excitement.

His gaze darted in every direction. "Where is your mother?"

"In the crowd," Sarah said, motioning behind her.

"You should not leave her alone."

"I longed for a moment with you, Mr. Banning." She grasped his forearm, and he brushed his fingers against hers for a heartbeat before moving his hand.

Sarah's heart fluttered beneath her bodice. Frightened of her emotion, she focused on the exhibit. "What displays have you enjoyed?"

"The new machinery. My mind flies from one idea to the next." Excitement rose in his voice.

"Sarah."

She jumped at her mother's voice. "Here, Mama."

Her mother's eyebrow arched. "I see. Please don't force your way through a crowd, Sarah. You must mind your manners."

"I'm sorry, but I find the displays exciting. See there." She pointed to an unfamiliar apparatus. "What is the strange device, Mr. Banning?"

"It's a press."

She raised on tiptoe, unable to see over the tall man blocking her view. "I can't see well. Can you see, Mama?"

"Let me assist you," he said, shifting to the side and allowing Sarah and her mother to have a clearer view. He stepped behind them. "It's called a hydraulic press."

Sarah's concentration blurred. Standing so close, she could almost feel the beating of his heart. He smelled of peppermint and body-warmed wool, and she longed to turn to face him and feel the prickle of whiskers beginning to show after the lengthy day.

"What is it called again, Mr. Banning?" her mother asked.

"A hydraulic press," he said, hunching over to lean closer so her mother could hear. "It's an amazing invention. Wonderful prospects."

His breath brushed against Sarah's ear and ruffled wisps of curls around her face. She tried to ignore the lovely feeling and ask a sensible question. "What is its purpose?"

His voice animated, John explained the use in simple terms. A flush of excitement rose on his face as he described how running water could be halted by a valve so the flow was forced upward, making a press function with little effort. Sarah made little sense of it, but she knew from his demeanor that this invention would be something important.

He had piqued her mother's interest. She listened intently to his explanation.

"We will be able to press apples with less manual labor," he said. "Less labor with greater speed, less monetary investment with more efficiency. It will work exceedingly well for your family's cyder business."

"An interesting concept, Mr. Banning. I'm sure Mr. Hampton will be most interested in your thoughts."

"The press will help your own family, also," Sarah added.

"The cost is too great for a farmer." He turned to her mother. "But for a man of Mr. Hampton's stature, it will make all the difference."

"Thank you, Mr. Banning," her mother said. "Sarah, let's move along. We'll leave you to enjoy the exhibit on your own."

He bowed to her mother and Sarah. "Mrs. Hampton. Miss Hampton."

Capturing Sarah's arm, her mother moved her through the crowd, while Sarah struggled for composure. She expected her mother's rancor for her improper behavior. But when she saw John she'd been stirred to forget propriety and station. In time, her mother would forgive her. Yet Sarah realized she treaded on unsafe ground. Not only could her disobedience bring retribution to herself, but her actions could cause untold distress for John.

Tonight in the quiet of her bed, she would ask God to give her wisdom to amend her improper behavior and guide her in the Lord's direction.

———∞———

"The exhibit was amazing, sir," John said, sitting in Edward Hampton's study. "You must go to London before the closing and see the hydraulic press. The invention will do wonders for the cyder business, and you could be one of the first to use it."

"You astound me, Big John. You have a creative eye. No one has thought to use the press for cyder?"

"No, not that I've heard," John said.

"You are brilliant."

John squirmed in the chair, uncomfortable with the man's compliments. "Thank you, sir, but I think others will envision the idea soon. If you approach a machine builder first, you will be ahead of your time."

"I will," Hampton said. "My lad, I will reward you for this. Once Sarah's ball is ended, I will leave for London. I cannot thank you enough for your resourceful thinking. Clever, that's what you are, Big John."

John lowered his eyes and nodded. He only wished he could share the knowledge with his father, but a project of this magnitude needed financing to make the presses, and for his family, the concept would be an impossible dream.

Sarah's comment rose in John's thought. *With God all things are possible.* Could Sarah be correct? Did God help farmers or only the lords and ladies of the world?

Hampton leaned forward over his desk. "Mrs. Hampton enjoyed the trip immensely. She has talked about nothing else since she returned—Belgian chocolates, majolica earthenware, French perfume." He arched a bushy brow and gave a chuckle. "But could you imagine what my Sarah has talked about?"

Fear rifled through John. Could her father suspect his fondness for his lovely daughter? John shook his head. "No, sir, I have no idea."

Hampton's chuckle turned to a full-bodied laugh. "Gummed envelopes. My practical daughter talked about daguerreotypes and gummed envelopes. She is amazing." His face glowed.

"She is amazing," John said, wishing he could open his heart and confess how Sarah had changed his tiresome life. Each day he filled with excitement hoping to see her for a fleeting moment. Her candid responses, her open mind, her intelligence completed the man he wanted to be.

"I thank you, John, for the care you extended my family and your stimulating information. My visit to the exhibition months ago had been so brief that—" He halted, hearing a tap on the door. "Come in."

The door swung open, and Sarah stood in the threshold. Her focus swung from her father to John, while a flush ignited her face.

"Don't be disconcerted, Sarah," Hampton said. "Mr. Banning and I are nearly finished. Come join us."

Sarah hesitated, then crept into the room, her hands folded in front of her.

"Come here, my girl," Edward said. "I have only now thanked Mr. Banning for escorting you and your mother to London."

"It was very kind," Sarah said, her gaze evading John's.

"Is this a private matter, Sarah?" Hampton asked.

At his question, John rose and backed from the desk. "I can excuse myself, sir."

Giving John a sidelong glance, Sarah paled. "No, Father, my gowns have arrived from London and Mother thought you would like to see them." Her timid gaze shifted to John.

"The pleasure of being a father, Big John. A man must look at fabric with ribbons, ruffles, and lace that has cost a small fortune." He patted Sarah's arm. "But admiring my daughter brings me much joy. One day you will know such joy."

John quaked at his direct gaze, fearing an inference in the man's comment.

"One day," Hampton continued, "you will have a daughter of your own."

Relief bathed John's fearful guilt. "One day in the distant future, sir."

Hampton smiled. "I must follow this lovely young lady and view the trappings that will capture some young man's heart."

"I'll be on my way then, sir." John backed away, his emotions whirling like a dervish. Futile, but true: he longed to be the young man who could offer his heart to Sarah and proclaim it to the world.

—⁓—

John returned from the orchard on foot. The morning had been cool, hinting rain, and he wanted the exercise. On hot days, he rode his horse, but the overcast sky and invigorating breeze urged him to go on foot. In the distance, he spied a tumble of skirt and parasol sitting on a stone outcropping. His stomach knotted, seeing Sarah waiting for him.

The four days he had accompanied her and her mother to London had been a paradox—a rapturous torment. Despite Mrs. Hampton's obvious scorn at learning he would be their escort, she had acquiesced and appeared impressed with his knowledge and fortitude. Though Edward Hampton admired his faithfulness, he could never presume to be accepted as an equal.

"Mr. Banning," Sarah's voice called as he neared.

John tipped his cap. "Good morning."

She eyed him from beneath her white wispy parasol. "I had a lovely holiday in London. Thank you for your gracious company." She sent him a beautiful smile.

His strong legs staggered, trembling beneath him as unstable as apple pomace.

She lifted her hand upward for assistance to rise. John inspected her soft, slender fingers extended toward him and longed to press them to his lips, to taste the sweet rose attar she rubbed on her skin to keep them soft. He'd smelled the aroma on days she had followed him to the garden, and he could no longer separate the flower's fragrance from the blossoming woman who lingered in his sight so often. He could not forget the moment in London when she clung to his arm and he dared to brush his hand against hers. Again, with caution, he propelled his arm forward and grasped her tiny fingers in his giant palm.

She rose, and her gaze dwelt on the incongruity of her hand swallowed in his. Then she focused on his face. "You are a Titan, Mr. Banning. A giant. . .in heart as well as size."

Her flattery caught him unaware, and he faltered before making light of her comment. "Do not say such things, miss."

She withdrew her hand, clasped it to her parasol, and took one step forward, then stopped to gaze at him. Time ceased as he basked in her admiring eyes.

"You are a handsome man, Mr. Banning. I must share a secret. In my mind I speak your name. John."

The sound of his name on her lips sent joyous shivers down his sun-warmed back. *I am a daring fool,* he thought, knowing he should not allow the remarkable sensations to remain in his thoughts. "You should not think of my name."

"But it pleases me," she said. "Would you speak my name, John?"

Her question stopped him like a man who has spied a coiled viper. He desired to bolt from the charming woman. "That is impossible. Totally improper. Please, don't ask."

"But—"

"Your father would discharge me. You are the daughter of gentry. I am little better than a servant."

Her eyes lowered, and he could barely hear the whisper of her voice. "Please let me hear you say Sarah."

Longing swelled in his chest, and he closed his eyes to control the sweet feelings that rambled through him. "I. . .I cannot."

"Only once, John. Please." She rested her hand against his forearm. "John."

He struggled to sound the name against his tongue. The sweetness of the tone filled his breath, and he could only murmur. "S. . .Sarah."

Their gazes met, and he clung to the moment like a baby bird ready to leap with faith into the air.

"Thank you," she whispered. She stepped back and appeared suddenly shy. "Please return alone, John. I'll be along shortly. I know you have work to do. . .and you would rather reach the garden without me at your side."

He could only nod, for his lungs had disregarded his command to breathe.

Pulling his gaze from her fair face, he moved off, his long strides creating distance between them. He could not look back for fear he would turn around and run back to her, lifting her in his arms and carrying her away. She had captured his mind and heart.

—⁓—

In the lamplight, Sarah gazed at her elegant ball gown. She eyed herself in the glass, admiring the delicate pink silk frock fashioned with balloon sleeves graced with deep lace epaulets. Her gaze swept along the demure rounded neckline, and she caressed the darker pink ribbon serving as a sash and admired the same shade bows along the lacy hem. The gown was exquisite.

She had pulled back her hair with a satin bow, and Dulcie had combed it into banana curls that brushed against her bare neck. Her only jewelry was pearls at her throat and small pearl earrings, a gift from her father.

Carriages had been arriving, and music drifted up from the parlor adjoining the small ballroom. Beyond, the conservatory had been readied where the dancers could retire and sit on benches among the palms.

She slid into her white satin evening slippers and lifted the delicate ivory fan trimmed with pink lace. She fluttered it in front of her face, reviewing her mother's prodding to display the fan properly. Without her mother's knowledge, she had practiced twirling it in her left hand. A young man knew it meant *I love another.*

If only John were one of the eligible young men of the village, the evening would be perfect. Instead, he had spent the day toting in bouquets of flowers from the garden and adding palms and fern along the terrace. In the frenzy of her ball, Sarah had only seen him through her window and caught a glimpse of him in the conservatory. Her knees weakened as she remembered the afternoon he'd whispered her name. *Sarah.* The word filled her heart like a glorious symphony.

Calming her thoughts, Sarah took a deep breath and opened her door. If she didn't make her entrance soon, her mother would appear to escort her down the staircase.

Laughter and voices drifted from the ground floor, and she crept forward, forcing her legs to carry her to the wide steps. She hesitated at the top, as her mother had insisted, until enough eyes were drawn to her entrance. Then in the growing hush, she made her way down the staircase.

A young man she had seen on other social occasions waited for her, taking her hand as she neared the bottom. Applause rang through the entrance hall, and joining her parents, she stood in the receiving line until her legs trembled and her face grew weary from her forced smile.

The music livened, and when the first reel began, another gentleman led her to the dance floor. One by one, the possible suitors took turns asking her to dance, bowing and scraping with an attempt to leave her with a lasting impression. All failed miserably. Sarah could only envision the chestnut-haired orchard keeper with his tender, dark eyes.

The meal seemed an endless series of tiresome conversations while Sarah nibbled from each course—julienne soup to boiled salmon followed by lamb cutlets and spring chicken served with her father's best cyder. Desserts were on a sideboard to be enjoyed later by those who wished. Sarah had eyed the fresh fruit, cherry tarts, custard, and her favorite charlotte russe, but her stomach had no interest in the food nor her heart in discourse.

At the appropriate time, Sarah invited the guests to return to the ballroom. The older guests settled in the parlor, leaving the young men and women to dance. Her face flushed from the heat, Sarah excused herself and hurried through the conservatory, then slid through the door into the moon-filled night.

Strolling away from the conservatory's glow, Sarah drew in the fragrance of the night air and looked into the sky. The lilting music filled the soft night, and her longing tugged at her heart.

"Why have you left your guests?"

Sarah gasped, then recognized John's voice emanating from the shadow of the privet fence. She rushed toward his voice as he stepped away from the shrubs into the moonlight.

Without hesitation, Sarah fell into John's wide-opened arms. He clasped her to him, her head pressing against his heart. "John, I am so glad you are here." She clung to him, her pulse racing at the delight of his presence more than the fear of discovery.

"Sarah," he murmured, his heart thundering against his chest, "my sweet, dearest Sarah. I am wrong to hold you in my arms, but I can no longer contain my joy at seeing you. You are an angel in the moonlight."

"You have acted with honor," she whispered into the linen of his shirt. As if providence decreed, a slow waltz drifted across the grass, and she swayed to the music.

John joined her, gliding and swaying together with only the stars as their witness. She spun away, and he brought her back into the fold of his arms. Together they spun in three-quarter time, their darker silhouettes melting into the night's shadows.

Washed with wisdom, John slowed and eased her deeper into the darkness, his eyes drinking in her ethereal loveliness. "You are the lovely dreams that fill my nights, the sun that warms my days, the stars that light the heavens. I do not deserve to even speak your name, dearest Sarah, but I cannot stop myself from the delight."

Her voice muffled against his chest. "I aspire for no other man to come courting, John. I desire only you." She lifted her hand and pressed it against his cheek. "Your hair as black as the night sky, your eyes as deep and mysterious as the ocean, your heart and soul as tender as a babe's."

Cautioned by reality, John faltered. "I fear God does not approve of my feelings. You know the Lord so much better than I, Sarah. I remember you said with God all things are possible. I yearn to believe it is true."

"It is true, John. God has guided me to you, and I believe the Almighty Father approves. Now we must convince my earthly parents. . .and that is the more difficult task."

Her words struck a chord of truth in John's heart. When he had attended church, he'd heard the vicar proclaim God as good and merciful, and if that were so, God would truly perceive the purity of his heart and his intentions. John cherished Sarah, and if God approved, he would swim oceans to take Sarah as his own. "I long to say the words that lay on my tongue, dearest."

She looked into his eyes. "Say the words, John, for I long to hear them."

"I love you," he whispered. "My life is incomplete without your gentle spirit in my care."

"I must speak what my heart has known forever. I love you, John, and God willing, one day we will proclaim it to the world."

In his peripheral vision, John saw movement near the conservatory door. He stepped deeper into the shadow. "Go, Sarah, before we are discovered."

She reached toward him as he slid through the privet.

"What inappropriate behavior has urged you to leave your guests, Sarah?" Her mother's voice pierced the night.

Sarah swung around and approached her mother. "I am enjoying the fresh air, Mama."

Her mother looked beyond her toward the privets.

Sarah's heart sank to her feet.

Chapter 6

Riddled with guilt, Sarah stood before her mother. "Isn't the night beautiful, Mama? I am mesmerized by the full moon and the scent of roses drifting from the garden. The ballroom is stuffy. Could we bring the music outside?"

"Don't be foolish. No one has a ball on the terrace. Now come inside with your guests. You'll catch a chill and catch your death."

Relief washed over her as she took her mother's arm and entered the glass door into the conservatory. With a sigh, she slipped from her mother's grasp and paused to speak to a friend and her beau. The distraction gave her a reprieve, and Sarah's mother wandered back to the ballroom, away from Sarah's fear-filled eyes.

If her mother knew the truth, she would send her away. . .to India or worse. Turning back to the glass walls, Sarah could not see into the garden. The reflection of light from the oil lamps painted images of ferns and palms mingled with a wash of color from the young ladies' gowns.

Still, she knew beyond the hedge John stood in the shadows, loving her.

—⚬⚬⚬—

John waited for three days, praying Sarah would find him to relate whether or not they had been discovered. The longer he waited for her to appear, the more he feared she had been locked in her room or sent away. His gaze lingered on the empty garden bench, and he forced himself to turn and tend to the plants. His mind, however, tangled around a dainty woman who had declared her love for him.

With his back to the gate, John heard footsteps and spun around to face Edward Hampton. His stomach knotted, fearing why his employer had come to find him.

"Good day," Hampton said, approaching him.

"Good day, sir." He averted his eyes, imagining he could read his guilt in the man's gaze. But the man's friendly face did not fit John's speculation.

"We are on our way to London, my lad. I pray when I see you again the news will be good." He extended his hand toward John.

Looking at his soiled fingers, John drew them across his trousers and grasped Hampton's hand in a firm shake. "I pray your trip is successful, sir." But his mind whirred. His employer had said *we* are leaving, and John's heart twitched. Would Sarah accompany them to London?

"My wife is waiting for me, so I must be off." he said. As he stepped away, Hampton called over his shoulder. "We'll return on Monday, John. I'll speak with you then."

My wife. Had he meant only Mrs. Hampton would travel with him? John observed the man until he vanished beyond the gate. His curiosity piqued, John edged forward and neared the garden wall, hoping to see who would pass in the carriage, but only a blur flashed past through the carriage windows.

He wiped his brow with the back of his hand. Five days he would wait for the news of Hampton's success. . .and perhaps to see Sarah again. He returned to the beds beyond the garden shed, his mind twisted in thought. While he bent over the plants, a shadow fell across his hand. Startled, he bolted upright.

Sarah stood before him, a look of shyness on her face.

His mind propelled forward, but he demanded his feet to remain still. "You didn't journey to London?"

She shook her head. "I remained behind. We have five days, John. Five days that we may become friends. Tomorrow I will inform the cook I desire a picnic in the meadow." She drew nearer. "Will you meet me there?"

Five days. Confusion rattled his brain. Good judgment restrained him, but opportunity nudged him forward. Casting wisdom aside, he answered. "I will, Sarah."

"May we walk a moment?" she asked.

He rose, and they followed the lane to the meadow. John held her securely, lest she stumble in the long grasses. When they reached the edge of the woods in the speckled shade, he bade her rest on a fallen tree trunk.

Facing her, John's gaze lingered on her dainty hand, her long tapered fingers resting against the folds of her skirt, as delicate and white as angel wings.

"May I touch your hand, Sarah?" Anxiety sparked with his question.

She extended her right arm toward him. "I have dreamed of your touch."

With caution, he wrapped her hand in his, reveling in the softness of her silken skin. She raised a finger of her left hand and laid it against his cheek, and he captured it beneath his free palm.

A shudder ran through him, but caution rose in his consciousness and he withdrew his hand. "Sarah, I must guard against my emotions. You are a lady. A Christian woman, and I respect you."

"No man has held my hand or been so near. . .except my father." She sent him a shy smile. "I have only imagined such joy."

John grappled with good sense. "I cannot be in your presence without longing to kiss your lips, but propriety and station restrain me."

"You may kiss my hand if you will. I would delight in it."

Overcome by her tenderness, he lifted her satiny hand and pressed it to his lips, feeling as if his heart would burst.

"Your lips are soft, John. One day I pray they shall touch mine."

"If God blesses us." He rose and walked away to calm his rising pulse. But a new request rose in his thoughts—one more pleasing to God. Sarah's love for the Lord had grown in John's thoughts and fired his heart. Eagerness rose to understand her faith.

"Tell me about God, Sarah. I believe, but I'm afraid my faith is not as strong or unfailing as yours. You're like a mountain. Your voice is filled with trust when you speak of the Lord."

He studied her profile as she looked across the meadow.

Her voice rang like the bells on Sunday as she spoke about her relationship with God. "He is my friend. Jesus walks with me daily and guides my feet. Though I feel secure and safe with you, I am more than sheltered in God's presence. The Lord promises His children eternal life if we believe. You stated you believe, John."

"Yes, I believe, but now I want to know the personal relationship you do, Sarah. I yearn to have a confident faith and to trust that God cares about someone as unimportant as an orchard keeper."

She shifted to face him. "John, don't say such things. Remember where Jesus was born?" Her gaze penetrated his.

"In Bethlehem."

"But *where* in Bethlehem?"

"A stable."

"Yes," she said, a smile lighting her face. "And to whom did the angels first announce Jesus' birth?"

"Shepherds." His heart tripped at his answer. "Shepherds," John repeated, the meaning of her questions becoming clear. "Christ was born in a humble stable and welcomed first by lowly shepherds."

"Yes. Yes." She leaned forward and pressed her cheek to his. "God does not create one person more important or precious than another. We are equal in God's sight. . . and in my sight, John."

His heart lifted at her words. "I don't know why the Lord has so wonderfully blessed me, Sarah." Turning his eyes heavenward, he noted the sun dropping to the west. "The time grows late. You must return before the servants come looking."

He slid from the wooden perch and helped her rise. With a watchful eye, John guided her across the meadow. When they reached the path to the garden, he halted. Benefited by his height, in the distance he witnessed a man walking their way. He hurried Sarah to the side of the barrel shed, his body trembling. "Someone is coming, Sarah."

Concern filled her face. "What shall we do?"

Their solution stood beside him. He dug into his pocket, extracted the key, and yanked the lock from the shed latch. "Inside, quickly."

Sarah scurried through the doorway as John followed and slid the door closed. "Withdraw behind the kegs, Sarah, and I pray whoever comes will not notice the unlocked shed."

In silence, he inched his large frame backward. When he reached Sarah cowering in the corner, he filled with shame. What man would endanger the reputation of an innocent woman as he had done? Only a fool.

He retreated into the darkness and waited.

The door swung open and a long dark shadow haloed by sunlight extended along the floor. "Now what fool left this shed unlocked?" a voice mumbled. Instead of leaving to find a key, the man lumbered into the shed, while Sarah's body trembled behind John.

Responding with haste, John stepped into the light. "What are you doing, Devon?"

The man stumbled backward, as if a ghost had risen from the shadows. "Big John, is it you?"

"You can see, it is." John strode forward, deterring the man from entering farther.

"But what are you doing in the barrel shed?"

John lifted a large cask and shook it, a faint slosh of water moved inside the barrel. "What does it look like, Devon? Soon we'll harvest the apples and press them into cyder. Where do you think we will store the cyder?" He frowned down at the smaller man.

Devon edged backward. "I'm not challenging you, Big John. I only feared—"

"Where do we store the cyder, Devon?" He repeated the question, mustering his confidence.

Devon clutched the doorjamb. "In the barrels. You know that, Big John."

"And what if our barrels dried out and cracked? What then?" He moved forward as Devon stepped outside into the sunlight.

"I only asked," Devon said, turning on his heel and continuing his march down the lane.

Ashamed of his bullying, John remained in the doorway until the man vanished from sight. With haste, he beckoned to Sarah.

She hurried forward and clasped John's arm. "Thank you, my dearest."

"You are safe now. Return to the manor. I shall linger behind before returning." He lifted her hand and pressed it to his cheek. "I will await you tomorrow at the edge of the woods."

"For our picnic?" she asked, stepping into the light.

"Yes. It is safer than the meadow."

"Until tomorrow, dear John." She hurried away down the path.

John braced his back against the wall, staring into the shadows. Tomorrow he would tell her he could no longer endanger her reputation. He cherished Sarah and would do nothing to lessen her purity in the eyes of man or God.

Chapter 7

Sarah lifted her basket higher above the long grass, her eyes directed on the woods. She didn't see John and wondered if he had been delayed or feared discovery. The servants, she sensed, kept a close eye on her.

Reaching the woods, Sarah paused. To her joy, John appeared from behind a broad tree trunk and hurried to meet her. He grasped the basket and guided her along the root-filled pathway.

"I've found a secluded spot," he said, leading her deeper into the shelter of the trees.

Before her, sunlight broke through the trees, and in moments, they stepped into a private glade speckled with wildflowers. The beauty prompted her to break from John's arm and bound into their private sanctuary. Her legs tangled in the cross-leaf heather, and her skirt brushed against the fading purple thistle and goldenrod. Breathless, she stopped and beckoned him to follow.

Joining her, John rested the basket on the ground wherein Sarah opened the lid and pulled out a cloth. Tossing it on the shorter grass, she sank to the earth, spreading her skirts over her ankles. John joined her.

Delving inside the wicker, Sarah eyed the picnic fare. "I hope the meal meets your pleasure, John. We have cold meat and bread. Fruit," she said lifting the items from the basket. "And cyder."

As she gazed at John, a magpie moth settled on his shoulder. She gasped in delight. "Don't move, John. You've been visited by a butterfly."

John shifted his head to view his winged friend and chuckled. "It's only a moth," he whispered.

"But it's a lovely moth."

He grinned as the moth fluttered away.

Relieved by his less strained face, she returned to the cold meat, and John grasped a hunk of bread and wrapped it around a morsel of chicken. The picnic fare vanished, and while Sarah sipped cyder from the drinking glass, John swigged from the jug.

The sun spilled warmth over their backs, and Sarah looked into the bright sky, admiring the clouds floating overhead. With pleasure, she pointed to shapes of sea creatures and ladies with long tresses.

"I'm overwhelmed by your vivid imagination," John said, "but life cannot always abound in fantasy."

"Look there. That is not fantasy," she said, pointing to a thrush feeding on the rowanberries.

"No, the bird is real, my sweetest."

"It's lovely, John. A glorious day. Would you help me rise?" The wildflowers had captured her attention, and Sarah yearned to gather a bouquet. When her feet touched the grass, she darted away, filling her arms with blossoms—heather, lavender, harebells, and Mayweed. Then to her delight, she came upon a cluster of wild red poppies. Without a word, John waited in the distance, observing her.

With her arms overflowing with flowers, she ambled back, filling her lungs with the scent of sun-warmed meadow grass and watching the white moths flit across the blooms.

"I should return before the flowers wilt," she said, yearning for the day to last forever.

"Yes," he said, his face weighted with concern.

Fear rifled through her. "What troubles you, John?"

"Before you return home, I must speak with you, Sarah."

Her hand trembled as she nestled the flowers against her bodice. "What is it?"

"Us."

"What do you mean?" Sarah's chest constricted and she struggled to breathe. "You declared your love for me, and I, for you. What could be wrong?"

"I do love you, Sarah, but our love is as much a fantasy as the cloud pictures."

His words stabbed her heart, and her thoughts flew back to the comment she'd ignored earlier. A comment wrought with nostalgia she'd been afraid to understand. *Life cannot always abound in fantasy.*

"I have made a decision," he said. "Our friendship must cease. If God wills it, then it shall be. My heart breaks with my resolve, but I see no other way."

"I believe God wills us to be together," Sarah whispered. "I have prayed, and the Lord has moved me to love you."

"I believe our relationship is insurmountable, Sarah. But God is the ruler of all things, and His will makes the impossible become possible. You said those very words." John brushed her cheek with his fingers.

The flowers tumbled to the ground, and Sarah crumpled against his chest, tears streaming from her eyes and dripping to her bodice.

"Don't cry, Sarah. You have led me to understand the Lord. Now where is your faith? With God all things are possible. Say it over and over." He tilted her chin upward with his knuckle. "Say it, my dearest."

"With God all things are possible. With God all things are possible." She murmured the words, while John gathered her bouquet and returned them to her arms. Her eyes blurred with tears, and she gazed at the bright blossoms against her chest, their colors merging shades of a rainbow. Without the man whom she perceived God had given her, life would be like the fading flowers—joy obscured by sadness.

—⁓—

"But Mama, please," Sarah begged, "I've no desire to entertain these gentlemen. I shall send them my regrets."

"Stop sniveling, Sarah. I must insist you accept an occasional gentleman caller. Let us examine their calling cards again. You may choose the ones you favor, dear."

Sarah curled on her bed, unwilling to look at even one card but to dishonor her parents hurt more deeply. Without proper escort, she'd held conversation with John and allowed him to kiss her hand. By loving a man beneath her social standing, she had already erred gravely, dishonoring her parents, thus dishonoring God. Her remorse had become unsettling.

Yet she loved John. How could she tell her mother where her heart lay? "Are you so anxious for me to depart my girlhood home?"

Her mother wagged her head. "I do not understand you, daughter. Young women await the day they reach adulthood—to be courted and wed. But you. . .you are impossible. I must consult your father on this matter." Marching from the bedroom, she closed the door.

Sarah longed to vanish, to hide, anything to stop her mother's insistence. Thoughts tumbled in her head as she slid her feet to the floor and sat on the edge of her quilt. She would select one young man and make him so miserable that all the eligible gentleman of the village would withdraw their cards. Shame filled her at the vile thought. What had become of her good sense?

Why had she given her heart to John? A farmer, yes, but a man of honesty, a man with vision, a man of simple pleasure who loved the earth and laughed at her delight in a butterfly. Sarah recalled the hours she'd wearied with the eligible bachelors she found pretentious and tiresome. Would God have her marry a man she didn't love because of social breeding?

Falling to her knees, Sarah pressed her face against the quilt and wept. She had dishonored her parents with her clandestine meetings and endangered John's character. She regarded him blameless. He had captured her heart, but she had pursued him. Utterly improper for a young woman of her standing. Yet in her heart, she perceived the heavenly Father understood and approved. Could she have misjudged the Lord's bidding?

Everything had changed since the picnic weeks earlier. The lovely afternoon lingered in her thoughts—the sky painted with cloud-creatures and her arms weighted with wildflowers. She pictured John's pensive face, and loneliness blanketed her.

Since that day, John had kept his word. She had not seen him alone. Sarah dried her tears and bowed her head. If a solution to her problem existed, God would have the answer.

—⁓—

John strode toward the cyder house. The apples hung ripe on the branches, nearly ready for harvest, and the presses required inspection. Gratitude filled him as he thought of his conversation with Edward Hampton. His employer had ordered a new apple press, and as a gift to John's family, he had purchased another for the Bannings' farm. Smaller in size, but a hydraulic apple press just the same. The gift reached beyond John's expectation and served as his only bright moment since Sarah's picnic.

John unlocked the cyder house door and entered. In another week, workers would arrive to harvest the apples, and with Mr. Hampton's encouragement, John had already selected maiden trees—the new varieties—to be planted in the early spring. One day, Hampton cyder would be proclaimed the best in the country.

Working in shadows, John unlatched a shutter to chase away the gloom. He inspected the wooden hopper, then examined the bladed cylinder attached to the handle. Before he reached the gears, the room brightened as a gust of wind caught the door and flung it open.

John hastened to the door and looked outside. A wind tossed the branches, then subsided as quickly as it had appeared. The intoxicating scent of apples drifted on the breeze, and John felt drawn away from the cyder house toward the orchard. What prompted him he didn't know, but a deep sense of purpose sped his feet along the path.

The cyder apples hung deep red on the branches awaiting the harvest, and he plucked one from the branch. He breathed in the rich, ripe scent, but the puzzling urge compelled him deeper into the orchard. Reaching the Morris apples, he faltered, his heart thundering.

"Sarah."

She stood beneath the tree, gazing into the branches.

"What are you doing here?" he asked, amazed he'd been drawn here.

"John." Her foot moved forward as if to run to him, but she stopped. "Something has. . . I–I have been longing for an apple."

"Here," he said, handing her the fruit he had picked.

She eyed it and shook her head. "That one is for cyder. The Morris apples are good for cyder and eating."

Surprised at her knowledge, John agreed. "Then I shall pick you one of these."

"I desire one in particular, John. Please, lift me so I may reach it."

His chest ached against his hammering heart. He gazed at the delicate woman for whom he would give his life. Would he not grant her an apple?

His caution vanishing on the breeze, he bent down and boosted her to the branches. The rustle of her skirts, her petite frame beneath the layers of cloth, the nearness of her overwhelmed him.

She plucked the apple, shined it on her bodice, and bit into it. The snap of the pulp sprayed, and the juice rolled down her chin.

John marveled at the dear woman in his arms and lowered her to the ground. Should he be deemed a coward? Should he march into her father's study and demand Hampton's precious daughter? Foolishness.

With downcast eyes, Sarah fingered the half-eaten apple. "I have missed you, John. But I have prayed."

Unable to resist, he caressed her soft hair fragrant with lavender. "We must both be steadfast with our prayers."

"You have acted with good judgment, I know. We must await God's bidding."

"Sweet Sarah, you are truly the apple of my eye. We shall continue to pray. . .and God will provide. The Lord has already answered one prayer."

Her sad eyes brightened. "Which prayer, John?"

"For my family. Your father has requisitioned a cyder press for the Banning cyder mill. His generosity is beyond expectation."

With hesitation, she rested her hand on his arm. "My father finds you worthy of good things. He has spoken highly of you. . .even at our dinner table."

"You're dinner table? In your mother's presence?" The thought left John unsettled.

Sarah paused, her eyes flashing. "John, do you think. . . could it be?" She clutched the neck of her bodice. "No, I cannot believe it, but perhaps. . ."

"What, Sarah?" He drew her closer, his eyes basking in the bloom of excitement lighting her face. "You have not spoken a full sentence."

"You must wait, John. If I speak it, my dream may be only a dream."

Chapter 8

S arah stood in her father's study like a criminal standing in a court dock with her father the judge. Her mother, the prosecuting attorney, paced the carpet in front of the desk, her arms fluttering like a frightened bird.

"It is mid-November, and she's refused every suitor." Mary stopped and sent a disparaging look toward Sarah. "Now the holiday parties begin. . .and what will she do?"

Edward hadn't uttered a sound since the evidence against Sarah had been laid before him.

"You must speak with her, Edward," Mary said.

Edward peered at Sarah over his spectacles.

The desire to defend herself charged through Sarah, but in her parents' eyes, she knew she had no defense. She sat like a condemned prisoner, unable to speak.

Two pairs of eyes condemned her, but her father's held a look of tenderness.

"Mary," Edward said, "would you leave Sarah with me?"

Her mother's gaze shifted like a searchlight before she answered. "Whatever you say, Edward. You know what is proper and expected."

He only nodded.

With a last look, Mary headed toward the exit.

He rose and waited for her mother to close the door before he turned to Sarah. "Come, Sarah," he said, sinking into an armchair, then gestured to one across from him. "Sit with me. We must talk."

Sarah crept to the chair and lowered herself, expelling a deep sigh.

"Why do you struggle with your social responsibilities, daughter? Your mother does not understand. . .and, frankly, neither do I."

Looking into her father's sincere eyes, Sarah felt tears pool in hers.

Her father leaned forward and patted her hand. "Do not weep, child. Tell me why you cry."

Searching for the appropriate words, Sarah toiled to form the sentence.

Her father's face grew heavy with concern.

"It is my heart, Papa," she said finally.

"Your heart? I don't understand." His countenance darkened. "Has someone. . . wronged you, Sarah?"

"No, Papa, never." If she confessed the truth, how would her father respond? His disconcerted tenderness assured her he would listen and understand.

"I don't have a heart to give another, Papa. Without my bidding, I love an honorable man."

"You what?" He drew back, his face pale and contorted.

Seeing his despair, Sarah could no longer look into her father's eyes.

"Tell me who he is Sarah? Did this man. . .behave improperly?"

"Oh no, not he. He has done nothing but endeavored to protect my reputation and to encourage propriety." Tears spilled from her eyes and dripped to her knotted fingers.

"This man is concerned with propriety?" Edward asked, his voice calming.

"Oh yes, Papa." Sarah rose and dropped at her father's feet. She prayed, asking God to grant her a solution, and she found it in her father's eyes.

"Daughter, don't cry. Is he a young man of the village? Where did you meet him? At church? Tell me his name."

Her mouth opened to answer, but the words stuck in her throat. "You will be angry," she murmured.

"Not angry, but startled. Bewildered. It is improper to be alone with a young man before you have a commitment."

Sarah brushed at her tears. "He expressed the same, Papa. But God was our chaperone."

His face flickered with concern. "Society asks for more, daughter."

"More. . .than God?" she questioned.

He shook his head. "You amaze me, Sarah." He rested his hand on her head. "Now, tell me the name of the young man who has captured your heart?"

"I love John, Papa."

"John?" His voice softened to a whisper. "I recall no young man named John."

She lowered her head. "The orchard keeper. You have spoken highly of him, Father. You have said he is clever, and he will be a success one day." Slowly, she turned her head, and seeing her father's expression, her heart ached.

The room hung with silence until her father spoke. "Yes, I did say that. He is a man of virtue and intelligence. One day he may find success, but. . ."

Rising, he took Sarah's hand and drew her to her feet. "You are my most precious daughter, but. . .I must contemplate this, Sarah. Your mother will be distressed." His piercing gaze caught hers. "Are you certain? Have you considered a lifetime with this farmer?"

"I am sure, Papa."

"Then I will do what I can." His face ashen, he sank into his desk chair and buried his face in this hands. "Leave me, Sarah, and let your papa decide what is best."

—⁓—

The choir and clergy filed past the worshipers, and when the pomp ended, Sarah followed others down the aisle and into the brisk autumn air.

The family carriage waited nearby, but Sarah hesitated. With her father away on business and her mother indisposed with a headache, Sarah had a rare opportunity to be alone in the village. Though the wind nipped beneath her cloak, she asked the driver to wait and hurried away on foot.

At the far end of the street stood a small country church. Its white clapboard siding and pointed steeple made direct contrast the gray stone of the Anglican church graced by an elegant bell tower. As she neared the smaller church, she prayed John had attended worship that morning. Weeks earlier, she'd learned he'd begun to attend the small church. The conversation with her father necessitated her desire to speak with him. It seemed imperative he be aware of their discourse.

In the park square across from the clapboard building, Sarah waited. When the doors opened, parishioners exited and made their way on foot toward their homes. Trembling with cold and her purpose, Sarah waited until John stepped into the sunlight. Pulling the cloak's hood over her head, she followed him along the opposite side of the street. When she felt assured no one would hear, Sarah called his name.

John's head swiveled, and he faltered before crossing the street to meet her. "Sarah. Where are your par—"

"I'm alone. I must speak with you a moment." The wind sent a shiver through her.

"It's cold in the street. Please return to the carriage."

Sarah grasped his arm and drew him under the shelter of a large oak, its wide trunk minimal protection from the breeze. "I have spoken with my father. . .about us."

His face paled. "I was wrong to allow our indiscretion to continue so long."

"Indiscretion? Please, John—" His words pierced her heart.

"After I complete the final inventory tomorrow, I will speak with your father. I must leave his employ."

Tears welled in Sarah's eyes before her faith caused them to subside. "Do you not trust God, John?"

He shifted and tucked his hands deeper in his pockets. "Why do you ask me now?"

"You told me God's Word has touched your heart. Yet, you do not have faith in the Lord's promise." She clutched the cloak around her, the damp cold shivering through her body.

"I am trying to rely on God, but I'm not foolish. God provides for our needs. . . not our fantasies." He drew her cloak more firmly around her. "You are chilled, Sarah. You must go."

"God makes all things possible, John. No matter what you say, the Lord can move mountains. If it is the Lord's will, we can be together."

She stepped back, and he caught her hand and pressed it to his lips. "My dearest, Sarah, I pray you are correct."

She backed away. Turning, she hurried toward the carriage, feeling John's gaze on her back and his love in her heart.

—⁓—

John strode through the cyder house, checking his figures and taking stock of the barrels. The apple harvest had been outstanding, and Hampton cyder had been carried on large wagons to the markets while John rotated barrels, allowing the new cyder to age or become vinegar.

His days at Hampton Manor were over. If Sarah had not spoken to her father, John would have returned to the manor on occasion to siphon the cyder into large crockery jugs and clean the kegs. His chest weighted with the memory of the trees he had ordered to be planted in the spring. . .and the new hydraulic press. But now, he would have to leave forever. The gardener, Charles Benson, had returned to mulch the plants for winter, and the older man would be there to plant and prune in the spring.

Still, life would go on. . .at the manor and for John. He knew vanishing from Sarah's life would be for the best—the only way, but a hole the size of heaven tore through his heart. His life, which had become a joyful adventure, would now return to drab, plodding hours.

Finishing his inventory, John closed the ledger and turned toward the doorway. When he stepped into the clouded daylight, a house servant hailed him at the threshold.

"Mr. Hampton requests your presence before you leave today."

"Thank you," John said, turning and locking the door.

"He is in his study," the servant added over his shoulder as he strode away.

John raised the collar of his lamb's wool coat and mounted his horse, his spirit weighted by the messenger's words. He would be discharged before he could offer to leave the Hamptons' employ. The concern affected only his pride, he realized and shook his head at his vanity.

The horse whinnied and stomped his hoof; John pulled the reins and trotted up the path. He passed the servant and, in a few moments, reached the house. Climbing from the mare, he dismounted and tethered it. Heavy-hearted, he paused before trudging up the steps.

Inside, he knew Sarah sat somewhere filling her time with womanly tasks, learning to be a good wife and mother for some lucky gentleman. The thought tore at him. Already, he missed Sarah's smile and determined ways. At twenty-five, John knew he should think of taking a wife, but his mind could not erase Sarah's glowing countenance.

He rang the bell and waited. When the servant arrived, he led John to Hampton's study. He viewed the familiar scene, knowing after his meeting he would walk out the manor door for the last time.

Standing in the middle of the room, Hampton motioned to a chair. "Sit, John."

John sank into the seat and rested a hand on each knee, eyeing his employer's steady gaze.

Hampton clamped his hands behind his back and paced. "Have you completed the accounting?"

"Yes, sir. Here are the figures." Pulling the ledger from his pocket, he held his notations toward Hampton. "Cyder barrels, vinegar barrels, jugs ready for the market."

He grasped the ledger and scanned it. "You've done well."

John's head shot upward. *Done well?* Tension knotted in John's shoulders. Why did the man not state his purpose and end it? "Thank you," he mumbled, waiting for the condemning finger to point the way toward the door.

Placing the book on his desk, Hampton focused on John. "You've done well," he repeated, sinking to his chair. "Months ago, I promised you a reward, John, and—"

"Please, sir, you have been most generous providing my family with a new cyder press. I expect nothing more." With downcast eyes, John waited for a response.

"But you've already accepted more, John. You've stolen something precious," Hampton said, his voice rising.

"Stolen? No sir, I am a poor but honest man."

"I know you are honest, John, but no matter, you have stolen my daughter's heart." Sadness reverberated in the man's voice.

Fear and sorrow seeped through John's veins like ice water. "I have tried to contain my feelings, sir, but Miss Hampton is. . .she did not heed my warning. . .and my own heart would not obey my good counsel."

Hampton shook his head and rose. "My daughter is a stubborn young woman, John. When she desires something, she is not easily dissuaded." He rounded the desk and stood before him. "I am as guilty as any for giving her all for which she longs."

With no need to respond, John held his breath and waited, confused as to where the discourse might be headed.

"My daughter told me of your concern for social proprieties, and I thank you."

John rose and stepped toward Hampton. "I would do nothing to harm your daughter or her reputation, sir. I have her best interest at heart."

"I have no doubt. . .but my daughter says she loves you." Hampton's gaze riveted to John's.

As if shrinking, John's large body seemed no bigger or worthy than a pesky mouse as he spoke from his heart. "I love her. . .with all my being." His words sounded frail and meaningless. "Yet I know it is impossible except if God wills it."

"You are a Christian man?" Hampton asked, his eyes narrowing.

"A new one, sir, but Sarah has helped me to know God in a more personal way. I believe in God's sovereignty and in Christ's saving grace."

"That is a blessed understanding, John. Do you know how difficult earthly life would be if I grant you my daughter's hand?"

"I do." His stomach churned as he saw the pain in Hampton's eyes.

"I cannot make things right, John, but I can give my daughter a secure life if nothing else."

John's heart stopped, then lurched while he waited for his dismissal papers.

Hampton walked behind his desk, opened a drawer, and pulled out a document. "I will give you this." He extended it to him.

John grasped the paper, his pulse coursing through him as he eyed the certificate. Confusion spiraled in his mind. "What is this, sir?"

"It is a deed to the apple orchard, John. It is yours. I have made a public notice to appear on the *Barnham and Norwich Post*. You may read it here." He slipped another paper into John's hands and tapped his finger on the spot.

John scanned the text.

> Whereas an advertisement appeared in this paper informing the public that the Hampton apple orchards have been granted to Edward Hampton's future son-in-law, John Banning of Barnham, Norfolk, declaring that following the wedding of Sarah Hampton and John Banning, the Cydermaking Business will be carried on by John Banning aforesaid by whom all orders will be thankfully received and readily executed.

The words ran together in tears of gratitude and disbelief. John opened his mouth to express his thanks, but Hampton detained him with his hand.

"No need to say a word, John. I have witnessed your labor. I have admired your creativity and fortitude. I proclaimed one day you would be a successful businessman. If my daughter loves you and you cherish her, I will not let society stand in your way. But you must be a good husband to my daughter."

John's hand trembled as he clutched the deed. "I could be nothing less if she will have me."

Chapter 9

Sarah looked across the table during the Christmas Day meal, unable to believe John sat across from her. Once her mother had accepted the inevitable, she had been quiet but cooperative.

Sarah loathed hurting her parents, but she had put her life in God's hands and God had led her to John—a farmer, a man of lower station. Though she did not consider herself an intellect, Sarah could not but wonder if God were proclaiming a statement to the world about inequities. John Banning had been born as worthy as any man. . .and far more worthy of Sarah's love than any other.

"We must plan the guest list," her mother said, eyeing Sarah as if waiting for her to reject the idea.

"Yes, as soon as possible," Sarah agreed. "But the list will be smaller than my coming out, don't you think?"

Her mother nodded, a look of distant sadness in her eyes. "But it will be as lovely."

Sarah yearned to rise and kiss her mother for her rallied thought. Though Sarah's marriage would not be without obstacles, with God it would be possible and blessed.

John listened to the discourse of his future mother-in-law and his betrothed. He'd been astounded when Sarah revealed her dowry would be a small house at the edge of the orchard. Small now, but one day, with the Lord's continued blessing, he would acquire a larger home for his wife and children. An abundance of children, he prayed. . .if it were God's will.

His own family had been startled by his announcement, but being kind and honest people, they were delighted for John and prayed only the best for each family member.

John rejoiced in the blessings God had sent him—intelligence, ingenuity, and a good business sense. But the greatest gift was Sarah's unquestioning love and her parents' acceptance. His life had been filled with the unexpected. Having eaten the holiday meal of goose and a joint of roast beef, John moved aside his plate and enjoyed a dish of delicious Christmas pudding.

Hampton smiled and drained the last of his cyder. "I shall offer a toast to my daughter, to John, and to their happiness." He tilted the decanter and poured a splash of cyder into each glass.

"Before our toast," he said to John, "share what further wish would bring you joy."

"I have dreamed, sir, that Hampton. . .Banning cyder would receive a Royal Warrant one day. That would honor you, sir, as well as your daughter."

"To happiness and a Royal Warrant," Hampton said.

They lifted their glasses and sipped the sweet cyder.

"And now," Hampton said, "I'm certain you young people would enjoy time alone."

While Sarah sent her father a grateful smile, John's spirit lifted with his offer.

"Thank you, Father," she said. "May we be excused? We will join you later in the parlor."

With Sarah's parents' blessing. John rose, clasped Sarah's hand, and escorted her from the table. Sarah urged him forward until they wended their way into the conservatory where ribbons and ivy adorned the circumference of the glass room. Looking into the moonlit garden, John's thoughts flew back to the August evening Sarah danced with him in the moonlight.

He drew Sarah into his arms, engulfed in new emotion. "Sarah, I love you more than life itself. You are my sun and moon. Stars glow in your eyes." He cherished every look and touch of the angel who would soon be his wife. "Tell me the day you'll be mine."

"Do you agree April is a good month for our wedding, John?"

"Tomorrow would not be too soon, dearest Sarah."

She laughed. "But we must appease my mother. The wedding will be small. . .not the social event she envisioned, but I will be happier and more content."

Happier and more content. Those words filled his heart. Gazing at his future wife, John surged with joy. Looking toward the entrance, he spied the green sprig pinned above the door.

"Come with me," he said, guiding her to the greenery.

"Are we joining my parents already?" Sarah asked beneath the doorway.

He smiled and pointed upward. "No, sweet Sarah, I am only claiming the last berry on this sprig of mistletoe. One kiss is left."

"Only one?"

Plucking the white berry from the leaves, John looked down at the demure woman at his side, her chin tilted upward, her lips soft and waiting. Cautiously, he lowered his mouth and brushed his lips against hers, feeling his heart melt and his knees grow weak.

"I love you, my dearest," she said, placing her fingertip against her lips as if holding on to his kiss.

"I'll love you forever, Sarah."

Though he had spoken, no words could truly express John's devotion and deep adoration for the woman who would soon be his wife. He had once said Sarah was the apple of his eye, but today he remembered the same phrase in God's Word. *"Keep my commandments, and live; and my law as the apple of thine eye. Bind them upon thy fingers, write them upon the tablet of thine heart."*

Sarah had not only brought contentment and happiness to his uneventful earthly life, but through her example and love, she had led him to realize that in Jesus, he had life eternal. No one could have given him more peace and joy than the unlikely woman God had chosen to be his.

John drew Sarah against his chest, feeling her heart beat in rhythm to his own. God willing, he would hold her in his arms forever.

Epilogue

William Banning stood in his office at Attleborough Station, staring at the document clutched in his hand. He'd been the managing director of the Banning Cyder Company since his father's passing in 1952. The business had been in his family since the middle of the nineteenth century when his great-great-grandfather John Banning married Sarah Hampton and received the apple orchard and cyder business as a wedding gift.

After John and Sarah married, they continued to make their home in Banham, perfecting the cyder and raising seven children—six sons and one daughter. The hydraulic cyder press had made all the difference. The business grew and prospered, and when John died, the business was handed down from father to son. The pattern of ownership—from father to son—continued for four generations.

As the business grew and transporting the cyder became expensive, William's grandfather Richard Banning moved the cyder business in 1906 from Barnham to its present location nearer London.

William had heard the story many times from his grandfather and his father how Big John Banning had made a daring proclamation—an admission of his bold dream—on Christmas Day 1851, the day John, a farmer, and Sarah, a woman of position, were officially engaged.

Adjusting his spectacles, William studied the document again, both amazed and satisfied. If only his great-great-grandfather were here, he thought as he gazed at the official document bestowed by Her Majesty, Queen Elizabeth II.

Banning Cyder had been granted a Royal Warrant.

MOONLIGHT MASQUERADE

by Pamela Griffin

Chapter 1

Dense, yellow fog shrouded the empty streets, causing Letitia to feel as lost as a soul in the tower's darkest dungeon. The night was wretched, unfit for man or beast. Yet for Letitia, her cousin's word was law.

Cautiously, she walked over the slick cobblestones, feeling as if she were nothing more than a fetching hound to a cruel mistress. A thankless slave. An unappreciated servant. It was a shame she didn't possess more than two feet on which to travel— like the cat that suddenly appeared out of nowhere with a screech that stopped her heart cold. It raced across her path toward the River Thames, which she assumed to still be on her left from the trickling of water she heard.

Shaking off the fright, Letitia drew the sack of pastries deeper within her cloak. She yearned to be soaking up the comfort of a warm coal fire. An uncomfortable tapping had begun just behind her left eye. Not quite an ache, as her hip was now aching, but a discomfort most certainly.

Through the fog, halos of light shone from the lamps along the streets, but not until she came upon them did their tall iron posts become apparent. Now and then, black hansom cabs rattled past, the creaks of their wheels and clacking of horses' hooves sounding far off. Head downward, Letitia pressed on, silently bemoaning her quandary.

A frantic whinny shrieked to her right followed by the jangling of harness. Hand flying up, as if to ward off an attacker, she twisted around. Her leg crumpled beneath her, and she fell. Heart frozen in terror, she watched a horse emerge from the fog like a phantom, rearing upward. Its lethal hooves crashed down within inches of her cowering form.

The driver cursed at Letitia, ordering her out of the street as he fought to regain control. The beast's hoof had landed on the edge of her cloak, trapping her.

Unexpectedly, someone stooped beside her. Large, warm hands covered her shoulders. "Are you hurt?" a masculine voice asked near her ear. The man looked down where the horse trapped her, and with slow grace, he stood. Speaking quietly to the horse, he took hold of its bridle. The beast calmed and eased backward off her cloak.

"You there!" the driver yelled. "Away from my horse. The fool wench has made me late as it is."

The man said nothing, only dropped his hands away and looked at the driver, whose heavy-jowled face could be discerned in the wagon's torchlight. Letitia wished she could see her rescuer's expression, also, for certainly it must be fierce. The driver averted his gaze as though cowed and drove away through the narrow margin of space that remained, with the great iron wheels rolling dangerously close to her head.

Letitia began to push herself off the cobblestones. Her rescuer was again beside her, assisting her to stand.

"I was unaware that I'd wandered into the middle of the street." She felt the utmost fool. The fog had captured sound and tricked her into believing the wagon was farther away, but had she not been engaging in self-pity, she might have been more attentive.

His hands were gentle; she wondered why he wore no gloves. Surely this must be a man of distinction, as noble as his character appeared.

"This isn't fit weather for you to be out walking. Come. My driver will take you home."

Hesitant, Letitia looked up. She could see little of his face, since his hat was angled low over his forehead. "No, truly." She took a few steps backward. "I can manage."

He frowned. "You're hurt! See there—you're limping. I insist you allow my driver to take you home." He took firm hold of her elbow and began leading her to the other side of the street where a torchlight's glow pierced through the curtain of fog. A coach emerged. "I'll hear no more on the matter."

"Really, I—I shouldn't." Letitia stopped. "The pastries!"

He left her and returned with the parcel, smashed from where she'd fallen atop it. "I'm sorry. Your pastries appear to be ruined."

Letitia refused to think of her cousin Lady Marian's reaction when she discovered there would be no sweet cakes for her late night tea. The merchant had surely left with his cart once the fingers of fog thickened while the lamplighters had climbed their ladders and lit the streetlamps.

"Come, let us remove ourselves from this place," the stranger said, again steering her toward the coach.

In a daze, Letitia took scant note of her movements yet managed the awkward step up into his coach. He released her elbow, and she sank to the bench seat. "I'm grateful for your kindness, sir, but I've no wish to trouble you."

With stealthy grace, he moved to the opposite seat. "Nonsense. No trouble at all."

Letitia gazed fully at the countenance of her benefactor. In the flickering light of the globed torch near the window, his eyes appeared a soft bluish gray, the color of a storm-washed sky on a gentle dawning, when the earth stood quiet as it struggled to breathe again. If peace had a color, his eyes would be the bearer of it. She noted the coarse weave of his drab clothing and assumed him to be a servant such as she. Perhaps he was some fine lord's gentleman and a man of great worth. A servant whose master deigned important enough to send out into the night with proper transport. Indeed, the coach in which she sat with its crimson leather seats, gold fittings, and the intricate brocade lining its inside walls appeared that of a nobleman's.

His finely chiseled lips curled into a smile revealing even teeth. "One problem remains. For my driver to take you to your place of residence, you must tell me where you live."

"*Sí*—yes, of course." Letitia felt flustered that she should be caught so boldly staring. "I reside on the other side of Covent Garden, in Belgrave Square, at Lord Ackers's manor."

"A fair piece for you to be walking," he said in some surprise. "This district isn't safe."

"I was on an errand for my mistress while it was still daylight. The fog thickened upon me unawares and evening came."

He alerted the driver of their destination, and then before she was aware of his intent, he shrugged out of his woolen cloak and wrapped it around her shoulders. "This may help to take the chill off. You're trembling, poor child."

The garment felt pleasantly warm from the heat of his body, and Letitia's cheeks blazed at the intimate gesture. She darted a glance his way, noting his fine breadth of shoulder and trim build in the simple clothes. Aware of her own unsightly appearance, with her fog-dampened hair plastered in clumps against her face and her skirt filthy with mud, she lowered her gaze.

"You're very kind, sir," she said as the coach jounced along the cobbled street. "I pray my fall won't be the cause of your finding trouble with your master. Will he mind your tardy return?"

A look of incomprehension crossed his features before a glimmer of realization entered his eyes. "Don't be concerned for my welfare. I shan't suffer at the hand of Lord Dalworth." He glanced toward the window, putting an end to their conversation.

Soon the carriage rolled to a stop. The driver opened the door to the familiar sight of the Ackers's four-story manor apparent through the veil of fog. Letitia shrugged out of his cloak to return it, but his hand on her arm stopped her. "Keep it. I'll send a messenger for it in the morning."

"Oh, but—"

"I insist. You're still shivering."

Not knowing the proper way to respond to such benevolence, she nodded. "*Vaya con Diós*—God go with you."

Drawing the man's cloak about her, Letitia hurried to the side of the house. The lonely, hollow sound of hoofbeats trailed away on the cobblestones. Before taking the stairs down to the servants' entrance, she turned to watch what little she could see of the coach's slow retreat.

———

Edward pondered the encounter as the driver transported him home. Home. A far cry from India, to be sure. Already he missed the hot, sunny days and the glorious, royal sunsets above the perimeter of jungle that enclosed the plantation. England's weather was abominable compared to the exotic land of sunshine from which he'd come. True, India had its monsoon season, but it seemed as if rain made a permanent home over London. If it wasn't raining, fog as thick as treacle smothered the city. Days of clarity were few, and the countless coal fires belching black smoke into the air did little to help. Still, his place was not to disregard orders given him, and so he'd undertaken the journey to England alongside the man who'd proven to be a trial, the man to whom he must answer for the next few weeks.

As the coach rattled forward, his attention drifted to the slight indentation the girl had left on the leather cushion. Never had he seen such big brown eyes ringed by such thick lashes. Her skin had been pale from shock, but in normal circumstances he assumed the color to be as creamy and white as a dove's breast. Her slim jaw had been pronounced, her nose narrow, her cheekbones high, though without the usual rosiness he'd perceived on other girls of her youth.

From the little he could see of her face within its gray hood, she'd been a comely lass, and her Spanish accent gave her soft husky voice added delight. Still, it did no good to dwell on pleasures of which he could never partake. The duke had given him an order, and Edward must see it through, however taxing the mission might be.

Heaving a resigned sigh as the coach traveled alongside St. James's Park toward his destination of Mayfair, he directed his attention toward the upper story of Buckingham Palace appearing above the fog. His brief stay in London had brought him no closer to resolutions. Nor did the prospect of a week in the country assuage the guilt of taking on the challenging role he soon must play.

Chapter 2

I t was always said of Scrooge, that he knew how to keep Christmas well, if any man alive possessed the knowledge,'" Letitia read. " 'May that be truly said of us, and all of us! And so, as Tiny Tim observed, God Bless Us, Every One!' "

Little Sally lay on her mother's cot, looking up at Letitia with shadowed dark eyes. "Miss Ticia, why did God let ye get huwt like Tiny Tim?"

Letitia closed Dickens's story *A Christmas Carol*. With Michaelmas Term recently upon them, it just being October, the selection of the child's favorite story might seem odd to some. But the novel was the only one her mother possessed, a gift given to her by the Dowager Viscountess Ackers. The cook couldn't read but treasured the book, nonetheless.

Letitia brushed back limp flaxen strands from Sally's pinched face, thankful the child's eyes were no longer fever-bright. "God wasn't the cause of my injury, Sally. I chose not to heed wise counsel and was confident I could jump a wall though I'd learned such a maneuver mere weeks before." She didn't add that she still often had difficulty obeying those in authority.

"And they had to shoot the ho'se?" The little brow creased.

Letitia nodded. "His foreleg was broken. There was nothing left to be done. I was but three and ten, and the harrowing incident served to teach me a difficult lesson. We must listen to those older and wiser. Had I listened to my *papá*, I would walk without a limp today." Letitia smiled. "That said, it's time for you to rest."

Sally's eyelids were already drooping. The straw mattress rustled as Letitia rose and covered the child with a woolen blanket. She lowered the flame in the lamp and left the servant quarters, taking the stairs to her room.

Before her hand could touch the glass doorknob, quick footsteps padded toward her.

"Where have you been?" Cousin Marian asked, a bite to her words.

"I was reading to the cook's daughter."

Marian sniffed. "Why do you waste your time on that urchin each night when you could be attending me? I don't know why Papa doesn't dismiss the cook; her pastries are horrid. Speaking of which, have you brought my cakes?"

Letitia silently counted to three to compose herself before answering. "I'm sorry.

273

I had an accident. The cakes are ruined."

"Ruined, are they?" Marian's green eyes flashed sparks. "Can you not carry out even the simplest of tasks?"

"It was the fog; a horse nearly ran me over—"

"Never mind." Marian stalled her apology with an uplifted hand. "I don't wish to hear excuses. Really, Letitia, you shall need to improve on your serving skills if you're to accompany me to the country in two weeks and attend me there."

"The country?"

"Yes." Marian's chin rose in a patronizing manner. "My family received an invitation last week to the Duke of Steffordshire's estate. Father has said we shall accept. The duke is my father's second cousin, as you must know since he was discussed at Lady Filmore's tea three days past. Everyone of importance will be at the ball he'll hold. It's considered quite an honor and a privilege to attend one of his affairs. . . ."

With half an ear, she listened to Marian rave on. Letitia viewed the ladies' teas as an excuse for idle gossip, and she assumed she must have excused herself from the women's company prior to them discussing the duke. Though she couldn't partake in London's social season, having never been presented to the queen, once she turned seventeen, Grandmama had insisted Marian take Letitia on informal outings. Yet she often escaped any tedious gatherings to walk the grounds or visit the stables. Her absence never resulted in anyone's undue distress. She was only allowed to attend because of Grandmama's influence. No decent member of society would have her otherwise.

". . .And such a scandal it caused!" Marian's expression hinged between disgust and excitement. "Of course, no one dares speak of the matter in good society."

"What?" Letitia's attention became fully aroused. "What scandal?" Surely she wasn't rehashing the so-called folly of Letitia's mother once again.

"The duke's son—Lord Dalworth. Have you not been listening to a word I've said?" Marian frowned. "Really, Letitia. I was bringing up the fact that the marquis' intended, Lady Anne Salinger, was discovered to have a lover whom she frequently met on the high moors. When she didn't return to the manor, her maid, who knew of their nighttime trysts, went in search of the lady and found her horse to have thrown her. Since that time, she's been destined for Bedlam, though her father will not relinquish her. She carries a china doll wherever she goes and speaks to it. The incident created a fine scandal, especially since Lord Dalworth had recently returned from abroad for the wedding. It's been said they quietly dissolved the engagement, and the marquis will be looking to take another wife. I'm confident that this is the reason for our weeklong hiatus to Hepplewith Manor."

Marian extracted a fan and cooled herself, as if what she'd just divulged had shocked her into vapors, though Letitia knew better. " 'Tis rumored the marquis will look for a wife from among those guests invited. He's destined to inherit a silk plantation in India and so much more."

"Poor Lady Salinger," Letitia murmured.

"Hardly! Letitia, do you not yet understand?" Marian looked put out. "Lady Anne Salinger was with child, unwed since she and the marquis were yet to be married. And she'll not give the name of the man whom she took as her lover."

"Oh!" Letitia felt the heat of embarrassment's blush. "But why should she do such a thing when she was promised to the marquis?"

"Oh, you truly are hopeless." Marian's gaze swept to the ceiling. "You might as well have lived on the other side of the moon than in Spain. And I'd heard the people were so passionate in your homeland. Never mind. I'm retiring to my room for the evening and won't require further assistance. But I'll want those tea cakes on the morrow!"

Marian whirled to go in a froth of ruffles and lilac scent. Before Letitia could retire to her own room, Lady Ackers's petite maid hurried her way. "Her ladyship'll be wanting a word with ye, miss."

"Thank you, Bertha." Letitia moved down the corridor to a bedchamber, the largest in Windham Hall.

Dowager Viscountess Regina Ackers stood in her sitting room, facing the fire, with her gnarled hand cupped over a mahogany cane and her back to Letitia. Dressed in a blue satin bed robe and white nightcap with lappets hanging down either side, she hardly looked intimidating. Yet appearances were deceptive.

The elderly matriarch had once dined with queens and princes and had lived a thoroughly fascinating life. It was said that Queen Victoria greatly admired this woman, who spoke her mind and did as she pleased, and in the days before age robbed her strength, Lady Ackers received many an invitation to the royal court. Everyone stood in awe—and many of those, in fear—of the great dowager viscountess.

She turned regally, her posture as erect as it must have been in her youth when she dazzled the courts with her beauty. The portrait hanging above the mantel claimed testimony to that.

"Tell me, Letitia, when will you desist in allowing my granddaughter to make a spectacle of you and speak to you in such a manner?"

"Perhaps when I'm crowned Queen of England," Letitia returned wryly. "Yet even then my coz will doubtless consider herself more lofty than I."

Lady Ackers's mouth twitched at the corners. "Come, sit by the fire. I have a matter of import to discuss with you."

Letitia did so, relaxed in her company. They shared a strange bond, one Letitia never fully understood. With Lady Ackers, she could be herself. She was allowed and encouraged to lapse into her native Spanish tongue, which Marian, who didn't know the language, forbade. Due to her fond feelings for Lady Ackers, who herself could converse in Spanish, Letitia had given in to the woman's desire to call her Grandmama, though they weren't related.

"You shall go to Steffordshire," the woman declared, sitting across from Letitia on her settee. "But not as a companion to Marian. No, indeed. You shall arrive as a lady, the lady you were meant to be. And you will be the one to win the heart of the handsome marquis."

Letitia laughed. *¡Seguro que bromeas!* The woman was dear to her heart, but Letitia presumed that senility often robbed her of sound reasoning.

"I? Jest? No, Letitia, I'm quite serious."

"I very much doubt a marquis would show interest in a poor relation of the Ackers, and a woman coming from a background of scandal at that." Especially after what Marian had divulged about the unfortunate marquis and his recent state of affairs.

The old woman harrumphed and banged her cane on the plush rug. "The earl was a fool to disown your mother. He would have had her wed to a cruel old codger destined for the casket. Indeed, Lord Rotsby died of old age not six months from the day Kathryn eloped with your father."

Letitia remained silent, not wanting to speak about what the nobility viewed as her mother's fall into disgrace.

"I've decided. You shall go. I will write Beatrice, informing her of the need to prepare for an extra guest."

That she referred to the duchess in such familiar terms bespoke her close ties with the woman. "And will you also attend, Grandmama?"

"I?" The woman gave a shrug that might have been considered graceful if her expression weren't so dour. "Perhaps, if I'm well. Perhaps not. But you shall go, Letitia, and do not change the subject as I sense you are doing. You will be provided with adequate frocks, of course, and I shall send my Abigail along to assist you."

Her lady's maid? "But who will serve Lady Marian?"

"Rose did before you came. She can do so again."

"What of my aunt? Who will dress her hair if not Rose?"

"Hester is indisposed. She cannot be seen in public until her time arrives."

"Sí, of course." Letitia's cheeks flamed at the reference to her aunt's delicate condition.

"No, Letitia. I've made up my mind. You shall go as a guest, not a servant. And I'll not hear another word on the matter." Lady Ackers banged her cane once more before she stood. "I am weary; the hour is late. We'll speak more of this another time."

Letitia rose and kissed the soft, wrinkled cheek. If she could have chosen a grandmother, this was the woman she would have chosen. Still, Letitia wondered what Marian would say to this new development, given that Lady Ackers's will was rarely crossed.

—⁓—

"Papa was a fool to give in to Grandmama's wishes," Marian fumed two weeks later as the coach in which they sat rattled along a lonely country road bordered with stately poplars. "You'll never pass as a lady of breeding; never mind that you were tutored alongside me. Our family shall be made a laughingstock, and all because of Grandmama's ludicrous directive."

Withholding a sigh, Letitia stared at her cousin. Marian had dispensed with the usual sober traveling dress and had clothed herself in a splendid brocade gown, wanting to make a lasting impression upon those at Heppelwith Manor, as she'd earlier told Letitia.

Beside Marian, Rose stared out the coach's window, as if to dissociate herself from her lady's ranting—which had gone on for the better part of half an hour— and Bertha sat quietly beside Letitia. Normally, Lord Ackers would have shared the coach with his daughter, but he'd chosen to ride astride his horse and given the lady's maids access to the interior.

Letitia envied him and was certain at this moment neither Rose nor Bertha counted it a blessing to ride within.

"If this change of plans distresses you so, I could attend in disguise," Letitia suggested lightly when Marian paused to breathe.

"In disguise?" Marian frowned.

"As a friend of the family. I could attend under a different name rather than be introduced as a relation."

Marian scoffed. "Really, Letitia. I should think you might recognize the gravity of the situation rather than jest about it. 'Tis a shocking turn of affairs, and one that could well put an irreparable blotch on the Ackers's name—if you were to act in a manner unbefitting of the role you shall temporarily possess."

Letitia sighed. "I assure you, my lady, I, too, am not overly pleased with this arrangement." Most of her life she'd helped her family with farming, and then she'd lived three years in servitude as a companion to Marian. Now she was expected to take on the role of a lady of leisure? The prospect was daunting.

"You say you're not 'overly pleased,' which leads me to believe there is in fact some amount of pleasure involved." Marian's green eyes were calculating. "A word of caution, Letitia. Do not forget who you truly are. A pauper you were born, and a pauper you shall remain. And keep away from the marquis!" The last directive came out clipped.

Letitia had no interest in hooking a marquis's attention; the thought was absurd. Even if he were to show interest, such an emotion would wane once he realized her true state of affairs. Although her family could hardly be considered paupers, they did possess little. Yet if love had been a commodity by which to live, her parents would reign as king and queen, and she and her siblings as princesses and princes. For the measure of love, they possessed in abundance.

"Why do you smile so?" Marian's eyes narrowed in suspicion.

"I was thinking of my parents and my brothers and sisters. I miss them."

Marian gave a disdainful little huff and looked out the window.

Letitia relaxed against the seat. Minutes of blissful silence elapsed before a commotion erupted outside and galloping hoofbeats were heard.

"You there," a shout came. "Pull aside!" The jangling of harness and creaking of wood ceased as the coach jolted to an abrupt stop, almost sending Letitia into Marian's lap.

"Stand and deliver!" came another command.

Letitia's eyes went wide.

Highwaymen!

The door flew outward, revealing a man with a black kerchief tied around his jaw. In one black-gloved hand, he aimed the barrel of a pistol in their direction.

"Well, and what have we here?" he sneered. "Come out, my pretties."

Rose crossed herself while Bertha uttered a low moan of despair. Letitia's own heart seemed to have lurched to a stop.

Chapter 3

When no one made a move to alight, the highwayman grabbed Bertha's arm and heaved her from the coach. Shrieking, she went flying to the dirt and landed on her knees.

"Come out, and no trouble will befall you," he instructed Letitia and the others.

"Do as he says, daughter," Lord Ackers's shaky voice came from without.

"Go on," Marian whispered to Letitia. "You first."

Bottling up her fear, seeking to be courageous, Letitia moved to step down. Marian assumed a stance behind her.

The late afternoon sun blinded as Letitia struggled to see who waylaid them. Three men, one on horseback, circled the carriage. One had his pistol trained on Lord Ackers and the driver, now absent from his box seat. The other bandit watched from his mount. All had black silk kerchiefs tied around their faces and wore broad-brimmed hats. Their manner of clothing appeared as if it had been pulled from a trunk of a bygone day.

"Come, hand it over," commanded the man who'd ordered them out. He held open a large drawstring pouch.

"What is it you wish from us?" Letitia asked.

"What, indeed?" he mocked, his glare cutting into her. "Your jewels, of course!"

Marian clapped a hand to her elaborate necklace. "No," she breathed. "You shan't have them."

"Do as he says, Marian," her father instructed, "and they'll let us go in peace. Their leader has given his word."

Letitia doubted the word of a highwayman but remained silent. The clink of metal and Marian's sniffle informed Letitia the girl had done as ordered. While one of the bandits tossed the luggage from the carriage's boot and began sorting through it for valuables, the first highwayman approached Letitia. "Your jewels, also, if you please."

"I have none."

"A lady traveling without gemstones to flaunt?" He stepped closer, and Letitia forced herself not to recoil. "Be warned, if you don't remove them from wherever you've hidden them on your person, I shall remove them myself."

"And I tell you, I have no jewels. Moreover, if you lay a hand on me, I can promise you it will be a decision sorely made and one you'll greatly lament."

He raised his hand to strike her. Letitia, having endured the sting of Marian's hand a number of times, was not cowed.

"Enough!" the mounted rider called, the first time he'd spoken. With languid grace, he dismounted and approached. The first highwayman stepped away.

"Have I your word you carry no valuables?" The leader spoke almost in a whisper, as he took his stand in front of Letitia. His blue-gray eyes above the kerchief gleamed with something akin to admiration, amusement, and more.

"Yes." Mesmerized by his stare, she could find no voice to protest when he lifted his fingers and stroked her neck. Something cold and rough rubbed against her skin—the feel of a gemstone—and she realized he must be wearing one of his ostentatious rings backward.

"Ah, but what have we here?" His smooth fingers plucked from her high collar the thin silver chain upon which hung a cross. He held the minute symbol of her faith against one fingertip and rubbed the bottom half with his thumb.

Letitia swallowed. "A jewel such as you covet, this is not, as you can plainly see. It is but a token *mi madre* gave me. Worth little save for its sentiment."

He looked up into Letitia's eyes. A strange mix of fear and excitement made her blood pound in her temples. There was something strangely familiar about those eyes. . . .

At last, he released his hold on the cross.

"You speak rightly. 'Tis of no value to me. Keep your talisman, my lady." Swiftly he turned and addressed the others. "Come away. We've tarried too long."

He mounted his chestnut mare while his two lackeys did the same with their horses. As he settled on his saddle, his focus again went to Letitia. Removing his hat, he swept it over his breast and out to the side, effecting an elaborate bow. "And so, without further adieu, we bid you good day."

Spurring his horse, he took off in a cloud of dust, the other highwaymen trailing him into a distant copse of trees.

"Well, I never," Marian fumed. "Papa, why do you stand and stare? Are you not going in pursuit? Those were some of my most exquisite jewels."

Lord Ackers moved to his horse. "I shall report the matter once we reach Heppelwith Manor. Until then, there's little to be done."

Pouting, Marian ordered Letitia and the other servants to retrieve the remaining contents of the luggage strewn over the ground. Once they completed their task, the driver again secured the trunks in the boot.

The remainder of the journey passed in relative silence. By the time the coach reached its destination, it bore a somber party indeed.

Letitia stared at the multistoried, gabled structure of Heppelwith Manor. Welcoming light poured forth from tall windows along the ground floor and a few smaller arched windows on the floors above. Half-full, the moon had arisen beyond the sprawling country manor, outlining the expansive rolling grounds and silvering a still pond flanked by trees.

Letitia sensed a shadow at a window and lifted her attention there. The broad-shouldered form of a man looked down upon them.

—⁓—

Edward watched the tardy guests alight from the carriage with the aid of the footmen. Four women stepped down, one wearing a splendid gown that appeared ill-suited for travel. Light from the lower windows illumined the face of another lady as she turned her attention upward. His breath mired in his throat, and he stood stock-still.

"Edward?" The voice of the duchess interrupted his thoughts. He turned from the window as her plump form filled the entryway. "There you are. Tell me, are you still determined to go through with this outlandish scheme of yours?"

He nodded once.

She sighed. "Very well. I've only just now learned that thieves accosted Lord Ackers and his party during their journey. This makes the second daylight robbery by highwaymen since you and William arrived from India two months past. See about fetching the constable, will you?"

"Of course. No one was hurt?"

"There's no need to summon a physician, though poor Lady Marian is beside herself with the loss of her jewels."

"I'll leave at once."

"Edward?"

He halted his rapid trek to the door.

"You are aware I don't approve?"

"Yes, well aware," he said quietly, not needing her to elaborate. "But as things stand, I see no other recourse."

Before she could detain him with yet another homily about trusting God, he left her presence.

Upon descending the curved stairway, he caught sight of the new arrivals near the foyer, one woman in particular. The same who'd looked up at him while he'd stood at the window.

She stood near twin oil lamps bracketed to the wall. Their muted glow brought out the shine of her dark curls within the beribboned gray bonnet. Her manner of dress was tasteful, simple. While a servant took their cloaks, she turned impossibly huge, dark eyes Edward's way.

A jolt of familiarity struck—he assumed that's what robbed him of breath—before she dropped her gaze to the black-and-white tiles. Hearing the duchess descend the stairs behind him to see to her guests, Edward continued to the servants' wing.

Yet all during his mission, the girl with the haunting brown eyes never left his thoughts.

—∿—

Letitia was shown into the bedchamber she would share with Marian. Her cousin's disparaging gaze darted about the large room with its modicum of furniture. "The canopy is small." Placing her palm against the high mattress, Marian pushed down twice as though to judge its softness, then pulled at the braided cord holding back the bed curtain. The olive-green drape whooshed alongside the bed. "It will have to do, I suppose."

"It's a delightful room," Letitia said. "I'm well pleased."

"Yes, you would be." Marian's mouth compressed. "Really, Letitia, must you be so gauche? Your behavior downstairs was reprehensible. One would think you'd never viewed a fine estate with the way you gawked at the furnishings, yet you've resided at my father's estate for the better part of three years."

Letitia held her tongue. Windham Hall, with its slightly worn furnishings, could hardly compare to the splendor of Heppelwith Manor. For Marian to wed the wealthy marquis would benefit the Ackers. If her cousin was correct about their reason for being here, such a manner of choosing a bride—by inviting eligible women from all over the countryside and choosing from among them—seemed odd to Letitia. Yet she'd long ago learned of the eccentricities of the titled and wealthy.

Marian preened in front of a standing oval mirror, pinching cheeks already rosy. "Our dreadful encounter with those robbers delayed us from a prompt arrival, but it worked to my advantage. We're the talk of the evening." Her eyes gleamed as she turned from the cheval glass. "Mine will be a name the marquis shall not easily forget. Did you see him? Was he not dashing?"

Letitia recalled the tall, fashionable gentleman, a trifle brusque and loud, with wavy brown hair and long sideburns. He'd been standing surrounded by a bevy of fawning, chattering women.

"I saw him." She poured water from a widemouthed pitcher into a matching porcelain basin to wash her face and hands.

"He's so debonair." Marian clasped her hands beneath her chin and came close to swooning. "The duchess mentioned that except for those functions they've planned, we're free to do as we wish during our stay. I have no doubt the marquis will be keeping close watch over those women presently unattached so as to choose his bride.

And I plan to be in his vicinity often. I will be the marchioness."

Weary of the incessant talk of the marquis, Letitia dried her hands on a linen towel.

"How do you plan to amuse yourself?" Marian's words bore a sharp edge.

"I noticed a maze in the gardens. Perhaps I shall also visit the stables."

Marian softly snorted. "One would think that your childhood fall would leave you wanting nothing more to do with the creatures. Very well. Ride the horses. I care little what you do as long as you stay away from the marquis." So saying, she flounced away and called for Rose to tend her.

Expelling a lengthy breath, Letitia touched her cross and its comforting ridges. At least Marian didn't require her presence throughout their stay. The thought made Letitia's lips curl upward. There might be something to be said for Grandmama's idea, after all.

Chapter 4

The next morning passed without much to distinguish it from any other and certainly without the excitement of the previous day. A prisoner to her cousin's never-ending monologue, Letitia spent her early hours in the bedchamber she shared with Marian. A servant brought them scones and thick cream at Marian's command. Letitia grabbed one from the platter and bit into it with delight.

"Really, Letitia," Marian scoffed. "I do hope you conduct yourself in a more suitable manner when we're in the company of the duchess. You eat like one of the hogs."

As always, Letitia chose not to respond. In the privacy of their room, she didn't consider her behavior so horrid, especially since she was quite ravenous. A creature of habit, Letitia had been dressed since dawn in a soft plum day gown with wide pagoda sleeves flaring out from the elbows. Marian rose much later and took extreme measures with her appearance—over an hour to have her hair styled by Rose. Yet Letitia was usually the one on the other end of the brush. With nothing to keep her hands occupied, the minutes seemed to drag by like aged souls tottering on the verge of eternal sleep. Marian had expressly forbidden Letitia to make an appearance downstairs without her. She supposed it didn't matter. Years ago, she'd learned of the habit of the nobility to break the fast late in the morning and assumed customs at this country estate would be no different.

Half past eleven, Marian declared herself presentable, and they made their appearance downstairs. A servant showed them the way to the breakfast room.

Silver chafing dishes lined the sideboard, and guests served themselves. Letitia filled her plate with kippers, sausages, and eggs. Throughout their meal, Marian scanned the entryway, and Letitia assumed she searched for the absent marquis. Except for one doddering old gentleman with a chain fastened to a monocle that had the habit of falling into his plate, all the men were absent. Likely, they'd taken their meal earlier and now gathered in the smoking room or were off on a pheasant shoot.

Across the table from Letitia, next to the posy-papered wall, a servant in dark livery stood surveying the room of frivolous females. Letitia observed him, experiencing a peculiar recognition. When a guest inquired something of him, his benevolent smile made Letitia catch her breath. Before she could collect her thoughts, he turned on his heel and quit the room.

Letitia took note of her surroundings. Each of the eleven breakfast patrons was engaged in conversation, including her cousin.

Silently Letitia rose from the table and advanced in the direction she'd seen the servant go. The room in which she found herself opened to a small room with a fireplace. Spotting the manservant standing with his arm against the overmantel, she relaxed. Unaware of her presence, he lifted his hand, frowning as he looked upon it, then closed it into a fist and stared into the fire. How odd. . .

The duchess suddenly appeared at the door in another part of the room.

"Edward," she said with authority. "I must speak with you."

So her rescuer's name was Edward, for Letitia was almost certain that this was the man who'd come to her aid on London's foggy streets. She watched him approach the duchess; then together they disappeared into the next room.

Disappointed that her query would have to wait, she pivoted to return to the breakfast room and almost collided with a man behind her. She jerked back to avoid contact, but her leg gave way. A gasp left her lips, as his strong arm wrapped about her back. She, in turn, grabbed his other arm to prevent her fall.

She blinked in astonishment as she met the marquis' dancing eyes. He held her close a moment longer than appropriate. A wave of heat rushed to her face. She made as if to move back, and he dropped his arms to his sides. Quickly, she retreated.

"Have a care," he said. "The flooring is slick."

"Sí, I will try to remember." She didn't look at him again. Surely, her mind must be playing tricks on her. "*Gracias,* my lord."

He made no move to go, and she couldn't leave since he blocked her path.

"Have we met?" he asked.

"I am Letitia Laslos. Viscountess Ackers is my aunt."

"Of course. You arrived with the unfortunate Lady Marian who lost her treasured emeralds and diamonds to thieves. Pray tell, did you suffer a similar fate at the highwaymen's hands?"

His words sounded glib, and curiosity compelled Letitia to lift her gaze. Was he truly so unfeeling? "I was happy to escape a similar misfortune. The jewels stolen from my cousin had been her great-grandmother's. It is a difficult trial for her to bear."

The marquis offered a little shrug, then tilted his head in a manner both indifferent and assessing. "You've given report to the constable?"

"Yes. However, I'm distressed to say that the sun blinded me, and I couldn't see the men clearly."

"Ah well." His smile was tight. "Fear not, dear lady. I'm certain these blackguards will be caught in due course. I must take my leave, but I hope we shall have opportunity for further discussion in the future. If you require anything, you've only to ask.

It is my humble wish that your stay here at Heppelwith be an enjoyable one." Before she knew what he was about, he reached for her hand and bowed over it, holding it a fraction from his lips.

Letitia watched him stride away, his head high. He seemed anything but humble. Handsome, surely. Charming, debonair. But he lacked character. Letitia had been able to perceive that in the few minutes she'd conversed with him.

She stepped from the room—and halted in shock.

Marian stood outside the door, her eyes murderous.

―⁓―

Edward left the private parlor, his conversation with the duchess concluded. He heard a woman's voice raised in anger.

"How dare you defy me? Did I not explicitly tell you to stay away from the marquis? Be warned, Letitia. I'll not be crossed. Grandmama may have had her say in the matter of allowing you to masquerade as a lady, but you're still my servant."

"Yes, m'lady." These words came quiet, meek.

Curious as to what poor soul was receiving such an undeserved diatribe, Edward rounded the corner. The lovely woman he'd glimpsed the previous night glanced at him, her eyes widening. Her stance haughty, the woman he remembered as Lady Marian Ackers looked over her shoulder at him, then turned her attention to the timid girl who evidently bore the brunt of her ire. He assumed his servant's attire had summarily dismissed him from the lady's mind.

"We will speak more on the matter later," Lady Marian said in dulcet tones. "I've other affairs to which I must attend." She flounced away, the bell skirts of her yellow gown swishing with her actions.

Edward did a quick study of the other woman. Her huge eyes had narrowed, and her rosy mouth was pinched as she looked after her departing mistress. Ah! What's this? Perhaps the fair maiden was not so timid after all.

Before he could walk past, her hand lighted upon his sleeve, and he halted in surprise.

"Please, sir." She dropped her hand away with a becoming flush. "If I may have a moment of your time? Two weeks past, on a foggy night in London, I had the good fortune to receive aid from a stranger whose nature was the epitome of benevolence. Are you that man?"

Edward started in surprise. "The girl with the tea cakes." But this was no child, as he'd thought her then!

She awarded him with a most beatific smile. "Sí, 'tis I. Your kindness is surpassed only by your consideration, sir, if they're not one and the same. When the servant came to Windham Hall to fetch the cloak you'd lent me, I was amazed to receive your gift of tea cakes as well."

Edward inclined his head. "I'm delighted to hear the act brought you pleasure."

"Such a word seems inadequate, given the circumstances. Your thoughtful deed spared me a second chastising, since I was unable to replace them the following morning due to the rain."

"After witnessing the behavior of Lady Marian Ackers, I don't doubt it."

Her long lashes swept downward, and Edward realized he'd intruded where he had no right. "Forgive my lack of decorum. My only defense is that I detest seeing anyone mistreated." In India especially, he'd been appalled by the manner in which Lord Hathaway's servants were dealt. Perhaps the man could run the silk plantation upon which Edward lived, but he was not a merciful lord.

"Please don't misunderstand me. Lady Marian isn't so dreadful. Not compared to some of the nobles I've met." Her eyes grew large at her gaffe, and she swept her gaze to the tiles once more.

Edward was delighted. Not only was she loyal, she was also sweetly naive. Not polished to a hard sophisticated sheen like most of the women he'd met. "And you're not one of those greatly esteemed?"

"Indeed not. Surely you heard what my lady spoke?" At his slight nod, she continued, "I'm but a poor relation and, except for this week, my cousin Marian's companion. But please don't reveal this. It's supposed to be kept secret."

"Indeed?"

She nodded. "The Dowager Viscountess Ackers arranged it."

Ah, that explained it. "Your secret is safe with me. But tell me, why the intrigue?"

"She expressed her desire that I be treated as a lady this week. I almost was a lady, you see—" Her words abruptly ceased, as though she'd just become aware of what she revealed. Shock dissolved, the small chin went up, the slim shoulders straightened, and Edward received a glimpse of her proud, indomitable spirit. "My *mamá* denied her father's choice of a husband and eloped with the youngest son of a Spanish count. My papá. Because he's the youngest son, according to law he received nothing when his papá died. All the land and monies went to his eldest brother."

"I see. So you traveled from Spain by invitation to become a companion to your cousin?"

"Yes. Three years ago." Her shoulders wilted. "Oh, but why do I tell you this? Marian is right to say I'm gauche."

"Nonsense. I see nothing amiss in your manner, but then, having lived in India for six years, I'm accustomed to a more straightforward approach in conversation than that which is employed here in England."

"Then you were with the marquis? You are his valet?"

Edward hesitated. "Yes, I was with him. And now, dear lady, I have matters to which I must attend. Fear not; I shall keep your family secret. Nor will I reveal your little masquerade." He chuckled, thinking how her predicament mirrored his own trial to a degree. "Indeed, I believe the Dowager Viscountess is correct. You should be treated as a lady. And so, I hope you'll not deny me the pleasure of addressing you as such during the remainder of your stay." He stopped short of taking her hand, instead giving her a deferential nod. "If there's any way in which I can be of service, anything you require, you have only to ask."

"I'm already indebted to you, sir."

"Edward, please. And it would be my pleasure."

"Edward, then."

The image of her smile stayed with him long after he entered the marquis' chambers.

Chapter 5

The ten-course evening meal proved to be a formal affair. Served *à la russe* with footmen in constant but discreet attendance at the guest's elbows, everyone was given their choice of whatever dish was at hand.

On Letitia's right, a rotund man with a mole dotting his nose spoke with a French accent so thick Letitia struggled to understand him. Feigning interest, she nodded at times that seemed appropriate but had little idea what was said. To her left, a gentleman with a bulldog jaw seemed more interested in tippling his glass of claret and viewing the lovely flaxen-haired dinner guest across the table than in trying to partake of conversation, though he did manage a few amiable words. In between continual nods toward the talkative French count and a brief response on the rare occasions the other gentleman spoke, Letitia managed to swallow her serving of lamb cutlets and buttered asparagus with peas.

Once dinner ended, the gentlemen left for the smoking room, the women for the drawing room. A piano sat near closed curtains. At the ladies' urging, the duchess's daughter, Lady Eleanor, went to it and claimed the seat. Letitia found a chair near the open door, which was removed from the others. While listening to Lady Eleanor play, she was alerted to the noise of men talking in the corridor.

"His *lordship* requests our presence." The low words came with swift contempt.

"Now?" His companion sounded no happier. "Why now?"

"Ours is not to question, but to obey. Has he not told us that often enough?"

"Huh! Let him issue orders for the present. One day we shall exact vengeance."

The first man agreed, and Letitia heard their footsteps depart but could scarcely think.

Those voices. . .she'd heard one of those men before. When he'd ordered her to hand over her jewels.

Capturing a deep breath, she slipped out of her seat as quietly as her wide crinoline skirt would allow and hastened to the corridor—to find it empty.

She pondered her dilemma. She must find Edward. He would know what to do.

A servant stood in front of the doors to the men's smoking chamber, and she moved toward him. "I must speak with Edward. Can you tell me where to find him?"

The man's snow-white brows hitched upward. "Edward, m'lady?"

"The marquis' servant."

He motioned with his white-gloved hand down the corridor's left.

"Thank you." Letitia moved that direction, her hip again aching, and soon found herself faced with three scrolled doors. Two were closed, one stood ajar. She chose the latter.

The room lay in darkness save for branched candelabra flickering on a table against an opposite wall. Birdsong lilted to her ears. A partition of the two-story outside wall had been removed and replaced with a hexagon of glass, against which a light rain pattered. Inside the aviary, trees grew to the ceiling, their trunks rail-thin. Lush foliage dotted with multicolored birds decorated the somber room with color. Flutterings of wings filled her ears as she exhaled in wonder and moved forward.

"You dare mock me?" came a booming voice from a shadowed corner.

Letitia spun in surprise. Her leg went out from beneath her. She grabbed the back of a curved settee to curb her fall. "Sir! You gave me a fright." Her heart slowed its frantic pace. "Why should you accuse me of such a thing? I don't even know you."

Her eyes now accustomed to the scant light, she noticed a bearded gentleman reclined in a wing chair, one leg outstretched and resting on a low stool. With his walking stick, he pointed to his bandaged foot. "Can you not see? Are you blind as well as impertinent?"

"Are you always so rude?"

"*What?*" he sputtered.

Letitia drew herself up, despising the tears that threatened. With Marian, she'd resigned herself to take the abuse and not strike back. Otherwise, she might be sent home to Spain, which would surely cause her parents distress. Yet she refused to bear anyone else's cruelty.

"To answer your query, sir, I could not see when I first entered the room. But I assure you, I would *never* make sport of anyone with an infirmity." Shaken, Letitia turned to make her escape but trembled so that she could barely walk.

"Stay, girl," he said gruffly. "I meant no harm. 'Tis this accursed gout that sharpens my tongue." When Letitia made no move toward the settee, he barked, "Sit down, I say!"

Although she wanted nothing more to do with the rude guest, she found herself doing as he said. Three years she'd been in servitude; following orders came naturally.

He peered at her beneath thick winged brows. "You say you're not mocking me, so I presume you've injured yourself in some manner?" When she didn't answer, he bellowed, "Well, speak up! I know you've a tongue in your head."

Letitia dug her nails into her palms to prevent herself from responding in kind. "My limp is due to an affliction I suffered as a child."

"Indeed? And does your limb pain you? You walk with great difficulty."

"Only during foul weather or when I've walked overly much."

"How did you come by it?"

His questions hinged on boorishness, but an air of authority cloaked him, making it impossible to deny his request. "When I was a child, I was given a horse by my uncle, one he no longer wanted. My father farms for him. In Spain."

She ignored his raised brow and continued. "It wasn't an extraordinary horse by any means, but it was mine. One day, I raced her and tried to take a low fence but failed. My hip was injured due to my fall."

"I see," he said thoughtfully, then grimaced as he shifted and jarred his foot. "You say you're the daughter of a laborer. Yet you speak as one well educated."

Letitia thought about not answering his pointed statement but sensed he would bully it out of her if she remained silent. She chose to tell him as little as possible. "What my mamá did not teach me, I learned alongside my cousin."

"Indeed?" he raised his brows. "And your cousin is. . . ?"

"Lady Marian Ackers."

"Then your mother must be Lady Kathryn Bellamy."

"She was."

Further conversation halted as Edward entered the room. "I must speak with you. . . Your Grace." His last words came vaguely when he caught sight of Letitia.

Blood froze in her veins. If the color of her face could be seen in the dim lighting, it must be the cast of death. *Your Grace?* Oh, let the floor rip open and swallow her whole! The rude stranger with gout was the Duke of Steffordshire. Her host.

Letitia opened her mouth but remained mute. Should she rise to her feet and attempt a curtsy, or should she apologize for her former argumentative behavior?

Edward seemed to discern the cause of her discomfort. His glance was sympathetic before he turned to the duke. "The marquis wishes to speak with you on a matter most urgent."

"Oh, he does, does he?" The duke gave Edward a measuring look. "Very well, you may inform my son that I shall see him presently. First I wish you to assist this young woman to her room. Have one of the servants give her something for the pain. Perhaps some of that laudanum the physician left on one of his infernal visits."

Edward swung his gaze to Letitia. "You're injured?"

"No. Please, Y–your Grace." She stumbled over the title. "I need no special favors."

"You'll do as I say, Edward. You may both go." The duke glanced her way, a gleam in his eye. "At present, my condition leaves me in a most foul temperament, and I'm not fit company. Depicted as rude even."

Humiliated by the entire episode, Letitia felt the need to redeem herself in whatever small way possible. "I would presume to say, Your Grace, that such is the trial of everyone at one time or another. At times, I've been described to have a most horrid temperament. Grandmama Ackers has taught me to count silently before I speak."

"Indeed?" His lips twitched.

She clamped her mouth shut, aware she was allowing her tongue to outrun her thoughts again. Thankfully, the warmth of Edward's touch as he helped her to stand reassured her, sending pleasant tingles through her arm as he solicitously moved his hand to her elbow and assisted her to the door.

"Gracias," she said a little breathlessly once they were in the corridor. "I can manage."

"Perhaps, my lady. But I've been given my orders. I'll locate a servant to help you to your room where you can rest."

"Really—no. 'Tis only a trivial discomfort. I don't wish to return to my room."

"Then I shall find you a comfortable location in one of the sitting rooms."

She agreed and walked with him to a room decorated in yellows and greens. Gold drapes of damask were partially drawn, exposing the cold drizzle, but a fire in the grate welcomed her.

"This is the duchess's favorite room," Edward said.

"Will she mind me being here?"

His countenance gentled. "She has expressed her desire that all rooms on the ground floor be open to the guests."

He settled Letitia comfortably on a plump brocade sofa, propped a tasseled pillow behind her back, and went in search of a servant to make a medicinal tea. She felt ridiculous but had to acknowledge her pleasure at being waited on for a change. She would be dishonest if she didn't admit to enjoying this bit of pampering and the concerned attention Edward gave her. Settling her head against the cushion, she listened to the soothing crackle of flames.

Soon Edward returned with a dark brew of bitters and made Letitia drink every sour drop. Once she handed him the empty glass, she remembered her reason for leaving the drawing room.

"The highwaymen—they've come," she said.

He started, taken aback. "What?"

"The highwaymen who accosted us. They've come to Heppelwith Manor. While I was listening to Lady Eleanor play, I heard two of them converse in the corridor and attempted to follow."

A black thundercloud crossed his face as he sank to the edge of the cushion beside her and gripped the curved back of the settee. "And is it they who harmed you?"

"N–no." She blinked, astonished at the change that came over him, grateful she wasn't the recipient of his ire. "No one harmed me. The injury is an old one."

The stony tautness left his features, but his eyes remained grave. "You were right to inform me of the matter. Be assured, I will tend to this. However you must tell no one what you've told me. If you're correct, and these are the men who waylaid you, you could be in grave danger if they suspect your knowledge of their presence here."

She stared.

"Do you understand, Letitia?"

Her name on his lips was enough to startle her into a nod. "Sí. I—I understand."

His shoulders relaxed. He studied her a moment, the look in his eyes indefinable, before rising to his feet. "I must leave you now and carry out the directive His Grace has given me."

Hand pressed to her bosom, she watched him go. It wasn't fear that caused her heart to race within her breast; from the little she knew of Edward, she sensed he would never strike a woman. Rather, it was the sense of believing she'd always known him. The strength of his manner, the warmth of his tone, the gentleness of his eyes...

Her breath caught as a pebble of truth smashed into her mental assessment of his character.

From a distance, his eyes appeared darker, but up close in the yellow light of the lamps, his eyes were blue-gray. And now she understood why they'd seemed so familiar.

They were the eyes that belonged to the leader of the highwaymen.

Chapter 6

Perhaps she was mistaken; she must be mistaken. No two men could be one person.

Seeking solace, her mind a cacophony of conflicting thoughts Letitia strolled through the maze of tall yew hedges angling off in intricate bends and scrolls in the center of the garden. She mulled over her encounters with both the marquis and Edward the previous day. Each time, she had thought she was looking into the eyes of the highwayman. Now she realized such a concept was absurd. Likely, the strain of these past two days had led her to believe things that didn't exist.

Inhaling deeply, she pulled her mantle further about her shoulders and lifted her face to the brisk air, just washed with morning freshness. Whatever tea Edward gave her yesterday had helped, and this morning a servant girl had brought more of the same, along with a salve of goose grease melted with horseradish juice, turpentine, and mustard. Dreadfully odorous, but it had relieved the ache in her bone to a great degree.

A ladies' tea had been scheduled for the afternoon, but Marian forbade Letitia to attend. The intended punishment for yesterday's unexpected encounter with the marquis was actually a reprieve. Letitia didn't wish to sit among strangers in a stuffy room, sipping weak tea, eating iced cakes, and listening to gossip.

Coming upon a wall of yew, she rounded the corner and almost barreled into the marquis.

"Oh!" She stepped back, putting her hand to the bush to maintain balance.

He also started in surprise, then smiled, though it seemed a trifle forced.

"My dear Lady Letitia Laslos." He took her free hand and bowed over it. "This is indeed a pleasure."

Ill at ease, she pulled her hand away and used it to smooth the flounces of her skirt. "I thought to take a walk through the maze."

"You need not explain; you may go wherever you like." Instead of allowing her to pass, however, he took her elbow and turned her around the way she'd come. "However, areas toward the center are slippery with mud, and I wouldn't wish you to fall. Allow me to escort you back to the manor."

Letitia had no say in the matter as he moved with her toward the entrance. She thought she heard rustling from within the maze and wondered if he had been alone, but no one followed. Likely the stirring of bushes had come from a bird or small animal.

He asked personal questions, and though Letitia was not as forthcoming as she'd been with Edward and the duke, he learned of her love of horses.

"You must ride with me," he said. "I happen to know of a gentle mare that would suit you well."

"No, Lord Dalworth, I cannot—"

"And you must call me by my given name, William."

"Again I must decline. Surely you realize that doing so would cast an aspersion on my character if someone were to overhear?" Even if that weren't the case, she didn't feel comfortable enough in his company to comply.

"Blasted nobility and its rules," he ground out before his face resumed a pleasant cast. "Nevertheless, I insist you ride with me. I'll not take no for an answer."

Letitia was flummoxed. She dared not further exasperate the marquis by refusing, yet at the same time she feared Marian might find out. But oh, to ride again. . .

Marian tolerated the sport only when social functions demanded it. Letitia hadn't been seated on a horse in months. Desire won out over wisdom, and she nodded.

She was hard-pressed to keep up with him as he accompanied her to the stable, his hand at her elbow as though he thought she might change her mind. Brain in a muddle, she forced her legs to move. This was madness! Apparently he wasn't going to give her opportunity to change into her riding habit. What if someone should see?

A short time later with the cold wind whisking her face, making her feel wholly alive, and the strength of the galloping mare's muscles bunched beneath her, Letitia forgot her former worries. Laughing, she agreed to his challenge of a race, and both horses flew across the waving fronds of a wide meadow. The hood of her mantle flew back, her hair bounced free from its loose chignon, but she didn't pause or care. Her horse reached the thicket first, and she gaily laughed her victory as she turned the mare's head around and reached down to pat its glossy neck.

"You're an accomplished horsewoman." Approval tinged the marquis' tone.

"I've not ridden much."

"Perhaps. But some are born to the saddle and need few lessons. I presume you are one of those gifted few. You must ride with me again."

His words knocked the exultant breath from her, and she shook her head. "I cannot, but I've enjoyed our outing. I must return before the ladies finish their tea."

In her delight to ride again, Letitia had lost track of time. She could see by the sun's position that afternoon was upon them.

"Of course," he said lightly. "We wouldn't want aspersions to be cast upon your character."

Discomfited by his wry words, Letitia glanced at him, but he'd already turned away. She prodded her horse to follow.

Upon reaching the stables, Letitia was surprised to see Edward outside, his face a mask of disapproval.

—∾—

His smile wide, William dismounted and strode over to Edward, clapping him jovially on the back. "Edward, old man! What brings you to the stables?"

"His Grace wishes to speak with you, my lord. At once." Somehow Edward managed to keep a civil tone.

"Does he now?" He turned his attention to Letitia. "A more faithful manservant one cannot find in all of England or India, I'll wager. Imagine. Standing out here in the muck and awaiting my return. What loyalty!"

William laughed, but Edward remained sober. His gaze shifted upward to Letitia, and his breath caught. She was lovely.

Her thick, glossy hair had broken free of its restraints and waterfalled down her shoulders and back in wavy abandon, while soft tendrils caressed her face. The healthy color, once absent, now bloomed from her cheeks, reminding him of blush-pink roses kissed by morning dew.

"Boy!" William addressed a stable hand. "Tend to my horse." He then affected a ridiculously flamboyant bow to Letitia. "Alas, I must leave you, dear lady. Duty calls. But I hope to again have the pleasure of your company."

Gratification thrummed through Edward to hear Letitia's noncommittal reply. Once they were alone, he held up his hand toward her.

"Permit me?"

Letitia hesitated before nodding. He placed his hands at her waist and helped her to alight. When her feet reached the ground, she stumbled into him.

"Oh! Forgive me." Her words a mere breath, she turned her face upward. "I'm unaccustomed to the saddle. That is—it's been a long time."

His own legs as shaky as a rice pudding, he nodded. His thoughts ebbed as he continued to stare into her luminous, wide eyes.

"Edward?" she whispered in quiet entreaty.

The dictates of propriety fled. Sound judgment escaped, hot on the heels of trained wisdom. Before he could change his mind and call them back, Edward lowered his head and brushed his lips against hers. No more than a feather's touch. The kiss of angel's wings. Of earthly sweetness encapsulated in what must resemble heaven.

—∾—

The shrill call of a hawk sliced through the air and startled them apart.

Letitia's face flamed. "Oh." She pressed her fingers against her cheeks and stepped back. "Oh!"

Concern filled his eyes. "Letitia—"

"No." She retreated another step, backing into the mare. "What have I done?"

"Please, don't take this to heart so. The blame was entirely my own. You've done nothing of which to be ashamed."

Wanting, needing to escape his quiet words and gentle eyes, she abruptly turned. Familiar weakness shot through her hip. Edward caught her as she staggered and almost fell. "Letitia!" Worry colored his voice.

She pushed from his arms. "Please—don't." Being in his embrace caused her heartbeat to escalate. Caused her to evoke the soul-stirring touch of his lips against hers. . .and hope for another kiss as sweet as the last.

If news of this were to reach Lady Marian or any of the guests, she would be in disgrace, cast away from decent society as her mother had been. Perhaps even sent back to Spain. While she would cherish seeing her family, she didn't want to be a disappointment to them or add to their trials by giving them another mouth to feed. Her mother wrote that the crops had been bad this year.

Picking up her skirts, she made haste for the manor, ignoring Edward's plea to wait.

Thankfully, he didn't pursue her, nor did anyone waylay her as she took the stairs to her room. A housemaid dusted within the bedchamber, humming. She bobbed a curtsy. "La, miss. I didn't expect you." With downcast eyes, she moved toward the door.

"Please," Letitia said. "Don't go."

The girl halted, uncertain, and Letitia realized her request must seem strange. After all, the girl didn't know Letitia was a servant, too.

"I don't mind if you stay and finish your chores," Letitia explained, unable to bear the solitude of her thoughts another moment. "And please continue your song."

The girl's eyes brightened. A slight smile shone on her freckled face, and she nodded, again flicking her feather duster along the wardrobe while she resumed humming.

The door banged inward.

Dismay pierced Letitia's heart. Marian stormed into the room, then caught sight of the maid. "Leave us."

The girl bobbed a half curtsy and scurried out the door, closing it behind her.

Marian stormed toward Letitia and slapped her. "How dare you!"

Letitia raised a hand to her stinging cheek. "I—I didn't mean—the kiss happened before I was aware—"

"You *kissed* him?" Marian backhanded her across the other cheek. "You kissed the marquis? Spanish strumpet!" She grabbed handfuls of Letitia's hair and pulled hard.

"No, it was Edward! Not the marquis!"

Tears stinging her eyes from the pain, Letitia struggled with her cousin. She clamped her fingers around Marian's punishing ones, trying to break their tension and pull them away.

"You rode with him," Marian sputtered. "Did you think I wouldn't hear? You willfully disobeyed orders, you wretched girl. You're no better than your mother. She was a strumpet, too!"

"Marian," a voice roared from the doorway. The rapid thumping of a cane followed. "Desist such unseemly behavior this moment! Do you hear?"

Marian loosened her hold and turned, shock draining the color from her face. Gratitude streamed through Letitia.

The dowager viscountess stood in the doorway, her countenance formidable.

Chapter 7

"What is the meaning of this?" Grandmama Ackers's voice brooked no refusal.

"She has disgraced us," Marian cried. "She defied all convention and rode with the marquis—alone—then kissed him!"

"Not the marquis," Letitia cut in. "Edward."

"Edward?" Lady Ackers's brows lifted.

"You rode with the marquis. Lady Sedgeworth saw you!"

"Sí, but I kissed Edward." Heat seared Letitia's face, and she swung her gaze to Grandmama. "But I did not mean to kiss him," she added in a whisper.

"Hmm." The dowager viscountess studied them both, a speculative gleam in her eye. "Marian, I will speak with you later. Letitia, come with me."

Fearing a well-deserved lecture, Letitia followed the woman to the bedchamber she'd been given. Lady Ackers sank to a chair, her hand wrapped around her cane, but no chastisement followed. She did, however, study Letitia with a discerning eye.

Letitia shifted, uncomfortable. "I'm happy to see that you changed your mind about coming, Grandmama."

"Yes, I presume you are." The woman's words were wry, but Letitia didn't miss the amused twitch of her lips. "The trunk at the foot of the bed. Open it."

Letitia knelt to do so and fell back on her knees, bedazzled. A mound of shimmering satin embellished with silver and gauze of the same color met her eyes.

"It's the gown you're to wear to the masquerade ball at week's end, and below is the mask. Bring it to me."

Letitia retrieved a white silk mask. Tiny seed pearls had been sewn along the edge. White feathers winged upward from the top. She gave it into Lady Ackers's hand and sat on the floor beside her chair. The gnarled fingers brushed over the stiff mask while a softness touched her time-worn face.

"I was seventeen, your age, when I wore this to my first masquerade ball," she said wistfully. "It was the week of my coming out, and the night I met Phillip."

Letitia's mouth parted. Lady Ackers's husband had been named Gerard.

"Our love was forbidden. His social status was beneath mine—he, a mere scholar and poet—and my father had higher aspirations for me. Still, we couldn't deny our love and sought for moments together throughout London's social season. We spoke of eloping, but days later Phillip was killed in a duel by a brash and prideful count who was skilled with weaponry. Poor Phillip wasn't as well-versed with a pistol." She sadly shook her head as if lost in another time.

Letitia was stunned but finally understood why the dowager viscountess had become her dearest ally. She must have seen traces of the girl she'd once been in Letitia's mother.

"My aunt gave me this mask," she continued, her attention drifting to its shimmering front. "Lady Leighton. She wore it to her first masquerade ball, where she saved her true love, my uncle, from his cousin's evil scheme. The man pretended to be my uncle, hoping to get him killed by instigating a duel, and thereby receiving the title and lands that were Lord Leighton's. Ah, yes. In truth, this mask has quite a history. It's needed to be mended due to age, but it was said to be worn the night a young couple escaped Paris during the revolution. And also at a masquerade when a mysterious woman in red attempted to wreak havoc between a couple. But these stories I shall tell you another time."

Awed by the little she'd already heard, Letitia dropped her gaze to the mask.

"I want you to have it, Letitia. For your first masquerade ball. Perhaps you, too, might find your true love there."

Caught up in its past, Letitia took the proffered mask.

"Now, tell me about this Edward."

The abrupt change of topic brought Letitia's head up. "He's the marquis' manservant. A good man, kind and gentle. He's come to my aid twice."

"Do you love him?"

Taken aback by the abrupt question, Letitia only stared.

"Come, come. Do you love him?"

"I. . . Sí." Amazement swept through Letitia to realize the truth. "I think I might. But there is a matter that disturbs me." She smoothed her skirt's flounces, uncertain how to proceed. "His eyes, they. . .remind me of one of the highwaymen."

"Indeed?" Lady Ackers's brow furrowed as if in deep thought. "Have you shared this with anyone else?"

"No, I—I could not be certain." Letitia felt foolish. "The sun was bright, and the marquis possesses eyes of the same color."

Lady Ackers steadily regarded her. "Perhaps the strain from the ordeal confused you."

"Perhaps." Relief cloaked Letitia to hear the assumption she'd reached stated as fact.

"As to the matter of my granddaughter. . ."

Letitia stiffened. The mere mention of Marian brought back the pain of the attack.

"You needn't tell me what I witnessed was a rare occurrence; I know otherwise. Mayhap I should have spoken sooner." Lady Ackers straightened. "Be that as it may, I've talked to Hester and have decided to give to you early what I'd planned to bequeath to you upon my death. One hundred pounds, to be used as a dowry, if you wish it, or to sustain you until you find another position. If such is your preference, I shall do all within my power to find you gainful employment upon our return to London. Lady Fillmore seeks a governess for her children, and that family is mild mannered. You'd do well to find a position there."

Tears clouded Letitia's eyes. "You're dismissing me?"

"There, child, don't cry." Lady Ackers stroked Letitia's head, as if she were a small girl. "I cannot bear to see you further mistreated. I only desire your happiness."

"But I shall miss you. How can I be happy without your presence in my life?"

In a rare display of emotion, the old woman let her cane drop to the floor and gathered Letitia into her arms. "There, there. You're the daughter of which I've dreamed. Your name comes from the Latin and means 'joy,' did you know? And you've brought such joy to me in my old age. In thought and in heart, we'll never be far removed, no matter the distance that separates us. We're kindred spirits, you and I."

Closing her eyes, Letitia laid her head against Grandmama's shoulder, allowing the woman's slow rocking to soothe her. Letitia could only hope that this was indeed God's will for her life, but that didn't ease the ache within.

—⁓—

Catching sight of Letitia, Edward strode into the sitting room the family used for times of private worship. She stood looking at a framed portrait above the mantel. Uneasy, Edward followed her gaze.

Letitia glanced over her shoulder. Her expression grew stunned. "Edward."

"My lady." Since their kiss, he'd thought of little else but her. Yet his best recourse would be to keep that moment buried and not air apologies again. "The family came by that painting years ago. William Holman Hunt is the artist. The duchess requisitioned him to paint it after having viewed the original. She highly favors it and paid five hundred guineas, though I venture to guess it's worth far less."

"Oh, but who could put a price on anything so splendid? I believe some possessions are worth more in value than any monies can provide." Letitia returned her gaze to the painting. "It gives me such warmth to see our Lord Jesus standing near the door and clothed with lantern light against the darkness, His face so entreating, His hand raised to knock. He's always there for us, is He not? Always waiting for us to open the door to Him, assuring us that He's there."

"I wouldn't know."

The saddest expression clouded her face as she faced him. "You don't know or believe in the Savior, Edward?"

"He's never done much for me."

"Oh, but that's simply not true." Her smooth brow creased. She lifted her hands to her sides in supplication, stepping forward, as if in an effort to make him understand. "He died for you and gave His all so that you might live with Him for eternity."

Her beautiful eyes begged him to grasp her words. Despite his resolve to remain rigid in his unbelief, he was moved. She'd endured a lot, but so had he. How could she hold on to such faith? Why should she care that he did not?

"Sadly, the artist made a mistake," Edward said. "Have you noticed there's no handle on the outside of that bramble-covered door?" He'd stared upon the painting enough times to know.

She looked back to see. "Perhaps Mr. Hunt did so on purpose, to convey that one must open the door from within. The Lord is too much of a gentleman to walk inside uninvited."

Her words disturbed him more than he cared to admit. He gave a little bow. "I must attend to my duties." Before she could further argue her point, he left her company. An important meeting awaited, and he could tarry no longer.

<hr>

"Lady Letitia, will you take a turn about the room with me?"

Letitia looked up from her book in surprise to see Lady Eleanor, the marquis' sister, smiling down at her. A bold jaw resulting in something of an underbite and small eyes did little to detract from the woman's gentle beauty.

As always, Letitia was amused by the English nobility's tradition of strolling about the room when one wished to speak in confidence to another. No one sat near her on the settee, and the room was large enough that the four playing whist in the far corner wouldn't overhear. But she didn't wish to injure Eleanor's feelings and kept her thoughts to herself, setting the book aside. "Of course."

As they began to walk, Eleanor pulled Letitia's hand through her arm, drawing her close as if they were sisters.

"Dear Letitia, I've grown quite fond of you over this past week. You speak little, but when you do, your words are a delight." They walked past the duchess, the dowager viscountess, and two other women, all engrossed in their card game, past the fire blazing within the shoulder-high grate, and on toward the window that overlooked the manicured lawns. "I would venture a guess that my brother feels the same. He appears quite besotted by your company."

"The marquis?" Dismay pricked Letitia as she recognized the truth of Eleanor's words. These past three days William had sought her company often enough that his behavior must be noticed. Strangely, Marian said little when they were alone, for the most part ignoring Letitia, but the frown between her eyes indicated her displeasure concerning the situation.

"You appear distressed. Tell me, I must know. Is it only my imaginings?"

Letitia hesitated. The marquis' sister had become a friend, and Letitia didn't feel comfortable continuing the charade with her. "Lady Eleanor, forgive me, but I've not been forthcoming with you."

"Oh?"

"My station in life isn't as grand as I've portrayed. I'm but a simple companion to my cousin. An English earl's and Spanish count's granddaughter by blood, yes, but my father holds no title."

Halting her steps, Eleanor studied her. The pressure on Letitia's arm didn't decrease. "You have one day left with us. You could have kept silent, and I would never have been the wiser." An intelligent light filled her hazel eyes. "You have a reason for telling me this."

"Yes, I . . ." Letitia faltered, averting her gaze to the window and the maze beyond. How she had twisted things. "I ask pardon for baring my heart to you in what must seem an inappropriate manner, but I don't love your brother and fear I should have spoken earlier so as to discourage his advances."

"Indeed." It was a moment before Eleanor spoke. "Your heart belongs to another?"

"Sí." Relief seeped through her to tell the truth. "I hold. . .an affection for the marquis' servant, Edward. I've made his acquaintance such a short time, but I feel as if I've known him all my life." The frequent occasions she'd come across his path were some of the most precious to Letitia.

"Really? Well then, poor William will just have to pine his loss, eh?" Eleanor slyly smiled and squeezed Letitia's arm as they again took up their stroll until they came full circle to the settee. "Edward's a fine man. You could do no better."

"Yet his refusal to acknowledge God troubles me."

Eleanor's features clouded. "I understand. . . . Yet with you and me to petition the Lord on his behalf, he'll have no choice but to succumb to the truth. Yes?"

Letitia smiled. "Yes."

Once Eleanor left her, movement outside the window attracted Letitia's attention. She watched, puzzled. Though the men were supposed to be off on a shoot, three had just entered the maze.

Chapter 8

Letitia stared in wonder at the vision in the full-length cheval glass. Around her neck, Lady Ackers had hung a silver chain with the most brilliant opal.

"It reminds me of the moon," Letitia whispered. "The entire costume resembles moonlight."

"Ah, behold the moon," Grandmama said from behind her. "A shy maiden benevolently tending the earth, she sheds her pale light; a beacon to the weary traveler, a gentle radiance to a world laden with darkness. Daily her sister, the sun, blinds with her brilliance those who gaze upon her countenance. Attracted to her fire and magnificence, many pay little heed to the moon's gentle comeliness and disregard her when she visits the earth. Only those with a discerning eye observe the moon's hidden splendor, the splendor which the Creator bestowed only to her."

Letitia's cheeks flamed. Doubtless, Marian was the sun; yet could Letitia really be compared to something so beautiful as moonlight?

"Phillip wrote that," Grandmama said with a sigh. "An eternity ago."

Sensing Lady Ackers wanted to reminisce, Letitia kept silent. The voluminous ball gown of palest lavender satin bore fine vertical lines of sparkling silver that caught the light through the gossamer gauze she wore as an overlay. Layers of ruffles frothed from the gown's sleeves at the elbows. For the occasion, her hair had been curled, coifed, and powdered and now matched the gown—a shimmering soft lavender with strings of pearls for a headdress. The effect made her appear almost ethereal.

Letitia lifted the mask to her face and fastened its satin ties at the back. Her thoughts going to her cousin, she pivoted to face Lady Ackers. "May I ask a question?"

"Of course."

"I know it's none of my affair, and instruct me to mind my own business if you'd rather, but what did you say to my lady Marian?"

A sly smile lifted Grandmama's lips. "Relations between you have improved?"

"Tremendously. Oh, she still dislikes me; I can see that in her eyes. But the occasion is rare when she insults me or raises her voice."

"I told her the truth, a truth I shall tell you now. But it must never leave this room, Letitia. I stated that had your father preferred her mother over yours, she might be the one whose family had been disgraced and farming in Spain."

"What?"

"My dear child, Hester loved your father from the moment she set eyes on him, and a more dashing man I've never seen. She was jealous that her young sister had so wholly captured his affections. It was for spite that Hester told the earl your mother eloped with Roberto to Gretna Green before Kathryn had a chance to return home and soften his heart. I have no doubt your mother would have succeeded; she was the earl's favorite. But Hester hardened him against her. I learned the details years ago; she confessed her faults to me, admitting that in time, she'd grown to love my son. It was then that she asked permission to send for you since she felt she must do what she could to make reparation to her sister."

Amazement numbed Letitia's mind; she couldn't respond.

"Let us speak no more of the matter. Tonight, you shall shine like the Maiden of Moonlight for which Phillip penned the poem. But remember this, Letitia." She clasped an edge of the filmy gossamer. "These are merely outward trappings; forget not what is of true worth."

Letitia vowed not to forget but anticipated the evening. For one final night she would masquerade as someone greater than herself.

—⁂—

Bejeweled ladies in richly hued gowns of satin, silk, and velvet flitted past, introducing themselves by such allegorical titles as "Frost," "Last Rose of Summer," and "Evening Star." Stately gentlemen had dispensed with their normal black frock coats to don colorful garb for their oftentimes garish costumes, depicting characters from books and plays. All the guests wore matching masks or carried them on long sticks.

Letitia swept into the ballroom with Marian, whose shimmering gown of cloth of gold turned heads. With hair of deepest auburn and creamy-rose skin, even without her jewels, Marian as "The Golden Lorelei" was a sight to behold.

Discreetly hidden behind a decorative curtain of evergreens, a band of musicians played while couples performed a quadrille across the oak floor polished to a mirror gleam. The cloying scent of beeswax hung heavy in the air. Tonight, the gentry had flocked from the surrounding countryside. More than a hundred people were packed into the huge ballroom lit with candelabra, massive chandeliers, and wall sconces.

A short man in a moss green costume approached Letitia, introducing himself as Puck from Shakespeare's *A Midsummer Night's Dream*. He asked her to dance, but she declined. His affronted eyes stared at her through the slits in his mask, yet he bowed and departed. If she could dance, she would. Such dances might be considered effortless due to their mere walking, but the constant figures would be difficult to maneuver, and she didn't wish her leg to give way on the ballroom floor.

She socialized with the marquis' sister—robed in flowing white, with a garland of leaves and flowers woven in a circlet round her hair and a chain crossed over her waist as Tennyson's tragic "Lady of Shalott"—and with her stood Lady Carolyn Vaneers, a shy, sweet girl dressed in the deep gold and brown of "Autumn."

Suddenly, the marquis stood at Letitia's elbow. Instead of holding his glittering green mask to his eyes, he held it down by his side. "Will you dance with me, fair maiden? Or are you a sprightly fairy, having visited the earth to capture my heart?" He surveyed her ensemble. His own costume of counterchanged dark green and black stockings and tunic resembled a character from the Middle Ages.

"Neither, my lord." Even though he was unaware of her identity, Letitia raised her fan to her lips, recalling her resolve to discourage him. "I am Moonlight, and I prefer not to dance."

"Indeed?" His mouth firmed, but he turned to Carolyn. "Perhaps you will do me the honor?"

She curtseyed and accompanied him to the dance floor.

French doors to the moonlit terrace stood open in the next room, beckoning Letitia. The press of bodies had raised the room's temperature, and tendrils of hair stuck damply to her forehead.

The night air felt cool. Grateful no one else stood outside, she looked upward to the full moon. Glowing like a great pearl in a misty dark gray sky, it hovered over a grove of oak trees.

Footsteps on the paving arrested her attention. Startled, she turned.

"My lady?" Edward asked. "You are unwell?"

In his full livery of dark blue trimmed with gold, he was handsome. A moment elapsed before she captured enough breath to answer.

"I am well."

He nodded and made as if to go.

"Please, wait." At his evident surprise, she explained, "I should like the company."

His brows sailed upward. "You would rather converse with a servant than mingle with the fine lords and ladies gathered in disguise?"

"If that servant is you, I would." The words were bold, but behind the costume she felt safe from discovery.

He stared at her a long moment. "Might I have the honor of knowing whom I address?"

An imp of mischief took over, and she briskly fanned herself. "This is a masked ball, sir. To reveal my identity would break convention."

"Ah, a pity." He appeared amused. "Still, I don't wish to break convention. Henceforth, I suppose I shall have to address you as 'The Lady of Moonlight' since I have no other name to go by."

Letitia inhaled deeply as though struck. "For tonight, sir, indeed, you may call me Lady Luna."

"Luna. . .the Spanish term for moon. Is it not?"

She gave a slight nod.

Dawning light entered his eyes and he stepped forward. "Letitia, is it you?"

"Yes, Edward." She gave up her pretense and lowered the fan, suddenly grateful that he knew her identity.

"How stunning you look. When I heard the lilt of your accent, I should have known. You have a beautiful voice."

Letitia felt the kiss of a blush touch her face.

"But stay, why are you not dancing? Don't tell me it's from lack of partners."

"I cannot dance," she said simply. "But I love the music and watching the dancers. And I've found dressing up in costume to be most pleasurable." Indeed, she felt like a little girl again and giggled.

The softest expression drifted over his face. "There's much I wish to say, Letitia, so much I wish to share. . ." He blew out a frustrated breath. "Hang it all, I will speak. I've come to feel strongly about you. Dare I hope my feelings might be returned?"

"I. . ." Shock robbed her of words, but any reply was eclipsed as the duchess swept onto the terrace. She seemed astonished to see Letitia, with Edward standing so close, but quickly regained her composure.

"His lordship requests your presence, Edward." The duchess lifted her beaded mask on its stick, casting a curious glance Letitia's way before she regally entered the ballroom again.

"I suppose our conversation must wait." Edward's words were tense, though he produced a smile. "Tomorrow, before you leave for London, may we speak further on this matter?"

"Of course."

To her shocked delight, he lifted her gloved hand to his mouth. The gentle pressure of his lips on her fingers caused her heart to palpitate madly, and the steady look in his eyes captured her breath. "Until tomorrow, dear lady, I am your servant." He inclined his head in a slight bow.

Long after he entered the manor, her gaze remained on the last place she'd seen him.

Their encounter adding an extra layer of warmth to her overheated skin, Letitia strolled in the coolness of the night. Flickers of torchlight caught her attention at the front of the manor where blazing flambeaux illuminated the walkway and couples gathered.

She could scarcely believe that Edward cherished her as she'd come to love him. Was it possible? Could he find her a position at Heppelwith so she could remain by his side forever? Lady Eleanor would surely speak for them.

Buoyant as a crested wave, she drifted toward the maze. A flicker glowed through the bushes. Curious, she moved toward the flame. Men's voices rose in furious whispers.

"We shall proceed with the robbery after dawn as planned."

"I don't like it. Since that Spanish wench opened her mouth, there's been nothing but trouble. Mark my words, it was her who alerted the duke to our presence here. We should have done away with her when we had the chance."

"And I told you, I don't condone murder. I've taken care of the matter. She's not as acquiescent as the dear Lady Salinger, but doubtless I'll win her over. Once I claim her heart and have brought his lordship to ruin, nothing will stop us. I'll have what I want, and you'll have your gold."

Pressing her fingers to her open mouth, Letitia retreated a step. The gauze of her dress caught the bushes. She tore it free.

"What was that?" one of the men asked.

Letitia spun around in alarm. The familiar weakness struck her hip, and she staggered, grabbing the yew wall. At the loud rustle she winced and attempted to hurry away.

"Stop her!"

An iron-muscled arm wrapped around her, stalling her escape and her breath. She blinked back fear as the leader of the highwaymen came to stand before her.

No. . . I—it cannot be.

He pulled the mask from her face. A pained but resolute expression firmed his jaw.

"Ah, Letitia. Why? Why could you not have made this simplest for everyone by merely accepting my advances and minding your own affairs? If you had, I wouldn't need to do what I'm forced to do now." He nodded to the men standing behind her.

Each of them grabbed one of her arms.

"No!" Letitia fought to get free, but she was no match for their strength. "What will you do with me?"

His hand lifted, and the backs of his fingers stroked her cheek. "That, my lovely Letitia, is up to you." His fingers traced down to her jaw.

Angry tears glazing her eyes, she wrenched her head away from his touch. She never should have trusted him. He possessed the power to do whatever he willed with her. There was no one to stop him, no one to save her. Save for one.

Sálvame, mi Diós. . . My God, save me.

Chapter 9

"Edward?"

Upon hearing Lady Ackers's voice, Edward turned and affected a slight bow as the dowager viscountess came to stand before him.

The woman harrumphed. "Now then, none of that. I seek Lady Letitia Laslos, who tonight bears the name of 'Moonlight.' No one has seen her for some time."

"I was with her more than an hour ago."

"Hmm. My Abigail found this near the maze." Lady Ackers handed him a white mask that appeared to have been crumpled underfoot. His heart plummeted when he recognized the bent feathers and seed pearls.

Letitia.

"I will get to the bottom of this. I assure you, she will be found."

"With you in charge, I don't doubt it. Notify me the moment she's located, Edward."

"Very good." He inclined his head.

A wry look entered her eyes. "You do that too well."

He was saved a reply as she turned and made for the stairs. Recalling Letitia's talk of overhearing the highwaymen, he alerted the house servants, and the search for Letitia quietly commenced.

One hour passed.

Two.

Then three.

After the fourth hour, Edward was beyond concern. Had he acted sooner, had he dispensed with his foolish scheme of which few approved, she would be by his side now. He was certain she'd been taken—but where? Was she alive? She had to be! He couldn't endure it if he lost her, too, the only woman he'd ever come to love. Now he realized how immense that love was. Could it be possible to feel so strongly about another on such short acquaintance?

Once Edward was so confident, attributing his position in life to his hard work and little else; now he felt utterly lost. Earlier, he'd combed the maze and grounds. Unsuccessful, he took his search to the manor. Room after room. Nothing.

Entering the empty chamber with the painting, the last place he knew to look, he glanced toward it. He could envision her standing there, her dark eyes wide, her hands lifted in entreaty for him to recognize and share her faith.

Moisture rimmed his eyes. "She belongs to You!" His heated words addressed the silent figure in the painting. "Why has this happened? If You're a merciful God, as she says, help me to find her—if You truly care so much. I cannot lose her, too!"

The lone figure wavered before him, and Edward dashed the tears from his lashes until the portrait was steady again. The expression of Christ in the portrait was so understanding, tender, compassionate. . . . The eyes seemed to beckon to him. . . to assure him that God's hope was the anchor on which he must now rely.

Inside Edward, something broke.

His palms hit the mantel, his head bowed low, while great gulping sobs he couldn't contain bellowed forth from the depths of his soul.

—⁓—

Letitia awoke to darkness most foul. Her arms ached where they'd been roughly handled, and what felt like strips of leather sawed into her ankles and wrists. Her jaw smarted from the scratchy gag bound across her mouth. She struggled to collect her senses.

The odors of horseflesh and hay led her to believe she'd been secreted away in the stable; there was no light to see. As if in answer, a horse's soft whinny and snort ruffled the air close by. She lay upon dirt, the chill seeping into her bones. A shelter stood overhead; she could hear the rain's patter strike wood and trickle through a crack. Water dripped onto her skirt with frequent splats. Its uncomfortable wetness had seeped through her skirt and petticoats. Shifting her legs, she winced as they strained against the tether, which cut more deeply into her skin.

Her mind couldn't grasp the truth. It made no sense. Why should he consort with unsavory characters? There appeared to be no rational explanation.

Closing her eyes, she succumbed to weariness.

When next she awoke, darkness still pervaded, but she could hear someone shouting far away. Calling her name.

Against the gag, she cried out, then raised her bound feet and kicked the wood. But her shouts came muffled, her actions weak. Frustrated tears burned her lashes and ran into her ears.

Please, Diós mio, let them hear. Forgive my foolishness in desiring to be someone I'm not. I've harbored bitterness because I wasn't one of the peerage, because I'm considered an underling to my cousin, something only You've known, something I was too ashamed to confess even to Grandmama. If I could again be given opportunity to serve Marian—and be warm and safe—I would be content; I would be obedient. Never again would I complain about my lot in life. Deliver me from those who would harm me.

Time passed. The rain ceased. Again her mind drifted.

Light behind her eyelids woke her, and she opened them to see dim gray light filtering through the cracks. She weakly moved her head and saw that she was nailed into a crawl space smaller than a closet and couldn't lie straight without her feet or head touching the walls. Focusing on the light, she tried to form prayers.

Cheery whistling broke her concentration. Her limbs stiff with cold, her hip aching fiercely, she raised her legs and kicked the wall. The thump was hardly effectual, and she tried again. And again. The whistling stopped. Footsteps crunched closer.

Letitia kicked again, forcing her raw throat to emit grunts. She saw wide eyes peer through the crack.

"Blimey, I'll have you out in a jiffy, miss." More footsteps, then the creaking of wood being pried, and a rectangle of daylight appeared as a plank tore away. The young stable boy stooped to look. "You stay right there, miss. I'll fetch help."

Where would she go? Letitia closed her eyes, assured her rescue was at hand.

Soon she heard more boards being torn away with fury, and blissful light covered her. Pressure weighted her wrists and ankles as a knife sawed through the cords. The gag was unbound from her mouth. Strong arms lifted her with ease and held her with supreme gentleness. She laid her cheek against the muscled shoulder beneath a coat that felt like serge and forced herself to look at him.

The eyes of peace stared back at her.

"Edward," she rasped, her throat like fire. Weary, her eyelids fluttered closed again.

"Shh." His lips brushed her forehead. "You're safe."

She was barely aware of him carrying her to the manor or upstairs to the room she shared with Marian. But when Edward laid her upon the counterpane, she roused enough to grab his sleeve. "You must stop him."

"Who?"

"The marquis. He robs Lord Bellingham this morn." With that, she fell back, and her fatigued mind and body relinquished themselves to rest.

Chapter 10

Inside the carriage, alone, Edward grimly recounted the facts. How could he have been so blind? Despite the little information he'd gleaned, he hadn't wanted to believe the truth, had avoided it for weeks. But there it was, staring him in the face. He'd been a fool! And he'd almost lost the woman he loved because of his folly.

To find Letitia bound and gagged. So pale. . .at first he'd thought her dead. The sick feeling returned, the abject fear that he might have lost her, the terrible ache in the center of his being, but he forced such memories away. She was safe and warm, and he must keep his mind on the present situation.

Almighty Father, I'm new in my service to You. I humbly ask that You help me to be successful this day, to remember Your Son is the anchor to which I must hold. I cannot accomplish this in my own strength.

When the shouts of riders came, Edward was ready. Before Lord Bellingham's carriage rolled to a full stop, he withdrew his pistol and flung open the door. There was a scurry of surprise, but he aimed his weapon at William before he or his men could get a bead on Edward.

"It's over, *Lord Dalworth*," he stiffly addressed the kerchiefed rider on horseback, who wore a brace of pistols, one on each side. "Tell your men to throw down their weapons."

Instead, William made a frantic grab for one of his guns. Edward was saved shooting him when five riders burst through the trees on horseback, pistols aimed at the three.

The two highwaymen threw down their firearms. William lifted his hands in the air, his chuckle terse. "Bully for you, Edward. You win. This time."

Instead of rising to the bait as he'd done all his life, Edward walked toward him. "You possess something that doesn't belong to you. Allow me to relieve you of it."

William glared but pulled off the loose ring that had slipped around his finger and placed it in Edward's outstretched hand.

"You almost killed her!" Edward tightened his hold on the ring, attempting a calm he didn't feel. What he desired was to pull the man from his horse and knock him senseless.

"I was confident you'd find her in that storage area where we played as children. And you did, didn't you? Otherwise, you wouldn't be here. But if not for me, my men would have killed her."

As the constable led him away, hands bound, William called, "She's not the type to wink at lies and deceit as Lady Salinger did. She'll never forgive you, Edward."

He bit back a reply. In his heart, he prayed such wasn't the case.

—⁓—

Letitia dressed, anxious as to why she was being summoned. Three days she'd remained bedridden to regain her health and strength. Except for Grandmama, the Ackers party had returned home to London. Soon, Letitia must go, too. Yet she'd learned a hard lesson. Just as the marquis had hidden behind his title to do evil, she'd hidden behind her masquerade, desiring to be someone she wasn't. Well, no longer. From this day forward, she would accept her role in life, whatever that may be. She would be content and embrace each day cheerfully. Having almost lost the opportunity, Letitia was grateful to receive a new start.

She'd been shocked to discover Marian had imparted helpful information to Grandmama, telling how she'd observed three men with Letitia near the maze. Later, she'd recognized one of them by his fairy-like costume as Puck on the outside steps and had eavesdropped on their conversation. Both men were upset that William prevented them from killing Letitia, and they'd quietly discussed returning to end the deed. Near dawn, Edward learned the information and met the stable boy running with news of finding her.

While Marian's farewell to Letitia days ago had been devoid of emotion, Letitia knew she had her cousin to thank for saving her life and told her so. Marian had flushed as if uncertain how to respond but hadn't pulled away when Letitia gently squeezed her hands in farewell.

Following a servant, Letitia entered the private parlor in which she'd glimpsed Edward walking with the duchess on her first morning at Heppelwith. The duke stood near a gold-veined marble fireplace, and Eleanor sat on a damask-covered chair. Edward stood near her. Seeing Letitia, the girl smiled and moved to embrace her.

"I'm pleased to see you fully recovered, Letitia, and I'm confident there are others here who share my sentiments." She glanced at Edward, whose face had reddened. "Alas, I must attend to my morning correspondence. We shall converse at tea, as we have much to discuss. Father?" She went to him and affectionately took hold of his arm.

The duke sternly eyed his daughter, though Letitia noted he patted the hand at his sleeve. "Very well, Eleanor. I'm not dim-witted. I'll leave you to it then, Edward. I must tend to my songbirds." The two left the room.

Puzzled, Letitia waited. Edward pulled at his cravat, looking ill at ease. For the first time, she noticed he wasn't in his livery. Had he been dismissed?

She sank to the cushion. "Edward?"

He moved to the opposite chair, looked at her, then shot to his feet and began to pace. "First, it's imperative you know I'm not a man who practices deceit. I had a sharp blow dealt me shortly after my arrival from India. My betrothed had proven to be a woman of immoral character."

Letitia swallowed over a dry throat. This had been the first she'd heard that his heart was attached to another.

"So as to avoid her further pain, the engagement, arranged by my father, was quietly dissolved, but the experience bred caution within me. I don't intend to return to India without a wife. No one of eligibility resides there—the few English women are married or are too young—and it's time I settle down."

Again he nervously pulled at his cravat, so hard, it went askew. "I devised a scheme to select a woman I could love who could love me in return. For such a plan to succeed, I had to take drastic measures. My family wasn't in favor of the idea, but neither did they prevent me from following through with it. The recent robberies aided in their acquiescence, due to the fact that the first victims who'd been robbed are dear family friends. In my role, I was able to investigate the matter, piece together facts. That's why I was in London."

"Oh," Letitia managed to breathe. She tightly clasped her hands in her lap. A sense of unreality teased her mind. Perhaps she was dreaming. This must be a dream.

He returned to his chair and brought it closer to hers. "My desire was to find a woman of virtue. One loyal and true. A woman who would bestow the same consideration to a servant that she would to a nobleman. However, in order to seek such a woman, it was imperative that I conceal my identity. How else would I know she wasn't playing me false for selfish gain? I'd been deceived once and couldn't let it happen again. Do you understand, Letitia?"

Face afire, she could only stare. Her spinning mind desperately rejected the words he had yet to say.

He leaned forward, covering her cold hands with his warm ones. "I am Lord Edward Dalworth. The marquis."

His face blurred. She desperately tried to force rational thought, to force any words to her lips at all.

Alarm lightened his eyes. Grasping her shoulders, he settled her back against the cushion and poured something into a glass. He put it under her nose, but she shook her head.

"Drink," he commanded.

One small sip of the bitter brew burning down her throat was enough to revive her. Disgusted with herself, she pushed his hand holding the glass away. She wasn't one to swoon. She must still be weak from her ordeal.

"What of Lord Dal—I mean, Lord William? Or. . .whoever he is?"

"He's my cousin. We both work for our uncle in India. My father and my uncle, Lord Hathaway, own a silk plantation there. William's father also had a smaller share, but he died of malaria."

"He robbed us." The words were inane, but Letitia couldn't think of anything intelligent to say.

"I apologize for the harm William caused. While he masqueraded as me, I learned of his plan to implicate me in the robberies."

"But I'd seen him, heard their plans! I knew he was the one."

His eyes were grave. "It would have been your word against his. He knew of my feelings concerning you and could have easily turned your words around to suggest that you were protecting me."

Letitia dropped her gaze. He needn't elaborate; no English court would believe the word of a domestic over that of a nobleman.

"He desired to take everything I possessed. I learned quite recently that he was the one to rob me of my fiancée by wooing her. Poor Lady Salinger." Edward sighed, briefly looking to his hands clasped between his knees. Letitia could now see his ring with the family seal, the same ring William had worn all week. "I should have suspected his involvement, but he covered his tracks well and pretended to be a friend. Doubtless he hoped to rob me of my title by having me sent to prison and achieve a higher position with our uncle in managing the affairs of the plantation."

"Is that what you do?" she whispered.

He smiled. "I manage the accounts. You would love India."

"I?"

"Of course. Don't you understand what I'm saying?"

She shook her head.

"Dearest Letitia, I wish to marry you."

Again her mind grew vacant. She sought for words. "But I'm not. My mother—"

"Was a lady who committed no crime. I know all about your so-called family scandal. I've talked long with the dowager viscountess this past week. As have my parents. You've won my father over with your spirit; you're the only one besides family who's ever exhibited enough courage to stand up to his bluster." He grinned. "And my patient sister was forced to hear the workings of my heart these whole miserable ten days."

"But"—Letitia shook her head—"I cannot marry you. I've never been presented to the Queen."

He chuckled. "That can be arranged. Lady Ackers seemed confident you would be agreeable. She sent a letter to Her Majesty, Queen Victoria, three days past."

Letitia stared, hardly daring to believe what was happening.

"Yet perhaps the lady dowager erred, and you don't return my feelings?"

At the worry in his eyes, she was quick to speak. "No, Edward. I've had great affection for you since the night you rescued me in London and took me into your coach." Her cheeks warmed. "It was *your* coach?" Of course it was. The knowledge that Edward was the marquis and not William still bewildered her.

"Yes." He shifted his gaze, again looking ill at ease. "Letitia, can you possibly forgive me for deceiving you by letting you assume I was a servant?"

She gave a faint smile. "It seems we both engaged in a masquerade. You as a servant, and I as a lady of worth."

"Ah, but Letitia. . ." He took hold of her hands, bringing her up with him as he rose to his feet. "You are indeed a lady of great worth."

He gathered her close to his heart, and Letitia relaxed her head near his shoulder. There was much more to say, much more to learn, but for now she was content to be held by the man she loved.

Epilogue

Clothed in a gown of silver, Letitia stood beside Edward on the plantation's open verandah and watched their guests dance. From behind, a night bird called out from somewhere beyond the fringe of mango trees. A monkey chattered, setting off a chain of jungle music as the strains of violins produced their own melody in the ballroom. The air was warm, the scents heady with nearby branches of frangipani. Letitia loved this beautiful, dangerous, exotic land, which no longer seemed foreign to her after having lived in it for almost three years.

"I would say that our first masquerade ball is a success, wouldn't you, my love?" Edward took hold of her gloved hand and kissed it.

"Oh yes. Quite."

Childish giggling reached her ears, and Letitia looked to see their curly-headed daughter peering round the wall, bare toes peeking from beneath her white night-dress, a crumpled costume mask of the same color held to her eyes.

"Regina," Edward warned, "shouldn't you be in bed?"

"Don' wan' bed, Papa." The girl scampered to her father's arms, and he hoisted her up. She kissed his cheek with a loud smack.

"Memsahib!" A young native woman with copper skin and a colorful tunic rounded the corner, out of breath. "Little missy leave her bed. She play in *memsahib's* trunk with pretty dresses, then run away from her *ayah* when I was not watching."

"Never mind, Yanni," Letitia told the child's nurse. "I'll tend to her."

"And you will read to the servant children again about the miracles of Jesus? I like to hear them, too."

"Tomorrow. I promise." Letitia was happy that Yanni had recently accepted the Lord. After two years of difficult communication and improving on the servants' English, Letitia had finally gotten through to them with the message of the Gospel while learning their language, too.

"I will tell them." Before leaving, the girl smiled and pressed her palms together, bowing her head and bringing her fingers to her forehead in a respectful *namaste*.

"As for you, young lady, you're being very naughty." Letitia studied her two-year-old daughter.

Regina gave the sweetest pout, wrapping her plump little arms across her chest. "Don' wan' bed."

The all-day excitement of preparations for the ball had buoyed everyone's spirits, especially the children's.

"If Mamá tells you the stories behind the mask, will you try?"

"Sto'ies?" Interest lit Regina's big brown eyes. She laid her head against Edward's shoulder and yawned. The hand holding the white satin mask hung down by her side.

"*Sí, mi niña.* The mask is almost one hundred years old and has many wonderful stories of adventure, including mine and Papá's. But you must be a good girl and do as you're told. Then I'll tell you all its wonderful stories." She kissed the small dimpled hand.

Regina's eyes drooped, the long lashes sweeping over rosy cheeks. "Mamá tew sto'ies."

"Tomorrow you shall hear them," Edward promised then smiled at Letitia. "I'll put her to bed."

During his absence, Letitia again looked from her place on the verandah toward their thirty-eight costumed guests. Eleanor was visiting from England and was dancing with a British officer, a titled lord in whom she'd recently expressed interest. Judging from his unwavering attentions, Letitia felt certain the girl's affection was returned. Eleanor brought news from home, too, of Marian, who recently gave birth to her firstborn son, having married a wealthy viscount twice her age. And Grandmama Ackers, as feisty as ever, had sent word that she planned to visit India for her upcoming sixty-first birthday, bringing Letitia's parents with her.

Letitia smiled, eagerly anticipating the celebration she would hold. She hadn't seen her parents or the dowager viscountess since before Edward and she had left for India directly after their marriage. First, they'd visited Spain, and with Edward's consent, she'd given her parents the hundred pounds Grandmama had given to her.

Hearing strains of a waltz begin, Letitia swayed to the music while staring up at the huge moon on its velvet canvas of black sky, bigger and brighter than it had ever been in all of England.

Sensing Edward behind her, she smiled when his hand slid around her waist then gasped as his other hand went beneath her legs and he swung her up into his arms. Automatically her arms flew around his neck. Nearby torches caught the mischievous twinkle in his blue-gray eyes.

"Edward, what are you doing?" She laughed. "What will the guests say if they see?"

"I don't care," he said. "Ever since I saw you that night three years ago on my father's terrace at the masquerade ball, I've wanted to dance with you. Conventions denied me the pleasure of holding you in my arms then. My one regret is that I waited this long."

She smoothed her hand along his lean jaw. "I've always wished I could dance," she admitted. "And to do so with my husband whom I dearly love would please me."

"Then, my Lady of the Moonlight, your wish is my command."

He brushed a tender kiss across her lips before beginning to waltz with expert grace. While in the starry skies above, the great disk of the moon bathed them in its gentle glow.

FAYRE ROSE

by Tamela Hancock Murray

Dedication

To my husband, John
My knight in shining armor for twenty years.

Chapter 1

P lease, Laird Kenneth. Have mercy!" Witta Shepherd touched one knee to the ground and bowed his head. "If I had the few farthings ye request, I would hand them over without question." He trembled despite the summer heat.

Why do they ask for more than we can give? Fayre felt her own body tense and then shake as she witnessed the scene between her father, Laird Kenneth, and two of his knights. The longer she watched her aged father's humiliation, the hotter her emotions became. Rage and fright threatened to display themselves, but as a mere serf, she couldn't afford such luxury. Only a fine lady of the king's court could dare express displeasure to an exalted laird and his vassals.

Mounted upon fine stallions, the knights were an intimidating lot. The animals looked grand, dressed as they were in horses' cloaks depicting the familiar plaid cover the laird wore, a yellow background nearly covered with horizontal and vertical stripes of varying widths in red, black, blue, and green. Whenever Fayre saw the cloth, she couldn't help but feel prideful that her father's land was part of such a powerful and prestigious kingdom. Yet she chafed under the complete obedience the laird demanded.

She didn't mind so much for herself. A woman's lot in life was to be considered nothing more than chattel. Didn't the priest say that the heavenly Father commanded men not to covet their neighbors' wives? If she doubted a wife's status as property, the Lord God's words left no uncertainty.

She knew that several of the men in the village had an eye for her, but Fayre returned none of their interest. Her friends thought her silly and vain. They tried to convince her that marriage wasn't about affection. The arrangement was a contract made between two families for the betterment of both parties. She knew her friends were right, but even watching them take their vows—the first one when she was twelve—left her with not enough envy of their status to convince her to follow. Why would she want to leave her father, who in his kind ways would never lay a hand on her, for a rough man who would think nothing of beating her should she oppose his will? Fayre shuddered and said yet another silent prayer of thanks to God that even though she was nearing the age of twenty, her father hadn't demanded that she wed.

Witta Shepherd didn't deserve to be embarrassed, to be treated by the laird as nothing more than a stubborn beast. Fayre had never hated the tartan as much as she did at that moment. Her eyelids narrowed so much that they hurt. She could just see out of the slits they had formed. She widened them before the laird could see her sign of ire and command his men to kill her, too.

Laird Kenneth, wearing a suit of light armor minus the headpiece, sat bolt upright, surveying the flocks and fields that Fayre's father had tended all these many years. He placed a flat palm and extended fingers above his eyes and studied the rolling hills, covered with fine grass for the sheep to feast upon. His gaze stopped and rested upon the two-room cottage in the distance where Fayre and her father had lived as long as she could remember. She thought back to the days when her mother sang songs—happy tunes she remembered from the traveling minstrels playing in the village—as she spun wool at the wheel. Those days, the ones before Fayre's mother went to live with the Father in heaven, were the happiest she had ever known.

Ever since Fayre's mother had died, sadness had followed Witta. His hair turned from gray to white almost overnight. The skip left his step. Her death extinguished the fire in his eyes. He was left with a gentleness of spirit, but one that was more resigned than joyful.

Fayre forced herself to stop daydreaming, to bring her attention back to the present moment. The knights wore contempt on their faces, regarding Witta like a faded flower whose time to be discarded had arrived. If only he would say something, anything, to defend himself and her. But Fayre knew he didn't dare. A serf, even an elderly male serf who enjoyed respect among the local villagers, dared not speak against the laird.

Fayre watched Laird Kenneth's appraisal travel from the hut to the vegetable and herb garden Fayre maintained for their subsistence. She could just make out their rooster strutting near the garden and hut. Hens clucked and scratched at the ground, unaware that one of them would be snatched for the evening's dinner come sundown. The two goats they depended upon for milk and cheese bleated in between chomping on clumps of thistles and grass.

Such a humble existence could hardly be the envy of a prominent laird, yet the greedy look in his eyes was unmistakable. He would gladly seize everything the poor shepherd owned so he could grant the land to one of his arrogant vassals, no doubt. The thought caused flaming ire to rise in the pit of her stomach, leaving her feeling volatile. She forced herself to put aside her feelings long enough to send up a silent prayer.

Heavenly Father, dinna let the laird take away what little my father has left.

At that moment, Fear tapped its icy finger on her shoulder, reminding Fayre that humble possessions were the least of her worries. The laird and his knights could easily slaughter the two of them on the spot, leaving their lifeless bodies to wilt in the sun-drenched field, undiscovered for days. Even then, Laird Kenneth and his vassals would go unpunished. Who would dare approach such an important man, a member of the landed gentry, a member of the king's court, with accusations concerning an insignificant shepherd and his virgin daughter?

With a renewed attitude of humility, Fayre murmured, "Blessed Savior, my divine God from whom all courage and strength is gathered, protect us."

"How dare you challenge me!" Rich with authority, Laird Kenneth's voice cut through the air.

Fayre startled. Was the laird forbidding her to utter a small prayer? She wondered how to respond until she realized the great man was looking directly upon her father. Her plea had gone unnoticed, at least by Laird Kenneth.

"King David has a war to fight," the laird said. "Victory will ensure he is granted his rightful position as king of France. Do you not see that by neglecting to pay your taxes, you are denying His Majesty's army the means to fight for the independence of our fair Scotland?"

Fayre could see the distress on her father's face. "My laird, I would happily give every coin in my possession to the king if I were in possession of any." He sent the laird a begging look. "Wouldst ye accept as payment my best ewe?"

The laird straightened himself in his saddle, his body stiffening into a rigid line. "I know we settled on a ewe as payment last time, but I cannot accept an animal in exchange for your rent on every occasion. In any event, you cannot afford to give away so much livestock, and the king needs gold to exchange for supplies and men."

A frantic light pierced Witta's dim eyes. "My laird, the season hasna been good. The Black Death has taken so many people that the need for wool and mutton is less. The marketplace stays empty." He looked at the goats. "Nanny will be giving birth soon. Her new baby will take her milk, leaving even less food for us." He bowed his head. "I beg yer forgiveness."

After making his plea, Witta allowed his other knee to fall to the ground. With agility uncommon for one so elderly, he leaned his head, sparsely decorated with white strands of hair, over his bent knees until his nose met the ground. Outstretched palms, touching the soil, trembled. The sight caused Fayre's heart to feel as though it were tumbling into the abyss of her abdomen.

"Silence!" Laird Kenneth raised his hand. "Perhaps a few weeks in the dungeon will teach you a lesson." He nodded once to his knights.

In haste, they drew their lances from their leather sheaths. The long poles were now trained forward in the direction of her father. The knights readying themselves to commit murder, their eyes took on a cast as cold as Fayre imagined their hearts must have been. She gasped and looked in the direction of her father. He prostrated himself on the earth.

"Nae!" Shouting, Fayre hastened toward the men with such fury, she felt her long braids slap on her back with each step.

The unexpected motion scared Laird Kenneth's horse into rearing. The others startled and snorted in response. As the riders soothed the animals with comforting clucks of their tongues, Fayre was thankful she had stopped the vassals from taking her father into custody—at least for the moment.

After his white stallion's front hooves returned to the ground, Laird Kenneth snapped his head in her direction. His gaze caught Fayre's, the metallic silver hue of his eyes matching the point of his javelin. His unremitting gaze left her feeling no less wounded than if she had been stricken by the forked lightning of God's wrath. He addressed Witta. "Who is this maiden?"

Fayre curtsied so low she thought she might topple.

"My laird." Though he remained in his obsequious position, her father's voice was strong as his eyes met Laird Kenneth's. "She is my daughter, Fayre."

Rising, Fayre looked into Laird Kenneth's face. Golden eyebrows arched, indicating his interest. A straight nose gave way to full lips that were parted to reveal a nobleman's even, white teeth. Fayre averted her eyes to the reed basket in the crook of her arm. It contained a lunch of milk and a sliver of cheese, plus bread and mutton baked in ovens provided by Laird Kenneth.

"Fayre," she heard Laird Kenneth say. "Fair indeed."

Fair? Her rage and fear liquefied into curiosity and unfamiliar stirrings. *How can he think me fair? I am but his serf, and my plain brown garment tells him so.*

Her doubts seemed to be confirmed by the knights' boisterous laughter. "Aye, my laird," one of the vassals agreed. His voice was hearty in a way that made her wish to throw her arms over her body in a vain attempt to shield herself from his lusty stare.

Feeling her cheeks flush, Fayre nevertheless summoned the courage to hold up her head. She deliberately ignored the plainspoken knight and set her gaze upon Laird Kenneth's face. Where she expected to see a vision of greed and desire, she saw instead the soft look of compassion and kind interest. His benevolent expression gave her the courage to speak.

"I most humbly beg yer pardon, my laird." Fayre wondered if her voice, soft with fright, was loud enough to conceal the sound of her racing heart. "I bring my father his food each day when the sun is high in the sky."

"And the flower you hold?" Like his countenance, Laird Kenneth's voice was soft. Was that a flicker of tenderness she spotted in those steely eyes?

She had forgotten the rose from her garden, even though she brought one to her father each day. "Fayre Rose," Father always said. "Ye bring beauty tae the world around ye."

"My laird," she answered, "the rose is from my garden."

"Never have I seen a rose with such brilliance, the color of the setting sun," the knight with reddish hair observed.

"Nor have I," agreed the other knight.

Laird Kenneth extended his hand to take the bloom, which Fayre willingly sacrificed. He studied its petals, touching each one with the gentleness a besotted bridegroom would reserve for his beloved damsel according to songs she had once heard traveling minstrels sing in the village. An approving smile touched his lips. "Lovely."

He tossed the flower back to Fayre. Too frightened to move, she allowed it to land at her feet. Filled with compassion upon seeing the bruised bloom, she bent and retrieved it. She felt the eyes of the men upon her but ignored them.

"Do you have a brother who can tend these sheep?" the laird wanted to know.

"Nay, my laird, she doesna," Witta answered on her behalf.

Laird Kenneth nodded for him to rise to his feet. "And why not?"

"The plague," he whispered and bowed his head toward the ground in a manner of defeat.

"Aye." Laird Kenneth nodded to show he understood. He redirected his attention to Fayre. "Then I fear you shall be spending less time among the blooms in your garden. You shall need to take your father's place here in the fields. Perchance you can produce profit enough to render his debt. Only then will he be released from prison."

"Then he shall never be released!" Her voice rising in pitch, Fayre motioned toward Witta. "Can ye nae see my father is old? Ye, my valiant laird, are a man whose honor lies in following the teachings of our Lord and Savior, Jesus Christ. How can ye consider taking a man so well along in years tae a filthy prison? Surely the Lord would not wish my father tae die in the dungeon! And die he will, if he maun spend even a moment among the dirt and rats!" Passion intense, Fayre stamped her foot. At that moment, she realized her hands had fisted so tightly that her fingernails dug into her palms. She knew she looked like a tempestuous child, but her anger was too great for her to exercise more self-control.

"Then perhaps the bonny lass has favors she would care to exchange for her father's freedom," the redheaded knight offered.

Fayre shivered despite the heat. She glanced sideways at Witta. Her father was too feeble to defend her. She would be forced to submit to whatever they desired. And with Witta so near, yet so helpless.

Father in heaven, please—

"Please!" Witta's voice, stronger now, echoed aloud her silent prayer.

"Enough!" Laird Kenneth's voice slashed through the innuendo. "Have you forgotten the knight's code of honor?"

"Nay," the redhead admitted. He nodded toward Fayre. "But this one is a mere serf."

"Do you not remember Saint Paul's epistle to the Galatians?" Laird Kenneth reminded him. " 'There is neither Jew nor Greek, there is neither bond nor free, there is neither male nor female: for ye are all one in Christ Jesus.' "

Fayre was just as quick to recall a pertinent verse: *"Hypocrite, cast first the beam out of thy own eye; and then shalt thou see clearly to take out the most from thy brother's eye."* She wished she could tell Laird Kenneth then and there about the large beam in his eyes, but her life depended upon her silence. She swallowed.

To her relief, the laird's words brought a shamed look to his knight's face. "I beg pardon," he muttered.

Fayre breathed an inward sigh of relief. Perhaps he was a hypocrite, but the laird's words had saved her from an unspeakable fate.

Despite Fayre's previous display of temper, a soft light flickered in Laird Kenneth's eyes as he returned his attention to her. "And my apologies, Fayre. My vassals can be obtuse at times." He paused.

"I beg pardon, woman," the knight said.

"Very well." The laird nodded to his knight. "As for the matter at hand, I do not wish the death of your father. But since he cannot pay his taxes, I fear he leaves me no other choice but to confine him to the dungeon until the debt is paid."

"But of course ye have a choice!" When she heard the shrewish tone of her own voice, Fayre knew she risked her life with such words. Nevertheless, she held herself upright, to her full height.

"Nay, I do not. If I were to favor your father, every serf in the kingdom would expect leniency."

"Then I shall go," Witta said.

Fayre shook her head at her father, despite the disobedience the gesture represented. "Nay," she whispered.

"But the rose, my laird," the second knight interrupted.

Laird Kenneth turned his attention to the knight. "The rose? What of it?"

"If I may be so bold, I am of the opinion that the royal court would be pleased by such lovely blossoms."

Laird Kenneth returned his gaze to the rose that Fayre held. He nodded. "Indeed."

"I propose we take the maiden to your estate," his vassal said. "Let her cultivate the roses in your garden. When you present them to the ladies of King David's court, the whole of them shall be delighted and look upon my laird with even greater favor."

Laird Kenneth's expression became thoughtful. He turned back to Fayre. His eyes searched her face. "Could you do that?"

"Aye, my laird. But. . ." She hesitated to raise an objection, but the thought of leaving her father alone so she could go live in a castle was not agreeable.

"But?"

"Ye need not cultivate the roses at yer estate," Fayre offered. "Ye may take as many as ye desire from my garden, any time they should offer ye and the ladies pleasure."

"Of course. But your cottage is far away from my castle. And having such roses in my personal garden would please me more. Can you grow them for me?" His voice held more humility than she had ever imagined was capable of a laird. His question seemed more of a request, a plea, than the demands and edicts so commonly dispensed from rulers.

Even though a feeling of disappointment engulfed her being, Fayre nodded. "I am certain of it."

"But my laird," Witta objected. "The lassie did nae harm. I am the one who has wronged the king. Take me and spare my child."

"Nay." Laird Kenneth stiffened. "The decision has been made. Your daughter will go with me in your place." He gave a nod to his knights, but before they could seize her, Fayre rushed to Witta and embraced him.

"God preserve ye," he said.

"And ye, my father." Breaking away, she looked into Witta's aged eyes. "Dinna despair. I shall be back as soon as the first roses bloom in the garden of Kennerith Castle."

Before he could answer, Fayre felt the grip of a knight squeezing her forearm. Witta tightened his hand around her fingers. His eyes misted as the knight drew her closer to his white steed, forcing her to break the hold. With a nod, he instructed her to mount the horse.

Before her bare foot reached the stirrup, Laird Kenneth intervened. "The lass shall ride with me."

To Fayre's surprise, Laird Kenneth mounted his steed and then gestured for her to come near. After she obeyed, he placed his hands on each side of her waist and lifted her with an easy motion until she sat in front of him on the horse.

Though his victories in battle were fabled, Fayre hadn't expected him to be so strong yet still handle her with a tender touch. His gentleness was small consolation when Laird Kenneth clicked his tongue, commanding the horse to trot away from the shepherd's field, away from the only home she had ever known. Terror knotted inside the pit of her abdomen and sent an ugly wisp to the base of her throat. Fayre turned and glimpsed her father one last time. As he waved farewell, she prayed she could keep her promises.

Chapter 2

Not far into the journey, Kenneth discovered that he enjoyed the sensation of his arms loosely enveloping the serf maiden. Her body was rigid, as though she was afraid if she moved, Dazzle would throw them both. As a serf, she would naturally be unaccustomed to riding upon any steed, let alone a beast of such quality and experience as Dazzle.

Though as a serf, she was far below him in station, Kenneth sought not to take advantage of her. He wouldn't be so bold as to hold her more closely than necessary for her safety. Since he could only see the back of her head, he had to content himself by forming a portrait of Fayre in his mind. Long, reddish blond hair, unencumbered by hats and jewels, was appealing in its free style. No woman he knew, whether maid or titled, would think of letting her hair catch a breeze. Perhaps that is why when wisps flew away from Fayre's face, they framed it in such a way as to make her seem fresh. And fresh she was. He could tell by her countenance, her innocent and questioning looks, that she was not yet cynical, not yet acquainted with the ways of the world. Perhaps such a young spirit wasn't meant to become as hard as some of the women of his acquaintance. He let out a breath. Was he wrong to expose the virgin to the wiles of the king's courtiers?

Yes. Yes he was.

But what of the roses? Without Fayre, there was no hope that he could ever impress the king or his courtiers with such brilliant orange blooms.

I shall just keep her away from King David's castle, that is all. I will keep her confined to Kennerith. That will be easy enough to do.

He nodded once. Even as he made his resolution, he drew a second internal portrait of Fayre. This time she was dressed in the ornate clothing of a member of the court. He pictured her in blue. No, not blue. Gold. Yes, cloth the color of gold would suit her and would reflect the light brown of her eyes. Her hair had disappeared under a conical-shaped hat decorated with a crimson cloth that hung from its tip and was caught up again on the back side of the corded brim, then allowed to flow partially down her back so that it blended with the red girdle she wore in his imagination. And shoes. Fayre couldn't be permitted to run barefoot in the castle, as he had found her in the fields. She would wear wooden clogs or shoes tailored of kid leather. One pair of each would be in order.

A pang of guilt lurched through his belly. When he first glimpsed her that morning, Fayre had seemed happy enough amid the squalor that she called a life. Not that her surroundings were worse than any other serf's. If Kenneth could have provided grand houses for all of his people, he would have done so gladly. If only he weren't obligated to extract what little money the serfs had to finance this war.

"My laird." The knight with hair the color of ebony pulled up alongside them.

"Yes, Ulf," Kenneth answered and drew Dazzle to a halt. He heard Walter, the other knight, stop his horse not far behind them.

Ulf followed suit. "We are just upon another house that is delinquent in tax payment."

Kenneth knew the house of which Ulf spoke without even looking. Like Witta Shepherd, these serfs were poor, too poor to pay what the king wanted. No surprise that Ulf pointed out the hut. He always viewed the prospect of a conflict, even a joust with an unarmed serf, with more vigor than Kenneth liked.

"We might stop there upon our next journey, perhaps," Kenneth answered.

"But my laird, we didn't spare Witta Shepherd. Or his daughter." Ulf peered at Fayre in a bold manner. Kenneth controlled the urge to give him a lashing with his tongue. Most men of Kenneth's rank wouldn't care in the least how his vassal looked upon a serf maiden.

But he did.

"Ulf is right," Walter, his second knight, agreed.

"Right," Kenneth blurted. Walter's observation brought him back into the present, a present that was none too savory.

Kenneth let out a sigh that he knew all around him could hear. Of the two knights, Walter was the one who didn't let emotion rule the day. If passing the next house offended Walter's sense of fair play, then Kenneth had no choice but to stop. Especially since Fayre was privy to his actions and decisions.

"All right, then." Tiredness colored his voice. Not only was Kenneth in no mood to undertake a disagreeable task, but also he was eager to return home. The longer they journeyed, the more he noticed that Fayre leaned more heavily upon him. Obviously, the long ride was taking its toll upon her body and spirit. But he couldn't ask her if she wanted to stop. If he did, his knights would never let him forget that he let a woman make his decisions for him. No, they would have to visit the cottage.

He pulled on the bridle. Obeying, Dazzle veered to the right. As they neared the house, a young woman exited the hut. Kenneth imagined she wasn't much older than Fayre, but her sunburned countenance and rough hands suggested her physical appearance had been hardened by work. She held an infant, and four children followed behind her. The smallest clutched at her drab wool clothing. Judging from the heights of the children, the woman had given birth annually over the past five years. A protruding belly suggested another new arrival was imminent. Despite her girth, she managed to drop a curtsy.

"Good day, lass. And where is your husband?" Kenneth asked.

Her face clouded and she tilted her head toward the ground. "He is ill in bed, my laird."

"I am sorry. May he soon gain robust health. Shall we pray for him?"

Her eyes lit as she looked up at him. In her obvious gratitude, years seemed to melt from her face. "Would ye?"

Kenneth nodded. He bowed his head, along with the others, and made a brief petition to God.

"Thank ye, my laird," the woman said after the prayer's conclusion. She paused. "But ye dinna come here tae pray. You are here tae collect the taxes we owe."

"Aye. But I can return when your husband is better."

She shook her head. "But I ha'e the money. We sold a sheep at market just this past week tae pay ye."

Her words caused him to feel a pain no less sharp than that of a piercing lance. Yet he had to do his duty to his king.

"May I approach?" she asked.

Kenneth nodded. Still holding the child, the expectant woman took a few steps toward the horse. The effort left her winded, her breathing audible. She extended her hand. When she opened her palm, he counted the coins owed by the master of the house. He extracted them from her sweaty palm and then secured them in his pocket. "Very good. Tell your husband he owes no more for now."

She nodded and curtsied. The woman's glance darted to Fayre. The light in her eyes bespoke curiosity, but she didn't ask questions.

Guilt caused a lump to form in Kenneth's throat. Would the whole kingdom believe he was apt to steal women away from those who didn't pay? Yet every time he felt regret about his decision, a feeling of gladness that she was with him soon washed it away. Kenneth had a nagging feeling that God planned for Fayre to come to the castle. Divine intervention or wishful thinking?

—∿—

"Twenty farthings and a pretty lassie," Ulf declared two hours later into their journey, as twilight fell. "Not much to show for a day's ride."

Fayre shuddered as she felt Ulf's stare bore into her. Yet his boldness seemed the least of her problems. Her precious rosebushes, gathered earlier when they stopped by the garden next to her father's cottage, had made an arduous trip. How could they survive?

Against her will, her thoughts returned to the prospect of her own survival. How could she elude Ulf while she lived at the castle? And were the other men even worse? What about the laird? Was he hiding his true reasons for wanting her to come and live in his castle?

No. He was not that type of man.

Fayre had been touched by the laird's gesture to the woman whose husband lay ill in bed. The idea that such a great man would bother to pray for one so far below him in station was sobering to her. Perhaps the laird really was sincere in his love of God.

She wondered about the spiritual state of his vassals. They seemed so different from one another. One was eager to collect all he could from each house, while the other expressed no feeling one way or the other. Fayre resolved to pray for them both.

If stopping at the first cottage wasn't enough, Ulf had convinced the laird to make yet another stop. The last cottage they visited had been in even worse condition than the one she and her father shared. She couldn't imagine the laird and his knights could collect any coins from its inhabitants. When they could find no one at home or in the nearby fields, she had breathed an inward sigh of relief. The knight called Walter seemed reasonable enough, but Ulf was too quick to draw his lance. Fayre could only pray that she and her party would arrive safely at the castle, despite her fear and dread.

She had selected four of her best bushes in hopes of transplanting them in the laird's garden. Fayre had no idea that the journey to the castle would take so long. The break for a meal had taken up a good part of the day. Not that she minded; her stomach had been begging for food for a full hour before they finally stopped. Her belly was rewarded for its wait. Rather than a humble meal, the men had in their satchels delicacies she had never seen, let alone eaten. Breads and meats flavored with exotic spices and herbs she could never afford to buy. They tasted odd to her palate at first, but she quickly realized she enjoyed the pungent flavors. She hadn't expected Laird Kenneth to share his fruit tart, but when he offered her half, she didn't hesitate. Such sweetness! The expression on her face must have shown her delight, for as she let the pastry melt in her mouth, the knights let out bawdy laughs. She didn't mind that she appeared unwise to the world. Let them laugh. Truly, the lairds and ladies feasted upon delicacies fit for the Lord above.

Perhaps the scrumptious food was but little reward for their travels. After bouncing for hours on a rugged pathway that could hardly be called a road, Fayre's backside reminded her with an unrelenting ache that it would not soon forgive such abuse. Fayre had clung to Laird Kenneth as though her life depended upon it during most of the journey. When the horse's hooves hit ruts and stumbled over rocks, she thought she might be tossed to the ground. She had no intention of falling so the knights could laugh and make sport of her, even though that meant holding the laird more closely than she wanted. At least he didn't flinch at the touch of a mere serf.

A waterfall flowing out of the gray rocks caught her ears with its sound. Since her eyes had adjusted to the dark, she could still discern its beauty. She pointed. "Might we stop for a bit?" she asked the laird. "I would welcome a drink of water, and I would like tae water my rosebushes, if I might beg your indulgence."

"Nay. We all must wait for refreshment. Darkness is upon us, and we are close to the castle now," Laird Kenneth answered. "To stop now would merely be an unnecessary delay. I promise you may drink of all the water you like once we arrive at the castle in but a wee bit of time."

Fayre didn't argue. The thought of reaching the place she would be calling home, at least until she could coax new blooms from the bushes, was welcome. Her tired and sore body needed a bed no matter how uncomfortable or modest. Aye, she could sleep on a bare floor this night.

As the laird promised, she didn't have to wait long. With a grateful eye, Fayre caught sight of the castle she would be calling home until the roses blossomed. Modest though it was, her own little cottage, the one she had shared with Father since Mother's death only a few months past, seemed like a piece of paradise in comparison.

Kennerith Castle loomed immense. Stones the color of tan comprised the building. Fayre counted four towers, one on each corner. She imagined herself in one of the overlooks, her gaze drinking in the land that was her beloved Scotland. If Laird Kenneth would let her roam. She cast a brief gaze at his shoulders, obviously broad even though they were protected by armor. Someone as powerful as he could squelch her as easily as a horse tramples a cricket. She quivered, almost wishing she were anywhere else.

What was my poor mind thinking, tae promise the laird perfect roses? What if there is a drought or too much rain, or what if the bushes simply fail tae bloom? What fate will befall me then?

She stroked a wilted petal of the vivid orange flower she held, the one originally meant for her father to enjoy over a simple meal of bread and cheese. She remembered stopping by the garden long enough for the two knights to wrench her beautiful bushes from their place in the soil. Hard and rugged warriors, the men seemed not to notice how lovingly the soil had been plowed or how each plant had been pruned so the blossoms bloomed on them just so. If they had been more observant, they would have never tossed the tender plants carelessly into leather satchels meant for the provisions of war.

Now her roses would delight the ladies of the court. Titled ladies who would otherwise have no use for a mere shepherd's daughter. The beauty of the flowers she devotedly tended so that none could compare would be wasted on them. How she wished the flowers would still offer joy to her aged parent. But instead, they had become a mere tool to gain the laird newfound respect. She almost wished she could destroy each blossom, just to prevent Laird Kenneth's mercenary wishes from coming to fruition. But for the sake of her father, she kept her feelings in check.

After the brutal assault upon her roses, none of the men had spoken to Fayre. Even Laird Kenneth had remained silent as she rode with him on his horse, whose name, she had since learned, was Dazzle. She had observed the way Laird Kenneth said the name, his intonation lying lazily on the zs, but curtly enunciating the rest of the letters so his voice sounded like a whip slashing through the dusk.

The tired horses seemed to gain momentum as they drew closer to the castle. Perhaps they anticipated a warm bed of straw and plenty of oats to eat. The watchmen were obviously adept at their job. A massive wooden drawbridge descended so the travelers could cross safely over the murky moat. Fayre surmised the water was deep and wide enough to house the fabled Loch Ness monster, reputed to live in the loch beyond the Grampian Mountains that rose up behind the castle. She had often fantasized about Nessie, first seen centuries ago. To have Nessie herself protecting the castle! Ah, but no doubt Laird Kenneth had plenty of vicious sea creatures lying in wait should an enemy fall into the water.

They crossed over the bridge and into a large courtyard, where three stable boys awaited to tend to the horses.

"Welcome to Kennerith Castle," Laird Kenneth said as he dismounted. He extended his arms to help her dismount as well. "I promised you water to drink. Are you hungry as well?"

Too apprehensive until that moment to think about her growling stomach, Fayre suddenly realized she could use a bite to eat even though the delicacies she had enjoyed at dinner had tamed her appetite throughout most of the journey. So as not to seem eager, she merely nodded.

"Come, then." Though he stood beside her, Laird Kenneth loomed over her, reminding her once again of his might. She wondered if this were an intentional ploy until he smiled. Under other circumstances, she might have thought him handsome. But not now.

"Might I first see how my roses fared? The journey was no doubt as difficult for them as for us."

The smile didn't leave his face. "Indeed." With a silent nod, Laird Kenneth commanded his vassals to retrieve the four plants from their satchels. The first had shed the petals from each blossom, with the exception of one or two on the stray bloom. Fayre felt her body tense as the remaining plants were taken from the bags. Each had suffered the same fate. Anxiously she touched their roots. They had become parched over the course of the day. She was unable to conceal her distress.

"Ah, my lass. Do not despair," she heard Laird Kenneth console her. "Surely someone with your skill can revive the plants, aye?"

Fayre didn't answer. She had made too many promises already.

Thankfully, the squire chose that moment to distract his master. "Laird Kenneth," he said as he bowed. "I pray your journey was a success." Lifting his head, the squire sent an admiring glance in Fayre's direction. "I can see my prayers were answered."

Kenneth cut his glance her way and then answered, "Would you have Fayre shown to the most agreeable guest bedchamber in the castle? She will remain with us for some time." Laird Kenneth looked at Fayre. "At least until the roses bloom."

"Aye, me laird." He handed Laird Kenneth a letter. Burned into the sealing wax was the outline of a coat of arms. Was it the herald of the MacMurray clan?

"From Lady Letha, no doubt," Ulf taunted Laird Kenneth.

The look that crossed Laird Kenneth's golden face was one of satisfaction. Could Lady Letha be the one whose favor Laird Kenneth sought?

Chapter 3

If Lady Letha was the one he wished to impress, Laird Kenneth showed no indication of his intent on his face. Not a muscle moved.

At the mention of Lady Letha, a strange feeling hit the pit of Fayre's belly. She didn't remember feeling that way before. She wasn't sure she liked whatever it was.

For an instant, Fayre wondered what Lady Letha looked like. Surely if she had attracted Laird Kenneth's attention, she was fine and lovely indeed. Would her roses please Lady Letha? And if they did not? She didn't want to think about that possibility.

At that moment, Fayre realized the urgency of her situation. Under normal circumstances, she would never have uprooted her flowers, but the laird had no patience to wait for new bushes to grow from slips. If she were to be honest with herself, Fayre would have to admit that she had no patience for such a wait, either. Fayre wanted nothing more than to return home. The more quickly she could grow beautiful roses for the laird, the more hastily she could return to the life she knew. In the meantime, her father would have to make himself content remembering her by the two bushes, planted beside the small window of the cottage, that she had left to bloom in her absence.

"What is the matter, Fayre?" Laird Kenneth asked.

She swallowed. He must have seen the distressed look upon her face. "The roots. They are a wee bit dry." She wasn't given to understatement, so her conscience pricked her. Fayre sent up a silent prayer for forgiveness.

The laird stepped beside her and investigated the plants for himself. "Are all of them this dry?" He touched the roots with his fingertips.

"Aye." She tried to keep her countenance from revealing the depth of her distress. She looked into his silver eyes. "I maun plant them right away. Please, show me the spot in the garden where they might grow."

Laird Kenneth peered west, in the direction where she supposed the flower garden was planted. He shrugged. "That is for the gardener to decide." He returned his attention to her face. "You and Norman can meet tomorrow morning and make your plans then."

"Nay, my laird." Then, realizing she was out of order, Fayre gave a curtsy so low that she feared she might tumble. "I beg yer greatest indulgence, my laird, but my task canna wait. I maun plant the roses tonight, even in the dark."

Otherwise, they will surely die. Then Father will be thrown in the dungeon, where he will surely die. What will I do then?

She looked up in time to see Laird Kenneth's eyebrows shoot up. "Indeed," he said, "I promised that you would have water for the roses as soon as we arrived here. I shall keep my word." He nodded toward the squire.

"Yes, my laird," he responded. "I shall summon Norman right away."

Relieved, Fayre stood upright.

"Perhaps you shall have some fortification as you wait," the laird suggested.

"I offer tae ye my greatest gratitude, my laird." Fayre forced her sense to overrule the rumblings of her belly. "But I canna. I maun plant these bushes as soon as I can."

"Then at least allow me to accompany you to the garden."

The laird's generosity surprised her, but she accepted his offer willingly. Fayre had never ventured more than three miles from her own little cottage. She couldn't remember a night she didn't sleep in her own bed. Humble though it was, her home offered comfort in its familiarity and warmth in its love. Fayre did not yet know whom, if anyone, she could trust in her new surroundings. Of those she had met, Laird Kenneth had shown himself the most compassionate thus far. She was willing to stay near to him as long as he was amenable.

Laird Kenneth took a lantern from one of the servants and led Fayre to the garden. As she expected, it was located in the courtyard behind the kitchen. Yet she didn't expect the garden to be so grand.

He chuckled.

"What do ye find so amusing?" she asked.

"Your eyes," he answered. "They are so wide they nearly constitute your entire countenance."

She bowed her head in shyness. "I–I just have never seen such, such. . .glory."

"Indeed?" He chuckled, then his face turned thoughtful as he surveyed his surroundings. His eyes took on a light that suggested he was seeing his garden for the first time, although Fayre knew full well that couldn't be. "I suppose you have not." He turned a kind gaze toward her. "This bailey garden is rather modest, in actuality. This is nothing in comparison to the king's."

Fayre gasped in wonder. "Then he maun have many gardeners."

"Aye. Many more than I."

"Will I be expected tae help tend the rest of the garden?"

"Nay. Norman is quite proud of his work. Do not be surprised if he resists your encroachment. I must caution you. He has worked here, alone, for many years. Those who help him are all men, so he is unaccustomed to working alongside women. Do not expect to be welcomed." He sent her a smile of assurance. "Do not fear. He is harmless enough."

Fayre nodded. She was all too aware that her position as a serf woman caused many men to look upon her as little more than a beast. If a man was rough and uncouth, he might not think twice about taking advantage of her tenuous standing. Her spirit calmed as she determined not to call attention to herself. "I shall try not tae be the source of any trouble."

To her amazement, Laird Kenneth took her chin in his thumb and forefinger and lifted her face so that her gaze met his. The gentleness in his touch astounded and delighted her. "How can one such as yourself instigate any trouble? Nay, such a prospect would be impossible."

She let out a little gasp, then an uncertain laugh escaped her lips. For the first time, she gained a glimmer of understanding as to what her friends meant when they tried to tell her about marriage.

Marriage? What am I thinking? Never.

No laird would marry her. No, she was here to coax life into the rosebushes so that the laird could find favor with the king. Or with a lady. Or perhaps both. The thought left her unhappy.

"Ah, here comes Norman now." The laird took his fingers away from her chin, leaving Fayre feeling even more unhappiness than before. With the other hand, he lifted his lantern to greet a wizened old man whom Fayre surmised was the gardener.

If the man noticed the laird's quick motion, he made no indication. He bowed. "My laird. Why summon me tae the garden after fall of night?"

"I know this is an unusual request, but the matter is of the utmost urgency." The laird held the rosebushes up for the gardener to inspect. "You see, these must be planted with the greatest of haste."

Norman rubbed his chin, which was decorated with dark but scraggly hairs. "Fine roses, they are. Such color!" He leaned closer to study the plants. After a moment, he shook his head. "They're dry, they are. Even though I'll be fetchin' water right away, they will never survive."

Fayre's intake of breath was louder this time. She clamped her hand over her mouth. "Please. Do not say that."

Norman took in her plain brown frock and decided he could address her without fear of reprimand. "And who might ye be?"

"She is Fayre. She is here to grow these roses upon my orders. You are to treat her with the utmost respect and see to it that the rest of the servants do the same."

"Aye, my laird." Norman touched one of the fading blooms. "I can see why you desire such a flower. I have never seen such a color."

"Nor have I until today," Laird Kenneth agreed. "You must give Fayre the best spot in the garden to assure that at least one of these bushes survives."

"But—"

"I care not how long the planting takes or even if you must uproot other bushes to make room for these. You are to assist Fayre in any way possible."

"Aye, my laird." His obedient words denied his sour expression. Fayre almost felt sorry for him.

"Likewise, I will assist ye in any way I can," Fayre told him.

"Humph." He twisted his mouth into a doubting line. "Come on with you. I think I know a good spot ye can have. I had planned the row for some of my best roses, but I can see that is not to be."

"Thank ye."

"Don't bother to thank me. Any favor ye get from me, ye owe tae my master."

As she helped Norman dig, Fayre wished he could find a way to be congenial. Laird Kenneth was right; the gardener was a wee bit grumpy. She decided that her best course of action was to ignore him. For that matter, perhaps her best course of action would be to make herself as invisible as possible. The less trouble she caused, the more likely she would survive her stay at the castle.

Heavenly Father, please grant my roses life so that my father and I might also live.

An image of the expectant woman whose husband lay sick in bed came to mind. She realized how self-centered her prayers had become ever since she had been taken upon Laird Kenneth's horse that day.

Lord, heal the ones who are sick. Protect those in this house, so that they might be spared from any sickness. Especially the plague.

She shuddered at the thought of anyone close to her being stricken with such a deadly disease that had already taken so many lives.

"Cold?" Norman asked.

"Cold?" She snapped back into the present. "Nay. I am nae cold."

"Then why do ye shiver?"

"Just praying."

"I never shiver when I pray." Norman shook his head as he tamped dirt around the roots of one of the bushes. "Who can understand a woman?"

Fayre thought better than to challenge Norman. As long as she was expected to work with him, she saw no need in angering him. He was already grumpy enough. Yet underneath his gruff exterior, she could see his love for the garden. Perhaps he was a gentle soul in his way.

As soon as the roses were planted and Norman had bid her an unenthusiastic good night, Fayre exhaled, letting out pent-up emotions of uncertainty, fear, and exhaustion. She didn't care whether her quarters were as magnificent as the laird's or a stall shared with Dazzle. All she wanted was to lay her weary body in a horizontal position and fall into a deep slumber.

Eager to reach this goal, she ambled to the back door and entered the palace through the kitchen. Not even the smell of the night's dinner, long since served but its delicious aromas still filling the air, enticed her to ask for sustenance. She hadn't been at the castle long enough to know the cook from the chamber maid, so she addressed the first person she eyed, a portly woman who looked as tired as Fayre felt.

"May I be shown tae my quarters?"

The woman folded her arms, cocked her head, and inspected Fayre. "So, would ye be the lassie that my laird brought home with him?"

"Aye."

Her gray eyebrows rose so high that new wrinkles were temporarily added to her forehead. "I can see why."

Fayre felt color rise to her cheeks as she squirmed.

"He'll be seein' ye now."

"Seein' me?"

The woman nodded toward a younger version of herself who was entering the kitchen, apparently having finished some task unknown to Fayre. "She's here."

"Good." The servant motioned for Fayre to follow her.

Fayre didn't bother to look at her clothing. She knew the dust needed to be shaken from it and that her face was surely smudged with dirt. She rubbed her fingers together in a vain attempt to whisk away a few particles of soil. "But I am in no condition tae enter a fine room, much less tae see the laird. Might I take a moment tae refresh myself? Can you nae show me tae my quarters first?"

The maid shook her head. "He wants tae see ye right away. Follow me."

The kitchen door led to a narrow and dark passage. After they passed through, the servant opened a door that led into a large hallway. Fayre stared upward at the arched ceiling that loomed high above her. The passageway was so wide that she and four other women could have stretched out their arms and touched fingertips and still not made contact with the opposite walls.

"I have ne'er seen such," Fayre noted.

"It don't seem so wonderful when ye're the one that's got tae scrub the floors and do the dustin'," the maid observed.

Fayre peered at the walls. "No, I suppose it wouldn't."

The maid paused in front of a massive wooden door. "Here we are. The laird awaits."

Fayre swallowed. Even though she had been with him all day, the prospect of seeing him again left her anxious. The maid's expression offered neither sympathy nor compassion as she announced Fayre to the laird.

Fayre could see she had no choice. She had to face him.

What did he want?

The laird was standing when she entered, a gesture she didn't expect from one of such elevated rank. She marveled at how she had seen him treat others with kindness, even serfs. But then, Laird Kenneth was well regarded in the land. She had heard talk of his fine countenance and fine form. Light hair was exposed, forming longish waves that made him appear young and carefree. Aye, and his silver eyes! She watched them reflect the nearby flames. The flickering light made his eyes glisten even more than they had in the sunshine earlier that day. Softened features suggested his mood was relaxed. Perhaps he was as tired as she. What would it be like to be a lady, to sit by the fire with Laird Kenneth after a long day and to touch his cheek, comforting him?

Is my mind unsound tae think such a thing?

She shook the thought from her head and curtsied.

The wooden chairs in front of the fire looked appealing, but he didn't offer her a seat. Fayre hoped that meant the visit would be brief. A wooden table by one of the chairs held a mug along with a plate that was empty save a chicken bone.

"I trust all is well and that Norman showed you a good and proper place for your roses?"

"Aye, my laird."

"And you have had your sustenance?"

"Nay, my laird."

"What? No sustenance?" The edge of anger that entered his voice unawares left her taken aback. This was a man who could be brought to ire in an instant. Fayre realized that if the laird were to do battle, he was sure to emerge victorious.

"Food was offered, my laird. I declined."

"Do you mean to say that nothing in the kitchen tempted you to eat? Surely my cooks could prepare something to your liking."

"I am quite certain any food in yer home is much finer than anything tae which I am accustomed. The midday meal was evidence of that. I am too tired tae eat at present, if I may be permitted tae say so. I am sure I shall regain my appetite tomorrow."

"I know you must be exhausted from such a day. I would not have summoned you here if it were not important. I surmise your expectations are to be treated as a servant while you are here."

"I–I dinna ken what my expectations are, sir."

He chuckled. "I suppose not. So much has happened today. I want you to know that as long as you remain here, you will be treated as a special guest."

Fayre felt her mouth drop open. A guest!

"Tomorrow morning the seamstress shall set upon sewing you a decent frock."

Fayre looked down upon her garment. The brown wool was plain, but no plainer than any other serf's. And it was clean. Well, as clean as it could be considering she had been on a horse all day. She swiped at the loose soil that had penetrated the cloth on the two spots where she had knelt in the garden to plant her roses.

"There is no need for that," Laird Kenneth interrupted.

She stopped. Perhaps he didn't want her to dirty the floor. For the first time, she noticed the stones were covered by a runner woven in a fine botanical pattern of threads in hues of red, purple, and gold, colors that could only be afforded by the rich. She looked up long enough to apologize. "Forgive me, my laird." She returned her stare to the floor and added, "But I am nae deserving of such honor."

"That is for me to decide." His voice conveyed a request rather than a command. "Brona—that is the seamstress—shall meet you in your chamber tomorrow morning."

—⁓—

When Fayre awoke the next day in a strange bed, her stomach felt as though it were leaping into her throat. Where was she?

Just as quickly, she exhaled and placed her right hand at the base of her throat. "Kennerith Castle."

She studied the room. In the light of day it proved larger than the entire hut she shared with her father. Tapestries depicting festivals and celebrations of lairds and ladies adorned the walls. And the fine fabric under which she lay! She had never dared try to barter with merchants to purchase soft material dyed in rich hues. Fayre imagined them throwing their heads back and laughing with unbridled mirth at the thought that someone as inconsequential as she would dare think she could own such luxury. The fine things in life were reserved for royalty and gentry. Still, she wished she were back in her humble dwelling all the same.

She heard a knock on the door. Before she could answer, a servant she had never seen entered. Somehow the servant managed to balance a tray loaded with food while opening the door at once. Fayre leapt out of bed and rushed to assist her.

"There's no need tae help me. I'm here to serve ye. At least, that's what I ha'e been told." She surveyed Fayre with beady eyes and sniffed through her hooked nose as though she smelled an odor. She set the tray on the small, oval-shaped table beside the bed. "I'm Murdag, your ladies' maid."

A ladies' maid! Fayre had never fantasized that she should enjoy the services of a ladies' maid—ever. Judging from the way Murdag frowned as she scrutinized her, the servant was none too happy with her new mistress.

Not knowing what else to do, Fayre resolved to be friendly. She caressed the sleeve of her lightweight night shift. "So ye are the one who left this for me?"

She nodded.

"Thank ye." Fayre smiled.

Murdag turned away and regarded Fayre's brown clothing. The garment was neatly folded and left on the bed. "Ye won't be putting that thing back on, are ye?"

"I most certainly am." Fayre's voice reflected her indignation. "My duty here is tae work in the garden. I am aware that Laird Kenneth will be sending the seamstress this morning, but I canna imagine that I would tend tae my roses wearing a fine frock." When Murdag didn't answer Fayre's logic, she continued. "And I know Brona will nae possibly sew a garment in a matter of minutes. I maun wear something while she works on my new clothing."

"As ye wish. Is there anything else, or may I leave you tae your breakfast?"

"Ye may go. Thank you." The words felt and sounded strange falling from her own lips, unaccustomed as she was to giving anyone permission to do anything.

Fayre shivered as she watched Murdag exit. She wasn't sure which of them was the more unfortunate: Murdag, for being forced to serve a woman below her own station, or herself, for being looked down upon by her maid.

Despite her hunger, Fayre didn't want to greet Brona in her nightclothes. She donned the simple frock that shouted her lack of position. As she slipped the rough woolen garment over her shoulders, she felt defiant. Why should she be ashamed of who she was? God had known her since she was formed in her mother's womb. He had put her exactly where He wanted her to be, for His own purpose.

The door creaked.

Fayre controlled the urge to display her ill mood.

Why didn't the seamstress knock?

She looked in the direction of her visitor and gasped.

"Sir Ulf? What are you doing here?"

Chapter 4

Ulf ran his tongue over his lips and leered. Even though he wasn't close enough to touch her, Fayre stepped away from his outstretched arms.

"What is the matter, my pretty lassie? You should be grateful that a vassal, especially one as close to the laird as I, would even look at you twice."

"If ye are of such importance, would you nae be able tae find many willing ladies tae do yer bidding?"

"Aye, I can have my way with any lady in the king's court." Ulf ran his fingers through a few strands of his curly hair. "But you! You are exceptionally fine, exceptionally fair. Fair like the roses you grow." He took in an exaggerated whiff with such force that his nostrils folded almost shut. "You are honest, of the earth. The smell of God's soil clings to you, to your hair, tae your frock."

He regarded her brown clothing, and then let his gaze travel to her bare feet. "Aye, you are different from the fine ladies I am accustomed to. I am expected to woo them with poetry and words o' love." He opened his mouth and patted it three times, feigning a yawn. "But with you, I need not display pretense." The expression on his face as he watched Fayre reminded her of how a lion must look when surveying his dinner.

Fayre shook her head and stepped back. Her bare heel made contact with the foot of the bed. Her heart made her aware of its presence by its rapid beating. Since she had nowhere to go, she stood in place, trembling.

Father in heaven, protect me!

Ulf swiped his arm toward her waist. She stepped aside, evading him.

Please, Father, hear my prayer!

"So you want to put up a fight, eh?" The glint in his eyes grew more evident. "I like a lass with spirit!" His chortle made her squirm.

Her answer was to make a run for the door. To Fayre's dismay, her foot caught on the end of the bed covering. She tripped. Although she managed to keep upright, she stumbled long enough for Ulf to catch her in his arms. Red lips puckered and made their way toward hers.

Nay! My first kiss canna be like this!

She screamed, her voice high-pitched with urgency.

Obviously surprised by her resistance, Ulf jerked his head back. "What are you making such a fuss for, lass? 'Tis only a kiss." An evil smile covered his face as Ulf brought his lips closer to hers.

Fayre moved her head away from his, but caught up in his grasp as she was, she knew resistance was in vain.

A welcome sound of footsteps was followed by the door creaking open.

Ulf stopped in midmotion, cursing under his breath.

"What is the meaning of this?" Murdag's face held an expression of curiosity and disbelief.

" 'Tis none of your affair," Ulf answered. Still, he let Fayre go and stepped back.

Murdag's beady eyes shifted so that her gaze bored into Fayre. "Is he here by your leave?"

"Nay," she whimpered.

"She lies!" Ulf protested.

Murdag's eyelids sharpened into narrow slits. She said nothing for a moment, then nodded. "Nay, I believe she speaks the truth, sir."

"How dare you accept the word of a mere serf over the declaration of a knight! If I werena a gentleman and you were a man rather than a maid, Murdag, I would be forced to draw my sword in my defense."

"I beg pardon, Sir Ulf." She curtsied and withdrew.

Nay! Now I ha'e no chance at all. Fayre's uncontrolled trembling resumed.

"Where were we?" Lust returned to Ulf's eyes.

Fayre watched the open door, hoping against hope that Murdag would return.

Ulf's gaze followed hers. "Aye. 'Twould be a good idea to shut the door, would it not? We cannot have everyone in the castle knowing our secret."

Fayre glanced around the room. Where could she run? Although the room was large, it had no hiding places. The only door was the one Ulf was shutting at this moment. Could she jump out of the nearest window? No. Shaped like keyholes, they were too narrow. And even if she could squeeze through one, surely the jump to the ground would kill her. Perhaps she could pick up an object and throw it upon his head? Nay. That would be too rash. Besides, Murdag had already seen her with Ulf. Her quick exit indicated she accepted Ulf's story that Fayre had invited him to be in her bedchamber. If she injured Ulf, he would have her thrown out of the castle, and her father was sure to go to prison.

"Nay!" she shrieked, more at the thought than at her captor.

"Silence!" Ulf cautioned.

At that moment, she heard the door fly open with such force that it hit the opposing wall. Fayre gasped when she realized that Laird Kenneth stood in the entryway.

"Ulf?" Laird Kenneth planted his feet on the floor and stood erect.

Ulf blanched, then bowed. "Aye, my laird?"

"So it is as Murdag said." Laird Kenneth lifted his chin and surveyed his vassal. Tightened lips suggested disapproval. "What do you have to say for yourself?"

"She wanted me to be here."

Wanted him to be there? How could Sir Ulf, a knight who was sworn to valor, bear false witness in such a blatant manner? The words flew off his lips as though he lied every day. She wouldn't have believed it possible had she not heard with her own ears.

"Nay!" Fayre objected. "He entered my bedchamber without my permission or my desire."

"The wench lies," Ulf said.

"Does she?" Laird Kenneth asked. "Then why is her body shaking?"

"In fear of your ire, no doubt," Ulf retorted. "She knows you can never believe the word of a serf over your own devoted vassal."

"It is my hope that you would not lie, but I fear you disappoint me."

"Why would I lie about a mere serf?" Ulf looked at Fayre as though she were a dead rat, before returning his attention to the laird. "And even if I did, what does it matter? She is but property."

Fear gripped Fayre's torso. Ulf was right. According to the law, she was nothing more than the laird's possession, to do with as he pleased. In spite of the fact that the laird had ordered the seamstress to sew her a new frock, in spite of the fact that she was ensconced in a guest chamber, she was his servant. The word of a chattel would never override the declaration of a knight.

Fayre braced herself to be punished. What would the laird decree? Fifty lashes? Banishment to the servants' quarters, where she was already resented? Or would she be spending her stay in the dungeon, no doubt among rats that would fight her for a piece of molded bread and unclean water—the fate she had tried to spare her father? She struggled not to shake.

"I shall not have any untoward behavior toward a woman who is in my care, regardless of her station." Laird Kenneth paused, studying them both. Finally, the laird looked his vassal in the eye and proclaimed, "Ulf, you may return to your home to await my summons."

Fayre's heart beat faster, but this time with victory rather than anguish. The laird believed her over his own knight!

Ulf's mouth dropped open in obvious shock and upset. "But my laird—"

"You heard what I said." The laird's tone showed that he would brook no argument. "I am the laird of this manor. You shall obey me."

"Very well." Ulf threw a hate-filled look her way, then bowed to Laird Kenneth and exited.

Ulf was gone! Fayre clutched her hands to her chest in relief. As soon as she realized she was safe once again, curiosity overcame her. "What will happen tae him now?"

The laird's eyebrows shot up and he folded his arms. "Do you really care?"

She wasn't sure how to answer. "I–I don't wish tae be the cause of hardship for anyone."

Laird Kenneth's eyes widened and he shook his head slowly. "How can you be so forgiving?" He paused. "Unless you really did wish his presence—"

"Nay, my laird. Ne'er." Fayre felt her face flush at the thought that she would ask a knight into her bedchamber. At the thought of what might have happened, unwelcome tears streamed down her cheeks.

"How scared you must have been." The laird's eyes were alight with compassion. He closed the gap between them and took her in his arms.

Nay! Not him, too!

She looked into his silver eyes, thinking she might protest. Anything she could say would be feeble since she was in his complete control. But when she studied his face, she saw no leer, no untoward lust, no puckering of the lips—just kindness. Truly he sought to comfort her, not to take advantage. At that moment, she realized she liked the feeling of his arms around her. Never had she felt more protected, more safe.

How can that be? I was once afraid of Laird Kenneth. Now he is my redeemer?

Gently she broke the embrace. "I praise my heavenly Father that ye entered when ye did."

"Only because Murdag told me."

"I praise God that she believed me."

"How could she not? Honesty exudes from you."

The compliment would have pleased Fayre any other time, but Laird Kenneth's words were too close to Ulf's earlier observation to give her solace.

"I only regret," he said, "that my vassal is not as chaste as you are. And he is not likely to be as forgiving either."

Fayre shivered.

"I assure you, he will not be permitted near you again as long as you remain here." A light of kindness entered his eyes. "You are righteous to forgive him."

"The Lord said for us tae forgive offenses, no matter how often they occur."

"You know much," the laird said. "You must listen to the priest rather than daydreaming during worship as many young girls do."

"My favorite uncle was a cleric. He taught me at his knee." Fayre felt her eyes mist. "He is gone now. Gone tae a better place, where the Lord has built many mansions." She bowed her head. "Perhaps even one for Sir Ulf."

The laird thought for a moment. "He seems to repent not. Remember, we are not required to forgive unless we are asked." The laird's voice was soft.

"Nay, but I choose tae forgive him nonetheless."

Laird Kenneth shook his head. "You are a stronger person than many who reside in the king's court."

A knock on the door interrupted them. A young woman stood in the entryway and curtsied.

"Brona," Laird Kenneth said. "Good. I want you to begin on Fayre's frock immediately. Her garment should be fine but sturdy enough for every day."

"Aye, my laird. In what fabric?" Brona inquired. "Is the gold cloth we already have suitable for your pleasure, my laird?"

"More than suitable. Perfect." With his broad smile, Fayre had never seen him look so happy. She realized how handsome he appeared when his expression was touched by glee. "But we have no fabric for the second garment, I am sure."

"Second garment?" Brona gasped.

"Of course. What colors do you prefer, Fayre?"

Fayre didn't know how to answer. In the past, her only decision regarding the color of the wool she spun herself had been whether to dye it with vegetable juices or to leave it in its natural state. "I–I canna imagine, my laird."

His mouth twisted into a sympathetic line. "Nay. Nay, I suppose not. Very well, then. You and I shall travel to the marketplace on the morrow."

Fayre was struck speechless. Travel to the marketplace with the laird? She couldn't imagine such a privilege!

"Brona," he was saying, "discuss with Fayre what type of frocks she would prefer and determine how much fabric I should purchase." The laird turned his attention back to Fayre. "Once you begin to dress in a more suitable manner, you shall be treated in a more suitable way. With respect. The type of respect a godly woman merits."

Respect? Could he think of her as more than mere property? His words seemed to indicate that he did.

"Brona," he said, "consider what you will need for three sets of clothing."

"Three!" the women exclaimed in unison.

For an instant, Fayre thought she might faint with joy. Never in her wildest fantasy did she think she would ever own one fine garment. But three? Had she heard the laird correctly?

"Aye," said Laird Kenneth. "Two shall be for every day and one for the king's ball."

Fayre gasped. "The king's ball?"

He nodded. "The event will be held two weeks from today. You, Fayre Rose—and your wonderful blooms—shall be present."

—⁓—

Later that day, Kenneth felt a pang of guilt as he left the castle with his falcon to meet his hunting party. Because of his actions, a serf maiden had been whisked away from the only home she had ever known and taken to an imposing castle that must have seemed strange and forbidding. His decision, made in a fit of tough compassion, had placed her in jeopardy from one of his vassals.

Father, forgive me!

Fayre was the only woman ever to inspire him to experience such an extraordinary number of emotions in such a short time. Certainly, her outward beauty showed through her mean garment. Yet he didn't fully see her inner spirit until she forgave Ulf so quickly after he displayed himself to be a beast. Had his vassal, a man he had trusted for years, always treated women as such? Or was Fayre subjected to his disdain just because of her low status?

Kenneth knew that his own father would chastise him if he had been present. A man given more to the material world than the spiritual one, his father would have found Ulf's pursuit of Fayre a source of amusement. What was a pretty serf if not a diversion?

The idea of following in his deceased father's footsteps repulsed Kenneth. He could not look at any woman and think she was something to be trifled with. The Lord Jesus Christ had made plain in His teachings that women were valuable in His Father's sight. Kenneth couldn't bring himself to treat any woman as chattel, no matter what the laws of the land said he could do.

Especially not Fayre. Fair as the roses she grew, she had caught more than his fancy. In the briefest of times, she had captured his heart.

—⁓—

The following day, Fayre ventured out into the garden to check on her roses. Yesterday she wished they would live to assure her father's survival. Today she wanted them to bloom into mature beauty to please her laird.

Her laird. He had rescued her, had believed her word over a trusted vassal. Her word! She never thought she would be of any value to a laird, but Laird Kenneth treated her as a prize. And to think, he wanted her to enjoy respect, so much that he was willing to buy her pieces of fabric at the marketplace. The thought was so lovely that it pained her to imagine it, to dream of such privilege.

She touched a green leaf of a surviving rosebush with a gentleness she reserved for her flowers. Of the four that had made the arduous journey, only one looked as though it had any hope of survival. Yet that one remaining plant looked hardy. Hard green balls on the tips of several branches promised flowers for the future.

Father in heaven, please allow my flowers tae bloom and for Laird Kenneth tae be pleased.

"Prayin' won't get ye anywheres with the flowers," Norman's sharp voice interrupted. "Only good soil and fair weather will get you good blooms."

She opened her eyes. "Prayer always helps, even if the Lord dinna see fit tae answer as we might wish."

"If He dinna answer as we like, then I dinna see how it helps much. That's how I see it."

"I am certain that God will change your mind one day. At least, I hope He will."

Norman shrugged. "I doubt that. Nae with this awful plague. It has struck the castle now. All of us are doomed."

"The plague? Nay, please say ye speak in jest." Fayre clutched her throat in shock and despair.

"I would never speak in jest aboot such a thing."

Fayre could tell from his monotone that he spoke the truth. She ran down a mental list of those she knew in the castle. The list was short. Since the laird had decided for reasons unknown to her to treat her as a guest, Fayre wasn't permitted to socialize with the servants. Yet Ulf and Walter, the vassals who had been with the laird the day he brought her here, told all they knew of her lowly status. As a result, the laird's friends treated her with civility, but no warmth. Her only real companion was her maid, Murdag. Even she had been unsympathetic to Fayre until the incident with Ulf. Contemplating what could have occurred was still enough to make her shudder. "Then who among us is sick? The dairy maid? Or one of the squires?"

"Nay. Much worse." He leaned toward her and whispered. "'Tis the laird himself."

Her stomach lurched in distress. She took in an audible breath. "The laird himself?"

"Aye. He was feeling ill last night. This morning, he dinna rise from his bed." Norman shook his head. "'Tis a shame. No one will go near him. Nae e'en his most devoted servants."

"They mustn't be devoted enough if they refuse tae help him in his time of need." Fayre remembered a time, not so long ago, when the laird had come to her rescue.

"The servants love him very much," Norman argued. "But tae go near him the noo is t' write one's ain death sentence."

Fayre imagined the laird, so strong, so bold, now lying helpless against a dreaded disease. "I maun see him!"

"See him?" Norman laid his hand on her shoulder. "Dinna be more foolish than the court jester, lass. If ye go near tae him, ye are sure to die."

"Perhaps I shan't die."

"Men of God have died while nursing plague victims. What makes ye believe ye are stronger than they?"

"I make no such claim. But if I die, so be it. I will go and see tae him now."

Chapter 5

Ye canna go in the laird's bedchamber," Murdag cautioned Fayre. "Not e'en his most loyal servants dare enter except tae get food tae him with the greatest of haste."

"They hurry in and out without a word? Does he nae deserve better?"

"He has been the image o' kindness tae me," Murdag admitted. "No finer example save the Lord Jesus Himself, I expect."

"Aye. Ye have witnessed his compassion toward me as well," Fayre said.

"I know. And I ken ye want tae repay him," Murdag said. "But the laird is already sick, and ye arenna. Maun ye make a deliberate effort t' place yourself in danger, thereby further endangering everyone else in the castle? Did I save ye from Sir Ulf only tae have ye die of the plague?"

Fayre looked down at the hem of the fabric that concealed her legs. She had already expressed her gratitude to Murdag, and she could understand the maid's distress. Yet she had to listen to her own heart. "Ha'e ye so little faith?" Fayre asked.

"Faith I ha'e, but certainly no more than men of God. Even some of them ha'e died while ministering tae victims in their flocks."

Fayre swallowed when she remembered how one of the priests in her parish had contracted the disease after praying over dying plague victims. "So no one is ministering tae the laird?"

"Our priest prayed o'er him this morning," Murdag said, "I imagine for the last time."

Fayre wondered whether Murdag meant that the laird had so little time left or if the priest feared returning to the bedchamber, or both. She decided that either thought was too dreadful for words and held back her urge to inquire.

She herself had been in prayer since Norman first told her about the laird's illness. Fayre was well acquainted with the power of prayer. God had chosen thus far to answer her puny petitions with mercy. Her father remained in their hut rather than being thrown into prison. Her best rosebush had survived uprooting, a long journey, and transplanting. Those who lived in Kennerith Castle had been kind. Even the one person who meant her harm had been thwarted. How could Fayre not follow

Scripture's admonition to pray without ceasing?

She had no intention of giving up now. But if a priest was not immune to death from this gruesome sickness, why should she be? The heavenly Father did not promise anyone tomorrow. How long would His mercy endure?

Questions, questions. Her priest said that the faithful should not ask questions but should trust in the Almighty. Obediently, she shook the questions out of her mind long enough to answer Murdag. "The laird, for reasons unknown, has treated me far better than I could have expected for someone in my lowly station."

"He is kind tae everyone, but I think he has taken a special liking tae ye," Murdag said.

Unaccustomed to flattery from anyone except perhaps her own father, Fayre looked at her lap to keep from answering.

"Word is all over the castle aboot how the laird defended ye," Murdag informed her. "If Laird Kenneth finds ye worthy, then so do I."

Fayre looked into Murdag's eyes. "Then ye understand why I maun return the favor."

"But tae sacrifice yer life—"

" 'Tis no sacrifice, when I feel such a strong leading tae be with him."

Murdag raised her hands in surrender. "I can see there's no talking tae ye." She motioned to the low-backed wooden chair in a nearby corner. "Come now. Let me fashion yer hair. Brona may not have finished your garment yet, but ye can at least have a few pearls woven through yer pretty locks."

"Pearls?" Fayre inhaled so strongly in delight that her breath whistled between her lips.

"Only a few. Nothing too fancy with that awful brown garment." She wrinkled her nose. "Even one of mine would look better than—" Murdag stopped herself for a moment. "Would ye like tae wear one of my frocks?"

Although Fayre knew that under normal circumstances a ladies' maid would never dare make such a suggestion to her mistress, Fayre was grateful for the gesture. "Do ye think. . ."

Murdag inspected her. "Aye, I believe one of my garments might do. 'Tis only for a while. As soon as Brona sews yer own frock, ye'll be wearin' that one. Let us hope ye can wear the one she sews at least once before you are laid t' rest in yer grave."

"Ye cheer me so."

"I beg pardon. 'Tis my fervent prayer that ye will wear yer new frocks for many years. And that most especially, ye'll be able tae dance in the gown at the king's castle someday." Murdag sighed.

"Someday. I am only glad that the laird discovered his illness before we went tae the royal palace."

"Aye." Murdag sent her several quick nods. "I shall retrieve the pearls the noo. And my best garment." The maid smiled with more warmth than Fayre had seen from her. "Surely the laird will believe he has seen an angel before he makes his final journey intae heaven."

———

Despite her faith, Fayre couldn't help but feel a twinge of fear as she approached the imposing door that led to Laird Kenneth's bedchamber. She set down the tray, burdened with a light meal, on the table beside the door.

Since she had never adorned her hair with anything other than the occasional wildflower, the elaborate braids with pearls woven in her locks felt strange and new. She touched the side of her hair now and again, fearful that one of the pearls might fall out. But Murdag's expert skill assured that they remained anchored in their splendor.

Murdag's clothing was heavier than she expected and fit tightly around her midsection. The garment had uncomplicated lace on the collar, ornamentation that made her feel as though she were wearing clothing far above her station. Two layers of white undergarments, wool stockings, and simple leather shoes with a button cover flap finished the outfit. The fabric of the outer garment was far less scratchy than the brown wool she had been wearing. The color reminded Fayre of the color of the Highlands on an early summer morning—a deep but muted green.

The kitchen maid instructed her not to knock; the laird was too feeble to answer. Fayre peered into the room. Her gaze traveled to a large canopied bed situated on the other side of the unlit fireplace.

God in heaven, I pray that I shall find favor with Thee. I ken I am selfish tae ask, but I ask Thee tae heal Laird Kenneth and t' protect me as well.

A lump underneath a pile of covers moaned. "Luke?"

The weakness of his voice made her feel as though she had been pierced through the heart with a lance. The magnitude of Laird Kenneth's illness struck her at that moment.

Lord, grant me courage.

"Nay, 'tis I," she answered aloud. "I ha'e come tae bring ye dinner." Fayre leaned partway out of the entrance and retrieved the tray.

"Fayre?" His voice sounded stronger. "It is you?"

Even in his puny state, the sound of his voice lifted Fayre's spirits. "Aye."

The covers moved and Laird Kenneth emerged from underneath them. He tried to sit upright, but only managed to prop himself upon his elbows. His hair was tangled and damp from fever. Fayre worried about his ashen skin and how he shivered, though she tried not to show it.

"I am glad tae see ye are feeling well enough to sit," Fayre noted as she set the tray on the table beside his bed. "I was expecting tae feed ye lying doon."

"Lying down, sitting up. In either position, I want no food." As if to demonstrate that he spoke the truth, he let his body fall back onto the pillows. "You should not be here."

"Aye, I should. I am determined tae nurse you back tae health. Whether you feel like it or not, ye maun eat." She lifted the cover from the largest dish. "Pheasant and turnips." She inspected the second dish. "And bread. Surely that will tempt ye."

"Nay."

She eyed a dessert. "Here is a fruit tart. If you dinna eat it, I surely shall."

"Go on with it. Why should I bother to eat? All is lost. I am doomed to die and take my entire castle with me."

"Do not speak like that!" The strength of her voice, daring to issue a command to her superior, surprised even herself.

"But it is true, is it not? I am doomed to death?"

"Nay. Ye arenna. By God's great mercy, I shall help make ye well." She pulled a chair up to the side of his bed. After she sat, Fayre tore a piece of bread from the small loaf and brought it close to his lips. "Here."

He shook his head. "Drink. May I have a drink?"

Saturated strands of hair hung above his eyes. He looked like a little boy who had just gone for a swim rather than a powerful man stricken with a dreaded disease. If only...

"I shall give ye drink," she said, "and then bathe your face with cool water."

Through half-closed eyes, Laird Kenneth looked upon her. "You are an angel."

She smiled. If only Murdag's image of her were true. If she were an angel, she would look upon the face of God each day. She could not.

Or could she?

"Thank you." Laird Kenneth's faint smile was her reward for cooling his face. She hadn't noticed until that moment, but his features were fine, as fine as any of the sculptured statues in the laird's gardens. Yet even in sickness, his eyes sparkled with the promise of fun.

He coughed.

Fayre could hear wheezing in his chest. The sounds frightened her. "Ye maun sit up. Ye maun clear yer lungs."

"Nay, it is too hard to sit," he said in between coughs. "I want to lie back down. Please." He let his head flop back onto the pillow.

"Nay. Ye maun let me prop you up."

"Nay." He pouted.

Fayre chuckled in spite of her frustration with him. "Did ye use that pout tae charm yer dear mother?"

"Aye, and she always let me have my way."

"Surely yer jesting is a sign that ye're feeling better already. So you should nae mind if I do this." She yanked the pillow from under his head.

"Say, what do you mean by that?"

"I mean tae rearrange the pillows so ye can breathe better. When I am through, ye'll feel so comfortable you will nae realize you are no longer lying doon."

"Since the plague has not killed me yet, you plan to finish the task?" He coughed as though for emphasis.

"Ye arenna a very good patient. 'Tis a sign ye're getting well." Fayre looked toward one of the small windows. Judging from the rays shining through, the sunlight was at its strongest. "Every minute ye live is a good sign. Many people are dead within hours of falling ill, ye know."

"I think of that every waking moment," he assured her. "God would not grant me a quick death. He decided I should suffer."

You should remember that the next time you collect the rents.

Fayre didn't dare speak aloud her private thoughts. Did the laird really deserve to suffer? Probably not. She had heard nothing but good about him since she arrived at the castle. Why else would she subject herself to the chance of becoming as ill as he?

"I'll have ye t' know, I've been praying for the whole castle," Fayre told him. "I dinna ken everyone's name, but the Savior does, and He answers prayer."

"You are praying for the whole castle?" he muttered.

"Aye."

"Then let us hope that the Father in heaven will indeed answer your prayers. Not a finer woman than you would be found among the ladies at the king's ball." His voice was soft. He gasped. "The king's ball. You should be there, dancing the night away, instead of here with me."

"Nay, I wouldna think of such a thing. What festivity would a ball be without ye?" Immediately she regretted her outburst. What was she thinking?

She was just about to apologize when his smile stopped her. "Next time, then," he murmured.

Perhaps her true feelings were what he needed to hear after all. She smiled in return. "Next time."

—⁂—

The next day, Kenneth opened his eyes. He could tell by his increased strength and improved humor that the plague had left his body.

Fayre's petitions to God had worked!

Imagine, the pleas of a mere serf. Then Kenneth remembered how Jesus healed the multitudes. Certainly everyone He touched wasn't a leader. And He listened to the pleas of women, even prostitutes.

Of course He heard Fayre!

Despite Kenneth's improvement, he felt weak and feverish and thought it best to remain in bed. As he recovered, shadowy nightmares haunted him before he awakened to the sound of singing and then fell asleep to the sound of sweet melodies. Fayre's voice was much prettier than any bird's song. She chose to sing psalms. The words comforted him, reminding him that the Lord was near. Her hands tended the withered laird much like they must have cared for her roses.

Too near, perhaps. Some nights, he thought for certain that he would be touched by death's icy hand. But that hand was stayed. Surely the heavenly Father heard his cries in the night. Cries in petition to preserve his own life—and Fayre's.

Kenneth barely remembered the first day he fell ill or when Fayre first arrived. All he knew was that she provided a constant presence for him, a presence of love and caring that confounded his reason for her sacrifice and courage in facing the unknown course of the plague.

"Fayre?" he called softly.

"Aye?" She left the window from which she had been peering and traveled swiftly to his bedside.

As she walked toward him, he noticed she wasn't wearing the brown garment. The new one wasn't as fashionable as the ones he'd seen in the king's court. Fabric dyed an indifferent shade of green hung on her small frame yet seemed tight around her waist. Even in such condition, the clothing was an improvement over the mean frock she once owned. "Is that the frock that Brona made for you?"

She looked downward. "Nay. It is Murdag's."

"Murdag's?" He laughed, filling the room with the sound of his mirth. "I never would have thought she would do you any favors."

"Neither did I, at first. She was a wee bit chilly toward me. I think she was insulted tae be assigned to one as lowly as I. Yoer high opinion of me encouraged her tae do me a good turn." She averted her eyes to the floor. "I ne'er did thank ye for taking my word over Sir Ulf's. If ye hadn't entered just at that moment..."

The thought of his boisterous knight clutching at Fayre as though she were a pawn in a game rather than a woman to be cherished enhanced his fever. "Let us not mention it again." His voice grew strong with resolve.

She sent him a smile that displayed the comely shape of her mouth. "What do ye need? A bite tae eat? Or drink tae quench your thirst?"

"Neither. I should like for you to summon my knight Walter."

She paused. "Why do ye need him? If there is something I can do for ye—"

"I doubt it. Unless perchance you can read." He made the suggestion knowing the prospect was unlikely at best. "I might try, only I still feel a bit weak."

"I wouldna ha'e ye try. Ye are still too ill."

"Walter, then. . ."

She answered with several rapid shakes of her head.

Why was she so reluctant to summon his knight? He had to admit, he hadn't missed his servants and squires much since he took ill. The past few days were nothing more than a fitful memory. Then a frightening thought occurred to him.

"Walter is not. . ." He didn't want to give voice to his fears. "He is not. . ."

"Nay," Fayre answered, obviously reading his thoughts. "He is well, as far as I ha'e been told."

"Thank our Father in heaven for such a blessing." He exhaled with relief.

"Aye, I prayed for him by name."

Kenneth felt his eyes mist with gratitude. He turned away so Fayre wouldn't see him in a moment of weakness. "So you will summon him?" he managed.

"There is no need. I can read to you," she answered.

Shocked, he turned his face back toward her. "What? But you—pardon me—are but a serf maiden." As soon as the words left his lips, he regretted them.

She lifted her chin in pride. "I am quite aware of that fact."

"Surely you cannot read Latin."

"Aye. Latin is the only language I can read. I told you aboot my uncle, the cleric. He taught me tae read."

So that is why her speech was closer to that of a lady than a serf! Certainly, her voice lilted with the Highland dialect, but it was nothing like the rest of the servants. Fayre's speech showed she was educated.

"Well, then," he said aloud, "would you be so kind as to read a bit of Scripture to me?"

"I wish I could. I ha'e not a copy. We were too poor tae have one of oor ain."

Of course they were. No serf was wealthy enough to own a copy of Scripture. Fayre was a prime example of what a person of low birth could achieve with the guidance of someone who cared and with the desire to learn and to remember.

Kenneth pointed to a wooden coffer in the corner of the room. "You will find one in there."

He watched as Fayre followed his instructions. When she opened the heavy chest and looked inside, she stopped for a moment. She reached for the book, but her motions were hesitant, as though the Words of God might impart judgment upon her in just the touching. She stroked the leather cover and took the tome in her arms, then held it to her chest as though it were a small child. Her excitement over touching a copy of sacred Scripture ignited his own.

"Open the book before me." Kenneth could hear the pitch of his own voice grow higher.

She complied, sitting in the chair beside him and examining several pages. Each one brought a gasp of delight. "I–I dinna feel worthy."

He understood. He knew from his own reading that the illuminations were startling in their detail. The monks at the monastery at Dryburgh had labored over the artwork for years. Kenneth extended his hand and touched hers. "You have come to nurse me at great risk to yourself. Surely you know I never would have asked that of you."

She nodded.

"Yet where are the others? I have many in my employ. Do you see them?" He paused. "That is the real reason why you were reluctant to summon Walter, is it not? You knew he did not want to take the risk of being too near me."

Fayre looked at the Bible in her lap. Her reticence only confirmed his suspicions.

"I would have expected as much from Ulf but not Walter." He pushed unwelcome thoughts from his mind and grasped Fayre's hand. Her fingers seemed so tiny in comparison to his own. When he gave them a gentle squeeze, she did not resist. "You nursed me all this time when no one else would. In my eyes, you are indeed worthy."

"Let us not be too quick tae judge the others," she answered. "Fear is a powerful emotion, and perhaps they dinna rely as fully upon God as I do. Nevertheless, I ha'e kept everyone in the castle in prayer. As of yet, I ha'e heard of no one's death."

"That is a blessing indeed. Thank you, Fayre," he said. "You are wiser than most learned men. I would be honored if you would read to me."

As Fayre's gentle lilt passed over the familiar words, Kenneth prayed for himself but said an especially fervent prayer for her.

Chapter 6

"The rosebush has many blooms," Kenneth said weeks later as they inspected the flowers in the garden.

"Aye. Norman took good care of them while I tended tae ye," Fayre agreed. "And they have flourished under my continued care, if ye dinna think me too vain tae admit."

"You are never vain." He observed the bright orange blooms and then looked into her eyes. "They are beautiful, but not nearly as beautiful as you."

Fayre felt herself blush. "Are ye delirious once again? Shall I return ye tae yer sickbed?"

"Never." He shuddered. "I have better plans for my future. Now that I have a future, thanks to you."

"Dinna give me such honor. 'Tis the heavenly Father who saw fit tae save ye."

"Your humility is charming in its sincerity." Kenneth took her hands in his. She liked the feel of his fingers wrapping themselves around hers in such a protective manner. "Fayre." His voice was almost a whisper. "I have a question to ask."

The way his voice dropped in pitch on the last word indicated he had turned serious. Her heart began thumping. "Aye?"

"Though I have never given voice to my feelings, surely you know by now how much I love you."

"Dinna say such a thing. I ken ye believe what ye say, but we have just seen the miracle of healing together. Ye were close to death, and our Creator breathed fresh life into ye with His ain breath. I believe that with all my heart."

"But you prayed for me."

"Aye." She averted her gaze to the roses, although the blooms no longer held any interest for her. "I ken yer love is felt only out of gratitude."

"Nay, 'tis not." With a gentle touch, he took her chin in his strong hand and tilted her face toward his. "My love for you is strong, Fayre. Stronger than any I have ever felt."

His cloaked reference to another stirred an unwelcome memory in Fayre's mind. "Even for Lady Letha?"

He jerked his head slightly, as if she had slapped him across the face. "Lady Letha?"

"Aye." She looked down at her feet, now shod in kid leather. "Dinna ye want me to grow the roses for her?"

His mouth dropped open. "For that foolish and idle woman?" Kenneth threw back his head and laughed. "Is that what you thought?"

Surprised by his reaction, she looked back up at him. "Aye. Yer knights said so on that first day ye brought me here."

"Did they now?" He chuckled. "Why did you let a little bit of jesting toward me throw you into such speculation? Nay, a match between the lady and me is but wishful thinking by my vassals, who value outward beauty far more than a lovely spirit. A marriage to her would add to my earthly riches but leave me hungry for spiritual food. Nay, such a woman will not suit. I am a free man, unwilling to tether myself to any but the finest woman." He looked her squarely in the eye. "No matter if she must barter a rosebush for her father's freedom."

The gravity of what he proposed struck her. "And if we were tae wed, I would be free."

"Aye."

"I could be marrying ye just tae gain my freedom," she challenged, although she knew her tone and expression indicated the opposite was true.

"I shall know you are not because your freedom does not depend on our marriage," he said. "Fayre, I grant you freedom now, whether or not we marry."

She gasped. "Truly?"

"Aye."

"Then I shall return the favor by releasing ye from any sense of gratitude. Ye need not marry me. By yer leave I shall take my freedom and depart." She curtsied.

Kenneth did not answer right away. He knew he had not asked her hand only out of gratitude for her devotion to him during his illness. Yet if she believed as much, he could only set her free. "Why, aye, you may depart," he managed. "I shall instruct Walter to escort you home."

"Thank ye, Kenneth," she said as she curtsied again. "I shall always be grateful tae ye."

Before he could answer, she ran back to the castle. She was free! She was going home!

—⁂—

Kenneth's countenance fell and his feet felt heavy in his boots. Fayre had run away from him. Was his company so horrible that she could no longer endure him? Had she been patient with him as a nursemaid during his sickness, praying for him to recover only so she could leave his presence?

Father in heaven, did I misread her? Was our time together of no more significance than that of a laird and a faithful servant?

Kenneth felt no sense of peace after his prayer. But he knew there would be even less serenity in his heart if he insisted on a wedding to a woman who ran from him.

He looked at the rosebush once more. Seeing the flowers brought rage to his being. Kenneth couldn't remember a time he wished he could tear an innocent plant from the ground by its roots and destroy it with his bare hands.

Resisting the urge, he turned away and headed toward his bedchamber intent on retiring early. To keep his promise, he was obligated to instruct Walter to escort Fayre home. Walter was the only knight that Kenneth wished to see. He was too proud to face anyone else in the moment of his darkest defeat.

—⁓—

Several hours later, Fayre and Walter approached the mean hut. Her heart pounded with joy. To see her father again! How many times had she thought about him and petitioned God for his continued health and well-being? Finally, she would look upon his face and hear his voice again.

Walter had barely stopped his horse when she jumped off, thanked the knight, and ran into the cottage. "Father! Father!"

"Fayre!" Witta rose from the small table where he was eating bread and vegetable soup and hurried to greet her. "My lassie! I ne'er thought I'd lay eyes on ye again." He wrapped his arms around her and squeezed her in a loving embrace. "This can only mean the roses bloomed, eh?"

"Aye, and Kenneth granted me freedom! I am free! Our debt has been paid." She stretched out her arms as though she could fly.

"Free! It canna be!"

"But 'tis!"

"Then we dinna pay rent t' the laird any longer." Witta's smile faded, and he furrowed his brows. "Free or not, ye maun call the laird by his title."

Fayre glanced at her feet in embarrassment, which only caused her father to look at them as well.

"Shoes!"

"Aye. A gift from the laird." She returned her gaze to his face. "I tended tae the laird when no one else would. He told me tae call him by his Christian name. I ken 'tis a privilege."

"A privilege!" Fear and suspicion entered his eyes. "What other liberties did he try to take?"

"None. I promise."

"Are ye sure, my lassie?"

She decided to omit the incident with Ulf. Why anger Father with a story about how she hadn't been entirely safe during her stay?

"Aye, Father," she responded. "Kenneth never touched me except to take my hands in his upon occasion." The memory of his strong hands holding her smaller ones sent a feeling of warmth through her body. She would miss such gestures, their conversations, and the life they shared however briefly. She couldn't think of that now. She was home.

"What, then?" he prodded. "Every gift from a man bears a price."

"A price! Many women would be happy tae pay such a price as he asked." She paused. "He asked me tae marry him."

"Marry him!" Witta chortled and slapped his knee with an energy she had no idea he could summon. " 'Tis no need tae jest with me, though the laugh has done me good, it has."

" 'Tis nae jest. He asked me tae marry him."

" 'Tis no jest?" He scratched his balding head, then smiled. " 'Tis no jest! My bonny lassie, 'tis a dream come true! And ye have come here tae take me to Kennerith Castle."

Fayre shook her head.

The happiness drained from Witta's face. "I see. 'Tisn't fitting for a lowly man like me tae be present at such a time."

She put her hands on his shoulders. "Nay! I told Kenneth I wouldna marry him."

"What? You denied him?" Witta's eyes widened. "And ye live tae tell the tale?"

"I dinna wish for a marriage based on gratitude alone. His gratitude, Father. I ken I do love him."

―――

In Kenneth's eyes, the castle seemed desolate since Fayre's departure. Its dreary stone ramparts seemed even darker on this day. Walter had returned without Fayre, unable to convince her to change her mind. How could she think that Kenneth had wanted her only out of appreciation for what she had done, however brave and good? Naturally, he felt grateful. But never would he propose marriage to any woman on such a weak foundation.

He loved her well beyond gratitude. How could he make her see? Desperately he wanted to chase after her, to make Dazzle gallop to the little hut she and her father shared. But when he asked the Lord for permission, he did not receive the Savior's leave. He would have to wait.

Father in heaven, what is Thy will for me? Surely the feelings I have must be love. But I wish not to marry her without Thy leading. I pray it is Thy will to send her back.

―――

A month later, Fayre was silent as she brought the day's milk into the hut. She set the worn wooden bucket on the table. "Care for a bit of warm milk, Father?"

"Nay, 'tis better tae save all we can for the cheese."

"The cheese." Fayre sighed.

"What's the matter? Ye ne'er minded making cheese before. Why do ye mope aboot, lassie?" her father asked. "Ye seem more enslaved than e'er, instead of the free lass ye are."

"Aye, but I dinna feel free."

"I ken. 'Tis love that enslaves ye, 'tis. Love that ye canna live the way God intended, as a man and wife should. Yer sitting here, all silent and miserable. That's nae way to be." He finished stoking the fire and came closer, then took her hands in his. "I remember how much I loved yer dear mother. I'm sure your laird is just as unhappy as ye, all alone as he is in that big castle."

His words brought a smile to her lips. "You dinna believe he proposed only oot of gratitude?"

"No man in his position would ask ye tae marry him out of thankfulness alone. Yer freedom would have been enough if that's all he felt. Nay, my lassie, he loves ye. And ye love him. Why dinna ye accept his proposal, Fayre?"

She looked around the hut. "But ye would be alone."

"I've been alone before, and I can be alone once more. 'Tis better for an old man set in his ways, anyhoo." He surveyed the tiny cottage. "This little cottage is all I've e'er kent, and I'm right fond of it. It's always been my life, and 'tis my life the noo. I know it was once all ye kent, but noo, there's nothing here for ye."

Fayre swallowed. If only he didn't speak the truth!

"Go," Father prodded. "I beg ye."

"Oh Father." She hugged him around the neck. "Yer guidance is what I've been praying for all these weeks. Now I know I ha'e release t' return tae Kennerith Castle."

When she broke the embrace, she saw tears in her father's eyes.

———※———

"There we go, Dazzle. Good boy." Kenneth stroked the horse's neck. "Time to survey my properties toward Loch Tay." Despite his cheerful demeanor, he'd been dreading this day for weeks. He desperately wanted to visit Witta's hut, but should he? Could he?

No. Fayre had fled at the prospect of wedding him. All was lost.

Kenneth and two vassals exited the courtyard, crossing the drawbridge that kept them safely out of the moat. The day promised to be long and hard.

They had only traveled a mile or so when in the distance, he heard horses' hooves clomping on the crude path ahead. "Halt," Kenneth instructed his vassals. "Let us wait and see who approaches." He stiffened, ready to draw his lance for battle.

When he recognized the coal black steed favored by Sir Rolfe, tensions eased. His knight and the two others who were with him, approached.

"A profitable day at the marketplace, I presume?" Kenneth asked.

"Aye." Rolfe's smile told him that he had a surprise that would please Kenneth.

"Good bargains, eh?" he guessed. "You always were good at bartering."

"Better than that. I found quite a prize." Rolfe tilted his head toward the last knight. At that moment, Kenneth realized that a woman rode with him. The last knight disembarked and assisted her.

Fayre!

He drew a sharp breath and leapt off Dazzle. "Fayre?"

The maiden he had come to love ran toward him. " 'Tis I!"

"You have returned!" He wanted to take her in his arms with more passion than he had ever displayed, but he hesitated. If he was mistaken, if she hadn't returned to accept his proposal but for some other reason, to greet her as a lover would make him appear foolish.

"Have I waited too long?" she asked.

He noticed that she trembled slightly. "Too long?"

She opened her lips to speak, but then seemed to remember that their actions were being witnessed by five knights.

" 'Never' would be too long." Kenneth extended his hand. "Lead on, my faithful men. Your lady has my favor. To Kennerith in haste that this joy may be welcomed to all within and beyond."

—⁂—

Despite the rapture she felt at riding upon Dazzle with Kenneth once again, Fayre quivered in anticipation and dread as they approached Kennerith Castle. What would he do once they were inside the castle?

The courtyard they entered was now familiar. Memories of her first encounter with the castle flashed through her mind. The circumstances were so different, yet the stakes were equally high. Perhaps even higher.

Kenneth helped her from the horse. "Are you in need of sustenance?" he asked as her feet touched the ground.

Fayre couldn't have eaten had her life depended upon it. "Nay."

"I wonder why you do not waste away to nothing," Kenneth teased. He snapped his fingers at a nearby squire. "Tell Cook I want the midday meal served to Fayre and myself in my private quarters."

"Aye."

"And have her send plenty of fruit tarts." Kenneth smiled at Fayre. "Before we retire to dinner, I want to show you something."

He walked in the direction of the garden.

My roses!

The brilliant blooms shone from the entryway. Sunlight filtered through the clouds above. Fayre quickened her pace so she could examine them more closely. As soon as she neared the bush, she touched one of the rose petals. "These blooms are beautiful! Even more beautiful than before." She turned to Kenneth and saw that he wore a pleased expression. "The king will love them."

"Aye. But I care less about what the king thinks of them than what you think. I am glad to see you are delighted with the care they have received in your absence." He motioned his hand toward the bush. "Go ahead. Pick one for yourself. Such a bloom would look pretty in your hair."

Fayre hesitated.

Not one to wait, Kenneth plucked the largest bloom and placed it over her ear.

Just the simple movement bringing him in such close proximity to her filled her with anticipation about the future.

Kenneth escorted Fayre to a small sitting room within his residence. When they entered, she knew she was home.

The fire was lit, and this time Kenneth suggested with a wave of his hand that she take the seat opposite his. She obeyed, though she was unaccustomed to the pillowed bench. She noticed that Kenneth shifted forward in his seat.

"So," he said, his voice a wee bit too cheerful, "Rolfe found you in the marketplace?"

"Aye. Father and I searched until we found one of yer knights." She hesitated.

"You did?" He leaned toward her, his eyes bright.

"Aye. I–I wanted to return." She peered at the stone floor and studied it to avoid his inquisitive gaze. Fayre couldn't bring herself to look him squarely in the eye. Not yet. "I hope my return doesna distress ye."

"Nay," he whispered.

The one word gave her courage to look at him. "I am here for a reason." Not knowing what else to do, Fayre stood and then curtsied so low that her nose nearly touched the floor. "If I am not too late. . ." She lifted her eyes toward his face. "I would be honored to accept yer proposal of marriage."

Her legs quivered and her heart beat wildly. What if she was too late? What if he had already found a lady? Or worse, become betrothed in her absence?

No, she would have heard.

"Fayre?" he said. "Why do you not answer? Can you not understand what I say?"

She had been so busy thinking terrible thoughts that he might not want her anymore, she must not have heard him nor noticed that he was standing before her. Suddenly unable to utter another word, Fayre managed to shake her head.

He took her hand and guided her to her feet. "Aye, I still want to marry you. This castle is nothing but a shell without your shining presence. I am the one who would be honored for you to be my wife."

As Kenneth entwined her in his strong arms, Fayre looked into his handsome face and saw that his lips were nearing her own. Again she quivered, but not with dread. Rather than the fright she had felt with Ulf, she welcomed her first kiss—a kiss from the man she had grown to love.

As his warm mouth touched hers, the heat of love filled her. At that moment, she realized that her sacrifice, which now seemed so small, had given her rewards beyond her most treasured hopes and dreams.

FRESH HIGHLAND HEIR

by Jill Stengl

Prologue

Crash! Thunk.

Icy air ruffled the bed curtains like groping hands.

"Papa!" Celeste shrieked. Visions of tattooed, spear-brandishing savages slithered through her imagination. Clutching her blankets to her chest, she pulled aside the bed curtain and felt about on a table until she found her eyeglasses.

Her father rapped at the door connecting their chambers before he entered, bed-shoes flopping, nightcap hanging in his face. "Are ye safe, lass?" He held up a candle and studied the shattered glass on the inn floor.

"No harm has come to me, but look." Celeste pointed, still hooking a wire behind her ear with the other hand. "Another message. Someone follows us."

A rock lay amid the shards beneath the window, wrapped in paper and tied with string. Her father picked it up, slid the note free, and read. The candle highlighted frown lines on his brow.

"Papa, what does it say?"

He threw the rock out the window and crumpled the note. "Come, let us trade chambers until morn. Have a care for your feet."

"Papa, is it another threat? Why didna ye let me marry Roderick and remain in Edinburgh? He would have protected me."

"We'll discuss this another time. Be off with ye now."

Chapter 1

Through the thick lenses of her lorgnette, Lady Celeste Galbraith studied the passing landscape with avid interest. White clouds cast fleeting shadows across high green hills. Pine-scented air brushed her face. The heavy carriage swayed and bumped over ruts in the primitive road, its wheels passing alarmingly close to a steep drop-off. She looked behind, searching for pursuit, but the winding road lay empty in the wake of the earl's procession of coaches and riders.

"Sit back, please, my lady," moaned Mr. Ballantyne.

Celeste turned her lorgnette to survey her traveling companions in the opposite seat. Mr. Ballantyne covered his mouth with a lacy handkerchief. His wig sat askew upon his bald head, and heavy bags hung beneath his faded eyes. His daintily shod feet dangled above the floorboards.

"I am sorry ye're ill, Mr. Ballantyne, but I've an interest in our surroundings." She focused her gaze upon the earl. "This is a desolate land, Papa. These mountains roll on forever like the sea."

Mr. Ballantyne moaned.

A twinkle appeared in the earl's dark eyes. "I forget that ye dinna remember our last visit to Kennerith Castle, my dearie. Ye were but a lass."

"I remember Uncle Robert from his visits to us in Edinburgh." Celeste recalled a stern gentleman.

"Aye, 'tis not a year since last we saw him." Her father looked pensive.

"Struck down in his prime, he was. A judgment from God." Mr. Ballantyne shifted his handkerchief to speak.

Celeste saw a cloud cross her father's face, but he said nothing.

"D'ye recognize these hills, Papa?" Celeste found it difficult to imagine him as a lad. Over one shoulder she regarded his narrow face and scholarly brow.

"Aye, that I do. This fresh Highland air nurtures many a hearty lad and forms him into a doughty warrior." She saw his gaze slide to Mr. Ballantyne. "Else it breaks a man's health, and he retires to the fireside, books, and ledgers."

"Doughty warriors," muttered Mr. Ballantyne. "Heathen barbarians, more like. These hills teem with painted, kilted savages. Nary a step up from the beasts, most of them." His watery eyes focused upon Celeste. "Tales abound of their treachery. How they'll skin a man alive and drag his woman into the hills and—"

"Fireside tales and legends. Enough, Ballantyne." When Malcolm Galbraith spoke in that tone, few men dared oppose him. He coughed into his fist, frowned, and subsided into the corner. Ballantyne retreated behind his handkerchief.

Celeste returned her attention to the scenery framed by the carriage window. Did danger truly lurk amid these rocky peaks and sylvan glens?

The warble of a horn caught her attention. Craning her neck to peer forward, she saw the attendant riders ahead disappear over a rise. The coach horses strained, their sweaty haunches driving upward. A whip cracked, and the postilions shouted encouragement to the six-horse team. A lurch, and the carriage leveled out.

The earl joined his daughter at the window. "Kennerith Castle." His voice held a breathless hush.

Beside the windswept surface of a loch, ancient stone turrets glowed against their emerald backdrop of hills. Then scudding clouds hid the sun, and the fortress plunged into gloom. With a great clacking of hooves upon paving stones, the entourage swept over a bridge and through a stone archway. Ahead, servants lined the castle's stone steps and curving drive, shoes polished, wigs brushed, buttons gleaming. The brisk spring breeze turned coattails into banners and skirts into sails.

Celeste blinked and lowered her lorgnette, wondering at her sense of dread. "So many servants."

"Ye're the daughter of a laird now, my lady," Mr. Ballantyne reminded her. "Remain seated until a footman places the step. Let me disembark first so that I may make proper introductions."

As soon as Mr. Ballantyne looked away, Celeste rolled her eyes. Irritating little man. He seemed to have made a miraculous recovery when the castle came into sight. Papa should put Mr. Ballantyne in his proper place. Papa was the new earl; Mr. Ballantyne was a mere secretary, related distantly to the family.

The carriage stopped. Celeste heard a confusion of barking dogs, clopping hooves, laughter and shouts of greeting, and the rumble of the baggage coach arriving behind. Servants in the earl's scarlet-and-silver livery passed the windows.

The coach door opened, and a footman placed the step. Mr. Ballantyne climbed down, his spindly legs tottering with fatigue, and began to speak to a waiting lackey.

"You next, Papa," Celeste requested, dreading the scrutiny of so many servants. How did they feel about a new earl taking over Kennerith Castle? Would they welcome the earl's daughter? The hand gripping her lorgnette handle trembled, making it difficult for her to see clearly. Vanity forbade Celeste to wear her eyeglasses in public, but the stylish lorgnette had its disadvantages.

Her father descended from the coach and surveyed his new domain. Mr.

Ballantyne's reedy voice announced into a sudden hush: "Malcolm Galbraith, fifth earl of Carnassis, seventh viscount of Dalway, and tenth baron of Kennerith."

Cheering broke out, and Papa bowed. Still smiling, he turned back to the coach and reached a hand to Celeste. "Keep your head high and win them with your smile."

Celeste followed her billowing skirts out into the sunlight and wind, holding her straw hat to her head. Everything was a blur until she let go of her skirts and lifted her lorgnette.

A middle-aged servant stepped forward and bowed. "Welcome back to Kennerith Castle, your lairdship. I am Crippen, the house steward."

"Good afternoon, Crippen. May I present Miss. . .uh, Lady Celeste Galbraith." Papa had not yet adjusted to his own august role, let alone to his daughter's honorary title.

With Mr. Ballantyne leading the way, the earl and Celeste passed along the line of servants, nodding with polite reserve after each introduction. Celeste felt as if she were an actress playing a part. She did not catch even one name, and not one servant looked her in the eye. As they passed the lead coach horses, amid the animals' heavy breathing, Celeste heard a whisper. Curious, she turned with a swirl of skirts and lifted her lorgnette.

Mr. Ballantyne gripped the sleeve of the manservant holding the bridle of one lead coach horse. Scrawny neck extended, standing on tiptoe, the earl's secretary attempted to whisper into the servant's ear, "His lairdship has need of ye."

Celeste took one backward step and twisted her foot on a cobblestone. Stumbling sideways, she gave a little squeal. Someone caught her by the elbows, and she scrambled to regain her footing. The world was a blur of scarlet-and-silver uniforms except for the wrinkled face inches from hers. "Air ye hurt, me lady?"

The old servant released her elbows and backed away until he, too, became a smudge. Celeste tried to laugh. "This terrible stony road! Just call me 'Your Grace.'" She quelled rising panic. "I seem to have dropped my lorgnette."

"My lady." One scarlet figure detached itself from the general haze. Celeste took a step forward and discerned an outstretched arm. "My lady, your spectacles."

She reached to accept them, but her hand closed upon empty space. A gloved hand gripped her arm, and she felt the handle of her lorgnette press against her palm. Her face felt hot. Now everyone knew her infirmity. "Th–thank you." She lifted the lorgnette. Silvery gray eyes met her gaze and widened. She caught a flash of amusement before he bowed.

"A pleasure it is to serve ye, my lady." It was the man to whom Ballantyne had been whispering.

"Be thankful the lenses didna break," her father remarked, then shifted his address to the helpful servant. "Ye've a familiar aspect. Have ye been at the castle long?"

The man bowed again. "I served the late earl many years, your lairdship. Perhaps ye've seen me attend him during visits in Edinburgh."

"Ah." The earl moved on. Celeste followed, her chin held high, bestowing a regal nod upon each person in the remaining lineup of servants. Her forearm still felt the firm grip of a leather glove. Was he watching? Her posture was perfect, her smile bright as she turned on the top step for one last overview of the serving staff.

Her eyes sought the coach horses. Her hopes drooped. The carriage was just disappearing into the stable yard below.

—☸—

"Come in, lad. Come in." Mr. Ballantyne and the earl lounged beside the hearth, smoking clay pipes.

Celeste did not look up from her needlework when the manservant stepped inside and stood at attention, but her heart picked up its pace.

"I've been telling his lairdship about ye," Mr. Ballantyne said. Celeste distrusted the old man's hearty manner. She pulled through a stitch of gold thread and arranged the strands with her thumbnail until they lay flat.

"Strong enough, aye, but he looks o'er-young. Are ye sure he's the man we want?" Celeste recognized her father's evaluation voice, usually reserved for oral examination of university students. For what task did he require this servant's strength?

"Certain-sure. Take a seat here, Allan." Ballantyne waved a withered hand. "Despite the lad's Highland lineage, the late earl favored him. Sent him to school in Aberdeen, where Allan distinguished himself. After the lad's graduation, the earl hired him as bodyguard."

"Where was this Allan the night my brother Robert died?"

"No bodyguard could have saved his lairdship. The coroner said 'twas a stroke. If it means aught to ye, I saw this lad weep for your brother that night. I wept meself, if the truth be known."

Celeste glanced up to see Mr. Ballantyne wipe his nose with a handkerchief. He would be wearing his sanctimonious expression, she was certain.

The servant named Allan perched on the edge of a chair. Celeste picked up her lorgnette and sneaked a look. He was as comely as she remembered. Those black brows and fine gray eyes! He must have dark hair beneath his wig, she decided. His hand picked at the buttons at the knee of his breeches.

He glanced right and caught her staring. He smiled. The lorgnette fell to her lap, and she picked up her needlework, holding the fabric mere inches from her nose.

"Are ye a supporter of the Jacobite cause?" the earl inquired gruffly.

"Nay—" His voice cracked. He coughed. "Nay, your lairdship. Some of my relations sympathized with the Stuarts, but I couldna support the cause. My loyalty and service are yours."

"Which clan?" the earl asked.

"I have taken the name Croft."

"I asked which clan."

A pause before Allan said, "MacMurray."

At her father's exclamation, Celeste hastily retrieved her lorgnette. She could not interpret the earl's expression, a combination of disgust and amusement.

"Och, Robert!" The earl shook his head, then pinned Allan with a glare. "Lad, ye must ken that we Galbraiths are sworn enemies to your clan these two hundred years and more. Blackmailers, thieves, pillagers, and worse are the MacMurrays."

"I've heard equally dire account of the Galbraiths. I disapprove the violent acts of both sides. Before her death just ere my ninth birthday, my mother advised me to come to the earl of Carnassis."

"And your clan didna object?"

"My mother's wish overrode any objection. I believe some connection existed in the family, though I am unaware of its nature. Your brother, his lairdship, once told me I had no need to ken."

The earl wiped a hand across his mouth and studied his slipper-clad feet. His gaze lifted to the portrait of his late brother that hung above one door. Celeste's blood ran cold as she read her father's thoughts, and she gazed upon the servant with empathy.

Mr. Ballantyne cleared his throat. "One reason I called ye here, Allan, was to deliver this. I found it among the late earl's effects." He produced a note with a broken seal and handed it to Allan MacMurray.

Celeste watched Allan turn the note over and over, then unfold and scan the message. His gaze lifted to the large Bible upon a reading stand in one corner of the room, and his face went red.

"Can ye tell us its meaning?" Ballantyne asked.

"Nay. It seems. . .out of character." Allan read the message aloud. " 'My son, all ye need to know is found in the Holy Scriptures. C. IV'" After clearing his raspy voice, he interpreted the signature. "Carnassis the fourth."

"So my brother turned to religion before the end," the earl said.

"Yet ne'er did he confess his sins," Ballantyne added with a lifted brow. "Now what do ye think, your lairdship?" He seemed to stress the term of address.

"I think ye've a brilliant mind," the earl replied.

Celeste laid aside her sewing and arose. The three men started to rise, but she shook her head. "Prithee, pay me no mind." They settled back into their chairs.

She began to stroll about the room, running her fingers across the spines of priceless volumes. Because of her voluminous skirts, she had to turn sideways to fit between the bookcase and an armchair.

"Are ye married?" the earl asked Allan abruptly.

"Nay."

"Pledged?"

"I have ties to no woman or man."

"Ballantyne tells me ye're trustworthy with women. Is this true?"

"In God's strength, I strive to treat all people as my kin in Christ Jesus."

The earl sat back. "Ah, a sincere man of religion. I am satisfied. This is a delicate situation, Allan MacMurray."

"Croft, if ye please, your lairdship."

"Croft it will be. Ye see, lad, I neither expected nor desired to become a peer. I am a man of books, not of politics nor business, and the responsibilities that come with a title are odious to me. My brother, James, was Robert's heir, and he had two sons. All three perished last year of influenza."

Celeste pulled out a book and fluttered its musty pages. A silence and conferring whispers brought her attention back to the men. Unfortunately, her lorgnette lay on the table, so she was unable to read their expressions. At times she wondered if appearing more beautiful was worth being unable to see.

"Celeste, 'twould be best if ye retired," the earl said, sounding ill at ease.

She closed the book. "If this concerns me, Papa, I wish to hear your arrangements." Too many secrets had been kept from her already.

"Very well." He turned back to the servant. "Allan, I wish to hire ye as personal bodyguard to my daughter."

"I?" Allan's voice cracked again. "What could anyone hope to gain by harming the lady?"

"I dinna ken. But twice I have received threatening letters. One arrived in Edinburgh ere our departure, the other last night at an inn along the way. Both poorly written, as ye'll note." He handed something to the servant—presumably the letters.

"Papa, why do I need a bodyguard?" Celeste asked. "I thought the threats were against you."

"The first threat demanded that I remain in Edinburgh and abdicate the Galbraith family claim to title and lands. Last night's note threatened your safety if I dinna return immediately to Edinburgh. The rogue knows the vulnerability of a father's heart."

The sincerity in her father's voice startled Celeste. Did he truly care so much? A month ago she would have taken his love for granted, but now. . .

The earl addressed Allan. "I want my daughter attended at all times, night and day."

Celeste turned back to the bookshelf lest the servant behold her crimson cheeks. Whatever was Papa thinking?

"At *all* times? Would not a woman be a more appropriate custodian?"

"I'm hiring ye to guard my daughter, not to question my judgment. I'm sure ye'll come to a balance 'twixt protection and propriety. Her safety, not her convenience, will be your primary concern. I'll so task ye only until the day Lady Celeste is wedded."

Wedded? Celeste's heart took wing. Papa must be considering Cousin Roderick's matrimonial offer after all! Soon she would be married and living back in Edinburgh, far away from this castle. Closing her eyes, she pressed one hand to her throbbing bosom. *Roderick knows me better than anyone, and he loves me.*

"That day may yet be years away, your lairdship," Allan protested.

"Ooh!" Celeste whirled about, and her skirts knocked a candlestick to the floor. Wax spattered in an arc across the rug. The flame extinguished.

"As ye see, I have other reasons for requiring her close supervision," the earl replied calmly.

"Papa!" Mortified, she hurried to her worktable. Her groping hands knocked her embroidery to the floor. Her lorgnette—where was it?

Allan knelt at her feet. "My lady." Once again he caught her arm and placed the lorgnette handle against her palm.

She lifted it to give him a baleful stare, but he was busy picking bits of embroidery thread from the Oriental rug. Folding her needlework, he replaced it on the table. Sweat beaded his brow and upper lip. His irritatingly angelic grin had vanished.

As Allan returned to his seat, Celeste confronted her father, ready for a fight. The earl wore a bemused smile. To her surprise, he lowered one lid in an affectionate wink.

"Ballantyne tells me scattered bands of Highlanders hide out in my hills," the earl said, "and these heathen folk dare to raid local villages and farms despite the military stationed nearby."

"They raid because they would otherwise starve." Allan shifted in his seat. "Are ye certain, your lairdship, that a guard need be put upon her ladyship while she is *inside* the castle? And what of your own safety?"

"I am armed. With numerous servants in my employ, many of them no doubt Highlanders, the danger to my daughter could arise from within these walls. I can take no chances. While Celeste is well educated for a woman, she lacks practical understanding. Her fortune has made her the desire of more than one impecunious scoundrel, and her artlessness leads her to believe them sincere. She canna see beyond the end of her nose either figuratively or in fact."

"Papa! I am no fool," Celeste protested in a choked voice. "And I need no armed eunuch at my gate as if my room housed a harem." She approached Allan's chair and glared down at him. "Be warned that should ye choose to become my guardian, I shall make your life miserable!"

Chapter 2

Heels clicked on flagstone floors. "Sirra?"

A dark figure appeared above the back of a bench. "It is arranged?"

"Aye, and his lairdship suspects naught. 'Twill keep the rascal under our eyes and the peerage safe. Ye're keeping your part?" The smaller figure glanced around fearfully. Moonlight shining through stained glass turned his wig orange and blue.

"Trust me. Meet here again in a fortnight."

―∽―

"Ye'll be comfortable in this chamber, m'lady. 'Twas furnished by your grandmother, Lady Elizabeth Galbraith. Your aunt Olivia died in that bed at the tender age of eighteen. Her portrait hangs beside the door." The house steward, Crippen, spoke in a monotone brogue.

"Indeed." Celeste knew the steward's inspection was mere protocol. A complaint from her would produce no change—the earl had insisted she occupy the chambers in the east tower, which were accessible only by use of a spiral staircase. Celeste's legs already ached from ascending and descending those narrow stone steps.

"Beryl Mason will be your personal maid," Crippen continued.

Celeste nodded at the white-capped woman beside him. "Aye, we met earlier today."

The steward said, "If ye have any need, m'lady, dinna hesitate to ring. Our desire is to serve ye well."

"Many thanks, Mr. Crippen," Celeste said in her best lofty manner. "This bedchamber is chilled. I require a larger fire."

" 'Twill be attended, m'lady." Crippen bowed and retired. The wooden door closed behind him with a hollow boom, and a small chunk of plaster fell from the wall.

Shivering, Celeste glanced around her bedchamber. It looked, if possible, worse by candlelight than by daylight. Faded tapestries lined the outer walls. A high, four-poster bed hung with brocaded curtains nearly touched the mildewed ceiling. One of the lathe-and-plaster interior walls seemed to bulge inward, and the floor had a definite slant. Nevertheless, aside from its architectural flaws, it was a chamber befitting a princess. . .a consumptive princess doomed to pine her life away in seclusion, or maybe a doddering maiden princess whose one lover died sixty years earlier on the eve of their wedding.

Pushing her glasses higher on her nose, Celeste met her maid's gaze and forced herself to smile. "I am certain we shall suit each other, Beryl."

The maid appeared to be in her early twenties, a few years older than Celeste. Her square face was handsome with its full lips and black-lashed blue eyes. A large knot of red hair and a generous figure completed her somewhat earthy attractions.

Someone rapped at the chamber door.

"Enter."

The latch lifted, and the heavy door creaked open. "My lady? I bring fuel for your fire." Celeste's unwanted bodyguard carried a sack over his shoulder. His beatific smile was back.

"I am grateful." Too late Celeste remembered to remove her eyeglasses. With an inward grimace, she realized that he would often see her wearing the ugly device during his stint as her guardian. She might as well swallow her pride and pretend unconcern. The admiration of a servant was inconsequential, after all.

Celeste watched him kneel beside her hearth and poke at the smoldering peat. He added two additional bricks of fuel and blew until they began to burn.

Beryl joined Allan at the fire and slowly ran a finger across his shoulders until her body pressed against his. "Meet me in the rose garden tonight?" she murmured in a seductive tone. Feeling her face burn, Celeste turned to arrange her hairbrushes on the dressing table.

"I have duties, as have you." Allan's voice sounded friendly yet detached. "Why not ask Dougal?"

"Wherefore would I be wanting to meet me own brother?" Beryl snapped.

He ignored her. "My lady?"

Celeste met his direct gaze and felt as if she should curtsy. "Aye?" *He is a servant,* she reminded herself, lifting her chin.

"By the earl's command, I shall sleep in your drawing room to keep watch o'er your chamber door. Should ye have need of protection, my sword and my life are yours." He bowed and made a hasty exit.

"As if I need a bodyguard," Celeste said. "Where do ye sleep, Beryl?"

"In the servants' quarters o'er the kitchen."

Celeste studied the maid's flaming hair, met her fiery gaze, and decided not to inquire further. "Assist me with my gown, if ye please."

Beryl lifted the gown over Celeste's head, then unlaced the corset and helped her mistress step out of the hooped bustle and underskirts. Celeste tried not to stare at

Beryl's arms, which were hairier and more muscular than many a man's.

While Celeste sat in a padded chair, Beryl unpinned her mistress's hair and brushed until it crackled. Celeste closed her eyes and groaned with pleasure. "Ye've a gentle touch, Beryl. After the tales Mr. Ballantyne told, I expected a wilderness inhabited by half-naked, tattooed savages clad in kilts. I was almost disappointed to find ye civilized."

Beryl remained silent, so Celeste chattered on. "I ne'er had a personal maid until last autumn when Papa hired Marie. She refused to leave Edinburgh, professing fear of the Highlanders, which is purely nonsense. Certain I am that ye'll be an excellent replacement maid, Beryl."

Celeste tipped her head back to smile at the Highland woman.

"Why d'ye wear that?" Beryl pointed the brush at Celeste's glasses.

"I canna see without them," Celeste admitted.

"Not at all?"

"Only a blur. Have ye lived at the castle long?" she asked. Establishing rapport with this maid would require concentrated effort.

"Nigh a year. Allan got me the work. We are soon to wed."

"Ah," Celeste said, concealing her skepticism. "I, too, intend to wed soon. Roderick is my father's heir. I first met him only last month, yet I feel as though I have loved him always."

"In his mate, Allan requires strength and courage to match his own. He despises weakness and timidity—such women he uses and tosses aside." Beryl's tone implied that Celeste was the useless type.

"Ye wish to marry a man who uses and discards women?" Celeste turned in her chair. "Allan claimed high principles. I must inform my father of his deceit. Perhaps he'll be relieved of this ridiculous duty. I should prefer to have ye near, if attended I must be."

Beryl's gaze traveled over her mistress in a way that made Celeste uncomfortable. On further consideration, she would prefer not to have this fierce maiden too near. Wishing she had donned her bed gown, she drew her chemise up over her shoulders and tightened its drawstring. "Roderick will come soon and marry me. He promised to love me forever."

Taking Celeste's hair in her hands, Beryl divided it into three sections and began to braid. "He is rich?"

"Nay, but he is fine and good." Smiling, Celeste recalled her cousin's burning dark eyes. "In his presence, I feel womanly. But Papa insists he courts me only for. . ." Her voice and her smile faded.

Roderick was not her only beau. Lord Werecock had also promised eternal fidelity; and, but a fortnight past, the viscount of Downeybeck had knelt at her feet in the university gardens and composed a sonnet "To the Ringlet Upon Her Shoulder."

Papa insisted these admirers cared solely for her fortune. It was true that no suitors had approached Celeste until news spread of the comfortable inheritance in English funds left to her upon her eighteenth birthday by her mother's mother. Celeste preferred to believe that her youth and reclusive lifestyle accounted for the gentlemen's previous lack of attentiveness. Surely such tender admiration could not be feigned. They must truly love her. . .mustn't they?

Beryl tied off the brown braid with a ribbon and dropped it over her mistress's shoulder. "I'd advise ye to make haste and marry ere ye join the ranks of maidens who've perished in this tower. Your aunt wasna the first."

Startled, Celeste looked up. An enigmatic smirk curled Beryl's lips. "I changed the water in your basin, and I'll bank the fire. D'ye need aught besides?"

"I–I think not."

When Beryl had retired, Celeste paced the chamber's warped floorboards. Pausing before Lady Olivia's portrait, she wrinkled her nose. "Ye're no true relation to me, my lady. Which fact disturbs me not at all, for either the artist had no talent or ye were a bloodless weakling. I'll be fearing not your haunt or any other."

She rubbed her upper arms. "Bodyguard, indeed. Personal maid, indeed." Disappointment at her failed efforts to befriend Beryl pushed out her lower lip. "I need no friends; I need no one. When Roderick comes for me, I'll run away with him if Papa refuses his consent."

Not even to herself could she speak aloud the doubts that gnawed like mice at the fringes of her self-respect. Only recently had Roderick brought to her attention certain disturbing truths. Celeste had often heard her father relate the tale of her parents' whirlwind romance—they had married within three weeks of meeting. He also frequently told of his joy at Celeste's birth. The one fact he omitted was the two-month interval between these important dates.

She opened one of the casement windows and leaned upon the sill. The castle rooftops below lay in shadow. Only a squirrel could escape by that route. Flashes of lightning glared upon hilltops far beyond the fortress walls and revealed lowering black clouds. The drapes billowed behind her, and several candles snuffed out.

Celeste's chin lifted. She spread her arms wide and felt her chemise whip about her legs. Heart pounding in strange ecstasy and defiance, she laughed aloud. "I am strong!"

A knock at the door whipped her around. "Who is there?" She grabbed her bed gown off a hook and slipped it on, buttoning with shaking fingers.

"Are ye alone, my lady?"

The bodyguard. Celeste pressed a hand to her racing heart and hurried to lean against the door. There was neither lock nor bar.

"To whom were ye speaking just now?" he persisted.

"Am I not allowed a soliloquy?"

A pause. "Ye needna fear me, my lady. Sleep well."

She hardened her heart against his beguiling voice. "Beryl says ye plan to wed her."

Silence.

"Allan MacMurray? D'ye hear me?"

His reply sounded distant. "Allan Croft is my name. If ye must ken, I hear your every word. The walls and door are none too sturdy."

"So ye o'erheard my conversation with Beryl? How impolite!"

"I coughed and made noise, hoping ye'd take the hint. In future, please say naught ye'd desire no man to hear."

Celeste recalled what he had already overheard, and her face flamed. "Are ye pledged to marry Beryl? Ye told my father otherwise."

"Beryl may say what she will, but I won't wed her."

Celeste blinked, uncertain which report to believe. "God give ye rest this night." She hesitated over his name. Nobility addressed most house servants by their first names, yet Celeste felt shy about treating this man with such informality. "Regretful I am that ye're saddled with this nonsensical post, but. . .but I dinna promise to be an easy charge."

"I ne'er expected ye would be."

Celeste nearly jerked open the door to demand an explanation for that remark but decided to wait until morning. After extinguishing her remaining candles, she climbed into bed. Firelight from the adjoining chamber shone through cracks in the door and beneath it. Celeste laid her eyeglasses on a bedside table, knelt on the counterpane, and tugged at her bed curtains. They refused to move. Rather than relight a candle and discover the reason, she gave up and left the curtains open.

Beryl had forgotten to warm the bed linens. Teeth chattering, Celeste waited for her body to heat them.

Could he hear every little sound from her chamber? How embarrassing!

Sometime during the night, she awakened with a start. Only after a moment of terror did she remember her whereabouts. The castle lay in deadly silence except for a strange noise. Celeste lay rigid beneath her coverlet. Rats? Bats? Ghosts? Fear made her hands clammy and formed a lump in her throat. "Mr. Croft?" she squeaked.

No reply. Had some assassin dispatched her bodyguard? Did a threat to her life lurk in one of the room's dark corners? Or had everyone else vanished in the night, leaving her alone in the ancient fortress? "Allan MacMurray!" She panicked, sitting bolt upright. "Where are ye?"

The sound stopped. Had her cries frightened it away? She heard rapid steps, and the door creaked open. "Did ye call, my lady?"

"I heard a noise. It has stopped now," she admitted, holding her coverlet beneath her chin.

"D'ye wish me to search your chamber?" he asked in a groggy-sounding voice.

"Please." She found her glasses and hooked them over her ears.

Allan knelt at her hearth to light a candle at the banked embers. He cupped one hand around the flame as he rose. His cropped hair, no longer hidden by a wig, appeared dark. Celeste watched him check behind her curtains and screens, then lean out each of the two windows. His bare feet padded silently as he returned to the doorway and faced her. He still wore his knee breeches and a full-sleeved white shirt, partly untucked and unbuttoned.

His white teeth flashed as he spoke. "Naught to fear. Perhaps ye heard the call of a wild creature in the hills." Dared the rogue laugh at her?

Celeste swallowed hard. "I thank ye," she managed to say.

When he was gone, she lay back. How strange to have a man in her bedchamber, and at her father's behest! "He wouldna dare touch me," she whispered to calm her turbulent emotions. "I needna fear him. He is my servant. Mine to order as I will." The idea had its attractions. She imagined him wild with desire for her. How she would laugh and spurn him, her devoted slave! He would learn that woman was not intended solely for man's amusement. He would learn not to speak to her in that contemptuous tone, as if she were a silly child having night terrors.

And again she heard the sound—a rasping, rhythmic purr. She opened her mouth to call, but then a suspicion entered her mind. Slipping into her bed gown, she braved the darkness and crept to the door. Sure enough, the noise came from her drawing room. She pulled open the door.

Allan stretched full length on his back beside a freshly stoked peat fire. One arm pillowed his head. His mouth was ajar, and he snored.

The snoring ceased. Celeste froze.

" 'Tis hazardous to creep up on an armed man, my lady." She saw silvery eyes glitter between his lashes.

"Ye were snoring."

"Ye're mistaken. I wasna asleep. Go back to bed."

Stunned by such arrogance, she returned to her room. While lying in bed, she heard movement in the drawing room. Inconvenient though his presence was, she felt secure. A giggle welled up and spilled over. *Not asleep, he says. Ha!*

Chapter 3

Y ou have been paid for the job; get on with it." The cultured voice held a dangerous edge.

"I need more. 'Tis a risky piece of work. I willna take the chance of holding the blame." Green-and-gold moonlight shining through stained glass patterned the speaker's cloak. Silver eyes glittered beneath his hood.

"I've pledged you my protection."

"And what value has the pledge of a traitor, I'm asking meself?" Disgust colored the man's thick brogue.

—⁓—

Instead of working her embroidery, Celeste watched Allan prowl the library. His wig was askew. He pulled out a book, thumbed through it, and replaced it. Rubbing a hand over his scalp, he jerked off the maltreated tie wig, dropped it on a chair, and stalked the length of the room once more. Celeste admired the glint of his auburn curls. Never would she have guessed that his hair would be a hue entirely at odds with his thick black brows.

Sunlight barred the carpets, and birdsong wafted through the open windows on a balmy summer breeze. On such days, even Kennerith Castle seemed to echo with songs of joy.

"Will ye read to me while I do my needlework?" Celeste requested, lowering her lorgnette. " 'Twould pass the time and employ your idle hands."

He spoke with a hint of asperity. "My lady could endeavor just once to exercise something other than her tongue and her hands. Ye've been at Kennerith these four weeks, and not once have ye ventured farther afield than the rose garden."

Celeste lifted her lorgnette and attempted to intimidate him with a cold stare. "If my indolence vexes ye, 'twould trouble me not at all if ye were to seek gainful employment elsewhere."

Allan met her gaze. His lips twitched.

"What amuses ye now?" she asked.

"Naught, my lady."

Her irritation increased. "I insist upon knowing the source of your amusement."

He gave a little bow. "If ye insist, your servant must obey. Each time ye gaze at me through those lenses, your eyes startle me—like an owl's they seem, huge and solemn. Why dinna ye wear the wire eyeglasses to do your fancywork? They stay put upon your face so ye needna forever be picking them up and putting them down."

"I see well enough to do needlework without spectacles." Celeste pouted. An owl? "Eyeglasses make me appear scholarly while the lorgnette is stylish."

Allan grunted. "I shall read." He approached the stand holding a large Bible.

Celeste picked up her embroidery and discarded the lorgnette. She heard Allan turn pages, then begin to read: " 'In the beginning was the Word, and the Word was with God, and the Word was God. The same was in the beginning with God. All things were made by him; and without him was not any thing made that was made. In him was life; and the life was the light of men.' "

"What are ye reading?" Celeste interrupted when he paused for breath. "This is from the Holy Bible?"

"The Gospel according to John. Chapter one. Ye've ne'er read it?"

Although his voice held no derision, she felt defensive. "I must've heard it in kirk, but I dinna recall. Is it. . .important?"

His tone softened. "Listen and see."

"This Word it speaks of was a person?" she inquired.

"Aye. So ye did listen. God communicates truth about Himself through the Word—the written word, the spoken word, and the living Word, who is Jesus Christ, God in the flesh. 'So then faith cometh by hearing, and hearing by the word of God'—that is a verse from the book of Romans. Let me begin again and see what ye think."

He read several chapters before his voice began to crack. "My throat is dry."

Celeste laid aside her neglected needlework, rose, and tugged the bell-pull. " 'Twas thoughtless of me, but I became engrossed in the story. . .and ye say this is true? It happened just as ye read?"

A servant appeared in the open doorway.

"Will ye bring us refreshment?" Celeste requested. "Are ye. . .Dougal?" From this distance she could not be certain.

"Aye, m'lady." He bowed and disappeared from view.

Allan answered. "Every word I read is truth. I should be pleased to read each day with ye, my lady."

Celeste wished she had worn her eyeglasses so she might better assess the facial expression accompanying his tentative offer. "If it pleases ye, I'll not object," she said. "As I expected, your assignment as my bodyguard has proven tedious. I quickly repented of my promise to make your life miserable, yet every day I unwittingly make good the threat. We've few interests in common, I fear." She smiled wistfully.

"I could wish ye admired me a wee bit."

"My lady, 'tis my honor to attend ye."

The servant returned with a tray, which he set upon the table.

Celeste's skirts engulfed her tiny chair as she sat down. "Thank you, Dougal." She poured soft cider from a flagon.

Motion caught her eye. Allan appeared to be shaking his head. She thought she saw the footman direct a rude gesture at her bodyguard, then exit in haste. "Is it my imagination, or does that man hold ye in disfavor? Papa recently spoke to Mr. Ballantyne about discharging those of the servants whose manner seems. . .insolent. I believe Dougal was mentioned."

Allan approached to take his mug. "Thank ye, my lady. Dougal and I are presently at odds, but I trust the rift will mend." Sipping the juice, he moved toward one of the rectangles of sunlight upon the faded rug.

The sun's reflection off his brass buttons nearly blinded Celeste. "Dougal. Mason? Is he brother to Beryl?"

"Aye." Allan appeared to be gazing outside.

Nodding as she mentally connected facts, Celeste sipped her drink. Dougal resembled his sister. For that matter, the footman was a rougher, wilder version of Allan. The two shared identical coloring and height, yet there the resemblance ended. Cynical lines bracketed Dougal's craggy features, and bitterness clouded his silver-gray eyes; Allan emanated poise and control.

Tired of viewing only Allan's vague outline, she once again lifted her lorgnette to study his profile. Her gaze shifted to her uncle Robert's portrait hanging over the doorway. Although Allan's ruddy, freckled complexion in no way resembled the swarthy Galbraith men, his classic features and graceful carriage suggested a strong influx of noble blood.

Every servant, every townsman—everyone who sees him must know his origin and pity him. He is Galbraith to the core. And I am not.

Rising, she flounced toward the window and stared out at high green hills beyond the castle walls. The manor grounds extended for miles southward, although only the first half-mile consisted of gardens and lawn. "This land—wild and barren, yet its intensity could break your heart," she mused aloud. "Ne'er before have I seen a sky so blue or grass so green. Though I fear these Highlands, I could learn to love them."

" 'Tis a bonny summer day. Nary a cloud in the sky." She felt him behind her. Not close enough to touch, yet near enough to send tingles down her spine.

"If ye could do aught ye chose this day, what would it be?" she asked in a rush of generosity.

"I would ride among those hills and let the sun beat upon my head, the wind beat upon my face, and my heart beat upon my ribs," he said without hesitation.

Amazed by this poetic outburst, Celeste turned. He still stared out the window. For a moment the longing in his eyes filled her with jealousy, but she shook off the unworthy emotion. "I shall ask my father to release ye from duty this afternoon," she said. " 'Tis cruel to keep a wild creature penned like an ox."

"I'd prefer to have ye along," he said.

Celeste's heart swelled. She lifted her hand to her throat and turned away.

"My lady? If I spoke out of turn, accept my apology."

She waved a hand. "Nay. 'Tis only. . ." She could not tell him. He would think it ridiculous of her to become choked up because he desired her companionship. "I dinna ride well."

"Then we shall ride slowly." The anticipation in his voice quickened her blood.

Celeste spun around. "Order the horses while I change into riding attire. I'll meet ye at the mounting block." Whatever the cost to her pride and comfort, Celeste determined that Allan MacMurray deserved one afternoon of happiness.

Allan's smile gleamed. "Aye." Halfway to the door, he stopped in his tracks and turned back. "Nay, I'll send word to the stable."

Celeste sighed. He took this bodyguard role far too seriously.

"And, my lady, kindly bring your eyeglasses."

―⁓―

A breeze caught the ends of the wrap holding her bonnet in place and sent them streaming over her staid mount's hindquarters. Celeste dropped her reins to tighten the silken knot under her chin.

With a startled exclamation, Allan leaned over and caught the falling reins. "My lady, no matter how gentle the steed, ye must keep hold."

She retrieved the leather straps and shifted her riding whip to her other hand.

"Ye also must hold the crop in your right hand. 'Twill do ye no good in your left."

Celeste gave a disdainful huff as her dignity ebbed. "I canna see that it matters. My steed follows yours no matter what I tell it. I thought ye wished to enjoy the day." She waved a hand to indicate the surrounding vivid green turf, Scots pines, tufts of broom, and rocky outcroppings topped by blue sky.

"Will ye not heed your horse so I may give notice to the day?"

Celeste's horse dropped its head to graze, jerking the reins from her gloved fingers. "See what the beast has done now!" Surely Allan must recognize the animal's malevolent intent.

He dismounted and hauled her horse's head up. Patting the cob's speckled gray neck, he gave Celeste a rueful look. "We might enjoy ourselves more on foot."

She wilted. "Ye're sorry ye brought me."

"I am not. Come. We shall tie up the horses and continue on foot. Ye've a treat in store."

Celeste placed her hands upon his shoulders and let him lift her down. But when she stood before him, looking up into his face, he immediately turned to the horses. "I'll give them loose rein to allow grazing. That will please your Robin and my D'Arcey."

"Robin certainly seems content to eat," Celeste observed.

"His one joy in life." After attending the horses, Allan dropped his tricornered hat and his wig on a rock.

Celeste looked up at Allan as he approached. Smiling, he met her gaze. Her heart leaped. His smile faltered, and he veered off toward the hill. " 'Tis a stiff hike, but the view is worth seeing."

He strode on, leaving her to follow. Tripping over rocks and ridges, she held up her skirts and silently grumbled. The trees became more numerous, shading the pathway. "I hear running water." Celeste gasped for breath as she emerged from the trees.

Allan stood tall, chin lifted, curly hair blowing in the wind, fists planted on his hips. "That ye do." His smile mocked her gently.

Then she saw it. White water cascaded through a gap in the hills, swirled over rocks, deepened, and flowed past just inches from Allan's boot toes. "Oh!" she gasped, expressing both awe at its beauty and chagrin at her tardy perception. Wildflowers grew in profusion around her feet. Rising mist dampened her face and fogged her eyeglasses.

Allan spoke above the water's roar. " 'The earth is the Lord's, and the fulness thereof; the world, and they that dwell therein. For he hath founded it upon the seas, and established it upon the floods. Who shall ascend into the hill of the Lord? or who shall stand in his holy place? He that hath clean hands, and a pure heart; who hath not lifted up his soul unto vanity, nor sworn deceitfully. He shall receive the blessing from the Lord, and righteousness from the God of his salvation.' "

Celeste listened with a sense of awe. To Allan, God seemed real and present. She looked upon the rushing river and felt God's presence for herself. She closed her eyes, then opened them to marvel anew at the beauty of creation. " 'Who shall stand in his holy place?' " she echoed. Not Lady Celeste Galbraith, if clean hands and a pure heart were requirements.

Bowing her head, she pulled out her pocket and searched it for a handkerchief. "The mist," she muttered, although he probably could not hear. Rubbing her glasses dry gave her a chance to blink back tears.

"My lady, pleased I'd be to instruct ye in the ways of God's salvation, if ye've a mind to learn."

He wore a distant expression and avoided her gaze. Was he truly concerned for her eternal soul? "I am so minded," she confessed.

Allan turned toward her, glanced away, started to speak, and faltered. Finally he nodded. Celeste followed him back to the horses.

Throughout the ride home, she felt the warm imprint of his hands upon her waist. It was worth coming out for a ride if only to have him lift her into the side-saddle. She determined to make this a daily occurrence.

Chapter 4

Ye must do this tae defend my honor."

"I'll do naught of the kind, woman. Do the deed your ainself." He shoveled porridge into his mouth between sentences. "I'll show ye a secret way to the tower, and none will be the wiser. Ye slit her throat in the night, back down the steps ye go, and ye're avenged."

A strong hand gripped his shoulder and gave him a shake. "Nay, 'tis ye must do this thing. If ye'll rally the clan to take the earl's carriage on the road to Aberdeen, ye can slay the twain at once, plus Ballantyne, too."

"*He* will be angry if she dies, but then, die she must since she's a Galbraith." He paused, then crammed in another spoonful of porridge. "A pity."

"Hellooo?" Celeste stepped through the open doorway. Instantly she backed out, waving off flies. Despite the open doors at each end, the atmosphere within the stable was pungent. She straightened her bonnet. "Is anyone about?"

"M'lady, ye dinna belong here alone."

The sound of that reedy voice spun her around. A man with a face of wrinkled leather sat upon a bench, leaning his back against the stone stable wall. A harness lay across his lap. Squinting in the sunlight, he touched his cap but made no move to rise.

"Quentin." Celeste acknowledged the old servant who frequently assisted her to the mounting block for her rides upon Robin.

"I'm guessing ye've come in search of the lad." Quentin smiled, revealing a few lonely teeth.

"The lad?"

"Your bodyguard."

The shrewd expression in his faded eyes annoyed Celeste. "D'ye ken his whereabouts?"

"That I do. He went for a gallop while ye took luncheon in his lairdship's chambers."

Allan's only private moments occurred while Celeste spent time with her father. She fingered the lapel of her riding habit, feeling guilty. "Mr. Ballantyne complained of the gout. We made a hasty meal of it. Besides, 'tis too bonny a day to remain indoors. I had begun to think we'd ne'er see the sun again."

Quentin let out a cackle. "So ye dinna keer for the fog, m'lady?"

"I thought 'twould never lift." Even the thought of the depressing mist that had shrouded the castle for weeks on end made her shiver and rub her arms.

"Ye'd best enjoy this sunlight while ye may."

Rhythmic hoofbeats caught Celeste's attention. "He returns. Dinna tell him I was here, please?"

Quentin looked quizzical, but he agreed. "If it please m'lady. And I'll give Robin your respects."

Celeste nodded. "Many thanks, Quentin." Picking up her skirts, she slipped into the stable, intending to escape out the far end.

The sound of Allan's voice hailing Quentin stopped her. Poised with one hand against the stone stable wall, she eavesdropped without compunction, hoping her name might enter the conversation.

"How was D'Arcey today?" Quentin asked.

"Prime for jumping. 'Tis a pity the new laird has no taste for the hunt." Celeste heard the slap of leather and clink of metal.

"Seems his lairdship has taste for naught about Kennerith. The crofters ne'er see him, and they with harvest coming soon."

"His lairdship enjoys his studies. The man loves his daughter, and he takes thought for the needs of others," Allan said as if in defense of his master. "At present he watches o'er my lady's safety to give me time to myself."

Celeste cringed. She had left her father and Mr. Ballantyne dozing in their chairs.

"Tell me how ye fare, lad. I've sensed trouble in your spirit."

A long pause. Celeste leaned forward, straining her ears to hear Allan's answer.

"My life is like unto riding a green-broke horse on the edge of a cliff."

"The lady is difficult tae guard?" Quentin sounded surprised. "I expected the worst of a highborn wench, but her ladyship fooled me. She seems agog to please. Her eyes follow ye, worshipful as a hound pup's, though they be blue as the summer sky."

Celeste smothered a gasp. How dare Quentin say such things!

Clop, clop, clop.

The men must be walking the horse around the stable yard, for their voices receded into the distance. Celeste caught only the end of Allan's reply: "...fright the first night, she's given no alarm. Except for our horseback outings, she does little but read, sleep, sew, and stroll about the castle gardens."

"Then why the cliff?"

"Between my lady and Beryl, I'm apt to lose my sanity. Women!"

Never before had Celeste heard so much animation from her stoic bodyguard. His frank opinion stung her pride.

The voices grew loud again. "And how does Beryl torment ye?"

"She spins tales—entirely her own inventions—about me. I hear every word through the chamber walls yet can say naught in my defense. If my lady believes these tales, she must think me the most reprobate of men."

"And ye think she believes them?"

"I fear she is uncertain what to believe," Allan said. "I have spoken to her of my faith in Christ and my desire to live a life pleasing to God."

"And?"

"Each morning while we sit in the library, I read to her from the Holy Scriptures. She has a lively mind and an interest in things of the Spirit. But then Beryl regales her with tales of my supposed exploits, and. . ." The voices faded out of hearing.

A horse in a nearby stall snorted, and Celeste nearly yelped aloud. Her chest heaved in the effort to repress emotion.

" . . . Galbraith?" She heard Allan's voice as the men and horse approached the stable.

"I have," Quentin answered.

"She desires to wed the scoundrel. I canna remain here to see it." Allan's voice cracked. "The earl plans to take her with him to Aberdeen tomorrow for a gathering of his academic friends. I should run while she is away and ne'er look back."

Celeste shook her head. Allan could not leave! Panic filled her at the thought.

"Escape, then, while ye may," Quentin said.

Celeste scampered out the far end of the stable. Pinching her lips together and shaking her head in denial, she sought a path through the outbuildings to the castle gardens. Which way? Brilliant orange roses draping over a stone wall beckoned her onward. After shoving open the garden gate, she rushed between flower beds to the castle's kitchen door. Already panting for breath, she ran to the great hall, up the main staircase, along the gallery, up the spiral staircase, and then burst into her sitting room. Darkness and flashes of light alternated within her head as she collapsed into a chair. With a thin wail, she dropped her head back, pulled off her glasses, and began to gasp.

"M'lady?"

In reply to Beryl's startled inquiry, Celeste could only shake her head and whimper. She felt as though her body must either burst the bonds of her corset or expire.

Beryl grabbed her by the arm, hauled her into the bedchamber, and began to strip off her riding habit. Only when the constricting corset had been removed could Celeste weep freely. She flung herself across the bed and let loose her anger and frustration. Articulate speeches took shape in her mind, words she would never dare speak aloud to that exasperatingly reserved man. Above all, she resolved he must not leave. Not ever.

Beryl brought in warm water, a sponge, and soap, leaving them on the dressing table. She laid out an afternoon dress of fine white lawn sprigged with forget-me-nots. "Ye'll recover your spirits after ye freshen, m'lady." Beryl's tone was gruff, but Celeste appreciated the thought.

"I dinna ken how I would ha' survived these months at Kennerith without ye, Beryl. Ye're more a friend to me than a maid." She caught hold of Beryl's callused hand, squeezed it, and smiled.

To Celeste's surprise, tears sparkled in Beryl's eyes, and her lips quivered. She tugged her hand away and retired, leaving Celeste to bathe alone as she preferred.

While she sponged her body, Celeste pondered. Despite Beryl's tales of his immoral exploits, Celeste knew Allan to be a man of high principles and strong character. The maid's lies sprang from insecurity or misplaced jealousy.

Celeste dried herself and donned a clean chemise, her busy brain planning a rendezvous with Allan. She would summon him to join her in the garden, and there she would assure him of her absolute faith in his integrity and inform him that she would not be traveling to Aberdeen on the morrow.

—⁂—

Celeste positioned herself on the garden bench and arranged her skirts. If Allan entered from the west gate, he would see her framed by sunset-hued roses. But no, the late afternoon sun shone full in her eyes. She hopped up and sought a better venue. A small alcove near the gate held a curved bench. Ivy would make a lovely backdrop for her gown. Smiling, she hurried to position herself upon the bench, leaving room for him at one end.

An angry male voice from beyond the garden wall reached her ears. Someone approached from the stables.

"My sister is a comely woman, but few wenches could compete with that dainty piece o' yours. I've a mind to tell his lairdship about the way ye've wronged Beryl, just as your worthless father left your mother alone and with child."

"Beryl's wretched tales come out of her blighted imagination." Allan's brogue was more pronounced than Celeste had ever heard it before. "I've heard her tell enough of them tae my lady whilst I was helpless to defend my honor."

"Ye'd accuse your ain kin of lying?"

"Has the whiskey scorched your brain? Beryl delights in mangling the truth. She's done it since we were bairns together. Ye must understand that ne'er will I wed a first cousin—I canna think it right. Beryl is as a sister tae me. Can ye imagine marrying your sister?"

Celeste heard the sound of clashing steel. "Ye're a traitor tae the clan. We all suspected it when ye ignored the call from our bonny Prince Charlie and left my father, Angus, tae lead the clan tae glory at Culloden. Beryl pled for ye, so we left ye be, thinking ye'd rally to the cause in good time, but now your true colors show through. Ye've turned traitor—a Galbraith lover. First cozening up tae the old laird and now breaking your pledge to marry Beryl."

"Put the knife away. Ye dinna understand, Dougal." Allan's voice sounded sad. "I love my clan. It nigh broke my heart tae refuse Uncle Angus's command and watch ye all ride off tae battle, but I couldna fight against the rightful government of Scotland. The Jacobite cause was doomed tae defeat ere a man set foot upon the battlefield at Culloden."

"Prince Charlie would ha' returned Kennerith Castle tae the MacMurrays," Dougal said.

"Perhaps, had he the power. But that is neither here nor there. The Stuarts lost the throne during the Glorious Revolution, and our clan lost its castle hundreds of years ago after an inglorious battle. These are the facts, plain and simple. And short of a miracle, thus the case will remain."

"Ye're no Highlander and no MacMurray. Ye're no longer one of us." Dougal spat noisily.

" 'Tis a lie!"

"Then prove your loyalty and join us in taking back our own!" Running footsteps faded into the distance.

Celeste sat with one hand pressed over her mouth, breathing hard, staring at a dandelion in the lawn.

Steps crunched on the garden path. Allan passed her alcove, moving toward the rosebushes at the center of the garden. Celeste hopped up and hurried after him.

He turned at her approach, smiled, and bowed. "My lady. I trust your luncheon was pleasant?"

"It was." Uncertain where to look or what to say, she touched a vivid rose and bent to inhale its fragrance. "Some of the roses had a second bloom this summer. Are they not lovely? Quentin once told me a legend about the lady who planted this garden. Have ye heard it?"

"The tale of the beautiful serf? The laird she married was a MacMurray."

Celeste pushed her glasses higher on her nose. "Your ancestors owned this castle?"

His eyes seemed to search her soul. "Ye o'erheard Dougal at the gate."

"I did." Her fingers tugged at the curl lying upon her shoulder. "I am truly sorry your family lost the castle. And to think, my father doesna' want it." She studied the effect of afternoon sunlight upon the castle's turrets and experienced her first genuine affection for the place.

"The Lord gives, and the Lord takes away. In His wisdom, He removed the castle from my family and awarded it to yours. I yield to His will. Would that my family might shake off its obsession with the past! Many MacMurrays have emigrated to the colonies or to the continent and started life anew. But others bide their time amid the hills, ever hoping fate will once again award them lands and titles. My uncle, Beryl and Dougal's father, perished at Culloden. Since I had no father, Uncle Angus had helped raise me until my mother's death."

"I am sorry. I wonder why my father allows MacMurrays to work for him. Not you, of course," she amended. "I meant your cousins."

"They use assumed surnames, as do I." Allan paused, frowning. "I wish I hadna recommended them to Crippen."

Celeste seated herself upon the stone bench in the middle of the garden. She reached out to pull an overhanging rose close to her face. "I received a letter today from my cousin Roderick, who is shortly to arrive. He tells me to trust no one, that my life may be in danger."

"He knows of the threats your father received?"

"He tells me to beware the MacMurrays." Still sniffing at the rose, she studied Allan's impassive face.

He opened his mouth as if to speak, then closed it.

"The day I arrived here, Mr. Ballantyne gave ye a letter from your. . .from my uncle. Have ye discerned its meaning?"

"I hope he meant to tell me that he'd made his life right with God. Ye canna be unaware of the rumors concerning my birth. Despite the evidence, I find it difficult to accept. My mother was a godly woman. She ne'er revealed my father's identity. To anyone."

"Uncle Robert claimed to be a religious man?" Celeste brushed the rose's petals against her cheek.

"Nay. He turned his back on God during his youth. But in later days he seemed ridden by guilt. Whene'er I spoke to him of God's forgiveness, he would shout me from the room. I believe he felt himself beyond redemption. Although he ne'er told me of his conversion, I hope he and God were reconciled."

"I begin to understand your meaning," she said, looking up at him. "The Bible says 'tis sin that separates us from God, and 'tis Jesus' sacrifice upon the cross that reconciles us. Ye read me the passage from Romans, and yesterday I read it again for myself. The Bible is a dusty old book—yet when I read it, my spirit comes alive. Since I arrived here at the castle, I have felt alive in a way I never knew before."

"I, too."

"Ouch!" Celeste released the rose, and it swung back into place. She popped the stinging finger into her mouth and leaped up. Her heart pounded as if to escape her ribs. Bending over a bush of delicate white blooms, she asked, "What d'ye mean, 'I, too'?"

He said nothing.

"Ne'er did I believe the vile tales Beryl told. Your virtue contradicts her lies."

Silence.

Rattled by his lack of response, Celeste allowed her mouth to babble on. "I'll not travel to Aberdeen with my father on the morrow. I shouldna be surprised if Mr. Ballantyne, too, remains at Kennerith. He is unwell." She feared to meet Allan's gaze lest he read her heart. "Thus your trial continues with no end in sight."

"I thought ye desired a respite from my attendance. Why d'ye choose to remain?"

She kept her face averted. "I abhor traveling." The lie stuck in her throat. Her skirts snagged in a bush as she spun to face him. "Truth be told, I feel safest with you, despite Roderick's warning. Though I ken ye dinna watch o'er me of your free will."

Allan released her dress from the rose's thorns. He snapped a sunset-orange bloom from its stem and handed it to her. Celeste accepted the flower, lifting her gaze to meet his. She sucked in a quick breath. Clutching the rose to her breast, she moved closer until her skirt brushed his boots. "Allan." His given name tasted sweet upon her lips.

A muscle jerked in his cheek. He blinked and broke their gaze. Taking a step back, he bent to pull a weed from the black, crumbly soil. "Would ye care to help me tend the roses?"

Celeste felt as if she had run up yet another flight of stairs. She drew a deep breath and smiled. "Like the fair lady of legend? I shall be pleased." She knelt at his side, shoving mounds of fabric out of her way. "Perhaps I should change clothing so I can find the ground."

Chapter 5

"My plan has gone awry! She remained here."

He rumbled a humorless laugh that reeked of whiskey fumes and shrugged off her clutching hands. "Then ye must kill her." His horse shifted and sidled as he mounted heavily. "Or leave her for my pleasure. She must die in the end whether ye do the task or nay."

"But *he* wants her left safe!"

"Many things he wants, he may not get." He chuckled again.

"So ye intend to betray him, Dougal?"

"No more than he intends tae betray me."

"Allan would turn back tae me if she were safely wed to another."

"Ye've gone soft on the wench, and Allan is a traitor." He attributed a few filthy epithets to Allan and spat on the ground, narrowly missing his sister's skirts. "Ye concern yourself with a lover, while I've a realm to reclaim. I go now tae rally the clan tae my side! Death tae all Galbraiths!" He reeled in the saddle and grabbed his horse's mane to right himself.

"A realm? Whiskey has addled your mind! Kill the earl, take the money, and let us all flee this cursed place! Allan will join us once she is lost to him."

"Allan must die with the rest of the wretched lot, since all ken he carries Galbraith blood. Why not wed Adam MacKinnoch, who's pined after ye these ten years, and rid your mind of our misbegotten kin?"

At her cry of protest, he kicked his horse into motion and jounced off into early morning darkness.

—⁓—

Celeste drooped while Beryl unbuttoned her gown. "The house seems empty with Papa away."

"Poor man. He'll be missing your care and company." Beryl shook out the gown with a snap and laid it over a chair.

"And I'll be missing his." Concern for her father's safety creased Celeste's brow. "Why'd ye stay?"

Pulling pins from her hair, Celeste met the maid's gaze in the mirror. "Why does it concern ye, Beryl? I thought ye intended to remain at Kennerith whether or not I left. Perhaps 'twas the prospect of arranging my own hair again that stayed my wanderlust." She let her hair fall over her face in disorder, then pulled it apart to reveal a grimace.

Beryl's lips twitched in response as she reached for the tousled locks. "If ye've a mind tae snare the viscount for your husband, ye'd best leave the task of hairdressing tae me. He's one with an eye for a pretty face, and we'd best see that he pays heed tae yours, my lady."

"Roderick? I hadna realized ye knew him."

A furtive expression crossed Beryl's face, and for the first time Celeste could recall, the Highland woman's cheeks flushed red. "I. . .ye must have spoken of him. . . or Dougal," she sputtered.

"Ye seem to ken more of him than I do. Roderick is a handsome man. He must attract many women." While Beryl prepared her for bed, Celeste tried to recall Roderick's flashing dark eyes and sardonic smile. During his brief but assiduous courtship, not once had she considered the implications of his evident romantic expertise. She had been too flattered and thrilled by his attentions to think clearly.

"Ye should marry him quick and make him take ye tae London or Paris where ye'll be safe."

"Safely away from Allan," Celeste concluded. "Are ye certain ye love your cousin as a woman loves the man she would take as husband, Beryl?"

Beryl's lips tightened into a pink slash across her freckled face. "I'll see him dead ere he weds another. What's mine is mine!" She spun Celeste around and vigorously brushed out her hair.

Celeste considered her maid's proprietary attitude. Despite Beryl's shocking lies and brusque comments, Celeste was fond of her. Yet Beryl, her brother Dougal, and Allan were all MacMurrays, members of the ancient clan that had once owned Kennerith Castle. If even half the accounts of clan battles and feuds held truth, the blood of a Highlander must run hot as molten steel, making a jealous woman such as Beryl a dangerous enemy. Although a clan uprising sounded like the stuff of legends and ballads, the venom Celeste had occasionally seen in Beryl's vivid blue eyes and heard in Dougal's gruff voice warranted caution.

"Will ye be needing aught else this night, my lady?"

Celeste blinked and turned. Beryl waited near the door.

"Ye'd ne'er harm me, would ye, Beryl?"

Beryl's jaw dropped. Her gaze shifted to one side. Her lips trembled, then set into a firm line, and her gaze met Celeste's. "Nay, my lady. I'll ne'er cause ye harm."

Celeste sighed. "I thought not.

The door closed behind Beryl with a hollow boom. Celeste heard her speak to Allan but could not make out their words.

Celeste extinguished her candles and climbed into bed. The castle's dank chill seemed to seep into her bones. She rose to pull the curtains and glimpsed the glow of firelight from her antechamber. Allan gave a little cough. He must have overheard her conversation with Beryl. He must overhear all their discussions, but Celeste hoped perhaps he could not distinguish every word.

Allan. To Celeste, he had become the embodiment of Jesus on earth—kind and selfless and considerate. His polite conduct allowed her to enjoy privacy despite his constant physical presence. Last night in the rose garden, her hopes had flown higher than the clouds, for his eyes had seemed to speak to her of. . .

But his subsequent behavior put the lie to her imaginings. Pleasant, friendly, yet detached—that was Allan.

Roderick's warning about MacMurrays returned to haunt her. Did Allan detach himself out of respect for her, or did he maintain emotional distance because he anticipated her imminent demise? She shook her head in denial even as her hands crept up to grasp her throat. *Can anyone be trusted? Do the MacMurrays all desire my death? Even the earl may plot my death since I am not truly his daughter.*

Her pulse pounded beneath her icy fingers. A sense of her own weakness swept over her. What chance would she have against a woman like Beryl, let alone against Dougal? She rubbed her hands up and down her arms. Skinny arms. No muscle there. No strength anywhere.

Jesus, are You here with me? Please, protect me from mine enemies!

A realization struck her. All the qualities she had seen or imagined in her bodyguard were exemplified in the Jesus of the Bible—kindness, strength under control, and selfless love. Allan might offer her protection, but Jesus had already sacrificed His life for her eternal soul.

A soft snore reached her ears. Allan slept. A little smile curled her lips, and her body slowly relaxed.

God had guided the earl to choose Allan as her protector. Allan, despite his MacMurray blood, was the best human protection Celeste could have. And even if Allan failed her, Jesus held her safe within His mighty hands. Because of Jesus, God would forgive her sinful self and make her His child. At that moment, Celeste put her complete trust in God's salvation.

—⁓—

It seemed mere moments later that Beryl swept back the bed curtains to admit morning light. "Arise, m'lady. A guest has arrived and is eager tae see you."

"A guest?" Celeste mumbled. She rubbed her eyes, stretched, and yawned. "At this hour?"

"Nay. He arrived late last night and slept in the southwest tower chamber. 'Tis the viscount."

Celeste sat up, blinking. "Roderick is here?" Ignoring the bed gown Beryl held ready, she hopped up and ran toward the blurry door. As greater awareness dawned, she turned back. "Last night he arrived? I must dress in haste and greet him. I must be hostess while my father is away."

Beryl handed over her spectacles and assisted her into the bed gown. Her mind spinning, Celeste buttoned its bodice carelessly while Beryl unraveled her braid. Allan must be told. What would he think of Roderick?

"My lady," Beryl protested as Celeste rushed back to the door. "Your hair. . ."

Celeste flung open the chamber door and nearly collided with her sentinel's back. He turned around. Eyes like polished silver regarded her coolly.

"Oh, I–I. . ." Her startled gaze took in his flawless livery, his brushed wig, and his hand resting upon the sword hilt at his side.

He bowed. "My lady."

Heat rushed to Celeste's cheeks. Allan's magnificence made her own state of dishevelment seem the greater. Hair straggled around her shoulders, and her bare feet cringed upon the threshold. She gripped the door, ready to slam it shut.

"Pardon if I intrude." A voice broke the silence. Roderick Galbraith paused in the drawing-room doorway. "I climb the tower to awaken my lady with a kiss and find another before me, a jester in scarlet raiment. Pray, introduce us, my love."

"Ye must know by the livery that he is my father's servant, my bodyguard," Celeste said. "Allan Croft is his name."

Allan again bowed.

Roderick's full lips curled in scorn, and his voice held mockery. "Aye, that I do know. Such irony! A misbegotten Highland knave in my darling's chambers, beholding her unbound hair? He'll soon rue the day."

"What nonsense!" Celeste's attempt at laughter sounded flat. "Roderick, why ever didna ye tell us the date of your arrival? Now Papa is away a fortnight, and ye've caught me unawares." She ran one hand through her braid-kinked locks. "But welcome, dear cousin." Extending her hands, she tried to smile.

"My love, you look ravishing. How many nights have I lain awake, imagining the glory of your hair? Yet every dream fell short of its resplendent reality." He brushed past Allan and lifted her hands to his lips. "As I explained once before, those eyeglasses mask the glorious hue of your eyes. For my sake, resume the lorgnette."

Celeste stared at the curling black hair on his ungloved fingers. A faintly fetid aroma rose from his bowed head, and she saw grime ingrained around his neckcloth. When had the man last bathed?

Giving Allan a sideward glance, Roderick yanked Celeste into a close embrace and buried his face in her neck. "And where is the kiss I've dreamed of all these lonely weeks?" Strong arms squeezed her body against his, and hot breath moistened her throat.

Burning with indignation and shame, Celeste pushed at Roderick's constricting arms. "What kiss is that, cousin? Ye've ne'er coaxed one from me! Unhand me ere my bodyguard rends ye limb from limb!" She tried to maintain a teasing tone.

"I'd run him through ere he took two steps in my direction." Although Roderick released her, his grin resembled a sneer. He patted his sword. "I'll soon put an end to this farce."

Celeste trembled in every limb. Sustaining a pleasant expression and tone, she sidled closer to Allan, noting that he gripped his sword hilt. "Enough talk of violence, Roderick. Allow me time to dress and welcome ye properly in the great drawing room."

Roderick moved in. "Why not send this boor away and welcome me properly right here?" He trailed a finger down her cheek. "Ye've no need of a bodyguard now that your Roderick has come." A hint of brogue crept into his cultured voice.

Sensing Allan's strength at her back, she shook a chiding finger under Roderick's nose. "Such a thing canna be done, even if I wished it. Papa hired Allan to watch o'er me, and only Papa can order him away."

Roderick scanned Allan dismissively. "I could knock him over the head and dump him down the garderobe hole if you but say the word. I'd have done it years ago if that rat Ballantyne hadn't caught wind of the prank and stopped me." He chuckled. "My own, to see your mane flowing free nigh takes my breath away!" He reached out a trembling hand.

Flinging her hair behind her shoulders, Celeste backed up until her heels bumped Allan's boot toes. All pretense left her. "Enough, Roderick. Your intimations insult me! Begone. I shall greet ye downstairs within the hour, and we shall pretend this scene ne'er happened."

Eyes flaming, Roderick appeared to deliberate between challenging Allan upon the spot or biding his time. Caution prevailed. "Within the hour, my own. And leave the churl behind lest I slay it before your tender eyes." He paused to give an ugly laugh. "Keep in mind, Highlander, that those who lift their eyes too high oft fall to ruin."

When she heard Roderick's shoes upon the spiral stairs, Celeste slumped back against Allan. His forearm slid across her back as he released his sword. "What has happened to Roderick? He is a stranger, not the man I thought I—I thought. . ."

How could she ever have imagined herself in love with Roderick? That dirty, lecherous, shifty-eyed beast! No wonder Papa had objected to the match. She shook her head. Turning, she gave a yelp of pain and nearly fell against Allan. Her hair had tangled on his waistcoat buttons.

"Alas, I appear to be trapped." She attempted a jest despite her heart's pounding, but he did not respond. With quaking hands, Celeste unwound her snarled hair, trying not to touch him any more than necessary. Allan's gloved fists clenched at his sides. His rapid breathing ruffled the curls framing Celeste's forehead.

—⁓—

Allan stood like a statue, enduring the exquisite inferno caused by Celeste's touch. As soon as her hair was free, he stepped back. "I shall call Beryl to help ye dress." He scarcely recognized his own voice.

"No need. I'm here." Beryl waited beside the bedchamber doorway, staring daggers into his heart.

Beryl knew. She had always known.

Celeste turned and dashed into her room. When Beryl would have followed, Allan caught her attention with a wave. She closed the door and approached him, her eyes hooded.

"D'ye wish my lady harm?" he whispered.

Beryl lowered her gaze and shook her head.

"Will ye aid us?"

A slow nod.

His tension lightened, and he whispered directions into her ear. "Can ye do this for me? For her?"

"Beryl?" Celeste opened her door and peeked out.

Allan stepped back, met Beryl's gaze, and received another nod. Beryl entered her mistress's chamber. The door closed, and another chunk of plaster hit the floor.

—⁓—

The next morning, Beryl did not appear in Celeste's chamber. Celeste dressed herself and wound her nighttime braid into a fat bun. Her eyes burned and her stomach ached. Evidence continued to mount that Allan did not return her growing attraction to him. He was impervious to her feminine allure, if she possessed such a thing. Slipping on her spectacles, she studied her reflection in the mirror.

Roderick was right—the glasses did hide her eyes. Not that her eye color could compare with Beryl's anyway. Her simple gown matched her eyes, but its gray-blue shade seemed to lend her cheeks a deathly cast, and her mouth puckered in a distinct pout.

Placing her hands on her hips, she twisted from side to side to examine her figure. Even without a corset, her waist appeared trim. The lace ruffles of her chemise peeped above the morning gown's low neckline and fringed its elbow-length sleeves. A ruffled cap topped her brown hair, its lappets dangling at the back of her neck.

How was a woman to know whether a man preferred willowy grace or plump curves? Celeste was uncertain which description suited her best—probably neither. Did Allan admire a petite woman or a lady of elegant height? Celeste's gloom deepened. Her height was somewhere in between.

She clasped her hands, bowed her head, and squeezed her eyes shut.

Dearest Jesus, my Friend, please help me! Keep Allan here to protect me and teach me about You. Beryl does not love him as a wife should, so please do not let them marry. Keep him safe, and do not allow Roderick to mock him today. And keep Roderick from touching me. I fear Allan will feel obliged to kill Roderick, and that would cause such trouble for him. For Allan, I mean. Amen.

Even while praying, she remembered Allan and Beryl with their heads close together, his gloved hand brushing ruddy curls from Beryl's ear. Had he reconsidered his objection to marrying a cousin? Had Beryl and Allan run off together? Did Allan believe his duty ended now that Roderick had arrived?

Lifting her chin and throwing back her shoulders, Celeste opened her chamber door and stepped into the antechamber.

Allan rose from an armchair and laid aside his book. "My lady." He bowed.

Celeste's face crumpled, and tears began to pour down her cheeks. She covered her face with her hands. Sobs lurched her body.

"My lady." His breath tickled her forehead. "Are ye ill? Have I failed ye in any fashion?" Distress colored his voice. "Come and be seated. Shall I send for wine?"

She shook her head.

He grasped her upper arm. "Please, come and sit. Can ye tell what ails ye?"

She allowed him to seat her in his chair. He pressed a handkerchief into her hands. "Where," she gasped while dabbing at her eyes, "is. . .Beryl?"

He went down on one knee and peered into her face. His thick brows met in the middle of his forehead, and his gray eyes looked dark with concern. "Beryl has gone, but I shall care for ye as best I can. Shall I summon a physic? D'ye hurt anywhere, my lady?"

She nodded and pressed one fist to the center of her chest beneath her bosom. "Here."

He started to reach toward her, clenched his hand, then returned it to his upraised knee. "Is it something ye ate? Is the pain constant, or does it throb?"

"Both." She tried to draw a deep breath, but another sob snatched it away. "I–I was so afraid!"

She saw his eyes flicker back and forth as he studied her face, which must look dreadful after her bout of weeping. "What did ye fear, my lady?"

"I prayed that God would keep ye here. . . ." Her body jerked with leftover sobs. "That ye wouldna leave. . .me, but I feared ye'd gone. . .gone away with Beryl."

"As ye see, I am here. Aught else?"

"Roderick. . .he frightens me. I–I dinna think I can con–control him long, and Papa. . .Papa willna return for many days!"

He switched knees and rested one elbow on the upraised leg. The tip of his sword scabbard rapped the floor. "My lady, in honesty I canna tell ye that your fears are groundless."

"Ye do intend to wed Beryl?"

A smile twitched his lips. "Nay, I willna marry my cousin, and I believe she now accepts it. Her temper is as fiery as her hair, and she indulges in unseemly fantasies, yet her heart is tender toward you, my lady. Against fearful odds, ye've won her loyalty by being a friend to a servant maid. I pray the Lord will reach her heart through your love."

His eyes narrowed. "I believe you intended, at one time, to wed the viscount."

Celeste squirmed. "I believed it myself until I met him again. He had convinced me of his sincerity, and he claimed to love me despite unpleasant family secrets. I now wonder if the tales he related held any truth." Her breathing gradually became more even. "I had even begun to wonder if you, Beryl, and Dougal intended to kill me." She tried to chuckle.

"D'ye trust me now?"

She met his gaze. "Entirely."

He thumped his hand upon his knee and arose. "Pray that good will prevail o'er evil, obey my every command, and dinna allow your cousin to touch ye. Can ye do this?"

"Aye."

"I'll escort ye downstairs when ye're ready, my lady."

Chapter 6

Pacing back and forth across the library, Celeste glanced toward her cousin and wished for the hundredth time that he had never come. The three days since his arrival had seemed endless. Roderick divided much of his time between secretive meetings with the ailing Mr. Ballantyne and intrusive encounters with Celeste. His dark eyes held mysteries that seemed to give him great amusement and satisfaction. Only when he looked at Allan did his face harden and his self-assurance waver.

Roderick's nose was deep in a book, but Celeste suspected him of feigning interest.

"Where did ye go this morn, Roderick?"

"On an errand. Be seated. You make me dizzy."

Celeste sat and picked up her needlework. The first stitch jabbed her finger. "Did ye go to o'ersee the harvest? Is it true that the villagers are unhappy because this recent wet weather spoiled much of the harvest?"

He gave her a disbelieving look and flung one elegant leg over the arm of his chair. "Why would I care? They'll pay rent out of their own lazy hides, if need be. If you must know, I was researching records at a nearby kirk. An ill-favored edifice. I prefer a fine cathedral or even Kennerith's wee chapel."

"People matter more than the building. Vaulted ceilings and intricate woodcarvings canna substitute for fellowship with other believers. I've learned to enjoy the simple services at the village kirk. I understand much more than e'er before, and understanding brings me joy." Celeste glanced toward Allan, who stared through one of the tall windows as rain drizzled down its panes.

"Some people would benefit from greater understanding, but others would only come to realize what they had lost." Roderick aimed the remark at Allan's back.

"There is hope for a man's repentance so long as he draws breath," Celeste said.

"If such belief comforts you, I'm glad of it."

Celeste blinked. "Either a thing is true or it is not."

"Aye, but some will believe it true and others will not."

"I believe Jesus is the Savior of the world, as He claimed."

"How charmingly archaic of you, my love. Religion is good for a woman as long as she doesn't let it harden her." Roderick closed the book over his finger and yawned, patting his lips. "Anything taken too far is a fault, including religion."

"But Jesus is not a religion—He is the Son of God."

Roderick rolled his eyes. "Women are more agreeable when their mouths are closed. Do you not agree, Highland scum? Especially that wench you plan to wed—the one with manly arms and womanly charms. A fitting bride for a weakling knave who would allow his wife to run the house. Do you know his origins, cousin? It seems our uncle took a passing fancy to—"

"Be still!" Celeste cried, standing up and rounding on her cousin with a swirl of skirts. "You take every opportunity to mock him. Canna ye see that he turns the cheek as Christ commands? My Allan could slay a feeble gentleman like you in an instant, but he is above senseless killing."

"*Your* Allan? What talk is this? I will not have it!" Roderick leaped from his seat and grasped her arm with iron fingers. "Remove those spectacles and use the lorgnette I bought you." He grabbed for her face, but Celeste twisted away. Spouting imprecations, he spun her back to face him. "You're mine alone, as will be this castle, the title, and all!"

A squawk of pain escaped before she realized what was happening. She heard the ring of steel and felt Roderick's body stiffen. A sword point hovered near the cleft in her cousin's chin. Roderick stared down the shimmering length of the saber. With Celeste pressed against him, his own sword was out of his reach.

"Release the lady."

Roderick swallowed hard. "She is my intended." His voice wavered.

"I am charged with her protection. Unhand the lady. Now."

Roderick let go and backed away. Celeste had thought he might draw his own sword, but he kept his hands lifted. "You'll regret this. I'll neither forget nor forgive." Once out of reach, he regained insolence. "When I am earl, all MacMurrays will die painfully or be deported. I swear it!"

He bumped into the door, turned, and made a hasty retreat. Allan sheathed his sword.

Celeste let her questions spill over. "How does he know you're a MacMurray? What mean these threats he shouts? Has he gone mad?"

Allan frowned. "The viscount spent much of his childhood here. He and I are auld acquaintances. He might ha' learned my true identity almost anywhere. The secret is no real secret."

He turned away and stood with arms folded across his chest, his jacket pulled taut across his shoulders. "As for his threats, I darena' leave your side long enough to discern their significance. The serving staff whispers, yet none will speak openly.

Dougal disappeared the morning his lairdship left the castle, and now Beryl is gone."

Celeste shivered despite the fire's warmth. "I wish Papa hadna gone away. E'er since Roderick's arrival, I've had a sense of impending doom. Something dreadful will happen, I ken."

When Allan did not respond, Celeste sank into a chair, remembering conversations she had overheard concerning the indolent tendencies of her uncle Alastair and the disagreeable repute of his son. Alastair had lived off his eldest brother, Robert's, reluctant largesse most of his ill-spent life, leaving Roderick to run wild.

"Papa has never cared for Roderick," she said. "Until this past spring, I had seen my cousin only twice before, and then I was a small child. When he came to pay me court, he seemed agreeable. I thought Papa was mistaken." The memory that Roderick's attentions originated immediately after Celeste inherited a small fortune obtruded itself once again.

"Allan, did he truly nigh stuff ye down the garderobe? I should think the holes too small." The idea made her shudder. In her mind, the shaft beneath the castle's antiquated latrine terminated somewhere near the center of the earth.

"He might ha' succeeded but for Mr. Ballantyne's intervention. I was a wee lad of ten; the viscount was fifteen." Allan's tone was matter-of-fact.

"How despicable!" Celeste whispered. "This castle would frighten me if you werena here. Almost I expect to become lost someday and happen upon a skeleton in a dungeon. Where is this chapel Roderick spoke of?"

"Ye've not seen the chapel?" Allan turned.

Celeste shook her head. "Will ye take me there?"

"With pleasure." A smile flickered across his lips. "At your leisure, my lady."

She hopped up and followed him from the library and down the main staircase. When he opened the front door, she asked, "Shall I need a bonnet?"

"Nay. 'Tisna far, and the rain has ceased."

He led the way down the castle's front steps and turned left. Then up another set of broad stone steps and along a covered walk beside the partially crumbled curtain wall. "Take my arm, my lady. Many flagstones are broken or missing."

Celeste gladly laid her hand upon his forearm. "It has a musty, moldy smell, this walkway." Large gaps in the sidewall revealed the castle courtyard and outbuildings. A cat stared at them, wide-eyed, then drifted up the wall and out a window like a gray mist.

"I suspect it supports a thriving population of mice, hence the cats." With that comment, he hauled open a wooden door. "The priest's entrance in days of old."

Celeste stepped inside, then waited for Allan to lead the way. A vaulted ceiling with arched enclaves displayed five intricate windows of stained glass. "How beautiful!" Celeste forgot the smell and the cold, gazing upward in rapt appreciation. Her fingers caressed a velvety walnut bench.

Allan strode down the aisle and stepped behind the raised lectern. An enormous Bible lay open before him. "We might have our daily readings here, my lady, if ye can bear the chill." His voice rang hollow in the expanse.

"Is the chapel nevermore used for services?"

"Not to my knowledge. Your ancestors—and no few of mine—lie beneath us in the crypt."

Celeste shook her head. "Not mine." Instantly regretting the slip, she turned to read the inscription on a brass plaque. " 'In memory of Adelaide Ballantyne Galbraith, beloved wife.' I wonder how many generations back are these ancestors."

"Many of the monuments bear dates."

Celeste read the verse inscribed beneath the name. " 'When Christ, who is our life, shall appear, then shall ye also appear with him in glory.' I pray these people were true believers in Jesus. I should be pleased to meet them in heaven someday."

Allan spoke at her elbow, his voice soft. "Did ye mean what ye said to your cousin about Jesus, my lady? Have ye accepted His salvation?"

She rubbed her upper arms against the pervading chill. "Aye. When I hear ye read Scripture aloud, my heart tells me 'tis truth. And your life is proof to me that God exists. I know that Jesus willna fail me, no matter what men may do or say."

He swallowed hard, stared up at a magnificent rose window, fingered his sword hilt, and looked back down at Celeste. "Naught ye could say would please me more. The Lord will keep ye safe, whate'er happens."

"I canna imagine a man hearing the Word and not believing," she said.

She saw his chest expand and deflate in a deep sigh. "I and my mother before me have oft spoken with family members about the Christ. They listen to the Bible stories, debate theology, decide which kirk the clan will support—and apply none of it personally. Only the Holy Spirit can convict a man of sin and persuade him to accept redemption. This I ken, yet my heart aches at the emptiness and hatred I see consuming my people. 'Twas not always so, and I pray God will once again reach the MacMurrays."

"Ye dinna hate my family, do you?" Celeste touched his arm.

He avoided her gaze. "My lack of hatred alienates my clan. If I am reviled for the sake of Jesus Christ, so be it. I loved your uncle, and I—" He broke off, strode away, and bowed his head, gripping the back of a bench with both hands until it creaked.

"And?"

When he turned his head to answer, she again saw him swallow hard. "I canna betray his trust. My lot is cast with the Galbraiths, though it cost my life."

He bent farther over the bench, eyes narrowing, then reached down and hauled a plaid woolen blanket from beneath it. Mutton bones, fruit pits, and a knife clattered upon the bench and floor. "Someone has been living here."

"Who?"

"I canna tell, unless he died and these be his bones. If so, he was a sheep."

Celeste grimaced then smiled. "Ha-ha. How droll. But what shall we do?"

"Depart in haste." He replaced the items and hurried her out the chapel's main door. "Turn back and exclaim o'er the windows again. We may be watched."

She obeyed, shivering. "But the windows appear dull from the outside. I have lived here for months, yet I know little about Kennerith Castle. What other wonders does its forbidding exterior conceal?"

"Perchance ye'll learn more of its secrets, but not now. It commences to rain again, and, fool that I am, I advised ye tae bring no bonnet. Make haste." He plopped his tricorn hat on her head and rushed her back to the castle as a sharp wind blew the mist into their faces.

—∞—

That evening, while dining with Roderick and Mr. Ballantyne in the small dining room, Celeste noticed her cousin's boisterous manner. Coming as it did so soon after his humiliation at the point of Allan's sword, this behavior struck Celeste as peculiar.

She felt Allan's presence at her back like a solid wall of reassurance. If she had noticed Roderick's odd behavior, it would not escape Allan's detection.

"A good day's work, eh, Ballantyne?" Roderick said around a mouthful of venison. He sopped oatcakes in the gravy.

Mr. Ballantyne seemed more wizened and miserable than usual. He picked at his food and drank quantities of wine. "The gout," he murmured. "Canna abide this rich fare. I keep telling his lairdship, but he doesna wish to disturb the servants. . . ."

Candlelight flickered in Roderick's eyes. "Uncle Malcolm was never meant to be earl. The value lies not in the castle but in the land! These crofters pay half the rent they should and could if the Highlanders didna steal our rightful earnings."

"My father will be fair and good to his tenants and to the Highlanders," Celeste said. "They owned this land before we Galbraiths did, at any rate."

A cruel smile curled Roderick's lips. "*We* Galbraiths? Have you forgotten your true parentage so soon, my love?"

Giving a start, Mr. Ballantyne spilled wine on his waistcoat. "Sir, ye've ne'er told the lass that tale? 'Twas intended a secret!"

Roderick chuckled. "And you've now confirmed its veracity. Ah, Mr. Ballantyne, what an invaluable source of information you are! Drink up, aged cousin. Enjoy what pleasure is left you."

Celeste clenched her hands together in her lap and felt Allan shift his weight behind her chair. "If ye'll excuse me, I believe I shall retire early this night." Her voice trembled despite every effort to control it. Rising, she curtsied to the gentlemen, who both rose to bow.

"Sweet dreams, my love. Soon you'll be mine in every sense."

Allan closed the door behind her. She rushed into the great room, stopped, and stamped her foot on the flagstones. "I hate him!" Her voice echoed among the beams high overhead. Immediately she repented of the childish display. "But it is wrong to hate."

"My lady, I grapple with the same sin. God is able to deliver us both."

Chapter 7

The new maid assigned to Celeste's service plaited her hair silently, warmed her bed linens, regarded her with proper respect, and curtsied before she left the room...yet Celeste missed Beryl. She lay awake with one candle burning long after the maid retired. Light from Allan's fire glowed reassuringly through the cracks in the heavy door.

Lord Jesus, forgive my hateful thoughts. I know I should love Roderick as You do, but I find it difficult. Allan is easy to love because he is like You. I wish to spend every day of my life with Allan.

Her eyes popped open. An idea slipped into her mind. She could bundle up in blankets and join Allan on the floor in the antechamber. They could sit beside the fire and talk. So many things Celeste wished to learn about her bodyguard, her dearest friend. Which foods did he favor? What were his fondest childhood memories? What was he thinking when he gazed at her, as he sometimes did, with his eyes of softest gray like lamb's wool and a hint of a smile about his lips? How would it feel to be held in his arms? Would he wish to kiss her? Roderick's caresses made her flesh creep, but the thought of Allan's hands upon her skin produced entirely different thrills.

Lord, my mind wandered again. Is it evil for me to have such thoughts? Surely I may sit and talk with Allan in the antechamber...and yet, somehow I know You and he both would disapprove. Perhaps this is the wisdom You promised to give me if I asked. I know it is impossible that Allan and I could ever marry, but if he could even be with me for the rest of my life, I think I should be content. Or would I? You know my heart better than I do. Please do with me, with us, as You deem best. I beseech You in the blessed name of Jesus.

Oh, and please help me to sleep. I am frightened to the depths of my soul this night! Since I mayn't have Allan's arms about me, I ask You to hold me in Your hands. Amen.

Despite her earnest prayer, Celeste's mind merely wandered in and out of consciousness, and strange dreams wafted through her thoughts. True sleep eluded her.

Sometime during the night, her eyes opened wide. A sound had awakened her. Allan still snored in the antechamber. The banked embers of her fire occasionally popped, but that ordinary sound would not have disturbed her peace. Someone was breathing nearby, breathing heavily but trying to muffle the sound. A footstep scuffed on the rug beside her bed, and the bed curtain rings scraped along the pole.

Summoning all her strength, Celeste rolled over and over to her right. She felt a blow upon the bolster, and a gruff voice cursed. *Thunk.* Cocooned in blankets, she fell off the far side of the bed and tried to roll beneath it. Heavy footsteps rushed around the bed.

Dust filled her eyes and nose, yet she freed her mouth of blankets and rug long enough to scream with all her might. "Allan! Allan! Please God, help me." Her screams turned to weeping, and her imagination felt a knife slide between her shoulder blades.

With her ear against the floor, she heard footsteps like crashing thunder.

—m—

Allan rolled from sleep to his feet and drew his sword at the first thump and angry shout. Celeste! The warped door boomed against the wall as he burst into her bedchamber.

Darkness. Silence but for Celeste's muffled sobs. Did the invader have her in his clutches? Allan's bare feet padded on the hardwood and rug. He sidestepped left to avoid being backlighted by the fire. His sword point drew tiny circles in the dark.

Glass shattered to his right. He turned, recognized the distraction ploy, and feinted left, sword extended. Something struck the wall behind him. His sword point caught on—flesh?—then sprang free. A shadow deeper than its surroundings passed between Allan and the hearth. He lunged low. His saber slashed. A grunt. The assailant landed prostrate on the floor. Allan pressed his sword point against the heaving mass. "As ye value life, be still."

"Allan?" Celeste's voice quivered.

"Aye, lass. Rise and give us light."

Shuffling sounds from the area of the bed.

"My lady, are ye injured?" Allan inquired, becoming restive.

"Nay, I am tangled in the bed linens until I can scarce move."

"Make haste."

"I'm making all possible haste, if ye please. I must find my eyeglasses!"

Her testy response pleased him.

"I'm coming now. Dinna slay me!" Her footsteps padded behind his back. She tossed a peat block on the fire and poked the embers into a blaze. Allan focused on the man beneath his sword.

"Allan, look!"

He glanced up. Celeste pointed to his left.

He returned his attention to the would-be murderer. "What is it?"

"A door in the wall."

"Close it, please."

"But should we not first learn how it works?"

"Later, when danger of this rogue attempting escape through it is past."

She obediently closed the door. "I see how it works! A lever hidden beneath the—"

"Clever lass. Now stay back near the bed." He nudged the invader with one foot. "Rise slowly and turn about."

The man clambered to his feet, lifted his gloved hands, and faced Allan. "I'd ha' killed ye both had I been whole, cousin." A sneer disfigured Dougal's countenance. Dark stains upon his breeches, hose, and coat glistened in the firelight and dripped to the floor. "Two days past, the earl's outrider caught me with a ball in the side, but not ere I'd shot his lairdship!"

"Ye're insane!" Celeste said. "Why would ye want to kill my father? Why would anyone kill Papa?" She began to weep again, and Dougal laughed.

"This castle belongs to MacMurrays by right of inheritance! The young master schemed to inherit, but I had my ain plans. Death to all Galbraiths! Death!"

Knocking Allan's sword aside, Dougal stumbled toward the chamber door. Only then did Allan see his objective—the point of a dagger was embedded in the wall. In one motion, Dougal gripped the dagger, spun, and flung it at Celeste.

Allan's sword knocked the knife aside. But in that moment, Dougal had staggered to the window, pushed open the casement, and climbed upon the sill. Allan dropped his sword and dove after him, catching his cousin by the coattail. "Dougal, ye're mad! 'Tis a rainy night—the roof will be slick. Come and let us tend your wounds."

"Ye'd heal me to hang me, traitor that ye air!" Dougal punched Allan in the head, then beat at his grasping hands. "I'll run to the hills or die a free Highlander!"

A kick caught Allan in the inner thigh, and pain made him see stars. Dougal left his coat in Allan's grasp and slid through the window. *Thud!* He hit the roof ten feet below. His scrabbling attempts to catch hold ended in a despairing scream that faded into the distance.

Celeste wailed.

Allan gripped the stone sill and pushed himself to his feet. Grief for his cousin and for the earl weighted his heart, but first he must see to comforting Celeste.

She was a wraith in white beside the bed, her eyeglasses reflecting the firelight, her hands clasped beneath her chin. She took one step toward him, then another.

The antechamber's outer door slammed open, and a stream of servants poured into the tower. Roderick entered last, dazzling in a violet-striped banyan robe. "What has happened here? We heard shouts and screams. . . ." His gaze fell upon Celeste, and his eyes widened. He then studied Allan, the open window, and the disheveled state of Celeste's bed.

He pointed at Allan. "Arrest that man for the attempted murder of Lady Celeste Galbraith!"

"Nay!" Celeste ran toward Allan. He caught her in one arm and grabbed her bed gown from its hook on the wall. Keeping his gaze averted, he wrapped her in its concealing folds.

"Roderick, ye dinna understand!" Celeste slipped her arms into the bed gown's sleeves. "'Twas another man tried to murder me. Allan saved my life!"

"Murder? Where is the body?" a strange voice asked.

Celeste buttoned her bodice, staring up at Allan's face. Why did he not refute the charge? She whirled about. The village sheriff stood at Roderick's side, looking almost as confused as Celeste felt.

"The body of the murderer lies in the courtyard," she said. "He fell off the roof while attempting—"

"The darkness and the late hour have bewildered your thoughts, my lady," Roderick said. "I sent for the sheriff when word of a heinous scheme reached my ears." He stepped forward, keeping a wary eye on Allan. "Sheriff, this man is part of the MacMurray plot to steal Galbraith lands and title. Are you a man of the law or not?"

The law officer wavered. "I am, but I see no evidence of murder, and the lady says—"

"If you neglect your duty, I'll have the wretch thrown in the castle dungeon until a scaffold can be built. The laird of the castle's word is law, and I am he. Charlie? Ian?" Roderick beckoned forward two young men, strangers to Celeste, who grasped Allan by the arms.

"Nay, ye canna take him!" she cried, but a large hand shoved her aside, and they dragged Allan toward the door.

"My lady!"

She met Allan's gaze. He glanced at the dagger on the floor. Celeste quickly seized it. When she looked up, he was gone. Heavy footsteps sounded on the stairs.

"Clear the chamber, the lot of you!" Roderick shouted. "Dumb sheep." Several servants glanced in evident bewilderment from Celeste to Roderick, but obeyed without protest.

Roderick fixed Celeste with a glittering stare. His silken turban and robe gave him the aspect of an Oriental potentate. He extended a hand. "The dagger, my love."

She clutched it, turning away, but he caught her and wrested the knife from her grasp. "I canna allow you to despoil either your breast or mine." She struggled to free her arm. His smile twisted into a sneer. The point of the dagger snagged in her lace chemise as he traced it along her neckline. Celeste stilled but could not restrain a shudder.

"Perhaps I'll keep you alive after all, safe in this tower until I tire of your charms.

Come what may, I shall inherit your fortune, for you have no other living relatives."

"The Lord knows your black heart, Roderick," she said.

"More religion. I have used God's house as mine these past months, and it served me well. Either He doesna care, or He canna intervene, or He doesna exist."

"Ye've been living in the chapel?"

"Aye. Accomplices inside the castle saw to my care and feeding. The MacMurrays played easily into my hands; I fed upon their resentment and superstition. Dougal killed your father, but it should be easy enough to switch the blame to your bodyguard, since Ballantyne will back my word that Allan Croft went missing these past three days. A prompt hanging, a few legal ends to secure, and all will be mine. Including you. If you'll join me, I shall marry you. If not, I fear you'll pine away for loss of your father and die here in the tower."

Celeste studied his features and wondered how such a heartless soul could exist. "My heart pities the void it senses in yours, Roderick, and I pray the good Lord will touch ye ere 'tis too late."

He swore and flung her away. "I'll give you until the morrow to ponder your fate. A laird of the castle has many tasks to occupy his time, but I might think to visit you. Be grateful for small mercies—I might have chained you in the dungeon with your lover. Dinna attempt to leave the tower; I've set my loyal guard upon the tower stair."

Celeste stared at the closed door and listened to his footsteps on the spiral staircase. As soon as silence met her ears, she sprang into action. First, a warm woolen gown and cloak. Sturdy shoes. A simple candle would not do; she lighted two lamps.

Then, standing at the closed portal, she pressed the lever inside a recessed candle sconce.

Chapter 8

With the grinding of stone, a black crack opened in the wall. Narrow steps led down a stairway barely wide enough for Celeste. Blinking and taking deep breaths, she lowered her chin. Dougal had traversed it; so could she. The air tasted dead. She bent to keep from bashing her head on jutting rocks. With a lamp in each hand, she could not balance herself against the walls. The staircase must wind around the thick outer wall of the tower, leading down—she would find out where. Her legs shook from fatigue by the time she reached the bottom step. A stone-lined passage lay before her. Something ran ahead, squeaking; its feet pattered on the uneven floor. Her own shadow loomed double on the walls, moving as she moved.

What lay at the end of this eternal tunnel? Dougal had entered it; she could exit it. The temptation to run back up the stairs to her familiar bedchamber passed through her mind, but she dismissed it. Allan was imprisoned in a chamber possibly less cheery than this. She must find a way to rescue him.

The tunnel ended. Celeste glanced around. Had she missed a door? The walls seemed solid. Perhaps another hidden door? She set her lamps down and searched for a lever.

Nothing.

Lord Jesus, please give me aid! She backed up and bumped her head. When she reached up to rub the spot, her hand connected with a hanging metal ring. A wooden door lay above her. She remembered to say a quick word of thanks for God's guidance before she pushed upward. The door gave, but its weight frightened her. Although the tunnel's ceiling was low, she might lack strength enough to push the trapdoor all the way open.

Allan. She could do it for Allan. Groaning with the effort, she gave a mighty shove. The door popped open but slammed back down. "No!" she shouted and pushed again. This time, to her surprise, the door lifted easily and swung back to hit the floor above.

A white face gazed down at her. She shrieked.

"Lady Celeste! Thank the guid Lord above, ye're alive!"

"Mr. Ballantyne? I thought ye were a specter!"

The little man reached a shaking hand to take the lamps from her. Celeste feared she might pull him into the tunnel if she accepted his aid, but for his pride's sake, she allowed him to assist her. Once seated on a stone floor with her legs still dangling into the tunnel, she glanced around. "Where are we?"

"In the crypt beneath the chapel."

Celeste froze. The stone blocks had a different aspect once she knew their contents.

"Why are ye here?" she asked.

"Where is Dougal Mason?" he asked at the same time.

Celeste looked at Mr. Ballantyne with sudden suspicion. "Ye waited here for him?"

"Aye. I told him of the secret passage, to my regret. I didna tell Roderick." His shoulders bowed. "Come into the chapel, and I shall reveal all. I must atone. You carry one lamp."

Celeste gripped his elbow and let him lead the way among granite monuments and marble effigies. He seemed barely able to climb the steps into the chapel. Once in the sanctuary, he dropped upon a bench and covered his face with his hands.

"I carena if they kill me; I must confess all. God has granted me no peace since the business began, and I canna spend eternity in such torment of soul!" he moaned.

"Mr. Ballantyne, what have ye done?" Celeste laid a comforting hand upon his shoulder.

" 'Twas Robert's doing. Had he not looked upon a MacMurray wench, none of this would have come about." Mr. Ballantyne sounded angry.

"Uncle Robert?"

"Aye, lass." Mr. Ballantyne lowered his hands. "He loved Laura MacMurray and married her in the village kirk, with me as witness. Fearing the wrath of his father, the third earl, he kept the marriage secret, promising Laura to own her as his wife once he became earl. But the hatred against Highlanders in these parts kept him silent even after his succession to the title, and ere he made up his mind to claim his bride and wee son, Laura died. She sent her innocent lad, him not knowing his ain father, to Robert's care."

Celeste felt a strange heaviness in her breast. "He never acknowledged his right-ful heir!"

"Cowardice destroyed him from within. He nigh burst with pride and love for the lad, yet he couldna look Allan in the eyes and tell what he'd done to the lad's mother. Robert laid the charge upon me to set up Allan as heir upon his passing."

Celeste shook her head. "Why did ye not? My father doesna care to be earl."

"Ah, lassie, the shame of it! I couldna bear the thought of a MacMurray taking back Kennerith! A Highlander." He nearly spat the word. "I told Roderick where to find the kirk marriage record so he might expunge it."

"Roderick knows! No wonder he hates Allan. He is—Allan is our cousin."

"Not yours by blood, my lady. Yet I'll not have ye thinking shame on your mother. She was married and widowed ere she wed Malcolm. Your father was a French army officer."

Celeste grabbed Mr. Ballantyne in a quick hug. "My mother and Allan's were both good women. I knew it! Truly, I did."

" 'Tis all accounted in the family Bible there upon the stand. I didna yet reveal that record's existence to Roderick."

Celeste stared at the huge book, visible now in the morning light streaming through stained-glass windows. "Uncle Robert told Allan in his note: 'All ye need know is contained in the Holy Scriptures.'" She ran up the steps to the lectern and turned to the family record in the front pages of the huge Bible. A sealed paper lay inside the book's leather cover. It bore a spidery inscription. Celeste read aloud, " 'Allan MacMurray Galbraith.'" With a thrill of satisfaction, she slipped the letter into the front of her gown.

The ground seemed to rumble. "Horses arriving. A carriage." Mr. Ballantyne tottered to open the chapel door.

In the courtyard, a sea of mounted horses surged around the earl's carriage as it slowed to a stop. "Papa!" Forsaking caution, Celeste ran down the stairs, across the cobblestone drive, between startled horses, and flung herself into her father's arms as he stepped down. "Ye're alive! They told me ye were dead."

"I might ha' been, but for Dougal's ineptitude with a firearm." Malcolm's voice held the ring of steel. "Thank the guid Lord, ye're safe! That maid Beryl warned me of a plot against your life. Where is Roderick?"

Celeste glanced around, noting uniforms, guns, and swords. The earl had returned to Kennerith in the company of a military unit. Her heart sang. "Papa, ye must hear Mr. Ballantyne's tale. Ye'll be thankful."

—⁂—

Cold from the stone wall seeped through Allan's torn shirt and drove deep into his bones. No matter how he strained his eyes, no glimmer of light relieved the dungeon's darkness. He wondered if he would live long enough to lose his power of sight.

Heaving a sigh, he tipped his head back. *Protect Celeste from that monster, Lord. I cannot see Your plan in this adversity, but I must trust that You remember Your children.*

He heard a clank overhead and running footsteps echoed. "Allan?"

"Celeste!" Was he dreaming?

Light appeared as a tiny square in the door to his cell. "Where are you?"

"Here." He rattled his chains and a moment later heard a key turn in the rusty lock.

The door creaked open, and Celeste stopped to stare. "Oh Allan!" An iron key ring hung from her hand.

He blinked in the brilliant lantern light. "Ye're safe?"

She set the lantern on the floor and began to try keys in his wrist shackles. "I am well. My father returned safely, and I used the secret door in the tower to escape and—oh Allan, how could he abuse ye so?"

Losing patience with the keys, she knelt upon Allan's bench and wrapped her arms around his neck. Smooth, lavender-fragranced skin filled his senses. He tugged at his fetters. "My lady—" She cut him off with a kiss that eradicated the dungeon's chill.

Her hands caressed his hair and rasped over his stubbled chin and throat. "Allan, I love you."

Helpless, he simply savored her kisses. As soon as he was free, he must run to the hills and never again lay eyes upon his beloved lady—but at the moment, this dungeon cell was paradise.

"Allan, I have a letter for you from your father." She slipped a note from her bodice and held it before him. "He married your mother! Ye're his true heir, not Papa. We're to hurry upstairs and hear Papa's announcement."

Allan wiggled his hands. " 'Twould help if ye'd release me, my lady."

—⁓—

In Kennerith Castle's great hall, Malcolm Galbraith confronted his two nephews. Soldiers gripped the arms of Roderick, whose twisted features expressed rage and defeat.

Allan stood alone. Despite his bare head and filthy, tattered clothing, the assembled company regarded him with evident awe.

Anxiety pinched Celeste's pounding heart. Since he had read his father's letter, Allan had spoken not one word. Heat seared her cheeks, and she avoided his gaze. What had compelled her to declare her love while he was unable to escape her advances? Nevertheless, come what may, she had memories to treasure of Allan eagerly returning her kisses.

Malcolm spoke. "After hearing Mr. Ballantyne's testimony and reading the surviving record of my brother Robert's legal marriage to Laura MacMurray, I declare Allan MacMurray Galbraith the true fifth earl of Carnassis. Let each man present stand as witness."

A murmur rose among the assembled servants and soldiers, quickly breaking into a roar of approval.

Epilogue

A carriage stopped before a modest row house on a street near the university. The coachman placed the step and held the door. "Shall I wait, your lairdship?"

The earl of Carnassis stepped down. "Ye needna stand about in the cold. Return for me in three hours, John."

In the entryway, a maid took his cloak. "Step into the study, your lairdship. I'll tell the professor and miss that ye've arrived."

"Thank you, Beryl. A certain crofter of mine asks about ye regularly—Adam MacKinnoch. Fine fellow."

She returned his smile and blushed. "I'm thinking I'll soon be following my lady back to Kennerith."

He grinned and chucked his cousin under her chin.

Beryl left him in a book-lined study. An embroidery, partially completed, lay on the arm of a chair.

"Welcome, your lairdship!" Malcolm Galbraith stepped into the room. He clasped the earl's hand and shook it.

"Ye look well, Uncle," Allan observed.

"Pleased to be where I belong." Malcolm drew his daughter forward. "I know ye've come to see my lass, but first I'd hear the news. What has come of Roderick?"

Allan bowed over Celeste's hand and lifted it to his lips. "My lady."

The lacy fichu crossed upon her chest seemed to flutter, and her face turned pink. "I am no longer to be addressed so, your lairdship," she said. "Kennerith Castle has a fresh heir. I am simply Miss Galbraith."

She sat down and picked up her needlework, but her gaze remained on Allan. He relaxed upon a horsehair sofa and attempted to direct his attention to her father. "Roderick has run to the Continent. I thought it best to show mercy."

"Did the minister at Dalway testify that Roderick rifled the kirk's marriage records?"

" 'Tis true enough."

Allan could scarcely keep his eyes off Celeste after three months' deprivation.

She appeared rosy and healthy. Her blue eyes glowed behind their thick lenses.

"What happened to your MacMurray kinfolk?" she asked.

"Dougal, of course, perished that night. Many of my kin decided to emigrate to the colonies; others I have granted crofts on the manor. I pray God will reclaim the MacMurray clan, starting with Beryl."

"She is an amazing woman," Celeste said. "We are fast friends now. She favors a young man from Dalway, however, so I may soon lose her."

"Perhaps." Allan restrained a smile.

"And Mr. Ballantyne?" Malcolm asked.

"He remains at Kennerith. His health deteriorates; he seldom leaves his rooms. Although I have forgiven him, he seems consumed by remorse. Only the Lord in heaven can remove such a weight of guilt. 'Tis joy to know that my father did accept God's forgiveness before his life ended, according to his letter. I regret he didna find courage to confess to me; nevertheless, all is forgiven."

"Your poor mother," Celeste sighed.

"Aye, yet now she lives in paradise and suffers no more earthly pain. I moved her body to lie beside her husband's beneath the chapel."

"Although their story is sad, I trust their son will have great joy in this life as well as in the life to come." Malcolm laid his pipe upon the mantelpiece. "If ye wish to address me, lad, I'll be in my drawing room. God bless ye both."

As soon as the door closed, Allan knelt at Celeste's feet, enveloped in her voluminous skirts. "My lady, how I have missed ye!"

"And why should the earl of Carnassis miss the likes of me?"

"Because he loves ye more than life itself."

"Och, I dinna believe it. All those months guarding me, and nary a word ye said." One dainty finger touched his waistcoat.

He caught her hand and clasped it to his heart. "Nary a word, but ye must have read all in my eyes."

"I'm short-sighted. I must hear these things to know them."

"Every time I said 'my lady,' I claimed ye as mine."

She leaned forward to touch her lips to his forehead. "Ye seemed cold at times. I thought ye loathed me."

" 'Tis a fearful thing for a servant to love his mistress. How I prayed for immunity to your beauty and charm!" His arms slid around her waist.

"Ye speak as if I were a disease." She framed his face with her hands. "And now ye're a great laird. What would ye need with a clumsy, sharp-tongued, bespectacled lass like me?"

He ignored her question. "The castle is cold and dank and falling to pieces about my ears. Without ye, I'd soon take ill and die of loneliness. I need ye to help turn a fortress into a home. I need ye with me to ride in the hills and to work in the Lady Fayre's rose garden. I need ye to read Scripture and to pray with me and to raise our children to love and serve the Lord Christ. I need ye with me to shine the light of God's love upon this dark world."

"I prayed. . .that ye'd want me," she confessed. Her lips met his, warm and soft.

Allan nearly lost his balance in the effort to bring her closer. Admitting defeat, he rose, gripped her hands, and pulled her up with him. Now he could hold her close without hoops digging into his thighs. She twined her arms about his neck and melted against him.

"We'd best ask your father's permission to marry," he murmured between kisses. "He's expecting us."

"Be warned that should ye choose to be my husband, I shall try to make your life wonderful," Celeste said.

ENGLISH TEA AND BAGPIPES

by Pamela Griffin

Dedication

Thanks to all those who helped and encouraged me,
especially to Mom and my local crit group.
And to Tracey, Tamela, and Jill—my online critique partners and fellow writers in
this collection—
it's so wonderful to be in a novella anthology with you lassies! *grin*
In the beauty of the gloamin',
in the dismal gray of storms, my God is ever faithful.
It is to Him I devote this story.
For without the Lord in my life,
accepting me when few others would,
you wouldn't be reading this now.

Only by pride cometh contention:
but with the well advised is wisdom.
PROVERBS 13:10

Chapter 1

Scotland, 1822

Fiona moved up the slippery path with care, clutching a plaid underneath her chin to block her head from the light shower. The long rectangular cloth did little to keep her completely dry, but then, she was accustomed to rain. It was her previous talk with the Finlays that gave her distress. Frowning, she paused to look up and study the familiar landmarks.

Endless steep-sided hills speckled with gray granite rose on either side and before her in the deep glen, adding their distinct signature to the untamed beauty of the region. Peaks of distant snow-covered mountains could be seen in the gap between hills at her right. To her left, a loch glimmered as drops ruffled the surface of the lake's waters. The cool, soft rain touched the rugged land, watering the earth of her Highland home.

Directly ahead, Fiona spotted a man sitting bolt upright on Ian MacGregor's shaggy nag, Dunderhead. From the navy coat, top hat, and black shiny boots he wore, the man must be a stranger, though she could only see him from the back. Why he was on Ian's horse was the real puzzle. Still, Fiona kept herself far removed from her neighbors' affairs, and likewise they left her to her own. The gentleman didn't seem the type to be a horse thief. What's more, who would want to steal old Dunderhead?

Fiona pulled her plaid farther over her hair as she walked past, her shoes squelching in the puddles.

"I say—wait a moment!" he called.

Fiona grimaced in her distaste for anything English.

"Can you help me?" he yelled more loudly over the tapping rain.

"There's nae need t' screech like a banshee." Fiona pivoted to face him. "I'm no' deaf."

She forced herself to calm. Often, when she was excited or upset, the thick Highland brogue rolled off her tongue rather than the proper speech she'd been taught as a child. She took her first real look at the dark-haired rider. Even wet, his countenance and form appeared pleasing to the eye, she had to admit. For an Englishman, that is.

"Thank you." He tipped his hat, civilly inclining his head. "I have twice been given erroneous directions to the place I seek and feel as though I've traversed this entire countryside. To make matters worse, I made the dreadful mistake of purchasing this nag that seems to know only one speed. Slow. So if you could assist me, I would be most obliged."

Fiona hid a smile. "Any halfwit knows just t' look at the beast that Ian's horse isna worth a shilling."

"Yes," he said, his voice bearing a slight edge. "I, too, have arrived at that conclusion. However, as much as I would like to stay and hold a discussion concerning the idiosyncrasies of the locals, I don't relish doing so in a downpour."

"What? This wee bit of rain?" she asked with an innocent smirk, lifting her palm to shoulder level to catch the drops.

He shook his head slowly, as though dealing with a backward child. "In that assessment we most assuredly differ, miss. Yet perhaps my view is colored by the fact that I've been traveling in this 'wee bit of rain' for a matter of hours. That said, I would be most grateful if you could tell me, is this the way to Kennerith Castle?"

"Kennerith Castle?" Fiona repeated in bewilderment.

"Yes," he said wearily. "Kennerith Castle."

Suddenly suspicious, Fiona took several seconds to examine his upright bearing and expensive attire. She gave a curt nod. "Aye. 'Tis that."

"Thank you *ever* so much," he replied, sarcasm coating his words.

Narrowing her eyes, Fiona left him and took a shortcut near a stand of birches that forked off the road. Englishmen! He could go and get lost in a bog, for all she cared.

When she reached home a short time later, she hurried through the entryway of the crumbling gatehouse to the living quarters beyond and slipped off her plaid. Squeezing the water from the tartan wool, she hung the cloth over the back of a chair near the peat fire to dry, all the while assessing her meager surroundings. Her grandmother huddled in a chair close to the hearth.

"Gwynneth has not yet come down from her chambers, and it's nearing noonday. Go and see what keeps her."

"Aye, *Seanmhair,*" Fiona said, using the Gaelic endearment for *grandmother.* Though the language had trickled away and all but disappeared, her family had passed down the dialect over the generations. Fiona was proud of that, intending never to let it fully die.

Exasperated with her irresponsible sister, mostly because searching her out was an interruption she didn't need, Fiona headed for the east tower. If Gwynneth were immersed in one of those idealistic novels with which she wasted her time, she would receive an earful from Fiona—that was certain!

The repeated bangs of the doorknocker resounded through the area, halting Fiona's steps. Deciding that Gwynneth could wait, Fiona whirled around and hurried to the entryway before old Agatha could get there. Checking to see that her tunic was properly tucked in, Fiona noticed that mud covered the bottom of her ankle-length skirt. She grimaced, but there wasn't time to change into another. Smoothing her damp, riotous curls away from her face, she straightened her shoulders and, as she opened the huge, heavy door, assumed the dignified air befitting the granddaughter of the earl of Carnassis.

The Englishman stood in the rain and stared, shock written in eyes that Fiona could now see were blue-gray. An impish hint of satisfaction swept through her, but she struggled to keep her face expressionless and inclined her head graciously. "Welcome to Kennerith Castle."

—∞—

The rain continued to beat down on Alex as he took in the smug expression of the bright-eyed wisp of a woman standing inside the door. Her eyes, a shade lighter than the overcast sky, glistened silver. Briefly he wondered how the slim column of her neck could hold up her head, as weighed down as it was by the mass of ginger-colored ringlets trailing to her waist. The plaid she'd worn earlier had hidden them. Yet what she lacked in size, she made up for in spirit.

"You could have told me," he said, giving her a mildly reproving look.

She shrugged. "You didna give me the chance. You were not exactly of a cordial mind."

"Nor were you."

She gave a grudging nod. " 'Tis true enough, I suppose."

Despite his irritation, Alex couldn't help but appreciate the lilting way she spoke and rolled her Rs. Of course everyone in Scotland spoke in such a manner, but with her smooth, pleasantly pitched voice, it sounded especially nice. If only her disposition were as sweet.

"I am Dr. Alexander Spencer, recently arrived from England, and I have need to speak with your mistress, Miss Gwynneth Galbraith, on a most urgent matter."

She straightened to her full height—the top of her head still only coming to his shoulders—and glared at him with disdain. "Now see here, Dr. Alexander Spencer of England—Gwynneth Galbraith isna me mistress, nor will she ever be. I am Fiona Galbraith, Gwynneth's elder sister and the granddaughter of Hugh Galbraith—the sixth earl of Carnassis, eighth viscount of Dalway, and eleventh baron—and laird—of Kennerith. If ye have need to speak with Gwynneth—though for what reason I canna ken—ye will need t' speak through me."

Her sister! Alex sobered. "Forgive my error. Actually, the matter concerns Gwynneth. It is your audience I desire." He motioned with one hand. "Might I come inside, out of the rain?"

The mystified expression on her face proved that she'd not yet heard the news. A measure of relief swept through Alex. Perhaps he wasn't too late.

Her manner still suspicious, Fiona stepped back, allowing him entrance. With a quick, calculating glance, he pulled off his hat, shook water from its brim, and surveyed the interior of the drafty citadel. The imposing exterior of the stone fortress, with its four square towers, moat, and keep, didn't reveal the true condition of the ivy-covered castle. Furnishings appeared worn and in need of replacement. The flagstone floor was in dire need of repair. Everywhere he cast a glance, evidence of neglect and poverty was visible, and Alex imagined the other chambers fared just as badly.

As though she discerned his thoughts, Fiona stepped into his line of vision, blocking his quiet perusal. "Ye wish to speak with me?" she asked, narrowing her eyes.

"Fiona?" a woman called from somewhere nearby. "Who is that you're talking to?"

"Only a strange Englishman who wandered here in the rain," Fiona retorted, her rigid gaze never leaving his face. "He soon will be leaving."

"Bring him to me!"

Fiona blew out a breath. "Aye, *Seanmhair.*" Her eyes narrowed at Alex. "Come on with ye, then. But I warn you, if it's mischief you're aboot, you've come t' the wrong place!"

The woman was impossible. Alex just managed to hold his tongue and followed her to a nearby chamber. The obvious scarcity of furnishings made the room seem larger. Near the fire, an elderly woman sat in one of four chairs in the room and looked at him, narrowing her eyes over her half-moon glasses. Two portraits hung side by side over the mantel. The one on the left was of a kind-faced gentleman in a plain, gray tie-wig, the other of a fierce-looking warrior with curly ginger-colored hair much like Fiona's. Both men and the girl shared the same feature of silver-gray eyes. The warrior in the painting wore a kilt with a long plaid of matching red, black, yellow, blue, and green clasped to his shoulder, and he bore a broadsword in his hand.

"That is my grandfather, Angus MacMurray, once a clan chieftain," the old woman said, following Alex's gaze. "And the first portrait is of my husband's father, Allan, who was also Angus's nephew." Her sober gaze turned his way. "Angus MacMurray fought—and died—at Culloden."

The stern words carried with them a warning Alex recognized. He was English; they were Scots. And though close to a hundred years had passed since the battle at Culloden Moor, these people had not forgotten it. That being the case, they would never approve of what Gwynneth Galbraith had done. Alex's lips turned upward in a dry smile. Without the women realizing it, they were on his side.

He quickly introduced himself to the old woman and withdrew the letter from his coat pocket, grateful to find the message only slightly damp. "While on an unannounced visit to my brother, Lord Beaufort Spencer, a scholar at the University of Edinburgh, I did not find him but came across this instead," Alex explained. "My brother had delivered it into the hands of a friend along with directions to mail it to our father next week. In short, the letter states that Beaufort met a woman visiting there, fell in love, and they have eloped. He doesn't say where they've gone."

"I dinna see what that has to do with us," Fiona argued.

"The woman is your sister—Miss Gwynneth Galbraith of Kennerith Castle." At Fiona's gasp of disbelief, Alex added, "It's all here in the letter, if you care to see it."

Glaring, she covered the short distance between them and snatched the paper from his outstretched hand. She scanned the missive, her face paling.

"Fiona?" the old woman rasped. "Tell me it's not true, lass."

"Aye, *Seanmhair,*" she murmured. " 'Tis that."

"Perhaps it's not too late," Alex said, understanding their shock, for he'd been rocked by the same emotion. "Beaufort left only the day before I arrived, and surely, if this is as much a surprise to you as it was to me, then there's a strong chance Gwynneth might still be on the premises?"

Fiona's countenance lightened. "Aye! She must be. I was on my way t' talk with her when your knock came."

Without waiting for a response, Fiona whirled around and headed for the opposite end of the castle. She took the winding and narrow tower stairs, passing a portrait of the ghoulish-looking Olivia Galbraith, who'd once occupied this same tower chamber. Many female ancestors had stayed in the well-fortified east tower, including Fiona's great-grandmother, Lady Celeste, whose love for a servant brought peace between the once-feuding Clan MacMurray and Clan Galbraith, and her other great-grandmother, Beryl, who'd been a simple ladies' maid. Now Fiona's sister occupied the tower that legend said had a reputation for bearing doomed women.

Fiona threw open the door to Gwynneth's sitting room. Seeing it unoccupied, she moved to the adjoining bedchamber, disheartened to find it empty, as well. She mustn't jump to conclusions. Perhaps the lass had gone to the crag that jutted out near the loch. She often enjoyed sitting there and looking out over the lake's waters.

On a nearby table, atop a copy of Sir Walter Scott's *Ivanhoe,* lay a novel Fiona had never seen—*Pride and Prejudice.* Beneath its title, the cover only said: "by the author of *Sense and Sensibility.*" Fiona grimaced at the book, whose script lettering seemed to accuse her, and wondered how her sister had come by it. She spotted a paper rectangle peeking from within the pages. With heavy heart, she slid it out and read her name on the parchment in Gwynneth's flowery hand. Fingers trembling, she opened the note.

Dearest Fiona,

When you read this, I will long be gone. I have fallen in love with a most wonderful man, Lord Beaufort Spencer of Darrencourt. Aye, he is an Englishman. I met him when I visited our cousin in Edinburgh last spring. I knew you and our grandmother would not approve, so I thought it best to keep our acquaintance secret. Beaufort also thought it wise not to inform his family of our wedding plans. Yet the love we share is strong, and we'll not be denied a life together due to prejudices that are centuries old. As you read this, we are on our way to Gretna Green, and when next you see me—if you will see me—I will be Lady Spencer. I pray that you can look beyond your intolerance for anything English and can share in my happiness. . . .

Fiona's hand holding the letter dropped to her side as she sank against the four-poster bed. After awhile, the stunned feeling dissipated, and she marched to her chamber, resolute.

There was nothing to be done but go after the foolish girl. And Fiona was up to the task.

—∿∿—

Wondering what was keeping the young woman, Alex stood, clasping his wrist behind his back, his hat in his hand, and gazed at the paintings, though he was very aware of the elderly matriarch's stern eye on him. The musty scent from the smoky fire coupled with the faint odor of mildew fit in well with these primitive surroundings. From the little Alex had seen, it was a wonder the castle still stood.

A quick, light tread on the flagstones made him turn, and Fiona rushed into the room. She stopped short at seeing Alex, as if just remembering he was there, narrowed her eyes at him, and moved toward her grandmother. Alex noticed Fiona had taken time to change from her muddy clothes into a serviceable dark blue wool dress. He wondered why. Certainly she hadn't done so for him.

"Well, child—speak." The old woman leaned forward. "Dinna keep me in suspense."

Fiona's woebegone expression told all. "She's gone, as he said. I found this letter in her room. She must have taken the secret stairway."

The woman put a hand to her heart, skimming the parchment. "Gretna Green! Such news may give your grandfather another stroke. . .though likely he's beyond understanding."

"She willna get far," Fiona assured her grandmother, retrieving the letter from the woman's limp hand now lying in her lap. "I'll see to that."

"Excuse me." Alex stepped forward, earning him a cold stare from both women, as though he'd been the one to steal their relation away and not his brother. From the little he'd seen of the castle, he doubted Gwynneth Galbraith had needed much enticing. "Might I see the letter? If I'm to find them, I'll need to know what it says."

"That willna be necessary." Fiona folded the letter and stuck it within the high neckline of her dress. "I'm capable of findin' my own sister."

Alex could barely restrain a laugh. "You? Surely you jest. Traveling to Gretna Green in this weather could take many days, even weeks."

"Perhaps for an Englishman," Fiona retorted, a gleam in her eye. "But no' for a Scot."

"I'm sorry, Miss Galbraith, but I simply don't have the time or the inclination to act as companion—which is preposterous in any case. Surely you realize the impropriety of a man escorting an unmarried woman without a chaperone present?" He didn't add that should she produce such a chaperone, the two would only slow him down.

Challenge sparked her eyes. "Who said anything about me goin' with the likes o' you? I'm perfectly capable of findin' the place on my own."

"What?" Alex couldn't believe what he was hearing. "You can't travel alone!"

"And why not?" She faced him, hands balled on her hips. "Because I'm only a wee slip of a lass and not a laddie?" she challenged.

"Yes—no." Alex twisted his hat around in his hands. The girl was confusing him. "It's a hazardous journey. You might not be safe."

"To be sure, I'm well able to take care o' myself."

"Fiona, you are certain?" her grandmother interrupted.

Incredulous, Alex glanced at the old woman. Surely, she couldn't be in favor of such a preposterous plan!

The expression in the girl's eyes softened. "Aye, *Seanmhair*. I'll find her."

"And how do you propose to get there?" Alex inserted triumphantly. "Obviously you've no horse, or you wouldn't have been walking in this downpour. And I certainly won't give you the nag I was saddled with, poor beast that she is."

After a long silence, Fiona lowered her head in evident defeat and turned her back to him, shoulders slumping. "Aye. Perhaps ye speak wisely. Perhaps 'tis best I stay. For surely, I canna walk across all o' Scotland and make it there in time to stop the wedding."

A little off balance by her unexpected change of heart, Alex paused before replying. "I'm relieved that you see things my way at last. It's best for all concerned. Do not fear; I shall see to it that your sister returns safely."

"How good of ye."

Alex stared hard at the mass of ginger-red curls flowing down her back. Had he detected a note of mockery in the words?

"Grandmother, ye've not yet had your broth," Fiona said, as though the thought had just occurred. "I'll see what keeps Agatha." She directed a cool gaze toward Alex. "I suppose you'll be wantin' food as well before continuin' your search?"

Alex considered the prospect. "That would be splendid. Also a cup of tea, if you have it."

"Ye'll not be findin' English tea at Kennerith Castle," she said proudly. "As to the other, I'll see to it."

Alex watched Fiona whisk from the room. Though the offer for refreshment had been less than charming, Alex looked forward to a quick, hot meal to warm him before heading into the chill rain again. Moreover, somewhere he must find a better piece of horseflesh if he were to catch up to his brother in time. Alex's father wouldn't tolerate failure in accomplishing this task.

Minutes passed, the low crackle of fire in the hearth the only sound heard. The old woman sat upright, staring out a nearby window as though looking for someone. Evidently she desired no idle drawing room chitchat, if this indeed could be considered a drawing room. Alex eyed every object in the sparse chamber twice, fiddling with his hat, turning it round and round, wishing the girl would hurry so he could be gone from this place.

From outside, the clatter of galloping hooves followed by muffled pounding—the sound of a horse exiting the drawbridge and tearing up sod—caught his attention. He rushed to glance out the same window the woman stared at. Through the paned glass, he made out a cloaked figure astride a fine gray mount flying like the wind. The hood fell away, and an abundant banner of long red hair unfurled behind the rider.

The old woman chuckled and turned her proud gaze toward Alex. "My granddaughter isna easily crossed, Dr. Spencer. She has the spirit of her forebears. You would do well to remember that."

Alex stared in disbelief and watched Fiona ride away along the high moor.

Chapter 2

Hours had elapsed since Fiona's escape. She still grinned when she thought of how she'd outwitted the annoying Englishman. Imagine, telling her what she could and could not do! The need for a hasty departure had been crucial; otherwise they would have wasted precious time arguing the matter, and Fiona didn't take kindly to anyone ordering her about.

Nigh unto two years had passed since her grandfather's stroke that left him an invalid and void of his mental faculties. Since that time, Fiona had needed to unofficially assume any pressing duties that her frail grandmother or the earl's secretary couldn't handle. Fiona and Gwynneth had been orphaned at an early age and had come to live at Kennerith with her mother's parents. Her fondest memories were the nights of the *ceilidh,* when young and old in their household, along with any visiting family or friends, would gather cozily 'round the fire while outside the fierce winds howled.

Grandfather had played the part of the bard and regaled them with stories of their long-dispersed clan and of battles fought, once against the Vikings and more recently against the English, passing the family history on to the next generation, often in Gaelic song. Fiona's head barely reached the kitchen table so she could help Agatha whip the cream and add the raspberries and oats for the delicious *cranachan* she favored, before she knew all about the noble Bonnie Prince Charlie and his final victory at Falkirk, followed so swiftly by his defeat at Culloden Moor. Fiona's courageous ancestors had played a vital role in those battles.

After Grandfather wove his tales, Grandmother played the ancient *clarsach,* a triangular harp whose use disappeared many years ago along with the clans—thanks to British interference. Her uncle sawed on his fiddle, her cousin played the pipes, and there would be dancing and singing.

Fiona missed those days.

Seeing a white ribbon of waterfall in the craggy hills ahead, Fiona prodded her mare to climb that direction. The gentle spraying sound of water was pleasing to her soul, and she slid off the gray's back. She stroked Skye's soft muzzle before trudging to the edge of the rippled water, white with froth from the pounding fall. Kneeling on the damp loam, Fiona dipped her hands into the ice-cold pool and drank her fill. The rains had stopped long ago, the weather a fickle companion to this ruggedly beautiful land. One minute the sun kissed the earth, causing the mountain burns and lochs' waters to shimmer as though jewels hid beneath their crystalline depths. The next, rain slapped the ground, streaming from beneath low-lying clouds that often skimmed the heather hills and glens and broad, rolling straths—all of which looked as if they'd been covered with an abundance of rich green velvet, whose nap waved in the constant breezes.

A soft whinny—not Skye's—ruffled the air behind Fiona. She stiffened and looked over her shoulder.

His bearing rigid, the Englishman sat atop a cream-colored steed Fiona recognized as Barrag, a horse belonging to the castle stables. The interloper tipped his hat, inclining his head her way. A most peculiar heat bathed her face, and she hurriedly returned her gaze to the pool. While she shook her hands free of drops, she heard him dismount. The rustle of his booted steps came close. She sensed him crouch by the water's edge and tensed.

"I wish to make a suggestion," he finally said, making her jump from the suddenness of his voice—closer than she'd thought. She darted a glance his way. He stared over the pool, his eyes seemingly on the tall waterfall in the rocks ahead.

"Aye?" The word came warily.

"It would be folly to escort you back to the castle. I would lose a half day's ride at least, and I have as fervent a desire to prevent this wedding from taking place as you do."

Fiona bristled at his inference that, had there been time, he would have forced her to return home. As if he could! She narrowed her eyes. "Go on."

"I propose we band forces and journey together. For reasons earlier stated, I was formerly opposed to such a plan. However, now that matters have changed and you've taken it on yourself to set out alone, I see it as the best recourse for all involved. Together, we might reach Dumfriesshire that much faster. You know the lay of the land better than I, and in return, I could offer you any protection you might need."

"You?" She stood and laughed. "An Englishman offering a Highlander protection? If I should need protection—and I dinna need any such thing—perhaps 'twould be wiser t' seek someone t' protect me from you!"

He let out a weary breath and stood, facing her. "You have my word, I'll not touch you. You've no reason to fear me."

"Hmph." Fiona crossed her arms. "And how am I t' ken that you're not cut from the same cloth as your brother? I'm certain 'twas his talk of trinkets that led poor Gwynneth astray."

"Is your sister the type of woman to marry a man solely for his money?"

She balled her hands at her sides to prevent herself from slapping his aristo-cratic, planed cheek. Raising her chin high, she said, "Ye dare speak ill of me sister after your brother has committed so heinous a crime as t' snatch her from her home?"

"By her letter, your sister was willing. It was no abduction, this."

"Oh!" Fiona spun around and made for her horse.

"Besides protection, I can think of another reason why we should accompany one another in our search," he called after her.

Curiosity at what he would say next compelled her to stop. Yet she didn't turn or address him.

"Though Beaufort and I are not cut from the same cloth, as you suggested, I know how he thinks. You do not. Should he and your sister encounter problems during their journey, I can better surmise the steps he may have taken to meet them. Also..." The sound of his footsteps came closer until he was standing before her. She met the disturbing blue-gray of his eyes and looked away.

"You may be disinclined to hear this," he continued, "but the truth of the matter is that I, being an English gentleman, likely will receive more aid from the villagers than will you, being a Highland lass. We shall be traversing country different from your own. Especially in the Lowlands, from the little I've witnessed, the Scots do not abhor the English. Neither do they hold any ancient grudges against them. Indeed, they've come to recognize the benefits of living under British rule. Yet I've also heard it said there are those Scottish Lowlanders who think poorly of Highlanders. For that reason, you may find it difficult to retrieve any information you seek."

Fiona stiffened, thinking of the land clearances, still in progress. Tenants were being driven from their homes in droves to make wider sheep runs so that the lairds could grow wealthier. Kennerith Castle needed to do the same but for different rea-sons. They could no longer support their tenants and thrive. Bad crops and the ten-ants' inability to pay rent had forced the decision neither Fiona nor her grandmother wanted to make. Both realized that to keep the castle and remain in the Highlands, there was no other way for them but to raise the money-producing sheep, which thrived well on rocky soil ill fit for farming. This morning, when Fiona broke the news to the Finlays at her grandmother's request, she'd given them several weeks to move, even offering to help relocate them to crofts by the sea or to the Lowland's cities to work in the factories there—unlike other lairds whom she'd heard gave their tenants only an hour's notice, even burning their homes so they couldn't return to them.

" 'Twas you English who encouraged the land clearances," Fiona stated in an effort to assuage the guilt. "So why should any Lowlander be opposed t' me or my kinsmen—and no' to you as well?"

"It's not merely the land clearances that make them prejudiced." He hesitated, as if he would say more, then shook his head and moved toward Barrag.

She followed him. "Speak, then! What is it that would turn my country-men against me?" Another thought struck. "Or perhaps ye lie t' seek your ain way, Englishman?"

He stopped walking and abruptly faced her. She barely refrained from barreling into him.

"I speak no falsehoods," he said. "I merely do not wish to repeat ill words spoken about another."

"If ye dinna tell me, I'll be sure 'twas a lie, and I'll go nowhere with you." Fiona was surprised by her words and quickly added, "Not that I plan to go with you in any case."

He released a breath, clearly exasperated. "Very well. If speaking will persuade you to join me, I'll make an exception this once, though to do so goes against my nature. Those Lowlanders of whom I spoke are of the opinion that all Highlanders are a wild, brutal, and uncouth lot."

"That's a lie, if ever I heard one! A Scotsman wouldna have said such about another Scot."

Or would he? Fiona had no idea. She only had knowledge of those things that her grandparents told her, mainly the history of her clansmen, but very lit-tle about the land or people outside her Highland home, except to say that the Lowlanders were weak for so readily giving in to the English and making their homes in cities there. Nor had her childhood nurse or tutor taught her anything but the rudiments of a girl's learning.

Alex looked at her with pity, and Fiona marched back to her horse.

"Will you accept my offer of protection and aid?" he called.

"No!" she fumed, mounting Skye. She guided the mare closer to the Englishman. Lifting her chin, she stared him down. "I need protection from no man. Especially if that man be you!"

Bouncing her heels into Skye's flanks, Fiona urged the horse into a full gallop. She needed no one's protection except the Almighty's. Her grandmother had raised Fiona to fear the Lord, and Him only did she serve. Her own people feared her, in the truest sense of the word, and some had accused her of being a witch or possess-ing an evil spirit until she saved a tenant's son from the loch's deep waters. Then the hurtful words finally ceased from all except the older children. Yet the people kept their distance. And their superstitions.

Sadness enveloped a heart Fiona thought fully hardened against the taunts she'd endured since childhood. No, she needed no man's protection. Likely, all would flee in the opposite direction should the curse visit itself upon her while she was in their midst.

—∞—

Alex guided his horse south, far behind Fiona's gray. Whether she was aware of his presence or not, he didn't know. She gave no outward indication. To allow a woman to travel unaccompanied went against his nature, and he'd appointed himself her guardian. If she wouldn't travel with him, then he planned to follow her—all the way to Dumfries and Gretna Green if necessary. She made good time and didn't dally, so perhaps she wasn't the burr under his saddle that Alex had thought she would be.

He frowned when he remembered her firm declaration of needing no man's protection. Stubbornness had made her eyes glint like a sword's honed edge. Yet her proud bearing was in direct opposition to the betraying tremble of her lower lip, which hinted at her vulnerability. Her ancestor may have been a fierce clan chieftain; however, Fiona wasn't as tough as she pretended. What had put such pain in her heart—enough to make her almost crumble when she spoke of needing no man's protection? Had someone hurt her? A lover, perhaps?

Irritated with his mind's wanderings, Alex shifted in the saddle and assessed the scope of treeless moors they crossed. Different from his home in Darrencourt, these primitive surroundings possessed a wild, eerie beauty—dangerous yet beguiling. Mauve-colored heather, wild bracken, and tufts of yellow broom carpeted the ground while barren crags etched a murky sky. High above, a golden eagle sailed. A breath of silver mist uncurled like smoke in the air for miles around, yet Alex could see well enough to travel safely, and his charge showed no inclination toward stopping. Soon, they would need to find somewhere to rest for the night. Hopefully a village would emerge before twilight fell.

A thick batting of angry gray clouds loomed closer, shadowing the land and bringing with it rain. When the drops grew more furious, Alex was relieved to note Fiona guide her gray toward an outcropping of rock. She sought shelter under an overhang, and Alex did the same, glad for the respite, though his cloak helped to keep some of the moisture off. Like these Highlands, his English home was known for its frequent rain showers.

In the cramped twelve feet of dry space with a recess no more than six feet deep, Fiona went as far to the other side as possible, and Alex stayed on his end. The cream-colored steed nudged his shoulder, as though looking for a treat, and Fiona gave a disgusted snort.

Alex looked her way. She leaned back against the rock wall, chewing on a hunk of bread. Remembering his own meal, Alex withdrew a wrapped napkin from inside his coat. Unknotting the cloth, he saw a crust of bread like Fiona's, a single smoked piece of fish, and a hunk of hard cheese.

Wondering if the woman only had bread, he held out the napkin. "Would you like to share?"

"I want nothing from you, Englishman," she said in a voice rivaling the cold rain.

He lifted his brows in a shrug and began to eat the cheese.

"So tell me, did ye steal that food from Kennerith, as you stole our horse from the courtyard stables?" Fiona's words held rancor, as did her expression. "Your kind makes a habit of ripping away what belongs t' others, is that no' so?"

"My kind?"

"You English. You stole our way of living, our traditions, even our dress. Why no' steal our food and horses, as well?" She tore away a large hunk of bread with her teeth, no doubt wishing it were the back of his hand instead.

"I seem to recall that much of what you named has been reinstated to your kinsmen. The dress, the traditions—"

"But no' the clans," Fiona interrupted.

"No, not the clans." Alex knew his history. The clan system of which she spoke had been considered too dangerous and was abolished decades ago after the Scots' defeat at Culloden. Likewise, all Highland customs and dress were done away with and stiff penalties invoked on those who opposed the ordinance, except on those soldiers who'd given over their loyalties to serving Britain. Approximately forty years ago, Highland dress and customs were restored to the people. Yet evidently that wasn't enough for this fiery slip of a girl, who stared at him with daggers in her eyes. Alex thought it wise to change the subject.

"Your accusation is false. Your grandmother gave me the horse in exchange for a few pounds."

"My grandmother wouldna have sold Barrag! Nor anything else belonging t' Kennerith—no' to an Englishman!"

"The horse is only borrowed. I shall return it to the castle upon completion of my task. Your grandmother was naturally anxious about your sister's welfare. Her primary concern was that I find her in time to stop the wedding."

"I dinna believe you. She knows I went after Gwynneth."

Alex decided it best not to repeat that a well-traveled Englishman would likely entertain more success than a girl who'd never left the Highlands—and her grandmother had realized that. He trod carefully. "She arrived at the conclusion that two seeking out the couple would garner more success than one. At any rate, she did grant me use of this horse and, while I saddled the beast, also had your cook prepare food for me—food, I will remind you, which you so graciously offered before your hasty departure from the castle."

Fiona smiled sweetly. "Let's hope she poisoned it."

Alex withheld an answering grin and brought the smoked fish to his mouth. He stopped short of biting into it, her words fully registering, and stared at the silver morsel. He thought he heard her softly laugh, but when he looked, her focus was entirely on the rain.

Alex discreetly sniffed the fish, then, feeling ten times the fool, bit into it. Fiona might be as wild as the buffeting wind and as obstinate as the endless rain, but Alex was certain neither she nor her frail grandmother would be an accomplice to murder.

At least he hoped such was the case.

Chapter 3

With the vast ocean on their right, Fiona and her unwelcome escort approached a scattering of white crofts shortly before nightfall. The Englishman inquired about a place to sleep from an old man mending a net, and he and Fiona were directed to a humble stone croft nearby. A thatched roof topped the single-story dwelling, and a large bundle of cut and dried brown peat lay stacked high against a wall. Plots of farmland ran right up to the front of each cottage, unhindered by boundaries of hedges. Even flower gardens were absent, and Fiona thought of Kennerith's beautiful rose garden started centuries ago by a serf maiden who married a laird. Girls like Gwynneth swooned over such a legend, but a romantic, Fiona was not. Still, she loved to stroll through the well-kept garden and breathe deeply of the roses' sweet scent.

At Alex's knock, a rotund woman came to the door. She nodded to Alex, who explained their need for a place to stay. Casting a cursory glance over both of them, she offered shelter and food for ten shillings, including lodging and feed for the horses.

"Have another couple like us, an Englishman and a Scottish woman, been through here?" Alex asked, handing over a gold half sovereign, which the woman eyed greedily. "The gentleman is approximately my age and has fair hair. The woman looks much like my companion, except her hair is dark." At Fiona's gasp of surprise that he should be so knowledgeable about Gwynneth's appearance, he glanced her way. "Your grandmother told me."

"Sich a couple rode through here late this mornin'," the crofter's wife responded.

Alex smiled. "Thank you. If you have separate quarters for us to sleep, I would be most obliged."

"Give him a bed," Fiona inserted. "As for myself, I'm in need of a fresh horse and lantern, if you have them."

Alex faced her, incredulous. "Surely, you jest. You cannot mean to travel by night."

"If ye feel the need for rest, Englishman, dinna let me keep you from it." Fiona drew herself up. "We Galbraiths are a strong lot. My ancestors endured many a night without sleep while in battle, and I will do the same."

"A foolish lot, I daresay," Fiona thought she heard him mumble. She peered closely at him, but his attention was focused on their hostess. He addressed her with a polite smile. "If you'll excuse us a moment?"

She looked back and forth between them and nodded. "I've bu' one empty bed, since my Sean jist married. The lady can sleep wit' my daughter." She moved away.

"Thank you, but I dinna need a bed," Fiona called after her. "I need a horse."

The woman gave no sign of hearing.

Frustrated, Fiona snapped her gaze to Alex's. "Now see what you've done?"

Alex's eyes were serious. "Miss Galbraith, it would be most foolhardy of you to continue in the black of night with no moon to guide you. Rest the evening here, and we'll leave before dawn. Beaufort isn't an early riser. Wherever the two have chosen to stay the night, I doubt he'll break that lifelong habit. Especially since it's doubtful he knows he's being pursued."

His words, "Wherever the two have chosen to stay the night," struck an icy shaft of awareness deep within Fiona's heart. Her expression must have betrayed her, for Alex quickly spoke. "I assure you, my brother may be many things, but he is a gentleman and will treat your sister as a lady." A flush of red crawled up his neck. "They'll have separate quarters, as will we."

"I told you, I'll not stay."

Alex exhaled a weary breath. "At least come inside and allow me to buy you a meal."

The hunk of bread she'd thought to grab before fleeing the castle had done little to sustain Fiona. Good food did sound appealing. Deciding that to tarry one hour wouldn't hurt, she brushed past him and through the door. "I have my own money, Englishman. I want nothing from you."

Inside, a warm peat fire welcomed her deeper into the room. A wooden table filled the area, with a bench on either side. On the other end of the big room, two beds had been built into the wall, each with a curtain for privacy. At one end of the table sat a red-faced man, seeming to enjoy the barley juice he tippled more than the steaming bowl of soup before him. He directed a cursory glance their way, nodded, then looked back to his cup.

Alex took a seat across the table from Fiona. Immediately her attention went to the peat glowing red in the stone pit. A rosy-cheeked young girl stoked and blew on the smoldering fire underneath the kettle that hung on a hook, urging it, until it burst into yellow flame.

The woman set a platter of oatmeal bannocks between them followed by two steaming containers of *partan bree*. With Fiona's stomach close to rumbling from the pleasant smell of the peppery crab and fish, she picked up her wooden spoon and dipped it into the rich, creamy soup.

She trained her attention on her food and noticed Alex also made quick work of his meal, even asking for a refill. Halfway through the meal, he leaned closer, as though about to confide a secret. "Miss Galbraith?"

Fiona looked at him over the spoon she targeted toward her mouth.

"I propose we call a truce."

"A truce?" The uneaten spoonful plopped into what was left of the soup, and she scoffed at him in disbelief. "Tell me. How is it that a Galbraith can make peace with a Spencer?"

His brows lifted slightly, as if surprised she remembered his name. "The century-old battles on which you dwell are recorded in the annals of history. They shouldn't affect the present in which we live. Even Almighty God has commanded that we not strive with our fellow man but learn to live peaceably with one another."

His words made Fiona uncomfortable, almost guilty. She shook the undesirable feeling away. "Did your ancestors fight at Culloden?"

"Truthfully, Miss Galbraith, I do not know."

"Ye dinna know?" The admission surprised her. "Did ye have no bard to tell you stories 'round the fire about your family history?"

His loch-blue eyes gentled, and an awkward lump rose to her throat—probably due to the thick soup. She tore away a hunk of bread and ate it, hoping to dislodge the discomfort.

"That is solely a Scottish custom, I do believe," he said. "However, my father did speak to us of recent ancestors, as well as briefly outlining the Spencer history and our lineage, time and again. Since I'm not in line for the title, he chose not to prepare me as thoroughly as he did Beaufort."

"Title?"

He studied her before speaking. "My father is the earl of Darrencourt. My brother is viscount and shall inherit the title and all that goes with it one day."

"Hmph. No doubt he enticed Gwynneth to her destruction with his talk o' wealth. Poor simple lass that she is, t' fall for such a trick."

Fiona hadn't realized she'd spoken her thoughts aloud until Alex narrowed his eyes. "And is your sister so easily enticed, Miss Galbraith? Perhaps, to her, wealth is a matter to be pursued, even grasped?"

Fiona stiffened. "Are ye implying that my sister would marry a man for his title and money?"

"Such a prospect is not unheard of. It has been done before this," Alex said soberly. "After living in such, shall we say, meager conditions, it's understandable that she should want to seek a better life."

Fiona swiftly rose to her feet. "So ye think us t' be wallowin' in poverty, is that it? That we're so destitute as t' snatch whatever morsels we can from whoever'll give them—even if it be from our foes?"

She drew herself up, reached into the small drawstring bag she carried on a belt around her waist, and slapped down onto the planked table two silver shillings for her meal. "Ne'er let it be said that a Galbraith took anything from a Spencer, in this lifetime or in the lifetime t' come. If Gwynneth be guilty of any folly, 'tis in believin' the lies of a cloven-tongued Englishman, who likely dallies with every poor lass he meets!"

Realizing what she'd just spewed in her anger and seeing Alex's mouth drop, as well as the other man's, Fiona felt humiliation's fire scorch her face. Her eye began to twitch and grow heavy. Swiftly she turned and headed for the door.

She would find another horse or die trying! She would not tarry another moment in *his* presence.

—⁂—

Before dawn the next morning, after a filling bowl of porridge and cream accompanied by oatcakes, the grain of which Alex thought better suited to a horse's food intake than a person's diet, he hurried to the stables. He hadn't ceased thinking of the Scottish spitfire since her hasty departure last night. When a heavy thunderstorm began only minutes after she left, Alex felt obliged to go on foot in search of her. Yet the wind had proven too beastly, blowing the slicing rain at a slant into his eyes and causing the ocean's waters to crash high upon the rocks. Soon Alex returned to the cottage, assuring himself that Fiona would know how to take care of herself, having lived in the Highlands all her life. Surely she would have found shelter elsewhere and not attempted to ride in such weather.

In the predawn light, Alex made out the building that housed the stables. He moved across the muddy ground and, not seeing anyone about, pulled open the ancient wooden door. It gave a low, protesting squeak. A horse's whinny greeted him, but it was a woman's sleepy groan that stopped him cold.

In the dim shaft of blue light forcing its way into the darkened building, Alex noticed a blanketed form on the ground at the end of a stall. The blanket undulated, the form rose, and a pair of half-open eyes underneath a matted tousle of ginger-colored ringlets blinked his way. The apparition sneezed.

"Miss Galbraith," he said in surprise.

She clapped her hand over her nose and mouth. "Be it mornin' already?" The voice came groggily through her fingers.

"Yes. Just." Alex hesitated, awkward. "I came to ready the horse for departure. I shall do so now." Hurriedly he moved toward the cream-colored steed.

Fiona put her hand to the wall, using it for balance, and rose to her feet, clutching the blanket to her throat. Alex wondered if he should excuse himself and give her privacy, but before he could speak, she turned her back on him and loosely folded the blanket. Alex was relieved to note that she wore not only her dress but her cloak as well. By her nervous actions, he feared she'd been clothed only in her undergarments.

"The crofter's wife has porridge bubbling on the hearth," Alex offered.

Fiona shook her head. "There isna time. And I'm no' that hungry. There's. . . there's something I must say. I–I wish. . ."

"Yes?" Alex prompted, curious about what incited such self-conscious behavior.

She faced him. "I wish t' go now." With awkward steps, Fiona moved to her gray, threw the blanket over the horse's back, and reached for the saddle. "What do I owe for lodging Skye?"

"The debt is paid in full."

"I canna take money from you," she all but whispered.

"And neither can I receive payment from you." He injected lightness into his next words. "So you see, it seems we've reached a stalemate. Now we can both stand here and argue all day about who will concede, or we can leave things as they are and continue on our journey—which is the reason we're here in the first place, I'll remind you. To reach my brother and your sister in time to stop the wedding."

"Aye." She nodded but still didn't look at him.

He returned his attention to the horse. The steed tossed its head when Alex tried to slip the bridle over its muzzle. Alex tried again but got the same response.

"Barrag can be irritable of a mornin'." Fiona came up beside Alex. "Sometimes, when Grandmother used to ride him, she would first stroke his nose and sing to him. Like this."

Bedazzled, Alex watched Fiona rub the horse between the eyes and down its muzzle, softly crooning to it in a language unfamiliar to him. Dawn's pale light streamed from the stable's open door, making her face glow. Indeed, her countenance had softened as she dealt with the horse and slipped the bridle over its head. A peculiar twinge clutched Alex's stomach when he noticed the red splotch on her pale cheek where her arm had evidently pressed against it while she slept. Her hair was frizzled with wild ringlets, an indentation at the back coupled with the way it bunched up on one side making it appear as though she'd lain down while it was wet.

"You should have taken shelter in the cottage," he said quietly. "You could have caught your death of cold sleeping on the ground after having been out in the rain and with no fire to warm you."

Her gaze flitted to his, surprise making her light gray eyes shimmer like precious metals. "I've slept in a stable before, when Skye birthed her foal. You needna worry, Englishman. I'll not slow you down."

Alex stood, rooted in shock, and watched her lead the gray outside. So she had changed her mind and decided to ride with him. What spurred such a decision? He wondered if this was another of her tricks, but what purpose would it serve? Even if she did slip away, she must know by now that he would follow.

—⁓—

Fiona rode silently beside the Englishman, aware of his frequent glances her way but unable to explain her behavior. Earlier, when they stood inside the stables, the apology concerning her ill conduct last night had shuddered to a stop.

An admission of guilt was often difficult for her. She'd been raised to believe that a Galbraith or a MacMurray apologized to no man—and she still felt rattled over the dream. The dream captured her attention, left her confused. Her grandmother had taught Fiona that the Lord sometimes spoke to people through dreams. Yet surely such a dream could not have come from the Almighty Himself!

Last night, when the affliction came over her and she'd been caught in the rain, Fiona slipped into the byre with the cows and horses to hide. Unfortunately, an older lad, a simpleton who cared for the animals, was inside mucking out the stables. She pleaded with him to let her stay until the storm stopped, when she would be on her way again. But he only gaped at her, as if she were the frightening, rarely sighted creature from Loch Ness, and backed out of the building.

Shivering and wet, Fiona had grabbed the blanket off her dry horse, thrown it around her shoulders, and huddled in a corner. A pervading cloud of despair loomed over her, making her feel as weak and hopeless as a starving kitten. Why had God made her this way? Why? Did He not accept her either?

Over and over she asked herself those questions before falling into exhausted slumber. The dream revisited her, as it had many times over the years. She was fleeing across a barren heath—at first on Skye, then on foot—while clouds boiled overhead and some unknown pursuer chased her. She raced toward a shimmering loch, knowing that if she could cross it, she would be safe. Always, before she could swim across, a monstrous shadow fell over her from behind and rocklike appendages encircled her, squeezing the breath from her lungs. This time, however, the dream ended differently.

Before she could reach the loch's cool blue waters, feeling the pursuer's breath hot on her neck, sensing his shadow creep over her, Fiona unexpectedly ran into a pair of open arms that closed around her back. Only these arms weren't cruel or harsh; they were gentle and comforting. The shadow lifted, the sun broke through the clouds, and Fiona raised her head from the man's strong chest to thank him.

Again, as had happened when she'd abruptly awakened from the dream to see the Englishman standing in the stable entryway, Fiona experienced a breathless, almost dizzying sensation.

Her rescuer's face had been his.

Chapter 4

The road took them beyond one of numerous hills, and Fiona heard the lonely wail of bagpipes. Up ahead, she saw a line of people. By the look of their clothes and the belongings they carried over their shoulders, they were tenant farmers. Several men guided beasts of burden that carried woven baskets and other goods. Midway up a nearby hill, a Highlander stood wearing a kilt and tartan plaid. The wheezing yet shrill notes of his bagpipes from the slow, haunting *pibroch* he played swept through the deep glen, as though bidding farewell to the people and the way of life they'd known.

Tears stung Fiona's eyes, and she blinked them away. "Likely they've been driven from their homes and seek new ones. Such has been the way of it for many years." She threw an unsmiling glance Alex's way. "Behold the 'improvement' of which ye speak so highly."

Without waiting for Alex to remark and feeling a twinge of guilt that she and her grandmother were forced to do the same with their tenants, Fiona tapped her heels into Skye's flanks and guided the horse along the road. Once she drew closer to the refugees, she saw what appeared to be five families, nearly twenty people, all with a lost look in their eyes.

"Where do you travel?" Alex's voice came from behind, and Fiona looked over her shoulder to see him address an old, bent woman.

"Tae the first burgh in the Lowlands we come tae wi' a factory," she said tiredly. "Tae seek work. Five days o' walk we've had."

"You must be weary," Alex said. To Fiona's surprise, he slid off Barrag. "Ride my horse. My companion and I are traveling in the same direction, if you don't mind the company?"

Relief swept across the woman's features, and she nodded. Alex helped the woman mount, then took the reins, leading the horse. A blond-haired giant of a man moved Alex's way.

"Thank ye fer helpin' my *mathair*. You're welcome t' travel with us as long as ye have a care to. I'm Hugh MacBain, formerly of Inverness near Moray Firth."

"And I'm Dr. Alexander Spencer of Darrencourt."

"A doctor!" the old woman exclaimed from atop Barrag. "The Lord love ya, laddie, fer surely He sent ye tae us this day." She motioned behind her, and Fiona saw two children pulling a small cart where a little girl lay. Her head was nestled on a collie's sleek fur. "My gran'daughter isna well. She fell while runnin' doon a hill."

"I shall see to her." Alex offered Barrag's reins to a fair-haired youth and moved toward the cart. Hugh announced to the others that they would stop for a rest, and Fiona reined in Skye as well, turning her horse so that she could watch Alex inspect the wee girl's foot. He asked for a strip of cloth and bound the dirty, bare foot tightly. " 'Tis only a slight sprain," he announced to her family, who stood nearby. "I recommend she stay off of it for a few days."

"She can ride my horse," Fiona found herself saying. Everyone turned to look at her as though just remembering she was there. Heat crept up her face. "There's room enough for the other two children as well. They look in need of a rest."

Alex's eyes were gentle as they studied Fiona. "Her foot should be elevated, but since that's not possible under such circumstances, perhaps riding atop your mare would be more comfortable for her than having her leg jiggled in the back of a cart."

Hugh nodded as though Alex's word were law. "The wee ones would ride best bareback. Ne'er have they used a saddle the likes o' yours."

Fiona dismounted and readied the horse. The injured child's eyes widened as another man, obviously her father, set down the straw container he carried and lifted her from the cart. An older boy picked up Fiona's saddle and threw it where the girl had lain, then took hold of the cart handles, preparing to pull it. Gently the man set the child atop Fiona's horse, placed the small boy behind her, and the other girl in front. None of them looked over the age of eight. Their little legs stuck out to the sides on Skye's wide back as each wrapped their arms tightly around the waist of the person in front of them and the older girl gripped Skye's dark mane. The boy turned Fiona's way.

"Thank ye, miss. I'm Kiernan, and these are my sisters, Rose and Mary. Mary is the one who was hurt. She's but three and is forever runnin' o'er the place. Like a wee fairy, she is."

Rose giggled, and Mary stared at Fiona with huge eyes, the same misty green as the other two children's.

Fiona wasn't certain how to reply. She was unaccustomed to speaking with people, except those at Kennerith, of course, and she rarely spoke to children. The tenants' offspring habitually taunted her, and Fiona found it best to steer clear of them.

She offered a hesitant smile to the MacBain children, then directed her attention to the long road ahead.

—⁓—

Hours later, the gloaming painted the sky with rose, blue, and amber once the sun dipped below the horizon. Twilight followed the lengthy afterglow of the sunset and purpled the glen, and they stopped for the night. Fiona had no idea of the expanse they'd covered nor of the distance yet to go, but she strongly was beginning to feel the discomforts of traveling and wished for a vat of steaming hot water with which to bathe. She felt so dirty, and her hair was a matted, frizzled mess. One kind woman had given her a piece of soft leather so she could tie her hair back, and Fiona gratefully did so. Now, as the chill night cloaked them, the white stars winking from a thankfully cloudless sky, Fiona drew close to the fire one of the MacBains had built.

"Dinna worry, lass," the elderly woman said. From a basket she plucked up a smoked herring and an oatcake and handed both to Fiona. "Ye maun eat. Yer sister will be all right. If it be God's purpose that ye find her, ye will."

The words hardly comforted Fiona, but she nodded. Shortly after Fiona and Alex had joined the MacBains, Alex had inquired if they'd seen other travelers on the road, and Hugh admitted to seeing a man and woman, each on horseback, ride past a few hours prior to Fiona and Alex's arrival.

"Which means," Alex told Fiona in an aside later, "if the riders were our siblings, we should be catching up to them soon. Hugh mentioned they weren't traveling with speed, so Beaufort must be unaware that we're following them. He had no idea I was coming to Scotland, and I'm sure he doubts you would pursue them either. Before meeting you, I never would have believed such a thing possible."

Fiona wondered if Gwynneth suspected. Surely she must know Fiona wouldn't have simply stood by and done nothing.

They had lost some time since joining the MacBains. Still, Fiona was glad they'd done what they could to help these people and were now all traveling together as one large group. Such a situation was preferable to sharing Alex's sole company, though Fiona grudgingly had to admit the prospect of being with him hadn't been entirely distasteful. There'd even been times, such as when Alex offered his horse to the old woman or when he'd so tenderly bound the child's foot, that she'd actually found herself drawn to him.

"The doctor is a grand man," Hugh's mother abruptly said, as though discerning Fiona's thoughts. "Ye could do nae better."

"Oh, but—" The words shocked Fiona into raising her head. "We arenna together—that is, we only ride together in search of his brother and my sister."

The woman chuckled. "With the way I see him starin' at ye an' ye at him when neither of ye think the other is looking?" She chuckled again. "Ye could ha'e fooled me, t' be sure!"

Fiona quickly rose, brushing off the back of her dress. "Such an idea is—is bizarre. Why, 'twould be like having English tea and bagpipes together. And anyone kens, the two dinna mix."

"An' why not? Others ha'e done so. 'Twould appear ye are well suited."

Fiona made a sound of disbelief, somewhere between a snort and a laugh. She couldn't help herself.

The woman eyed her. "What aught have ye against him, lass?"

"He's English."

The woman let out a scoffing sound that matched the one Fiona had just given. "Is that all that ails ye? A more foolish excuse I've ne'er heard."

Fiona drew her shoulders back. "My *Seanair* raised me on stories of what the English did to our clan."

"Aye. I, too, have heard sich stories in my day, an' from my ain gran'father as well," the woman replied softly. "Perhaps ye think I've nae right tae be speakin' t' ye so. Bu' I'm the oldest in what's left o' my clan, and I speak t' everyone the same." She eyed Fiona, her blue eyes wise amid the wrinkles. "Ye can take what I be tellin' ye t' heart, or ye can forget the words ever were spoken—'tis a choice you alone maun make. But I've found it wise no' t' blame the sons for the sins o' their fathers—especially for sins nigh unto a century old."

Fiona kept her gaze on the crackling fire.

"The doctor is a braw man, undeservin' of yer scorn. I kenna the two of ye, but I've two eyes with which t' see. Instead of judgin' through auld stories spoken in days gone by or lookin' at himself with only yer eyes, see him as he is, lass. From yer heart. 'Tis said, the heart is the best judge o' matters, showin' things as they truly are."

Some time elapsed before Fiona spoke. "I must be away to my bed of heather if I'm t' rise before dawn," she said quietly, more disturbed by the woman's words than she let on.

"Aye." The woman nodded and bit into her fish. "Sleep well."

Fiona moved toward Skye, intending to bed down near her mare. On her way, she met Alex, who'd just left the four MacBain men.

"Are you all right?" he asked, concern evident in his tone. "You look upset."

"I'm fine!" Fiona clipped out, walking past him. She was grateful he didn't follow.

Wrapping her cloak more tightly about her to ward off the chill, Fiona sank to the damp grass, spotted with heather, and looped an arm around her upraised knees. She ate the fish and bread while staring above the steep hills at the numerous stars in the blue-black sky and tried to sort through her thoughts. That many of these musings contained the Englishman didn't sit well with her, and Fiona scowled. Despite her weariness, a long span of time elapsed before she lay down and fell asleep.

—⁓—

Three days had passed since Alex and Fiona had joined the MacBains. The steep hills and rolling straths were beginning to level out, the expanses of valley becoming flatter and easier to travel, with thicker stands of trees spotting the hedged land. At a wide river, they crossed a long stone bridge single-file, and Alex watched Fiona guide her gray ahead of his horse. Each day, she gave all ten of the MacBain children turns riding Skye, usually three at a time, then took a turn as well.

Alex watched her now, sitting as regal as a Highland princess atop the gray mount, the setting sun transforming her hair into blazing ringlets of fire, and thought to himself that even dirty with her face lightly sunburned she was more attractive than many fine ladies of his acquaintance. Fiona possessed passion. Spirit. Strength. If the sister was anything like Fiona, Alex could begin to understand why Beaufort had done such a thing as to elope with a Highlander. Yet the earl, their father, would be less forthcoming, of that Alex was certain.

He could almost hear his father rant and rave, see him throw his arms about and declare, "If Beaufort marries this miserable Scottish wench, I shall disinherit him! Go to Edinburgh. Watch him. If he defies me and again meets with this wild creature, bring him to me!"

Alex had gone gladly. If Beaufort were disinherited, Alex would receive the title—a title he didn't want. He'd spent ten years watching and aiding his uncle in medicine, fascinated by the prospect of healing, until, at the age of twenty, he took up the profession as well. Now, at twenty-six, Alex was satisfied with his life and didn't need the burden of being next in line. From what Alex had observed of his father's duties, an earl must oversee his land and tenants and would have scant time to pursue doctoring. His father certainly had little enough time for his family, though any anger Alex once harbored for his father's neglect had long since passed.

Once they crossed the bridge, Alex glanced toward Fiona. She stared at him, a mystified expression on her face.

"Miss Galbraith, is anything the matter?"

It took her a while to answer. When she did, it was as though she'd just heard his words, and a deeper pink enhanced her already rosy face. She gave a slight shake of her head. "No. 'Tis nothing." Hurriedly she turned Skye southward and resumed following the others.

Alex was curious but didn't pursue the matter. She'd been acting peculiar all day.

A band of pale gold stretched across the hilly horizon, the thick clouds above it deep indigo blue when the group crossed a narrow, high stone bridge that stretched over the River Forth and left the Highlands behind. Lush, flat land bordered with trees cloaked the area. Pillars of smoke erupted from factories and marred the pale sky. Nearby, a huge stone fortress loomed on a crag ringed by a thick patch of trees, the town spread out below it.

"We'll be takin' oor leave of ye," Hugh MacBain said. "A place t' live I must be findin', before I seek work at a factory."

They said their farewells, and Alex inspected little Mary's foot one last time. To his surprise, she clasped him around the neck. "Thank ye, Dr. Spencer, fer makin' me foot all better," she whispered, then hurried away. He watched as she skipped beside her sister, no sign of injury evident. The young always did mend quickly, at least in the physical sense.

Alex's gaze drifted to Fiona, who couldn't be more than twenty, if that. Sometimes he caught a wounded look in her eyes, one she quickly masked, and again wondered who'd hurt her so deeply. Fiona prodded Skye to a walk, and Alex guided Barrag beside her.

"We also should seek shelter before nightfall," Alex said. "I shall see to securing each of us a room at a hostel, then will make inquiries about town concerning Beaufort and your sister. There's a chance he might have decided to stop here for the night. Beaufort never was one for long-distance traveling, and I presume that he chose the destination of Gretna Green for the marriage due to the fact that it's on the way to our home in Darrencourt. I suppose you and I should count ourselves blessed that they decided to wait and marry there. With Scotland's lax marriage laws, they could have married anywhere in the country, so I've been told."

"I would think my sister had her say in it," Fiona admitted rather grudgingly. "Gwynneth is idealistic. Gretna Green has quite a reputation, I've heard, and is just the type o' setting she would fancy for a wedding."

Alex held his tongue. He didn't see how an irregular marriage outside the church could be considered romantic but knew English literature had made it seem such, and there were those who sought the small village as sanctuary. Many mismatched English couples whose parents weren't in favor of a union eloped to Gretna Green on Scotland's border, near neighboring England, to exchange marriage vows. Oftentimes, they were pursued by irate fathers or vengeful brothers or even wronged suitors in a mad chase of horse and coach. Yet all too often, the rescuers were late in arriving.

Alex hoped he would reap better success. To push the mares harder would be folly, because a horse could go lame from such ill treatment. Now that they'd reached the Lowlands and better roads, perhaps he should seek out a coach and fresh horses, like he had used earlier in his journey. At that time and with no explanation, the driver had taken him no farther than the rugged Highland border, and Alex had to continue on foot until he'd bought the old horse that took him the rest of the way to Kennerith Castle, where he'd met Fiona. That was an encounter he likely would never forget.

Soon they entered the bustling city. Crowded rows of multilevel stone buildings faced one another across the long street. Narrow alleyways branched off the cobbled lane. Alex found an adequate hostel with two rooms, but no available stable for the horses. Nor had the innkeeper seen Beaufort.

"It might be wise for you to rest here while I try to locate accommodations for the horses," Alex said to Fiona. "Upon my return, we'll search the city for another mode of lodging where your sister and my brother may have taken rooms." If he found the errant couple, Alex realized that Gwynneth might not agree to come with him, since he was a stranger. With Fiona there, he hoped the sister wouldn't make a scene. He hadn't yet decided what he would say when he confronted Beaufort.

At the sound of men's boisterous laughter nearby, Fiona's eyes darted to the street. She drew her cloak more tightly under her throat and clutched its black folds together. She seemed anxious, and Alex realized she'd probably never seen a crowded city.

"I shall return as soon as I'm able," he said, regaining her attention. "You'll be safe here."

Her gaze snapped to his, then lowered, but she remained mute. Apparently she didn't want to admit her fright.

Alex took his leave, wishing he didn't have to go. It took him longer than he thought it would to find lodging for the horses, and at a steep price, though he handed over the silver crown without arguing. He quickly left the stables and hurried toward the inn, anxious to rejoin Fiona.

Once he arrived at the hostel, alarm grabbed hold of him. She wasn't where he'd left her. He made inquiries to the pleasant-faced woman inside and searched the first floor's public rooms, but to no avail.

Fiona was gone.

Chapter 5

A light shower watered the cobbles as Fiona hurried along the narrow wynd. She stayed close to the buildings that towered on either side of the road and away from the livestock and carts that clattered through the area. Nervousness propelled her feet faster, and she gripped the damp woolen cloak around her at the waist, keeping her arms crossed.

Not long after Alex left, when she'd first seen the woman enter the building up the road, Fiona had been sure it was Gwynneth by the cloud of dark hair and familiar-looking green hat she wore. However, having hurried in that direction to reach the place where she'd seen the girl, Fiona was uncertain which of the close buildings the young woman had entered. She knocked on a few doors, earning her one or two grumpy replies but no sister.

One kindly woman suggested she try the inn three streets over. Fiona gave her thanks and hurried in the direction the woman told her to go. She didn't need Alex's help and still felt a little miffed that he thought her so weak as to require protection, leaving her behind and telling her she'd "be safe" at the hostel.

Two streets down, the shower grew heavier. Fiona drew the cloak over her head, muttering at the unpredictable weather. With the rain impairing her vision, she darted into an open doorway shrouded in welcome lantern light. Maybe whoever owned the building would allow her to stay close to the entrance until the rain let up.

Boisterous talking trickled to murmurs, and Fiona saw that she'd entered a tavern. Three youths walked from the long bar toward her, interest putting a gleam in their eyes. Anxious, Fiona flattened her back against the wall. She searched for a sly remark, to show them that she wasn't afraid of them, when her right eye began to twitch. . . .

―⁓―

Alex hurried along the wet pavement in the direction the hostel worker told him Fiona had run. Whatever possessed her to leave the shelter of the inn and dash out into the rain, into an unfamiliar city? Did her desire to leave his presence compel her to engage in hazardous forays in the dark of night, the moment his back was turned? Frowning, Alex pulled his hat farther over his brow, though it did little to keep his face dry, and stalked onward.

He should leave the foolhardy girl to her own devices. She was so determined to prove herself capable of going it alone. He should give her the benefit of doing so and resume his task, giving no further thought to her whereabouts. He should allow her to do as she pleased and forget her existence. He should. . . But he couldn't. Her safety had become imperative to him, and he would tear this town apart, if need be, and knock on every door, until he found the strong-willed vixen and assured himself that she was all right.

"Witch! Begone frae here!" a man yelled into the storm.

Alex halted, shocked, as a cloaked figure with downcast head quickly stumbled from a nearby tavern, as if thrown from it, and lurched into the rain. A man appeared on the stoop, cursed, and bent to scoop up some mud. He lumbered after the cloaked person and threw the clod at the slender back. The figure staggered and almost fell but continued running in Alex's direction. The hood fell away.

Alex gasped and rushed toward Fiona. She barreled into his arms before she saw him. He closed his arms around her trembling form, raw anger pumping his blood and making him wish he could slam his fist into the cruel drunkard's face, though he'd never hit a person in his life.

"Fiona, look at me," Alex insisted, pulling an arm away from her back and trying to lift her chin. He thought he'd seen a trickle of blood near her brow. "Did he hurt you?"

She kept her head down. "Nae—please. . ." Her shaky wisp of a voice could scarcely be heard over the rain. "Leave me be."

"I'm afraid that's impossible," Alex retorted staunchly. She seemed determined to shield her face. Nevertheless, he realized, standing in the middle of the street in a downpour was not an acceptable place to hold this conversation. Seeing no coach or wagon nearby, he draped his cloaked arm over her shoulder, drawing her chilled, wet body close to his side, and steered her in the direction of the inn. "We must see to getting you dry. Then I shall want to examine you."

He felt her slim shoulders jerk then tense. "Nae—you canna—please! I'm—I'm all right."

"Miss Galbraith, as a physician, I shan't get a good night's rest until I'm assured that you are indeed well."

She said nothing more, and Alex chose not to press the matter. This time, he would have his way.

Once they reached the hostel and he turned her over to the innkeeper's wife, ordering her to see that Fiona change into dry clothing, Alex waited until he was sure she would be presentable, then tapped on her closed door. The innkeeper's wife opened it.

"If you'll stay," Alex said, "I think it will ease the lady's qualms."

"As ye wish." The woman moved aside to let Alex pass.

Fiona sat among the pillows on a high, four-poster bed, engulfed in a voluminous white nightgown with a neck-high collar, obviously belonging to the stout innkeeper's wife. Her head was lowered, her fiery, damp ringlets cascading to the ivory sheet.

An invisible hand gripped Alex's heart. She looked adorable. . .and vulnerable. . . and altogether too frightened. Switching off his emotions before he said something he shouldn't and aroused her ire, he adopted his clinical doctor-patient attitude and proceeded with the examination. He wished he'd at least thought to bring his bag with his stethoscope, but when he'd left Darrencourt, he hadn't known he would need it.

Tapping her back and chest through the gown and placing his ear close to her heart, Alex heard no matter that could point to pneumonia or other illness. As many times as she'd been caught in the rain since they'd met, that was a relief. Seeing purple bruises the shape of meaty finger marks above her tiny wrist where the wide sleeve of the nightgown had fallen back, Alex tensed, trying to keep his anger in check. How dare that drunken sot touch her!

Frowning, he brushed his finger along the marks and felt her startled jump. "Did he hit you?" Alex asked softly.

Fiona shook her head. "One of them pushed me, and I fell against the wall, but no one hit me."

Alex closed a gentle hand over her wrist to take her pulse. Again, he felt her give a little jump. "Relax, Miss Galbraith, I'm almost finished with the examination. Please lift your head so I can look into your eyes."

"My eyes?" she asked, her words soulful.

Alex was confused by her behavior. "Often matters can be determined about a patient's health by looking into their eyes."

Underneath his fingertips, her pulse quickened, and he felt her arm begin to tremble. My word! Was she crying?

"Miss Galbraith?"

"Tell her t' leave," she whispered at last.

"The innkeeper's wife?"

Fiona nodded.

Puzzled, Alex motioned for the woman to step outside. She did so, leaving the door partly open.

"She's gone," Alex assured.

Slowly, Fiona lifted her head. Her right eyelid hung halfway down, as though stuck, and twitched madly, causing the thin ivory skin around it to pulse.

"Did something get into your eye?" Alex asked, at once concerned. He brushed his thumb near her throbbing temple and was startled when she jerked backward, as though he'd struck her.

"It oft happens when I grow upset and weary. Ever since I was a child. It starts and stops withoot warning."

"Have you been to see a physician?"

"There isna one near Kennerith."

Alex considered her words and hoped she wouldn't get angry by the suggestion he was about to offer. "Miss Galbraith, I know little about afflictions of the eye, though I suspect this has to do with the nerves and not the actual eye itself. However, my uncle has studied the subject in depth and is a good friend of Dr. Thomas Young, who is quite knowledgeable in matters concerning the eye. Perhaps they could be of service to you. There is still much in the field of medicine that we as physicians do not understand and are only just discovering, but if anyone would know how to help you, these two men should."

She sat very still, her one good eye looking at him. He was relieved to see that it was clear and alert, the pupil normal. She appeared in fine health despite her earlier encounter. If there had been any blood on her brow, it was gone now. Looking closer, Alex discerned a shallow scrape near her temple.

"You dinna think me cursed?" she asked quietly. "Or a witch?"

"Of course not!" Alex wondered how she could arrive at such a conclusion. He smiled. "At times I might think you overly determined and a little reckless, but I've never thought evil of you." He cupped her face, his thumb again brushing the skin near her eye above her cheekbone, and was relieved to note that the twitching had slowed.

Her good eye lowered. "Thank ye, Dr. Spencer."

Suddenly he became aware of how soft her skin felt, how silky her damp curls were as they brushed his fingers. He withdrew his hand from her cheek and stood. "I prescribe a good night's sleep." He hoped his tone sounded professional. "I shall see you in the morning."

She looked up. "Will ye search for them this night?"

"No. To seek them in such weather would prove fruitless. I've given some consideration to the matter. Chances are, Beaufort continued on to Glasgow, in the hopes of finding better accommodations since that city is quite large—much larger than this. Perhaps with God's help we shall waylay our siblings on the road tomorrow. And now, I shall bid you a good night, Miss Galbraith. Pleasant dreams."

He moved to the doorway, barely hearing her wispy "good night" in return.

—◊—

Fiona watched Alex's back as he rode ahead of her. They were in unfamiliar territory and had been since they'd left Glasgow two days ago where he'd taken the lead.

Just like her brief interlude in the small burgh of Stirling, Glasgow was a frightening experience for Fiona. Thousands upon thousands of people hurried amid huge buildings that loomed in all directions, making her want to flee the teeming city and run back to her empty, wild Highland hills, where only deer and sheep and what amounted to fewer than fifty people dotted the burgh near the castle.

Alex had seemed to understand how overwhelmed Fiona felt, for he paid solicitous attention to her without belittling her. It came as a shock that she hadn't minded his courtesies one bit. Since the night Alex had rescued her from those drunken men, showing nothing but kindness after learning of her affliction—and not calling her evil, as others had done—Fiona had moved past the point of merely tolerating Alex's company. She actually was starting to like it.

If her great-great-grandfather Angus knew, he would roll over in his grave.

Uneasy, Fiona fidgeted in the saddle, focusing her attention beyond Alex to the scenic area they'd entered only that morning. The gently rolling hills were mostly uniform in size with trees at their base and granite at their tops—but nothing like the untamed beauty of her Highland mountains. Black-faced sheep spotted the fertile grasses, the white wooly animals as plentiful as they were at Kennerith.

She looked ahead to a river they were approaching. At this point, it wasn't wider than any others they'd crossed, but the bridge was in sad repair, the stones soft and crumbling away at a few places, and it didn't look capable of bearing their weight.

Fiona guided Skye beside Alex, who halted his horse and stared at the flowing peat-brown water. Here it must be deep, for Fiona couldn't see bottom. Alex's expression reflected the doubt she felt. He looked up and down for another way across, then guided Barrag along the rocky bank. Soon, they saw a lad of about eleven years. He was crouched near the water's edge and appeared to be looking for something. At their approach, he lifted his head.

"Do you know of another way across?" Alex asked. "The bridge doesn't appear safe. We are headed to Gretna Green."

The lad eyed them a moment before he straightened and pushed a tangle of wild, barley-colored hair from his eyes. "Aye, that I may, bu' it'll be costin' you." He spoke in the familiar Highland brogue, making Fiona feel less homesick. For the past few days she'd heard nothing but the broad Lowland way of talk from a Scotsman.

Alex raised his eyebrows. "What is your price?"

"I dropped me reed in the river." He pointed to a slim stick with holes, floating out of his reach. It was stuck against some tall grasses growing in the water. "Fetch it, and I'll show ye the way across. I even ken a shortcut, if ye've the stomach for it."

"My, but that does sound intriguing," Alex said with an amused smirk. He swung down from Barrag. "Very well. Show me this reed, and I'll do my best to retrieve it."

The boy again pointed it out, and Alex hunched down, putting one hand to a rock on the bank and reaching toward the reed with the other. His fingertips barely brushed the stick. He stretched farther, lost his balance, and fell into the river with a loud splash.

"Oh my!" Fiona chuckled and nudged Skye closer. She watched Alex surface, then grab the bank and hoist himself out. He snatched up his hat floating nearby and stood, river water streaming from his clothes.

The boy let out a delighted whoop. "Me reed!" He plucked it from the water. Alex's thrashing about had caused the stick to move within the lad's reach. "It's thanks I'm owin' t' ye."

Alex's expression was stiff. "So happy to oblige," he muttered, removing his coat and waistcoat and wringing out the dripping material. "And now if you'll show us your shortcut?"

"Aye." Smiling, the boy raised the reed to his mouth and fingered the holes, producing pathetic gurgling notes. He shrugged. "It needs only t' dry. Come along then."

Alex moved to Barrag, his polished black boots making squishing sounds. "How well I can relate," he said under his breath, and Fiona chuckled. Once he mounted, he looked her way.

She couldn't prevent the grin that flickered on her lips at the sight he made. His dark hair was plastered to his head in little waves. His pantaloons and shirt clung to him, outlining upper arms and a chest that looked surprisingly toned and accustomed to a hard day's work. Fiona would have thought that doctors engaged in little exercise except to visit their patients.

Alex returned her smile as he donned his dry cloak. "Indeed, judging by your expression, I must look a sight. Happily, the sun is shining, and the day is quite pleasant."

Fiona was certain his explanation of the sun's warmth must be what made her insides glow. She couldn't remember feeling this light and carefree in a long time. Forcing her focus on the wee piper leading the way and not on the tall Englishman riding beside her, Fiona sobered, reminding herself that she was on a mission. There was no place for foolish thought.

They followed the lad through a cool forest. Here, a shallow burn bubbled over gray rocks, and birdsong filled the trees. A woodpecker's taps clattered from somewhere upstream. The boy continued to lead them, playing his gurgling reed.

"Christopher!" A fair-haired girl with freckles burst through a stand of firs and came running toward them. "The bairn comes, and Mam says I maun fetch Daddy. There be trouble. She canna stop screaming." Terror etched the delicate features of the child smaller than Christopher.

"Am I to understand your mother is in childbirth?" Alex asked.

The girl looked his way, surprise in her eyes—whether from his drenched condition or the sudden realization that her brother wasn't alone, Fiona wasn't sure. The child nodded.

"Is there a midwife present?"

The girl shook her head, her lower lip beginning to tremble as her eyes filled with tears. "An' we havena doctor, either."

Alex hesitated, pensive. His gaze went to Fiona, and in his eyes, she sensed an apology. He looked at the frightened girl. "You have a doctor now. Take me to her."

Chapter 6

With little recourse, Fiona also decided to delay the journey and followed the trio. Her own mother had died in childbirth, and Fiona's heart ached in empathy at the fear she'd seen on the children's faces. If she could do something to help, she would. She could still remember Gwynneth and herself as wee children, huddled in each other's arms as they listened to their mother's screams from a far-off chamber. Later, their father came to tell them that the baby and their mother were dead. Months later, he was killed in an accident—his neck broken from a fall off his horse, an accident no doubt aided by the endless drams of ale he'd drunk in a futile effort to numb his grief.

Fiona hoped these children weren't to experience a similar childhood. She had lived a pleasant life at Kennerith, once she and Gwynneth moved in with their grandparents, but rarely a day went by that she didn't miss her mother or wonder about her.

They approached a small cottage. Instantly Alex dismounted and hurried inside after the boy and girl. Fiona followed.

A glance in the next room revealed a woman who lay deathly still on a crudely made bed. At first Fiona feared it was too late, but when Alex took her hand, the woman stirred. "I'm Dr. Spencer," he said reassuringly, "and I'm going to try to help you."

The woman said nothing, only closed her eyes. As Alex bent over her, Fiona turned to the children behind her. Beside Christopher and his sister, a child of approximately three years stood, her curled index finger hanging from her mouth. The wee tot stared at her mother's inert form. Fiona closed the door and gently drew the small lass away. She studied the humble dwelling, noticing the distinct smell of cooked *haggis*. Obviously the woman had been preparing a meal before her pains struck.

"Are you hungry?" Fiona asked the children.

All three shook their heads no.

A low, eerie moan from the next room quickly grew into a pitiful wail, then a scream. The small child ran to her sister, throwing her arms around the girl and burying her face in her frock. After the scream died away, Alex stepped outside, closing the door behind him.

"Miss Galbraith, if I might have a word with you?"

Fiona moved his way, the grave look on his face sharpening her apprehension.

"The baby is turned around," he said, his voice low, "and I must confess, I've never been faced with a breech presentation. Your prayers would be most appreciated."

"Of course."

Alex eyed the three sober faces of the children. "Perhaps it would be best if you took them outside. If I need you, I'll call."

He reentered the small room, and Fiona herded the children outdoors. The sunlight warmed her shoulders, chasing away the chill of death that seemed to pervade the hut. The children stood as though uncertain. She must give them something to do to get their minds off what was happening inside the cottage.

Fiona looked at Christopher. "Have you any idea where your father might be?"

The boy nodded. "He went to a nearby burgh."

"Perhaps you should fetch him?"

"I am no' allowed, bu' Garth may do so."

"Garth?"

"My brother. He tends the sheep in the high pasture."

Fiona felt a measure of relief. "Fetch Garth, then, and be quick aboot it."

"Aye." The boy raced toward one of the nearby hills.

Fiona felt a tug at her skirt and looked down at the smallest girl.

"Please t' tell me," she whispered, her blue eyes huge. "Is my mither t' die?"

A rush of emotion swept through Fiona, threatening to close her throat. She crouched low and took gentle hold of the girl's shoulders. "We'll pray for her—aye? And for the bairn. My grandmother oft spoke that the Almighty protects what is His own and listens t' the prayers of His children. Will ye pray with me?"

The girl nodded.

"What's your name?"

"Marget."

"And I'm Sadie," her sister said.

"I'm Fiona. Sit ye doon, the both of you, and let us pray."

"Are we no' t' kneel?" Sadie asked.

Fiona's limbs were tired from the long ride, and the cool grass felt good. "I dinna think the Lord should mind this once."

The two girls sat cross-legged on the ground with Fiona, the three of them forming a circle. Closing her eyes, Fiona murmured a heartfelt prayer. She felt first Marget's cool hand slip into hers, where it lay on her lap, then Sadie's slid into her other one. At the unexpected contact, Fiona's words abruptly stopped, and she almost lost all train of thought. Then with eyes still closed, she continued the prayer and gently squeezed each of the girls' hands.

Alex released a weary breath. He wiped off his hands and arms with a spare cloth he'd found, directing a smile toward the exhausted but happy mother and the sleeping babe beside her. There for a while, he had thought he might lose them both. He'd heard of physicians' attempts to manually turn the child while in the womb, but most all such cases ended in death for both mother and child. Alex had stood, uncertain, as he debated on the right course to take, trying to reassure the tortured woman, do his work, and pray at the same time. Miraculously, the babe turned of its own accord—or perhaps the Lord's hand had nudged it? In his profession, Alex occasionally witnessed wonders that couldn't be attributed to medicine, and with the many prayers being lifted up on this woman's behalf, Alex wouldn't be surprised if divine intervention had been the cause this time as well.

Now, many hours after their arrival to the cottage, Alex pulled down his rolled-up sleeves, fastened them, donned his wrinkled and damp waistcoat and overcoat, grabbed his hat, and stepped into the next room.

A stocky man with a red face immediately rose from a chair, fear written upon his features. Earlier, when the husband arrived, he had rushed into the room, paled, and stumbled back out.

"She's dead," he now whispered.

"She's alive and well," Alex contradicted. "As is your son."

"Son?" A radiant smile crossed the man's craggy features. "Might I see them?"

"Of course. She's weak, as is to be expected, but she's awake."

The man walked into the next room, closing the door behind him, and Alex took a chair at the table. Fiona set a bowl of stew in front of the oldest girl and then eyed him.

"You look wearied," she said. "Are ye hungry? There's a good barley stew t' fill your belly. . .unless you would prefer the *haggis.*"

At the spark of mischief in her eyes, Alex couldn't resist. "Which is. . . ?"

"The liver, heart, and lungs of a sheep cooked in its stomach, along with suet, oats, and onions. Make no mistake about it, 'tis a food for warriors. All my ancestors ate *haggis* before doin' battle."

He didn't point out that the sheepherder and his wife hardly looked like warrior material, though after what that woman had been through the past several hours, perhaps they were. The ingredients didn't sound appealing, but Alex had a fondness for steak and kidney pie, which was somewhat similar, he supposed—though baked in a crust and not a sheep's stomach.

He watched her walk to the fire pit in the middle of the room and dish stew into a bowl. "I shall take a serving of the *haggis,*" he said.

She spun around in surprise, then gave a slight nod. "Very well."

When she began to tip the stew back into the hanging pot, Alex added, "No—I'll take that, too. I'm quite famished, actually."

Fiona set the food before him and sank to a chair. Alex looked at the shiny brown and unappealing mass, a mix of mashed potato and rutabagas on the side, tentatively took a bite of the *haggis* and chewed. She watched him as though waiting for him to retch or explode, Alex wasn't sure which. The dish wasn't as tasty as the favored kidney pie, rather gamey with a strong distinctive flavor, but it was edible. He took another bite.

"You like it?" she asked in surprise.

"I wouldn't ask our cook to put it on Darrencourt's menu, but it will suffice." He smiled at her, and she looked at the fire, seeming uneasy.

"About this delay, you have my apologies, Miss Galbraith, but I simply couldn't ignore a woman in need."

"You didna hold me here. I stayed of my own accord."

Wishing to reassure her, Alex said, "I'm reasonably certain we still have a chance to reach our siblings in time."

"Aye," she said quietly.

But the next day brought with it a pelting rain that seemed bent on attacking the small dwelling. Lightning flashed through the one window of the cottage and thunder rumbled. Water trickled in through the roof in a far corner, and together Fiona and Sadie cleared the large kettle of the last trace of porridge left and set the black pot underneath the small stream, emptying it outside as needed. They ate smoked fish and bread that day.

"Do not fret, Miss Galbraith," Alex said, hoping to console her. "This same storm will keep Beaufort and your sister from traveling if they are in the area."

From where he stood near the window, Kyle, the man of the house, looked at Fiona and Alex where they sat at the table. He pulled his pipe from his mouth and stared. "Do ye seek an Englishman and a Scottish lass?" he asked.

"Yes," Alex said in some surprise. "You know of such a couple?"

"Aye. Yesterday, when I was in the burgh seein' aboot my wagon, I saw two such as they in the smithy's shop. From what I ken, and it isna much for I came as they were leavin' the place, one o' their horses threw a shoe, and they were seekin' a coach. The smithy told them there was no' one available, and they maun wait 'til he finish with Laird MacClooney's horse."

"How far is this burgh?" Alex asked, encouraged by the news.

Kyle appeared to consider. "Two hours' journey by foot."

"The shortcut I be showin' ye is faster," the boy said with a pout.

"Christopher," Kyle admonished. "I'll no' have ye speakin' in sich a disrespectful tongue, or it's boxin' yer ears I'll be doin'."

"Bu' it is faster, Daddy. They ride t' Gretna Green."

"Gretna Green?" Kyle asked in surprise.

Alex shared a look with Fiona. "Yes."

"Then it's congratulations I'm offerin' t' ye," Kyle said, a huge smile cracking his weathered face. "Though you needna wait to reach the Green. We have a priest who'll marry ye in the kirk. 'Tis the least I can do t' fetch him, if ye have a mind t' wed."

Fiona blushed. "No—I—"

"We do not wish to marry," Alex inserted, as flustered as she. "We travel to Gretna Green to stop a wedding."

Kyle's smile dissipated. "Och, I see." He stared at both Fiona and Alex. "Are ye for a certain ye dinna wish t' marry? I've been watchin' the both of ye this day past, and ne'er have I seen two people who seem so well fitted t' another."

Fiona choked on the cider she was drinking. Alex listened to her cough while Sadie slapped her back. Bewildered by a new revelation, Alex couldn't pose an answer to Kyle's comment. He realized as he sat watching Fiona fan her face and try to catch her breath that the prospect of having her for a wife wasn't at all unappealing.

She'd been a tremendous help to him during the birth. Strong and steadfast, she stood at his side near the end, often seeming to read his mind and bring him those things he needed before he asked. Any of the English young ladies of his acquaintance would have probably fainted dead away at the first signs of labor. A doctor needed a strong, loyal wife who would aid him in his profession, if necessary, as well as be a good mother to his children, if the Lord should bless them with any. He observed the kindness Fiona bestowed on these young ones, the tender care, and he had witnessed her unswerving loyalty to family. Moreover, he and Fiona had been talking civilly with one another for a few days now, and he found himself enjoying her company.

Alex was thankful when the baby's sudden crying from the next room put an end to all thoughts trailing through his mind and Kyle left the table, letting the matter drop. Yet Fiona wouldn't meet Alex's gaze, and he couldn't draw her into conversation.

Christopher merrily played his reed, masking the uneasy silence that fell in the room.

Chapter 7

C ross that bridge," Christopher said, pointing to a stone arch on the far side of the forest, "and when ye reach the other side, go on 'til ye come t' the gap between hills. Turn t' the left, and ye'll come back t' the road. If ye be followin' my lead, ye should reach Gretna Green by nightfall."

"Many thanks," Alex said with a tip of his hat.

"Mind ye, take care of your mother and your sisters and the new wee bairn," Fiona said, feeling strangely choked. "And help your father and Garth with the sheep."

"I will," the lad promised.

As they rode over a vista of rolling farmland, Fiona felt strangely sad to leave the sheepherder's family. In caring for the children these past two days, she had discovered a part of herself she hadn't known existed. Always, she had tried to shield herself from people, hiding within Kennerith and its surrounding mountains to protect herself from the scorn others might show. During this journey with Alex, she had been forced not only to converse with strangers but also to live among them, with no thick castle walls to protect her. In taking a chance by reaching out to others, she, in turn, had been blessed.

Last night, when her eye unexpectedly began to twitch while she tucked the children into the one bed they shared, little Marget hadn't run away in horror but instead placed her wee hand against Fiona's face, her blue eyes wide with concern, and asked, "Does it hurt?"

Tears had choked Fiona as she grabbed the little hand and kissed the palm, her heart full with the knowledge that the child didn't fear her. Nor did Marget think her affliction a curse, but instead had shown love and concern, as had Sadie and Christopher. Perhaps there were people outside Kennerith like these children, like Alex, who wouldn't reject her and might even come to accept her. Through his patient ministrations and kind words, Alex had shown her an acceptance she'd never known. And through them, Fiona came to realize that God accepted her also. Just as she was—flawed and all.

She watched cool, blue shadows slant across the flowing hills while confectionary-white clouds crept past a low sun. Alex was different than she'd first thought. Indeed, if Beaufort were as kind as his brother, perhaps it wasn't so horrible that Gwynneth had eloped with an Englishman.

The random thought shocked her, and she quickly spoke to cover the confusion she felt. "Tell me about your home at Darrencourt. What's it like?"

If Alex thought it strange that she should so suddenly ask such a question, he didn't show it. "The manor is a brown-and-white, sixteenth-century Tudor with elaborate gardens and a deep forest beyond, where I often go to hunt." He directed a look her way. "Darrencourt is in the country, with an abundance of green meadows in which to ride."

"No moors or mountains?"

"There's a stretch of moorland within a short distance of Darrencourt, but no mountains. Only wooded hills, much like these, only not so barren at the top." He motioned to the slopes on either side of them.

"And what do you hunt?"

"Venison, pheasant, quail—whatever meat my mother expresses a culinary desire for at the moment." He grinned.

Fiona was surprised. "Do you not have servants to take care o' such matters?"

"We do. Yet I enjoy the hunt. Fencing, too."

"Fencing?"

"Swordplay."

"Aye." That would explain why he was in such fine shape. "Are you accomplished?"

"I can hold my own."

Fiona studied his aristocratic profile and proud bearing, then looked to his strong hands holding the reins. She didn't doubt his words for a minute. "And have ye found the need to also treat your opponents?"

He looked at her curiously. "Treat them?"

"From the cuts o' your sword."

He let out a loud, delighted laugh. The sound cheered Fiona. His eyes sparkled with mirth, and she noticed attractive creases bracketing his mouth. Had they always been there?

"I assure you, Miss Galbraith, the points are tipped for safety's sake. Fencing is considered a sport, and we use stilettos, not swords."

Fiona thought about that. From tales told at the *ceilidh,* her ancestors fought with weapons to kill, not for game play. "The only time I've heard of a sword being used for purposes other than the battles for which it was made is in a dance o' my kinsmen—but even that dance is connected with war."

"Oh?" He sounded interested.

She nodded. "Centuries ago, King Malcolm slew a chief of MacBeth. Afterward, he laid his sword o'er the chief's sword and did a victory dance—what my kinsmen call a sword dance. My cousin David is adept at that, though he canna toss a caber for the life of him." She chuckled when she remembered David's attempts at carrying and throwing the upright tree trunk during the games of skill and strength her kinsmen played.

A comfortable stretch of silence settled between them before he spoke again. "Tell me about Kennerith. What do you do there?"

"Often I climb the hills. On a clear day, you can see the ocean and some of the islands while standing atop Mount MacMurray."

"Mount MacMurray?" he repeated with upraised brow.

"What our family named it generations ago. 'Tis the steepest mountain on our land. Pines and alders cover its base and trail upward, but at the top lies nothing but granite."

He nodded, his expression meditative.

"We also named the roses in our garden MacMurray Roses," she added. "Gwynneth and I take turns tending them. 'Tis a family tradition we dinna leave t' the servants. The garden is ancient, as ye can see by the Celtic cross in its midst." She thought back to something her grandmother had said. "I was told the roses began through an ancestor named Fayre. And legend has it that throughout past centuries, no matter what hardships Kennerith underwent, every new owner of the castle found at least one bush still living. The roses are lovely, of the most unusual color ye will find. Like the sunset before the gloamin', they are."

"The gloaming. Twilight?" Alex questioned.

"Aye." Fiona smiled. " 'Tis the afterglow once the sun disappears beyond the horizon. The gloamin' lasts a long while."

The day passed in pleasant conversation as they continued southward. They reached a pass where the road narrowed, and they had to travel single file. Fiona felt almost saddened to end their discussion. When Alex pulled Barrag to a sudden stop, Fiona walked Skye closer to the trees crowding the lane so she could bring her horse next to Alex's. A small village could be seen in the distance.

"Is something wrong?" she asked.

He didn't answer for a moment, then looked at her, his eyes no longer laughing. "We have reached our destination. Beyond lies Gretna Green."

—∞—

Fiona said nothing, but Alex sensed by the faint frown on her lips that she hovered in a state of indecision, even remorse. In an instant, the sober look was gone, and she bounced her heels into Skye's flanks, prodding the horse into a wild gallop.

Alex followed, wondering if he'd imagined her earlier hesitation. She seemed anxious to reach the small village, whereas Alex now had reservations. What right did he have to tell his older brother not to marry? Certainly the fact that Gwynneth was not merely a simple peasant girl but the granddaughter of an earl must hold some sway with his father. Indeed, if the sister was as amazing and lovely as Fiona, Beaufort should count himself blessed.

It was then that Alex realized he was smitten with his redheaded collaborator, though he couldn't pinpoint the exact moment she'd found her way into his heart. Little did it matter; she considered him as repulsive as the filth scraped from the bottom of his boots. Alex withheld a sigh. Duty to family prevailed. He might have experienced a change of heart, but it was of no account. He would remain loyal in carrying out his father's wishes.

Gretna Green appeared to be no more than a cluster of white cottages at a crossroads. Alex spotted an inn, a tavern, and other places of business. People walked through the streets, going about their daily duties. Alex slowed his horse to a walk, and Fiona did the same. He guided Barrag up to the first person they met, a short man with a bulbous nose and large ears.

"Excuse me," Alex said. "Could you tell me where marriages are performed?"

The man cracked a wide smile, showing several gaps where his teeth had been. "Where'er ye like. Most are wedded at Gretna Hall, others at the Sark Tollbar—the first cottage ye come to when ye cross the border and pay the toll. Especially if the pursuit be hot, ye may want t' go there. Others share vows in private cottages or e'en here, outside among the gorse bushes." He spread his arms wide to encompass the village. "There's nary a place a weddin' canna be performed in all o' Gretna Green."

A slight man wearing an apron strode from a cobbler's shop. "If it's a marriage ye be wantin', come this way," he called out to Alex.

"Nae," a stout man on the other side of the road cried out. "He has just come from the asylum this week. I can show ye t' a respected man t' give ye yer vows, a Robert Elliot."

"Nae," the other man cried out good-naturedly, "my friend is drunk on ale. Bishop Lang is the man ye seek."

The two continued their easy, competitive bantering, and Alex questioned the man they'd first met. "You have a bishop presiding over weddings?"

"In name only," the man said. "David Lang was but a peddler in his youth before he served in the British navy. He's been in the marriage trade thirty years and has performed many a ceremony." He scratched his head. "Come t' think of it, he was called on only minutes ago to wed a couple."

Alex grew alert. "Where?"

"Gretna Hall. Many a fine lord and lady ha'e married there. Ye will be in good company." Chuckling, the man gave them directions, and Alex prodded Barrag into a fast gallop.

Fiona stared after Alex, then urged Skye to follow. Heat bathed her face at the villagers' assumptions that she and Alex had eloped and were looking for a place to wed. Even more shocking was her discovery that the idea was not detestable. Quite the opposite, really. And Fiona realized that somehow, at some point, she, Fiona Galbraith, a Highland Scot, had fallen in love with Alexander Spencer, a noble Englishman.

The abrupt awakening nearly unseated her from her horse.

Her grandmother might one day forgive her, but her grandfather, God bless him, never would stand for such a match, if he were cognizant of his surroundings. Fiona creased her brow, thinking of all she'd learned from those she'd met on their journey. Indeed, a whole new world had been opened to her, one not entirely without merit. The elderly MacBain woman's sage words were accurate. This was a new era, a time for change. Surely, then, it was time to let go of prejudices almost a century old as well as of the pride that had fostered them.

Perhaps Gwynneth wasn't as foolish as Fiona had reckoned her. Indeed, she might be the only intelligent Galbraith alive.

With each pounding of Skye's hooves on the road, Fiona felt more uncertain. What right did she have to try to stop her sister from marrying the man she loved? Gwynneth was seventeen, of marriageable age, and if Beaufort were as wonderful as his brother, as kind and considerate of others' feelings, then surely Gwynneth would enjoy a happy life. Wasn't that all that mattered?

Yet Alex's family considered Gwynneth unfit, and Fiona didn't think he'd understand her sudden change of heart if she were to speak. She didn't wholly understand it herself. After the rudeness she'd shown him those first days, Alex probably was anxious to be rid of her, though he was too much a gentleman to say so. Fiona only had herself to blame. Never mind that she was unaccustomed to strangers or the art of being sociable. She knew what the Good Book said about being charitable toward one's fellow man, and no excuse would erase the fact that Fiona had acted shamefully. The revelation was sobering, and she issued a silent plea for God to intervene and steam out the wrinkles in her rutted character.

Soon, they approached a long carriage drive. A wide, lush lawn covered in hardwood trees and evergreens fronted a white stone manor with gray trim along its many windows. Numerous chimneys rose above its gray roof. In front stood a shiny black coach, empty of its passengers, and a team of fine horses, prancing and snorting, their red coats glistening as if they'd just come to a quick stop. The driver worked to steady them.

Alex hurriedly dismounted, and Fiona followed him inside Gretna Hall. He threw open the door, looked around the empty foyer, and hurried through the open door of a parlor. A man, approximately in his late sixties with black clerical robes and broad-brimmed hat, faced a couple who had their backs to Fiona. The woman wore a bonnet, but the dark hair was familiar.

"Stop this wedding at once!" Alex cried.

The couple turned in terrified shock, and Fiona felt strangely relieved.

Alex's face darkened a shade. "You have my apologies," he told the unknown couple. "I thought you were someone else."

"May we continue?" the young woman said, her fearful gaze on the door. "I'm afraid Papa might come charging in here at any moment." She slipped her hand into the fair-haired man's, they exchanged a few words, saying they agreed to take one another for man and wife, and the older man officiating proclaimed them married.

It was over so quickly, Fiona wasn't certain it had happened, but she couldn't miss the joyous kiss the man bestowed on his blushing bride before escorting her from the parlor.

Alex moved toward the old man. "Have you wed an Englishman and a Scottish woman today?"

The man's full face beamed and his dark eyes sparkled. "Aye. I married them an hour ago. Sich a fine couple. They took a room here as well."

Alex quieted. "May I see the register? If we speak of the same couple, the man is my brother."

The old man nodded and pointed to the open page of a thick ledger where names and dates had been penned. Fiona stepped beside Alex and read the last entry:

On Wednesday 22nd inst at Gretna, Lord Beaufort Spencer of Darrencourt to Gwynneth Galbraith of Kennerith in Scotland. A polite young lady and a dignified nobleman. Paid one hundred guineas.

"Then we're too late," Fiona murmured.

"You sound almost relieved," Alex said in surprise.

Fiona turned her gaze fully upon him. "If the truth be told, I am."

He showed no astonishment, but his eyes intently focused on her, as though looking deep into her soul. "Might I ask why?"

"Aye," she responded just as softly. "When first we met at Kennerith, you were just a name, a class o' people I'd been taught to dislike, and I was bitter about other things as well. But during our journey, you've become a person t' me. One I greatly admire." Fiona tried to keep her words blithe, yet her heart pounded madly at the light that entered his eyes. "To be sure, if Beaufort be anything like you are, Dr. Spencer, then Gwynneth couldna have made too horrid a match."

"Miss Galbraith, if you'll permit me to speak?" Alex seemed suddenly flustered, searching for words. When he took hold of her hands, Fiona forgot to breathe. "Before setting out for Scotland, I never dreamed I would find a woman I might grow to love, if that is indeed what this emotion is. All I know is that I desire to spend each moment in your presence, to walk by your side and learn of all that interests you, to never refrain from looking into your lovely silver eyes. . . ."

"I can marry ye this moment, if ye so desire," the elderly man suddenly said, reminding the two of his presence. "If ye have no ring, I can provide one as well."

Heat bathed Fiona's face, and her heart sped up with nervous expectancy. Her hands grew slick in his, but Alex didn't release his hold. This was so sudden, but it was what she wanted. To marry this man. It was as though the reason for her existence, for God putting her on this earth, instantly became clear to her. She was to become Alex's wife and bear his children.

"No," Alex said, never breaking eye contact with her.

"No?" Fiona repeated, her dreams spiraling to dust.

The elderly man tsk-tsked and left the parlor, leaving the two alone.

"My dearest Fiona—if you'll allow me to take the liberty of addressing you as such?"

Fiona nodded, confused.

"The love I have for you seems quite real to me at this moment. However, this swift change regarding our feelings toward one another should be tested with time. Before engaging in the holy institution of marriage—and it is a wondrous and holy institution—I feel we should spend time getting to know one another. I shall make it a priority to visit Scotland whenever possible. In time, if we should decide to marry, I would rather the wedding take place in a church, before God, with a true minister presiding, and with our families' blessings. Rather than on the sly, in the front parlor of an inn, with an ex-peddler speaking the vows—and against our families' wishes." He tightened his grasp. "Do you understand, my dearest Fiona?"

"Aye." Her earlier disappointment evaporated, and she smiled. "I've always wanted to marry in the castle chapel at Kennerith and have the reception in the rose garden there."

Alex grinned. "I'm anxious to see these famous MacMurray roses. Perhaps when I escort you home, you'll show them to me?"

The awareness that he would be returning with her to Kennerith made her smile all the wider. "Aye, that I will. It willna take you long to win o'er my grandmother. She never would have allowed someone she didna trust t' take her beloved horse. And my grandfather is no longer mindful of his surroundings, so ye'll have no problem with him. But what about your father? Will he come to accept me? Or Gwynneth, for that matter?"

Alex sobered. "I'll talk to him. It may take some time, but I'm convinced that my father eventually will realize what wonderful additions the Galbraith sisters will make to our family. He's an intelligent man."

Fiona laughed. "I once thought myself the same, but this past week I've come t' ken that I've much to learn."

"You're one of the most remarkable women I've ever met." Alex's expression softened, and he raised her hands to his lips and kissed them. "Shall we see about acquiring two rooms and then go in search of a meal? Before they leave, I have a sudden desire to wish my brother a hearty congratulations and your sister the best of wishes!"

Epilogue

In the midst of the castle chapel, decorated with an abundance of sunset-colored roses, Alex kissed his new bride. At the warmth of his lips on hers, the strength of his embrace, Fiona's heart beat with wonder that her beloved Alex was now her husband. She felt brighter than the streams of sunbeams that shone down at them from one of five stained-glass windows, encasing them and the Scottish minister in an aura of jewel-toned light.

Pulling away, she smiled and looked into Alex's blue-gray eyes with their familiar sparkle. She could never doubt his love; it shone from his eyes. He took hold of her hand, and together they moved to accept their families' blessings.

As Fiona predicted, her grandmother hadn't greatly argued the point that Fiona loved an Englishman. The fact that King George IV had visited Scotland during the same year Fiona first met Alex and they had embarked on their journey together had helped matters. It was said the English king had appeared in a kilt, and Fiona knew, thanks to the author Sir Walter Scott, that Highland dress and customs had been embraced by many of the British, even romanticized.

Alex and Fiona's courtship was more wonderful than Fiona dared dream. On the occasions Alex had visited the castle, he and Fiona climbed mountains, rode horses, and fell more deeply in love. The most amazing thing was that the twitching in Fiona's eye disappeared. She hadn't had an episode in months. Yet even if the affliction were to return, and Alex's uncle wasn't able to treat her successfully, Fiona was confident that her new husband would never cease to love her.

Gwynneth moved forward to hug Fiona. "I'm so happy for you," she said. "And so glad that you'll come to live at Darrencourt."

"I'll miss this castle and our grandparents," Fiona admitted, "but Alex assured me that we'll visit every summer. I canna explain it. I never thought anything would entice me to leave these mountains, but I look forward to living at Darrencourt. I canna imagine a life without Alex."

"Aye. 'Tis the same way I feel about Beaufort."

"I scarcely can believe it! Both of us married—and to Englishmen as well!"

They laughed, and Gwynneth glowed from the promise of the child she carried within her. Fiona was pleased that she would soon be an aunt and relieved for Gwynneth, whose first months at Darrencourt had been difficult. Beaufort's father hadn't disowned him, as he'd threatened, but he'd had nothing to do with Gwynneth at first and avoided her presence. Beaufort's mother, dismayed but resigned to Beaufort's choice of a bride, had insisted they properly marry in the Church of England, and they had honored her wish. As the months passed, both Spencers came to see what a delightful and polite girl Gwynneth was and apologized for wrongly judging her. Their acceptance of Gwynneth made Alex's announcement of his own impending marriage to Fiona easier to accept.

Gwynneth pulled away, brushing the wrinkles from the shoulders of Fiona's best gown of shimmering emerald green. Beaufort stepped forward to hug his new sister-in-law. "You're perfect for my brother. I'm confident after meeting you that Alex has found a woman who'll stand up to him and not always let him have his way." He directed an amused grin toward Alex.

"Shall we move to the garden?" Alex asked, his color heightened at his brother's ribbing.

Fiona slipped her arm through his. "Aye. I have yet to give you your gift."

They walked into the spacious garden, fragrant with MacMurray roses. So many of the orange-red roses still grew on the vines that the absence of the ones Fiona used to decorate the chapel didn't show.

"Sit ye doon," Fiona instructed, her hands impatiently going to Alex's shoulders to seat him in one of two chairs that stood by a table off to the side. Agatha had helped her move the furniture into the garden that morning.

Alex chuckled. "My, I am intrigued by what has my new wife so flustered."

"Hush now," Fiona said with a smile. She nodded toward her cousin, and he lifted his bagpipes to his mouth. Soon the wheezing wail of pipes erupted into a carefree jig. Two of her cousins began to dance in the center clearing, and others quickly joined in. Fiona was surprised to see Alex's father, Lord Spencer, attempt a turn beside her grandmother, though Lady Spencer only looked on with a smile. Caught up in the music and dancing, no one paid attention to Fiona or Alex, which suited Fiona just fine.

Agatha walked toward them, bearing a platter with a very English-looking tea set and a platter of small cakes, then left. At the curious lift of Alex's brow, Fiona smiled, poured liquid from the pot into a cup, and set it before him.

"I once told you that ye'll not be findin' English tea at Kennerith Castle," Fiona explained. "At the time, false pride led me t' believe that English tea and bagpipes didna mix—I even told others so. Well, I was wrong. Please accept this gesture as a token of my love."

"Fiona," he breathed and grabbed her hand, pulling her down to his lap.

"Alex!" she protested with a laugh. "What's gotten into ye?"

"Perhaps it's this wild Highland air or the realization that the woman I adore is truly my wife. I don't know. But I doubt there's a man alive who's as happy as I am at this moment." He kissed her until Fiona forgot about all else but him.

When he pulled away, his gaze sheepishly went to the dancing guests as though just remembering their existence. "Perhaps we should save this for later. If Mother were to see us, she would be scandalized—even if this is my wedding and the woman I hold is my wife."

Fiona laughed and cupped his face with her palms, brushing her lips over his once more. "Aye, Alex. I do love ye so." Smiling, she stood and took hold of his hands. "Come, and I'll teach you a Highland jig. Later, we'll drink our tea, when we're alone together."

He allowed her to pull him up. "Mrs. Spencer," he whispered near her ear before taking her arm to escort her to the dancing. "I must confess I eagerly await that moment."

Fiona shared a secret smile with her Englishman.

To be sure, so did she.

BONNIE BLYTHE is the author of thirteen inspirational novels that illustrate God as the true Author of romance. An Oregon native, she now resides in Tennessee and is enjoying time with her first grandchild.

PAMELA GRIFFIN is a multi-award-winning author who fully gave her life to Christ after a rebellious young adulthood. She owes that she's still alive today to an all-loving and forgiving God and a mother who steadfastly prayed that He would bring her wayward daughter "home." Pamela's main goal in writing Christian romance is to help and encourage those who do know the Lord and to plant a seed of hope in those who don't. She loves to hear from her readers and can be reached at words_of_honey@juno.com.

KELLY EILEEN HAKE lives in LA with the kitten she and her then-boyfriend, Jeff, rescued from a very tall tree. Semi, whose white fur, black spot between his ears, and black tail makes him a walking semicolon, is the grammar cat Kelly never knew she needed. She's decided the cat and the boyfriend are both keepers and is currently planning a wedding with her new fiancé!

GAIL GAYMER MARTIN, bestselling and award-winning author, has been blessed with 85 published novels and five million books in print. CBS local news listed Gail as one of the four best writers in the Detroit area. She is the author of "Writing the Christian Romance" published by *Writer's Digest*. Gail is a founder of American Christian Fiction Writers and a member of numerous other professional writing and speaking organizations. In her earlier professional career, Gail was a teacher of English, literature, and public speaking at high school and university levels. She still enjoys teaching workshops at conferences across the US. She lives in Sedona, Arizona with her husband, Bob, and is active in her church both as a writer and in the music program where she sings in the choir and is a soloist. Visit her website at www.gailgaymermartin.com.

TAMELA HANCOCK MURRAY is a bestselling author of both fiction and nonfiction whose work was honored with an Inspirational Reader's Choice Award from RWA. Tamela and her husband of 35 years are empty nesters who live in Virginia and love being the parents of two lovely daughters. Tamela enjoys time with her extended family, traveling, reading, and appreciating her readers! Please find Tamela on Facebook, where she is probably the only Tamela Hancock Murray, and on Twitter @Tamela_Murray.

JILL STENGL is the author of numerous romance novels including Inspirational Reader's Choice Award- and Carol Award-winning *Faithful Traitor*. She currently lives with her husband and two spoiled cats near Raleigh, North Carolina. Her interests include drinking huge mugs of root-beer rooibos tea, spoiling her grandchildren, and indie-publishing sweet fairy-tale retellings. Visit her website at www.jmstengl.com to see her current writing projects.